THE DISINTEGRATING BLOODLINE

Louis T. Bruno

iUniverse, Inc.
New York   Bloomington

The Disintegrating Bloodline

Copyright © 2009 Louis T. Bruno

All rights reserved. No part of this book may be used or reproduced by any means, graphic, electronic, or mechanical, including photocopying, recording, taping or by any information storage retrieval system without the written permission of the publisher except in the case of brief quotations embodied in critical articles and reviews.

iUniverse books may be ordered through booksellers or by contacting:

iUniverse
1663 Liberty Drive
Bloomington, IN 47403
www.iuniverse.com
1-800-Authors (1-800-288-4677)

Because of the dynamic nature of the Internet, any Web addresses or links contained in this book may have changed since publication and may no longer be valid. The views expressed in this work are solely those of the author and do not necessarily reflect the views of the publisher, and the publisher hereby disclaims any responsibility for them.

ISBN: 978-1-4401-2916-2 (pbk)
ISBN: 978-1-4401-2917-9 (ebk)

Printed in the United States of America

iUniverse rev. date: 3/20/2009

Permission Acknowledgements

Grateful acknowledgement is made to the following for permission to reprint previously published material:

Random House: Excerpt from *Until I Find You* by John Irving, published by Random House press. Copyright © 2005 by Garp Enterprises, Ltd. Reprinted by Permission.

Sanctuary Music: Excerpt from "Children of the Damned" by Bruce Dickenson from *Number of the Beast* by Iron Maiden. Copyright ©1983 by Sanctuary Music. Reprinted by Permission.

Thurd Eye Music: Excerpt from "Baby Fat" by Curtis Jackson from *No Mercy, No Fear*, Copyright © 2006 by BCD Music Group. Reprinted by Permission.

"In this way, in increments both measurable and not, our childhood is stolen from us—not always in one momentous event but often in a series of small robberies which add up to the same loss."

-John Irving,
Until I Find You

Contents

Prologue: "Chris's Emergence"   xi

Book 1

Chapter I: "A Favor for a Friend"   1
Chapter II: "The Protection Run"   20
Chapter III: "The Game to End All Games"   54
Chapter IV: "A Honey's Luck"   86
Chapter V: "The Field Trip"   102
Chapter VI: "Faces of the Fallen"   129
Chapter VII: "Blood Costs Lives (and Loyalty)"   148
Chapter VIII: "Death is Inevitable"   168
Chapter IX: "Inside the Office of Chris Mangini"   188
Chapter X: "A.J.'s Watch"   209
Chapter XI: "Bleeding Hearts and Runny Eggs"   248

Book 2

Chapter XII: "The Abattoir of Truth"   265
Chapter XIII: "Transcendent Dreams and Milky Way Lights"   289
Chapter XIV: "The Bear's Hibernation"   305
Chapter XV: "An Unfortunate Case"   326
Chapter XVI: "A Procrastinating Protagonist"   336
Chapter XVII: "The Massacre at George Bradley"   346
Chapter XVIII: "Scars Don't Heal"   367
Chapter XIX "The Woman inside the box"   386
Chapter XX: "A Secret in the Rabbit's Drug Den"   412
Chapter XXI: "The Shadow of Morte"   456
Chapter XXII: "The Wheels are in Motion"   488

Prologue:

"Chris's Emergence"

"Christ! Three fights that involved in three deaths and a crazy psychotic kid who nearly killed innocent students and did more than ten thousand dollars in damage to the glass windows. This can't be another Columbine."

At George Bradley high school in Upstate New York, Vice Principal O'Donnel was beginning to see George Bradley was dwindling not from the outside, but from within like a hollow tree, and his influence as an authoritative figure was being ground into soft powder by the hands of angry "concerned parents" and the school committee. Only he was more worried about his massive ulcer than the horrid state the school was in. His neatly kempt hair was dripping sweat down his brow and a stink was emitting from every pore in his body was staining his clean crisp shirt.

As he surveyed his desk, he began to think about the events, and every time he thought, the less of an appetite he had. But he knew what gangs thrived on, and it was fear. They used that more than they used knives or bullets, and he was armed with nothing but a pen and a list full of possible suspects that were responsible for the current chaos. Only he had questioned all of them, and no one was giving up anything. Not even the fiends who would give up anything just for their "precious" habit.

Only his morals would not let him go that far as to retrieving information. Only he had used all the resources he could possibly imagine. None of the gangs were talking, and the only thing that he had gotten was "they're handling with themselves." That wasn't going to help, but he knew that he had to keep pressing at the gang leaders, throw all their weight on them. But he knew that these gangs were hard, tough, and nonnegotiable in any kind of deals. No, they would not surrender to him, but to another.

"Chris Mangini." He thought with amazement, and then placed his hand around the phone. He hesitated for a moment, but then knew that only Chris Mangini, could be their only savior and solution to this mess. He had dealt with him in the past over a personal matter of a debt with certain "wiseguys" in the city. Chris hadn't vouched for him by all means, but had provided him the money to pay them back. But now, the chickens had come to roost, or the hell hounds have come for their retribution. He would repay his favor to Chris.

When he got hold of their bulldog, Gene Dov, he begged them with an outright plea to squash this violence this made Gene, this rather handsome swarthy Jewish boy, want to chuckle.

"You must remember, if we ever need any kind of assistance, you will not refuse us."

"Yes," he almost wanted to say, my lord, "anything. What is it that you want?"

"Total control!"

He wanted to laugh, but dared not to if he would send the slightest inclination of a joke. The Golden Jew, Gene, wasn't an enforcer but his influence was just as strong, and could affect the existence of his life. But he was rumored to be the reason behind the wrath of Chris Mangini. "Okay… when will I know the gangs have been stopped?"

"You'll know when. All those that owe an favor to Chris Mangini will always follow through. No bullshitting. If you welch or find yourself in a bind, you will have to deal with the consequences."

The line went dead, and he for once in his life, felt that the responsibility wasn't entirely resting on his shoulders. "It's okay to get some help." He thought, but in a way, silently regretting the whole phone call. He leaned back in his seat and stared at the ceiling above him. The currents of the air conditioner relaxed him, and he closed his eyes.

"Such merciless and almost barbarous behavior."

But he couldn't find any reason to blame them for doing what they were doing, and in a way, he owed at least that much to Chris for his own inadequacy as a Vice President. Some bull-dog he was, a poodle was more like it.

A dash of blush blood jetted up from the face of Jacob Barley as the sounds of bones colliding with Chris's fist sent small shockwaves of pain throughout his arm and body. It hadn't hurt after the multiple times of beating his face until every bruise turned into full fledged cuts that widened as Jacob started to taste large sticky gobs of blood inside his mouth.

Chris's fist had been unrelenting cannonball of pain that was turning Jacob, this small blonde haired Adonis into a piece of red meat. But when his fist had been covered in an inch of blood Gene handed him a small Kershaw knife that was gleaming above them in the moonlit sky. Gene was mortified by Jacob's appearance that he grimaced as blood dripped from every hole in his face, and a thought occurred that elated his fears.

"Better you than me." He thought, and then watched from the corner of his eyes as Frank Latitante hurried beside Gene and his eyes were taking in this blood lust.

"Fucking kill him!"

Then another one of his soldiers, Krazy, who had finished beating several of the Outcasts into a state of unconsciousness, and as he saw that they were knocked out cold, he threw the body of Clifford Barley into the grass and hurried over with a punch drunk, unstable walk.

"End that sorry piece of shits life for good." Krazy, whose bruises weren't from this fight, was still high off the violence that he had to punch invisible foes in the darkness.

Chris flicked the knife and then said, almost preaching than he was talking. The knife gleamed in the moonlight, and through the darkness, Jacob could see even though the blood was deep in his eyes.

"No, he shall live. But he will live in shame as he will tell everyone who did this to him. No one shall ever pass out drugs or sell them in my school. You tell anyone who does, is going to get a severe beating you wished you were dead. " Such power, such a deviant mind that bordered on outright lunacy that made Chris Mangini smile in a deifying way that made even Chris's own men skin start to shiver.

He managed to squeak out a threat that was heard above a whisper. "You'll never get away with this."

Chris stopped and then his clean cut face became hard as stone, his cleft jaw twitched as he then leaned forward and whispered, in a cool sinister breath against his cheeks. "You think I haven't thought of that?"

Jacob fell short as all the cuts made his skin sting in the same way as if liquor was poured on his face. Only then he poked the small Kershaw knife into his throat, and then pulled it out in one quick instance. Then he made one quick cut down his throat and pushed himself off his body. He tried to grip at Chris's shirt, but he tossed him back to the ground.

Out of the entire beating, it made him start to croak like a dying frog as he pushed his hand against his wound and tried to call for help. Blood kept leaking through his hands, and like a fish gasping for air, the blood started to jump from his mouth as he started to gargle and eventually…

They left Jacob and several members of the Outcasts to bleed, and their souls starting to leave there bodies, Chris dialed the three numbers 9-1-1 and then left the phone on the hook.

"Hello?" The police officer said into the phone. Only the officer became worried and said again, "Hello?"

Chris and his men left and it was on the day of October 14th 1997, they had let everyone know that there was a true certified gangster that was not going to take anyone's shit, including the Vice-Principals, or the rambunctious gangs. To be certain about the Vice-Principals trust, his son had been kidnapped and was delivered to his house just after they had asserted their power and required a weekly tribute that would more or less, make them break their own greedy piggy banks. Only that was Chris's law, and a god he became at that moment.

Only God's could feel fear, and the only time he had ever been afraid was when he had received a small package from Sicily. Long pain that he had buried deep within his mind had come back again from one of his liaisons in Sicily that was keeping watch over his property. The only thing that was inside the package was a sloppy reward letter that was written in paint in bold capital letters *Ricompensare per la testa di cugino del Mangini di Chris 1.000.000 dollari*. He was actually ignorant enough to give a million dollar contract on his cousin's head. Chris knew he should be scared because he and his cousin, whoever he was, were the rightful heirs to the throne of Sicily. But he couldn't understand why he didn't want him too, but then he read on with the awful note, *500.000 dollari per il Chris Mangini esiliato, condannato, e senza padre*. He felt a kind of sick gratitude from the fact that he wanted his head as well, but those words *exiled, damned, fatherless* hurt him more than the actual threat. It was all because of him that he had come to this god awful country without a father, and even his mother didn't even get to see him buried. The Don had not desecrated his body, but left it entirely pristine that definitely made Chris curious to go back, but there were spies in the hills. He wouldn't last too long until somebody found out about his arrival and would have a hit squad crawling underneath every kind of rock to kill him if he showed his face in any town. That was what he was not going to risk, but with the purse for more than a million five, he knew that assassins from all over would be vying for that kind of reward money. Only Don Mangiano was so vain that he wanted his own people to do it, and would not place that responsibility with any outsiders.

"Send your own to do your own dirty laundry."

And he had a thousand soldiers that would gladly do his bidding, but then he would probably kill them instead of paying them the promised amount.

"Scoundrel." Chris thought. "Coward. He thinks he can come after me?"

The Disintegrating Bloodline

"What do we do?" His friends, and soldiers asked.

"We let him come, and hope that he brings a thousand of his best to come at me."

"What about your cousin?" Frank asked, his cupid face made him seem more attractive when he was worried.

This definitely perplexed him, and in a way, it was like sitting in a crowded square and trying to meet someone for the first time when you hadn't met them in the first place. He winced for he was once, in his long life, had been robbed of an answer. Only he gave a lackluster reply that didn't make them think any different of him, but only increased their admiration for him as soldiers, brothers, and comrades in the fight.

"We will find him without attracting the attention of the family's, including Don Pescaro. He has enough on his plate, and I know his influence will hold the hordes at bay. For I fear that someone will try to uproot our family, but our friendship is solid, and through the shittiest situations, we will stay together."

"Until death to us part." Krazy yelled, and all of them joined in. Only Chris smiled and in that moment, they hugged in a joyous jubilee were bucking all that lay ahead of them in a naiveté that was perfect, but also dangerous, for time moved without anyone's permission and allowed nothing, not even the stars and the moon, to stay the same.

BOOK 1

Chapter I:

"A Favor for a Friend"

George Bradley high school is an hour away from New York city, tucked away in the arm pit of the state, and for all the kids that attend it felt they were from another galaxy away from civilization. There were prickly pimpled backward freshman to creamy alabaster doll face seniors waiting for the first period bell to send them off to their second period class. At 9:45 in the morning their faces hung low to hide their baggy, depressed eyes as they carried large stone tablet textbooks that felt like a small rock of Gibraltar were on their backs. In addition to the pain of the books, the students' stomachs were growling from the lack of food and minds were twisted as if they were drunk. For some time (if not most of the time) they wished they had been drunk, and some of them knew how to hide it with an air freshener. While the tired eyes mirrored the malcontent for their school lives, other students were trying to get by with the basic education George Bradley had to offer. They knew it could have been far worse—even though it had been normal for a while—but after Chris Mangini came to George Bradley, it was like nothing had ever happened.

Only the little hand inside the black rimmed clock was trailing slower than a slug disintegrating in an inch of salt. The students believed that someone was inside the wall delaying the little hand so that they could be trapped indefinably. While they were stuck to their chairs like flies on a sticky trap their teacher's rapid teaching pace would never stop if they were left without a bell. But lunchtime was the time where the students could get away just for a half an hour—rest their angry minds from the mental beatings—and provide a sort of relaxation before they went back to the flogging lairs.

As the students watched the clock for the next three hours, the big hand landed on the black numbered **12**, the bell let off a painful and loving sound—*bing...bing...bing...bing*. The students had readied there backpacks long before the bell rung. The students flushed out of the classrooms like they were about to shit themselves, and a refreshing wave of blasted air that washed the suffocating pollution that filled there school like muddy waters—violent, dirty, and seeped to the brim with distorted visions of a fixed, uncircumcised world. In this world, they would not have been slaving away, but that is life's cruel hand—the cards are never in your favor.

Chris Mangini knew what he could not control, and everything he could, he never released until it was time. He focused his oddly handsome Sicilian bred eyes on the Commons as he sat comfortably at a table in front of the long open hallway. Behind him was the senior courtyard window; the courtyard was already starting to be filled with brownish gold faded leaves—signifying that winter was on its way and that was what he couldn't change. His table overlooked half of the domain of Commons A lunchroom to more than five hundred hungry students while Commons B held as many as two hundred more finicky, remorseless two legged mammals. To Chris's east was the quadruple door exit and to his west was the bus ramp's smooth hill extension. In George Bradley there were the Five percent (counting the principal) that everyone looked up to—feared and hated—but no one touched because they were men of action, and there words rarely required a contract signature to ensure their loyalty. Chris Mangini's presence was like a ripple in a calm pond, and the affects of his presence were felt for miles if someone had disturbed the pond. Securing his reign, he met three other friends and comrades; Gene Dov, a money making Jew, Frank Latitante, a quick witted gunslinger and William Beans, A.K.A. "Krazy", a tough young thug. With their reign solidified, George Bradley was there's for the taking.

Long after the fourth bell tone finished, he saw the students scattering towards their tables with bags of packed lunches, sitting next to their so called "friends," and coming up with useless conversations that didn't add up to anything but filled the void of shortened time.

"Did you see Geri's tits?" One boy said, as his mouth made a gurgling sound as he chomped on his homemade peanut-butter-and-jelly sandwiches.

"Yeah," the other boy, with deep seeded freckles smiled with trite delight, holding his free hand out to his chest, "those boppers were like melons," and began shoving the bologna and cheese Kaiser roll sandwich into his mouth. The others had ordered turkey subs from Subway, and or cheaply made Taco's from Taco Bell.

Chris had never trusted Taco Bell, or any kind of food outside his own, and he always had a feeling about what was in their meat. But seeing them tear into their sandwiches, watching the Mayonnaise dripping from their sandwiches and licking their fingers so carefree just sickened Chris to the point of throwing up.

"Disgusting!" Chris thought, cringing as he turned his head, trying to shield his eyes away from this awful sight, but was already scarred by their bread and mustard stained incisors gleamed a yellowish pee color on their teeth.

Chris could never eat in front of these kids for a lot of reasons. It disturbed him to see these kids licking their fingers as if it were a lion licking their prey's blood off their paws like a grotesque fascination.

"*Chilllllllllllldreeeeeeeeennnnnnnnn of the daaaaaaaaaaaaaaaamed!*" At that second, a heavy metal eighties band "Iron Maiden's" *The Children of the Damned* was running through his mind, and hearing the lead singer Bruce Dickenson, screaming the lyrics into his head agitated him.

"Did they even care about walking into this school wondering if they were going to be shot?" Chris thought and knew the answer immediately. "No, they just want to sit and eat their fast food passing precious time away, not taking advantage of the freedoms they had right there." Chris sighed angrily, knowing it was true but then he knew that there were kids that were actually using the classes to their advantage, and it soothed Chris's bitterness, but it did not calm him. There were also teachers that he thought were more disgusting than a crack head, but that was a different story.

There was an endless and haunting issue hanging over Chris like an Albatross that continued to peck and sometime degrade him when he wasn't, or trying to think about his daily responsibilities. One missing member of his family was of importance, but he would not try to search through invisible smoke to find an answer. He feared that when his crew met him they would bring more bullshit to the table. Although it kept him alert, the stress of being killed was more than he could bear, and to not know the answers, was a sin.

Chris was starting to feel his sins flushing the life out of his system at an abnormal rate—like a curse that was withering him into a deformed cripple—doing the exact opposite—keeping his muscles tight and controlling all the veins in his body. Chris knew why, and that didn't even need to be said. His cousin was the reason his body tightened every time he moved. Every time he moved, Chris moved, and he could feel him move.

At that moment his mind became sidetracked from something in the corner of his left eye. A very handsome boy with wavy black hair and a rather short but muscular appearance: his triceps and biceps pushed against his long white T-shirt and his dark blue baggy jeans that trailed over his masculine legs and fell over his scuffed Reebok sneakers. While in the crook of his arm was a large zipper binder that had pages bulging out of the folder—a sign that a person did actually pay attention. And in his other hand was a brown paper bag that was about to break through the bottom. Chris saw him standing in the middle of the hallway, dumbfounded and confused, like he had been lost in a glass maze, and saw his reflection everywhere he went. Chris felt trapped in a glass maze himself, but the only reflections he would see were the dead men that haunted him every time he looked inside the mirror.

Chris would have mistaken him to be a sophomore, but he wouldn't have been surprised if he was a freshman, and would have been really amazed if he were a senior. He probably thought the boy didn't care about what grade he was in. "A strong handsome guy doesn't care really about a man's opinion's either way." Chris thought as he scratched his nose, pulling at his nose with his index and thumb fingers, releasing as it made a small popping sound.

The boy glanced at him, and then turned away in fear of Chris's presence. The boy stood for a long moment, staring into the distance of bobble headed students, but was obviously ignoring the few open seats beside him. Chris didn't really want to sit *next* or *offer* to him, because his stress was released through the silence, like leaking an odor through his pores and he just wanted to have some peace and quiet before his crew ruined it again.

"God—don't come over here," Chris thought, but he wasn't sure if this was God coming over to him as a little boy, he was blindly attracted to his presence, because like God he brought a person into this world and could take them away.

But when he saw him turning around, he decided that that he would play around with this kid, shake him up a bit.

The boy walked up to the table, the boy's muffled voice gave off an embarrassingly timid whisper, fading into the talking crowd behind them. "Can I sit here?"

Chris looked at him, seeing his blue eyes laying everything at his doorstep, the endless conversations of others blocked Chris's hearing, which like hearing the wind passing through his ear, and he belted, throwing his head closer, leaning his back off the light blue plastic chair. "What?" His muscles twitched in agitation, and he narrowed his eyes.

The boy shook his head, and then leaned forward and said in a louder voice, *"CAN I SIT HERE?"* Chris drew his eyebrows low, and he watched the boy put his hands to his side, and his voice attracted a few wondering eyes from the tables.

"As you can see there are no other chairs, and I was wondering if I could sit here." He replied in a louder and less aggressive tone, trying not to anger the savior of George Bradley.

Chris knew that he was being polite, and the noise fading out of his ear,

Chris narrowed his eyes, feeling the urge to laugh building up to his stomach, he finally said with a serious tone, "No you can't."

The boy shook his head, knowing that there were more than four chairs around his table, and then Chris came back with a vicious comment that exceeded far beyond sarcasm. "Get the fuck out of here!"

Then his voice became very sarcastic in a blink of an eye, "Why don't you look for some more seats since you weren't looking that hard!"

The boy hadn't caught his sarcasm he turned around hurtfully and walked away from his presence. He did not want to be dead for making a stupid remark to a cold-hearted killer so he felt it was better to leave than get killed.

But at that moment, Chris knew that he had pissed the kid off—far more than he thought—and his spiteful voice was what triggered the boy to walk away. All he had wanted to do was just give him a hard time, but he saw just from this one encounter this kid took jokes way too personally. Only from deep inside him Chris let out a yell that towered over all the conversations in the lunchroom.

"Hey," Chris scratched his thick eyebrows as he raised a hand and… looked like he was about to die from the overall joy that was secreting from his mouth, "Come back!" He smirked, and the boy, who stood for a moment, just looked at him with betrayed wonder. Was this cold hearted killer laughing for everyone to see, or was it just for show?

"For what reason?" The boy thought, but then decided not to let his anger get the better of him. "Don't get too hurt, but how would he hurt me?"

He walked back toward the table, and hoped that he would not be leaving with one of his limbs dismembered, but felt oddly attracted to his warm, unusual presence. What he wanted to talk about, the boy didn't know, or want to know. He just wanted to roll with it, and think about it later.

The boy walked over with a nervous caution for his life as he stepped two feet in front of the table, seeing Chris's laughing fit start to die down, he looked at him questionably, as if this whole scene was a trap.

"I'm not gonna bite!" Chris said, with a choking laugh as he pulled out one of the chairs, scraping the legs across the floor in an "scccchhhhh" ear piercing scratch, and pushing the back almost two inches to the mirror like window. The boy didn't know whether he should have been honored or frightened, and then, with a heavy heart sat down in the chair.

After he sat down, he set his books and almost destroyed paper bag lunch on the table, a moment of silence passed through them when Chris thought that he had to talk first. To break the tension, or just be friendly.

With a steady hand, Chris put his hand out to him and said with an honest smile, "What's your name?"

The boy looked at his hand, not knowing he should even be talking to him, felt a bit resistant to give him his name at all. Only he wasn't like half of the kids in George Bradley, and he wasn't going to ignore him when he had his hand out in respect.

"My name's A.J."

A.J. put aside all of his flights of paranoia, and then shook his hand. His hand felt warm, clammy to the touch, and A.J. kept his hand in his grip.

Chris could sense that A.J. was totally calm with which he was, and Chris thought that was unlikely for a person to be at his age. "Is he fourteen or sixteen?" But it felt tough by the way his palm touched his own. Chris could oddly imagine the dirt on his hand, and could feel all the stories resonating from his warm hand like he was in a living art gallery.

But A.J. could not judge him just on the basis on what he heard from everyone else and just on what his *hand* felt like. He had a chance to talk to Chris Mangini, the big boss, and he saw a few students watching him from another table in fear. If they wanted to be spectators, and watch from a safe distance, that was there business but A.J. was different, he was not like the rest of the herd. He had guts and brains, but he didn't know what that would get him into one of these days. But A.J. knew that people had to pay for being completely different.

Chris nodded and his dark green olive eyes stared into this boy's ocean blue eyes—trying to read his thoughts—when he said his name in his head, "A.J."

He did not want to forget about this kid, because he knew all these names just by repeating it in his head, and then started to introduce himself.

"My name is…" Chris said, still gripping his hand, wiping the sweat off his palm. It moved him in a haunting way. A.J. replied before he could even speak.

"Chris Mangini," A.J. interrupted, skipping the introductions, "I know of you and have seen you just walking by. I thought you never liked to talk to anyone." At that moment, A.J. could feel his hand tightening around A.J.'s hand, focusing his strength on his fingers, but he made no threatening gestures.

Chris's squeeze was almost harder than a king Cobra did when it was coiled around its victim, and then he said, "I guess you thought wrong."

The two let go of each other's hands, and then A.J. slowly reached down towards the ground, where he had set his bag, and pulled out a foil wrapped sandwich and a 12-ounce Coka-Cola can out of his bag. He fit his finger inside the seal, and leaning it upwards he sent the fizz up into the air like water shooting out of a geyser. The fizz flowed out like smoke rising out of an old man's cob pipe as the pain alleviated from A.J.'s hand. A.J. was somehow immune to that kind of pain, and aside from the pain, he wanted to know what he had done wrong to make him do that. A.J. knew that he had done nothing wrong, but he just decided to tear through his lunch—and quickly—because he knew that the time was going to not last long.

Chris saw him opening his lunch, and then looked toward the door where his comrades would be walking in a momentary notice—fucking everything up, including the time he had now.

"I have to let him know what's going on!" Chris thought, knowing now that he couldn't make him leave, but he needed him to know before his crew arrived and would give him the royal treatment, which would be like royal shit.

Chris turned his head, seeing A.J. tearing through half of his sandwich, sending chunks of crumbs all over the end of his shirt and a few crumbs were pushed into the corner of his mouth. "Listen!" Chris became a little disgusted, but then continued on like nothing had ever happened. "Do you know who I hang with?"

A.J. turned, and wiping the corner of his lips and brushing off his shirt, he said, "Yeah. I have seen them. Are they going to give me a hard time?" A.J. grabbed the Coke Cola can and took another sip of the syrupy liquid—the syrupy taste soothed his throat, sending his taste buds in a sugar frenzy that was about to travel faster through his bloodstream than a falling comet in the sky—where nothing seemed like a coincidence or an accident.

"No." Chris said, "Just let me introduce you, and they will give you some props, but don't be surprised if they do that at all."

A.J. nodded, feeling like he had made a mistake sitting here at all. "I won't!" A.J. said reassuringly, and took another sip of his Coke Cola.

Chris licked his lips out of nervousness when he looked down toward the quadruple exit/entrance door and saw his three soldiers, Frank Latitante, Gene Dov, and Krazy swaggering through the front door like some show boat gangsters with gold watches on their wrists and shiny pinky rings on their fingers with ridiculously bright suits. But the look that he wanted them to wear comfortable jeans and white T-shirts that showed no gang color and attracted no attention from the faculty. With that bit of reconstruction on the three, he gave them an entirely different lifestyle when they joined forces with Chris. Keep a low-key house; don't wear jewelry or any kinds of chains, and no talking to the police at all, except in matters of business. But their confidence and loyalty shined brighter than any diamond in the sand, and when they talked to anyone, they held there heads high and walked proudly.

Yes, these were the four that no one fucked with, and Chris was proud to have them a part of his team. But he felt like something was missing from this group, which was another member. He scratched the side of his head, and then watched as they approached them.

A.J. could see the first boy, Frank Latitante, a tall skinny fellow with a gaunt like face, long bony fingers, and was wearing a gray Wu-Wear T-shirt. Over his scuffed Nike shoes were long Khaki pants that were creased over the bottom. The Wu-Tang Clan were a popular group of New York Emcee's that were mainstream rap stars when they decided to put out their own clothing line after there music became underground because of the governments prohibition on CD's. "That's Frank," Chris whispered.

The boy in the middle almost had A.J.'s physical features, but had more stocky shoulders and an attractive ovate face. He was Gene Dov, and A.J. knew it by his long reptilian nose and his dark thick hair that was almost as thick as a crow's nest. Gene Dov was the financial reason behind Chris Mangini's success at George Bradley, but their personal relationship solidified it more than a woman's vagina. He was a reckless son of a bitch and a loyal one as well. But it almost set him back when he saw him in a fine leather jacket and a bright blue turtleneck shirt that almost made him look ridiculous with his thick bulging collar ride up his neck. "That's Gene," Chris continued, and A.J. nodded.

It was cold out, but the sun made it almost unbearable to wear a coat none-the-less wear a turtleneck, (that made his swarthy face seem glazed over from the shining sweat) but he knew that winter was approaching, and that was a good precaution. The boy on the far right was Krazy, but his real name was William Beans. He was their tough guy, their muscle, and the scars on his face showed the harsh realities of an alcoholic father who like to beat him and put cigarettes out on his eyes (which discolored his corneas). "That's Krazy," He stopped, and wiped his lips.

When the three were approaching the table, their eyes all focused on A.J., like sharks catching the scent of fresh blood swimming toward their table to feast on this boy. Even though they walked toward Chris and gave him a "pound," which was slang for a handshake, they narrowed their eyes and made smug eyes. He introduced A.J. to them, and out of all of them, Frank made the first introduction.

"What's up?" Frank said, and held out his hand.

A.J. looked up, and then held out his hand. Just as he was going to shake, Frank pulled it up and then laughed. A.J. still had his hand in the air when they were still laughing, and just shook it off with a shrug.

A.J. just stared at him irritated as Frank apologized, but not really. "Who said you could sit here?"

A.J. spoke rather proudly, and said, "Chris let me sit here when I had nowhere else to sit."

Frank nodded, wondering if he was telling the truth or wondering if his ears were really hearing this inconceivable notion.

"What is this?" Frank thought, "Was he becoming soft, or is this another side of him that we haven't seen until now…whatever? He welcomed us when we were on our asses." Only they knew that if Chris wanted this boy to sit here, they had to deal with it—like it or not, he's the boss—but Frank knew that business had to be settled whether or not this boy was present. Frank and Gene grabbed a few chairs positioning their chairs around Chris, and started to whisper what they found out. Only Krazy stood against the wall, surveying his surroundings, adding a layer of protection around Chris and his companions.

"Hey boss!" Frank whispered. "I think we found something that you might want to hear."

Chris's face grimaced with that of a deadly premonition, seeing Gene leaning over so that he could hear.

"Your cousin is alive."

Everyone's ambivalence was strong, but his voice stirred a confidence that spoke the truth.

"We thought it was false, but we checked out our sources." Frank continued to whisper, nonchalant, but couldn't help but feel a certain amount of excitement about this. If his cousin did exist, the stratosphere of New York would be perfected and the stars would be aligned again.

As they proceeded to continue talking, A.J. had not heard a word between Chris and his men. A.J. thought that was rightly so, because he didn't *want* to know what they were saying and anything that didn't involve A.J., wasn't his business. So, he finished his Coke-Cola with one quick gulp, and at that moment received a rush of energy to stay up for his next class.

Another fifteen minutes passed by, making it 12:20 when the long hand had moved on the dark black **4**. A lot of kids had been throwing away their food by this time—or had just gotten out of the cafeteria lines with their food—were just now sitting down now to eat. They pretty much had to scarf whatever they could—shoving down tacos or cheeseburgers in a mad hot minute—before the bell rung for them to get back to their class. But when A.J. thought he could have some peace, a face that he did not want to see was in front of the table peering with his ugly acne rash face pulsating with ignorance and his skin stunk of crusted dry milk.

A tall redneck boy, Steve Lee, who had stolen something precious to him. He played around with the fact that he wanted to rub the whole thing in his face, embarrass him to the highest level. "Maybe he is going to give it back?" A.J. thought, but then he knew that it wasn't going to happen.

"Hey bitch boy!" Steve burst out with a trailer trash voice that was alien as the holes in his pants, and his gray shirt was stained from old B.O. The smell was unbearable, toxic to the point of poisonous and the redneck boy's breath ranked of sewage.

"I guess not!" A.J. thought, and then spoke to him in an aggressive tone, "What do you want!"

Steve changed his tone, running a hand through his short hair and then asked A.J. innocently, mocking him, "have you seen my money clip? I seemed to have lost it?"

At that moment, his blood was boiling and he was ready to strangle him at this moment. "You motherfucker!" A.J. thought, and then making up his thoughts in one hot second he calmly said to him, "well, maybe it was because you took it, you cock biting, turd chewing, dog breath, pizza pimple face motherfucker!"

Frank looked at Chris, almost smirking from this strong comeback, but Chris did not smile. In Chris's solidarity he was studying him tirelessly, hoping to place this kid to the insane brother of Jacob Barley, but this boy was almost as tall as a basketball player, and Clifford, Jacob's brother, was a lot shorter. He watched as he laid his palms on the table, and moved toward A.J., opening his mouth his buck tooth was bright yellow. Chris could only lead it to smoking, but that stench couldn't be helped even with talcum powder and toothpaste mixed together.

But then Krazy stepped off the wall, and started to walk around the table, taking this as a drastic situation. But the boy flinched, and he pulled his hand out of his pocket a small, black leather money clip with the faded gold letters, *A* and *J* on it.

Clamped inside the leather clip was a small layer of dirty one-dollar bills, which held about fifty ones inside with imprints of his fingers on the leather clip. He was obviously trying to make A.J. jealous, but even though he would have denied it, it was true.

"That's too bad," Steve's voice bordered on proud idiocy as he stuffed it into his back pocket, in a polite but also in a vindictive sarcastic tone, "cause I was just gonna give it back to you. But it doesn't look like your lucky day. I guess you'll have to wait!" Steve walked away with childish arrogance, even though he was trying to insult A.J., he couldn't have imagined the damage he had caused himself. Chris did not like it when someone was insulting his own companions, but when someone was insulting one of Chris's friends, that deemed just as much cause for punishment.

"What was that about?" Chris asked very frankly, his eyes fell upon him with curiosity. "How did he get your money clip?"

A.J. sighed, wiping the sweat off his face—the boy's presence had deeply offended and angered A.J., but now he was blowing off real steam. Looking at Chris he saw a crazed look of demons ready to tear—bite and scratch—if he didn't tell him what was going on.

A.J.'s voice was dry and his heart was forcing the words out of his mouth, "What happened was…we were sitting across from each other in class, and twenty minutes before the class ended he asked me if he could see the clip. I told him he couldn't, but he kept on bugging me. But when I was taking out my money clip to get my money, he swiped it from me, and said if I told the teacher I was a snitch."

A.J. shook his head, and sighed with resentment, "I tried to get it back, and he kept ignoring my phone calls, and I tried to get one of the teachers to talk about it, but he keeps denying it. So he knows that I'm a…" He took a deep breath, and then his confusion took hold of his words, "This is just great. When you need the teachers the most they don't do a damn thing!" A.J. decided to stop talking as a long series of sighs exited from his system, toiling with his anger that was slowly eating away at his soul's very fibers.

Chris could feel his own anger bubbling in his system, and he felt like he wanted it as much as A.J. had at that moment. But when his eyes refocused back towards the boy, he saw him walking down the hill bus ramp, but he wasn't going to leave yet, he was going to get ice cream or a drink from the vending machine. They had to hurry now or they would never get his money clip back. He looked at A.J. again, and noticed a rather straight scar that stretched across his brow, and looked like it had faded into his skin. Being that this should have been important at the time, it was this boy's pain of not having what had been rightfully his.

"Do you want your clip back?" Chris asked in a rather plain base like tone. Chris saw in A.J.'s eye that he wanted his clip back, and no amount of hatred could contain him from denying the fact that he wanted it back.

"Oh fuck him!" A.J. thought wildly, and with a glint of fear and awe, he proclaimed, reassured in every way. "Yes!"

Frank shook his head, discouragingly but stopped when he saw Chris motioning to him with his eyebrows.

"Maybe its time we get your clip back?" He said, and then Gene and Frank rose up out of their seats and slowly walked toward the bus ramp, like a predator stalking his prey, in slow crawling strides down the halls.

Chris, Krazy, and A.J. watched them disappear into the crowds of and they waited for the results.

Gene and Frank stormed through the open doorways with mass amounts of smells, students all huddled around the vending machines, all kinds of body odor and wet vomit fart smells that made Frank and Gene's stomach cringe. The toxic wet-fart smell was another reason to get the hell away, but they needed to find this boy before he left this area or their opportune time to strike would be closed for good. They could never get a punch in without a teacher separating them before anything started but kids always loved to see a fight. If the crowd of kids could give them a layer of protection, they could easily get his money clip out of his pants, and give him a few quick punches while he was down. It would be so simple.

The two predators stood around for a moment, scanning the area with a keen eye, and saw that the tall galoot was in front of a Pepsi machine that sold twenty ounces of other sugary liquids as well as Kola, a marked down brand of sugar drinks. Unbeknownst to them, a small crowd was staring at them, as a barrier started to slowly form around them.

"Probably a Mountain Dew!" Frank thought, "But he's going to leave with few broken teeth."

They saw the boy taking out the money clip, and pulling out a one-dollar bill he put it inside the machine, watching the money being sucked into the black money sucker, and then spit back out. If were any time to take the offensive and make their attack on the boy it would be now.

The two stepped forward, with their finger nails digging in their rough palms, they saw him smoothing the wrinkled dollar bill out and stuck it inside the black slot, where it quickly sucked up the money. The machine made its wurring, buzzing sounds and the small screen let him know with the highlighted red words **VEND** so that he could pick out his desired soft drink. At that moment, it was like everyone knew what was going to happen, a larger wall of kids began to encircle them, as if they knew what was about to happen. When the two approached him, Frank was going for his back, and then Gene stealthily moved to the right.

Frank clenched his fist and then threw it into the boy's back, feeling the bones in his back crack and heard him wail in pain, and his body landed against the machine making a loud "ka-klunk" sound, shaking the contents inside the machine. Frank heard his bones ache underneath his fingers, and Frank grabbed the boy's neck shirt and pulled him off, feeling his shirt starting to rip, and then Gene laid into him good. Gene slammed his boulder fist into his pillowy stomach with such intensity that he knocked the wind out of him. The boy gasped and began gagging uncontrollably, but this was the perfect time to beat him senseless. Frank let him go, and threw him and he fell to the floor as if he was dead weight. He crash-landed on his side like a diseased baby that was left inside a garbage can.

The Disintegrating Bloodline

"Damn!" A few spectators burst out, and another said, "That shit has got to hurt son!" "Son" was black slang for pal or friend, and there were a few black kids to see and hear and groan from the sound Gene's fist smashed into his body.

"Fuck yeah!" The voices moved closer, and this is when the crowd started to move around them in droves. A few groans came from the student spectators who had felt his pain, after Frank dislocated his jaw, as blood began to ooze from the corner and treaded down his lower lip.

"You like taking people's shit! You like being a tough guy!" Frank yelled, and saw that the kids were starting to layer around them, and he knew what they wanted. So he decided to give them what they wanted.

But before he continued further damage onto the boy he leaned over, and began to search his pants for A.J.'s clip. The boy, who was rising off the ground with his bare palm he pushed his hand away, but Frank met his resilience with a swift forward punch to his ribcage, sending him groaning to the ground with pain. Sticking his hand inside his pocket, he could feel in his fingers some lint, and a greasy kind of oil sticking to his fingertips. But when he searched deeper his fingers came across leather, and the bills felt like dirty feathers from a ink soaked quill. Frank clutched it, and then pulled his hand out of his pocket.

Some people had laughed, but the remainder of them kept silent.

"A.J." Frank saw the faded gold letters, and he knew this had to be his. After he stuffed it in his pockets, they decided to give the crowd what they wanted. Gene used the souls of his Nike shoes to stamp on the top of the boy's head. He moved around like a boxer, and then stamped into his nose, sending gushes of blood across the floor, until they heard a loud *CRAAACK*, and that got a response out of all the spectators, that continued to grow with curious and terrified eyes.

"Awww shit!" A scared and amazed white boy yelped, and smiled with scared amazement. They weren't really excited from the blood flying out of his mouth, but embraced it with a perverse love, letting the sounds desensitize what there senses could take—letting everything roll of them.

"You like that shit! I don't see you fucking laughing now!" Frank hoped that he liked it, and kicked him in the stomach just to see him groan, but he couldn't groan nor think from the pain he was in numbing his bones. But then the fight was broken off, too soon for violence freaks to get there high and too late for the other bystanders to get there hooks in, which really wasn't much of a fight. Frank and Gene were torn away by two teachers to the vice-principals office. When they forced them down the long hallway Frank smirked with a proud feeling that he accomplished his order, and he did it well—almost too well.

Frank smiled, not even breathing hard enough to be out of breath. He saw the blood running down his lips and inside his mouth touching his tongue, and one could say that in this time—they thought that he wasn't breathing.

A.J. saw the two, pants partly covered in blood, and he wondered in his head about that smirk, what was he telling him. He turned toward him and said, "What's going to happen to them?"

Chris, with the most relaxed face, replied, and his green eyes meant it. "They are going to the Vice-Principal's office to talk."

A.J. nodded, and then laid back in his seat, watching the crowd dissipating into different directions as A.J. saw the boy, who had obviously fainted, being carried by two teachers on his shoulders. He cringed from the blood, but knew that the kid deserved it.

"Deserved to be beaten and his nose smashed for all to see?" A.J. thought, knowing that he had heard the cracking sound all the way to the B cafeteria, but then he did not care about this boy any longer, and smiled, grateful for what had happened. "Anyone that doesn't listen to me, should die." He thought, and wiped away his smile.

After the fight, Gene Dov and Frank Latitante were sitting across from the vice principal, Mr. O Donnel, with his long Irish face and paper white skin, who was looking over their files on his computer screen. After taking a look at their past misdeeds he closed the files and said in a clam way, avoiding any formalities. "How good to see you again!"

The two did not say a word, but he had to ask them what the hell was going on. He looked at Gene apathetically, and he could feel the lack of it resonating from Frank as well. "You know you broke his nose, dislocated his jaw, and almost killed the poor bastard!"

Gene said nothing, and then the Vice-Principal turned his attention toward them expelling his anger about the situation.

Mr. O'Donnel tried to break their icy silence by thawing out there block of icy nerves. "I could expel you two, or worse, send you to jail."

Frank smirked, and then Gene started to laugh as well, and deep down they knew that he couldn't do anything to them. "What's so funny! What did he ever do to you?"

"He offended us with his bad taste of pants." Gene said through his chuckles, getting to his patience.

Frank scoffed and added sounded a little more sincere, "I think it was about a pair of socks." The only thing Frank did was smile, but Gene couldn't help but smirk.

"Ah," Mr. O' Donnel shot a sarcastic remark, "So *Chris Mangini* sent you to beat him up over a pair of socks. Do I need to bring him in?"

These two knew everything about this man, all his vices, all his ins-and-outs, and all his personal secrets. If they wanted to get this guy early, then it wouldn't be too much fun but they weren't going to let him have the upper hand and try and involve Chris in anything.

"Listen!" Gene said, "You know you can't expel us. You know you can't pin anything on Chris. We keep everyone in line and you know it! Half of what you do is sit behind that desk and look at child pornography. I bet that's what you have on half of your hard drive, right? You wouldn't want people to find that out, and ruin your reputation would you?" He smiled with such deviance, revealing all of his teeth for him to see what he knew about him.

Then Frank interjected, devilishly. "They also wouldn't like to hear about your underage prostitute who had to get an abortion, that you paid for, because *you* did not want her to have the child. Did I forget that you *paid* for it as well?"

O'Donnell shook his head, clicking his teeth, knowing that everything they said was true. He saw his deviant all-knowing smile reflecting the truth of what went on inside his mind. He had vices, but if this got out it could mean prison time, and even if he got off, he would never recover from the mental torture that the media would do to his family. If he knew what Chris Mangini had done for him in the past, this would be a favor for him. He just gave them a three-day suspension, and told them that he would call his parents, but he knew he wouldn't; O'Donnell valued his life and the life of his *own* children too much to endanger them with this petty bullshit. With that business taken care of, he returned to his child pornography file. Clicking on the video icon, he deleted all of his files.

At that moment his phone rang, and the principal's voice quietly spoke, "Is everything all right?"

"Yes sir. It was just a stupid fight. I gave them three days suspension."

"Who were they?" The principal asked.

"Gene Dov and Frank Latitante." Mr. O'Donnell pronounced Frank's last name *LA-TEE-TAAAN-TE*, and Gene's *Dovvvv* because he was Irish and the words couldn't hide his New York accent.

A long moment of silence passed through the phone. Only the Principal knew who they were and everything seemed tense at that moment, "You took care of them?"

"Yes sir," Mr. O'Donnell replied with a comfortable sigh that made his blood circulate through his system, "everything's taken care of."

"Good," a long sigh blared into Mr. O'Donnell's ear, "then that's that."

Mr. O'Donnell looked over the two folders that had pictures and a list of the cirrocumuli of what crimes the two boys did, and knew these weren't just the only students, but he did not touch them, or keep them back. They had more offenses then their grades showed. "F's and D's…but they are slick… too slick." He scrolled past their list of failed classes one last time in the celled row, and knew that they more than capable of murdering him and getting away with it. "Too slick!"

"That's that then." Mr. O'Donnell closed the two folders, and hung up the phone.

With that he felt at ease, but knew that he had to let them go, because he knew he owed them. Stashing the digital folders back into the icon drawers, thankfully, he went back into his digital trashcan. He looked around him, feeling watched even though his door was closed. As the fear fizzled from his system he dragged a digital line over the various files, and with one click of the mouse moved all the child pornography back across his desktop screen. He placed them back into the files he had under "personal" and opened one of the files.

He began to watch a rather older looking boy molesting a young underage girl. His penis became erect, and he knew that masturbating right now wasn't good, but his vices were powerful than his own mind. He closed the curtains to the windows, and unbuckling his belt, the zipper came down next, and he began to masturbate to the sounds of the large boy spreading the young girls labia apart with her large box cutting penis.

The next day came, the classes were the same but in the halls, the climate had changed considerably. The eyes of all the students (even some kids that he did not even care to look at) were falling upon him like November rain. The large, oversized black gang members with their oddly oversized heads that wore their red gang bandannas in their back pockets cocked their lazy eyes at him with a smug look slouching against the egg white wall. Then there were big-breasted cheerleaders, black and white, creamy skins and beat red freckled cheeks stared at him with an incestuous sexy stare that said he was the next demigod. With young girls with wet lips, their curiosity always murmured questions like "I wonder how big his dick is" and "I want to jump all over him" crossed their mind, and felt that this fantasy might be coming true. A lot of people were thinking, eyes slanted and lips pouted, "What's so important about him?" and A.J. didn't know what they thought about him. And he didn't really care, even though it did embarrass him at first to think what other people were thinking.

He turned, leaving their prodding grey eyes behind him and left the English, History, and Science halls for the rest of the spectators, who never had the guts to talk to Chris Mangini. He pitied them because they envied him, and even his pity was less than he could do for them. He knew he wasn't God, but he had come to the conclusion that Chris Mangini was God.

As A.J. passed the library he saw out of the corner of his eye the abandoned senior courtyard. It's desolate surroundings looked eerie knowing and so distant to him, and for some reason, he knew that he was not going to have the privilege to sit in the Senior Courtyard, ever. He walked out of the hallway, and looked at the bus ramp where Frank and Gene went and destroyed that boy's face.

"The bloods gone, but the memory is still there!" A.J. thought knowing that no one will ever forget that, and he hoped that the beating seared their memories. He wondered what it was like actually beating the boy up. He knew that Gene and Frank did so he wouldn't have to. It burned inside him to know that they didn't do worse to him, but he was lucky they could embarrass him the way he had done to him. Turning away he felt that this was such familiar territory, and how everyone sat at the tables with such a carefree attitude. When he looked again, he saw some people were staring at him—staring with resentment. When he looked at Chris's table he saw Chris motioned for A.J.'s presence. A.J. smirked, and then went over to the table, ignoring the envious screw faces, and sat in the chair.

Chris's green eyes were full of fire when he saw A.J. walking with a chipper smile as his dark black hair glinted in the sunlight, revealing the small brown patches of hair.

"Hey A.J!" Chris said, and then shook his hand with a mighty, earth shaking force.

"What's up?" A.J. said, as he laid his backpack on the ground, and then patted his back like his friends had done. Chris smirked, not knowing how to take this pat, and rubbed his hand along his khaki jeans. But before A.J. pulled out his lunch, he said with a wondering thought, "Where are Gene and Frank? Did they get suspended?"

Chris's eyebrows raised, and then said with a serious tone, "Are you recording this?"

A.J. was taken back by this and shook his head, "No!"

Chris's sarcastic voice came back and said, "Then why do you need to know?"

A.J.'s shoulders raised in confusion, and then he said, "Just trying to make conversation that's all."

Chris laughed, and nodded, "I know what you want!" Chris reached into his pockets, searching deep within his pockets that contained secrets that no one knew of, and maybe no one ever knew—like the dark abyss. In that instant, he found it, passed all the secrets, he held it in front of him.

A.J.'s eyes shined brighter than any other flawed diamond, and saw in his hand his money clip, just like he said he would get back for him. What amazed A.J. was the fact that he stuck to his promise, and seeing it was the most unbelievable thing to him, it was almost astounding, but rather simple when someone finally got something done. Only he did not want to get in trouble, but then he didn't leave anything to doubt.

But when he held and inspected the clip, the leather had been cleaned from Steve's dirty fingerprints, and the old bills were gone, but were replaced with what he had seen were new bills. When he looked at it again, he saw that the numbers were not one, five, or even ten, it was a hundred dollar bill.

"A hundred dollar bill! What the hell?" A.J. thought and then lowered the clip underneath the table. Releasing the latch, he counted the fresh bills and saw that there were two of them in it.

"What the hell is...two hundred dollars doing in here?" He said, almost choking on his own tongue before he finished his sentence.

Chris smirked, and then said indifferently, "I guess he left his money in there."

"No man," A.J. said, not falling into his trap, "that redneck can't make this much money. I can't take it." He held it out for him, and Chris waved it away, but A.J. was not going to give up yet, because his conscience forced him to reject his kindness.

"I don't want it!" A.J. whined, and felt the tension growing between them.

Chris was irritated, but did not yell at him. "Did you want it in the hands of that redneck prick? Now, he's not ever going to bug you again, because *we* got you your clip back. And if he insulted you, he insulted me. I can't have my friends insulted."

A.J. lowered his head, but then felt Chris punching his left arm. "Don't put your head down! Look at people in the eye when you're talking to them. Now, just put that inside your pocket, and think of it as a favor."

A.J. nodded, looking at the crisp dollar bills, feeling the clip burning a hole in his hand, and eating away at his conscience every second he was holding it. So, he took his advice, and stuck it in his pocket.

After that, they fell silent. For fifteen minutes, which was already half of the lunch period, Chris was eyeing the lunchroom, studying everyone in the distance while A.J. was attacking his sandwich with little to no remorse, and drank his regular Coke-Cola with kickback leisure.

"I want to ask you something." Chris said, turning his body sideways, and facing him with that warrior like pose—as if he was in the killing position.

A.J. turned, with his sandwich in his hand, and some crumbs on his lips, and he brushed it away with the back of his right hand.

"I want you to join our ranks." Chris voice was like hot slugs leaving the barrel of a gun, and hit A.J. quicker than the sandwich hit his stomach.

"I think you have a lot of strength, and I want to test you out to see if you are one of us. If that's all right with you, we can talk more, but if you don't, we can't be seen talking anymore. I don't want you mistaken as some trouble maker." Chris turned back into his seat and let A.J. have time to think about his proposition.

"Holy shit!" A.J. thought and turned away, knowing that if he looked at Chris any longer, he would feel violated because he knew what he was offering was far surpassing his wildest wet dreams.

"Do I get left behind in the herd or do I separate from the pack?" A.J. had a lot on his plate already—but A.J. had secretly wished for this opportunity a long time ago—

since his freshman year. As he liked to think, "I have choice, and the choice is mine to decide." He knew what his answer was.

"Yes, I want to run with you guys." A.J. said with skittering anxiety. Chris nodded accepting his answer.

"So fucking be it!" Chris thought, knowing that he had not forced him to come along, he breathed easily, and then he spied the clock. The little hand was travelling toward the black **12**, as it became **11:55** the bell rang, and everyone heard its dinging, ostracizing call as they rose out of their seats. Now they could run to their classes or casually take a brisk walk.

Time seemed to move around them, passing by there bodies and travelling through their ears. While that happened, it was as if everything was silent, everything had kept playing like a loud musical.

"Go on," Chris said, waving him away, "Get to class. I will tell Krazy that you are a new recruit and to treat you like family."

A.J. rose out of his seat, not asking any questions, he slid his backpack through his arms and flopped it against his back. A.J. asked, "Aren't you going to show me?"

Chris laughed, and with certain graceful ease proclaimed with a wave of his free hand, "No. I can't tomorrow, but be prepared, and be open. Because tomorrow you are going to see the other side of this school."

A.J. nodded as he fixed the strap around his other shoulder, A.J. felt oddly detached by this news, but excited about the endless possibilities he was going to encounter. "I guess we won't see each other for a while."

Chris just smirked, and said with a wild certainty. "I guess we won't."

At that moment, A.J. walked away from the table feeling the whiff of a new life, fresh air, and another opportunity from his companion, friend, and Captain, Chris Mangini.

Chapter II:

"The Protection Run"

All Thursday night A.J. fantasized in his room when he wasn't worried morning about his expected test. Would he be initiated like the old days, or will it be some test of endurance? He fantasized so hard that if he thought about it any longer he would bust a nut from anticipation—like a long climax porno scene before busting a nut on a woman's breasts—but girls were the last thing on his mind. When all the girls that he knew were experimental drug users, he did not want to deal with a clinging, isolated, naïve head-case.

As A.J. walked through the halls, he felt the crowds' eyes hounding, descending on him like vultures ready to tear his flesh apart. He wasn't going to make it easy for them to spot him.

At that moment, he bolted through the line of kids pushing large and skinny kids out of the way, and even some people followed A.J. in a line like a long caterpillar. He speeded though a crowd of black students without saying "excuse me" like he was a unconscious ghost. A.J. Pushed past their large odiferous armpits, a large whiff of heavy cologne and sweat jumped off the black students' bodies and into the other students throats. It felt like he was in a gas chamber of sweet toxic death that smelled of heavy unburied carrion, and that smell, stained his narrow mind of what could possibly stink.

Even if there was no one in the hall, he felt that putrid stench of BO clinging to the walls like a plague, and infecting his organs with little restriction. He felt like he could never escape the students intoxicating odors, and images of concentration camp refugees peeling skins off their orange bodies ran through his head. But he felt free enough to escape it, and as he pushed through the next swarm of kids, he felt invincible, forcing the kids to depart like Moses and the Red Sea. But in all actuality, he was using his hands to part them like water bugs traveling down a small ravine.

A.J. enraged half the massive sweat stained congregation of students that blocked A.J. and his heart beat against the edge of his chest and his heart palpitated as if he hadn't had a cigarette for more than three days. But his own sweat formed (probably from the affect of being surrounded by other unclean constituents) and began to form at his large hairy underarms and his sweat traveled down his large body, and made a small dab mark against the side of his gray shirt. But it was a Friday morning before the first football game of the season, and everyone *at least not as much* as A.J. was, which was as much as a convulsing dead body. But A.J.'s emotions were stronger than his tiny brain could imagine, and a whole stadium full of kids could not detain his own happiness.

Once he made it down the hall he saw a few Senior's in the courtyard sitting with their lunches across the table with the wind blowing their hair into a frizzy or sending their bushy hair into a dance. The library he used sometimes (in a age of technological bullshit), which served as a safe haven for people that were on the run from the Assistant Principal, and could hide behind a book—even if it bored them to death. But when A.J. was in the library, it was a new experience every time. As the wind was blowing in the commons, throwing up the leaves in all directions in the air he saw that all the tables were desolate except for the third from the left, located exactly right in the middle. It was almost like an wood grain thrown that Chris Mangini had stolen in a *coup de tat* so that his friends, business partners, and his enemies could see him sitting behind his open table. A.J. imagined him a methodical despot king that could hoard anything, and across the commons—he was the king of all the land—and his thrown was securely settled in blood.

A.J. he saw, in the clear distance, Krazy—whose lips were cold and lifeless—pains that had formed into large untreatable bruises that made his purple veins pulsate painfully down his neck—arching over the seat leaning against the table with an uncomfortable grudge.

A.J. approached the table, and said, "What up?"

Krazy just looked up at him and glared with flaring suspicion as he said, "*U* the one that Chris told me to wait for?"

A.J. saw his large purplish bruises and felt that it was pulsating against his cheeks shaking A.J. off his readily tacked down thoughts. "Yea, where's Chris?"

Krazy, looking left and right for a lot of odd particular reason, "He thought that you should learn this without his help." He faced A.J., and looked more relaxed than he had been a second ago continued—disturbed by his own peaceful thoughts.

"You know," removing his elbows off the table, he then began to crack his index finger. "To give you a," Krazy then moved on toward his middle finger, bending it backwards, it gave off a loud *POP*, "good representation of how we do things." Before he could even breathe, he moved onto the next finger. A.J. couldn't stand this, because it was like scraping his fingernails across a chalkboard to him. Like someone that was eating cockroaches—it was just gross—and A.J.'s entire body cringed from every twig snapping second. A.J. closed his eyes and blocked out the cracking sounds as if he was a little boy pushing out a bad dream and opened his eyes, gritting the words on his teeth. "Yeah. I guess so."

Krazy turned and with that deathly derelict stare, "Well, don't get too excited, because now you start your training." His apathy was nothing short of a clever con man, and it was a good quality. "Maybe you were lead here for some far off reason, but the boss said you might prove to be valuable to us. I tend to disagree, but I'm not in charge."

A.J. was astonished that this kid was saying *anything*, and A.J. was also stunned that he heard this ruffian say any intelligent words. But he didn't see a ruffian now, and if he was loyal to Chris, he needed to follow the chain of command. "Nothing comes free," A.J. thought, ruefully, but got over the whole authority thing.

"So, we are going on what we like to call a," Krazy curled his pinkie and ring finger on the inside of his palm, extending out the index and his middle finger making a bunny ear, "a protection run." A.J. knew that this was a way for someone to make a quote, watching him crush his fingers together as he said in an informal "know it all" way. He lowered his hand as he continued talking. Even though he was being serious, A.J. couldn't help but chuckle from his dry sense of humor.

Krazy shook his head, making his large bloated bruises seem alive as if blood was filled in a soft socket on his face. "A protection run means that we go around collecting money that people owe us. We do this every two weeks, and everyone that knows will be waiting for us. Now, what Chris wants you to do is to collect the money that people owe us. The people we are dealing with are the Preps, the Outcasts, and the Bloods."

A.J.'s eyes narrowed with confusion, and then said with perplexity in his voice. "What do you mean by *Bloods*?" Even though he felt like he knew from somewhere in his past—no his own home life—he saw this hand gesture, but he didn't know what he was applying the gesture to, and would let it be.

Krazy's blank, soul sucking, stare began to petrify the living daylights out of A.J. so much that his commanding eyes could have told him to prepare an open apology for that piece of miscommunication, but then Krazy's deathly stare into a devious grin, and at that moment he gave a swiping motion horizontally along his face, and smiled, "You understand now?"

A.J., whose brain had not been properly running at the moment let out a understanding, yet confused laugh. A.J. finally came across the hint that Krazy was making a racial gesture that white or of European descent did in his parent's small town of Aliquippa whenever they were talking about black people, and that swiping gesture required no explanation. A.J. didn't know how Krazy would know that, but he decided to ask him anyway.

"How did you know about that?" A.J.'s smile stretched to both sides of his face, undaunted by his ugly features, but totally taken in by Krazy's smile.

Krazy smirked, and his eyes glinted with appreciation then said, "I know a lot of things."

After A.J. chuckled, and what seemed like a happy moment ended when Krazy rose up from his seat, his body possessed by his practical mind, and his matter of fact tone said, "But time is against us, and we need to hurry."

At that moment, A.J. was feeling anxious and ready to leave himself, but his legs weren't ready for him to move. He might have just blamed it on laziness as he thrusted his back into the air and pushed his chair back against the wall with the joints of his knees. His bones creaked with lack of coordination as he stretched his arms out above his head. He silently groaned as all the connecting air bubbles creaked up and down like a cat's spine being cracked in two.

"Man. What are you," Krazy looked at him with disgust, "an old man or something? You sound like you're going to break your back."

A.J. turned and chuckled as he cracked one more air pocket in his back, surprisingly enough scared Krazy, as A.J. said, "Nope. I can break the air bubbles in my back, just as you did in your fingers." He lowered his hands, closing the B.O. that radiated from his arms like shit out of a dragon's ass—which was a smell that could kill a Doberman—and then sighed from the relaxation his body was feeling when Krazy's stare that he had seen before returned. "Let's go."

As the two pushed the seats underneath the table, A.J. was about to pick up his backpack; Krazy waved his hand in an orderly, and pleasurable fashion. "No one's going to mess with it. This place is like Iraq, if you take something from us, we slice their hands off, or do worse, understand!" A.J. saw pleasure in Krazy's twisted eyes, and all that A.J. could do was trust him, because if he trusted Chris Mangini, then he could trust Krazy. A.J. put faith into his words, and there was nothing he could do—or say to reject—his word. He and Krazy left the table, and what A.J. once was back there too.

When A.J. and Krazy left Chris's thrown unwatched, the students in Commons A were all quiet—their footsteps steps echoed in the commons, like a drip of water falling into a cavernous well. As they walked around the brick table with small swivel seats where ten to eleven kids were dining on tacos that dripped feces and cafeteria Spaghetti covered in simmering month old sauce. Even if cockroaches were walking across the table, and a hammer smashed and sprinkled with glitter it in front of them, it would not have bothered them. As they dined on there shitty lunches, the crowd watched them with insidiously scornful eyes that ejected hate from their opened pore framed heads. The next hall on the right was another way straight shot into Commons B, but there was another larger space that if you were going to go through that, that would lead you straight toward the entrance/exit doors to the technical center.

Only as they passed another entrance toward another line to a cafeteria waiting for the large, STD filled lunch ladies served them miserable concoctions the cafeteria could pull out of their big fat-asses. The students viciously tapped their feet in a disheartened beat, but their irritated stance begged to be fed—and they stood for no other reason except to do this useless act of feeding.

A.J. could not stand these Neanderthal Cro-Magnon creatures, sinking low to the ground, wanting nothing else in their lives except food, a wife (or woman), and a job. A.J. knew that it wasn't a bad thing to want the simple pleasures in life, but A.J. also knew that these kids did not know the difference between a woman and a *skank,* misconstruing friendship and hormonal lust.

That's how A.J. knew how to deal with the simple heads, but he knew what a woman was, and he did not respect whores. But, even though there were some that were cool, he had to tolerate the presence of a whore or a *skank* for a long time. The reason why he held such hate for whores was because one had come between his father and mother's relationship. He knew not to spoil a good thing with uncomfortable news, even if it spurned his soul to think about.

When they passed the small lunchroom hallway by twenty seconds, Krazy grabbed A.J. by the shirt and tugged on his shirt and A.J. looked down at his hands, and then began to yell, "Hey, what are you…" and landed against the tile wall stand with a solemn *THUD*.

Krazy's grip tightened when he tried to speak after he pulled him to the side, but laid a hand against his mouth. A.J. didn't know why he had been pushed back, and Krazy's long fingernails were digging into his skin forcibly like an eagle's talons clenching into a small prey. Lowering his head so that he could whisper to A.J. on the sly, "There's where you have to go, to the Preps. You see them?"

"What do I need to do? Are they going to get hostile?" A.J.'s voice sounded different sounding incredibly frightening and worried, as if an incredibly disastrous situation was about to unfold. Even though A.J. did not realize his own voice, his own mind was just spouting off at the mouth. As Krazy's head moved side to side, his purple face became relaxed as his bruises seemed to fluctuate and come alive.

"Just go and get our money. They shouldn't give you a hard time." Krazy then moved to A.J.'s left side and laid his shoulder next to the grainy brick pillar. He scratched his cotton shirt, looking down at the ground, feeling fulfilled by being able to teach this boy the tricks of the trade.

"Okay. I'll be back." A.J. had become relaxed and transfixed in his hatred as he moved away utterly confused as if he had been drunk and then started toward the table, with a fist clenched together making his hate pulsating in his veins like a untrustworthy drug, ready to explode.

A.J. stared with naivete like a newborn that had seen their first light, and his naïve sense of perception told him that hate was the right way. The Preps were sitting at the second long table with three large jocks with their long shirts covering their ashy elbows, and their shirts tucked inside there pants making them look even more ridiculous, even more embarrassing was how it did not complement their gargantuan bodies. As if they could hide there large beer bellies with their dark red shirts that contained beer more than it did human blood. But it was the cheerleaders that made the group a little more alluring to the human eye (no fucking kidding), and A.J. saw a few cheerleaders that had caught his eye. The only thing that he had seen were the legs, smooth, no stubble's, and this made his penis tingle. Then after it tingled, his penis pressed against his underwear and pushing against his pants.

But then a cool, deceiving voice whispered, *"these people are not like him. They don't live in a slowly disintegrating suburb that is falling on its last leg. They don't know what it means to do hard work, if it wasn't handed to them. They don't know what its like to live in a house that wasn't built more than two years ago. They don't know what it's like to live with little to no money. They don't…"*

All these realities that they didn't know or comprehend spurned his ever beating heart, and he almost popped a blood vessel contemplating on others blissful ignorance. After his anger spell subdued, a pinging pain began ringing inside his head. But something in his mind began to strangely click. He was beginning to identify with a feeling that that he had always felt, but his emotions never wanted to acknowledge; it was hatred. He hated them with all of his being.

Jessica Albini, a beautiful blonde/brunette bombshell that had the most delicate skin, and curves to drive every man crazy when she walked past was sitting her perfect heart shaped butt in a glum, uncomfortable position. Even though she had naturally large round breasts for a girl of seventeen and was virtually unaffected by pimples or acne, she should have been happy about her beautiful disposition. But her beauty could hide her sadness in her small body. With the promise of the other boy's hand made the other cheerleaders jealous, and her dominatrix attitude was the reason why she could rob them of their money, and send them home empty handed. But, all that changed when she met her last boyfriend, Alan Firenze.

He was a common cake eater (who couldn't even be considered Italian) who like any pigheaded man treated women like any other objects of pleasure, and she was questioning why she had seen anything in him in the first place. He had left an impermeable scar trailing down the back of her right thigh. It almost looked like a dog had dug its nails into her skin after jumping up on her too many times, but this was not the first scar that she had to bear from the dumb brute. Alan seduced her to his bedroom one night while partially intoxicated when Alan's friends jumped her out of nowhere like horny animals all accosting her body, ripping her dress and rubbing there large hands up and down her body as they threw her onto his bed.

When she tried to resist, their large hands tightened around her skinny arms and legs as she continually bucked against there tight ashy grip. But, then she saw her boyfriend standing over her crotch, and her body thought he was going to rape her, but Jessica was ultimately wrong. Alan, with a sick sadistic grin, pulled up her shirt to reveal her small supple belly. Some of his friends laughed as some leaned their heads over her belly—while she was still in their grip—trailed their tongues across and inside her belly button, exciting and scaring her at the same time. Jessica thrust them off her stomach with a flick of her hip, as Alan's grin turned sour as he held a cheap switchblade that he bought from a Haitian boy that got it in Queens. The blade was peering out of its compartment like a sea creature peering out of the murky water, and it gleamed with such brightness that it frightened and attracted her with a raw unguarded pleasure.

Her eyes widened as he began to straddle her down to the bed with his hairy curled legs. Jessica wanted to cry but she couldn't, and all she could do was sob tears as he began to cut along her belly. He wasn't poking the knife into her skin he was trailing the blade just hard enough so that she could have a scar, "to always remember him by," he whispered to her as the long mark began to slowly bleed on her tight belly. Jessica didn't know if it was the fact that he couldn't get his penis hard, but the pain was so excruciating that she had urinated on his bed, and the urine sent the other boys scattering in disgust. He had left a long scar that traveled from the left side of her stomach past her rib cage. She was not the one to call the ambulance, and she did not tell the cops who had done the crime.

But before her stitches were taken out, she broke it off with Alan that very week, blocking all his phone calls and his unexpected arrivals to the house. And the leader of the Preps banished him from their group for good. As a matter of fact, this was the anniversary of the first month they hadn't spoken for the past two years.

She had tried to forget about the whole thing—completely put it out of her mind as if it was some failed Cesarean section, but she knew he had taken something else away from this drab situation. That was her happiness, her innocence, and worse, she felt like her soul had left too.

The scar would never fully heal, and that was another reason why she wanted to be single, to avoid the pain of opening up to another person, to never show her naked body with her scar to anyone *again*. Only she felt that her promise wouldn't last too long with the way her depression always caught up with her need for that attention, the need to be wanted, and that was not a bad thing but when she looked to her left, she saw something that kindled her nestled curiosity.

A boy, with scruffy hair, and a medium round head, a short pointed nose was standing at the edge of the table and called out to them in a resounding laid back voice, "What's up?"

Then a boy, who was sitting next to Adam said, "What the fuck do you want?"

Jessica shook her head in disgust as she saw the boy's face frown with complexity, but he then replied with coolness as he retorted, "It's none of your damn business what I want with you. I need to speak with your boss, Adam Reoni. It appears that you owe us money. I'm here to collect."

The cheerleaders looked at each other as their ears were open to a new found curiosity with there ears pricked and there mouths open like dogs in heat as they listened to what was going on, but Jessica knew that this was her catch.

"Young, rebellious, tough, and had a rugged bulky appeal." His broad shoulders made her eyes traipse off to his pants, noticing his bulge the corner of his jeans.

Jessica averted her curious eyes and saw that her friends were no different than panting dogs with adrenaline pumping urge to hump his leg. She would make her move in due time, because she knew that none of her friends would go beyond there own little fantasy realm, and she saw that he looked like a rather normal person, but that remained to be seen.

Adam Reoni looked at A.J. with his large brown eyes as he extended his open hand—his triceps bulged out from the sides of his arm—towards him, and said with a kind of compelling persuasiveness that made him stand out. "I'm Adam Reoni." When he looked at him, he was afraid because he felt some great disturbance coming from him, and knew that he was here to *seriously* collect Chris's money.

A.J. almost forgot his manners as he put out his hand, and then put his cold wet palm against his warm palm, and his thick fingers wrapped around his hand.

"I'm A.J." When they shook, A.J. almost felt that his whole body was being shaken by Adam's unseemingly large hand. A.J. pulled his own as they didn't break eye contact for a second, as A.J. felt that Adams gorilla body pushed out as if he was on steroids that made his body seem bloated with super-human strength. After they made each other's acquaintance, they let their hands go, and the table fell silent. Even though the ice had been broken, the hatred was still toiling with A.J.'s emotions.

"Well, *A.J.* Don't mind this asshole, he may look smart, but he's as dull as a rusty nail when it comes to manners. Are you new, I haven't seen you before?"

A.J. smirked and shrugged his shoulders, knowing the rituals of introduction was all bullshit (to see if he was a new student) as he said, "I just started today actually. But I'm just here to get the money so…if we could just get down to business, because I'm in a rush."

"What are you?" Adam asked, "some kind of speed demon? A pill popper?" Adam's hand slowly delved down into his pocket, looking for his money as he shook his bald head in a disapproving shake. His deadpan tone bordered on sarcasm, but to a person that was possessed by anger, violence was always an option when the brain's synapses shut down. A.J. would have seen red, but all he could see was a man with blood and tissue that he felt could tear through with his bare incisors.

"*Speed* as in the drug *Speed*." A.J. was uneasy by his smart aleck remark. His hatred started to rise again, and he felt that if Adam Reoni didn't follow what they were supposed to do, things were going to get real ugly for them. And even though his mind was telling him not to act on his emotions, his nestled ego was starting to make his strength become a possibility. His pride was on the line, and only a second's insult would send this situation into a shit storm depending on the strength of his anger. Everything around A.J. seemed to quiet down in the commons, and a eerie feeling that he was alone in his anger.

"Yeah," Adam held a long thick envelope underneath the table, and then held it out in front of him, and eyed him as if he was a dog, "cause you are acting like you are a fucking druggee."

"I don't do drugs." A.J. said with brash honesty, and his direct style could make people think otherwise, "nor would I ever touch them. You might want to get your friend off the *roids* though. His pimples are starting to show." He pointed toward the boy, and then everyone saw the boy that had made fun of him. Obviously the boy had been embarrassed from the crime as his cheeks blushed bright red as his muscles shook with rambunctious intensity, "Fuck you, man."

A.J.'s mind heard this boy's remark, and he met the boy's eyes head on knowing this boy was a punk, a stupid heartless little pill popping shit that could be intimidated like a fickle young girl when she found out her birth control and pills had not indeed protected her. A.J. stared with wide eyes burning with the hatred that had been stirring inside his heart, but had then made his face rumble, and if he couldn't control his anger, he didn't know what would happen. Oh how he hated him at that moment, and he never took his maddened eyes away from his sight, and A.J. dug his fingernails into his palm to stop himself.

"Maybe you weren't listening." A.J. said, taking in a deep breath and letting it out of his system with a laugh, the words flew out of his voice with such scorn that A.J. did not even realize that he was possessed. Then the conversations began to resurface around A.J., as he continued his assault against the dumb dim-witted jock.

"I don't give a fuck what you think or feel right now you *smack head*." He didn't really know if he was a drug addict or not, but he needed to make an example out of him.

The jock's face grew sour with his lips pushing downwards, and A.J. kept after him, leaning forward as if he was going to jump over the table. "And guess what? I don't give a rat's ass, but I'm sure on the hairs of your mother's cunt that you do not want to know me. So, don't try to think of something to say, and I didn't stutter if you didn't hear me so keep your mouth shut if you don't have anything to regret." A.J.'s words and presence was definitely felt throughout the table, and everyone was aware of the violence he was capable of commanding.

At that moment, the boy who had thought he had been rewarded with a comeback had been easily put down by a rather uncommon retort, and A.J. spoke with a smooth clear diction that derailed the jock's mental tracks.

A.J. was taking deep breaths of relief—his body and mind in control of his surroundings when he pulled his body away from the table. He saw Adam holding the money, more like palming it with his other hand so no one else could see it. A.J. eyed it with deep fascination, and then said, "Well, I guess

I'll be on my way then." Adam looked at him, and as he watched him snatch and flow out of his hands like skin lotion. Adam knew that he had been pissed, and even under that cool exterior, he could sense a dark cloud glowing around him as he watched A.J. stuff the money into his pocket, and patted it to make sure it was firmly inside his pocket.

When A.J. motioned to Krazy with a nod, leaving their sight, Adam looked at the hot headed boy, and chastised him with a cool warning that if he ever did that again he would cut his throat if he pulled that kind of stunt again. He assured him that he would do it too, if Chris didn't catch up with him first. The boy did not reply, and when that was settled, everything returned back to normal.

But a question was impregnated in his mind, and began to grow on him like a fungus. "For someone that was *new*, he sure didn't act like he was *new*." He didn't know the answer to this question, but he would keep an eye on his own business.

After the momentary silence, they started talking again, very quietly, but then very loudly so that they could be heard—without appearing intimidated—throughout the Commons. Laughing from some not really witty but not really funny jokes, and talking about some unimportant issue that was going on in their lives. Only Jessica was the only one that was silent and thinking curiously about when she would meet this *A.J.* again.

Her insides were passionately tingling from A.J.'s handsome physique, as she wanted to get up and follow him, and get inside his pants. Actually, she remembered that they were having there first game of the season, and there was enough buzz going on about it all day she might as well puke if she heard any more about it. At that moment, everything in her life that had been turned upside down had taken an unexpected upside—and she felt herself smiling, sending all her bad memories away if just for a eternal minute. She wasn't excited about the game of course, she was happy that she could recover from her tumultuous experience, and found some peace and happiness finally.

Jessica decided that if he would be at the game tonight she would talk to the boy who gave her newfound peace, and her smile withdrew from her face, turning back into that same down-and-out look she always had on.

"What's wrong?" A girl by the name of Catherine Redding said to her, wondering with a curious glowing in her small face of spastic joy.

Jessica looked at her, and gave her a warm, unfading smile. "Nothing." Then a great sigh blew out of her, and then said with reassurance. "Nothing at all." She turned her head, and then pretending to look away, she smiled again, hoping and longing for the chance to see the new boy again. "A.J."

The Disintegrating Bloodline

She thought leaning her head forward, and started to eat her lunch, feeling satisfied with herself again to eat solid food again.

A.J. and Krazy were already down the hallway that was a straight shot into Commons B, a rough area where the Social Outcasts hung there hats and people who were affiliated with no one at all rested, but not in peace. With their money tucked safely away, and with their next stop not too far away Krazy decided to make some small talk with A.J. before they entered another world that was unfamiliar to them.

"So, how does it feel?" Krazy's eyebrows rose with a kind of perverse excitement that should have meant something more sexual, but A.J. knew what he was referring to— the undeniable, heart thumping, lust empowering, *power*. He felt great, and he wouldn't try to contain his excitement.

"Yeah. I kind of felt a jolt running through me. Like I was on fire, and every second I spoke, I felt *powerful* you know." A.J. rushed a hand through his hair sending clumps of hair through his fingers and toward the front of his brow in a flip-flop kind of motion and let his arm fall to his side.

Krazy saw that A.J. was pushing his chest out, and he was starting to strut like he was some big time tough guy. Krazy laughed at this, and knew that A.J. was fooling himself even if it were just for a few minutes. He knew that it was time to get their money from the Outcasts, and the way they did business, and had no idea how they paid any of their debts. The only solution was to forget about there debts and denied all knowledge to their face. They knew that when it came to paying debts, he knew that they never played with Chris Mangini's money. Sometimes they liked to prolong the payment, but it was only a few times when they needed to get physical and they had to make sure he knew that they meant business, as always.

Now, if JJ, the official spokesman of the Outcasts were going to give him the run around again, he didn't know if his patience would last again.

As they passed by the two big fat teachers with thick moustaches, they gave a greedy looking smile that resembled 1860's Irish cops who were standing around an abandoned alleyway, ready to rough up some young hoodlum for no good reason. But A.J. thought that on all probability they were on Chris Mangini's payroll.

Krazy and A.J. took a left treading down the large five rows of blocks, passing by all the tables on the inside of the Commons, holding a little more livelier crowd than in Commons A. Students were talking, and doing what every kid should be doing, just fucking around and having fun telling dead baby jokes. But when they reached the last row, Krazy knew that at the end of the farthest reaches of Commons B; the Outcasts were next on their list.

At that moment A.J. grabbed his arm, and then pulled him over to the side, furling his eyebrows, eyes filled with worry. Everything grew quiet again. "Wait a minute, man. I know the leaders."

Krazy looked at A.J., and knew that he wasn't kidding. By the way his petrified face magnified the way he sounded the fear was already interwoven in his hard-boiled stamina, attacking his anger, and bringing his mind off the anger high.

"Who? Jacob and Clifford Barley?" Krazy rubbed his ashy nose, and then wiped the corners of his wet, salivating mouth.

"Oh yeeeeeeeah?" Krazy said, looking at him with a peculiar eye.

A.J. shrugged, regretting his decision to say anything at all. "No. They used to live down the street from me, and they used to borrow my stuff all the time. But, we've had a rocky friendship over the past year. We had a falling out since then."

"Well," Krazy replied, confused by his words. "Then you don't have to worry. We are going to talk to JJ, he's the one who is going to give us our money."

"Okay." A.J. felt relieved, but he still had more fear in his system, but the courage to keep moving was counteracting the fear virus. "Let's go."

Even though he did not want to go, he felt compelled to do so in a sort of rebellious way, but even more personal because of the hard times he had put him through. The occasions were numerous and the threats of him being expelled by the vice principal were very real, and he felt that payback was due.

A.J.'s heart beat vivaciously, making his blood pump faster than any waterspout, and he swallowed some formed spit quietly to keep his violent spells on edge.

Krazy shook his head away all notions of doubt, and then they started toward the table of Outcasts.

JJ—a scrawny, weak kneed, pointy nosed, young man was sitting at the table with the largest group of Gothic and Outcast kids in the entire state. Every time he breathed, it was like he was speaking through his cheeks. Even though he didn't know who was with him, he did not care about that. With his short black sleeve shirt already resonating sweat from beneath his bare armpits, he could not help but feel that all the deodorant companies were ignorant of his problems. He made his large clunky skateboard Van shoes tap against the ground as if he was wearing high heel pumps. He felt his long black pants trailing over the outstretched tongue and behind the back of his shoes, while the crease of his pants touched the floor. But he was really feeling his legs clutching together, out of fear and anxiety. JJ wasn't stupid. Krazy was coming for their payment. JJ should pay him, but he had a few debts to pay off, but JJ had so many debts it was ridiculous.

JJ was already *blunted* with seedless marijuana and had gotten an early start on his mother's cheap liquor and smelled to the point that he washed his mouth with it. He was feeling a bit woozy as he went to greet them, "Heeeey Krazy!" He yelled as Krazy went to receive him, and against Krazy's principals, he held up his hand, and received his "pound."

JJ pushed his body into Krazy's, but he did not accept his hug with the same kind of warmness he had with Chris. Krazy always felt like JJ, in his junkie look, was always trying to suck up to him. He did not acknowledge A.J. for a minute, and with that in mind, A.J. held his tongue because he did not want to be friendly with people associated with Jacob and Clifford Barley.

A.J. turned his head, looking around him but was silently listening as Krazy began to speak with the dullest of voices, like a fingernail tapping against a large concrete pipe, but his point was still made. "So, you know why I'm here." Krazy's face made no emotion from this moment on, his purple head centered and waved face on him so hard it was as if he was about to cut him as if he was marble.

JJ saw the emotions in his face express a clear persona, putting everything out without having to say a thing. He knew that it was time to pay up for the pills of exstasy, dime bags of marijuana, and huge quantities of Heroin that he and few of his other friends had dabbled with over the last few years. Everyone else's debt, was there debt.

"Um…" He raised a hand toward his face as if he had forgotten, looking toward the ceiling avoiding eye contact with him, and then looked back at him as if he had an epiphany, only secretly, he knew what day it was. "I know why…it's time to pay. Yes! I know, I know. It's time to pay, *all day under the sun makes JJ a bright clam in the bay.*" He made quick hand movements as he talked as if he was throwing things in the air.

JJ let out a loud snickering laugh escape him, which echoed all around them, as if he had been some demon—a deeply acne infected demon with round white heads moving along his cheek and neck—that was really reflecting how everyone really felt.

"Yeah…um…about that, there's something that you need to know." JJ whispered to him, his cheek flapped as if he had gills and made a flubbering sound in the back of his throat.

Krazy leaned over, irritated to hear what he was about to say, and he heard him say, "I can't tell you anything else, but this. I don't have the money."

Krazy's patience was that of an unlighted rope of dynamite harmless and docile—but at that instant became lit by JJ's wrong words, as his eyebrows flared, and he didn't want to cooperate with his deteriorating patience.

"What?" He wanted to scream this reply, but he knew that screaming would do no good now.

"Okay. Tell me again." Krazy's voice was irritated, and was definitely ruffled. "I don't think I heard you correctly?"

JJ's voice became very shaky, and his body began to fidget like some uncoordinated annoying rat dog that wouldn't sit still. "Come on man. I thought we were square last month? You know me, I'm having a bad month." JJ always tried to change the subject when Krazy's voice became irritated. The bright purple bruises looked as if it were going to pulsate.

Krazy shook his head in disagreement, "You always are having a bad month, and then after a few minutes, you somehow pop up with the money. It's probably in your pockets right now, as we speak," replied with a large dose of cynical apathy.

"No, man. I'm serious. I don't have the money. I swear I wouldn't lie to you!" JJ's hand started to shake, and then he snapped his fingers in a nervous manner. JJ was starting to feel the last of the dope leaving his system, and then paranoia and fear set over his collected thoughts. Then like every disaster, all his senses that he could coordinate dive-bombed into a pile of shit.

"Are you just lying to me," Krazy looked dead in his eye, inflicting his hatred onto JJ without touching him, and taking another deep breath, "because if you are lying you know what is going to happen, right? But if you aren't lying and you have that money in your pocket, I think that it would be a pretty wise choice that you give us the *fucking* money right *fucking* now."

JJ began to shake his head, snapping his fingers, and then knowing that if he gave in now, he would loose his respect with his crew (even though they couldn't care less). But, at this point, he knew that things were probably going to get worse for him. So he dove right in with blatant disregard for himself and the Outcasts all the same.

"Hey fuck you man." JJ shouted arrogantly, "I don't have to take this shit! I'm part of a crew."

"But I don't see them making an effort to protect you!"

"That's because they know I am in the right, so fuck off you purple headed motherfucker!"

At that moment, the last cindering rope that had finally burned up his last bit of thread, and now he had definitely exploded.

"*Fuck you, you whiny drug addicted little shit. You, or your crew, don't have the fucking say-so to give me any shit. You owe me, and you need to ante up. So ante up!*" Krazy's top had finally blown, and they started to argue with each other until their words intermingled over each other's voices, like two overlapping waves of traffic, not making sense at all. No one had bothered them, even though there yells were louder than the crowds, the crowd did not change, like a sibling who were watching there parents fight. They just sat there while they did not disturb them.

A.J. was listening to quite an earful of what was being said between the two. He thought this was just what JJ had wanted him to do all along. Pointing fingers, spiting at each other like two rabid bulldogs on a leash just waiting to maul each other to shreds, but this was just getting ridiculous.

But A.J., standing in his own pubescent silence, the arguing had drifted away, and a voice uttered very simple and practical words.

"Do something about this!" The voice thought, plotting, and wanting in his mind to break loose. Only A.J. considered two dangerous factors that were playing against them. First of all, there were the two "fat cat" teachers that were across the other side of the hall, eyeing them—but weren't sure if they would stop them or not—Secondly, there was the fact that Jacob and Clifford weren't present. A.J. thanked God for that, but then looked back at the two large teachers, and saw them slowly move down the hall where Frank and A.J. passed them down the hallway.

A.J. thanked God for that one, and knew that one factor was taken care of. While on the other hand there was Jacob to think about but knew that he wouldn't care if he knew what was happening. A.J. knew what must be done, and he had to do it, because there seemed like no choice in the matter.

A.J. acted on his quickest of impulses and clutching Krazy's shoulders he thrusted him into the large pillar slamming him against his right shoulder. Krazy landed like he was a slab of flesh being pounded by a large dirty mallet. Krazy groaned as he put a hand on his arm rubbing it, feeling a syringe shot force a small affect on his triceps.

As Krazy was getting over his momentary pain, he saw A.J. thrusting his fist into JJ's face, hearing the teeth in his mouth crackling like popcorn, and the way his fingers banged into his mouth amazed Krazy as he saw JJ falling to the floor, like a sack of flower, and his small face laid against the floor with a loud *SMACK*. JJ was lying with his bloody mouth wide open, swallowing and spitting out large globs of blood across the floor.

Only A.J. moved around until he stood over his head, and grabbed onto the front of his black T-shirt that said, "Life sucks, deal with it." Krazy noted that the message on the T-shirt was a rather fitting title for the predicament that JJ was in, and it seemed less comic and more ironic (and in a way, both were intertwined).

Gripping onto his T-shirt, A.J. leaned his head upwards, and yelled over to Krazy, teeth bare and lips drawn back. "Get your ass over here and grab his legs."

Krazy looked at him, and then peered around the corner where the teachers were standing. With his keen eyes, he saw that they were gone, not even in clear sight. Krazy thanked God that those teachers had their backs, giving them that window of opportunity. Also, he thanked God for the fact that Jacob was not present. Would he care? "Probably not?" Krazy thought, "no one would interrupt what they were doing, because no one could touch them. We rule this school."

Someone was really helping them from being caught, if that was anything to thank God for which he thanked at that moment. He turned around, seeing A.J. beginning to drag JJ along the floor, and yelled to Krazy, "Come on, get his ankles!"

Krazy shook off his moment of instability, and then ran up to JJ's fallen body, and gripped his long black pants, squeezing on his ankles as they lifted him up off the ground, and moved him down the hallway. Levitating his body off the ground they strengthened their grip as they took another right toward the next passageway. They felt that for a small scarecrow of a boy he was getting pretty heavy for them to carry, and when they took another left at the next hallway they had made their way toward their destination, the technical center bathroom (where the technical center students could go to). They regained control of his body, and the two moved him back and forth like a battering ram, and with a full swinging motion, the top of his head thundered against the large door, definitely cracking or damaging his brain.

JJ made a few groans, but his pain did not persuade A.J. or Krazy from proceeding as they disappeared inside the tiny dark bathroom, hearing the door close behind them as they knocked another small door with the base of his head. When they entered—it was as if they were in another time zone, and inside "Smokers and Drinkers Cabin" where the most cigarette butts, roach tails (ends of marijuana joints), and sometimes cheap liquor bottle caps were found mixed in with the array of shit smelling intoxicating fumes lurking inside the darkness of the stalls anything could happen.

When they entered into the small, dank smelling bathroom of "Smokers and Drinkers Cabin" they threw his wriggling body to the rather unclean floors that magnified more than four different pairs of brown shoe patterns, and its brown thickness on the white floor that seemed to seep and bubble out of the floor like something out of one of those old science fiction movies.

A small scream burst from his mouth as they threw him to the floor, his right cheek landed against the floor, smacking the side of his mouth sending electrical jolts through the half side of his face. A large red mark began forming underneath his swollen jaw knowing that the pain was not going to get worse, but it was just beginning.

A.J. walked over toward his lifeless almost dead body, like he was some fish that had been pulled out of its round bowl, and was breathing for dear life, his eyes were begging for a little bit of salvation, mercy. A.J. and Krazy hoped that the pain would be exactly the salvation that he needed for his offense. Looking at him lying there with his swollen face and blood dripping onto the cake-dirt floor, A.J. hated him more than ever at this moment. He didn't know why he hated him, but it was as if his body was on cruise control that was being steered by his anger, leading his emotions away from rational thought and into the realm of uncontrollable anger.

When he looked up at Krazy, he was waiting for him to give the order to unleash more hell on JJ. Krazy was leaning against a ring-layered faucet magnifying the artificial light shining down upon it, like it was the stained truth being shined upon from that dash of light revealing all the shit on top of everything a person ever believed. But if JJ had not been so smart to take the time to polish that lie, it would start to seep through their ugly round heads, and show that ugly stain upon their faces. That was like that ugly ring inside that faucet representing those lies that JJ was telling him all those times, and now it was time for him to pay the piper.

Krazy thought that his lies had finally just got so used up that it started to bleed through, like his blood that was dripping like beer from a broken bottle. Krazy was beginning to light a cigarette, his lips gently holding the end of the cigarette like a newborn baby resting inside a giant's hand, and pulled out a lighter as he held it underneath the cigarette. Licking the spark with his right thumb, a bright flame shot out of the metallic hole and the end of the cigarette began to burn up rather quickly, and a cloud of smoke puffed out of his mouth with one forceful blow, as if he was commanding the winds. The smoke disappeared into the darkness that was lingering, telling them what to do.

Krazy gave a stopping motion as he was taking in the tobacco with full acceptance, as he pulled it out of his mouth and a mountain of smoke came billowing out, "JJ, just give us the money, man!" Krazy's charming empathy made him seem mad, but also a person that knew the truth as the smoke disappeared into the abyss, "You'll make this so much easier on yourself."

JJ did not reply, and all that came from his lip he did was more hawking blood onto the floor as he tried to crawl away—like the dog that he was. But after they would be done with JJ, he would wish that he had ever refused to pay him again. Krazy was going to do just that, but it was A.J. that would execute his orders. This was the perfect way to break A.J. in, and the way it looked, Krazy didn't have to teach him a fucking thing about intimidation.

Krazy, like A.J., was waiting for him to give his answer; only A.J. began to see the ridiculous aspect of waiting to receive an answer from him, even though it pleasured his tainted sense of humor to see this rat crawl before him—weakened and afraid.

He was about to test his restraints until JJ stared at A.J., and he caught a crazy look in A.J.'s eyes, he stood beside the crawling worm that was heading nowhere as he swiftly kicked him in his rib cage. JJ let out a choked yell, and it echoed around the wall like the faintest voice in an abandoned mine shaft. With quick thinking, A.J. lowered himself next to JJ's choking mouth, and gripping him by the hair. He pulled his head off the floor, and then clamped his palm against his mouth. "Stop!" A.J. whispered into his ear, but the muffled screaming intensified as JJ tried to shake his head free of his clasping hand.

JJ began to feel his breath shorten, his thin cheeks were sticking to the inside of his mouth as JJ lowered his teeth over the whites of his fingers, and clenched A.J.'s fingers with his discolored teeth. AJ felt the bite of his teeth sliding across his wet palm, but when he withdrew his hand, JJ's screaming returned. With the quick pain that his teeth had caused his hand temporary pain, A.J.'s grip tightened against his greasy hair, and then threw his head down to the nasty floor. Slamming his head on the ground he heard his face make a loud *CRAAACK* as a few bloody teeth shot from his mouth and spun underneath his chin and nestled underneath his black T-shirt. JJ wanted to scream but all he could do was sputter out gargled words and blood from his nose, and a large part of it surrounded his mouth and covered the floor.

"Damn!" Krazy thought, almost choking on his smoke, "This kid's good." He regained his breath, not at all affected by the sight of the gushing blood ejecting from his nose like a jet of water, as he heard the loud cracking sound that made Krazy flinch a little, "He's damn good! He's incredible, but this kind of thing seems natural, it's not forced." He shrugged his shoulders, raising a questionable eyebrow that gave no hint of any kind of intelligence, as he felt his question was answered already. Returning back to his cigarette he chuckled away the awful sounds of blood cutting off the flow of oxygen.

JJ could not decide between cursing and coughing up more blood, but both seemed impossible for him not to do in this moment as A.J. burst out, "where is it? We want our money right now!" Only then, in a fleeting second, he felt like something had gone horribly wrong. "Maybe I killed him?" A.J. was not going to figure that out at the moment, but when he saw his arm limping along the floor, he knew that he wasn't dead yet.

Only JJ was very limited with his speech, and he wanted to save the rest of his breaths to recuperate from his brutal beatings. A.J. then began to pat the sides of his pant pockets; his palm felt something that was large and thick padding inside his right pocket that almost made his lower legs seem thicker than they were. Since his body was turned northeast toward the darkened wall, his head was heading toward the bathrooms he pushed him over on his

The Disintegrating Bloodline

back—almost breaking every bone if he pushed him over any harder, and then reached into his pockets to pull out the large thick envelope.

"This is it!" A.J. said with pride as he tossed Krazy the large envelope. Krazy acted with quickness as he passed the cigarette in between his fingers grabbing it like an outfielder catching a high ball, it fell right into his hands, and then felt that his nicotine craving was gone, and now another craving was about to be fulfilled. His craving was all wrapped inside this nice white envelope for him to relish, and salivate over like eye candy.

Krazy threw the still lighted cigarette into the faucet, and then pushed back the flap with his thumb. Looking inside the envelope, he picked through the layers of bills through his fingertips as the dirt climbed inside his fingernail as he flipped through each and every individual bill, counting beyond the speed of light as he ran up a tally of the money in fast whispers.

"Ten thousand, two hundred dollars." Krazy finished with a faint whisper, hearing his own inside voice bleed out from the safety of his mind like a pirate lusting over his gold, and if anyone heard his lust, others would see his jealousy. But he did not care if A.J. knew how much he had, he was just glad that he was able to count the money in front of him right now, and that was all thanks to A.J. Only they had gotten what they needed, and now they both knew that it was time to leave before someone got curious—especially the vice principal.

"Is it all there?" A.J. asked, his emotion's still in possession by the rage, but was breathing very calmly, constantly thinking of what he could do to JJ, and A.J. hoped that he had enough money so that he wouldn't have to do some more irreparable damage to him. Only A.J. felt relieved when he heard Krazy's relaxing voice alleviate some of the pressure. He felt his heart beating so hard that he couldn't remember the last time he been so overjoyed and was fearful at the same time.

Out of the corner of his eye he saw that the smoke was still circling from the sink, pulling his attention away from Krazy for a moment and then back at JJ whose body was curled like an infant. He then turned back on Krazy, and waited for his answer. A.J. figured that either way, JJ was not going to leave the bathroom the same again.

"Yeah," Krazy said, closing the envelope as he patted it, like the way some people breathe on money to see if it is real, and then placed it inside his pockets. "We're good."

A.J. nodded and then breathed in with some relaxation as he let it all out. "Its time to go." A.J. thought, and to his surprise they did, but A.J. was not done yet. He had stuck his head inside the toilet, making bubbles travel around him as he screamed inside the brown, covered toilet. He pulled his head out by his hair, and he was coughing—a good sign that he was still alive. A.J., glumly left his head in the bowl, and even though he wasn't dead JJ wished he had been. But when he got out of his bowl, he would get his revenge, but he would wait.

As they left the bathroom they started to laugh, elevating some of the pressure off their chests. With the money in his pocket, and all worries aside, Krazy felt like he needed to point something out to him.

"You know, A.J." Krazy sounded oddly amazed, "I can't believe you did that."

When A.J. knew that he was talking to him, he laughed again as A.J.'s bobble pulled up and grabbed his chest, "I can't either!"

JJ just smirked, and then he leaned over sneakily and whispered, "How could you not forget that you stuck his head inside the toilet? You could have killed him! But, that's what he gets. Why didn't I think of that long ago?"

A.J. looked at Krazy, and knew that his arching smirk was wide as a pulled quiver of a bow, and then in that glistening crystal moment he remembered how he was covered in the dirty, shit filled, toilet water. A part of A.J. hoped that the boy died and the other part of him wanted him to live but that was life, you either cheat death or death embraces you—and then depending on your belief structure its all a one way ticket to two places, no round trip flights either. Only A.J. didn't exactly know which place he would go when he would meet his end, and he didn't want to be thinking about this while he was on the job because it made him feel like shit.

A.J. just shrugged and sighed, uncomfortable "It's all in a days work I guess?"

Krazy just looked at him with that "I know, don't tell me that shit" expression and they continued on down the hallway—wide eyed and with little regard to no entity or spirit. They now passed the two big fat teachers leaning against the wall, and gave A.J. and Krazy a conniving, underhanded smile.

The two took a short cut where a wide gap that had its bathrooms on the left, and a large piece of artwork that was under a glass frame encompassed most of the wall on their right, which was a slopped together landscape picture, a heavy blue sky over large green hills with pastel like outlines. But that was like the art buffs in the art department that decided to show off the worst paintings while trying to promote it as their best art at the same time.

Once they left the large gap, they headed North, and then took a small sidestep as they walked down the hall that was on the other side of the library. As they walked a bright light cut through the glass blinding their sight, burning Krazy and A.J.'s corneas as they cringed with sheer discomfort.

"Man that sun is so fucking bright!" Krazy declared, as if it wasn't obvious, he waved a hand over his face, and A.J. did the same, as if a light at the end of a tunnel was blinding them as they headed down the hallway.

"I know." A.J. concurred as he moved to the middle of the hall, hoping to get rid the sun that was in their way, "and the winds are really out today. The snow's going to be a bitch this year!"

Krazy nodded, "I don't know, soon maybe" he said and by the way he was nodding, he knew this was just irrelevant talk to break some of the uncomfortable silence before they went to deal with the *Bloods*. A.J. knew about there reputation for peddling Heroin, Marijuana, Crack (a derivative of cocaine), and different varieties of ecstasy pills.

A.J. never liked to think about people using drugs, but remembered that people used different things to get rid of there pain, but a lot of times they became addicted and couldn't get off. But, those are the stupid chances that people take.

When they moved out from under the suns vindictive rays, they left the muddling conversations behind them and made there way down the white desolate hall, and Krazy pointed with his finger, "There," Krazy grabbing onto A.J.'s shirt, pulling him over toward the bathroom, "in there!"

A.J. looked and saw to where the large hand was pointing to, which was the hallway bathroom. A.J. knew that this bathroom was a lot nicer than the technical center's was, and this was a dangerous haven for young hoodlums like the bloods to get there "drink or smoke on", as they liked to say, without being hassled by the faculty. The time that they would usually flock to the bathrooms is when the lunches began. They didn't care if they were hungry or not, if they could just finish a small joint of their favorite weed until an innocent bystander were terrorized, taunted, beaten, and sometimes urinated on there victims.

The people that were responsible for this ghastly vindictive assault were never brought to justice, and students rarely ever visited the bathrooms, including A.J. People believed the rumors, and took that as a sign that the hallway bathroom belonged to them. Only the one place he did not want to go was to *this* bathroom and risked being severely beaten by thugs that knew nothing of compassion and mercy, and he didn't have a gun or anything.

"Hey one thing though?" A.J. said hoping to catch Krazy's attention, and he did, seeing the light shine flesh the purple—revealing what used to be his face was a normal cheekbone. His eyes were blinking, making his face look like some bruised and battered Bison that was beaten with a metal bat, making his matted long hair look like dark tangled braids. A.J. cringed from the thought, and then said, "Are you coming? Because, you know what goes on, you heard about what has happened to a few people that have traveled through there."

Krazy just shook his head, knowing full well of the rumors, and then said with honesty, "I know. Don't worry about that." He then dropped down to a whisper making him look at his mouthed words. "Look down!"

Before he looked even farther passed his shirt, Krazy flipped up his shirt and in his pants a large metallic pistol grip reflecting with the shining sun, like a watch face being shined by an overhead light. By the looks of it, its metallic grip and the grooves of it looked like an old version of a Colt .45 handgun. He could tell by the style of handgrip by how the black rubber grip arched outwards like a disjointed elbow, and saw the Colt Stallion leaping in the gold emblem. A.J. did have a fear about going into the bathroom alone, but a question popped into his head.

"Where are you going to be?" A.J. felt the fear creeping through his blood veins, cracking through his calm composure, filling A.J.'s mind with the fear that he might not walk out of the bathroom.

"Don't worry," he checked his back and looked over A.J.'s shoulder in a paranoid manner, "I'll be sitting right next to the door, and if anything goes to shit in there, just say, 'winter is to fall and spring is to summer', and I'll be in there with my Stallion."

Krazy's reassuring face and gesture toward his "piece" made A.J.'s fear dispel from his mind just for a second, which gave him a bit more encouragement to go in the bathroom headstrong. Thinking about the secret and rather simple phrase, A.J. didn't know what the significance meant, but he then wondered how fast he was with his "Stallion." Even though it felt weird walking into the lion's den, he knew that there would be a guardian angel just waiting to help him in a moment's notice. But A.J. wasn't about to go until he was ready.

After a bit of consideration, placing last minute doubts in the situation, A.J. finally belted in submission. "Okay. But I want you to jump at the second anything sounds fishy. You got that?"

Without even considering the thought for a second, "Yeah, sure. I'll be waiting for you. Now, go! Get in there before any more time passes."

A.J. heard the urgency in his words, and then knew that now was not the time to be messing around, now was the time to prove his true loyalty to Chris Mangini.

"Good luck," Krazy patted A.J.'s shoulder heartily, and A.J. was set. When he was walking away from Krazy he approached the large oak door that made him not want to go but knew he *had* to at the same time. He looked at Krazy one last time, and then when he glanced one last time, a quote that was very fitting of the situation arose in his head.

"Well," A.J. thought, "I guess we all have to go sometime. I just hope God has not found my intentions wrong."

A.J. was frightened, but he was already giving into the weakness that he did not want to slip in, and like a dark pool of oil, enwrapped in black of mud. Diving headfirst into his mission, he pushed the door with his own two hands, and emerged into the darkness of the bathroom.

Krazy stood watching A.J. with a newfound respect, and then walked over toward the door, standing inside the dark crack that was just beside the door. He laid his back on the other side of the door, and listened with a close ear. He just hoped that nothing went wrong, and if he heard his footsteps and his voice he could ready his itching hand to release his handgun from his pants, and rubbed his fingertips against the black grip. Waiting…waiting for his chance to intervene, but he hoped for the exact opposite as he massaged the grip with the tips of his fingers, waiting for anything to happen.

When A.J. left the hallway, the dim overhead light baptized him in a new and dark way that felt like an overweight shadow, pulsating against his brain, shaking his very confidence. But right now, in this jungle of darkness he could feel his soul be thrown in the bushes of this darkened forest. A fly circled around A.J. as he continued, smelling the ever-present perfume of shit that kept his senses tense. But A.J. began to imagine a slaughterhouse of pigs hanging with their intestines split open—hearing his footsteps made him imagine the way they screamed—dripping from their carved up bodies. He kept his wits about him as he walked passed the urinals mirroring a faint reflection of his body in the urinal. A.J. could hear the *glub, glub,* of the toilet water shaking from within the pipes, rumbling across the rim of the bowl.

All the bathroom stalls were closed, and they were blacker than a foggy eve—almost so foggy it made his mind trail off into the forbidden woods of his emotions—crackling leaves of itchy nerves and the soft moist ground that smelled of horse piss as he saw a puff of misty smoke rising from one of the stalls and heard a quick intake of inhaling and then puffs of smoke rose from around the stall and traveled across the floor, and left its rather tantalizing aroma around A.J., sending a quick message to his head.

"This was weed!" A.J. almost burst out, but then stopped as he heard someone standing up in one of the stalls, and the sound of a contracting zipper being pulled upwards and it was like there was a gateway for the devil to come out whenever he felt it was right, and it seemed ironic if the devil would come out, with his blunt in his mouth and a wide "fuck you" grin on his boulder face.

The door opened, and someone that he had expected, but never really saw, who looked like a large shadow, was Jailbird, was stumbling out of the stall with a large rolled up cigar crunching in between his teeth. The only things that he saw of him were his teeth sparkled like white pearls, and gleamed brighter than the full moon in its peak of a summer night. A.J. didn't like the smile, and then Jailbird spoke to him, testing his confidence and trying to falter A.J.'s self-being.

"So small fry," Jailbird sounded like a cannon—very demanding but very muffled. But that was probably because the blunt was in between his teeth, so that it made it harder for A.J. to understand, but he got the gist of what he was saying. Jailbird took another intake of his "blunt", sending the ashes in the air as he gripped the blunt with his index and thumb fingers and flicked it with a small swipe of his curling middle finger.

"What *chu* want? *U* want some action?"

A.J. saw his round face, and saw nothing but his big fat lips and smoke billowing out of his mouth like a steam engine as he walked into the overhead light. His soulless eyes were mirrored underneath the overhead light, and sent his smoke in a heavy force of gravitation. A.J. waved the smoke away as it traveled through A.J.'s hair, and felt like he was dealing with a zombie clouded by purple haze and aggression. He was wearing a long black T-shirt that had "Black Power" written across his barrel chest with many simultaneous fists in the sky. And he was wearing a pair of long black Khaki jeans that were released by some clothes designer with the company name "Be Cool" on the sides of his pockets.

But when A.J saw that Jailbird starting to advance toward him he braced himself, and cocked his head upwards, almost boldly yelling, "I'm here to collect for Chris Mangini."

Jailbird didn't even look angered by this off handed comment—more taken back by the sound waves that was disturbing his high and taking another hit of the large blunt and exhaled the smoke into his face *again*, "are *u* a spy?" He was now directly underneath the light, and his large ovate head leaned forward swiveling to each side.

"What do you mean?" A.J. was offended.

"*U* know what I mean!" Jailbird shouted, "Are *u* a fucking narc?"

He lowered the blunt toward the side of his pants, and then said, "No, I'm not. Just talk to me for a minute man, don't be so paranoid."

Jailbird shook his head and tisked, as if he was really just controlling his violent urges from tackling him into the wall as he said, "Okay man." Jailbird looked relaxed, but he wasn't at ease. "I haven't seen *u* before, so what's your name?"

A.J.'s voice faltered as he said, "My name is A..." He wanted to complete the last letter in his last name, but he could only draw a blank as if he had lost all his motor skills, "J." A.J. stated his initials together once again, "My name's

A.J." A.J. didn't know if he was really trying to remind himself of who *he* really was, but it felt reassuring to hear his own name, like he actually existed.

Jailbird just looked at him cleared his nose in that real addictive manner as he said, "Yeah, yeah, I got it. *Youse* a fucking parrot, ya fucking retard!" He had pulled back as he took a hit off his blunt, playing with fire.

A.J. didn't like his tone, and that made his blood curdle with a hatred that only made him think of the boy he had nearly drowned in "Smokers Cabin." By the way this baboon was acting A.J. knew he could not contend with more than twenty pounds of solid muscles in one arm. Only the fact that he said *youse* that didn't sound like he was from New York—he sounded like he was from Pennsylvania.

A.J. shook his head almost like a fidgeting jerk, and it looked like he had just set the situation on an axis that he couldn't set straight again. And then he let his courageous nuts swing in the air, "Listen. I don't have time for this shit! Just give me the money!"

At that moment, the blunt that Jailbird had been clutching in his hands suddenly slipped through his fingers, and fell to the floor. A.J. saw the smoking blunt land to the floor, and without taking his green eyes off A.J., his foot rose off the ground and he ground the cigar into the floor with his large black Timberland boots.

The sounds of his boot scratching against the floor echoed with intensity, shaking the entire bathroom, but it did not falter A.J.'s confidence, (even though it was like the giant Goliath running toward David) as it felt that an eclipse had just dropped over the room, and darkness had descended over the bathroom.

At that moment when Jailbird suddenly turned the darkest for him when Jailbird grabbed him by the collar, and thrusted him against the dirty wall—making his back smack against the wall—sending throbbing pain in his lower back. A.J. felt the sweat off Jailbirds hands tightening around his wool cotton shirt, and if he gripped even harder, he would tear a hole with his long razor blade fingernails. Jailbird reached into his pants, and then with all A.J.'s fears came true out came a large plastic 9mm Glock handgun out of his pants and pressed it against A.J.'s neck.

"*U* came to collect, *u* pretty *mothafucka u*," with a clear conscience that confirmed his violent nature as he licked his lips with his large tongue and his bald head was warming like a egg in the buzzing light bulb. "I should plug *u* in yo ass, pretty boy!"

At that moment, A.J. was thinking of everything at that moment, he did not cry or beg for his life. But the way the cold barrel jerked against his neck, it was almost like he was preparing a hole in his neck before he even pulled the trigger. Jailbirds trigger finger was radiating heat, just itching to release A.J.'s blood out the back of his neck. A.J. oddly kept his composure in the face of this strong, overpowering adversity that was literally pushing and crunching the life out of his chest.

"You better give me that money!" A.J. demanded in an rather brave and foolish tone, "Or my man Krazy's gonna fill you with so many holes you are gonna look like black Swiss fucking cheese!"

Jailbird just laughed, "Oh really," and at that moment, Jailbird pulled the gun away from his throat—taking two paces backwards he pushed the gun into his right eye socket. It was like he was in an eye doctors office, sitting on one of those plastic chairs, and A.J. was trying to look at the chart ahead of him, but all he could see through his right eye was just pitch black. When he was looking through the barrel of his gun it was dark, soulless, and represented everything that death stood for. As the barrel was positioned in his eye, an icky feeling crawled all over his body, like a million worms were just slipping and eating through his body, and Jailbirds hot breath almost made A.J. want to puke. He was thinking about his mother, his father, everyone, and hoped that God wouldn't send him to hell.

"If he is, why don't he come in and save yo ass?" Jailbird coaxed cynically, trying to fill A.J. with doubt, as he was pushing the cold steel farther against his eye as if he was trying to line the gun just right so the bullet would send his brains into the urinal beside A.J.'s legs. It would look like chunky red potato soup after the bullet exited his head but then he remembered what he was supposed to say if anything had gone haywire, and now was the right time to say it.

"Winter is to fall, and spring is to summer." A.J. yelled with a hoarse voice, moving his head impassively, not breaking his intimidating eye contact with Jailbird, nor shaking the barrel that was pressed so firmly against his eye. But A.J. was rather estranged by how odd it sounded, and by the way Jailbird was looking at him, his chin dropped, and his eyebrows cocked with curiosity. Only he couldn't understand it, and didn't want to understand it.

"What the hell is *u* talking about?" Jailbird was annoyed and aggravated by A.J.'s hidden distress signal, even though he did not know about it as he shoved the gun into his face even harder. "Is that some kind of faggot shit *youse* saying?" It was only a matter of time before Jailbird pulled the trigger, and just a matter of time Krazy could intervene.

Then at that moment the door swung open, and it was like God had answered his prayers, or A.J. had yelled loud enough for Krazy to hear himself say that stupid, but life changing signal. Krazy, as he promised, burst into the bathroom and A.J. watched Jailbird's face turn pale as paint, and his body was in a state of shock that could stop a clock.

"Put him down!" Krazy demanded, with his Stallion in full view "He's with me." Krazy's crazy, psychotic eyes flared as his fingers clenched the rubber handle until his fingers went numb.

But Jailbird had kept the gun directly pointed into A.J.'s eye and grunted as he slowly pulled the gun out of his eye, and then pointed it to Krazy, with his objective clearly changing. Krazy's guts sensed that he did this on purpose, like he wanted to just send him on the edge, but knew that Jailbird was a simple, dense person, and all he wanted now were answers even if his answer was right in front of him. He didn't really even know what a puzzle was, and never fully finished one in his life.

"What are you doing sending this newbie in without you. You want to get this faggot killed?"

Krazy didn't even smirk, but he scoffed, almost laughing. "The boss gave me strict orders to let him try to handle the protection routes, and besides, I was prepared for the situation. But now that you know, its time that you gave up the money that you owe us."

"Fuck you!" Jailbird roared, shaking the gun in a fleeting attempt to scare, or even taunt that proved no great affect on Krazy other than his finger cocking the hammer back, *ca-lick*. "You know I'm always high man. I get paranoid bout' *dat* shit."

"Yeah," Krazy thought, seeing that Jailbird was beginning to turn into an infant, mouth open for a tit and about to wet his pants. "Maybe if you remembered to get your fucking mind straight on a day when you have important things to do, maybe you wouldn't bug out when it came to paying your dues." His gut was thinking that, but his mind didn't want him to say what he was *exactly* feeling. He knew that he needed one thing, and it was the money—and getting out alive.

"Listen." Krazy said, his heels digging into the grimy floor, "just put your gun away and pay up."

"*U* put *yo's* away first, and then I'll give *u da* money." Jailbird's emotions were possessed by the sensamelia and his mind was going in circles from the way the herb was messing with his brains. He didn't know who to trust first, his gun or his instincts.

At this point, Krazy didn't care about this bullshit, and what he really wanted to do was pull the trigger and shoot this crack smoking gorilla straight to hell where he belonged. But if he was going to negotiate, he had to negotiate on agreeable terms—even if he had to meet the bastard halfway. "We'll lower them together!"

Jailbird thought about this and knew that this was going to be the only way of settling this affair, if they didn't kill each other first, because he saw that crazy look underneath his purple blush face. Krazy was ready to pull the trigger, if he really wanted to, and he knew he would do it to protect the new kid and Chris's honor. Jailbird also thought that he Krazy didn't care about hell or not. You don't want that type of person holding a gun when you just came down off a buzz. Jailbird made the agreement, as they lowered their weapons on the count of three.

"One…two…three!" The two lowered their weapons and then sheathed them back into their pants, and away from sight. Once the tension ended, Jailbird was not making any attempt to approach them as reached into his pocket and then pulled out an envelope—the paper crinkled by the money in it's enamored wrapping.

"Here it is!" Jailbird motioned, waving it as if it was his white flag, but he saw that they were making no intention of walking toward him.

"You don't want it?" He taunted, trying to get them angry enough to approach him, but it wasn't working. So, with little or no respect, Jailbird threw the envelope as it spun in a helicopter blade as Krazy made a quick grab for the envelope in the palm of his hand like an outfielder catching a ball in his mitt. Only the large part of the envelope landed in between his index and middle finger and a small slice mark formed between his fingers. He stuffed it into his pocket without even counting it—funny how he didn't realize a small dab of blood fell on the tip.

"Aren't you going to count it?" Jailbird asked, hoping to ease some of the tension, but as far as Krazy and A.J. were convinced, their business was done.

"No. Because I know you know how to count money and if there is anything wrong with it, I'm coming back for you. You know how I am!"

"Yeah." Jailbird moaned with discontent, agreeing with them at the same time. Only as A.J. and Krazy were about to leave, Jailbird called out to him. Krazy stopped and turned around as he safely stuck the envelope in his front pocket.

Jailbird looked at him with his green eyes, and then with a doltish curiosity, "What makes you think that there wouldn't be everything in there?"

Krazy saw that he was trying to be sarcastic, or it was just the fact that Jailbird was a simpleminded, numb-skull that could probably never read more than a sentence in a book, but was reading them anyhow. But this was just unlike him, because now he wanted to be sarcastic prick, and Krazy wouldn't let this shit-head get the best of him.

"I just know." He turned it around on him; his sarcastic tone meant to be spiteful and humorous. "Believe me, I know when its light. You have a spectacular fucking day, okay?" At that moment, A.J. wanted to laugh, and his teeth were biting his tongue.

After they left, Jailbird whispered, as if he was whispering a voodoo curse. "*U* punk ass mothafuckas are gonna regret that shit!" He turned, and then with his shoulders swishing back and forth he headed toward the other way, and started rapping to himself, like nothing had happened, just the same old bullshit, like on every other Friday. It wasn't a real defeat for him; it was just like this on any other Friday.

When the two left the bathroom, they felt the natural sunlight cleansing the darkness off their faces as they wiped the back of there hands upwards, pushing there faces back into their skulls—totally blinded and darkened as to what portal they had just been transported to.

"Whoa!" A.J. said looking back at the bathroom, feeling its presence calling out to him as if he had just been given another chance with his life, but then was deeply petrified—and how much of a mind fuck it was—to find out the world was on its axial when he found out that the world was indeed a fucked up place.

"What just happened back there?" A.J. pointed with an uneasy finger back to the bathroom, where that rather uncomfortable situation happened just moments ago. For a moment A.J. was stunned by the fact that it happened so fast—from standing five feet away—to being two inches away—and then having a gun forced into his face.

Krazy looked at him, not fully expressing the anxiety that was in his system, he replied in a rather solemn and comfortable tone, "I don't know?" Glancing back at A.J., he then stopped looking at him with a suspicion and then, "Why don't you tell me," his vindictive question left no room for sympathy.

A.J. felt rather stunned that he would ask him this question, but it was a just question that he didn't know how to answer being that everything had just went to shit in a blink of an eye. A.J. thought that telling him everything might have been a good idea to get the shit off his chest.

"Well, let's see." A.J. shook his head, shuddering from the bleakness and fear he had felt being inside that dark shitty bathroom of hell, "I walked in there, and I noticed that there wasn't anyone in there, so I waited, and who comes out Jailbird, blunted and stinking of weed."

Krazy smirked letting a little chuckle escaped him, amused by the use of A.J.'s clever wording, the smirk on Krazy's face quickly disappeared as he motioned for A.J. to go on, "Yeah, what else?"

A.J. took a deep breath, and then continued. "Well, when I told him I was here to collect, he just bugged out and thought I was someone else. Then he pulled that..." A.J. stopped and felt the end of the barrel rubbing against his eye again and everything in his system wanted to let everything go, or cry, but couldn't. It was like he couldn't find the right words to express it, and he fell silent again.

Krazy saw his eyes and knew that talking about it was not going to help him get over it as Krazy started to walk again, leaving A.J. standing with his thumb up his ass.

A.J. saw him, and forced his legs to catch up with him. A.J.'s mouth was open, and he was starting to say something when Krazy interrupted him, "I'm sorry I sent you in there," remorsefully, and then stopped, not looking at him, "I didn't know that was going to happen, ah hell, maybe I should have expected it. But I'm proud of you anyway, you went in there on my orders, and you came out a man." He then proceeded as a madman with his head cut off—totally disconnected like a mind/body schism—heading off into his laboratory to continue his disastrous experiment.

"It's okay." A.J. managed to say as he was catching up with him. A.J. followed Krazy toward the side doors, where the sun was shimmering down the hallway through the windows as they approached the side doors. With the way Krazy was walking, A.J. knew that he was leaving, and he called to him, rather strained, "Where are you going?"

Krazy halted, and saw the anticipated and frightened stare on his cheeks. Krazy gave him an unaware look, and then said, "Oh, I'm sorry. You're done. Chris Mangini is going to be at the game tonight, and he wants you to be his guest of honor."

A.J. acknowledged everything that he had said with a nod, but couldn't believe it. For being assaulted less than two minutes ago, A.J. felt an extreme amount of joy swelling up inside him about this invitation, "To be apart of the kings court." A.J. thought with a bright zealous filling his emotions with hot air until his body would pop with vivacious excitement.

But, when he realized that the danger was over, and his eyes were wide with that kind of curious anticipation in his eyes that made his face seem older—it must have been from the darkness. "What time is the game?"

"Why are you asking me?" Krazy sarcasm always made feel A.J. relaxed, even though his serious eyes were piercing him his purple bruised face Krazy then let a reassuring laugh. A.J. cocked his head, and even though he was perplexed, everything seemed okay that resolved any more questions. "I'm kidding, lighten up!" Krazy smiled, and it made his dimples press against his purple face, "its six o clock tonight, so be there."

"I will!" A.J. said, feeling the hot air in his mind deflating like a hot air balloon, relieving him of the uneasy air in his mind. "Where should I find you guys?"

Krazy just smiled, which it really made his bruised and purplish face rather handsome, like a smashed bullfrog that was staring at him and then burst into a million pieces as a car squashed it into oblivion. Then in a rather subtle and haunting response, and with that daunting smile, "Don't worry. We'll find you."

A.J. was now completely puzzled, confused and frightened him to the point of worrying about his personal safety. "Just take it easy," A.J. thought and then said, "this is it, this is your night!"

Seeing that this was a perfect time to leave, A.J. spoke with the presence of great fortune and thanks, "Well, I guess this is where we must part." A.J. turned around and just when he took two steps away from him, Krazy called out to him and saw that he had become agitated. "Where the fuck do you think you're going?"

"Huh?" A.J.'s upper lip rose in confusion, showing his bare white teeth.

Krazy sighed, and then stood with his arms swinging beside him as if he was holding his patience on a short leash. "Give me the fuckin' money you nitwit!"

A.J. groaned, and nodded his head out of embarrassment; showing him that he was caught in his own complacent stupidity, he then apologized, "Shit man, I'm sorry."

A.J.'s hand moved quickly and he pulled the large white envelope out of his back pocket, and then Krazy retrieved the envelope with certain cheetah like speed as he stuffed it inside his closest pocket and then patted it to make sure it was tightly in his pocket.

"Thanks," Krazy said, pulling his pants up over his belly, above a large stretch mark as he scratched his bunched up crotch, letting the blood flow through his privates again, waking up his hung, docile penis back to the world again.

"Wouldn't want to forget." A.J. eyes widened, and he gazed with amazement as Krazy reached into another pocket, and as he pulled out his hand. Krazy reached over and grabbed his hanging left hand, and squeezed with such intensity. Gripping his wrist, he placed his palm against A.J.'s, feeling clinging onto what he had in his hands all along. But he didn't want to see it, or accept it to know what it was, and hoped that it was a shocker.

For a moment, after the two pulled there hands away, A.J. turned his hand upward, and saw a crisp one hundred-dollar bill peering out at him like a newborn child that had just seen his mother's face. Only President Adams eyes were not so innocent, and when A.J. peeled it back he saw that there were more eyes staring up at him, with amoral intentions that could only be fulfilled by A.J. only. As a matter of fact, when A.J. opened the first bill there were eight more pairs of eyes rushing past each other as he saw that the amount added up to about four hundred dollars. A certain rush of embarrassment splintered A.J., and he said in amazement, "What's this?"

Krazy just looked at him, and then knew that he was a simpleton, a newbie, someone that hadn't learned all about the craft of business just yet. "Listen. You know what that is, it's your earnings, *your bread.*"

A.J. liked the sound of what Krazy was saying when A.J. closed his hand knowing that he was right in some respects, and then stuck it inside his pockets. Krazy started to silently whisper to him, edging up to A.J.'s side.

"But don't talk about it here because anyone with curious eyes will want to see it, so don't even take it out to even look at it, not until you are alone. You got that?"

When Krazy patted his shoulder he headed toward the door. He then disappeared out into the bright sunlight, being enwrapped by the large blanket of sun, and it blinded A.J. as Krazy blew through the doors, as if he was not allowed to see him go, like a passing memory he was not allowed to remember.

When the door closed behind Krazy, A.J. just stood still for a moment, trying to figure out what happened, the bell suddenly discharged its loud ear-piercing jingle throughout the school letting all the students know that it was time to go back into there cages for the rest of the day. But none of the monkeys ever got to go back to the African Congo at the end of the day. Humans had a few things over animals in that sense, but people who followed, never got ahead.

"Well, I guess its time for me to move on." A.J. whispered as he heard the trampling of the some hundred students pounding against the tile-checkered floors.

Patting his pocket, like Krazy had done, after he moved away from the doors he backtracked, taking another right, he headed down the next hall, and then toward the table where they had been sitting. Students were already starting to move in large herds, but there his backpack was, untouched and exactly where he left it. A.J. smiled as he thought positively, "This job pays good, and has a good protection plan."

At that moment, he felt like odd jobs for him that could get him some extra money here and there, and help his parents refurnish the house or pay for a new one, if he could afford it. Even though the ability to cheat death was like winning the lottery every time, everything that happened to him today would feel right tomorrow. Like he was born with an uncanny ability to be something more than he was given in his life and he wanted to take every opportunity they offered to the fullest. Only, he had to wait and see, wait and see what the sordid waves would bring to his beaches.

A.J. picked up his backpack at the table slinging it around his shoulders with some discomfort of the heavy burden of carrying these books. A.J. then headed toward his next class, but he had been in the most important class of the day, and that made A.J. proud…proud.

Chapter III:

"The Game to End All Games"

Three-o-clock came along at a snaillike pace than on any other day. The hallways were being crowded wall to wall toward the bus ramps, heading home to whatever life they had and would hibernate in it for the weekend—while blurring the lines of comfort and responsibility—before Monday—like a bad headache—came creeping up at six in the morning.

A.J. made his way down the ramp, feeling like he had broken a time barrier in his life. He did not know if it was the thick air rising over him like a grand tidal wave that was about to swallow him under bulging hormones and clapping shoes did not stop for him. But that time barrier was a definite split from his everyday grind.

With all these kids piling behind him, A.J. pushed through the doors, seeing the lines of buses that were arranged in no numerical order from numbers such as 33 and then 256 came next. If they were at the back or at the front of the line, they couldn't do a damn thing about it. Luckily, A.J.'s bus was the fifth from the round docking entrance like lines and this time he would find a seat perfect for him in this uncomfortable, odor stained "yellow cheese."

As he trampled up the black rubbery steps (the woman behind the seat smiled at him, but her body was sweating in agony) with a sense of freedom stirring in his chest, his pouncing feet rocked the bus as he traveled to the middle of the bus, and stuffed his backpack in the corner. Closing his eyes he sat his legs up against the plastic brown seat, and slumped against the metal paint. Even though there were students yelling apocalyptic words "get this fucking show on the road," and (with a rather quick reply from his busdriver) "shut your mouth, carver," A.J. closed his eyes, and everything turned silent. It was almost like a light switch that he turned on and off, blocking out all the bad and painful things and turning it back on when A.J. felt good. He fell to sleep, without bothering to give up the space next to him.

This was where he resided in his ride of hell, but it didn't really bother him that much now he had seen the light. As the ignition switch started the gears the engine moaned as if a cranky old woman who hadn't been fucked in twenty years shouted, "Give me some cock now!" When the engine started, the bus left the docking station—rumbling away, shaking every multicultural boy and girls—black, white, Hispanic, Asians, hormones' with the promises of seeing their homes but as A.J. opened his eyes, his mind played back the scene in his head. A.J. didn't want to analyze—or even imagine how he had missed that one chamber prescription—*brains splattered and shattered bones toiling in the urinal as if it were left over cheerios*—he combated those thoughts with thinking of the sexiest girl he could imagine, celebrity or porn star, but he couldn't. All he could think about at that moment was staring down that black barrel of death. But he forced his mind to do that, and smirked with his eyes closed, like some fool that had come across a grand idea.

And do you know what that grand idea was? "I'm finally apart of something grand," A.J.'s voice echoed, dancing in his head, "and this is the best thing that has ever happened to me!"

It was three thirty when A.J.'s walked into his house, and his surroundings would be peaceful and lonely until three forty when his mother would invade his privacy. His backpack collapsed to the floor like dead weight, shoes stumbled next to the door—one upside down and the other on its side like dead carrion. A.J. gracefully traipsed across the carpet and then jumped up and sank on it like it was his sandpit of comfort. Then at that moment, when his mind was clear, he began to think of what he was missing. He knew that without a driver's license and no car, hence he had to wait for a ride to the game. A.J. also knew that he had schoolwork to do, but the money in his pocket made him think less of his schoolwork, and having fresh clean bills in his hand felt more appealing. Pussy was also appealing, but he didn't know how it felt or tasted.

But as he thought about it, A.J. searched his pockets and pulled out the hundred dollar bills, "with no one around" like Krazy had ordered. The bills burned a hole in his eyes as he counted his day's pay glancing back to the door with an uneasy stance. Thinking about his entire total almost made him giddy like a young schoolgirl, and a boy with this kind of money, would feel the same way. He had now generated six hundred dollars in the past two days, and seeing that there was an easier way to make money, he knew that there was a loophole to life.

With that issue settled on his conscience, he jumped up and headed cautiously toward the window as he stared out through the cracks of the curtains, and looking through the crack of the parted curtain, he saw all the small houses standing in a row like doll houses, but he became angry. What angered him was a wanna-be thug white boy with a hoodie walking by with a smug carnivorous look on his face. He knew that his neighborhood consisted of "whiggers" with a lot of hard talk, but the infamous Jacob and Marley Brown were the exception. When the white boy was at the end of the street, A.J. turned away from the window and started toward his room scuffling his feet across the gray carpet sending small fragment of dust twirling up from the floor.

His room consisted of a nice bed, fresh covers, and new pillows, which was courtesy of his mother's quick way of returning back home on her lunch breaks.

When A.J. walked into his room, feeling calm in his own room, he saw his useless PC computer vegetating like a stubborn dog that would not budge or function—falling on their hind legs or shitting around until they ultimately died from a virus (such is the way of death's long fingers).

There was a desk next to his bed so that he could do homework and inside one of his drawers was the money clip in his top drawer, and this time he decided to follow his parent's rules (but really on his own decision) by never bringing his clip to school again. But instead of bringing money to school, he now needed to worry about how money would be coming *in*. He could never imagine making money like this in his wildest dreams—it burned so bad in his mind that he had to forget about it entirely.

At that moment A.J. thought about how that kid, JJ was going to be after he pulled his head out of the toilet. He knew he was set for life if he decided to keep working for Chris Mangini. But his parents were going to be another factor and if they couldn't get wind of his actions, they would never leave him alone anymore than they already did.

Suddenly, a loud crashing noise came bursting from the kitchen, and heard his mother's voice calling to him over the clattering dishes. A.J. quickly moved toward his desk, reached in the drawer for his money clip, stuck it inside his pocket, and closed it as he left the room to greet his mother. When he entered the room, he already heard the clanging of dishes being set aside, one on top of the other. He prepared himself to greet her by putting on his best smiling face, even though it might seem fake or forced, he needed to give the impression that he was fine.

The kitchen and the dining room were both connected, which had a large rectangular table. It had a large stove, four round burned grills, and an oven underneath, and he thought he saw a nice large kitchen, with a new oven, new stove. But the harsh realization of this burst his bubble, and he sat down in his wooden chair that had a small broken stick in the middle of the chair, squeaking when someone fidgeted in the chair. Obviously the chairs needed renovations, but that wasn't the only thing that needed renovations.

"Just be yourself." He thought to himself as he made his way down the hall, and laughed when he knew that he was right on the money about what she did when she got home. It was like a Catholic ritual with her cleaning the dishes that they seemed to forget about the night before. A.J. slowly crept into the kitchen not making a single sound from the floor—smelling the way she had been after a long day of work. A.J. felt like he was normal again. Even though he had been given another dose of reality, he loathed all one sided conceptions, perceptions, of life.

At that moment, A.J. quietly moved his hands outwards like a mountain cat ready to pounce on his prey and then with a single motion he clamped down on her shoulders, and whispered aggressively. "Hey, Ma!"

The overall force of his hands sunk into her shoulders sent shockwaves of fear into her system, "Hey," she yelled as she continued to wash the dishes, "how was your day?" She turned her head momentarily, not breaking a single swiping motion of her hand, she turned her spotty cheek and rather comfortably he leaned his head forward, and gave her a quick kiss (and deflated with a soft sizzling sound). She gave a warm, content smile as she returned back to her dishwashing, and A.J. removed his hands off her shoulders as he went over to the table and then plopped into one of the seats.

"I had a good day!" A.J. said, as an uncomfortable knot formed in his chest, "I went back to the teacher, Mr. Bennigan, and got the work I missed."

"Did he give you the right stuff to make up?" Mary sighed with disheartened disgust as she closed the cupboard door.

She walked over to the table and sat next to him, gently caressing his head as she then set her arm around his large shoulders.

"What do you plan on doing tonight? Do you have your counselor tonight?" Marie said brushing his shoulder acting openly affectionate to his needs.

A.J. thought about what he wanted to do, and going to the home game was number one on his list, but in that moment, he knew that he wanted to do something else. He had spoken an interest in getting a bank account, but then where was he going to get the money? "I'll get a job," he would tell her, hoping that he wouldn't sound too obvious. But, he knew that was what he wanted to do, so he decided to give it a shot.

"Well, I want to go to the home-game tonight," A.J. said, his heart beating on the edge of his throat, feeling worried that she might see through his lies, "and tomorrow I want to go to the bank and get an account, you remember we talked about that?"

"Yes, I do." Marie nodded her head in understanding, leaning her hand out to his and patted it for a few minutes, "Who are you going to the game with?" A.J. fell silent, and then his mother knew who it was going to be with, and she let it all his anger on him. "It better not be with those hoodlums."

A.J.'s eyebrows narrowed, and his forehead clenched upwards as he looked at her in a unchallenging way, "What hoodlums?" A.J. knew exactly what she was talking about, Chris Mangini and his band of ruffians. Only he did not consider them that way.

"Don't give me that shit, Anthony!" Marie (who always responded to her first name when she serious) was real matter of fact, "you know who I'm talking about, that boy Chris. The hoodlum!" Marie snared trying to bring him down with contempt, feeling her hand press down on him even harder, trying to weed out his lies through her usual motherly bullshit. She could always make him talk, but now he had to make an effort to lie to his mother over and over about his new profession.

"No. I'm not going with him!" A.J. replied scornfully, "And he's not a hoodlum. He got me my clip back, if it weren't for him I would be sitting around with my thumb up my ass waiting for him to give it back. So, he's all cool with me!" A.J. pushed his mother's oppressive arm off his hand, feeling the blood returning back into his fingers. He hated her when she did this to him, and sometimes wished that she had not come home at all.

"What do ya' mean?" Marie forced her eyes at him, trying to make him see whatever reality she saw felt right to *her*. "That kid could probably could care less about you!"

When any other day when A.J. hadn't known better, he would have agreed with her, but now his eyes were opened to the real truth. People like Chris Mangini did care about other people, and this was just some doctrine that Marie had been forced to believe and learned to accept in a "get-along" society, but A.J. was walking around with open eyes.

"Yes he does," A.J. shot back, and then controlled his anger, "if he wouldn't have talked to me, why wouldn't he give me money inside the clip?" A.J. said and then quickly shut his mouth.

"You have that money still?" Mary's eyes were shocked, and her mind was surrounded by the capable evil her son could be corrupted with, and one was…a secret. Her motherly feelings were in tune, and as strong as caste iron bars that prohibited her vision.

"And if you do, you should get rid of that right now! That's dirty money!"

"What do you mean? Get rid of six hundred dollars..." Then A.J. stopped talking again, knowing he fucked himself again.

His mother gasped and then clutched her chest in emotional shock. She now knew that his account had now gone up from two hundred dollars to six hundred dollars, making the grand total eight hundred dollars, and that's all she could see in his eyes...dollar bills.

Marie then saw that her son's facial expressions went cold and she saw that he went silent. "You mean you have six-hundred dollars now? When did you get that money?"

"From elsewhere!" A.J. belted out, unaware of how deep his grave of lies had been, and his mother was going to bury him in it. A.J. saw the rage stirring in her eyes as she then screamed, "Elsewhere? Where? If you don't tell me I'll slap your face till it hurts!"

A.J. laughed, and then smirked with a wily smile, resembling how Chris had laughed at his naivete before he was baptized again. Although Mary wasn't pleased, she was serious and her own face had grown cold, impenetrable of emotions, even though her anger was streaming currents that was not just heard, he *could* feel her currents. But her heart crumbled when she saw her son not giving into her demands. She let out a long sigh looking into his sweet blue eyes, innocent and blind.

"Listen, I'll let you go to the game, if you give me the money in your pocket, I'll give you money to go to the game," Mary held out her hand waiting for him to give her the money "how's about ten dollars?" A.J. looked sheepish, feeling that she was right for some reason, reaching and let it fall into her open and unclean palm.

The weight inside Mary's palms grew heavy and as she released the clip she counted the money with a weary, deliberate precision. The bills were crisp hundreds; she was still mesmerized, counting the bills as she finished in a blink-of-an-eye quickness.

She turned to A.J. and her lips puckered and eyes narrowed as if he was eight years old again, and said, nodding her head disapprovingly. "How did you get all this money? I thought you only had about two hundred dollars the other day?"

A.J. was silent, and was thinking of a good believable lie to tell his mother. If she could see through his lying face, it would be all over, and any boy that could withhold anything from his mother could act without thinking—but he wasn't a good liar.

"Did I say two hundred, I meant six hundred. I didn't count it all." A.J.'s making face was believable—eye lids wide, eyebrows not too far up the forehead—his face was the equality of angelic beauty, but demonic possession.

"Are you sure you didn't say two hundred just the other day? Or were you lying to us?" Mary's contempt was ready to bend A.J. to his will. But his darling face made her rethink her moves as if she was a chess player. She had to move her words strategically across the board of his childish antics, but she couldn't predict in his face the answer, and she had to predictably give up, only for a little while to collect her thoughts.

"Well, I think I can hold this for a while, and whenever you need something I'll give it to you, but don't carry all this around with you, it could get stolen. You'll be making everyone think that you're selling something." Mary's tone was harsh and cruel, but this sounded fishy, like she was using his money as bribery to keep her silence.

"What are ya' talking about?" A.J. wanted to rise out of his seat, but couldn't force his mother away from him—like a bothersome little sibling (A.J. knew how childish his mother seemed, and his hate was bubbling).

"You know what I'm talking about," Mary bitched about her reasons, "with the *drugs, the guns, the needles*, and all that other shit that people deal to kids. Does that clarify what I'm talkin' bout, or should I continue?"

A.J. became enraged with his mother who usually made him mad, but he possibly had no idea what his mother was trying to tell him. But he could feel the anger rising off his skin and bubbling as she continued ranting.

"Okay, okay, I get what you're saying. You can hold onto the money, but are we going to talk about this with dad?" A.J. asked feeling as if he made a mistake even saying anything to his mother. She didn't say, but what he couldn't find out, he couldn't make any judgments—but assumption was always room for question.

A.J. always knew that punishment would come through his father, Tony Cattiano who was a third generation of Cattiano's who resembled his grandfather—strict and to the point, always had a way with fear—and that was the way his father was. But he had his good points that were his father's most acquirable personality.

"Who are you going to see?" Mary's interested voice almost resembled that of a purring cat when they rubbed against your leg. "Somebody special?"

"No. Just goin' to see the game and see some friends."

Mary smiled, considering what A.J. had said, but then offered to go with him. "Are you sure that you don't need me to go with you?"

A.J. just looked at her and then said sarcastically. "No, I'm a big boy. I can go alone."

Mary shook her head, perturbed at the fact that her son rejected her offer. "I know you're a big boy, but I didn't want you to be alone tonight."

A.J. looked at the clock, and knew time was slowly passing for them, even though this might be a good reason for them to end the conversation.

"It's about five thirty," obviously changing the conversation, "I think it starts in about half an hour, twenty minutes. Should we start over to the school, now?"

Mary knew what her son was doing and she decided to drop the conversation. This usually happened with them and she never wanted to make her son mad. Mary could never give up on her son, not for a million dollars. A.J. was worth more than gold to him, even though he wasn't hers.

An hour had past when the fiendish short hand on the clock had passed five-o-clock he heard his mother's voice calling out to him letting him know that it was time to go. Outside the sun was beginning to set, shining its last bit of blood rays on his bed through the window as the way the sunset over the overburdened clouds with the burden weighing upon his soul. He knew he would have hell to pay and had to get away for a while before he faced the fire.

Mary's voice echoed throughout the house like a tremor of sound waves pulsating throughout the house—rumbling the thick walls. "You want to go to the game? Let's go. You'll be right on time for the game and you'll get a good seat."

"Yeah, let's go." A.J. said rising up from his chair, and then rushed out toward the hallway. His mother standing at the door with her long black fur coat ending at her knees, and saw her reaching over to get her purse that was on the floor. A.J. could feel the excitement in A.J.'s blood but was alert when he saw his mother reaching on the ground for her purse, and as she bent over, she groaned as if the pain of a thousand bloody knives had dug into her lower back, smiling with nervous agony. A.J. came to her side and pulled her up on her feet. The pain in her back had not gone away since the last time she had it. A.J. felt screwy about leaving his mother alone, especially with her back and knee problems. He felt like an idiot for treating her so bad.

"Are you sure you don't want to come tonight?" A.J. felt slight pinpricks of remorse, but a solace that he did not realize covered him from his own guilt. A.J. forgot about her problems for a moment and lowered his head down to her level, keeping eye contact with her as he pick her up on her feet.

Mary didn't want to see her son not smiling, which only made her pain thicken with the thought of her sons happiness be deprived of her petty back problems.

"Here are the keys. Start it up for me, I'll be out in a second." Mary said pushing her son along to the door.

"Can you get around without me?" A.J. asked hoping that she was fine to get on without him, but his mother's stubbornness did not give any room for compassion.

"Yeah. I'm fine just go! I'll be out in a minute." Mary leaned against the wall, catching her breath forcing the keys into her hands.

A.J. saw some kind of glowing strength resonating from his mother, and he felt like a total asshole *already* for lying, but he knew that she would never let him go if he let the guilt overcome him. It also hurt him because that his lie was already working on his mind, eating away at his conscience, and burrowing a small nest of guilt inside his soul so that later he would remind himself such a shit-head he was. A.J. forced a smiled out of him as he slowly stepped to the front door with the keys gripped inside his hands, he walked across the yard, and upon reaching the car he opened the driver seat. With her son starting up the car, Mary felt her back creak with udder agony, a long sigh left her mouth with great unease as Mary stood and took her first steps back to the kitchen.

Her feet scuttled across the floor with each improving step her pain sent her flying to the wall, catching herself with the palm of her hand. The pain filled up in her head, as if all her blood clots had come to take control of her system, and then ventured down in her knees. Mary groaned as her heart fluttered as she clutched her chest—thumping over her right hand as she felt those needles traveling through her body again. The panting became out of control, her heart was fluttering, and her veins were pulsating, begging for some medicine that promised to take the pain away, ignoring the fact that it always came back, eventually. Only that was until she reached into her purse pocket and held in her hand a prescription bottle for her back and leg pains, *Sirrillium*.

Her hands shook as her thumb pressed against the cap. The cap fell to the floor with a silent *pound* as she turned the bottle upside down spilling two green capsules into her palm and immediately threw the pills on her tongue, and swallowed them without any water. The instant painkiller was roaming through her blood stream running through her nerve endings of her brain, *shaking her, nullifying* her nerves as she felt her heart begin to beat normal again.

A.J. became impatient of his mothers tardiness and slammed the door behind him as he shaped footprints across the yard, and made his way to the cement walkway. There grass always grew into a wild safari with bugs and insects crawling up and around the blades of grass, looking up at them in fear, smashing on their territory, leaving large imprints of his gargantuan feet in the grass.

As A.J. opened the door, his mother, even though it looked as if nothing was wrong with her, he still felt he should attend to her needs.

Walking back into the house, he yelled into the empty sounding domain. "Are you okay, mom?" A.J. asked as he stepped on the round carpet to wipe the wet cum smelling grass off his feet as he stared into his mother's new and unfamiliar face.

Mary uprightly walked past A.J., who was obviously scared by the look on his face knew that something was certainly wrong with his mother, but she wouldn't give A.J. any inclination to how her pains really caused her.

"I'm okay. Just had to get myself going. Get my jump start." Mary chuckled, painfully, and waited for her son to stand beside her.

"Why are your cheeks red?" A.J. asked, hoping that his mother would talk to him, but she didn't.

She put a hand over his shoulder and A.J. and his mother walked to the car, opening the car door, letting her adjust herself in the blue furred Chevy Caprice, and as they pulled the door on the Chevrolet caprice and with each creak the door closed behind them.

Mary turned the keys in the ignition as she moved the gearshift down two *CLICKS* into Reverse as it started to back up onto the black paved road, until their car made a long *slurring* sound as it finally stalled out, stopping in the middle of the road. It was a perfect place to get into an accident killing them instantly. A.J. and Mary looked at each other in the comfort of the padded seats unsure of the car's reliability, but they didn't try to start a conversation that would never lead up to anything. And you know what that answer would be, "It's old, and it will never fix properly."

Mary turned the key again, hearing its old engine rattling like a person with Parkinson disease, as she slammed her foot on the gas pedal two more times. Then after one more push of her foot and turn of the key, the engine roared with perfection as if it hadn't had any problems at all. Mary sighed from her anxiety and proceeded into the middle of the road, and clicked the gearshift back into Drive as Mary pushed on the gas and went the easier way to the high school (left on Rosedale Ave., taking the intersection of Hilmount and Rosemill—passing a nice white house that he couldn't have) hoping that it would get them there without stalling out again, but that was no big deal, which was a big lie that she did not like to admit.

The thunder of the band rolled nearer when his mother turned on Mulberry Ave, like the belly of some awaiting beast that was growling for his dinner. The large thunderstorm of drums overlapped with the marching bands thumping footsteps echoed through the car windows, and his mother was humming the tune of the school song. A.J. was starting to get that sound stuck in his head, and he cursed himself for getting attached to a good beat—because it always faded away.

George Bradley High School consisted of one large building that broke off into a ROTC building for kids who participated in junior military training.

Every morning the drill team would be out on the black top near the far-left side of the court overlooking the areas behind the marble bleachers getting a clear view of the gated entrance for the buses. Mary traveled past the front entrance of the school, and took the next right leading into the student parking lot. The lot was crowded with one-hundred parked cars on top of the grassy field, as ten member families flocked (as two boys hopelessly darted) across the parking lot in hopes of beating the crowd. Only it was a fruitless victory when they saw that the line was exceeding like that of a line into a club bathroom.

"Why was this game so important?" A.J. thought to himself, but then knew that this was the first game without there original coach. A.J. thought he knew his name, but he didn't care about that shit until now. A.J. had a dark feeling that Chris needed him for a dangerous mission, since Chris wanted to enlist him *so fast* into his crew. In retrospect, he thought that it would take a long deliberation of political swagger, but he felt that the times were starting to move in a mind-bending, head trip that didn't really seem to stop for questions—everything was on the waves of everyone's word.

The lines were crawling a mile long with anxious football patrons and whiny children dancing around the pavement begging to "sit down" (while their parents kept pulling them off the ground) and chatty teenage boys and girls in long jeans and tight T-shirts talking about their personal issues of incestuous ideas were all were anxiously waiting to be seated inside the large Roman like coliseum. The stadium consisted of a long gated entrance ranging to the far-left side and across the far right side with an open gate for the band members and buses of the opposite and home team. One fenced in door remained on the right side under a gold lock that looked rusted and scratched from the elements of winter, rain, snow, and sleet. Although A.J. (who kept feeling his knuckles being a memento against his knuckles) was late, he suspected that Chris Mangini and his regime would be sending lookouts throughout the stadium to deliver A.J. into the hands of his mentor.

"Are you sure you don't want me to come with you?" Mary said overlooking the line; feeling worried for her son that he might not be able to handle this large occasion without her.

"No, mom. I'm okay, I'll give you a call." At that moment A.J. remembered that his money was with his mother, and he needed Mary's cell phone to call her if he was going to be there.

"Oh, yeah. I need to borrow some money, plus I need the cell phone, *please*." A.J. hated to borrow money from her since she was already having a hard time with keeping a job, but he wouldn't have to worry about that anymore since he was going to be making money now. Mary's eyes grew with readied excitement and smiled with a large endearing grin.

"Sure!" Mary replied, immediately digging through her large purse that looked like it could hold everything but the kitchen sink pushing her small journal aside, and beheld a bright gleaming metallic object that was peering out of one of the zipper compartments. When he looked at it more closely, he saw that in the dim light there was not one, but two, three, and four spikes.

"Why do you have a fork inside your purse?" A.J. said with a short laugh who always knew that she left something from her lunch inside her bag, usually it was a plastic fork, spoon, or knife, but today it was a dirty fork.

"A what?" Mary asked, as she kept searching through her purse, as if she didn't see it.

A.J. smirked as his domineering hand reached into her purse and held the fork right in front of her face. Mary stared with a pondering look, and remembered where she had the fork.

"Oh yeah," Mary said, "I had that when I ate my lunch today. I had peaches, they were okay."

A.J. handed the fork back to his mother, and with one hand she threw it inside her purse and continued for her pocket book.

A.J. let a short deep sigh letting his guilt hang on the edge of his lips, withholding the thought of owing somebody a favor, even to his own parents, irritated A.J. to the point where he wanted to bite off his own tongue, and die from the overall uselessness that he was by the way he treated his parents (and was resentful of how the world treated them). While A.J. was staring off at the overall presence of the crowd with miniscule curiosity until Mary found her pocket book snuggled at the bottom of her purse. Fingering passed the piles of receipts that were bigger than wads of cash until she found a twenty dollar bill that she had just cashed the day before and held it out for him to grab. A.J. saw the crisp bill just ready for him as his hand itched to feel his mother's money, but for a second he extended his hand to receive the bill, but then he stopped and would've given anything not to take her money.

"What, you can't take money from your mother anymore?" Mary persuaded A.J. with that forgiving ear-to-ear smile, "Just take it. I wouldn't let you go without any money to get into the game." A.J. quickly grabbed the bill, folded it up, and put it in his pocket as A.J. proceeded to open the door. Before he could leave his mother tapped him on his shoulder. A.J. turned, remembering that his mother always wanted a kiss before he left. He turned and gave his mother a kiss on her cheek.

The wind began calling to A.J. through the doors as the fresh full moon shined like the smile of a pale witch's toothless grin, and the way things sounded, the moon was calling to all wolves of the night to howl into the pitch black sky.

"I gotta go," A.J. said, in a rush, "the line's getting long."

"Okay." Mary whispered softly, embracing A.J. tight and then remembered that she needed to let him go. They let go of each other, and she gave him a look of remembrance as she stormed back into her purse, and handed him the phone. "Here's the phone, and have a good time, and don't hesitate to call me if you're bothered by anything. I love you."

A.J. looked at the phone, and noticed that it was beginning to wear down around the side, the paint already beginning to chip as he stuffed it into his pocket, making a bulge against the top of his right thigh. He looked at his mother, and then said with real emotion, "I love you too." He almost wanted to cry, but he couldn't at this particular moment, because the wilderness was calling to him.

This happy moment went sour immediately when a small tap hit Mary's window like a splattering rain drop, and Mary turned around and wasn't surprised to see a policeman was staring through the window, hiding his supposedly friendly eyes underneath dark shades. His lips looked parched and wet from a cigarette that had reeked on for days, and the cop's breath fogged the glass (almost forming into a crystal like substance that would break) as he tapped on the window, and motioned for her to move.

A.J. saw this cop, knowing that he was being a prick, and A.J. pulled on the door handle, pushing the large door with his knees, he jumped out of the car and closed the door behind him giving his mother a wave goodbye as he made his way down toward the back of the line. Mary glanced back to the police officer, giving him a not so friendly wave as she returned her hand back to the wheel. She clicked the gearshift into Drive, and pressed her foot on the gas, traveling at fifteen miles per hour. Looking in the rear view mirror she never endlessly eyed A.J., watching the puffs of smoke leave his sticky mouth as he stood with his clammy hands in his cold pockets. Mary took a right at the back exit from the stadium, and with a small whispered, "God help him." She felt a chill dance up her back as she drove away, back to her home with great unease that made her sigh and shiver in a new kind of fear.

After A.J.'s mother had left him on the curb, A.J. walked down the pavement as he saw the linked line was growing in considerable length by ten more students. A.J. sighed and stood at the far end of the line, standing behind many smelly people as noticed that the security was rather light, filled with teachers and New York's finest with walkie-talkies awaiting a distress call from one of the teachers on the lookout for any random fights to break out. The only policemen were the ones that greeted the patrons with metal detectors and pepper spray on their belts and a custom made Les Baer Custom Thunder Ranch 1911 45 caliber pistol with the Baer steel frame, dovetail, lowered and flared ejection point and a stainless steel 7-round magazine.

It had been ten painful, nail biting minutes and he was wondering whether time had stopped now or there were so many others it was ridiculous. The impatience was seeping from the restless and anxious patrons like invisible blood, purging from their system in agonizing pain as the thought of waiting in the line to lessen was almost funny to watch. Not to mention A.J. as he tapped his feet in rhythmic impatience.

"What is taking so goddamn long?" A.J. thought angrily as he huffed and he puffed and he bit his nails. After a few more minutes of waiting and listening to a crowd of people talking about the weather and the daily bullshit they were going through as the line slowly moved forward like a slow and tormented death but it only gave them one more step to the entrance. He leaned on the fence to rest his back, as angry patrons twenty bodies away they voiced their complaints with a raunchy taste of acerbic ignorance in the back of their throats, *"What's the fuckin' hoooooooldup?"* and *"Get this line started foooor Christ'sssssssssss sakes!"*

Other patrons in the line weren't bothered by these complaints, knowing that they were voicing their raw inner opinions, but did not have the heart to sound like these assholes. He leaned back, battling within a cage of hostility, against the fence and waited for the line to lesson up.

But when he thought that everything was going to stop, a quick hot breath jumped across his cheek, and touching his mouth and infecting his nostrils as he turned his head to feel a sweating behemoth body leaning against his back. No one was there, but a fast orgasmic voice caught him in his tracks, letting his quick whispering order A.J. into a paranoid stance.

"Slowly grab what I'm about to hand you through the fence, and I'll meet you at the front gate." A.J.'s head was still, though his eyes were feeling this person's rack of hair.

A.J. saw out the left corner of his eye with a piece of purple paper clenched with half of it between the large index and thumb fingers and the length of his fingernails were almost as a woman's and underneath was a layer of dirt bunched inside his fingers, like a dirty old woman. A.J.'s ability to hold his food was starting to take affect when he heard a gurgling noise as he slowly grabbed the end of the purple note, and begun to pull on it. It felt as if the two were playing tug of war inside a mouse hole, slowly and surely the weight of the paper became light as a feather and the weight had disappeared as all he heard footsteps traveling far away from him. "Probably heading to the other side of the wall," and A.J.'s senses became alert with full attention to his surroundings.

A.J.'s body, which felt like it had been in a clamped vice, finally turned with the freedom to move again, he saw in his hand the piece of small purple paper—that was his ticket to the game. A.J. held it out in front of him, and now knew that he didn't have to wait in this line anymore, and this most likely was a gift from Chris for all his good work. As the cold air whipped against A.J.'s body he turned, watching his back like a special ops receiving a package, as he readied himself to step out of line.

A.J. sidestepped and treaded with eager spirits as he passed the enraged patrons who were looking at him with dangerous mosaic eyes of greed and envy. Eyes from all around became attracted to A.J.'s footsteps as if he became a celebrity of some sort. When he approached the brick entrance a wave of uncomfortable pressure like bad Karma from a voodoo woman, and by the way he looked, he didn't know him at all. But his name floated through A.J.'s thoughts, not being able to make out who this fellow was from his scattered and free floating memories. A.J. started to approach the space until out of nowhere a shrilling voice screamed at the top of her lungs, "HEY!" as if a thousand crows were shrilling at him. He turned his attention toward a semi-tall blond woman who with very attractive features—pretty face with a personality of a heartless mind and fiendish prideful soul. She was Kathy Redding, a regular snobby uptown woman who was an avid member of the school PTA who always had something to add or say with comments that was trivial to the other needs of the parents. Only for her "precious" daughter and "handsome" son, who participated in a number of school activities and were deep into the prep world, not to mention the most unimportant kids in the entire student body.

"People without a ticket don't jump in front of everybody." Kathy sneered at A.J. with her snake tongue flaring as if she was ready to strike. "You can't do that!"

"Excuse me?" A.J. said, obviously putting her off, he gave Kathy a small wave for him to wait. Kathy was trying to see who he was waving to, but with her narrow eyes, she couldn't see too much of him anyway.

Kathy looked at him, not understanding what he was saying, and then shot back with her regular ignorant comeback, like a robot, "You need to get back in the back of the line."

"Why do I if I already have a ticket?" A.J. held the small purple ticket in front of Kathy, as if she was blind. Kathy's eyes rolled into the back of her head, her flesh curdled with embarrassed bitterness. "Another Dago!"

"Well, they were taking people who already had tickets two minutes ago." She said, trying to put up a roadblock against him. "I'm sorry, you're just going to have get in the back of the line."

He looked straight into her stone eyes and saw deep inside her was a pond of seedy pride that would be polluted with bio-hazardous animals that were dying of a prudish cancer-like malnutrition that affected the ego and the body. The affects were that of a sweltering ego and weakened body.

A.J. had given plenty of thought and Kathy's tricks were as old as her mascara, and after a moment of studying her motives, knew exactly how to put her on ice.

"If you don't mind," A.J.'s voice was in a calm and sensitive manner, "could I go in front of you? I'm meeting some friends here, and I'm already late if you don't mind?"

Kathy felt a slight sting of embarrassment towards herself, as her words slipped from her mouth in astonishment. Her voice suddenly changed into an upbeat pathetic tone that meant only she was stunned. He certainly didn't look like a "Dago", but his oily features made her give into his kind request.

"Go ahead." Kathy's unkind vehemence was ever present in her sour tone.

"Are you sure?" A.J. replied who was clearly trying to make her angry and throw another public fit. "I wouldn't want to be jumping in front of you." A.J. was now witnessing Kathy's face then turned sour as her skin curled back as if her toenails were being bent backwards with pliers. She now had fallen off her high horse and landed in a puddle of thick squishy mud. A.J. would have been surely pushing his luck if that actually happened, but to him that would have been the cherry on the top of his beautiful day.

She looked at him with a spiteful face, and then hissed, urging with adamancy, "Honey, Go before I change my mind."

"Okay." A.J. rushed passed her as he walked under the stone entrance, A.J. handed his ticket to the ticket taker to show he had proof to get in. Then the next degree was a cop to greet him with a metal detector and search him in order for A.J. to keep their social standards in check.

The policeman had a disenchanted smile, and a neat crew cut, and a stocky chest and large broad shoulders as high as a mountain ledge as his freshly shined badge number 717, which meant he was from the 71st precinct. He was armed with a .40 caliber Glock 21 series pistol and pepper spray clipped to his belt unhappily escorting shit-mouthed parents into a football game. But his mind was on busting up some local or out of state drug dealers, and moved up along the food chain so he can get his fat paycheck from Uncle Sam. His name was Officer Rose Kelley.

"Come on, do *ya'* want to get in this game or not?" Officer Rose Kelly argued, looking A.J. square in the face with his beady black eyes burning with rage underneath his protective identity changing glasses as A.J. extended his arms and stood with both legs spread apart to hear that beeping stick over his body. The noise gave off a slow *beep*, then another pulsing *beep*, and then it stopped, and the officer motioned for him to move forward with his laser stick.

When he saw the stick hanging down by his side, A.J. took one last glance at the officer's greasy but shiny impression in the overhead lights. A.J. now moved toward the messenger who was in the middle of the stadium—standing with his hands folded across his chest and his compact belly seeped over his saggy belt line—as A.J. knew searched his memory for his name. He was Danny Parello, an Italian that watched over Gene's crew—also subsequently could pass for a Jew—who was short in figure just like A.J., but he swagger was like a jelly snake slithering across the cement ground toward him. A.J.'s uneasiness escalated as he approached the associate who was under Gene's personal regime, but was a member of the DiAngelino family.

"Are *ya'* A.J.?" Danny voice was cagnesque and extended his hand to greet him, but before he interrupted him.

"*Ya'* took a long fuckin' time to get here, I'm Danny Parello." A.J. looked at his hand, with certain distrust and his grip made a loud slapping sound in the air. A.J.'s hand felt his large sausage fingers tightening around his fingers, and his eyes mirrored a malevolent glare. Once by the time they let go, both of them were anxious enough to leave at that moment.

"Let's go. The boss's *waitin'*, let's go!" Danny snapped his fingers demanding his attention as the two started off to the far-left side of the stadium.

The stadium was of marble color with a shade of light gray with four large blocks arching up the large stadium towering fifty feet that had large sleek brick that was as sheik and decadent as the Roman Coliseum, and it had sleek curves danced along the top of the walls, like a curvature in the spine. All the while, the greasy black sky lingered across the clouds, the stars waxed and waned, and the moons pale face blazed a hark hole in the dark sky. Although the sky blackened his mood it did not affect the marble. A.J. felt his body nudge into other people, about to excuse himself, but he then pushed forward, hearing the band start up again, and time was running away from his grasp.

The band pounding away, drumming into the air, like the belly of some beast grumbling, and the trumpets and clarinets joined in with a sharp scream for that hunger. But what made the band equally impressive was the sheer number of how many cliques were apart of the bands—some were preps, some were social misfits, and others just wanted to be apart of something, and that was what made a band. Even though the band was something of interest, it never interested A.J. to the point of joining. Now he had another life set before him like a platter of a large gourmet dinner—plump chicken and breasted Turkey, yams of delight, and beets of sorrow—he had to dig his teeth in, and ingest everything but the fat, gristle, could always interrupt the best part of the dinner, and A.J. had to deal with the fatty parts now and then to enjoy a meal.

The high school football team was now gaining attention in their once lousy loosing streak with the graces of another coach sweeping there presence, but also with a little help from Chris Mangini, this season would prove to be a very profitable time for him as well with the help of Adam Reoni they got the coach had went to resign from being the high-school coach at George Bradley. It was now that Chris called upon a new coach by the name of Dean Winslow, a champion leading coach that took NYU's team all the way to the college championships. With his alliance, he would put more play-time into the other team members, fairly and according to what all of them wanted, and life went on as usual for everyone else while Chris's profits tripled with each ticket sold.

Chris was deep in his dream state, remembering that situation so avidly in his memory, he felt the cold night wind whipping at his face, the noises of conversations were awakening him to the world that wouldn't go away, even how hard he tried to push it away.

He did not feel the wind at all after he woke up from his trance, and looked up, as a voice said, *"You are the one-most-high. You are the balance. But beware Chris, son of most high; a close friend shall bring about your destruction. And a younger boy shall take your place as leader."* This echoed in his head, burning as if hot branding irons were stamped into his brain, but then disappeared as he began to look around him, placing himself in the present, but in the distant most regions of his transparent head. Letting the cool wind hit him like an Advil after a long night of drinking mixed alcoholic beverages, he felt protected knowing that his most loyal and trustful soldiers were standing around him, and at that moment he felt A.J.'s presence approaching them. Even though he couldn't see them, he turned to Frank and quietly spoke into his ear.

"Is he coming? *Ya'* see him?" Frank looked beyond the crowd, not seeing anyone at first. But when he was about to correct Chris he saw A.J. in the distance with that snake in the grass Danny Parello beside him. Even though Chris was unsure, Frank felt that it was imperative to let him experience the freedom of the ocean, without confusing his shallow preconceptions.

"I see him boss!" Frank said, Chris was breathing in and out like a locomotive train, and glanced back at his leader, who looked like he was about to fall over.

"I don't want him exposed to the D'Angelino family." Chris said, controlling his long paces, "Like I said *get his feet wet*. The only time I want Danny in on something is tonight. I know he watches Gene's crew, but he's too close to the D'Angelino family, and I don't trust him." He felt the gun calling to him from his waist, as he rubbed his sheathed weapon as if he was patting a dog vying for affection. Chris drew back his leather coat to calm the vying Beretta and CZ handguns that scratched ever so diligently against his back in bubbling whining sound. As he covered his coat again, he was calm again, knowing his dogs were around him. The swelling in his head calmed down, feeling this great weight overtake him in unbearable anxiety.

Frank looked at him, feeling like that was a lie, but he couldn't tell if he had a weakness for A.J., since he had heard Chris telling Gene that he reminded himself of a teenager, being that he was 25 already. He knew about the missing bloodline, the cousin, but he couldn't draw on such an easy assumption. "It wouldn't make any sense, a coincidence as this would be of impossible to claim…but it's a start?"

Chris put his best-relaxed face on and then said, "Hey guys."

At that moment, all of his men turned toward him, and in that moment, he let a joke go. "How many cops does it take to push the *moolie* in handcuffs down the stairs?"

All of them looked at him, and Frank questioned, "How many boss?"

Chris waited a moment, and threw them the blow. "None, the son of a bitch fell down the stairs."

And in no time, the joke set a fire in their souls and churned a most awful wildfire that made everyone bust out laughing that they were unaware of their own tears streaming down their bulging, wet eyes of fluorescent puberty. But Chris kept a humble smile, making them know that he wasn't really trying to impress them, because in a way jokes made people feel *normal* again, and if this was a way for Chris to be normal, then it wouldn't be too far from being human.

As A.J. and Danny were passing the crowds of parents and students through every grade level from freshmen to senior, A.J.'s eyes bestowed upon a large group perched near the far side of the stadium on the opposite teams end. They were nettled and rustling in their nests—distant from the entire world, not paying attention to what was around them.

"Theirs the boss with the usual crowd, you can get along fine from here!" Danny patted his shoulder roughly as A.J. flinched, and Danny laughed in an arrogant for his sweet content self-absorbed life. A.J. looked into his eyes gleefully and joined his laughter. Everything—the talking students and the magnetic wave began to become one single minute ear-piercing screech.

"Hey, kid. *You scared*?" Danny's eyes intensified with a maliciousness that bred violence without ever saying a word.

The looming presence of the stadium was more frightening to A.J., because it was like a rising mountain and with each step, the more things became clearer, the more A.J. was becoming in tune to human nature's ways.

Whether it was lust, betrayal, or anything venial—the ways of human nature was that of a cesspool, and this cesspool was getting murkier by the second.

"Yeah, you need to be!" A.J. said with his best smart-aleck look, and then started toward Chris's circle. A.J. knew that he had been seen from the other side of the stadium and he pushed his back straight up and took a quick look behind him. He looked behind him and saw Danny had vanished in thin air.

A.J. saw Chris Mangini with the usual crowd with Frank who had a small three o clock shadow and neatly kempt sideburns whereas Krazy was sporting spiky haired look and Gene with his long turtle neck shirt rolling over his stomach and was just as groomed as well. But he saw a few other shady characters that made him feel very nervous, but there was no turning back for him at this point, and being nervous was important to him—*kept him on edge.*

As A.J. approached the circle a voice called out to him in a loudly, in a most enthusiastic voice, "Hey, It's A.J.!"

A.J. smiled, bashfully, as he approached them with happy appearance, and full of spirit but his smile disappeared when he saw the faces of the boys, cold and fierce, calm as the fake grass grew but deadlier than any Cobra about to bite and strangle his prey. Cobra's knew how to bite, and there venom could only kill once after the poison took its toll. These hard working Italian boys with tanned skin, brown and green eyes, curly and slicked back hair, only made there appeal more dangerous.

At that moment, Chris turned to see A.J., upright and tall with his chest outright in a proud statuesque manner of a lion detecting A.J.'s innocence in his eyes, and felt that part of him was still innocent as a lion cub.

Chris approached him and said earnestly, "You got the tickets from Danny?"

"Yeah, he found me. But I almost missed the game because of that bitch Kathy Redding always sticking her nose in places where it doesn't belong." A.J.'s defiant voice relaxed his body, making him quiver with the fresh cleansing air blowing through his body like burning tequilla down his body.

Frank yelled, fueled by the adrenaline rush unknowing that he was entirely too loud. "That Kathy Redding, her daughter's a piece of ass huh?"

"I guess she is. You would know, right?" A.J. replied with sarcasm leaking out of his pores.

Frank laughed and A.J. joined in the laughter. Then A.J.'s wondering eyes saw a bulge coming from Chris's left hip, and a metallic gun butt was peering out of his belt line making his every bone in his body tense up. A.J. knew that this it was a gun—"definitely," A.J. thought, and couldn't quickly decipher which model or make—even though he needed to see it to tell—he felt too intrusive to just ask for his gun.

"You see something you like?" Chris whispered under his breath.

"What do you mean?" A.J. replied meekly, noticeably scared, and was afraid of attracting any unwanted attention.

Chris looked down at him and knew that he was lying. Chris knew many liars, their tones shifted and there eye and body movements particularly were a dead give away.

Chris looked at him letting his word be heard, and cocked his head sideways. "You know what I mean. You saw it, didn't you?"

"I don't know what you're talking about." A.J. replied with his pits and palms beginning to sweat as his knees began to weaken, his heart was pounding against his chest, making things less clear for him.

"Don't worry, things like this are best kept to yourself. We don't want to frighten anybody, or alert any of my men." Chris's threatening presence was so strong that even the moon stood still for him as the clouds drifted across the sky.

Chris eased away from him and gave him room to breathe. He gave a short laugh that said he was playing with A.J.'s mind since he had offended A.J. before, he didn't want to make him mad again—but, "I guess he knows I'm playing around," Chris thought, nervous but at the same time happier as if he had just seen his first born son.

Chris bottled his raving happiness and looked to the three Italian boys, "I don't think you know these guys over there," quickly changing the subject and wrapped his left arm around his shoulder, and directed him toward the three boys he had passed by before.

"This is Antony, Guido, and Giuseppe." While Chris was making the introductions, A.J. saw that they made no attempt to shake his hand. "They are all from back home; all with the same backgrounds. So if you need any help from these guys brush up on your Italian. First things first, we'll get you through what's going on during the game, and the rest you'll learn along the way."

A.J. got the impression that they were cold fierce boys, but it was difficult to tell if they were or not. But, it was not until A.J. went to shake the first boy's hand, Antony. With A.J.'s hand in Antony's grip he instantly tightened around his fingers as if he was about to break all his fingers with one single shake—and felt death floating through his grip.

"The game's about to start!" Gene yelled over the whole congregation moved like a mighty flock of predators tracking their next meal. With their heads held high the mere sight of these boys were like giants that demanded attention or action would be taken—from the smokers to passerby's rubber necking to see them and someone yelled, "What's up Chris Mangini," and then Chris gave a broad wave. A.J. was behind Chris, and was almost hit by his swinging arm directly between Krazy and Frank's dominating bodies. A.J. secretly loved this attention, and he didn't have to say it, but this was better than he ever dreamed—it was like being with a celebrity. Although A.J. felt the presence of Rose Kelly's unwanted eyes gleaming toward him like his tobacco stained teeth when he smiled, but he left his sight when they walked through a large cement entry, which towered twenty feet with two arches running up both sides. The wind started to rise with a small gust as A.J. pushed through kids that stood in the hallways near the entrance. The sun's last rays set over the sky as the darkness began to set over them as the moon began to shed through the clouds as A.J. saw the outline of the full moon and didn't want it to come out, because it made him think of all the wolves that were crazed calling and howling to its pale face, trying to see what it will say to them. But indeed the wolves were about this very night, and A.J. was amongst them.

    The stairs went around both sides of the wall with a support rail that led to stairs around the outside arch and climbed for thirty or forty steps. At the top of those steps was a small block with that same metal railway coming at the top of the rectangle square arch. At the end of the long entrance standing on the tip of the stairs a young girl was chattering into her cell phone, the tuned band instruments with rumbled and clattered as the drums echoed through the stadium—pushing and thumping against their chests. A.J. followed Chris, pushing past snobby WASP students with tilted baseball caps with the L.A. Dodgers and New York Yankees symbols on all the way up the highest point of the stadium. Every ten steps he began to loose oxygen as the wind became thinner and less gusty, and to where they were looking down over both sides of the fields.

    A.J., catching his breath felt like his ears were going in and out, his eyes were wet and for a moment he felt the noises had disappeared, but then came thundering back in a pulsating, pounding and ear splitting intensity of the band. At that moment, everything in the galaxy didn't seem so distant, and when he looked up, he thought he could raise his hand and touch every planet in the galaxy but then he felt a great privilege to even being introduced a secret society that no one had told him about. A.J. had to find it, or felt like he wanted to find this way of life, and his search was coincidentally successful.

    Chris Mangini sat amongst his men with a kingly attitude—black jacket resting below his waist and his shirt was clinging to his rather muscular abdominal muscles—and cocked his marble sculptured head to the side as he and his Jewish brethren were condescendingly picking with their careful eyes which woman would be theirs, and who would die by their sharpened beaks. You could almost understand the flocks half broken accents that were floating around like an airborne transparent virus that starlets and harlots couldn't comprehend this beautiful choppy language was second nature to him, like a voice in the back of his head that wouldn't go away. The attraction was relentlessly prodding a deep sudden pleasure in his brain—to join—and cling to their flock.

Nearing the group, Chris was sitting on the long cold metal seat in between Krazy and Frank, but Gene was found in his group, "the ten lost tribes," on the other stadium seat not far from Chris's view. Strange how he wasn't in their group, but Chris knew he had to be around some Yids, if he really wanted to be normal, that is, for patriotic sake.

"Hey, Paisan!" Frank yelled from his seat and motioned A.J. to sit down. Chris saw A.J. from the stairs and scratched his chin, feeling flecks of sand chipping off his face, pondering many questions.

Then as A.J. eyed the ever-stretching field time shortly elapsed as his ear made one last popping sound, and as if a sharp knife had been forced inside his eardrum—vertigo seized him, swirling his mind like vodka tonic, turning his legs and body into viscid jelly. He beheld the field in awe and turned his head away from the lonely field, and saw one boy holding onto something underneath his coat. From the short distance, A.J. could see the metallic barrel peering underneath his legs like some fearful boy peering from the side of his father's coat, and A.J. stood shocked by this warm welcome of death. But since he was met with a barrel in his eye, he had become attracted to death, like it was his one true soul mate.

Then out of nowhere Krazy threw his hand over his shoulder and began whispering ferociously, and for a second, the boy looked confused. Then he became intimidated and fearful of Frank's words as he slowly hid the gun, and covered it disgustingly with his eyes narrowing with hatred.

Chris suddenly gave his men a reassuring thought as he said in Italian, "he's okay. He's a *friend of mine.*" Chris then told them his name and the men slowly turned their attention back toward the game with their hate projected toward the open field, as if he hadn't existed. A.J. swallowed his heart back into his throat and then saw that one of the boys rose up, moving around another boy, and then sat next to Chris Mangini smirking comfortably and then sat himself on the metallic lined seat, where his mind was set at ease. Only being squished inside a line of pubescent boys, he couldn't help but catch a whiff of their stench.

In his newly acquired seat, the oh-so certain feeling of almost being shot by someone he never knew or met left him, but it was always in the back of his head, watching—waiting to greet him again like a cackling old witch. A.J.'s eyes were focused on the cheerleaders who were chanting, exciting the crowd *"GO, GO, BULL DOGS"*, hands CLAP-CLAP-CLAP, *"LET'S GO"* CLAP-CLAP-CLAP, *"LET'S GO!"* throwing their legs and bodies into the air as the crowd replied with a roaring cheer. From his high perch, A.J. had noticed Jessica legs were more naturally tanned than the rest of her teammates burned and freckle skin. Her light blonde hair gave hints of a light brown color or could be dyed to dark black. His stomach grew tense and the thought of talking to her seemed nervous but he couldn't really tell what she was thinking, and all he could do was ask her how she felt, because women love to talk about what's on their minds. But his time was with Chris, and until they talked, silence was golden.

Chris saw that A.J. was eyeing the cheerleaders with a foolish and dumbfounded look of misplaced wonder and boyish awe. Chris knew such a look, and he remembered the same grin from when he saw this beautiful Italian girl walking past him in the city, fresh off the boat (or the plane) from the same town, with no family to accompany her. Even though they had lived under the same circumstances—and Chris constantly battled his own depression problems—instantly bonded and after a period of time—that never seemed slow or digressing—hit it off. But that was before she became his wife, and the nights when he was with her, he never regretted marrying her or the child that they bore together.

Then, out of the blue, Chris turned to him and whispered, "I want to tell you something that can help you throughout your life." A.J. looked at him with open ears, and then nodded, to let him know he was listening.

"I'm gonna be frank." He breathed in, and let everything out like a gust of wind as his breath flowed like a puff of smoke travelling from his lungs. "I think you have a big clue of what I do. And you have the assumption of what goes on, right?" The level of comfort in Chris's system went down, and the pain in his heart began to rise.

"Yeah, I caught a glimpse." A.J. said, but his words were suddenly cut off from Chris who had now looked furious, with a cold layer of stone covering his face. His eyes almost looked dead, lifeless as the dark sky above them.

Then he leaned forward, and then unleashed, "Forget what you know—the second you think you know anything, you're dead." When Chris spoke those words, A.J. became silent and his breath drew to a soft pace. A.J. saw in his face was clear from discomfort that he didn't want to lie to him, but from the way his voice was burning with discomfort, he didn't know his true motives—he was just being on the level.

"There's a war going on, and I'm not gonna bullshit yea', because you're smart, and bullshit confuses people, so listen up. Certain *friends of mine* want to kill my boss, and the world revolves around business so, in turn, they think that they can get a piece of the action on his contraband CD rackets."

"CD's," A.J. exclaimed, "why?"

"Because the government wants a piece of the action, and businesses aren't standing for it. So, they ban it, and that's where we come in. Businesses pay a lot when there's an inflation of goods, and that means more money. When you get more money, people start to act and think differently."

"Why would they want your boss dead then?" A.J. asked with curiosity. "Can't they split a piece of the action with him?"

Chris had barely eyed him, trying to avoid looking in his eyes, "No, because that's his rackets and he shouldn't have to bend to anyone's will. Everyone would be rich if we could get along, but Greed is the only thing that thrives business, and ruins people's lives," for fear that his past would rattle his spirits.

For a moment A.J. gave his word much thought and knew what he was trying to say. A.J. thought about it and stayed silent. Chris cursed to himself in a soft Sicilian dialect and looked at A.J. knowing that he had scared him, but Chris decided to have a bit of sympathy for himself.

"I didn't mean to intimidate you, but this is very serious, and you have to keep earning. That's how the commission lets us stay above water. In a nutshell, its sink or swim when it comes to the dues."

A.J. couldn't help but not keep silent on what he was hearing. His mother had told him how these people live, but he wanted to prove his mother wrong about Chris. A.J. had caught a huge whiff of the ugly truth, but the words he was saying were not dawning on him.

Chris's words were stern and strict sliding from his throat, tongue, and out into the air as if he was coughing up a hair ball—it congested his whole body to even say his words.

"Can I ask you something?" A.J. interrupted him with polite impatience, "but I couldn't say this if it wasn't on my mind."

Chris turned his head, his face parched, knowing he would say something rash. "Well, if it wasn't on your mind, then you wouldn't be thinking of it." Chris paced himself because A.J. was fresh and needed more of his help, but he motioned for him to whisper it. A.J. leaned into Chris's left ear and palmed it so anybody wouldn't catch wind of there conversation. A.J. was almost too nervous to ask him what he was about to say so he just decided to come out with it.

"Are you involved in drugs?" A.J. whispered with a nervous shudder, like a rabbit sneaking across dead leaves.

Chris pulled and looked at him sourly, and Chris's top lip drew up revealing his top teeth in a sour expression, and then faced the field, shaking his head disapprovingly. A.J. was waiting for his answer, on the edge of his seat as he waited. "Is this the way God gets back at me?" Chris thought, and knew that the truth was like that of an allusion. "When one takes a bath in a pond of lies, there's no way to tell where the discoloring on your soul begins."

Chris was brought back by the sounds of crashing football players echoed off the field with their helmets clattering against each other like rams ramming their numb foreheads into each other mindlessly. It fueled his head with the rage that he could muster against A.J.'s rather implicating question.

"Don't make me angry my friend, because you got another thing coming if you are trying to break me. What the hell is that supposed to mean?"

"I'm sorry, I didn't mean to…." A.J. shamefully replied and began to lean his head down.

Before A.J. could finish out his apology, Chris suddenly cut him off, seeing his head fall down to his chest.

"I thought I told you not to put your head down." Chris barked and tugged at his shirt. "Keep your head up, and since you asked it's only fair that I give you an answer." A.J. saw his anger seething from his eyeballs, but it occurred to A.J. that he wasn't going to give him an answer, and it burned him for a moment, but like all burnouts, it proved to be superficial, but still something to get mad about.

Then the buzzer suddenly rang ending the second quarter for the game. The two teams had met each other at the forty-yard line, with a staunch taunting from the each team. A.J. was torn by the sound and still awaited his answer, but only he could see a blank iguana stare on Chris's face.

"It's for your own good." Chris returned to his tranquil state, watching everything with his ever shifting eye and laid his back against the seat, wishing he could tell him the truth, but there wouldn't be any purpose in telling him now.

A.J. had about enough of this, he surely knew he had to be lying, but he didn't want to think about it. A.J. decided to take a walk and cool down from this issued propaganda.

"I'm gonna take five, do ya guys need anything?" A.J. said and sidestepped across Frank and Krazy. But before A.J. could get far from Chris's sight, Chris tapped Giuseppe and pointed to accompany A.J., and he followed right behind him.

A.J. felt someone's breath puffing against his cheek behind him as he walked away. A.J. thought it was Chris and reared his head to only find out he was disappointed when he saw that Giuseppe was standing right behind him. This only made A.J. nervous because how much he had to think over.

A.J. looked at Chris with the desire only to find out if he had half the heart to tell him the truth. But truth is certainly a myriad.

A.J. moved down the steps with cheetah like speed Giuseppe following behind him like he was his annoying shadow of protection and a woman flooring up the stairs like a mad steer with her kids not too far behind, and what looked like her youngest boy, fell on the steps. A.J. moved out of the way for the woman and the two smiled with a long grin, but moved passed them without paying their gratuity, and the two moved down the tiny steps, on toward the bottom row where they could see all the cheerleaders in full view. But before they moved any further, an angelic voice called up to him from the bottom ledge just beside the black top. It sounded almost the same as his mother, but to him, her voice was like the sweet calling of a sparrow, and he wanted to find the source of this beautiful sweet but disenchanted voice. Amongst the mad chattering and the blaring of trumpets and crystal showering of clarinet the band played "free ride", he was determined to find it.

A.J. felt Giuseppe's gargantuan hand sinking his fingers deep into his shoulder, and with his other hand pointed to him where that voice was calling and A.J. looked down the side of his pointing finger like a telescope and saw Jessica. In her joyful glee she was grinning happily with a twinkle in her eyes, and did a little three-sixty spin with her feet upwards and then landed. A.J. liked this, and the only thing he could see was her smile—making her doll face twinkling a happiness that resembled a punch drunk boxer—standing against the stone block, gazing with a sheer love struck eye as he approached the bottom of the stairs. As she leaned over towards the pillar, her friends pretended not to watch but it burned their skin and their subconscious to watch her be happy.

"Hey!" Jessica said, galloping, her feet stamping the track, almost leaping over the stone.

"Hi." A.J. leaning on the stone block gapping the track from the stadium, with his face two inches away from each other. Even though this seemed to be an accident, there emotions were nothing short of that as Jessica cautiously moved back, feeling her bubble being invaded on the first approach. She wanted to make his blood boil for her, but her heart was beating so rapidly that she felt faint from the excitement in her system.

"Fine," Jessica gasped, and then held her chest, the wind traveled up her shaky legs. "Im glad to see you. How have you been?"

"I'm better now, A.J. sheepishly smiled, "since I have seen you."

"Well. I'm always around." He tapped his foot, and then stamped the ground as Jessica leaned forward, and pulled him by the shirt. A.J.'s body shifted as his face turned and whispered in a rather brashly. "I wanna' know if this a trick?"

Jessica stood back alarmed by what he said to her, acting like the well played victim.

"Now why would you ever think of something like that? I just want to know if you have a girlfriend." Jessica batted her eyelashes as she stuck her chest out, making her fabric bulldog look as if it was actually running across her chest.

"Really?" A.J. said, pulling backwards, his eyebrows rose upwards from her protruding breasts, "I was just wondering why the most popular girl in school was trying to make a pass at me, and ask a nobody like me if I have a girlfriend."

Jessica scoffed from his naivete, "You've been the talk of the school."

"Whose been talking about me?"

"You know…word gets around." Jessica said, stamping her foot against the black top. The sounds around them seemed to magnify like a warbling television frequency, and they could hear there own thoughts getting muddled by everything around them.

"Well, I guess actions speak louder than words." A.J. said confidently.

"Then I wouldn't be standing here then?" Jessica smiled and then let out a small comfortable laugh.

A.J. laughed, getting the joke, but then said seriously. "I guess your actions are going against your principles?"

"Uh, I guess when I see a good thing, I go after it. Principles come second when I see a good thing." Jessica didn't know how that would come out (if he might mistake it for talking about Principals), but when she saw A.J. smile, she felt comfortable.

"I guess we can say that you did the right thing by ignoring your principles."

Jessica winked, and then whispered, "Don't tell anyone though."

A.J. felt like his heart was about to explode, and his whole body had become nervous again by her comment. He was deeply smitten by her personality.

"Then…" A.J. said, starting to accept the immediate disappointment, "I'd like to see you outside of school sometime. But if you're too scared or embarrassed about who I am, I understand." A.J. looked at her, his mouth starting to form some spit in his mouth, sweat dripping down his side, as he waited for her answer.

Jessica looked at him with certain suspicion, as she had wanted him to say that long after she had made his acquaintance.

"Yeah. Why would you say I'd not be interested? You're insanely handsome, and Adam really liked how you handled things. He even had to make that kid eat those words he said to you." Jessica said and gave him a more than friendly look.

"Sorry about that." A.J. said apologetically.

"Don't worry about it." Jessica shifted her body in a back and forth kind of motion, as if she was anxious to get back to her team. But she knew that wasn't it.

All A.J. could do was give her a smile back, and the two laughed it off, like they were in there own world. He bottled his laughter to a small chuckle, giving her a quick wink back. Jessica leaned over the gap, pressing her cheek against his, and she whispered so softly that it accentuated the tension pleasure as she wrapped a strand of hair behind her ear. A.J. couldn't resist glancing at it with quick timing at this beautiful human being before him.

"The only time I have to myself at the present moment is after gym practice. I'm practicing for the basketball games on Monday and meet me by the gym. Then we can go to your house. I can drive." Jessica kept her cheek still, and pressed her soft lips on his cheeks. Since Jessica may have been two inches taller on her tip toes that was the only way she could express her dominance—by clearly throwing her breasts into his face.

A.J.'s heart had begun pumping and his hand began to sweat profusely as soon as her lips touched his cheeks, a hard-on immediately formed in his crotch. Good thing he was pressing against the stone pillar.

"I can't wait." A.J. slowly spoke into Jessica's ear and Jessica moved her scrunched lips closer to his ear, to excite him, but then moved away, feeling his panting breath pushing against her cheeks.

"We'll get to that later." Jessica said as she fell into his blue eyes and wanted to get lost in his brain, wanting to know every move he made and be right with him. Something scared her for a moment, but she couldn't help it, this was all very new to her for some reason, even though the promise of sex shouldn't have—this was something more.

Then the sounds of kisses with soft moans festered beside them, and they turned to see who it was. It was a large tall boy wearing a large baseball cap with long baggy pants that went down to his waist revealing his underwear as a cheerleader with short curly hair was forcing her mouth inside her mouth, massaging her tongue inside his mouth. It looked like they didn't even care, and to the A.J. and Jessica, were provided them with some distraction from actually kissing, almost like watching pornography. While his hands caressing her breasts like they were round balls of dough he gently tweaked her nipples with his large sausage fingers. They could watch them for hours as Jessica heard someone call her from the track, and when she turned, she could see it was her friends trying to call her back to her duties.

"Jesssssssssssssssssiccccccccccccccca!"
Jessica heard her friends and heard there second call.
"Jesssssssicaaaaaaaaa, come onnnnnnnnnnnnnnn!" She couldn't ignore them for long and as the band played over the yelling, almost as if someone had sent the band to play and at that moment she felt that she was the most popular girl in school.

But the blaring of the trumpets and the sharp fingernail scraping clarinet screeching were calling to her like voices in the wind as her friends kept their incessant callings.

A.J. and Jessica stared at each other with an odd distant glance, like they had been apart of something special, but knowing in their heart of hearts that this happened all the time. It was something to watch two people kissing, and whether it's just in the heat of the moment or just an all out tongue slobbering fest, it's just special. The two suddenly heard footsteps marching so loud that it would have shook the calmest stone out of place.

It was Danny Parello and Giuseppe's brother Antony, who had a fury twirling in his eyes, looked disturbed by his brother's insolence.

Antony approached the boy and forcefully grabbed Giuseppe's hair, as his lips pulled off with a suctioning sound with his tongue hanging in the air, as the cheerleader bounced off the ledge and then ran back to her yipping friends. Antony motioned for the boy to leave, and he left.

"Don't worry about him." Danny said, letting a laugh escape him. "The girls are off limits when there are games. But I guess you wouldn't know that, would you A.J.?" A.J. laughed nervously as he shook his head, agreeing with what he was saying.

"The word is that we've been getting some complaints about our *star* quarterback." Danny was filled with such disdain. "We've been sent here because our business partner is airing his mouth about our business partner, yea know? I gotta' find a way to pull our friend away from his game, just for a moment. If you can lend your help that is?"

A.J.'s brain immediately started to work out a situation in his head. It wasn't really that hard for him, because whole scenes could come alive and in striking detail and lush colors. Then the thought occurred to him. What if one of Danny's cheerleaders were able to pull him around the side of the stadium, keep him occupied till Danny and his friends got him in their grasp. That's what prostitutes were for, and if he knew the right one, this cockamamie scheme could possibly lead to victory or defeat.

The wind was now blowing at a steady pace, and the moon steadily shifted in the dark abyss above them and the temperature was now falling as A.J. felt that he lost all of his humility, but he was confused about his innocence.

Danny saw A.J. staring at the quarterback as he strolled up and down the field, with an air about him, like he was better than they were.

A.J. looked at Danny with a cunning diviner, and both of them knew that he had an idea. By what Chris Mangini's crew had said this kid had the looks, guts, and cunning of being a Captain. Danny could see it, even thought he might not believe it.

"Is this guy a *fanook?*" A.J. asked, hoping that it sounded right when he said it. Danny saw his intentions, laughed and answered his question.

"I wouldn't know. He always pays me for a night with one of my girls after his big game. Why?" A.J. looked at the cheerleaders when one of them gave off a small laugh as his face lit with a renewed look, as if he had discovered pi. The gaggle whispered in heat waiting for a dominant male to chase after them at any moment, and claim them for their bodies as territory.

"What are you thinking?" Danny's teeth gleamed as he stretched his lips back, and stretched his whole face as if he was silly-putty.

"Get one of your girls to get that scumbag to the left side of the stadium," A.J. said, exhaling through his nose as his eyes were fixed in fury and might, like he had received this idea from the heavens. "Make sure it's for about two to five minutes until we can get through the stadium. And then we can settle the shit, and catch him with his pants down!" Danny watched as he continued on like a madman, explaining his plan, and thought about it, feeling that this was not going to work, or that the coach would be a problem as well.

Danny only knew him for no more than five minutes but he thought that his plan seemed realistic enough, but if Chris said he was bright, and anything that this kid said was golden. There were doubts in his own mind as he tried to grasp his mind around A.J.'s idea.

"What if the coach comes lookin' for him?" Danny said with little conviction.

"We'll deal with him if he comes lookin' for him." A.J. quickly counteracted his apathy.

Danny was then hooked as his eyes searched for the perfect girl to tempt his newly attained victim. He leaned over the stone gap and waved over to one of the cheerleaders who had been eyeing him since he arrived. One of his best girls was the one and only Kathy Redding's daughter, Allyson. With her dark brown eyes, pale skin, and blonde hair gave her better features than her mother's obese qualities. She had dark brown eyes and tanned skin that gave everyone the impression she was a frequent salon tanner.

But if she took extra care of her skin and had ritualistic sex with a few cheerleaders, she would be accepted in the Prep clan. With her hands combing her cheerleading skirt down Allyson leaned forward over the stone ledge and flung her arms around his large back. She released her arms from around his back (feeling his perspiration staining his cotton shirt) and stared with gleeful grin gave off a whorish complexion. But before she could say a word, Danny turned his cheek for *her* to kiss him.

His smooth guy qualities betrayed gentlemanly conduct, but Danny was far from a gentleman. Allyson rolled her eyes at him, and she leaned over the gap and affectionately kissed his cheek. Danny then swung his arm around her back, and forced her butt up, mooning all her friends, and hearing a riotous laugh. Danny whispered into her ear, giggling from her first reaction, but as his grip tightened around her waist she became nettled. And at that moment when Allyson thought he was being an asshole, A.J. gave her a rather charming smile, and flicked her open tongue sensually and whispered into Danny's ear, "you owe me," and flicked her tongue against his rather large ear lobe.

Danny's hand ventured down her hips, slipping under his skirt and palming her left butt cheek, his finger resting next to her tiny crack.

Allyson enjoyed his sweaty palm caressing her butt, and dreaming of his large finger caressing her sweet honeycomb. She pulled his hands off and ran passed her line of friends who were staring in burning fascination—eyes wide, thin lips open but Jessica watched with little surprise. Allyson, with her hard toe shoes, ran up to the quarterback who was shaking his shoulders in a cosmic rhythm, totally into the game. But when she tapped him on the shoulder he turned around, and saw Allyson's charming face, he relaxed as the distracting teeth shattering sound muddled her voice—disabling his field of hearing.

"I can't hear you!" He lowered his head as he steadily breathed his hot breath against her chest.

Allyson forced the most seductive whisper she could muster, and whispered with that of a tiger's purr—nodding with her head. "I want to give you some good luck." The quarterback arched his eyebrows, certainly perplexed about this offering, and gave an agreeing nod. The quarterback grabbed her hand in jubilance, and staring at her with quirky ideas no one would know. Only because he had given into her offer and the two made their way to the left side of the stadium, Danny knew that this was the perfect opportunity for them.

Chapter IV:

"A Honey's Luck"

"She's got him. Let's go before anyone catches them." Danny said and then darted up the stairs—huffing with short breath—quick as lightning—his fat shifted up and down underneath his shirt—leaving A.J. and Antony dumbstruck by his speed. Antony then moved forward as he picked up his pace after Danny who was pouncing on the concrete to catch up with Danny so that they could make their attack. A.J. felt a triumphant spark from this moment and he knew that time was quickly slipping through their fingers like sand.

A.J. pushed the bystanders that were standing in the entrance of the tunnel out of the way and he broke through the long concrete entrance, dashing past two bystanders who were standing around and talking like they had nothing better to do. As A.J. passed them he saw Danny and the two passed the policeman he didn't trust. The Officer flashed a very conniving smile, revealing his gold tooth in a conniving grin.

From his high perch of a seat from the stadium, Chris Mangini saw the quarterback being led around the side, and when he looked down at where A.J. was, he saw that Giuseppe, who was supposed to be looking after him, had evaporated from sight. Besides this strange series of disappearing acts, Chris knew that A.J. could keep up, and when he looked again, he saw that he was running up the steps with no trouble at all, as if he was moving along like a spirit in the wind that could not be left behind. Chris smiled, as he knew that it was time for A.J. to make his own experiences, even though he was worried for him, he knew he could take care of himself.

The offensive team, The Fighting Gerald's, were beginning to make there way with the foot ball toward the fifty-yard line, running with almost superb trained speed as he passed the forty yard line, and was suddenly met by a strong defensive linebacker, pummeling him to the ground, sending the crowd into a mixed uproar of cheers and jeers. Chris clapped his hands slowly, and the others around him did that as well. Chris waited, and watched as if nothing was happening, but feeling that actions were being taken care of.

Danny and Antony were walking out of the gate, and down the sidewalk entrance and they saw Allyson and the quarterback already fooling around exactly as A.J. said, *with his pants down.* They saw her slowly massaging his fleshy log with her right hand, and saw from that distance, his bulging head positioned bobbing underneath her skirt. But she hadn't pulled her skirt up for him just yet—becoming a distraction from the game as she slowly jerked his penis, sending fiery blood into his prim cock. His eyes were closed and groaned in pure lusting noises, breathing in total ecstasy (not exstasy) his body was taken in by deceit, crippling his legs and emotions all for the sake of a honey's luck. Allyson gave a quick glance by the bus entrance, and saw all if them were staring. She nodded for them to come and relieve her from these duties, but bought them more time by grabbing his head and forced her tongue inside his mouth, passionately massaging him with every lick of her swiping tongue.

Danny whispered to Antony, and every time he spoke, the words floated to their ears' in total secrecy, and with that came the warning, "don't harm him, just intimidation." Only if the situation called for it, they could show this quarterback how his privates looked unattached from his body real quick. On that note, the three made an approach across the pebbled ground like ghosts floating in the midst, and without kicking disturbing any of the pebbles beneath their feet.

The quarterback almost opened his eye, but Allyson put her hand over his eyes and she began to viciously bite, digging her two razor sharp front teeth into his pink lip, like a rusty nail piercing the soft lower flesh. Her teeth pulled out of it like a vampire bite, and then placed her mouth over it, as if she had hurt him and was sucking on his bloody wound. Of course she hadn't hurt him, but she could hear him whining as she then sucked his lower lip until she felt something quick and liquid-like jumping on her skirt. Allyson hated to even think of what it was, and she didn't even what to see what it was, knowing that her assumptions would be true. When she looked down, she saw a long white milky substance resting on the edge of her skirt.

"Damn it, like the Clinton scandal!" She thought and then pessimistically remembered how to get rid of a cum stain. He gave off a soft moan, and with that long eruption across her skirt, the pleasure in his body ended, sending all blood back to his brain, as the deceit began to leave his quivering pile of jelly.

Jessica pulled her moist lips off his, seeing that his penis was starting to shrink down like a turtle's arm and legs crawling back inside its shell.

"Thanks!" The quarterback moaned, as if she had done him a favor.

She scoffed, and then looked at the two, who were standing around her in their towering height, and she walked away, rubbing away his stringy jissom off her pants, making sure it was clearly away before she returned back to civilization. She looked one more time, and saw that she wouldn't want to be in his shoes right at that moment. Allyson returned back to the field, rubbing her hands on her skirt, feeling his cum sticking on her hands like caramel, and she didn't know how to get it off. But until then she would continue her steps with the team, and they just looked at her when she approached the line.

"What happened?" One of the cheerleaders said with a sparkle that knew everything—that annoying bratty whine that wanted in on what was going on or would resort to squealing.

"None of your business." Allyson, unafraid of her friend's intimidation, and hissed at her, "Now, get in the line, we need to work the crowd."

Antony and Danny were all standing around him with weapons of very large calibers in their pants: Danny was concealing a Berretta M29F and Giuseppe was carrying a black Glock 22, a handgun that could fit anyone's hand. The Berretta carried fifteen 9mm parabellum bullets, and the Glock carried ten, which was about five less than the Berretta. Inside Antony's palmed hand was a retractable switchblade that could cut a man's throat with no feeling or empathy at all. But, he didn't intend on killing him, just sending him into a state of fear he had never felt before, and if he did, he would make him feel it again. All of them looked at each other, trying not to laugh as he spoke to her, not knowing she had disappeared.

"Babe?" The quarterback said, breathing in large spaces of air, even though the wind was down, his body felt warm all over, giving his body that extra layer of protection, but not that kind of protection that could stop bullets or shatter a knife in two.

Danny looked at Antony, and he sent the blade out, and pressed it against his bulging Adams apple. As he slowly opened his eyes Allyson had disappeared, he now went from being excited to fearful since he had been lead by his own stupidity. Even though his body had now turned cold he could see these figures standing as if they were machines, but not there faces. It was the darkness, and not even the faint darkness could hide the fact that there was a blade sticking against his Adams apple.

"Don't make a sound, and we will make sure your parents won't receive your privates in the mail. Got it?" He saw all there eyes staring upon him like he was some kind of circus freak, something to be viewed, limp dick and all, like some clown that had just been caught naked in the woods taking a shit.

"Pull your pants up." Danny said, feeling the sensation of the knife in his hand was more than a feeling—to see blood pour out in large gushing spurts excited him. The quarterback slowly pulled his pants up along with his pants together and when he thought he was going to be afflicted by pain, the two stood motionless and blank, like a singing blade of grass. Danny slowly lowered the switchblade from his Adam's apple, giving him some room to breathe.

Then a snickering came from none of them except for Danny, who was taking real pleasure in watching him tremble from his sloppy embarrassment.

But the quarterback saw him, and stared with hatred as he said, "Fuck you, Danny." He voice trembled as he adjusted his wet package.

"Oh, come on hon." He mocked him in a very girlish/gay voice, and then his voice deepened again, "If you can keep it up long enough, but that's not your department, huh?"

The quarterback just shook his head when he felt the sting of his insult reach his heart like poison, "That's wrong man," but knew if he wasn't dead yet, they were keeping him alive for a purpose. With a daring but scared tone, he said, "I hear you got a problem with me."

Danny's eyes fixed upon him with pity and shame. " I don't got any problems with you. We think you're pretty cool, but I think it's you who had the problem by going to Chris and begging for his help, and then going around talking all this shit about him, like you're some fucking nigger. If I did have a problem, I wouldn't be talking about it, but I can't do that. We wanted to talk to you before this got out of hand."

This quarterback meant nothing to Danny, and the insurmountable amount of torture could be endless—silent, loud, a chamber full of explosives up his ass, anything. Danny looked back and didn't see A.J. "Hurry the fuck up, kid. Awww fuck it!"

Back at the exit/entrance way, A.J. was walking beside the barbed wire fence, feeling institutionalized by the wires, but rationalizing this as reality was something of a farce but as A.J. tried to avoid eye contact with the officer, but it was like he had heat ray, and as he was almost out the brick doorway, the officer grabbed his arm, squeezing as he stared him down. A.J. looked into his eyes, through those dark sunglasses, knowing the true corruption that lay in his heart, and did not want to see behind those sunglasses, because if he did, his eyes would be red. The officer clicked his teeth, and then leaned over to spit. The spit flowed out of his mouth like a rocket, and it hurled to the ground as it made a loud *splat* sound. Before the spit landed on the ground, A.J. pulled his arm away from the officer and he came free like a loose screw. The two looked at each other, A.J.'s arms tense and his fist was clenched ready to fight him. Officer Rose Kelly just looked at him, not moving, veins bulging out of his neck; everything that was telling him to cuff this boy and haul him away for fun. But he knew that he was with the three Dagos and the Jew boy that he had let go just two seconds before that. The officer let him go, and they didn't have to say a word.

    A.J. made his way on to the right side of the stadium, passing that same fence he was just outside and along his way A.J. saw a couple of smokers who were managing to make an escape away from the game and calm their nicotine addiction. Their attire looked very preppy, and A.J. felt that these two had seen him before. The smoke of their cigarette's blew past their heads and floated into the air, as they nodded to him out of respect. A.J. nodded and kept on his way.

    A.J. had reached the end of the stadium approaching the large open gate, looking over the gravel road to the bottom where the buses were parked. A.J. spied Danny and Antony from afar surrounding the frightened quarterback against the wall. A.J. was surprised that his plan surely worked, and he didn't know how to accept it. Whether out of happiness or fear as A.J. quietly walked down the pebbled walkway kicking up small patches of dust as he saw from the short distance the gritty details that were unfolding. The quarterback made a gargling scream as Danny threw his fist into the quarterback's face. Blood quickly left his nose in a large spray, almost like a tomato being smashed with a hammer, when another punch landed into his chin, adding insult to injury, the back of his head smacked against the concrete. The quarterback quickly grabbed his cheek, and felt for any broken teeth with his fingers. Surely there were, and he leaned his bloody face down spitting his two bicuspids and molars out in a milky red wad of spit.

    A.J. rushed over to the bullies in a slow walk, and saw the quarterbacks face glowing with orange blood and a line of white spit was leaving his mouth.

    "Did I miss anything?" A.J. said as he made the large bodies jumped as Danny thrusted another punch into the quarterback's belly out of surprised fright. The affect of the punch sent the quarterback's organs into a jumble of painful disarray. They turned and looked at A.J. with hateful murderous eyes, but A.J. thought that this torture was a little too extreme, but he didn't say a word against it.

    "Kid!" Danny said, breathing disproportionately, immediately laying another punch into the quarterbacks' face, making his mouth turn into a water fountain of blood, spewing it out in large puffs.

Danny looked at the others, and then said in a sarcastic way, "If you're gonna do that again, don't be so fuckin' loud!" After he was done talking to A.J., he turned his attention back to the blood soaked quarterback who was holding his jaw in agonizing pain, about to choke on his own blood.

A.J. daringly approached the quarterback and stood face to face with the quarterback giving him a tough relentless stare, but inside the quarterback A.J. could see the overwhelming amounts of terror and insecurity seeping as his tears streaked his blood stained face. A.J. knew that if he took a few more beatings from Danny or Giuseppe, he was sure that beyond his shattered face he would ultimately be dead—if Danny had his way. A part of A.J. liked seeing this quarterback being knocked around, watching his blood spraying from his face, turning him into that of a monster. They made him look like everyone else—scarred and ugly—and A.J. felt honored he beheld this transformation of how beauty became ugly.

Although his face looked like a bloody piece of rare European beef, A.J. didn't want to see him dead, this was enough for offending Chris's pride.

"Do you want to get hurt," A.J. centered his face right within the quarterback's eyes, feeling the quarterback's hot breath touch his face, as he braved the blood that flew off his face. "Or even worse be taken into the hospital for trivial shit. But I'll tell *yea'* something right now. If I was in your shoes, I would be listening to whatever we have to say and if *u* don't want to be six feet under. We'll take that risk, and I promise you we will."

A.J. continued in an elegant but straight fashion, if he was Jesus giving life to a sick and injured leper. A leper this football player wasn't, and he knew that Jesus wouldn't have threatened to put him in the ground, but he couldn't help but pretending to evangelizing this boy from his impudent darkness.

"We are all reasonable men here, and I'm sure you're not as big a loud mouth as people say you are." A.J. gazed menacingly at the quarterback as he spit blood on his shoes.

A.J. sighed unhappily, knowing that he was not getting his attention. "I'm sure we wouldn't have met under these circumstances if you hadn't let your feelings get in between your maturity." He sounded sarcastic, only A.J. was speaking in a dead serious tone to the decrepit, now smashed, monster of a quarterback. "But if you ever breathe a word about this or what went on right now, I'm sure you won't live to tell your parents what happened."

A.J.'s speech was interrupted by the loud *whomp* of a punch entering into the quarterback's stomach. The quarterback bent over, on all fours gasping for air, holding onto his chest and stomach as if they were about to fall out of his body. He crawled on the ground, and picked himself up from the ground, dusting off the grass from his pants. His confidence was now shattered, and now anger was the only thing he could feel. Speaking with a dagger edged tone his voice became higher than a whisper, and he intentionally wanted to cut there pride, as if he was on a plank about to enter the doomed waters.

"You *WOPS* ain't got the guts to try anything stupid. I'll tell everyone about what happened…" The quarterback's tone sounded uncontrollable, but was suddenly turned into a gagging choke as A.J. had been pushed out of the way. Antony had forced his Glock 22 into the quarterback's mouth cutting off his flow of words from his mouth. The pistol that Giuseppe held in his hand seemed small and undetected although A.J.'s first impression was that it was bigger in the dark. His voice was very stern and straightforward, and surprisingly good with a charming accent.

"Us *Dagos* have more guts than you could ever imagine. Don't think that we don't do what we say. Because no one, including your team members would ever come to your funeral from how fucked up you will be. So, this is our gift to you."

"Better him than me!" A.J. thought, and then concentrated on something more random but more appropriate—their backs and what there scene was like.

The Quarterback's eyes widened as he was being confronted face to face with a madman, sweat began to pour from inside his pits, a tunnel of shit began to cram in between his scrunched anus as the cold barrel clicked against his teeth and his tongue. Blood slowly dripped on the black slide of the firing mechanism. Only, A.J. couldn't help the feeling was all too familiar to him, but he remembered he wasn't the one underneath the wrath of a mad man's barrel, utterly helpless and scared shitless—under the mercy of his waiting trigger finger.

Giuseppe pulled the trigger. A.J. closed his eyes and covered his ear expecting to be deaf, and hear everyone around them start to scream in fear, but no sound of a gunshot or a firecracker was to be heard, just a solid toneless *click* of the hammer.

A.J. opened his eyes, lowering his hands, and saw that the quarterback was not dead at all. He wiped a sigh of relief as he saw a trail of urine traced through his tight spandex uniform and covered the side of his Nike air shoes. Antony now shrugged an evil smile and by the way he was forcing the barrel into his mouth looked like he was a doctor touching his tonsils with a wooden tong. But now it was time to show this quarterback the light from the dark, intelligence from ignorance, and life overpowering death.

A.J.'s veins were flowing with blood again after this happened, and spoke to him rather coldly and bluntly, far from the four-play, it was time they were heard. "Are you going to cooperate like a gentleman would? Because if there were any bullets in that gun, you would have been shot because of your pride, and since we have given you another chance, this is your penance."

"You are always now in our debt and you will have to repay that debt whenever you are called upon. I wouldn't care if you were fucking your bitch or if your grandmother just died and her wake was in five minutes, you skip her wake and go to the funeral. Understand?"

The quarterback was now defeated, and the epitome of all his emotional defenses was now depleted as a blood soaked tear cemented into his cheek, knowing that Chris Mangini was his God and after a mock execution, his conscious had plummeted through his stomach and vacated down his leg. He submitted to there power shaking his head with the gun still nestled, softening his mouth.

The quarterback was only a small part of the world, and his popularity would be a laughing stock of the entire school knew of his urinal accident, and his premature ejaculation. He would have to join the outcasts. His name would have been down the toilet and all the popularity he had worked for in two years would be a failure in one night, but he knew they would be good on their promise.

The three had succeeded in their humiliation and ruin of the quarterback. His life meant more to be humiliated than to his nonexistence.

Danny looked at Antony and gave him the signal to pull the weapon out of his mouth. Antony slowly pulled the steel slide out of his mouth as the front of the barrel touched the quarterback's top-teeth as he saw the quarterback flinching every second as the cold shaft left the quarterback's tongue. He bent over and grabbed his throat collecting air as his face had regained color, and the shit bunched up in his anus had then pressed against his clear white pants. Antony chuckled and swiped the spit-covered slide on his shirt—the quarterback looked at him with agitation look, like he was about to yell but all he wanted to do was cry. Antony bucked at him with a stoic, ungodly shift of his body as the quarterback cringed and put a blood stained hand over his head.

A.J. grabbed his arm and turned with a shocking surprise. After being face to face with Antony—each second was as if a nightmare of hell had spawned inside his head—he relieved his grip and let Antony go. But then Antony forced the 4 pound semiautomatic death machine into A.J.'s cold, clammy hands. At that moment, Antony and Danny started to walk back toward the open bus entrance, leaving A.J. with a broken down quarterback and the plastic piece of death. A.J. stood for a moment transfixed by what had happened, and then glanced at the others who were trailing off kicking up dust and pebbles as the pebbles rolled like falling comets and the dust swirled in the unknown galaxy.

A.J., who did not want to look down at his palm, felt nervous with the gun in his hand, after a moment he heard voices, *possibly looking for the quarterback!* He quickly pulled his shirt up and stuffed it into his pant line covering the handle with his shirttail. A.J. then took one last look at the quarterback, who was hunched over, crying in his own childish sadness, wanting everything that had happened to be gone from him like some unpleasant wet dream into a nightmare. A.J. felt sick at that moment like he had been apart of something wrong.

As A.J. moved up the dirt path he gave one last glance to the quarterback, and at least he could cry about it, and A.J. at least gave him some credit for that.

Mark Redding, Cathy Redding's son, was four foot two, sandy spiked blonde hair that was starting to fall back down on his nicely cropped hair was looking for the quarterback. Being that he was the team's kicker, he knew many people inside the Prep faction, and of their vices. He didn't see where he had gone, but he knew that it was time for them to go on the offensive, and they needed their quarterback to take them *to the goal line*. As he traveled along the front of the stadium, the blasting screams and constant noise that burned into the night sky also burned his eardrum. When he left, he felt the noise lessening, giving him a minute to regain his hearing, but it wouldn't last for long. But, when he started walking up the hill he saw a boy hunched up against the wall, and his hands wrapped around his legs, not ashamed but wrapped in his own apathy. For some reason, Mark felt that this was their star quarterback but he hoped that it wasn't and nothing was wrong. But for some good reason, he felt it was his man, and continued toward the crouched fragile being.

"What are you doing man! Are you all right?" Mark Redding carefully asked, seeing the dark puddle that was underneath him, and the long line of piss was forming down his spandex pants.

"What's wrong man?" Mark said, never really feeling any real sympathy for the quarterback since he never liked him, but a sting of sympathy gave him the benefit of the doubt.

"No!" The Quarterback yelled into his hand, becoming almost inaudible, "Nnnn…nnnn…nnnn…gg…ggg…ee…ttt…off" jabbering his words in a frightful stutter.

"Come on, tell me what happened!" Mark said, very calmly and then the quarterback pulled up his head and showed him.

Mark couldn't believe how his face was so bloody, and he didn't even want to ask him what happened, but he knew he should ask. With a rather fearful and a bright case of wonder on his face, he said, "What happened to you?"

At that moment, the quarterback began to cry again, sending spots of blood all over his arms and made his white pants bright red, but he did not care, because it was a relief for him. Mark Redding looked side to side anxiously up and down the hill and pebbled walkway. "No one," Mark thought and slowly pulled the quarterback's head out from in between his legs and brought his face upwards. Looking into his teammate's eyes, he knew that the damage had been done, not just by the tangy apple juice aroma—but his pond had been sucked dry and it had usurped the hardheaded bastard's soul.

"Let's get you cleaned up!" His teammate (and sadly) friend, put out his hand. The quarterback was amazed that he wasn't giving him a hard time but with his outstretched hand, a glint of knowledge crossed his brain. In this world of explosions and glinting promises in the universe, blind kindness was something of an accepted mystery—and when it happened, it was a bright solarplexus of colors that made everything okay—just for a minute. The quarterback finally accepted his hand and pulled him up, enwrapped and bathing in his open kindness.

"Come on. I'll take to the locker room and get you cleaned up." The quarterback was pleased, but he was silent, pressing his hands up against his battered face. Mark led him around the side when they walked out across the track, feeling the bright lights burning their eyes, fleshing his weakness out for all to see. But when they beheld their circus freak, the crowd went silent, and some threw up a cynical laugh. Jessica from her distance saw the quarterback with Allyson's brother, but she wasn't the one to ask about things that weren't her business, and that suddenly quelled her curiosity, only for a short time.

Back around the side, outside along the fence, A.J. hadn't realized how much it had silently bothered him. He was urging to get it off his quivering lip as he could feel the frosty tension and to breathe a word would sink the tension, and make them delve into their feelings, which were large waters for them to cross. It seemed good for a moment not to talk, but A.J. felt like the tension needed to be broken, releasing everyone from this pent up rage that was choking off all the air. A.J. felt the annoyance of the metal sticking to his sweaty back, was constantly putting him on edge, like a tick that was burrowing into his skin, biting relentlessly, not letting him forget what was in his pants. He walked beside Antony and spoke rather soft, still not comfortable, but coming to grips with this rather bloody scene.

A.J. put a hand over his shoulder and whispered on edge, "I thought you didn't know how to speak English?" Antony turned with his marble cut chin down, and replied with a calm but prudish heir about him. "There are a lot of things you don't know about me. But you handled things good, I like you."

"Really?" A.J. blinked his eyes, cocking his head oddly, and it surprised him a bit that he was getting a compliment from a killer on his nerves of steel that he didn't know he had. Giuseppe gave him a sarcastic stare—eyes narrowed, his brows cocked, then falling—turning away, knowing that he didn't need to repeat himself.

But A.J. felt the gun that Antony had put in his hand and asked him if he wanted it back, but kept it very vague since they were in the company of civilians.

"When do you want your… you know the thing back." A.J. said. Antony glanced back at him, and A.J. gave a small pat to his waist, where the gun was poking out of him.

He replied with an honest answer. "No. You keep it. Just think of this as experience."

"No, I can't. My mother could find it." A.J. protested, knowing that this was true in all circumstances, since he was no good at hiding anything.

"It's not my responsibility anymore." Antony shot back, spit flying from his mouth. "Just throw it in your neighbors trash, I don't give a fuck!"

A.J., for his own life, was not seeing the point of he had been dubbed the honor of being the trash man. As he was about to pull his shirt up they were already nearing the gate where the same cop that was ready to swipe people with the electronic beam of exploitation. A.J. now felt the fear of being caught with a gun that wasn't his, but if he just stayed calm—"yeah, right," with a stroke of his wand it would ruin everything.

He sped up next to Danny and whispered to him really petrified. "That cop was giving me a hard time before I left. I don't trust him, he might fuck up our cover and arrest me."

Danny's rotund body shifted unworried and untainted by what A.J. had said, and ignored him as the two—Danny waddled as Antony strutted—in front of him and walked calmly, when he lowered the wand in front of A.J., motioning for him to stop, as the wand began, with a mind of its own, *ticccccc… ticccccccccc…ticccccc…*as A.J. finally stopped, and Officer Rose Kelly started to wave the electronic stick attempting to shake him up by his large brutish stature. The stick started to make small beeps, *beep…*along his chest…*beep…*along his chest, coming dangerously to his pants. Danny yelled to the officer before the stick touched his waist…

"Hey!" Danny said and the wand was right above his chest. "He's with us!" The slow beep went off two times in a fast motion, but then Danny looked at A.J. with a tense stare telling him to be cool.

The officer stared at A.J. and A.J. gave him a posing smile. His large hawk eyes glared and he was about to be gripped in the *claws of justice* but his plans were thwarted as he pulled the stick out of A.J.'s way. He moved past the officer without saying a word, feeling the bitterness stirring his bubbling sticky pot that was beginning to make his chest hurt.

A.J. moved passed him and hurried toward the two, who were all standing in the middle of the stadium waiting and looked over their shoulders in a paranoid manner.

"You did good kid." Danny's creepy and honest smile actually made his darkened face seem less brutish, but normal it comforted A.J. to a point where his nerves were at ease. "You can come to my place in Queens anytime, you hear me, don't be strange, son." As he shook his hand, A.J. felt an albatross laying a big fat rotten egg in his open hand.

"See you in the future."

Danny let go of his hand and headed the same way they came through, shifting out the open brick entrance way and into the darkened parking lot. He had certainly hid well in the shadows, almost too well. A.J. watched him from inside the gate, and at that moment had to get back up and see Chris before he left.

From Chris's kingly view nestled in his stadium seat, he saw the three walking up the steps, admist all the screaming fans that were bellowing into the sky like commoners asking for more bloodshed in the coliseum. Chris was watching A.J. walk up the steps and saw something ultimately changed—his walk and posture had become stiff, like a plank of wood had been stuffed up his back. At that moment, felt a tap on his arm. Chris turned and arched his head and Frank spoke in broken Sicilian, even though it was a good effort, he cared about the privacy of their conversation.

"Are you thinking about taking him to the city soon?" Frank had been thinking about this for a while on how they were about to go about introducing him to the Commission. Chris felt a small ball forming in his chest as he spoke, and his eyes, the darkened well that could be the apocalyptic portal into his mind.

"I don't know. You go around and see if anybody knows where he lives so we can watch where he goes to which bus stop. Like every new soldier, he's not gonna be too innocent for long."

For a moment Frank put his mind to work and knew about something he could pull A.J. into. He broke away from his Italian since they weren't talking about important things. "You know that *thing*?"

Chris thought about it and was confused since he had many *things* on his agenda and being vague in his life was an everyday ritual. "What *thing*? That *thing* tomorrow or the *thing* next Saturday?"

"You mean the *thing* next Saturday. Yeah, maybe I'll bring my *friend of mine* along." Chris hinted, but Frank wasn't really sure why he was bringing a damn average "Joe blow from windy city" into their organization, but Frank didn't want to be jealous of him—that was the way women acted.

Chris motioned for A.J. to sit down as if he was an elderly grandfather calling his grandchild to keep him company when A.J. saw his welcoming gesture and sat right next to him like a grandchild, his black hair gleaming in the overhead beams like that of liquid tar. Only the two groups, Chris's and Gene's "Ten Lost Tribes," formed of protective layer of sixty people that looked little more than a platoon from afar. Chris was eager to hear what had happened, and so he would find out as Chris put a hand over Antony's shoulder and proceeded to ask him what happened when he left.

Chris laughed with a maniacal twist in his voice, relishing in the torture they inflicted upon him. Only he intervened with urgently with a distraction.

"Have you thought about what I said before?" Chris said with an eager impatience, as if he was leaving A.J. too much time to think.

"About my question or what you said to me earlier?"

Chris nodded, and A.J. surely meant his sage advice he had given him. It still didn't help him figure out who he was, but he knew that it would only get murkier with each day.

"I don't really know how to understand it all yet, but the last few days have been really good since theirs a lot of money involved and with the right guidance from the best in the league. I can say that now I really don't fear death or anyone else's bullet, because if God saw what I had to endure, then he wouldn't punish me."

Chris scoffed, agreeing too much with his tough talk, "Well kid," and nudged his elbow playfully, "that's a good thing. Don't worry about death, because once you conquer death, then you have nothing to fear. Listen and follow me, learn the ropes, and don't let anybody know what's goin' on in your head that can't keep their fucking mouths shut. And another big thing for you to learn is to speak when you're spoken to with me and my friends, but go with the program, and you'll do good things."

Now A.J. was seeing clearly, even though the complexion on his skin looked flushed, a beating drum was keeping A.J.'s body pumping with life, and A.J. felt lost in a myriad of mirrors. Every reflection seemed new, but unfamiliar, even though he could be lost forever, A.J. would start having long cases of insomnia forcing his eyes open as if his eyelids were glued to his skin—and the despair of sleep would be unbearable.

"I want to see myself in a house where the kitchen is bigger than my room." He sounded like a mad man that was living inside a trashcan, speaking of things that he would never have, but still had the right to dream about what he couldn't. "I want to help my family pay off their bills, and put myself at the top of the game. It's not bad to have some fear and respect…" he finally forced the words out, slowly, "I'll do whatever it takes. In no words or less, I'm down for everything."

Chris saw another side of A.J. that Chris thought he would never share *this early*, and that could be disastrous, because once the deal was signed, there was no turning back. *"Into the dark abyss, said the young man fishing,"* an apparition said echoing in the halls of his brain. "But for what?" Chris thought, "Fishing for what? Compliments, wishes, dreams, love, pain…what is the answer?" The voice disappeared, and nothing was solved, but he guessed that even the answers would be solved when things would be right.

"Are you sure," Chris smiled comfortably, bringing himself back to reality, "that's a broad list of goals on your plate. But take it slow, don't go cowboy on me. How about we get your feet wet first. You gotta serve before you can rule the throne. I can't deny your aspirations though, and that's good to know that people have aspirations…even in this age of information and false deities, you know, just a lack of ambitions. But, I guess everyone has a crusade, and we all have to persevere, and serve the cause." Even though he was being sarcastic—"he was beyond sarcastic," A.J. thought, "he's dead serious," totally enamored by his words. Chris finished and then looked off into the field, and off into the sky.

Then after that momentary pause, Chris spoke out of the clear blue, and turned his head, but did not eye A.J. "Why don't you call your pop or your mom to come and get ya'. I won't detain you any longer, you had a long day."

A.J. was stunned that he was letting him go this early, and the fourth quarter hadn't even ended yet. He didn't know if he offended him or said something wrong, but he needed to know for his own sake.

"Are you sure, I could stick around if you want?" A.J. was concerned; his eyes were filled with dismay and his body hunched over.

"Naw, you get out of here. Get some sleep."

"Is that okay?" A.J. hoped he wasn't fooling around, or had disappointed him in his inability to comment on his words. But A.J. saw that he was wearing all his worries on face, dragging his young face into that of an old man overcome by skepticism and fear for his soul. But Chris was worn out by skepticism and fear in which they had become room mates, inseparable from each other—not giving his soul too much room to breathe.

"Yeah. Go ahead. There isn't much to see now. You're doing good work.

Like I said, keep your nose clean and be a good earner, and keep the piece out of sight."

"Yeah, I got *cha*!" A.J. assured him loud and clearly, and that was what he made his good byes, while some nodded with respect, and then journeyed down the long flight of open steps. He walked down fifty steps before he got to the rail and hopped down the right side of stairs, and made it to the hallway, still crowded with kids, but as he passed them, he traveled down the long tunnel, looking upwards at the sky. The wind started back up with a howling *swoosh* as a chill ran up A.J.'s back as he heard the distant crowd screaming in a bloody uproar as the opposing team made a touchdown. A.J. would remember this night very well, that he finally had a group of friends that actually cared about him, and wanted him to be apart of their group. Maybe he was fooling himself, but he was pretty confident lately.

Ten minutes after A.J. left the arena Chris's tightly knit group of twenty Italian soldiers were migrating toward the stone exit. Police officer Rose Kelly was seen on the other side of the stadium, watching for any uprisings or fights, since they were filled up with ninety black students. If he had to beat any of them in the head he would, and didn't really need to worry about white kids starting any trouble. Chris and his friends walked through the gates quietly and quickly, as they walked toward their vehicles and didn't enter their car before Chris and his friends entered into their cars safely.

Chris, Frank, Gene, and Krazy all rode in the same car and it was Krazy's turn to drive tonight. Frank was in the passenger seat while Gene and Chris were sitting in the backseat. Antony and Giuseppe made their way into the vehicles on the other side of him.

"So what was with A.J. asking you about?" Gene said looking over at Chris. Chris became annoyed when anyone asked about this, but never showed his anger.

"It's nothing. I think he's too smart for his looks. Just keep this kid on the down low." Chris was looking out the window, tapping for the boys to go away, wishing he could do that to Gene at this moment. His bodyguards dispersed, and all of them entered into their cars with no trouble at all.

The three were sitting inside chewing on Chris's orders, but Gene's stomachs was aching and he refused to accept his word now and felt that in his gut it needed to be said, risking his honor.

"Why do you want to do that? This kid doesn't know jack beans, and no one is going to give a shit about what he is. The real question is can we trust him." Chris faced Gene, arching his face in a pinnacle that looked like a plateau of a cliff.

"Why do you want to know that?" Chris said, his voice getting curious, staring at him with curiosity surmounting in his system. "I thought you said he had a strong stomach?"

Gene stopped himself before he lost his temper, and then said with disgust. "I don't know how much he can handle, and if he's got a big mouth, people are going to know about shit that is not their business."

Chris just shook him off, and then said with total disdain, "He's not going to do that, start the car."

Gene just shook his head with disdain looking out the window, and then Krazy started up the beast, sending out clouds of air as they headed on their way. First to Chris's house where they dropped him off where he would slip some money into her purse so that she could spend it on whatever she wanted—food, clothes, personal expenses, whatever. To see his mother happy kept him going, and knew that happiness came with a price. He smiled wishing that his father was here with him, but then knew that he was in a better place. He laid next his wife's sleeping body for half the night before he finally slipped into deep sleep, with his eyes open.

A.J. went to sleep with his closed.

Chapter V:

"The Field Trip"

A.J. woke up in a major fright as a layer of sweat trickled down his head as water trailed across his eyes. Blinded from the disorienting sweat, the air conditioner was buzzing in a lone droll, and A.J. wiped the forming sweat from his forehead. A.J. would have remembered his dreams, but this dream seemed rather odd, so he had to remember it. A.J. decided to wash his face and prepare for the hard Monday ahead of him.

A.J. pushed the covers off with his feet and the cool air relieved him from the awful enclosure as goose bumps rumpled out of his skin as the cool air avoided him, as if his body had been disabled, his body's intrinsic switch to his hormones. The door gave a small *creaking* sound as he tiptoed down the halls. He had made it to the bathroom, slithering through the open crack like a snake as he quickly closed the door behind him, but the cold floor felt like three feet of snow against his bare toes. After he winced from the way the cold jumped on his feet like flaming coals, A.J. approached the sink and turned the knob that released the hot water. The water jetted out like rushing rainwater as he cupped his hands, sending sprays of steam against his tired. A.J. splashed his face once with the warm water and another with cold water so that the sun wouldn't blind him.

Dabbing his face with a towel, he thought about going back to sleep, even with the mix of boiling/cold water dripping down his thin but red cheeks. Closing his eyes, he was jabbed by a broken up scene that scared, intimidated his senses for a long minute. His memory was clouded almost as if he had forgotten about it as soon as he could remember it. Only A.J. closed his eyes and tried to piece his foggy dream back together. *"Clouds…a mist…a big man…and…"* He searched within his mind, and found it, but was fearful of what he saw. *"Another man on his knees…"* A.J. looked closer, seeing through the fog, his blood turning cold and worms were crawling all over him as he saw with such crystal clarity. *"The man above him is forcing a gun into his mouth."*

A.J. opened his eyes again; no mist, no big man, just the darkness of the sink, a confused, perplexed mess. With his face clean, he proceeded toward the shower, but for the life of him he didn't want to see that *big man* again. Inside the shower, the hot jets were beating against his body mercilessly as A.J. leaned against the shower wall letting the hot water soak his tired skin, as his mind went on autopilot, just talking about random stuff that had no real connection at all. After a moment of being beaten into submission by the streaming jets, he let his hand fall down his stomach and land on his crotch.

But he didn't want to ruin his performance with Jessica, and let his weaknesses consume his mind for the rest of day. If she was into him, she would respect his decision not to do anything, but things were the other way around, he would have no problems with her, but all dreams regarding the man had left him, but he wasn't rid of it yet.

Before he had gotten out of the shower, he had laid his dream to rest, grabbing the restless doorknob with a towel around his scarred black and blue belly, and pulled it open quietly so he wouldn't wake anyone up. A.J. quietly made his way from the bathroom and slipped into his room, and slowly shut the door behind him. He proceeded to his drawer and found a pair of dark blue jeans. He forced his head through a white long sleeved T-shirt as he slicked his long black hair with a fine-toothed comb, and grabbed a bottle of gel. Holding the comb below the end of the bottle he squirted it out, and ran it through his hair. After his hair was perfectly slicked back, another nagging feeling made him go back to the drawer where the piece had been stashed from the other night.

He opened the drawer very slowly and felt a tingling crawling rush over his body, and what he thought was there actually was not. The Glock was gone, out of sight, not even there. He thought about what he had done with it, and he almost went crazy enough to go everywhere and look for it. He remembered that he had dumped it in the trashcan of his next-door neighbors, the Silvios. From the distance of his room A.J. heard his fathers roaring yawn echo through the halls, and he closed the drawer in a comfortable manner, knowing that he had nothing to fear about the Glock. Feeling in a peaceful mind he felt obligated to accept the day before it even came, but he decided to lay back down in his bed before the sun rose. As he laid his on the other side of his bed, he closed his eyes, feeling the drowsiness of his eyes beginning to weigh on him, he fell into a deep sleep, for a small time.

Once the sun rose over all the houses on A.J.'s block, covering them in thick pulpy orange and red colors the clock read quarter to seven, and A.J. gathered his books together in one hand and A.J.'s ears caught the rustling of the pots and pans being stacked from the hallway. The sounds resembled a clamoring bell from a gothic cathedral, but he could hear those bells echoing that it was six fifty, and his bus would be coming to his stop.

A.J. opened the door and saw that the light had been turned on in the kitchen and a smell of Pam and the scraping of a fork was twirling a few eggs in the frying pan, as if fingernails against the chalk board. But A.J. was in a hurry and could only grab what he could carry and make quick timing for the bus stop. As A.J. approached the kitchen he saw his mother and father standing side by side over the oven quietly whispering soft fantasies to each other with his father's arm quickly sliding his fingers down his mother's side and palming her right butt cheek. A.J. smiled, and saw his father walking away from her proudly, pushing his hairy chest out while his mother worked diligently at the stove. He watched them as he took his pills, avoiding anything else to eat (thanks to the Adderal that caused him from eating), and he kissed them both goodbye.

Once A.J. left, the tension between them had finally left, and Mary started to shed out a few tears, rushing toward his wife giving her a compassionate hug. She wasn't crying about anything else except the fact that A.J. was going to leave them and start his own life, and in a way, *he already had.*

A.J. had started down the block with the suns rays burning his corneas, like the way a flame hits a tightened vein accentuating the pain arresting his nerve endings. It sent him into a state of shock as he covered his eyes and walked further down the road. As the gravel below him echoed with grieving pain, the group of trees in the foreground shielded the bright morning light from A.J.'s faltering vision. As the sun was peeking giddily through the green leaves A.J. looked to his watch, and saw that the second hand was nearing twelve, making it two minutes to seven, and thought that the bus had been late. He thought that he had been on time like every morning or had just late. He approached the corner of Belmont Ave and looked down the crossroads of his street. Each of the crossroads seemed to go on for miles, leading to other parts of the suburb, but he couldn't help but feel alone, in this neighborhood of a lost cause and hiding within these houses were the living skeletons that breathed, but were never really living.

A.J. stood at the corner looking down each way, nothing and nobody came around in the morning. Where A.J. lived his neighborhood didn't start up until eight thirty in the morning and the only vehicle around between seven o' clock and seven fifteen is the arrival of the big yellow "dick" cheese. And with a relaxing sigh he set his books down on the pavement, yawning throwing his hands in the air stretching his tired bones. For miles, the trees, in their tall mighty stature, were not going to last forever, and he knew this better than anyone. He was not going to be safe for long, imaging the trees falling down and men in suits who were bug eyed aliens underneath their sharp Armani.

He waited for another minute and the morning wind blow into his clothes, chilling A.J. to the bone, reminding him that he was such a big fucking asshole for not wearing a jacket. He tried to figure out what that noise was, unless he was hearing things, the sound of a car's engine erupted throughout the quiet, sleeping street. A.J. immediately stooped to the ground picking up his books as he was waiting for the large yellow cheese to come and pick him up.

But A.J. didn't see a bus, but only a shabby beat up car blazing down his street like he was on fire. He couldn't see the driver or the passenger's faces until the car was nearing Belmont Ave. A.J. had never seen that car before and especially in a condition where the bumper had been taped together on both sides and how the paint was discolored. Inside the car was Krazy, Chris's lieutenant driving the car but without Chris in his presence, A.J. knew that something had been up from the start. But as the car approached A.J. the passengers broadened A.J.'s view. Inside was Frank riding next to Krazy; Gene and Chris were seated very comfortably.

The car stopped with a screeching halt next to A.J. and jumped back alarmed, trying not to be hit, but had been definitely thrown off. A.J. saw that his friends looked refreshed and tired at the same time, as if they had been without sleep for days on end, only to shut their eyes for a moment would rejuvenate their senses. A.J. looked at Chris and saw that he had the face of a night owl—bags underneath there eyes and constantly moving. With a sharp wave of his hand, Chris motioned for A.J. to get in the car. A.J. felt hesitant for a moment and tapped on the window with the back of his finger, but Chris looked at A.J. and motioned him to go on the other side. A.J. got the hint as the door slowly opened as Gene lumbered out, holding the door for A.J. He stood for a moment jolted as if a bolt of lightning had struck him in his heart to jump inside the car.

The neighborhood seemed quiet enough and the denseness in the air gave him a feeling of isolation. He felt that if he stepped into that car, A.J. would never make it to the school, late or not. But if he had missed one day of school they would be making phone calls all day until they got one of his parents at work or at home. Although he thought maybe they would be going to school and was thinking too much. They were giving him a ride, and what could steer A.J. away from the trust of his *paisans* was fear. A.J. slowly walked around the car and approached the open door.

Gene sighed and became impatient with an enraged stare that made A.J. walk faster and with that final decision in practice, he moved past Gene entering into the center of the seat next to Chris. Gene laughed shaking his head and groaned in a calm growl.

Gene jumped in as A.J.'s body was inside the car as the car roared down the street while A.J. fixed himself in his cramped space. In the car, A.J. heard the engine huff out of a faulty starter, as a rickety ride at Six Flags would make if it was about to give out. He turned and saw that he had missed the bus by a few minutes.

A.J. shrugged and saw the moods on their faces that his companions weren't in the mood to talk, just like a dead choir in an abandoned church. A.J. opened his notebook and decided to finish some unfinished homework he had forgot to do over the weekend, while they sat in the silence. Holding down his pile of papers, which were never clipped in the holes, he set the paper above the other first month notes of his busy schedule as he pulled a pen from the felt pocket pouch where pens and pencils were kept safe He laid the pencil down to the paper, and then began to finish an answer to a question.

8. What was the largest population of Indians in the Northeast Colonies, and where were the connections?

In New York, there were the Unami and Munsee tribe that came from Delaware and settled into Manhattan. The Dutch had traded guns and ammunition with the Iroquois from Maine to the Mississippi and between the Ottawa and Cumberland Rivers. There was also a Mohawk tribe (now called Mohawk Valley) Schaunactada (in Albany) and the Onoalagona tribe, (Schenectady).

Chris saw this and held his laughs down to a small chuckle when A.J. darted his head to see what was so amusing, as his chuckle turned into a hoarse cough. A.J.'s head turned cockeyed and flashed him a wink, and returned to his thoughts back to the question on the twenty questionnaire assignment of US History.

"Too smart for a young kid," Chris thought, seeing him write down his answers as many things began to pop into his own mind. Chris had seen and heard from many outfits that wars internal and outside the family's proved that the streets were becoming open territory for slaughter houses, proving to become a real slaughter on all sides. The family's captains and soldiers of New York were fidgeting in their seats from anticipation of war with Don Pescaro. Someone needed to make the first move before the boss of another family was the target of another family. But when Chris had seen A.J. finishing his homework, he quickly stopped A.J. from finishing his homework, and had to instill something that he might not like, fear.

"What are you doin'? You finishin' something important?" Chris sarcasm turned ruthless and arrogant. A.J. peered at Chris with a confused stare, his eyes widened from his lashing comment.

"I'm finishing my homework so I won't get in trouble with that prick Mr. Mulland." A.J. said.

Chris nodded his head pressing his finger over lips with his thumb balancing against his cheek. "We are going to school aren't we?"

A.J. asked him again with an adamant look. In that second, four ears and eyes were listening and hearing their conversation quite clearly. Everyone inside the car had been used to the deviant strings Chris had to pull to get him off of school, which was easy as flicking his wrist. A.J. saw an evil glare seep through his face only putting A.J. in a tighter position. Chris only laughed arrogantly arching his brow arching in a daunting yet haunting tone.

Then confused filled his cheeks and felt a dangerous feeling within his very bones. They weren't going to school.

"Where *we* goin' you won't need to deal with that prick Mulland. Or have to finish that assignment." Chris made a crooked finger and tapped the top of A.J.'s homework, as if it wasn't as important as what they were about to do. It didn't take long for A.J. to get what Chris was hinting at, but he really didn't want to know what Chris had done behind the curtains just yet. A.J. didn't want to know that part of the equation, but the overall total was perplexing. A.J. now thought getting into the car was a choice he had made once that door was behind him.

"So where are we going…" A.J. replied but then closed his mouth, knowing that he subconsciously broke the first rule to never ask questions. But A.J. held his breath anticipating a well deserved chiding from Chris. But Chris didn't take this as any insult since he was going to give it to him good anyway.

Chris didn't want to get angry or let his rage slip from his calm fingers. He wanted to chide him like a father would do to a son, but he gave A.J. the benefit of the doubt with a subtle and chilling façade that became cold and clear as the ever-chilling winds of winter.

"We're going on a *school* trip, it doesn't concern you. You're going to learn some things that are not in those history books." A.J. looked at his half-done history homework with a half-hearted despair toward it. The reality of doing this work meant that after all his work, there would just be more, and that paper wouldn't be of any use to him.

"If you have to know, the city is where we have to be." Chris glanced at

A.J. conspicuously, cocking his eyebrows up and down as he felt the engine made a sputtering coughing sound.

"Goddamn it!" Frank yelled, and hit the dashboard. The starter immediately sprang back into action, and they continued on their smooth journey to the city. A.J. now felt Chris's words penetrate his open mind and saw into his nervous, feeble eyes—he could see he wasn't comfortable which was going to keep his mind stagnant, sticky like honey. Only if he could shield him from his weaknesses, he could be free from his worries and do the most impossible things. A.J. let his tense bones start to ease his clenched fingers all the way down to his shoes, and even though the air conditioner was on, small goosebumps popped along his arm.

"Come on, you look like ya' seen a ghost or something. I thought you were always this calm." Chris said nudging his shoulder giving him that all knowing grin letting him see the Chris Mangini he had come to know and respect, but still afraid at the same time. A.J. let a chuckle escape him as he came to realize a troublesome thought.

A.J. pushed aside everything, and opened his notebook turning to no particular section and A.J. zipped it closed. "Don't do it," his better judgment was saying, but as he A.J. leaned back in next to Chris in a certain wonder and amazement as they continued on toward the road.

"Now, Look at that. You got more room to breathe." Chris said eagerly yet redefined look at A.J. At this point he decided to change the subject. "So how's your mom and pop?" A.J. immediately heard this, turning to his captain, and spoke with a great ease in A.J.'s voice.

"They're okay. Everything seems okay. Only my mother looks sicker by the day and I don't know how they are going to pay for another operation." A.J. said with a terrible pain coming from his hurting heart that was beating ten times harder. And that sweltering pain started into churning flames as he heard, *"be afraid, don't try to claim the things you sold. Remember the dark abyss, and obey my orders."* He felt his mind starting to slip out of time frames and he then felt his brain slip back into this world—away from the darkness.

"My sympathies." Chris said, with little to no eye contact, and knew that there was nothing else he could do was said his peace and not say another word. He glanced at A.J. and knew that he would be facing his own problems, but could he wield a piece and carry out an order for him? Chris would find out when they reached the city.

Chris saw all of his companions gazing at him—with eyes of spurning thoughts— waiting for the question he was about to ask. Chris seemed interested but was worried, but nothing he seemed to envision was about to happen. Total power.

The Disintegrating Bloodline

Another few minutes past by when all of them including Krazy who never showed any sign of fatigue or sweat, wiped away his forehead repeatedly. Claustrophobia was also playing apart, and being in the cruel tiny space started to feel like a dead Turkey roasting inside an oven. Frank's head pulsated as all the nerves in his head was about to explode from a heat aneurysm—even though it was starting to get cold outside, the suns ability to give off heat wasn't weakened by the winds gusts. He turned the knob (after having accidentally turned the radio knob, disturbing them from there sleep) and felt the air conditioner brush past his face and refresh the small fabric compartment. Frank sighed; and the rest began to silently thank Krazy with their long sighs of contentment. As Chris let out a few puffs of air he felt the ever-lasting presence of the city streets calling out to him.

After passing a few more cars Frank got off the highway and passed through Queens. The city was ever restless crawling with homeless hunchbacks covered in a half torn blanket slung across his chest covering half his mouth as his face looked crushed and torn by fists and knives, including his aching body that was possessed by hunger. A.J. stared at him from the window for a brief moment and quickly turned not to make himself too obvious.

Chris, feeling the fake air being too weak against the heat, went to roll down his window and slowly turned the handle. As he turned the handle, the window let off a squeaky fart sound as he let the glass stop as the cool air floated throughout the car. Also the gritty streets and sewers let off a stench that made A.J. cover his mouth but Chris seemed to breathe it in, as if he lived off the toxic smells. He never saw the city how Chris had seen it through his eyes. He saw Chris's enlightened face and knew that he had a connection with the city A.J. couldn't understand.

Chris scoffed at the street hustlers from his window with his ever so cocky smirk. Chris felt Little Italy creeping around the corner as he heard it calling to him.

"Enemies wait behind gates of fortitude, perfect timing," The voice murmured. Only Chris bent his head out the window staring up at the large buildings as they towered into the sky, and knew that he was better than all those people inside those buildings, because he was doing what they really wanted to do. Also, in a way, they were both apart of the same symbiotic ritual of stealing and killing anything (and knowing when to drop a problem) for the highest bidder. Chris knew when to drop a problem, but Chris didn't know when the weight would get too heavy for him to carry…*"to deal death's bite,"* the voice hissed and Chris rolled the window back up.

As they were nearing Mulberry Street, A.J. noticed a situation that caught his attention, but would have gone unnoticed real quick if he weren't in this car. A.J. saw a police car and a black limo parked side by side in the middle of the abandoned lot. Their exhaust barrels were spewing smoke from the pipes creating a cloud that was both clear and hazy, and really awful to smell if someone was in a garage with it on. While both of the cars remained idle the windows slowly drew open, and in a quick flash darted from the open limo window ending up in the police car. Only A.J. couldn't distinguish behind the tinted windows as the cars bolted in opposite directions.

A.J. saw the limo creep into an abandoned street while the driver of the police car sped out of sight down another direction. The only characteristic that gave the driver away was a bright shiny curved egghead through the darkened window reflecting the shady character's sunglasses. For a moment A.J. felt a tingly chill creep into his body making his mind twist and turn in knots. A.J.'s mind could only paint a picture of one person that made him even more nervous than anyone he had met. That person might have been the police officer from the other night. It wasn't really that hard to say that some of the police were on their payroll, but A.J. didn't really notice it—not ever—until now.

In the passenger seat, Krazy saw a leveled lot where they could park the boss's car and give themselves some shelter. They would have to pay first, but that wasn't a problem at all. Krazy told Frank to go in there, and Frank turned the P.O.S. (piece of shit) toward the red and white striped access entrance bar between the outside and into the darkness of the lot, where many things happened. Frank rolled down the window; he reached into his pocket, and held an assortment of dirty quarters, dimes, and nickels. He picked up four quarters (two clean, and two discolored by water) and threw it into the round metallic tray. The money clinked and rolled around the machine and the bar rose up for Krazy. The bar moved up and Krazy pressed on the gas leaving the ever-bright morning light behind them entering into the dark surroundings of the leveled parking lot. Chris rolled the window back up, and pressed his back against the seat, waiting for this ever-tiresome ride from hell to stop. A.J. looked behind him catching his last glint of sunlight as a row of artificial lights shined in a long clear plastic case down upon them.

They traveled around a row of cars filled in each parking space, all new Lexus' with boomboxes and bubble eye headlights, and there eyes ate up the lines of Mustang's, Toyota's, Hondas, and Ford trucks. Frank, who was not paying attention to any of these cars, took another spiral exit deep inside the bottom level, bumping over a bridge as the car slightly jumped up and down as they slowly drove down the hill into the lowest parking lot and he felt the ground holding the car up and A.J. speculated that this lot was desolate compared to any other desert in the farthest reaches of the Middle East. *"Screams are nonexistent."*

Chris saw a spot near the elevator and pointed a finger toward where he wanted him to park the beast in this high pedigree stable.

"Park the car right there!" Chris said pointing to a spot adjacent to the elevator as Frank turned the wheel and lined the car perfectly aligned in the open parking space—pushing the bumper against the edge of the wall. Krazy put the beast in park, turning the keys, the engine stopped—making a few jumbling coughs—as he pulled the keys out. Since they had stabled the beast, it was time to leave, but silence filled the vehicle as everyone waited for Chris to give the word. All of them waited in silence as Chris looked behind him, in the bright coagulating light, seeing if the cost was clear from anyone in the underground lot. Chris finally pulled on the handle and stretched his legs out of the car and stood with a comfortable, yet cramped posture. Although he felt naked without his trench coat on he fixed the end of his shirt and let the door open for the rest to follow them. Then as if lines of dominos were about to crash on them, Krazy and Frank were the second to leave and slammed there doors giving off a loud slam. Although A.J. and Gene were left inside the car A.J. watched Chris, Frank, and Krazy approaching the trunk, and opened it with jangling of their keys, and put the trunk open. A.J. felt that he was kept inside the car for a reason and one of them didn't want them to see what was going on.

"Why are we here?" A.J. said extending his head all around him curiously. When Frank was opening the trunk, Gene pulled his head away and then said, "It's for your own good. Just wait, and you will see." Gene smiled sneakily as A.J. just shook his head, and then faced forward, looking at the brick wall, staring at a sign.

PRIVATE PARKING

As Chris and his two bodyguards opened the trunk, Frank and Krazy looked over their shoulders, fearful of anyone spying on them before they opened the trunk.

When the trunk finally opened, it was as if they had stuck gold, and no one else was seeing this except for Krazy, smiling like a bloodthirsty hyena that was covered in his victim's blood, and his gluttony was craving for more.

Inside the trunk, they surveyed a massive array of weapons all great and small just for his protection. Most were pistols that ranged from .45 calibers to 9 millimeters and down to the largest twelve-gauge "shorty", or "crowd control" covered underneath the felt of the trunk. With the felt rolled up against the back of the trunk, his guards began to arm themselves. Krazy and

Frank finished gathering their tools and searching for extra ammunition as Krazy fancied the .45 handgun, it was large and just the right fit for the size of his hands, and Frank had favored a black Military Berreta handgun that held about fifteen to sixteen shots, and Frank liked the smooth handgrip for a moment, and felt confident with it's sleek style. Then he reached back into the trunk and grabbed another clip of preloaded ammunition in a small camera bag. He was about to grab the bag, but then Chris stopped them.

"Wipe that grin off your face." Chris said with a rather cynical tone as he watched Krazy's smile drop faster than a fire-blazing meteor burning through the sky. He then spoke in a whisper. "This is serious, we are going light this time to see the Don. If we're doin' a piece of work today, A.J.'s going to be apart of it, but he doesn't carry one. One of you has to give it to him." Chris said and picked up another bag, grabbing a pair of shoes that rested next to the bag. After they were done with what was in the trunk, Krazy closed the trunk.

Chris let his hands fall to his sides, unraveling his fist letting the cool air travel through his sweaty hand. Chris felt a weight of the world pressing against his mind, and he let himself speak again, calmly but with a mellow without even cracking his stone face.

"Let's not give anyone ideas, because you know he doesn't trust anybody that's new. So, just hang onto it." Chris nodded with approval as he patted his shoulders.

Krazy and Frank nodded their heads in agreement, and stuffed their weapons inside their belts, and had the safety already on so their weapons wouldn't go off inside their pants.

Since he had become apart of his crew, he had nowhere close to being *made*. Chris didn't want anybody, especially A.J., touched by anybody, because if anyone was going to take his soldiers out, they had another thing coming.

At that moment, Frank shut the trunk, and after they covered their weapons with the ends of their coattails as Chris motioned for them to stay as he moved toward the door where Gene was, not noticing Chris's presence at all. Chris lifted up his hand, balling his fist, extended his pointer knuckle outwards; he tapped against the glass plate. Gene turned, and a quick dose of fear made him jump out of fear. Gene sighed, knowing that the coast was clear when he opened the door, shaking his head disproving of Chris's jokes, but then shrugged off his out of place scares. When A.J. started to move out of the car Chris tossed the black bag into A.J.'s lap. A.J. paused, feeling the plastic material brush against his face as he looked down at the bundle, filled with confusion, giving off a rubbery smell.

"What's this?" A.J. said with total lack of enthusiasm.

"Get dressed! We got to stop somewhere first!" Chris ordered as he nodded to the plastic trash bag that was positioned in his crotch.

But A.J. felt embarrassed by what Chris had told him and stopped the door before it could close. Chris looked at his tense face and thought he was going to become abrasive and attack him.

"Is there some dead cat in here?" A.J.'s sarcastic question should have made him laugh—at least chuckle, but it wasn't working on him. But when he looked at him, he knew he was being serious, and for a moment he saw something scary and frightening in his friend's eyes, and his sarcasm dropped like lead weight. Behind him A.J. saw Krazy moving behind him, and in his waistline a gun was peering out certainly not unveiled for no reason except for one thing, intimidation. The black metallic pistol instilled another known fear that he had met once before, but he was certain that Chris or his companions would definitely put a bullet in him.

A.J.'s defense flushed from his face as if Chris's love had not existed, only fear and malice stretched across them as A.J. leaned back into the seat staring into there eyes. Chris and Krazy weren't moved by his silence, but as A.J. spoke again with less enthusiasm, and more speculation.

"Why do I have to get dressed?" He looked into the bag, and saw a suit. He looked back up and said perplexed. "Are we going somewhere important?"

Chris saw this and he uttered in a remorseless, quick and hard response.

"Yeah, we are. Now get dressed." Chris's apathy gave him the strength to close the door in his face. Chris and his friends walked a few steps from the car giving A.J. little to no privacy at all. After Chris and his soldiers headed away from the car, A.J. thought it wouldn't do him any good to rebuke an order. As A.J. took his pants off, he felt the sweat from his underwear rising off his curly leg hairs, and buttoning the plastic button in the hole, it slowly sagged down his stomach. He felt that they were two inches too big in the waist, but he could tighten it with his belt. As he slipped his arms through the purple button up shirt, he felt the cold wind whipping against his bare chest, and stuck his arms through the sleeves, feeling the suit clinging to his sticky body.

The purple button up shirt fit perfectly and as he buttoned his shirt, his finger came across another hole. Only this did not feel like a hole that belonged to the shirt, and when he poked his finger into the hole he pulled it out. Looking at his finger, he curiously grabbed the material and faced it upwards so his eyes could see what it was. It was a round hole that was directly across where his guts were, and there was another perfect symmetrical hole right next to it—three inches in diameter—it couldn't have been anything else except…

"A bullet hole?" A.J. whispered, but then quieted his voice. But maybe this was something harmless maybe even a mouse could have been chewing through it. But a mouse never left holes that were never that clean. He just stopped thinking for a while and when he was ready, he grabbed on the latch, pulling it with all his might. He pushed the door open and then placed his foot out of the car.

From their circle they watched A.J. with a curious eye and what he would look like. They saw his oddly misplaced tennis shoes peering over the black satin pants, and knew that it wouldn't matter because the pants would cover them up. As he moved out of the car, he had closed the door, making the whole underground lot rumble with a soul-shattering KA-BOOM. As he straightened his eyes, he cocked his head back and shoulders back with a proud strut, he held out his hands, wanting their approval.

When A.J. made his approach, Chris gave him a small round of applause. Then everyone started to go along with his clapping, as Frank smirked, Krazy laughed, but Gene just looked at him with the same stoic face, expressionless. A.J. didn't know what to think of his light applause, and this gave him confidence flowing back into his body—and rejuvenated his wayward soul—in a bloody washed suit—that resurrected memories of Chris's long lost friend.

Chris spoke with a half-hearted laugh in his voice and threw his hands up. "Hey, now he's dressed!" Chris made A.J. happy enough to forget about school for a day. But A.J. saw something quite odd, as if he was looking upon someone else, and was totally enwrapped in his own thoughts, looking as if he was far off in the distant sands of his memory, slipping away into madness.

"How do I look?" A.J. asked turning around so that they could see how the suit looked on him. Krazy and Frank saw the holes in his shirt and saw his pale belly inside the holes. Gene really thought nothing was wrong with the suit and praised him all the same.

"It looks great, kid." Gene said, raising his arm, knuckles tightly clenched together and then put his arm around his neck. Krazy and Frank looked at each other knowing that he had to hide the holes that were not hidden very well, but the holes weren't really that noticeable, but had to question his boss's obsessive qualities. Only Gene could not believe that Chris had given him an outfit from his fallen comrade, Lorenzo, and if he could have given him a dead man's clothing Gene knew that he loved that boy. But when he thought about it, it seemed ironic, and like a curse, he would probably meet the fate of his own personal friend.

"Besides..." Gene thought. "Any man that wore the suit of a tainted man would receive the same punishment." Gene was delighted with all these delicious thoughts of evil as he quickly hushed them down as he smiled, *"for men never escape the blade,"* a new disturbance echoed, *"when the blade grows legs and chases you around the kitchen."*

Only all of them seemed to know that without one key ingredient that would hide the bullet wounds, he would never make it past the "Old Guards" sitting around the front of the Dons café. At that fleeting second, Krazy knew what would be needed if he were to make it without being undetected.

"Hold on!" Frank said as he pushed A.J. out of the way and walked back over to the trunk. "I'll be right back!" He pulled the keys out of his pockets and entered the key into the hole giving the key a quick twist as his pistol shifted inside his waistline, like a snarling pit bull waiting to tear his opponent to pieces. Frank opened the trunk and then pulled the latch over his head, looking into the trunk.

His fingers were tapping against the trunk repeatedly like a triple drum beat, pondering intensively while his eyes scoured every inch of the trunk, forgetting the shotgun and the extra pistols that were neatly clipped inside the trunk underneath the felt lining. He knew what he wanted something but he didn't know where it was that his intuitive eyes were looking for. A black leather jacket that looked very beat up, with no scratches that proved to be long lasting against nature's fury, but life's unexpected fast balls of snow, rain, and whipping winds seemed to imbed inside the fleshy material. It called to him he knew that this would have to do for now. Being that his outfit didn't adhere to any style code, he knew it wouldn't matter.

Krazy grabbed the folded jacket, held it in the crook of his arm and with one hand on the end of the trunk closed it down with one forceful swoop, filling the soulless lot with an echoing SLAM! Before Frank forgot, he pulled the keys out with a quick thrust emitting a light jingle that clashed together like small little bells that were tied around a Dobermans balls. He then walked back to his friends with the black coat in the crook of his arm, and a smile on his face that couldn't be replaced.

A.J., looking around Frank's thin exoskeleton, was especially curious with what Frank had in his arm. He had no idea what Frank was up to, but his curiosity was scratching against his neck like his curiosity rubbing against his pervading thoughts. But as Krazy approached A.J. he knew without a doubt it was for him, but felt like he should not accept it.

"Who am I kidding?" A.J. thought. "I'm on the ride, that I can't get off." A.J. sighed, but then held his breath as Frank pushed Krazy aside, standing toe to toe, looking at each other, as if they were about to turn around, walk ten paces, and obliterate into a thousand pieces. Feeling his intimidation radiating from his body, A.J. didn't like how Frank was looking at him. Only after that tense stare dissolved from the center of his eye, he picked up the coat from the crook of his arm and held it out for him, smirking as if it was a present.

Krazy never let his comfortable stare leave as A.J. looked at the folded coat and spread the coat apart peering through every nook and cranny, as if what he was offering was a trick. The inside was dark black and had two coat pockets on each side, and took it from him, slowly.

"Put this on! This is what you were missing." Krazy said as he let him have the coat, sniffing and wiping his nose with the back of his hand. A.J. took his attention away from the jacket glancing at Frank with a renewed look in his eye.

"Thanks. I'll wear it all the time" A.J. was appreciative, but still naive, as he threw the jacket around his back and Gene moved behind A.J., extended his hand out to fit his hand through his sleeves. Once he had the plastic jacket on, he threw his collar upward around his neck, and hid the part of the tie around the back. "You don't want to look like a Pollack!" Gene said giving him a sincere, quick pat on his shoulder.

Krazy and the rest of them chuckled from his kind, but incredibly politically incorrect gesture. Only he didn't know how he would react to another situation, and surely this was another test for A.J., and it would require nerves of steel and a stomach that could swallow all the unprocessed, unclean meat from a diseased slaughterhouse. Only they could feel an eerie presence from A.J. wearing this coat, and a small wind blew by him, *"death is molded from clay, and hardened until hollow."* This voice was starting to annoy Chris, and a love that he had forgotten, had just been remembered. But fear was also in the mix, and he could honestly feel fear. For that reason (a odd reason, surely) Chris held him in that high esteem, but he knew that A.J. actions were to follow A.J.'s talk, they would then have a final decision about A.J.'s future in the family. Chris knew that time was slipping through his fingers and his pride, and his crew's dignity was at stake.

"It's time!" Chris said gravely and then turned around starting toward the stairway that led up to the ground floor. In that moment everyone knew that Frank, who was the strongest of them all, followed regimentally behind Chris. The rest of them fell into place while A.J. walked up the darkened stairs, there shadows imbedding into the walls, like demons that were crawling through the pavement. Everyone except A.J. were all feeling tense about walking through Little Italy again, like they were going to be met with resistance along the way. Something worried Chris before they had even reached the top floor. *"The Virgin is here to protect you."* He felt calmer after this.

Frank and Krazy's breath flowed like mist as they yawned, sending spit into the air as the sounds of cars on the street strolled by kicking up dust, and a moments silence filled the street until it repeated again—along with loud thumping. When it was quiet for a moment, Frank approached the door, and threw it open, letting the sunlight pour in, blinding them for a moment as if they had been traveling through the darkness of purgatory, and they had found a backdoor into heaven. For being in the darkness so long, it felt pretty good to be in the light.

Chris moved out the door, approached the streets and welcomed the honking of the cars, the loud blasts of stereo systems, a rising stink that came from the morning sewers, and the restaurants that made up of Little Italy. The restaurants and small corner shops were the foundations of Little Italy. Chris saw the street corner and that reminded him where he had lived for the last ten year of his life. Chris had lived or had done business everywhere respected and feared him.

Frank and Krazy took a few steps into the light, feeling the oppressive decaying walls almost falling on them and on the corner Chris waited for Gene and A.J. to come out. The both of them stepped out, feeling both the sunlight and the wind push on his hair, pushing it sideways in a blow dryer motion.

A.J. was in wonder from the streets and corner shops with their flickering neon signs that the storeowners didn't even bother to take off. He could see through the decaying walls, a pride that still held this city up, even though it had grown old and lost it's allure a sort of jelly like aroma that elicited from the dilapidated pores. This didn't surprise him as they walked up another block A.J. as he saw something that he didn't know what to make out. The rows of apartment buildings had luminous large stairs that lead into small unaccommodating tenement apartments. A.J. couldn't imagine what kind of smells that were too grimy and too bleak that would surely drive a man to suicide.

They then moved into a large crowd slipping and greasing past them, like waves of sperm travelling into a polluted womb. They lost the attractions of the restaurants, cornershops that were probably under Don Pescaro's thumb. But as they approached another bar Il Café Italiano, it's chipped walls and dark windows suspended A.J.'s thoughts, making it seem new while it still preserved a feel for its old style. The window panels were dark; the tint bordered on a creamy gothic mix, and a romantic appeal that had all the ingredients for a place of Old world style and rage.

Outside the *Il Café Italiano,* sitting in a group of metallic chairs were several middle aged tanned men, two had brownish eyes while the other men had rich olive green eyes. Another old man, with a baldhead (with a small birthmark on the front of his lobe) sat with his leg spread out and his hands rested gently on top of his long khaki dress pants. Old and fleshy veins stretched along his once strong hands and made his dreary face turn as old and grave, like a wilted cabbage. His voice was cleaner than any blade, and his Italian sounded second nature as the words flowed out of him faster than poison being drawn out from a wound. At that moment, the men were now laughing, slapping their knees, shaking their heads, laughing unwittingly at his crude sex joke, but it was funny at the same time. Even though they were still telling dirty sex jokes, and even as old as they were, they still laughed like immature boys.

Though as normal as this group of men acted, something didn't seem right to A.J., as they approached the café, A.J. saw that these men instantly grew silent and gave them a rather observant stare as they walked past into the old men. A certain crooked quality was treacherous, discomforting as they walked into the restaurant. Gene gently tugged on A.J.'s arm, and fell back next to Gene, worried. What A.J. did not know was that these were the "Old Guard", Don Pescaro's oldest friends and trusted soldiers.

It seems that the group of older men had seen Chris and his crew from afar. The Capo of Don Pescaro's crew, Benny Shapiro, a large handsome man with the black hair and green olive eyes certainly gave him a cool feature with his large poncho sticking over his tight pants. His cool sensible nature always hid a deep malicious rage that revived the devil reincarnate. For when a piece of work or a contract came along he could make anything disappear. If it was friend or foe, he always got the job done, these rules always kept and survived inside the family's strict regime. His sharp temper and his deadly street antics earned him a name throughout the five boroughs, and the FBI (with a small pact they had made back in Post-Good Old days) never messed with them.

Chris and his company were approaching the door of the café, ignoring their good looks, and greeted the men with handshakes and they cordially shook his hands. They nodded to Frank, Krazy and Gene. But when A.J. gave these old men a nod of recognition they gave him an indifferent stare. A.J. felt hurt by their cold haunting stares, and A.J. shamefully turned his head away following his friends into the bar.

The bar was dank and empty with a few dim lights keeping the bar alive with a few early morning "slobs" who were making an early drinking binge and would be given a five-minute grace period until they kicked him out. But along the walls, dim sunlight peered into the window—as dust danced above the floor—and glowed on the line of stools at the bar. At a few corner tables next to the windows there were leather coats, drinking, chuckling over small talk, and the open floor was just a straight entrance—no tables or anything—resembling that of a dance hall.

Chris walked across the open floor and approached the bar. He sat on the stool, and rested his foot upon a metal bar.

Then a large bushy headed man, his rather pudgy stomach pushing against his black shirt, walked out of another door with a towel resting around his shoulders and his arm pits of his shirt were spewing in sweat. "What do you want?"

"Give me a Long Island!" Chris said, leaning backwards as he clamped his hands together, and smirked.

The bar tender nodded smugly, and pulling the towel from around his neck, he grabbed a glass, and all slowly filled it up with the right ingredients.

Chris lightly tapped his foot against the bar, anxiously waiting for the bullshit routine—*wait for the Capo to come out and bring me up*. They sat in the pedestal chairs, laying their hands across the table, looking at each other with complete and utter boredom, remembered that the bar tender was not asking for his ID. A.J. didn't know that Chris really needed to be asked, and A.J. was staring with awe that he wanted it just as the liquor swirled in the glass. After he laid the glasses back down on the table, he grabbed a small red straw, and stuck it inside the glass; he swished it around the drinks like interracial sexes forced to get along. Chris saw another set of stairs that lead up into a room where the don sat and lounged in his corner-room, planning everything.

Then the bartender set his drink in front of him and Chris picked up the round glass with his thumb and forefinger, swishing his alcoholic drink around, getting lost inside the liquor's thick dream. But when he would have indulged himself in that drink, he felt that the drink wasn't the same as usual. Its potency stung the strings of his nostrils, but he lowered the drink. He then looked at Krazy, he picked it up, and smelling it first. He smirked and then forced it down without touching his throat. But when Krazy took a big gulp, Krazy let the liquor touch his throat, and it burned him, but he forced it down without and smirked approvingly.

Chris nodded, and patted his back. Krazy pushed the drink down to Gene. Gene took a sip and then passed it down to Frank. Frank held the drink, but knew that he was driving and passed it down to A.J. A.J. looked at it for a moment, and then picked it up nervously. Frank watched him put the glass to his lips, but then felt a finger tapping against his shoulders. Frank turned and saw Chris leaning out against the seat, waving his hand against his throat in a cutting motion, signaling him to not let him drink.

Frank turned, seeing the liquor lean toward his open mouth, and Frank immediately put a finger over the glass and pulled it downwards. A drop had not even touched A.J.'s tongue as it slipped out of his hands.

A.J. looked at Frank, about to speak why he had taken his drink, but had stopped that when he took a large sip as he forced the drink down his throat and passed it back up to Gene.

A.J. just looked at him, and bit his lips and then looked around him—

totally pissed and had to swallow it—even though a drink would have made it better.

Then at that moment, from down the hallway, the door swung open as a breeze swooped through the bar sending goosebumps along their skin as the air conditioner came on at full blast. Chris turned and saw Benny Shapiro, strutting himself around the bar, walking up with a half-cocked strut and came up to the bar where the boys were sitting.

"Damn it!" Chris thought as he spread his hands through his hair, letting out a heavy breath escaping his lips. Chris surely respected Benny Shapiro; his good nature made him relinquish their strong positions when they were around certain powerful friends. Only his arteries were shriveling up like that of dead dogs penis, and he couldn't help but feel his body succumb to the warm pat—or the pat of deception as Chris thought of it—of this Captains deadly charm and come back with equal or more force.

Chris turned around noticing this short, round faced middle aged Capo's lower crooked teeth. His green eyes magnified a certain liquid ability to transform, and with that conniving grin—his teeth scraped like a chisel against a faulty plaster—and everything in that smile would say "fuck you," but then sardonically add, "and how's your mother?"

"How's it going buddy?" Benny said, as he gave him a warm hug. Benny's voice was pleasant and upbeat; no one could mistake him on the street, but if he were standing over you in your bedroom, you wouldn't have noticed it.

"What's so funny!" Chris said as they patted each other's backs respectively.

"Nothin'!" Benny said, letting go of Chris and he barked. "What is so funny?"

Chris shifted off his pedestal seat and his feet pounced against the green tiled floor, shaking the very tiles with the ends of his black tennis shoes. Everyone in the bar turned, and when they saw it was just the sounds of someone's feet, they returned back to there drink, swishing there lives away with every gulp, giving into their weaknesses, overshadowing the world only to the ocean of sadness ahead.

The two walked up the stairs toward the Dons room. Chris didn't look back one second at his boys for backup or anything. Chris had to do this alone the sounds of their beating feet echoed the halls, and inside the corridor hall. A.J. stretched his neck out across the table trying to see where Chris had been escorted. A.J. leaned back into the chair and sighed, remembering that Chris was a professional. The thought of being denied a drink spurned his hatred like that of a sizzling prod burning the top of his stomach. It was just ridiculous, but everything seemed stupid anyway—money and respect was the only thing he wished he had with the help of Chris Mangini.

Chris and Benny were walking down the hallway in silence as they approached the brown door to Don Pescaro's quarters—he could hear the door pulsating as if it were a still beating heart—and he could feel the voices talking loudly. This was where only his highest Capos, his Consigliere, a dons right hand man that always handled beefs with internal or external-family struggles, who was a key advisor to any of the dons decisions, and then came a main soldier, and also a main associate, who ran the lower echelons of the family food chain, but the one person in power that always accompanied the Don was the Underboss. To be an underboss was one level underneath the Don, and whenever it came his time to become "boss," loyalty between flesh and blood weren't barriers for reasons to stop someone.

Don Pescaro's Underboss, Joey Stefano, sometimes sat in on certain meetings with the Don and in times of need, gave their opinions, but the Don could veto any decision based on his own judgement. With those four loyal officials around him, he was no stranger to betrayal—even when he had been up for Boss, but his brother—Don Pescaro—had taken his place.

Chris and Benny approached the door as Benny stood in front of him first while Chris stood on the other side of him shadowed in the darkened hallway. Benny grabbed hold of the round knob, and standing sideways, "Are you ready?" Benny said, as his top lip rose, revealing his murderous pearly whites—and he .

"Yeah!" Chris said bluntly as he shrugged his shoulders forcibly, and Benny opened the door and the two walked into the room.

Inside the room, the blinds were closed around the room from any uncaring eyes, and keeping the light from heating all these old bastards up like Thanksgiving turkeys. Only a few dimming rays streaked across the shades and a few lamps shining up one side of the room as the one near the window, shadowing the natural light with its artificial rays. The apartment was shabby, while the walls were cheaply decorated showing the lack of refurbishing—decaying wall paper that was starting to loose its color and the designs were starting to turn white. Don Pescaro was resting on his leather sofa with his heavyset brother in law, Joey Stefano, who had a round pouch, which squeezed out some of his buttons revealing his belly. He was Don Pescaro's brother in law through another marriage, and even though they weren't related he loved him as if he was his own kin.

But inside this room, Chris noticed a very odd thing. He noticed that the Consigliere was nowhere to be seen, and everyone else was here, except for him.

For a split second Chris's nerves felt strain by Joey Stefano's presence, with his spotty skin shining like glycerin as his large eyes widened for a long moment, and rolled downward enviously.

As he loosely approached a seat next to the Don, he felt the weight of his eyes bearing down on him, as if he was ready to strap him down. The Don looked very weak and frail, as if he Chris breathed on him he would just fall apart, like a person that had been sprayed with sulfuric acid, and eaten through like rotted wood to a termite. As Chris sat in the opposite chair, and disengaging his stiff back against the chair. He wiped his hands on his pants cleaning the sweat from inside his palms.

The Don cocked his head moving his lips very fast as he spoke, charmingly smirking. "So," Don Pescaro said, brushing the sleeves of his shirt jacket. "How are things going with your crew? I hear good things coming from friends of ours."

Chris nodded, and answered him with the outmost sincerity grinning with a gracious underhanded courtesy as he replied.

Chris knew that the Don was in the middle of placing soldiers and captains in key spots where they could spot out rival opponents that were looking to juice protection rackets under another family's protection. So, Chris decided to be short and to the point, and be on his way.

"Good, Very good Don Pescaro. Things are going very well for us; business has increased ten points since the last month." Chris said as the Don nodded his head approving of Chris's loyal behavior, knowing whom he was talking about.

Only his brother in law Joey Stefano scoffed from the Dons fondness toward the boy. Slowly clenching his fist as all of his fingers cracked as he watched them laugh and talk as if the don was a young man, himself as if in his prime days of a young man with strong bones and quick hands, Joey Stefano could only sit back and watch this mockery go on. He would listen, and analyze everything, about his territory beefs with the D'Angelino family.

The Don raised his hand up to his face scratching his chin and gave a wave of disapproval with his hands, and Chris could only sit in his chair and do nothing about it. "You know, when I came into this, people had a little more respect. It helps when young people have a sense of duty and responsibility." Don Pescaro nodded, looking off toward the opposite side of the room, he lost himself in the wallpaper for a moment—letting the young man in him leave, and a grave bottomless feeling made his stomach cave in with despair.

After Chris finished, he reached into his pocket. As Chris leaned forward,

Joey's eyes saw him pull something out and hold in his hands a large thick envelope that broke through the seal, leaving an imprint through the white coloring on the stamp. Don Pescaro received it with a laugh, flashing a wide grin and reached across the couch, with a renewed strength in his eye although the pain of old age stretched his skin and twisted his bones, as if they were turning into dust.

Chris Mangini felt honored and gratified by the don himself, if this kindness was indeed false or just for show. Either way he trusted him as a business partner, or more like a friend. That was just Chris had wanted, his ultimate trust, and after years, he had finally had it.

Chris chuckled and thanked him. Then at that moment, he knew that something else had to be said. "How's that *thing*?" Chris asked in a vague tone that meant something very secret only between the people inside the room. Don Pescaro's eyebrows arched with his head cocked to the side. "Is that *thing* still on for Saturday?"

"What *thing*?" Don Pescaro said.

Chris wasn't sure if the Don had been aware of his situation with the war that was about to begin, and it was open stakes on the prohibiting of music CD's or contained programs for offices and anything that could be put on a disk was declared illegal to trade and sell for any reason in the Censorship law. But to every money-maker this was a dream come true since he had a couple of connections that knew where these trucks filled with music CD's and Windows, Mac, programs were heading. Chris knew that it was the time Chris and his crew would jump on the bandwagon before any of the other families got into it, and if they weren't, he would—with or without their permission.

"That really, really big *thing* that's supposed to happen very soon?" Chris persuasiveness was business like, but couldn't be duplicated when he was serious.

The Don nodded his head and gave a moment to think. Then it was as if his senses had come to him in a quick flash of thought and he gave a small but weak laugh, forcing spit from his hot mouth and filled the air as he bent over paralyzed as he cupped his hand over his mouth, catching the speedy spit in his mouth. Chris almost thought this was a sign of the Don's last breath on earth, and he couldn't have him dying just yet.

"Are you okay!" Chris jumped up, extending his hand behind his back. He slapped the dons back lightly, seeing him force one last cough from his lungs, torturously trying to gain his breath back—spit formed at the corners of his mouth. Don Pescaro swallowed his juice back down his throat and breathed laboriously trying to return to his stature, feeling the pain traveling through his body, his ribs pulling off his heart, sending blood back through his bodies, feeling the air in his lungs revamping his body.

"Listen." He took another long breathe, catching himself before he leaned over again. "What you're doing is good work." Don Pescaro said with a construed whisper, trying to catch his breath lowered his head next to Chris's. "Maybe you'll be running your own family someday? But to get where we are, we all have to take our turns in this lifetime. The only time to take action is when your family is in danger. That's what matters, *family*." Chris Mangini sat back down across from the Don, and then saw that Joey Stefano had not even flinched—spurning his hatred even more.

"Thanks," The Don said, as he leaned close for him to hear. "Old age has finally caught up with me. You're just like my nephew, always helping his uncle, even to pat my back. You were always good to me, even to everyone in our family. " Chris chuckled and took his flattery as a sign of his mellowing old age, and almost mistook it as being senile, but Chris knew that out of all his flattery, and accepted it with a grain of salt.

"Come here" With a wave of his hand Chris lowered his ear next to the Don's lips, and he told him everything, without uttering one word. Chris did interrupt him, knowing the rules and had to accept what had the Don had ordered to be done and went with what the Don said. Chris wasn't ultimately shocked for a moment but again, and said, "Okay."

The Don reared his head and saw Chris's reaction to be that he was distant but still yearning for their respect without any emotional attachment. The Don raised a hand to scratch his chin. The Don thought he would react childishly; full of glee and excitement to be given a piece of work, or blood thirsty. But the Don knew he was smarter and more mature about a situation this seriously and delicately.

"Do you think this is going to work? Do we have the right people, to you know, the right people to look the other way? If it needs to be done it's done."

The Don saw Chris's face turn dark and grim with his stoic eyes revealing his hollow barrel conscience—clean and without any remorse. That's why he could trust no other except Chris, business wise and personally—more than his own brother.

Figlio Mio" The Don said with great respect and love. "You have always been loyal to me since you joined our family and without question handled whatever we asked you to do. Don't worry about this problem with the other commission members, you have my permission to take care of this problem, and don't *let anything get in your way*, and don't forget what's coming our way, now go on." He gave him a small wave for him to go. Chris knew that it was time to leave, unfortunately, as he stood from his chair, he faced Joey

Stefano—a rat of a man, vying piece of shit know-it-all—and left with pure hatred in his heart.

Chris made his way toward the door, and before he could even speak, Benny Shapiro held the door for him, and Chris looked back one more time, staring into his deep green eyes. *"Your enemies stab your back, while your friends stab you in the front!"* The voice said, and Chris heard the door close behind him as Benny and Chris marched down the stairs beside each other. "Who's going to stab me first?" Chris thought, and then answered his own question. "The ones who are closest to you."

Don Pescaro sighed, feeling a quick rush of sweat forming on top of his skull, and rubbed his hands over his thin two stringed comb hair, and then fell back in his chair, contemplating many decisions. But his underboss and brother in law Joey Stefano looked at their Consigliere, Roberto Pesante, who had surveyed the entire scenes from the shadows in the corner of the room, like a fly on the wall. Only he wanted to clear his troubles while his Consigliere was present.

"What do you think of him, Don Pescaro? Has he changed?" Pesante said uncovering himself from the corner of the room sitting in another armchair.

Joey glanced at Roberto, hoping that he would be able to bring out the worst in him, make him show his ill favor toward Chris. Don Pescaro saw his brother in law restless looks explains his impatience.

"He's a good kid!" Don Pescaro said, his calm stable mind rippled, but wasn't disturbed.

Then, Joey's voice made Don Pescaro's calm pond turn into an oppressive wave of humiliating *assistance*. "Don't be foolish." Joey stamped his feet, and ran over to Don Pescaro, yelling like a school child. "He's using you for his gains. I know you like him, but his true nature is that of a snake and you can't fool a snake without thinking like he does. You have to kill him!" Don Pescaro kept silent, not saying a word, but his big green eyes glared with defiance.

Joey thought to himself " Damn it, how in the hell can we still keep Chris Mangini alive this long? And with the added pressure on the Don to be a target." Joey Stefano's patience was wearing low, and his very brain was about to explode if he didn't take a breath. He saw his old age melting his mind into a senile old fart but while the Don was still alive, Joey Stefano was not about to let the Don be fooled—their organization, families, and pride were on the line—even if he had to take his position away from him.

As Chris and Benny left the darkened hall behind them, Chris saw his friends were eating an early morning steak and cheese sub that the bar tender had special made for him and his crew.

Chris's crew looked as if nails poked through the cushions pushing their butts upward as all of them surveyed Chris's grave face. Even though he was happy to be out of there alive, Chris knew that it was time to leave. Chris looked at A.J. who was chomping down a big steak and cheese sandwich—a puddle of grease formed at the top right of the plate where chopped meat lay scattered with globs of gooey cheese stretched from the bun--dangling across the bun to his greasy lips. His soldiers, Frank and Krazy saw Chris's flare his eyebrows. That was it, and with that one suggesting glance, nothing else needed to be said.

At that moment, Chris turned around and saw Benny's large hand. Chris shook his hand and then the two of them exchanged hugs and patted each other on the back.

Benny let go of Chris and immediately walked over to the bar where the tender had been cleaning glasses out of the small sink. Chris saw them getting up, but he looked at their plates and said almost innocently, confused.

"You didn't leave any for me?" Chris sarcasm was hard to follow, but then he shrugged his shoulders when they looked away sheepishly.

"Don't worry. Let's go!" Chris joked and then they headed out of the bar in single file as they passed the "Old Guards" who were all still lounging in their lawn chairs, and watched them very carefully. None of them made contact with the brash group, and A.J. felt something very wrong in these men and gazed into the streets, because that's all he had as well. A.J. hurried past Frank and Krazy and halted next to Chris when they were at the end of the block. A.J. glanced at Chris with worry but Chris's relaxed face made A.J. better to himself. Although Chris knew what was going to happen, Chris gave him a grin and then turned back to the light that shined from across the street. "I guess there's hope for all of us?" A.J. thought, disheartened, feeling like the weight of the world was on his shoulders as they continued down the shadowy street.

The busy streets were almost turning desolate as Chris and his crew moved like a pack of predators, blending into their surroundings, totally into their zone. Chris had a piece of work to do, and he was going to follow it with every detail. A piece of work meant that the Don had given an order to handle a 'cockroach problem'. But who was going to do it? He wasn't going to tell.

The traffic began to worsen as the morning welcomed the busy afternoon traffic, and brought about the afternoon lunch hour. But after another minute Chris felt 10th Av. Nearing, and only now he began to almost dread bringing A.J. along with him. When he thought it carefully, there was no sense to keep babying him this long. After all, Chris knew he would have to be exposed to this, and now was the best time. He wouldn't be surprised if he wouldn't be sleeping at all, but that's what all of them lived with, the faces of the fallen.

Frank was approaching 10th Ave. and he could feel it calling to him like a crack child screaming from an abandoned trash can, and he was there to supply more vice to the possessed apartment complex. He remembered that parking in front of the building would look suspicious, but if they parked on the other side of the building where A.J. and Krazy could make their escape without causing anyone to see their getaway car—it could possibly work. Krazy or Frank would have to instruct A.J. on everything, where to walk into, and where to escape. In this case Chris had to hand down this information to Frank and they would have to hand it down to A.J. Chris leaned over to A.J.'s notebook where A.J. had placed it before and set it down in his lap. A.J. held the zipper notebook with furled eyebrows.

Chris unzipped the binder, seeing the bombardment of papers sticking out of the folder while Chris grabbed the thick line of papers and ripped a blank sheet from the binder leaving the holes dismembered and then closed the binder with his left hand. Chris looked around and felt in his pocket for a pen to write down the room number and the name. He knew the tool's he would need is a gun and a lock pick if there was trouble opening the door. Chris felt on a pen and pulled out a blue and red punch pen that he always kept. He adjusted the pen into his palms, and then clicked it open from the top and began to write down three numbers and after he was done Chris creased the top of the paper down, folded it again and handed the note to Frank. Frank received the note, tired of everything, as he read the name, and held his breath in excitement.

And the only thing that caught him off guard about this job was that this was a "Made Man" from the Farelli family, Salvatore Forello was a wild card to his family. This only brewed strange feelings between the two families, and it seemed too complicated for him to understand why he was doing this for him.

Salvatore Forello, who had turned forty two three days ago, was responsible for most of the disappearances of Don Pescaro's Capo's and their own soldiers and was producing too much heat from the cops with his constant run-ins on of trafficking charges. His constant loud mouth lawyer Steve Rosenberg always had to help him out of trouble. He was sacking out in this shitty hotel to stay out of sight, and resting in a prostitute's bed. There were rumors of him taking out the boss to expand his own power too, so it was working out for the both of them.

Only Chris thought that A.J. *shouldn't know,* so he wouldn't be taking things personally. But when someone takes a shot at another family, the other four families are forced on to take a side, because it will affect them—

financially and economically—sooner or later. Chris knew that Don Pescaro was fed up with trying to listen, and with that he was sending a message to one of the powerful neighborhood factions.

Frank glanced up from the piece of paper, and nodded to Chris in the window. He folded it into his pocket, and knew that serious look in his eye. Frank got out of the car and went around the back of the car.

At that moment, Chris glanced down at him, and then said, "Go!"

A.J. looked at him with his greasy lips shining like an old Chap Stick liner in the rearview mirror. "What do you mean?" Chris just shook his head, seeing that he wasn't getting it.

"Just what I said!" Chris ordered as his eyes weren't faltering, and his tone told him that he wasn't joking.

A.J. just looked away from Chris, knowing that he had to go, but something in his gut was telling him not to go. But, his word was his bond, and he didn't want to break it. "Okay." He sighed, and then grabbed onto the handle, and pushed the door open.

A.J. looked around the desolate streets with an odd sense of insecurity that something lurked inside the shabby and moldy apartment. A.J. got out the car, shut the door rather hard, and then followed Frank to the front door. Frank approached the door, and they went around the moldy apartment, and after they disappeared, Chris hoped that he wouldn't freeze up.

Back inside the car, Krazy was in the driver's seat and with a certain sense of excitement asked with his skewed discolored face shining as his whole head moved, "Why are we here?"

Chris shook his head, and then said, "I don't' know?"

Gene's calm face turned perplexed, his plucked eyebrow's narrowed, mouth and face grew tense as if he was about to ejaculate into a whore. "Is it a trap?"

Chris looked at Gene, his face emotionless, and said, "I hope not?" Chris turned away from Gene, and that was the end of the conversation. They sat and waited.

Chapter VI:

"Faces of the Fallen"

Frank had seen hotels like this in many scenarios. He noticed the hall lights flickered making the chipped walls noticeable for anyone that didn't even want to see it. He felt like this place had been possessed, where bruised, beaten, and sometimes toothless whores traveled up and down the halls, even in the lobby, strutting with everything except their bras and panties. In their uniforms, they searched for any man so that they could show them a good time. Frank grabbed a New York Time newspaper that was folded up on a lamp table and folded it underneath his arm. It was just thick enough for him to hide his weapon.

Frank saw the door that led up a windy second story stairs and approached the door, inconspicuously leaning against the wall. To add to this irony he covered his face with the front section of the Times with a right-side column screaming,

PREGNANT MOTHER STABBED! NO WITNESSES!

as a policeman came strutting through the front door—blue shirt pressed and his badge neatly shined. A.J. turned his back as the cop strutted with his hands on his sides, surveying the then utterly quiet foyer of wide-eyed whores dangling their phone chains off their fingers. They swung it both ways as they had long add-on glittery fingernails.

There was a policeman leave the hotel lobby Frank pushed into the door with his shoulder and A.J. rushed behind him.

The two hurried up the steps, seeing there shadows traveling alongside them and taking many forms in the darkness as Frank felt very odd about coming here. He looked behind him as their echoing shoes clinked like a falling pebble against an empty well and falling to the bottom with a small *dud*!

Then when Frank were reaching a good stopping point, he stopped in the middle of the stairs. Holding the paper open in his hand he pulled the Berreta 9mm from his pants. Palming the large black handgun, he stuck it horizontally inside the paper—with the butt facing upwards—and folded it back up like in a fish market, as if he was some kind of businessman of death.

Frank held the closed paper out to A.J., and his eyes grew with amazement as he opened the folded paper and beheld the shining metallic death dealer in the dim lamplight—like a father looking at his newborn. The paper felt heavy inside his hands as A.J. breathed anxiously, looking up at the blinking light, and at that moment, there was a clanking sound that echoed around them—as the sound of doors opening and closing—whores yelling hateful bashings to their pimps only to be yelled at, and then a resounding slap of the pimps ended the conversation. A.J. and Frank looked at each other and then Frank pulled out Chris's note and a lock pick folded inside the note so if the door was locked A.J. could force himself in. A.J. grabbed the note with his right hand holding the paper close to his ribs.

A.J. felt very sick and his conscience had been thumping constantly in his head. "Get out, now! Stop, leave right now! This is stupid, you're stupid for doing this, give it back and…" A.J. quieted that voice, hoping to never hear it again.

Frank saw that he had the tools, now it was time to give him the background. He had explained everything to A.J.

"Approach the room quietly and make damn sure to not flash it around. Also to be safe and silent, watch your back, and don't talk to him, even if he tries to intimidate you. If you have to, grab the doorknob with the end of your shirt. Got me?"

Frank leaned over to whisper the basic instructions, as the air sifted through the open hallways—as a large creaking sound stamped throughout the complex—as if a thousand rats were crawling through every hole, eating away the fiber of the building—pushing the tenement house.

"I don't have to explain what you do with the 'heater'. Do you think you can handle it? Say something right now if you need me to come along." Frank waited for A.J.'s answer.

A.J.'s mind was going left and right—waves of dilemmas splashing against both hemispheres—while his thoughts were shut down, keeping him from saying anything.

"Are you okay with this?" Frank said one more time, remembering all

The Disintegrating Bloodline

of his first time fears, giving him a chance to get out of it before he was sent on his way.

At that moment, A.J.'s mind turned on so quickly, that somewhere inside his mind had just made him belt out the first two words he didn't want to say. "I'm fine," A.J. said. "I got this under control." A.J. patted the paper with the gun tucked inside it, and the room number in his left. Frank looked into A.J.'s innocent eyes, knowing that his eyes would be opened now and forever—all compassion and everything Godly—gone forever.

"Don't worry." Frank's statuesque posture assured A.J., but it did not calm his sweating face. Frank gave him a quick hug, feeling the sweat from his body cling onto his shirt. Frank squeezed his body, and he whispered, feeling his ear starting to twitch in excitement. "Don't leave the gun, okay. Bring it back. Don't be seen." Before he released him, Frank lightly kissed him on the cheek.

A.J. didn't know whether to be horrified or just stand in awe from this unwanted, but affectionate attention. As Frank moved back, A.J. cocked his eyebrow, and then Frank moved back, and turned him around. "Get going. Don't be long, three minutes." Frank watched A.J. walk up the stairs lightly stomping up the steps and turned at the next corner to the second floor. Frank had no need to stay after he left his sight stand around and wiped his hands, hearing it clap in the hall as he walked down the steps flushing through the lobby like shit through a clean water pipe, playing it real smooth passing by lazy whores, who's faces were seeping from pubescent acne from every pore—legs with bruises and old whip marks from their Johns. As Frank passed the whores he left through the side door and the sun glossed over the building, covering the entire street—basking against the hot black cement until steam rose off it. As the sun started to move away from him, he felt his sight return back to him. Frank traveled around the back of the car, seeing Gene turn his head around, and opening the door for him and Frank jumped inside it, shutting the door with a loud *SlAM*, and the silence wasn't going to last too long.

"How's he doing? Did he get everything? Did you tell him what to do?' Chris was more than concerned—he was frightened for him.

"He looked like he understood what he was sent to do and all I know when I left him is that he is on his way to the room." Frank fearfully glanced over his shoulder. Chris nodded and returned forward—sitting in silent agony.

A.J. was strolling down the apartment hall, biding his time by searching for the door number, and after a while all the numbers in front of him were going backwards, and all the numbers were turning gray, like the black color was dissolving off the numbers.

After traveling down the hall for a while, he saw the crusty door numbers **344** that was scripted across the paper. For a moment A.J. stood and surveyed the hallway, looking back and forth—as the light at the end of the hallway shined in through the windowpane with a bias glare. A.J. looked at the wall and he could imagine the man from his dreams. This got him to thinking that whoever was waiting behind that door A.J. hoped for their sake that he wouldn't find them, because someone was going to die, and it wasn't going to be him. A.J. began to think that dreams were not all that far away from the truth.

A.J. began walking again, and saw the light traveling in and out of the window at the far end of the hall. His shadow danced and then disappeared as he looked at all the numbers.

"332," A.J. whispered, and then looked to the left side, "334." He glanced his eye across the hall and passed 336, 338, 340, 342, and then he looked at next door and saw the numbers that he obviously led himself to.

The numbers left a permanent scar in his mind as he approached the door without letting a single breath touch the door while A.J. listened to two voices rising and falling. Back and forth the voices began to scream as if an enthusiastic conversation turned violent, but this sounded different than that. A.J. listened, and listened carefully.

Inside room 344, there was no conversation going on between each other except the exchange of Salvatore's unprotected penis penetrating this Irish slut Jane Ferguson. He didn't really care if she was shaved or not, his life was already down the drain, and fucking this slut was the only thing he had left. He didn't even have the power and stature anymore, all he could do was make his penis push against her tiny triangle.

"Oh yeah," Salvatore Forello screamed, feeling their greasy sweat rubbing against each other and the sheets made a large wet spot as he screamed, in agonizing pill filled pleasure. "Take that you dirty bitch!" Feeling the heat of the apartment enclosing in on them, he continued pounding into her with every last bit of his strength, and slowed down—looking into her green eyes—he smiled, as if he was done and he whispered. "I'm not finished yet!" He clenched the white sheets, and began drilling his penis into her even more relenting vagina as the screams intensified as the bed holder moved so forcefully that it almost literally jumped if his back were to ever be the same again. He slammed into her again, and again, and again…

From outside the room, A.J. heard everything that was happening inside—the screams, the pleas, and the forceful punishments that came from within the room almost scared him, but he put two and two together that this was not violent, this was rough. Now, A.J. had never heard this kind of sex up close before until now, and he paced his breathing heart as blood began pumping to his crotch, and he had lift-off.

But he quickly pinched his arm, remembering that he needed to stay focused, and not eavesdropping on the sexual moans and groans of his target and a female prostitute. After a moment of listening to screaming and yelling, it ended when a great moan, like a lion that had discharged off into its female partner, and then rose off her with great pride.

A.J. listened as he heard the voices in a conversation.

Salvatore rose off the young girl with his discharged into her vagina. Jane, with her bright green candy paint fingernails just had this sour, expressionless face, as if she was expecting something more. Jane felt that a lead pipe had just penetrated her insides and left them open, and that was good because her body was hot when she was being taken by this forty two year old man. Even though this was the best sex she had had since her stepfather and boyfriend gangbanged her in her anus and vagina, she liked how this man handled her—gentle and caring.

"How was it?" Jane said, turning her head sideways, looking at this sweaty old man hoping that he was grateful.

A moment of silence passed as the noise of cars filled the streets and loud honking noises resonated around them as he breathed laboriously and said, "No." Jane just looked at his tanned and rather dark body, and said, "What?"

At that moment, Salvatore's body rose off the bed with his naked body turned toward her in full view—his tiny butt moved in a prance as he looked out the window—the sun shining against his hairy chest—and then screwed his face at her. "I had better *goomars* that were better than you!"

Jane's blood boiled faster than a coffee pot of crack as she pushed herself off the mattress—the springs sounded like a cricket's chirp—as she hoisted her body up with her elbows. "Then why didn't you go fuck them you fucking pervert!"

Salvatore would have been mad at this point, but there was nothing to be mad about an underage whore—"She's sounds like my daughter," Salvatore thought, frightened from his self awareness, and he didn't know if this was Freudian or not (if he had sex with a girl, was his thinking of his own daughter), but he pushed that strange self-awareness away along with her ignorant retort. "That's because fucking you was no different than fucking the bed."

The calm retort made Jane's body burn with hatred as she tried to fire, but her mind locked up, and jammed her usually quick witted thoughts. "You know what…" Then at that moment, she just shook her head, and looked out the closed wooden windows. Salvatore just stared at her as she looked out the window, trying to ignore him the best she could.

"Now, I'm going to take a shower," Salvatore's vindictiveness was more than he expected, but he dropped the conversation as he walked—his nude body strutting as his flat feet stomped into the bathroom, "so if you want to join me after you get over your bullshit, you'll know where I'll be." His voice made it definitely clear that he did not care about her, but as he closed the door, she clenched her palms against the bed. At that moment, she wanted to kill him, and maybe she could, "maybe stab him in the shower or cut his dick off with a piece of glass?" But if she wanted to kill him, she had to move fast.

A.J. didn't hear all of the conversation, but knew that the tension inside the room had escalated. He heard the slamming of the door breeze through the cracks as he heard water running and someone humming to himself. "Is it the whore or the target?" A.J. took one step to the right and left, as he slowly stuck the lock pick—jiggling and moving it—not really knowing what he was doing, "I guess I'll have to wing it, since I don't…" A.J. gave a small jerk as he pushed the tool up and down, then to the right and to the left. He heard the lock click- clanking inside the door as he pulled on the round door handle and felt the door slide open airing out a small puff of air, and the sunlight was peering through the crack of the door.

A.J. paused, holding all of his emotions inside and reached inside the paper for the Berreta, as he tightened the grip on the gun he lightly pushed the door open to behold a shear disgrace of a room. He saw a young girl covering her face with the white covers, breathing quietly, trying not to scream, her eyes were layered with dark bruises. A.J. just shook his head as the wooden floors looked like they had piercing splinters sticking that looked like nails that could go through your skin and come out the other side. He also saw a thong and a black belt with spiked bullets thrown on top of each other in a pile.

Only then the girl, threw the covers off her body, revealing her small breasts and short plump body in the peering sunlight.

"Just great!" A.J. hissed to himself "She pissed herself, and I have to kill my target in front of her." A.J. regretted ever coming up here, and his mind had to work fast before his target walked out of there with his pants down, or off in this case.

"Listen," the whore whispered, and then walked over to the pile. "If you're here to kill him, let me do it." She bent over, slipping her thong along her plaster-like jointed knees, and covered her freshly shaved bush as she then slipped on her brown cut kilted dress.

A.J. shook his head, face complacent, but his mind ultimately perplexed—like he knew that nothing knowing that the situation became complicated. "Get out of here!" A.J. ordered.

The water suddenly turned off while a tumble of voices sounded off all around him, like spirits, but knew that people were above him and around him, and knew that after he took his shots he had to leave, quickly. But he really felt like calling it off. "No, that lame fuck sticks his dick in me, and expects me to take it."

A.J.'s fears encircled his mind while he was waiting for the target to unveil from behind the door. But before the door would open, he reached into the paper, and then quickly gripped on the Berreta that was inside the paper, and pulled the Berreta from the paper. The whore gasped, but then reached for it in childish folly, and then pleaded, pressing her palm against the top of the slide, "Please, I want to do him. Let me shoot him, please…." She moaned, fiendishly, and A.J. pushed her hand away.

A.J. heard the water ending, as he saw the steam rising underneath the door, steaming up the wood.

A.J. lowered the gun to his side, but then a small humming echoed like a haunting melody, and A.J. did not want him to come out for he wanted to hold onto the last bit of his innocence, but the whore's offer was too tempting, but gripping the gun, *"accept your destiny,"* the voice then whispered, as the bathroom door began to slowly open while A.J. gripped the gun even tighter as the fog began to dissipate. The whore stood still as A.J. saw through the fog a large man walking out of the bathroom as A.J. beheld his scrappy beard had nets of water on his chin, sparkling like diamonds as his eyes of light brown met his and a short pointy nose sticking out, almost looking like a beak on a bird.

"What are you doing here?" Salvatore said walking out the door with a towel across his lower half, covering his curved penis and looking at him with his tired elephant eyes. A.J. looked upon this man, and said nothing, seeing this ignorant, foolish man not knowing that he had reached his end.

"What the hell you doing in here?" Salvatore said arrogantly with a nasal sound in utter disgust. "And what the hell is that smell?" A.J. wanted to laugh, but just smirked as he nodded toward the bed. His eyes spurned the young girl, and he yelled, "Are you Jane's pimp or something?" Salvatore said, hoping that it wasn't what he really thought it was. "Well are you?" He huffed as he sighed out of impatience and anger as he walked over toward the drawer, but then saw his drawer was open, his small .357 parabellum snub nose was gone. He couldn't help but stop in his tracks and then said, "You are here to kill me aren't you?"

A.J. coldly nodded his head, not saying a word. But then the whore pulled out his .357, and pointed, her hand trembling in fear.

Before he could move, the shots left barrel faster than he could breathe and Salvatore's body flew back like a gymnast doing a back flip, but he landed against the door. The sounds of the echoing shots cracked his eardrum repeatedly, and a draining fluid made it feel as if he was bleeding—enraged, and blood toiling—from the spinning barrel.

Back on the other side of the building where the car was still puffing out gas, the shots spilled through the buildings, and sent as they hurried toward the distress call.

Gene turned around and yelled, "That's him! Come on, man!" He turned around in angst and then looked at Chris. "Let's leave him!"

Chris looked at Gene, and calmly retorted, "He'll be here!"

"He's gonna bring the fucking heat down on us man!" Gene's worried voice almost sounded bitchy, hesitant.

"Since when did you care about the police?" Chris said, as he turned away, giving him the cold shoulder. "Come on kid!" Chris whispered, hoping that he was on his way, and slipped by them undetected.

Back inside the hotel stairs, A.J. held the prostitute's hand as they ran toward the stairs of the emergency exit, rushed through the exit door, and paced down the stairs pulling her body close to his jacket. He could hear her heart pumping with excitement. The lower door burst open with swarms of policemen toting pistols and calling for back up with flushed, scared faces, breathing into there shoulder walkie-talkies, out of breath, "answering to 187, need more back up." The voice called back, without hesitation, "all active police members head to Brooklyn...."

When A.J. walked down the stairs, he heard the beating footsteps, "probably cops?" A.J. thought as it sounded like they were inside the walls, and grab him at any second.

Only A.J.'s heart stood still when he saw seven policemen in bright blue shirts had turned the corner—pushing him and the girl against the wall not looking with no importance. A.J. turned his head down and started down the next flight of stairs. But when A.J. thought he was out of the woods, another police officer was standing with his dark sunglasses shining with a fabric cleaner glare and his bright silver nose shined like that of a fresh polished boot. He wasn't too sure until the second he looked down and saw his large monstrous hands and his bright shining knob of a forehead in the glaring overhead light.

"It couldn't be the blue suit from the game?" That worried him the most, and was pretty sure, but didn't want to bet on it (even if his odds were betting high on the ladder). A.J. had accidentally made eye contact with him. A.J. was sure that Officer Rose Kelly had certainly seen A.J. He gave him an evil smirk look as the both of them continued walking, and A.J. was the only one who glanced back, and then continued on his way.

He kept his head forward and didn't look behind him. Maybe Rose Kelly passed him and A.J. thought that he had been oblivious to what he had seen, but he remembered those harsh eyes, burning a hole through his dark sunglasses as if he had known he was the shooter all along, and if he didn't look at him, it didn't matter, that was all.

A.J. descended the stairs, and A.J. surveyed the lobby area waiting for the perfect time to make his escape. He beheld a squad of policemen walking around the lobbies, trying to talk to any of the prostitutes standing around, questioning everyone, "asking if they had seen anything?"

"*Nothin' u* would think is wrong, *offfffficccccaaaaaaaa*." A tall black woman replied, wearing a tight Gucci suit (that almost seemed like bubbly plastic) that stuck to her long frail body, and the two missing teeth made it hard for the officer to understand her.

A.J. then found another route to his escape, just walk out the front lobby. Since the front lobby was being occupied by the police A.J. could make his way around the side, slinking his arm underneath hers, and leaned into her ear, "Act natural."

But he took hold of his thought, and A.J. made his way down the hall feeling the musk of the cigarettes latch onto his clothing like old mud mixed with blood, and slowly walked out the side exit that they had parked beside. The two made their way out the side door, and the sun jumped over the building, and perched on their shoulders, "Act natural." A cold wind hit him fast when he opened the door. He closed the door, and approached the car.

From inside the car Chris thought A.J. was already caught by the police, and behold Chris saw A.J. walking—with a *pootan* in a skimpy black shirt and a dark brown skirt—with his hand looping through hers and strutting real smooth as Chris turned back and notified everyone of A.J.'s arrival.

"He's coming" Chris said, "He got out okay. Start the car" He sighed and Gene turned in his seat and saw A.J. opening the door—as he sent the prostitute away—and fell butt first in his seat breathing rather rapidly. Frank started the car, and let the engine rumble softly as he slowly took off. Looking into the mirror, Frank eyed six police vehicles, whose lights were turning, sending several different blue flashes as if they were spaceships from old television sitcoms, and then turned another block as he felt the pressure lighten, but they weren't away yet.

"It's about time," Gene said, hoping—and in some feeble way—to break the tension as they left the building in undying haste. "I thought you were caught by the heat."

Chris saw A.J. turning his head one more time before they left the block, and knew that he had left a part of himself back there.

He looked down at A.J. wondering, almost scowling in his cocky manner, watching his stone eyes—with water forming—peeling the entire car. Chris remembered vaguely, but his nettled face brought everything back like a bad dram—guilt, paranoia, shame, and by the end of the day, suicide would probably cross his mind.

"You okay?" Chris said, pulling his hand up toward his shoulder and then patting it sincerely, even though it wasn't his nature.

A.J. turned, and his face was impregnated with discomfort, "Yeah, I'm just a little shook up that's all." Chris shook his head, and then took his arm off his shoulder.

Chris just looked into the distance at the oncoming traffic when he said, "Don't worry. Everyone goes through this sort of thing. It will last for a few days, but then it will subside." A.J. just nodded not saying anything, feeling his heart beating rapidly, not wanting to say anything more.

"Did you kill him?" Gene abruptly barked.

A.J. glanced, but did not look him in the eye when he mumbled, "yeah." A.J.'s insides almost wanted to collapse on him, (his amino acids and synapses were starting to falter) and a disgusted feeling started to rise and the thought of being used had occurred—only he couldn't stand the situation he was in. Nothing had gone right for him, but one always bears the burden for their families, even if they don't always see your scars.

Two hours later, Frank had stopped at a corner restaurant to get a bite to eat. They sat in a corner table waiting for his friends while they ordered their food; Chris sat next to A.J. while Gene sat next to Frank and Krazy, giving the most strongest accessibility to any kind of danger that came there way.

When there pizza arrived, A.J. watched them scarf down the pizzas, ripping through the doughy bread letting a few pieces of pepperoni falling off the dough, occasionally grabbing a tissue to wipe their cheeks and lips. A.J. stared at them as if he was a white man gazing on cannibals—tasting and licking their fingers—chomping on their hand tossed pizzas. Only he shoved it down his mouth with a piece of pizza, nibbling away while he heard their lips smacking delight.

After they were done, leaving their waitress a big tip, almost oddly as they made their way out of the city and toward upstate New York. It certainly had been a long morning for A.J. and all he wanted to do now was relax and keep a low profile for the rest of the day. But then A.J. became more curious of the time and lightly tapped Chris's hand.

"You got the time?" A.J. asked curiously. Chris shook his head and with a flick of his wrist he flung the watch up to A.J.'s face making sure he saw the time. A.J. grabbed his hand and eyed the time on the face. It had been twelve thirty the last time he checked, now it was three forty five, quarter to four. Time had gone by faster than he expected.

"You got a date or something?" Chris said, almost laughing, a fiery glint filled his eyes. "You got somewhere to be?"

A.J. had no reason to lie to Chris since he was meeting Jessica after school, and they would surely understand. He thought—no he didn't want to—but he did think about her whole body. Not just the curves, or her flat pectoral muscles contracting when she kicked her legs up.

"Jessica asked me to meet her after school today." A.J. said almost whispering it, but proclaimed it loud and clear, so that all of them could hear him.

Chris cocked his eyebrows, and knew that he would either break his virginity or blow his pants before even took them off. Chris had no need to further A.J.'s assistance with anymore lame advice that his crew could offer. Even though he should have been loading his schedule with more errands, he decided to go easy on him for now.

"I know what you are going to do." Chris said in charming devilish laugh "Trust me, I know." A.J. laughed back, really surprised—and not so surprised—at the same time.

"Is she meeting you at school or at her place?" Chris quickly asked with the sharp fast eccentric nature of a clicking typewriter.

"No, at school, probably near the back where she practices for the games." A.J. replied, smirking but not really smiling.

Chris laughed, and then looked into the dirty rear view mirror. "Frank!" His commanding voice got the attention of everyone else as well.

Frank looked at Chris in the rear view mirror puzzled, awaiting his next orders. "Let's drop lover boy off at school" Chris said, "he's got a girl waiting on him."

Frank nodded, leaving the highway and after five minutes, A.J. became anxious again, nervously fidgeting inside his seat, waiting to be there at the school right now, with Jessica, holding her, caressing her, touching her…

When they were nearing the school, the shady bricks almost began to chip from the way the sun reflected off the rather neo-futuristic building—squared off roofs and buildings that looked squared off and polished like fine marble.

A.J. bent over in his seat looking out the side window as Frank lightly scoffed, shaking his head at A.J. Frank turned around the back of the building toward the gym, turning the corner opposite the bus exit turning right again passing the curb and the fence. A.J. had tried to forget about what happened behind the stadium that entire weekend—it bothered him a little bit—but then it bothered him less. When Frank approached the curb to the back entrance of the gym the car halted, violently there seats as the breaks gave off a shrilling, ear splitting screeching sound.

Chris shook his head in sheer annoyance.

"We gotta get the car looked at." Chris said as Frank nodding in tired disenchantment, putting the car into Park. Chris looked down at A.J. proudly while A.J. nervously smirked, cocking his head sideways. A.J. looked around the car sensing that this was A.J.'s last stop with them, and the would be done.

"Do you guys still need me?" A.J. asked in a last fleeting attempt, "I could help you if you still need me?" A.J.'s concern was actually making Chris reconsider his decision about letting him go.

But before he was about to let A.J. out he had to dispose of the gun, Chris didn't need to ask before because Chris was practical and would spare A.J. his lecture, and just lay it out for A.J. Only his hormones were raging and impure thoughts were manipulating his thoughts very easily.

"One more thing," Chris said, "Did you bring the weapon back with you? Because you don't want the cops to handcuff you when you walk out your front door." A.J. remembered the black metallic Berretta that was digging into A.J.'s side, like it had been attached to his body. A.J. searched around his pants, pulling up his shirt, he grabbed the black handle, taking it out slowly. A.J. almost didn't want to part with the gun as he slowly held the gun in his palm in front of Chris expecting him to receive the weapon. Chris arched his eyebrows very sternly as if A.J. was holding the gun incorrectly. Gene hunched over in his seat watching A.J.'s every move.

"Don't point the gun at any of us!" Chris said cautiously, as he held it sideways, with the barrel focused toward the front seat.

Gene extended his hand across Chris's waist he snatched the gun. He grabbed the gun with a small rag and immediately went to wiping down the entire gun, starting with the grip down to the barrel and examined the gun again for anymore fingerprints left on the gun. The sun magnified against the metallic slide as he finished rubbing the cloth as if he was trying to rub the metal off the gun, and when he was finally done, he stuffed the clean gun under the car seat, far enough for it to disappear.

Chris gave him the 411, so he wouldn't worry about what to do for a few days. "You won't see or hear from us for a few days. Keep your nose clean and don't attract any attention, cool?" Chris said, and then leaning over in his seat, and in his hands was his folder that he had forgotten about. Chris levitated his books in A.J.'s lap as A.J. felt his folder pressing against his groins. A.J. shook his head while he grinned, watching A.J. groan in pain. A.J. looked up at Chris not amused from the slight pain, but then Chris handed him his clothes that were thrown inside the black trash bag. A.J. looked inside it, and then he said, "Do you want me to throw the clothes away when I get home?"

Chris just shook his head, and then motioned him away, "Don't keep her waiting! She's over by the wall with her friends waiting for you." He said eyeing Jessica's group of attractive girls decked from head—rubber bands in tight ponytails to their shell toed sneakers—in their cheerleading outfits. Two of them were blonde and one with jet-black hair, the most gorgeous green eyes with the right kind of lips—dick sucking lips that is (DSL). All of them, except for Chris gazed upon these little girls—because he didn't need to get his pleasure from disease-spreading, malcontent underweight prostitutes that couldn't keep themselves tide to one man—with apathy when money was supposed to be earned.

Chris was glad for A.J. but he had a wife and was now a dutiful father to his baby boy, and didn't want more stress from a mistress giving him more stress than he already had, it was just preposterous. They talked for a moment, and they watched for a few more minutes as they left him holding her in his arms.

Inside the car Gene already knew that A.J. was about to become a victim luring into Jessica's web of attraction, giving him a taste of what would be one wild sexual experience that only porn stars knew of. Only Chris was disinterested with their childish spying and called to their attention.

"Let A.J. have some privacy huh?" Chris said, "because right now he is now apart of our circle." Everyone tuned in on what Chris was saying digging into like a mechanical drill altering everything that was human. Everything seemed right.

"He's proved himself and now he needs to know how to earn his daily bread. Now we have many things to take care of!" With a light wave Chris gave Frank the go ahead to leave. Frank pulled the clutch down, and pressed on the gas passing A.J. and Jessica. A.J. turned to watch the Chris leave feeling odd about leaving them. After the car past a row of cars, Frank took a right at the corner and another left at the football stadium exiting the back way.

At that moment, A.J.'s attraction suddenly ended when he heard the screeching of the car blaze through the afternoon sky. When he turned around, and watched them leaving he felt Jessica's arm touching his shoulder, and he turned, feeling a certain eerie chill go up and down his system. "Don't worry. They can take care of themselves." Jessica said still holding A.J. in her grasp.

"I know," A.J. said very concerned, "I was just gonna see if they needed anything else." He put down his head, but then Jessica reached toward his chin, and pulled his eyes away from—spacing his emotional distance away from Chris's reign. She pulled his head up, and Jessica saw something very disturbing—his eyes were hollow as a log, and what she could see was nothing…no life, no light at the end of the tunnel. Jessica took her fingers off his chin, and then dusted down the suit pretending she wrinkled his suit.

"I don't know what to say. Very professional and…" Jessica's train of thought trailed off for a moment to find a credible attribute toward A.J.'s thrown on suit. Jessica wanted to say something positive, but his overall handsome face stunted her words from saying anything as she stared at his beautiful, but paralyzed eyes.

"Handsome," She wanted to say something different, but she couldn't say anything else but "And handsome" again and burst out from her lungs a childish chuckle. A.J. grinned happily as they embraced each other in this moment of happiness. Jessica ended her chuckle in a weak cough as a small moment of silence drifted between them. The awkwardness began to dissolve as Jessica's hand began to release her from his grip, and A.J. leaned down—sweating from every pore—to pick up his notebook and his clothes that were in the black bag. With his left hand he grasped the trash bag, and with his right he gripped the tip of the binder, and on the way up from the ground A.J. slowly admired Jessica's legs, seeing if she would notice him.

"See something you like?" Jessica said in a sarcastic, yet seductive tone. As A.J. rose from the ground, he looked at Jessica with a tranquil stare as he felt his presence putting her in a fix. A.J. felt all too calm about his flirtatious behavior, just as a man should be when he was obviously looking at a woman.

"What!" Jessica taunted A.J., mockingly bringing her shaved calf in front of his face.

"Nothing!" A.J. shot back, smelling the perfume expunging off her tingling, raw flesh. "What *are you* looking at?"

"I know what I'm looking at." Jessica's green eyes told him the whole truth, even if she didn't want to admit it. "I have a funny feeling of what are *you* looking at?"

A.J. pulled himself off the ground, and stood over her, making her flesh crawl in ecstasy (not *exstasy*) "I know what I'm looking at, and you're right in front of me." A.J. managed to pull off a smooth compliment without being an asshole.

Jessica giggled from A.J.'s compliment and she reached out to grab his hand, and the two started down the concrete letting their friends take a good look at them. A.J. sheepishly glanced at Jessica just admiring her beautiful face—her hair shifting in the afternoon wind—and when he saw her as if she was in a mind-bending maze, and the less complex her face looked he wanted to explore this maze, through the deepest part of her soul—to the open crevice of her mind down to the very tips of her toenails.

He turned away as there hands pulled their bodies closer as their fingers began to intersect between each other. Jessica stole a glance, her quick senses perceived his movements, and turned. She smiled with an uplifting feeling as they continued into the parking lot.

"Didn't you say that you are practicing in the gym today?" A.J. asked breaking the silence. Jessica turned her head sideways trying to remember if she had practiced or not. As the answer juggled in her mind, the answer suddenly fell in her hands, and when she had all her balls in her hands, she remembered why she had been standing around with her friends.

"It got cancelled today," Jessica said, looking into his eyes. "You would have known if you were here today."

A.J. turned his head toward Jessica with sour eyes deeply perturbed by her intuitive nature.

"If you only knew what kind of day I had." A.J. thought angrily. Then A.J.'s emotions began slipping in between the cracks of his calm cool complexion. His face was steaming with rage—nose flaring in heat—and head cocked back as Jessica turned to look upon A.J. she became frightened and averted her eyes away his malicious stare.

"What's wrong?" Jessica spoke in a muddle voice as she raised her head up a bit to A.J.'s level. A.J. suddenly stopped in his tracks breathing in and out from his nose bottling up his anger—hearing it fizzle and pop until his nerves were turning into burnt joint roaches—and A.J. sighed with his cold silence, avoided the conversation. But Jessica was blocked by her naiveté, and with the outmost care for him stopped and then looked at him. He turned away, but then she decided to go out on a limb for him.

"A.J.!" Jessica shouted as she extending her right hand out and gently cupped A.J.'s right pale cheek. It was cold and clean, and when she finally thought about it, she felt his presence growing angry. A.J. looked upon Jessica's worried face as he started to breathe again and spoke very point blank to Jessica, trying to explain his odd silence.

"Jessica," A.J. said, putting his hand against the top of her hand. "It's what you said before, how did you know I wasn't here." A.J. sighed as A.J. started to walk again leaving Jessica's hand floating in the air. Jessica became disillusioned—everything that had come to this point had vanished with A.J.'s words—perturbing her comfortable emotions as spoke seriously.

"I was only making a joke," Jessica replied, her voice whining in keening high notes. "The only reason I said that was because I didn't see you today…in the commons. You and Chris are always sitting on the other side of commons A, that's why I said that." Jessica implied no regrets, or apologized for her actions but Jessica felt so lacerated by A.J.'s apathy that she felt something was wrong. Only the words she disliked so much came out of Jessica's lips. "I'm sorry."

A.J. looked into Jessica's eyes very collected, but a small unnerving paranoia kept A.J. on edge, like a knife carving underneath his skin, poking his insides and snapping off all connections to his muscles and brains.

"It's okay. Don't worry about it." A.J. made little to no eye contact with her, somewhat—no, *definitely*—embarrassed by how he was acting, but wanted to avoid anymore embarrassment. Only Jessica was embarrassed too, and a moment of silence cut off all form of communication—rendering them no leeway for comments about the weather or the day. They stayed quiet for the entire ride in her 1992 Corvette.

The two weren't that far from Mulberry Ave where the houses became replicates—carbon copies that really made no fine detail even that appealing in a suburban blueprint. Jessica's impatience began burning between her thighs as the Corvette slowly traveled at twenty five, cruising as the engines burned slowly sending exhaust into the industrious, scourge soaking sky—as she searched for Belmont Ave. Jessica turned right again and scoured out the window with her eyes scrunching together—feeling her eyes circling and narrowing on the houses like binoculars adjusting, but could not guess which house was his.

"Where is your house at?" Jessica asked as she used her right hand to block the sun and refocusing her eyes back onto the street. A.J. pointed to the left side of the street, feeling the envious rays trying to block his vision.

"I'm the third house on the left." A.J. said as the car slowly crept down the block, and stopped right in front of his house.

"Right here?" Jessica asked as she parked next to his rather small diminutive house even though the overall look of it was cozy, but she looked at it with pure face value appreciation. She could see a comfortable living environment, and she could sense it.

"This is it." A.J. said looking at his house, and when she turned back toward him. Only she saw that he looked jabbed and pronged by his inner conflicts.

"I knew the second you saw my house you were going to look down on me."

Jessica could not believe how he was acting, for the most part she apologized—nor even made an attempt—but this did not make any sense to her—like the clean insides of his corneas.

"Listen." Jessica urged forcefully, "I don't know why you are acting like this. I took you home without question, I noticed you, I couldn't have met you at all—and you want to criticize me…"

"I wasn't…" A.J. tried to speak.

Tears were starting to form at the bottom of her cup, and her lips began quivering, and like a sad bow string, she began to tremble. "I don't care about where you live and I don't care about your status. I could give a shit about half of what people say about me. I just want to be with you!"

"I saw your face. Don't act so self-righteous, the look on your face said everything." A.J.'s harshness added more hatred to the situation, and she coughed her words as the tears began to flow down her apple cheek.

Without any warning, Jessica jumped out of the seat, and moved over the middle seat, and stretched her left leg wide open. As she moved across the seat Jessica prompting her knees on the plastic seat and she leveled her crotch against his pants. With her arms she grabbed his neck as they looked at each other. She looked into his eyes and moving inwards she started to kiss A.J., slowly, but then the two became quickly acquainted with each other's tongues.

"I don't know…" She didn't let him speak as her tongue passionately, but not intentionally, blocked off his speech. His hand quickly fell against her dress, feeling, and instantly seeing the image of her butt in his mind. Perfectly centered, but he pulled away and grabbed her shoulders. Jessica's tongue stood out, and then wiped the slobber from around her mouth.

She closed, and looked into his eyes. Fear of not being good enough for her.

"I'm a virgin."

She did not chuckle, and she leaned her head forward, pressing the side of her head sensually and said, "Don't worry…" and then her hands traveled to A.J.'s zipper. Even though she was taking the initiative, she was impressed by A.J.'s thick penis. She began to pull down his pants, and then A.J. began to help her.

"Okay" A.J. said with a relaxed tone as his hands pulled his pants to his thighs. He did not see it, but his large stiff rod touched the side of her cold thigh. Jessica backed up off his legs, as she pulled her skirt up to reveal her soft wilted sunflower that had a long line of neatly cropped hair. She then slid it over his penis, and it felt tight at first, but then it was silky and wet.

Spreading his own lips, and smiled as she took control. She forced A.J.'s hand on her breast as she rode him, as his penis traveled deep into her insides. Jessica instantly pulled his hand up her shirt as she continued to move back and forth. A.J. rested his head against her chest, heaving and moaning, but a silent tear began to form on the side of his eye.

After five minutes, A.J. could feel his own climax beginning to build up, but he wanted to hear her scream a bit more. He grabbed her sides and forced her small and agile body on his monster penis.

Jessica didn't resist as she felt her climax beginning to take its form, and when she was about to come she looked at A.J., and said, "Don't come in me!" But then, it was too late, he already came. But the rush was the best part.

For a moment, the two did not separate for a moment, with Jessica resting her head against his shoulder, "You were great." Jessica panted short breaths as she kissed him on the lips. It felt sweet for the both of them, but as Jessica felt his rod not shrinking like most men, she pulled it out her self. Her vagina felt like it had been spread out like a thumb digging into a piece of dough, she pulled herself off A.J.'s lap and sat in the driver's seat.

"I don't know who I am!" A.J. thought, but then something else whispered over his shoulder, *"You are not alone, the one who asks, always sees a glimpse, a hint of new life."* A.J. guessed that Jessica was his new glimpse, even though over the course of this weird day, everything he knew had just flew out the window.

Jessica was very emotional from her experience and watched as A.J. began to pull his pants back up over his limp penis.

"What's wrong?" A.J. asked, "Did I hurt you?" A.J. said as he wanted to slap his own stretch of stupidity.

"No." Jessica said as she turned to show him her smile that spread from cheek to cheek, making her cheeks turn bright red and her body reeling in heat. "You were great." A.J. smiled, and knew that she was lying. A.J. nodded, and then looked out the window

"I know you want to stay and talk with me, but I got things to take care of too." Jessica said and, picking up his flattery, and began to put on her clothes.

A.J. was shocked, but he couldn't care either way. "Cool. I'll see you tomorrow." He opened the door, and then he said, just before he left. "I like you," and then he left.

Jessica didn't know if she was used by A.J. or not and began to pull her underwear back up her legs as she set her underwear around her waist and thought, "I don't care," Jessica thought, "even if he did make me reach my peak I still love him. Damn my status in school and whoever disagrees with me." Jessica thought angrily sighed as she turned the engine on roaring away taking the other exit out of Mulberry Ave. and was anticipating his arrival tomorrow at school.

While Jessica roared away, A.J. had already run to the bathroom, stripping himself of the suit, and emptying out the black bag with his old clothes. But before he could put them on, the food that he thought he digested was soon starting to curdle his stomach, and rushing toward the toilet, he then threw everything up. Leaning over the toilet with his naked body shaking like some addict in a bulimic drug loss, and like the addict, his mind couldn't analyze what his body was going through. The vomit looked like he had eaten soup, but the small black particles in the brownish green palate told him that it was the steak from the restaurant.

With a long line of spit forming from his mouth he wiped it off, and then pulling himself off the floor. He heard the engine roar off from the block, and then sat next to the toilet for a moment, getting his thoughts together. Only he couldn't think, and he was afraid to look in the mirror, because he felt like he wouldn't see his own face anymore.

He could rationalize things, but he couldn't rationalize his darkest fears. He saw the dead mans face, and his body spilling blood. The barrels were smoking, and both were to blame, for the man he would never ultimately know would be forever in his dreams.

Chapter VII:

"Blood Costs Lives (and Loyalty)"

After Chris had dropped A.J. off at school that very second, Chris was now off to finish his business in New York with the setting sun giving into the darkness giving them the power to do whatever they wanted. All of them were calm on the outside, but were contemplating, calculating each and every move. Each of them had ideas, but Chris had a surefire plan that oddly enough required no thinking at all. As Frank traveled down the road, the sounds of horns were blaring in all the lanes, but even though cars were honking there horns angrily, and with the outmost patience they waiting to receive orders from Chris as his other soldiers quietly anticipated.

Only the itchy trigger finger soldiers that lurked throughout the boroughs of New York City were going to be a problem. To the New York families, Chris Mangini was a threat, an almost incurable plague to his enemies that would lead to an instantaneous death.

Chris knew full well that he was a primary target becoming more cautious with every decision that he made and needed more than ever to watch everyone, even the loyalty of his own soldiers. And as the sun sunk down over the large skyscrapers this was an imminent sign for Chris to make his move down at the docks and discover who else was clouding over them. Even if his enemies did come at him, he had to show whoever was controlling his docks a thing or two in the matters of business.

Only he felt that one way his enemies would try to attack his fortress would be by sending a young, steadfast boy to approach Chris whenever he was strolling throughout the halls. He didn't want to endanger the students at George Bradley. The best thing for him to do was the time to leave the school scene for a while. He wasn't leaving permanently, but he needed someone trustworthy and strong enough to handle his rackets while he was away.

Anyone that was not blood related through his Capos or his Zips made him turn the other cheek. Although he had vouched for A.J. he didn't think that he should explain any of his decisions.

"We gotta go to the docks tonight." Chris said bent on his destination, carefully thinking out everything. "We need to contact a few of our Zips in Brooklyn or Manhattan. Know anyone?" Chris said, looking into the mirror, hoping that Frank could come up with anyone.

"Yeah, I could call a few people." Frank said, and focused his eyes back on the road, and had the perfect two that could be of some use on this mission.

But this struck a chord and Gene became defensive, "I could help."

With that thought, Chris sharply waved his hand in a empirical way.

"This is not your fight" Chris said pensively "I want you to see that our matters in business are well kept under control and call some of your friends to watch all of our bookies, because they might get pressured into joining them, so I think that might give them a good warning." Then Chris looked around the car, letting his words be heard, so that he could hear his words.

"Don't worry about it. You will not be left out of anything." Chris turned toward Gene, and tapped him on the shoulder. Gene just looked at him, and forced a smile under his scoffing breath become rather hot, and his mouth was dying for something to drink. Only he thirsted for something more, power.

Gene turned back toward the window, staring at the pink and green sky that always settled over the city like a plague cast on everyone. If you made your city shitty, then you had to pay for it.

Chris nodded with deep pain as he looked forward, not giving anything else more thought except for the mission at hand, and knew that one thing was clear. There was no favoritism in Chris's clan, and he treated them like they were his own brothers, just the same, and everyone in the group had there own specific function, and without him, this group couldn't last, but that didn't make there own presences inferior.

Inside the apartment, the two bothers that Frank called, Jerry and Niccolo, threw their coats over their shoulders as they slowly moved across the living room, kissed their mother goodbye and quietly closed the door behind them. As the two brothers traveled down the halls then down a flight of stairs with a rewarding sadistic smile as the two occasionally pushed each other playfully into the cracked, green apartment walls, smiling from the opportunity that they had.

As they went down the last flight of steps, the two pushed the doors wide open feeling the cool night air pushing against there coats, rebounding and swishing through their unshaven black chin hairs. They waited for a moment to see where Frank was.

Surveying the city streets, the corner lights blinked consistently from red to green, and he was dumbstruck, not by the lights. But the way the lights reflected on his eyes—glowing pubescent mirrors of hazy dreams—he could see the reflection of the lights on the streets. Niccolo tapped his brother on the shoulder and the two started walking proudly, very professional and not attracted by the sounds of the incessant conversations in buildings above him—stuffing their hands inside their pockets. A state of alertness came over them as they walked across the street, as Niccolo stopped in the middle of the street as if he was entranced stunning him from head to toe sending him into a state of complete and total shock. They were being picked up by Chris Mangini.

After he introduced the two for the first time, he knew that the longer they waited the docks were going to be swarmed by extra security from here to the Hudson. Frank turned forward in the driver's seat, and started the car with extreme haste as the engine began with a soft purr, and turning into a lion's roar. As Frank looked behind him he saw the impending traffic before them.

Frank suddenly veered out into the lane swishing them in their seats as stowaways in the bottom of a large vessel, and quickly pressed on the brakes as he reared behind a cars bumper with a screeching halt.

All of them were nervous down to the pit of their stomachs, barely speaking to each other. No one knew exactly what was about to happen, but Chris had an idea before they had even reached the docks.

Before they reached the Brooklyn docks, Chris had to make this clear before he would unleash a reminder to those lazy, bulging men with sweat pouring through their shirts, and faces the size of bowling balls. The dock owners were incredible pushovers for cash, beatings, and threats towards them or their families, but that was what made them easy targets—like an abusive mother with a young sissy boy.

Frank approached the docks, hearing the sounds of the water rushing up the dark malt liquor river with polluted, intoxicated fish. Jerry and Niccolo became fascinated by the gray flat stony pier that overlooked the endless surpassing amounts of rocky water that crashed and yelled against the sides of the blue walls. The whistling wind was calm as a desert night—everything coexisted on the branch of a wine vineyard—and they were on that vine. Only a few small blue and white lights were burning bright across the docks as they parked next to the edge of the pier where the barbed wire entrance with razor blade spirals wrapped around the top of the fence, but Frank had many ways to get through anything, and this was no discussion.

Chris was staring through the holes of the barbed fence, Chris saw to his dismay that two guards were aimlessly walking around a few crates, foolishly tapping the top of the crate with their flash lights duck-taped around the sides of their shotguns. These guards were probably over-night hoods dressed as police officers, but Niccolo and Jerry could handle this. Chris could not make out their faces and the clean cut, stereotypical fat guy resembled nothing of a policemen.

"If Frank and Krazy could make it across the docks without being spotted or taking out the guards without being noticed everything could run just as planned." Chris thought as he examined the dock guard's movements and tried to make another assumption of the police officers faces as they mysteriously disappeared behind another row of large crates.

Everyone was waiting for the plan, but what they were really waiting for was for him to give the signal. It wouldn't feel right to leave without the instructions, because he was like the blueprint for a building, the eraser to a pencil, a condom for a dick. If that was taken out, nothing would matter.

"Okay," Chris said and everyone sprang up from their seats and Chris immediately put them at ease. "Relax." All of the relaxed, laughing for a moment, and he laid out the instructions, choosing his words carefully. "I want Frank and Krazy to go and see what and who is pressuring our docks. I want you to bring your cousins on this job, and I don't want any gunfire coming from those docks, real quiet and subtle."

Chris turned toward his cousins, overlooking Gene, who was ultimately swelling with jealousy.

"Are you guys good with a knife?" The two nodded with a mish-mashed expression.

"Good, you're smart boys. Smart enough to listen to your mother once and a while, right?" Chris knew that this was a soft spot that could easily throw them off guard, feel ignorant and ashamed from their actions.

The boys knew what Chris had said was true, and unlike he did with A.J., Chris did not tell them to raise their heads back up, and he wanted them to learn, accept their error and move on. If they did not have any order nor rules to follow, chaos would then reign and the universe would then begin its circle on the fucked up axis.

"Don't say anything. Learn from your mistakes, and don't treat your mother bad. Don't be lying around all the time. Get up and make your way. You got that?" They nodded, and said nothing.

Chris spoke again more forthright. "Go. And don't come back until you find out who has been putting pressure on our docks." As he finished speaking Chris rested without having to repeat his orders and rested with silence floating through the car.

Suddenly the car door began to creak open slowly as Frank and Krazy began following his orders. The brothers confusingly follow each other as Frank leapt from the car and stupidly slamming the door behind him.

Niccolo with a frightened expression stared into his cousin's face—images of being beaten, thrashed and being lashed for his obnoxious behavior. He stared half-cowardly and Niccolo nervously looked away in fear. Frank scoffed and disappeared into the darkness like a ghost, and after he moved beside large crates. As Frank glanced around the corner, he noticed a few guards making small jokes "Now, my hands up the girls ass." The man took a break as he puffed on his late night cigarette, and exhaled a cloud of smoke into the air. He noticed a few more, but they were already falling asleep in their massive dosage of boredom. The only real threat was those two guards that seemed invincible as they turned their backs, continuing the joke, "as my son is blowing his teacher's cock," and faced the rear of the docks.

"But were there more," Frank thought, but would

As Chris sat from his safe comfortable position, he watched as Frank and the other three approached the side of the fence while Niccolo trailed behind them and landed against the fence. As Frank glanced behind him, he raised a finger up readying the awaiting soldiers then he threw up a second finger making his soldiers wait more.

Then Frank without warning suddenly burst around the corner without leaving an echo whispering in the air. As soon as Frank disappeared around the corner, Krazy began around the corner as the two brothers lagged behind Frank.

As Chris watched and waited to see if everything was okay, a subdued thud filled the foreboding silence and a smacking thud came from the pier with an unsuspected groan. Gene also caught onto this noise too, and wondered if he was playing favoritism with the Italians, or more like leaving him out of the action. But he was thinking of questions that he couldn't answer.

"Hey, Chris!" Gene said as Chris turned with a revived look in his eyes as he dusted off the blinding sleep with the back of his hand. It almost scared Gene to fixate himself upon his commander, friend, or boss. He did not know if he was on his side or pretending to be his friend.

Gene held his breath for a moment and let his words flow from his mouth very sharply and discreetly.

"I know you want me to make sure our business is okay. But, why do I always get the bitter end of the action. You know I put myself on the line just as much as Frank and Krazy do. No disrespect intended but all of us are in your debt for letting us become apart of your clan. You gave us something to do to make my life mean something, even if I am just a Jew."

Gene huffed and Chris's face became worried as if he had disrespected or angry. But this was what Chris had wanted, to let Gene ease himself off him, and let his venerability flow back into his veins as if he was a psychiatrist easing Gene of some trouble. But he wouldn't put him down for it.

Chris nodded his head and began to comfort his worried friend with a light pat on his shoulder.

"I know you might think I am showing favorites with Frank and Krazy, but I'm not. I love you just as much as those boys." Chris said, giving him what he exactly wanted to hear.

"That was fucking great!" Niccolo whispered, as he looked over the two bodyguards, lying next to an empty gas canister and their cigarette letting the last of the smoke travel in the air, and the cherry finally dissolved in the wind. They laid unconscious, mouth open, and starting to salivate. Frank had grabbed there silenced pistols, and put it his pant lines.

"Shut up!" Frank hissed under his breath, and then was eying the factory with great wonder. The large dominating castle had not lost its brightness, and then moved in a low crouching walk as a soft pulsating green light glowed above them. They landed against the walls, just below the windows bright lights and saw a shadow walking passed the windows. "Damn it!" Frank whispered, almost in pain.

"What?" Krazy uttered, wandering what he saw.

Frank lowered his head, and then said, "There are more guards." He knew what to do. "After I enter, follow behind me and spread out. You take Niccolo, and let Jerry go by himself."

Jerry and Niccolo looked at each other, knowing that they couldn't be apart from each other, and Jerry said, "Why don't you two go together, and we'll take the other side."

Frank turned, and with an impatient whisper, "Because he can be on the top, and get Jerry from the top."

Jerry and Niccolo looked at each other, and nodded, after a moment where the sound of the wind beat against the water as he clutched the round handle, and pulled it open. He could see the light peering through the door, and when he pulled it open, he slipped into the factory—a darkness upon a world of light.

Back in the car, Chris began to see that Gene was falling into the cracks of jealousy and bitterness, and the heat of his anger was confusing everything but there was nothing that he couldn't handle, let alone a person's confused feelings. Chris was not fooled by what he was saying, but now was not the time to give Gene the chance to put things out in the open without Krazy and Frank in their presence. He wanted to squash any nesting bed of restlessness that would accumulate until he would become so untrustworthy that he would switch sides.

"Like I said," Chris sighed, finding the right set of words, "I don't want to treat anybody else in my crew any different. We all have to do what we have to, and I show you lots of respect." He looked away for a moment, and then came back his face repugnant. "And those foolish notions of letting you have the bitter end of the action. You have most of the school lunch area, and some of our routes are covered by your crew under your flag. And most of your racket activities are in Manhattan, where I let you operate, also under your flag. Did you forget about that?"

Gene just shook his head, not saying anything. But Chris was going to make this perfectly clear, crystal.

"Like I said, when the time comes, I'll include you when your help is most needed, and it was never about race. Remember when I brought you around, and they doubted you, I vouched, I always have."

Gene nodded in an agreeing shake, remembering clearly. He let the tension in his arm slowly unwind his bones.

Inside the factory, piles and piles of boxes were loaded around the dark and muggy underbelly of the large, wheat smell of cardboard and plastic wrapping that was scattered around the floors like leaves resting underneath a large oak tree. But inside these boxes were a prize that no one even thought of, nor even dream of. It was the boxes of freshly packaged CD's that none of the stores could sell because it was illegal to own any of these disks, whether it was music or company programmed, the government was desperate. Frank and them had quickly relinquished the guards, and took there weapons too. But one of the weapons that one was carrying was a large butcher's knife that looked like it had been freshly cleaned for whatever purposes. Niccolo was the one who had it, and Krazy just scoffed as they made there way toward the stairs. There footsteps echoed around the factory, like water trickling in a well, and every haunting drop echoed intensely and loudly. When Frank approached them, they were all standing on the other side of the metallic stairs just moments away from walking in and taking him by surprise.

"What are you waiting for?" Frank said, looking across the metallic bridge and saw a bright burning light shining against the plastic door.

With his large .357 Revolver, Frank walked toward the door, and kicked it open. After he kicked the door he saw a large fat man putting some kind of files into a safe, and when he turned, the look of true fear entered into his system as the harbormaster yelled in shock terror. He started to run away, and Frank ran after him. Then when it turned into a struggle, everyone else joined in the pummeling.

The windows were fogging up and a dank warm smell began rising from the edge of the dock walls against the outside windows. A quick jabbing thought began to aim, and set off a newfound worry—and everything down to the inner-sanctum of Chris's scorched soul that could not be replenished. It was the murder weapon that they had given A.J. He would have Gene take the weapon, wrap it up in a handkerchief and take it to the edge of the pier. The he would tie a strong rope material around the handkerchief in a bowtie, and with that large rock tied at the other end of the rope it would drag the handkerchief to the bottom of the pier. As long as the rock was heavy and large, this plan could very well work, but even if someone wanted to look for it, it would either be on the other side of the Atlantic before he got through with it. As soon as this problem was taken off his hands, he could think about more important business matters for his boot legging venture.

"Gene!" Chris said in a slow paced tone as if he was going to recite epic poetry from his large memory. "Take the gun to the pier, and dump it."

Gene turned, and with an odd complexity, he puffed out in exasperation. "When, Now?"

"Yes, take it to the pier and find something strong to tie the handkerchief with. Then tie a rock. Use any kind of rock that is in your disposal, and tie it to the other end of the rope. Then when it is tightened, drop it into the pier and let it sink to the bottom of the ocean."

Gene felt odd about acting on such sort notice orders but did what he was told.

But he decided to thrust his pompous behavior down his throat feeling the strong taste touch his throat like vinegar residing in the back of his mouth—dissolving the very fibers that he once was, and would never be again. But for now, he had to scold Gene with a sooth scolding reminding him who made the calls.

"You know I apologized for putting Frank and Krazy in front of you. Like you said, I gave you a chance to make something of yourself, and that was one reason why I brought you along." Then he put his face into his face as if he wasn't hearing everything. "Why don't you just try and do what I say? I respect your opinion honestly. But at least do what I tell you to do, and like that Nike commercial said, *Just do it.*"

Gene lowered his head for a moment and cowered in disappointment. Chris decided to bring his conflicting friend back to his old self again that tough kid that went through a whole fight with three broken fingers. He saw a restlessness within him—*the starving are never satisfied*—the voice—which he had become fully comfortable and and annoyed by said. Something about this voice was right—but Chris felt that this voice had to be wrong.

"Okay!" He said coldly but without rousing Chris. In that moment, Gene leaned over the seat and bent down searching for the handkerchief that was right near his feet. Gene felt his way under the seat, and he palmed the large handkerchief in his hands as he rose from his hunched position and glanced around to watch his back.

When Gene finally mustered the courage to leave, he approached the door and gripped the lever with his nimble fingers, and felt the sifting fog that started to suffocate his throat. Gene made a daring turn on the lever and let the door silently creak open as the fog vanished within seconds of the fresh air gusting through the stale odor of the car.

As Gene stepped out of the car, the wind began whipping against the hood of the car with a loud howl. The door let off a rather loud SLAM from his force. As Gene walked around the car—more like piece of shit of the decade—the rear window fogged up again. As he began trailing down toward the ever-culling pier, he looked up at the stars, and saw shadows moving about, almost as if he could see demons running around the room.

The room was in shambles, the harbormasters papers were all over the place when they finally got him to calm down. But it wasn't easy though, it was like trying to suppress a wild boar with small needle shots. Jerry and Niccolo had been socked in the stomach and across the jaw. Even though it had knocked them down, they still had consciousness over their body, but they were guaranteed to feel it in the morning. It took all of them to hold his body down against the edge of his desk. Palming the weapon, he cocked the hammer (the Harbormaster inched backwards against the oak wood desk) and pressed it against the harbor manager's sweaty temple.

"Now will you listen!" Frank exasperated voice began to heave, and he felt the cold metal starting to rub on his palm like blood.

"That must mean," Niccolo said exasperated, "he'll listen." Nobody laughed, but everyone was so tired and pissed off that they would have laughed if they had enough energy to laugh.

"Now!" Frank said, "Tell me who are pressuring the docks!"

"I don't know what you are talking about!" The Harbormaster groaned, his large body pushed against the light blue shirt. The cringing odor expunged from how he smelled, but Frank was not hearing this.

"I think you know, you fucking punk ass!" Frank said, and then yelled, "Who the hell came and muscled us out of the docks! Tell me!" Frank maneuvered the weapon against the side of his head—his eyes and voice full of perturbed demons—as he buried the head against his head. Frank acted like one of the dead, giving him the straight facts through brutal force.

"Okay, okay, I'll tell you, just don't fucking kill me!" The Harbormaster repeated like a broken record, almost crying, his voice became hoarse.

"Talk, tell me everything!" Frank demanded. "Tell me right now!"

While Gene clamped the neatly folded clothed handkerchief inside his clammy sticky hands the wind began to attract the sounds of the threatening sea with taunting waves and small growls of the crashing sea against the onyx pier wall. As Gene traveled down the bleak pier, the stars bright points reflected against the water with the moon's gazing eye blazing right beside the patches of stars next to each culminating pack of stars, and he wondered when winter was ever going to leave them. Feeling the wind of the air brush his cheeks like a woman's cold lips, Gene approached the edge of the dock pier, and felt the wind almost pulling him down into the blackened water.

Gene's hand began to twitch as he grasped the smooth material arousing himself out of the state of fear. He rubbed his eyes with a free hand as he fixed his eyes on the clear moon, seeing that it was the only light that could awaken him.

Then out of nowhere, a flickering light began flashing on and off again. Two power towers stood with dreary wires almost drooping to the ground like sad faces. For a moment, it was almost waving to Gene as the wind had begun to stir up again—and he felt the wire cables sadness of always having to stay in one place. Never leaving or progressing until someone cut them down.

While the wind started up again, an eerie feeling rested on his neck, giving him goosebumps up and down his body. He lowered his head and stared down at the ground. As Gene fixed his eyes on the black ground, piles of useless junk were next to his feet as he kicked a small bowl to the side and grunted curses to the wind.

He began to wonder if trying to get rid of a weapon that would float right back up to the surface was a good idea. Gene struggled trying to see with the flickering lights, grunting curses to the wind again kicking another object that sounded dead and hollow, but proved to be full of life at the same time, and that—like the dead hollow object—was taking a toll on his conscience.

As he searched around the pile of junk at his feet, he saw a flickering light, and a small coil of rope in a circle like an awaiting snake that was sleeping, listening to the crashing of the waves sprinkle its rays against it's shedding skin. Only now Gene had to fulfill Chris's orders.

Gene leaned down to the ground, bending over on his knees, holding his weight with the soles of his shoes as he examined the small coil of rope and the handkerchief coexisting in his left hand, his mind was toiling with many ideas. Only the bitterness of envy began to cloud his judgement and he ran his hands through his head, remembering the thought of getting rid of the gun became hazed from all thought.

Gene rose from the ground, still palming the handkerchief in his hand, he burned with questionable doubt about his exact motives. He was not preserving his own life; he was helping Chris cover A.J.'s tracks from the police. And that little twerp had not even known them a week and he was already participated on murders handed down from Chris's boss, Don Pescaro. "I should be the next in line, Goddamn it! I've been working my ass off to get in his ranks."

Gene approached the edge of the pier, uncloaking the handkerchief and revealed the gun to the open moon as he was holding a sacrifice for God, and he could see the dirty reflection of A.J.'s prints. Holding this weapon, this made him want to do the impossible and take control…

"No, not that way!" Gene thought as he almost temptingly slipped the metallic piece into his pants. The thought of putting A.J. through that kind of torture would be too risky for Gene. But he was starting to think for himself, and he wasn't going to take anyone with him unless they were going with him to the black abyss. And if A.J. was going to be like the rest, then he would die with the rest of them.

Although he wanted to keep the weapon for some reason, he knew that getting rid of it was a better idea.

After the Harbormaster had explained everything to them, Frank was in a calmer state than he was before. Everyone else was glad, because they didn't want to see him kill anyone. "Is that all!" Frank ordered, holding the stacks of papers, looking over the long list of products (coincidentally in printed Excel format) "Virus protection systems from…" He scrolled down the list, rapidly, "Windows, and some other small companies?"

The large brooding man was laying back in his chair, wiping his head off with a moist cloth as he said, "No. Turn another page. We got almost every music artist in the whole borough to the Midwest and California. We got everybody."

Frank flipped the piece of paper over, and his eyes glazed over the impressive list of artists, and then folded the paper back over with an approving nod, and then said, "When are they going to make another shipment?"

The large harbormaster shook his head, and then said with contempt, "Jesus, man! They come and go whenever they please." He started to breath like he was about to faint, and held the cloth against his forehead dabbing off the sweat as if it was his own blood.

"Take a guess!" Frank demanded folding the paper back down.

The Harbormaster sighed, and then closed his eyes, trying to think of another day when they would probably be taking the stuff up to Boston and Detroit. "Probably this Saturday. They got a big order going to Boston and Detroit somewhere, if you meet them on the back roads, they won't be able to stop you. But they don't go without a lot of people. It will be like battling a friggin' army, you'll never win!"

Frank just shook his head, hearing everything, in a complacent manner not really paying attention. Only he needed him to remember whom they were with, and he as a person needed to be taught a lesson.

"We'll worry about that!" Frank assured him, and then walked over toward the man, and folded his hands together as he said with a smile, "What's your name?"

The man looked at him oddly, and then said, "My name is Henry, Henry…" But before he could continue Frank interrupted him, and spoke with total ferocity, "Well, Henry. The next time you decide to give up our docks to anyone other than *Chris Mangini*, I guarantee you, your families are going to be nailed to the wall, if you fuck up like this again."

The large man or Henry, was taken back from his deviant behavior, and had gotten the picture of the consequences. "I get it!" Henry said with moral repugnance that could be easily taken for sarcasm, and Frank saw this as the perfect opportunity.

Frank said, "No, I don't think you do." Then he looked over at Niccolo, and motioned him with his eyebrow.

He screamed, as they pushed there weight upon him as they laid his hand on the table. "What are you doing!"

He screamed it again, but Frank did not respond as he held the butcher knife above him. "Here's so you won't forget!" The man's eyes widened, as Frank gave Niccolo the signal, and it came whooshing down toward his finger, so swiftly like a guillotine cutting off a person's head…

Plop. That's the sound it made when the piece of steel echoed from the deep blue water. Gene slowly opened the folded handkerchief from his tight hand and with both hands, Gene let the handkerchief slip from his grasp, whisk down to the top of the ocean floor and landed like a thin piece of cut garlic thrown into a pre-heated pot, bubbling and soaking up the bottom only to disappear in a matter of minutes.

Gene scoffed as he turned from the pier with a satisfied grin and wiped his hands of burden, but only guarding another secret no one would know about. As Gene started back toward the car his calm attitude became induced by a surprise.

A loud petrified scream shrilled across the harbor lot and spread like an echoing burst of erupting tremors. It was a sharp disturbing pain from within the center of the earth, but he knew that came from somewhere. Gene kept moving as he darted his head to where the sound was coming from. He made another quick check around him and kept on toward the car. As he was just shaking off that strange sound and make it back to the car where Chris was waiting for him.

Then out of the darkness of the night—another yell filled the air—like a haunting crow screeching into the night, but it sounded like a baby just before it died—a soft dilapidating murmur. From the distance, a desk lamp was giving him a full view of the pantomimic scene. He could imagine what had happened, and it was almost like a violent shadow puppet game as he saw the shadowy hand rise up high and land pounding against the harbormasters face.

"You crazy sons of bitches" Gene huffed as he watched this scene from the farthest distance, picturing all the bloody detail that he did not want to see what was happening, and then moved on.

Frightening, a frightening pleasure made him only block that shadowy image from his mind, which only concerned whoever was in that room and what was going on. Gene did not doubt that Frank and his brothers were not at all behind those very windows carrying out Chris's orders with the assistance of Frank's dumb cousins following his orders.

As Gene scurried away from the docks, stuffing his hands into his pant pockets as the air smashed against his face, making his forehead and hair start to heat up, and form sweat from his forehead. The car began moving further, and further away from him as if he had been drifting through the cold desert night and a dark black oil pond appeared to him—obviously fooling his eyes and his mind—peacefully waiting for him to drink out of. Although as he began moving toward the car the rippling water began waving by as his impatience thrust his body toward the car.

Gene felt the tips of his fingers grip the edge of the cold metallic lever and pulling down with all his might he released the stale cringing air out as Gene brought the wind with him making a quick and grasping CLAP from the door.

"What took you so long?" Chris questioned, curiously. "Did you fall in the water and they had to bring you back to shore?" His dimples revealed a deranged person that was attempting to read his thoughts, and composing it in a list.

Gene just nodded his head with a small meek laugh. "Yeah, I guess so."

An itchy feeling ran through his pants like fleas on a dog's skin, and he couldn't tell what was wrong with himself as he wiped his face—he kept his eyes open—trying not to close his eyes—blocking the voices that tormented him so—he revealed his complacent face. His apple cheeks were a soft shade of green in the darkness—revealing his soft mellow attitude.

"Did you get rid of it?" Chris asked with a low guttural tone.

His lips were parched and he spoke uneasily as he breathed fiery words from his throat, shaking his head, "Yes," arching his eyebrows, grinning foolishly, "It's down at the bottom of the pier where it's supposed to be."

Chris accepted his answer with a nod, and calmly examined Gene's weird behavior leaving him to wonder what exactly took him so long—and glanced down at his pants to see if he had kept the gun—but couldn't see any bulge that he could see. He let Gene flash his white teeth, as a grinning joker would do for a sad child while he laughed. But as Gene glanced around the sides of his pants, he started looking toward the window pretending to look away for a moment—alarmed by a small ounce of paranoia.

But as Chris turned around again, Gene saw Chris's agitated appearance turn sour like a orange being squeezed into a dead bear's eye socket. Gene did not know what he was doing, and as he spoke he strung like a piano cord from his vocals with a sharp whisper.

"What's wrong?" Gene said turning in his seat glancing over his shoulder to see if anything was wrong, searching through the mystic steam covered window peering into the bleak dank darkness. As he searched needlessly he became worried that Chris was starting to suspect him of something—but couldn't pin anything on him.

"Don't worry about it" Chris said, eyes twinkling with a sense of madness that said he had taken care of everything.

"I thought I saw something that looked strange." Gene became agitated and wiped off the sweat of his forehead, making a nervous drumbeat against his legs.

Chris let a relieved breath of air travelling from his lungs and his chest pushed in and out like an overworked machine.

Gene was swept with an infuriated rage as if his mouth had been sewn shut from the inside, and his patience was sizzling like hot water over a bed of heated rocks whenever hot water was thrown—agitating his anger with every shocking detain.

Only time was against Gene as the steady footsteps of six feet and four bodies began to echo across the docks, Frank and the three soldiers were slowly passing the gates and past the gravel.

Their shadows made a dark reflection from the lamppost as shadows of Frank and his two cousins (the bumbling idiots) standing right outside the car, all with a stirring rage that was guiding them like a marionette puppet—blindly following their cue cards that was manipulated by a powerful being—Chris Mangini.

"What's going on?" Gene asked, his face was tight and narrow like a freshly sharpened spear and his eyes were determined while his hooknose crept over his lips. "Are you sure it's okay? I could go and comb the entire pier before we leave!"

"Don't worry" Chris said as he looked towards Gene with his beaded eyes. "It's nothing. You know how you see something in the dark that looks like it's moving, the shadows that play tricks on us."

Chris's answer quietly reassured Gene of his allusions and the two immediately went silent as the soldiers opened the doors. Frank took the driver seat while his cousins situated themselves squishing, packing against Gene and Chris like a can of sardines. Niccolo and Jerry were sweating an odorous hardworking smell of chipped paint and strong salty coastal smell leaking from their neck collars as they shoved beside each other. Gene tried to ignore this smell, but couldn't push it away.

Blood was on Niccolo's knuckle around the inside of his palm, and Gene was taken off guard when Chris had begun to speak. Chris stopped talking, and everyone except for Chris stared making Gene feel awkward for yawning.

Gene did not have to look around him and see why they had stopped. It was his yawning but they were sarcastically sending embarrassing messages through their faces. Niccolo and Jerry bent their heads down, for they were mere help and it was disrespectful for them to look upon Gene this way.

But before Chris started off his sentence, there was a small period of uncomfortable silence floating through the car and against the ceiling like a draft, letting them chill off that warm displeasure. When it had gone on for more than five seconds—eyes drooped and his voice echoed, commanding their attention. "What did you guys find out?" He felt like his voice only thickened in the silence as he became infuriated and yelled, "Hey! When do I have to ask you guy's a question. I don't have to wait for an answer *ever* again, not while I'm the *boss!* Now for the last time, did you guys find out anything that would benefit our war situation?"

It took only a few seconds for one of his soldiers to collect the information off the top of their heads, scan through the least important details of their mission and present to Chris the facts, and only the facts. So, the first lamb of the group to speak up was Frank because if Frank knew that no one would speak up, no one would say anything.

"The families are desperate. They want to corner in on all of the Don Pescaro's score, they don't want to spare anybody. Even the possibility of getting rid of their own wouldn't have kept them up at night. The only thing that we would have to fear is the notion of someone revealing everything, blowing everything sky high for all of us."

The Disintegrating Bloodline

"And also" Frank added taking a breath, "Treachery is brewing throughout our own affiliations. I have a few contacts checking in for me about something that perturbed me from the very beginning. Someone had spilled the beans on our plans and had our bootleg operations roosted from our labs. And after that, two more had been found out. Nothing was linked to us of course, but other friends of ours were named and are not happy about what has happened. Since this new law is coming into affect, we need to be really careful about who we talk to."

Frank sighed with a renewed discomfort as he exhaled, like he was on life support and Chris's ears perked upright and alert, his bones toughened and hardened, his ears burned like a thousand crystals under a Bunsen burner, crackling and sizzling as the rather disappointing but affordable news benefiting the rest of his operations around the city—one operation and everyone wants a piece.

"Who was trying to muscle in on our territory?" Chris asked, "Are any of the families moving in on our territory?"

"The Batista family of Manhattan. That's the only positive information I am sure about. We will have to find out what we can on our own. We did find out some really good news though…"

Chris jumped into the conversation taking Frank by surprise. "I hope you didn't have to pulverize someone for it. Did you?" As Chris said those words he immediately stopped, not wanting to know, because he would find out in the papers.

"No. I don't want to know yet." Chris said with a light laugh, and then he was serious again. "Go on," Chris folded his hands across his body in a swaying manner and his chin was hanging steadfast in the air. Slowly, everyone began taking the focus off of Chris, and then back on Frank.

"The good news is that we have hit the jackpot of all scores." Frank let out a resounding tone as his friends faces lit up with a polished glow as they listened to him speak. His excitement was more than joyous, he was ecstatic, "I have found list after list of arrivals from the music industry from Operating system companies such as Macintosh and Windows. And of course this guy had known way too much for an average Joe on the block. He deals with the family soldiers every time they come looking for their protection."

"Hold on," He pulled up his shirttail revealing a scroll that was hidden secretly inside his belt pants with the top tightly pressing against his neatly, shaven ripped pecks. Frank slid the scrolled list gently from his pants and rolled the scroll with both hands, and handed the scroll with a renewed look in there eyes.

Chris held out his hand to receive the scroll with his open hand and Frank gave Chris the list. Chris opened the scroll with both hands holding it first side to side, but as he saw the words running from top to bottom he turned it right side up, foolishly misreading the page. The words that were on the page were listed in Excel cell formula that had only a date, location, and what was being transported.

First Chris ran his eyes down the list of dates that was neatly typed on the far-left side

10/17

only meant that the first number was the month and the second number was the day when the truck was supposed to arrive. But to his surprise, the numbers continued onto the next page, all the way up to the last date,

12/21

Chris knew that the number 10 was this month, October and the last number, 12 was December. Then Chris flipped the page backwards, scrolling through the locations of where the trucks would arrive from Ohio and another through Pittsburgh, Pennsylvania, and all the way up to Boston and Detroit. But mostly all of them would run through Buffalo, mostly wooded or surrounded by large fields with no one around for miles. At least that was taken care of for them. Then to add more egotistical pressure on Chris's shoulders, it even included the time it would take to meet them at an intersecting point.

Chris knew that everything had been mapped out too well, and he had to praise his soldiers.

Chris rolled the list back up with a wide smile, grinning to his soldiers with an avaricious gleam like he had just eaten a great dinner and he had to "thank the chief" for the wonderful meal.

"You guys did really well. We can really put a chokehold on the competition. The only place where anyone is going to get anything on a CD is from us. This list goes on through December 21st. We can split the dates up between every one of us, except for Jerry and Niccolo since they are only getting started. But before we start dividing and conquering..." Chris began to conjure up words as if a dictionary was already in his head, and immediately started back to his sentence.

Chris saw his soldier's eyes salivating over every word he said and when he breathed for a moment, they awaited his answer, and then he let his words run from his mouth and dance off the edge of his tongue and take them by surprise.

"We should go on a few of these days before I want to let you guys take a piece of the action. See which family's are in on this deal. Also, we must call up somebody who can get us in with computers." He put his finger on his chin, and continued with his brilliant plan. "About ten or fifteen people, we'll need more computers later, and more computer whizzes, to copy the CD's onto another disk, or break into them. Maybe round up some of those associates that never get any sleep that are always thirsting for recognition. But what can I say? We did good tonight" Chris let a laugh escape him as his soldiers began sighing releasing the anxious air escape from the pits of their stomachs and letting the blood circulate back into their veins as they joined in with a chuckle and a small laugh—the only laugh he did not find funny—an additional work load of long nights.

"Let's go." Chris said, "We don't need to hang around here anymore. We have one more day until another truck is coming through so I want everyone to get their acts together, clean yourselves up, and do what you guys have to do before we see each other. Take care of business, fuck your broads, that's fine. If you go back home, let them fall asleep first, make anything up. I don't care, just be ready for the long night ahead."

That was Chris's words, and it was set in stone that no water could dissolve. His soldiers did not speak nodding their heads with a complacent smirk as if they did not hear a word he was saying.

Frank did not waste time as he went upstate. For the whole ride nobody spoke a word, only a few conversational words that lit everyone's attention, but did not explode into any great conversation. As they moved north of the city, their troubles had only begun since they needed someone to take hold of the school in their absence, but that would be the easy part. They knew someone had to watch over their thrown and the perfect person to do that was A.J.

As Frank pulled up to Gene's house, he pushed on the brakes landing right next to the curb, he steadied the brakes as Jerry and Niccolo filed out from the back seat one by one. Gene looked at Chris with a renewed look in his face, and nodded to them before he left, and decided to end their night with a good note.

"So, I'll see ya' later!"

Chris let comforting words put everyone at ease, and his legs quivered as he lost control of his edge as he tightened his fist in fear. Gene looked away for a moment as he felt his strong predator intentions gave off a demeaning devil like stare—totally complacent with his burdens.

"Okay." Chris said, "Be ready tomorrow. Finish any business you got with anyone in the streets, and see any of your girls that you always have on your collar." Gene wanted to laugh, but knew that he was being serious.

Gene nodded and made his way across the seats and made his way up the curb and across his lawn, as the two brothers (who kept staring at him as he left).

He watched the car move steadily down the street, and he watched as the car's glowing lights left from sight in the darkest night. Only then, he heard a buzzing from his pants, and he pulled out his cell phone. He answered it.

"What!"

Gene was expecting to hear a salesperson badgering him about buying a product from the television. He heard one of his associates screaming and cursing about, "how there fucking trucks got ripped off, get the fuck over here man!"

"Okay," Gene said, rubbing his forehead, "I'll be there soon, okay. Just hold on! Are you at the spot?"

"Yeah," Joey's voice felt strained, like a chord from a violin, "get the fuck over here man!"

And then a flat tone was all he heard.

Gene slowly walked down the street and saw no hint of dawn was in sight—it was only midnight—two minutes actually.

Shit. That was what was cropped in his underwear for the past hour being held and he felt like he was wearing a baby's diaper. His mouth had been taped shut by large duck tape and he had been tied down in a chair under a blazing hot lamp. The more he tried to break free of the tape he kept receiving blows in his chin and gut. He didn't know what hurt more, a fist shattering his teeth, or feeling his guts just ache to the point of wanting to throw up.

The voice leaned over the light, but he couldn't see him. "When's your friend gonna get here?" His hot breath was magnifying against his cheek. Joey thought it was so disgusting that it smelled like a fetus covered in shit, and this guy must have been stupid if he thought he was going to answer him while his mouth was taped shut. But that was what he wanted, and he had gotten the results none. Was he going to live, probably not. It was just a matter of time before he was died. Then, just when he was about to contemplated his destiny to the afterlife, he heard a small rattling coming from the other side of the club house doors, and he knew that was Gene, walking blindly into there trap.

Gene had become blinded by the darkness again, and the only light there was showing was in the middle of the lot, amidst all the piles of boxes of CD's that were "supposedly" gone. He yelled, "What the hell is going on here!" Silence and the sound of his own footsteps was the only thing that he could hear echoing in the dark. "Damn it, say something!" He suddenly reached for his gun, but couldn't feel anything on his waist because he knew that his weapon wasn't to be found. All he had was his fists, if he could use them.

"Don't people know how to listen?" The voice interrupted with cool persuasion, infuriating Gene's emotions.

"What are you talking about?" Gene yelled as he walked toward the light, but then his voice rose up out of nowhere, and pressed against him like a layer of heat. "Stop right there!"

Gene stopped, but was on the edge as he watched his best friend blood drooling down his pale cheeks, and his curly brown hair was matted with a layer of blood.

"Who are you?" Gene demanded, yelled into the darkness, confronting this omen—shapeless like smoke but ever present like fluid on his lips. "Tell me who you are!"

"I will. But I know you Gene. You are Chris Mangini's dog, running all his errands, watching the school and his protection runs. You came from a Jewish family in the suburbs, and you always had anger problems, pissed in your sleep until you were ten years old, and you saw a shrink for about a few years, but I'm sure Chris doesn't know that."

Gene was silent, totally taken off guard by the eerie elocution of the voices delivery, and felt violated by this person telling him his most vulnerable parts of his life. "How did you know that?"

"I know a lot of things! Look at my face and you will see how I know."

The voice walked out under the light, and Gene was so taken back, and shocked that he couldn't even describe who he was talking to. He couldn't believe who it looked like. The round head *looked* like A.J.'s but he couldn't tell from how the darkness's impressionable shadowed him. But his methodical voice was like Chris was speaking, covering his mind and he was dumbfounded.

"*Now will you listen?*" The voice demanded.

Gene had lost all the will to argue, and he decided to listen—against his bullheaded ignorance, "Talk!"

"Do you care about this kid?" The voice said, revealing a knife, and pressed it against the boy's throat. Joey's eyes widened as he felt the steel pressing against his skin—the cold blade touched against the caked blood—he felt his anus starting to pulsate as if it was an organ.

Gene looked at Joey, and knew that he was his friend, but knew that someone had to be sacrificed if there was going to be a revolution. "Blood costs lives." Gene sighed, grieving for his already lost friend.

"No." Gene stated coldly, and saw Joey's eyes widened with fear as the figure pulled his head back and quickly sliced his throat, blood seeping from his neck like a faucet all over his shirt and splashing down to his legs like a stuck pig, and let his head go. His head fell sideways as more blood poured from his neck, and his eyes stared at Gene. There was no expression in his eyes, and his skin was turning whiter than a ghost. He wanted to turn back now but he couldn't.

Chapter VIII:

"Death is Inevitable"

New York's morning lights crept through the foggy windows and hit the front of Chris's face (making him remember the way the sun hit his small town of Sicily), and wiped the lingering sleep that clung from his lids off with a swipe of his hand. As he stared at the blue chipped ceiling he lowered his head slowly facing the entire room. His large maplewood desk was filled with a few pens and tablets that were scribbled with a message. In his leisurely manner he had summoned one of his associates to take his calls on behalf of Chris Mangini.

He never trusted talking on any warehouse phones (or any as a matter of fact), and he always had an associate take down the message, so that his voice would be recorded for FBI men (they are the equivalent of pimps listening to their whores telephone conversations).

Chris scratched his chin holding the tablet in his hands, and threw it down against the table in a tired manner as the need to fall asleep next to his wife and child entered his subconscious thoughts—asleep next to his wife, protecting her, but was really endangering her.

With a great exertion, Chris leaned forward in his chair steadying his legs firmly planted on the concrete ground as he shifted his back up as if he was a bear in attack position and he slowly gritted his feet across the floor toward the two glass windows over looking the entire warehouse with one full perfect view.

The warehouse lot was filled to the brim with small desks that held illegal CPU systems and given flat LCD computer screens to complete their job. The busy associates—calm and alone in their work, busy as soulless ants thriving off each other gathering every speck of dirt to build on—moved back and forth staring into the flat screens of abyss—eyes were bloodshot and emotions were drained—moving the mouse over the **burn** button, taking out the original CD and inserting a blank disk to record over the ghost file placing the finished CD's into clear jewel cases, then into boxes where they could be sent off to the underground stores. They repeated this process for hours, burning after burning this went on, and after they finished burning more CD's they proceeded onto making another CD at twenty seconds top. This continued all through the night.

"So much money, but so little time to make it." Chris shrugged, exhaling pent air as he watched the sun cast its rays upon the eyes of the tired workers stopping them in their tracks zombified as they felt the suns rays whisk against their pale beaten cheeks.

But time had seemed rather slow for him as he wiped the ill-wanted sleep from his eyes—made an effort to sleep—shutting his eyes and turning his chair away from the windows—but the heat of his room kept him paranoid—kept his mind guessing about the day—the CD's—his enemies and men under lock and key but the fact remained that someone was going to turn on him. The fear and sadness that that it could come from any direction—the rival families, George Bradley gangs—but he knew it could come from his own family—his own poisoned tree—the person he owed his life to would want him dead. He lived with this like an ambulance medic who knew that he was going to be the one bleeding his soul on the ambulance floor. The men, who had fallen, would be waiting for him in Hell, and would probably tear his soul to pieces with long curled fingernails. He could feel their hatred spurning, but he would have to keep them waiting.

Nine o' o clock and it was more than a month since he had left A.J. off at the school—in that fleeting moment he thought his wife's sweet childish face of twenty—5'9 and beautiful black hair that could come alive in tentacles and grab him. It wasn't irregular for a woman of her age to get pregnant, but he was even more surprised when he found out his tiny wife had given birth to a *ten pound and two ounce* baby boy. No problem at all, and that day after Dino was born—it was like a white glimmering light had entered his life. Nothing could have meant more in his life—all the sleepless nights holding Dino in his arms—looking into the sky, knowing that God did exist.

He wanted to stay in his dream world, thinking about times that weren't so complicated, but decided to return his mind back to reality, seeing the large task that hovered over his head tonight.

Chris thought, and then lit a cigarette. Blowing smoke into the air he knew what he needed. "About three guys including him, and needed two more to steadily outnumber the opposition of whoever was accompanying the trucks. Just like small predators running beside the alpha beast to make sure he would have a layer of protection from attacking predators just as the Roman Empire's armies were based on, but with one weak point.

"A.J.!" Chris proclaimed, and leaned forward in his chair and pressed it against his ear, with his shoulder holding the receiver against his ear, and began to dial away at a number that had been itching to call—like a small twitch that had been pushing in his body, like a multiple sclerosis patient.

The phone tone pulsated tone, as he had to wait for Frank to lazily pick up the receiver. In that moment the tone ended and a patch began to open up in the phone like a flood of water that had reached through a through a fortified dam.

Frank's voice began to echo through the phone line and entered into Chris's ear with a dull and inattentive splash. "Yeah?"

It was Frank all right, and off the job as it sounded. He was probably trying to get some shut-eye long before he would ever see the morning sunrise, but he knew that it was time for him to wake up. "It's 9:00 o clock at night! Wake up for Christ's sake!" Chris thought, venomously.

"Get your clothes on and meet me at the factory. You still got your cousins along with you?" Chris said hoping that he had not dropped them back off at their house in Brooklyn.

Frank, sitting in his dirty covers, looked over on the floor, and looked at his lazy cousins spread out across the floor— on the opposite side of his Eiffel tower of porn. "Yeah, they're sleeping right on the floor next to me." He reached over and grabbed his pack of cigarettes that was resting on top of the alarm clock, and shook the package with a light chuck as the tubes of cigarettes pounced up and down like coins in a coffee can.

"I hope not next to you?" Chris replied with a soft jabbing tone in his voice, knowing that he was trying to wake him up.

"No, man. My girls don't even sleep with me!" Frank said quietly flipping the Marlboro lights cigarette top and reached for the first round cigarette that stared at him with his index and thumb and fitted it into his mouth. "What's the fucking point of a bed when you have to share it?"

Chris laughed lightly as if he was really touched by his joke—giving his idle mind a rest, and knew it was the time to really motivate him to get out of his bed. Chris glanced over toward the old-fashioned wall clock showing eight minutes after nine. Chris spoke into the phone with a clearer and serious tone, knowing what day it was.

"I want you guys out here before nine forty five, and get Gene on the way up. He's going to watch over the factory for us here, so we can go and retrieve a delivery." Chris said, hearing a flickering sound of a spark and long whooshing flame line giving off a whipping crackle into the phone.

A puff of smoke leaped from his mouth, blowing smoke rings from his lateral position in the bed. If this was unhealthy or not he was pretty good at this, and knew that he could be doing worse things than cigarettes.

The smoke from his throat was suddenly abrupt, as Chris interrupted him.

"Frank. I have some news for you and I can't tell you this over the phone." Chris added, being coaxed.

Frank heard this and held the cigarette between his index and thumb fingers and breathed in the cigarette—feeling the smoke rise through his gums and lungs. The smoke passed from his small teeth exhaling against the round receiver.

"Yeah, what do you got to tell me?" Frank said awakened but felt his body pulling him to the bed. "Can't you tell me over the phone?"

"Maybe if you get here before nine thirty and I'll tell you."

His eyes widened and his fingers held the cigarette limply as he heard his proposal loud and clear for he was going to be upped next to Chris, but he couldn't get his hopes up. Frank spoke upbeat but with that same weary lull that came with his voice.

"Sure, I'll get right over there. You're in Brooklyn right?" Frank said while taking a puff of the cigarette—arching his left eyebrow—and completed another circled O ring with some personal excitement in his mind.

"Yeah, so don't take all night." Chris taunted and the phone line went flat as a stale coke cola.

Frank pulled the receiver off his ear, shaking his head tiredly hanging up the phone as he wiped the deep sleep that had took hold of him for quite some time and put out the half smoking cigarette that was burning the end of his paper.

Five minutes had gone by since he had glanced at the clock and he thought he was dreaming.

"Nine forty three." Frank thought with dull encouragement. "Making good time." And after this—meanwhile getting his cousins up and picking up Gene—he was inspired by a memory guiding him toward a Brooklyn factory, a one that Frank had never frequented but where he had to go. He turned the corner and made his way toward a shady and deserted factory. No trees, no grass, only a mile of steel was paved across the factory lots as he rolled through the factory gates. Of course many factories were like this and this didn't surprise him because his father always worked in a factory that resembled this very one.

But as he approached the front of the warehouse delivery gates Frank saw two peculiar figures were standing bright headlight with an already preheated car, pumping exhaust fumes that formed into night mist. Although they looked like workers from a distance he wanted to see if the two were on an unannounced smoke break slacking off on the first night of the job—but that was in any walk of life. Frank approached the delivery truck gates flicking the bright lights on and off temporarily blinding the two figures forcing them to turn away for a moment, returning an unwanted gaze at Frank.

Frank now made a clear distinction between the two; one of them was Chris and the other was a mystery worker he had never seen. Frank was embarrassed clicking his tongue, shaking his head and smirking as he turned the wheel using a quick hand over hand maneuver toward a small plight of stairs leading into the factory domain. Frank did not suspect that Chris had been waiting outside for long.

As Frank turned off his lights he set the car into park, he opened the door springing out of his seat, and everyone did the same as he slammed the door behind him he felt that he was walking on unwanted territory. Being in some factory jobs, this one just felt creepy—the window lights shined as if this was a den for ghouls and goblins. Frank cautiously moved toward the two giving a light "what's up" nod as he saw Chris smirking wit laid back attitude.

Frank's bones quivered as he took two more steps and gave him a strong handshake. Frank's hands were warm and sweaty: a man's hands were always warm when one was extremely nervous or extremely confident, but Frank didn't feel confident, it was just the way he was. But Chris's was warm also, but what was he thinking, what was he going to say? Frank just went with it, and the two released each other from their strong grip.

His aggravated face looked sour and his teeth could feel no taste as he kept trying to ignore Jerry and Niccolo's boyish pushing game, but in a way seemed angelic in a way.

"So, you made good timing. I guess it didn't take much to get them up?" Chris saw the two brothers pushing each other until they stopped.

"Good. It only took a hot towel over his face to wake Niccolo up, but Jerry got dressed before Niccolo got out of the shower." Frank yawned as he turned and watched the two playfully push each other again. He shook his head as he said, "On the other hand" Frank continued with dissatisfaction on his tongue, "I could be getting some well-wanted sleep dreaming of some beautiful broad handing me a large sack of cash, otherwise, just fine."

Chris responded to this quip with great ease and lax, "Don't worry about the large cash part, just worry about the broad who's giving you the cash. You know what I'm saying?" Chris laughed lightly as Frank chuckled with him. The two were cold and watching their hands grow numb from the anticipation.

"Money cannot buy loyalty for all the cash in the world. You arrived right on time right on time. Do you want to know why I called you out tonight?"

Frank looked towards him again pulling his hands out of his pockets. "Why?" Frank started to rub his palms together warming his hands up.

Chris began to give Frank the right approach to tell him the good news. He had been upped up to Captain. Frank held the rewarding feeling inside only letting a smirk pass him by, but everyone else was smiling for him, and Chris patted him on the shoulder. Not only could he have a separate crew, Frank had his blessing and his permission to operate a small crew and start making his soldiers make the money for him while he answered to Chris. But he did not forget about properly respecting Chris Mangini—like a God he was.

But as a God always wants respect and order, Frank knew two things that Chris was not going to tolerate in the school, the operating and distributing of drugs. It was too risky, and the schools would not participate in looking the other way toward a drug dealer.

Frank thanked him for this tremendous privilege, and then ordered him "to meet out in the boon-docks somewhere where large cornfields grew beyond any man's height." That was where they would be and expect a roadblock with one car blocking the road. The signal was to click the bright lights off and on giving them that they weren't the enemy and would let him pull over. They were to stay with him while he went and picked up A.J.

After he was given his orders Frank walked over to the car, jumped in, and pulled the gears with haste and tore out through the factory entrance. Everyone watched as Frank had left without a trace, leaving Chris and his men not enough time to get to the fields and prepare for the trucks.

As the three began to move toward the inside of the factory, Chris tapped Gene on his shoulder, and he pulled Gene by his side.

"Come here, I wanna talk to ya for a second." Chris guided Gene away from the car and over to the flight of stairs. Chris began instructing his orders without one flaw in his voice.

"Watch out for the factory while I'm gone. I probably won't be back tonight so get one of my friends to drive you back to your place. Once you get inside call your mom and dads house and tell them you are spending the night at my house and will be at school tomorrow and will be home that same day. Got it?" He then proceeded to give his number to another warehouse and told him to freely call if anything came up.

Chris saw Gene's eyes narrowing without the proper respect. He must have been exhausted from the lack of sleep he must have been getting, but there was that bitterness that was burning again—like on the docks. Whatever this was, Chris was getting tired of this act he was putting on. He must have wanted to badly go on this mission since he was ready to go.

"You must have expected to go with us tonight. But I need you to watch over the factory because I can't trust anyone else to watch over something as large as this, except for you. You're dependable. If the cops arrive tonight and want to find me you know how to handle them, right? I trust you to watch over this place, until I figure out some things, you and your boys can operate on the routes. You got it?"

Gene looked at Chris with a rather decorated—dazed punch drunk gleam in his eye telling Chris that he had been granted to guard the United States Treasury—foolish teeth that shined like the moon.

"Got it, I understand." Gene's dedicated tone as he eagerly set out his hand and Chris's grabbed it, and his palm stuck to Gene like a fly stuck in a spider's web. Chris's strong web-like-grip almost cracked his fingers as he patted his back with sure fire sincerity. Then Gene threw his free arm around Chris's back returning the respect, but his hot arms fell against his back, and he thought that he was going to crumble with happiness—morbid sadness that he felt could only come with betrayal. The two let go of each other without fully understanding each other, even though they were alike, and Chris headed toward the car while Gene headed up the stairs and into the building doors.

Chris saw that everyone was ready to go and he took his appropriate seat riding beside Jerry. But Chris started to feel Gene "The Golden Boy" was starting to loose his shine—and the bitterness was starting to discolor his ego—bleeding insane pride into his thumping, pulsating mind.

"Let's get going. We only got a few minutes before we find a good spot."

All of them nodded as Jerry fiddled with the gearshifts placing it into Drive, pressing his foot on the gas pedal he headed toward the factory gates and turned a right at the first opposite highway leading him down the far side of New York. They traveled for fifteen to twenty minutes, wondering down the roads with the plain fields around him and passing a few railroad crossings. As they hurried a few more railroad crossings, they began to disappear behind the black of the endless pitch-black night. All roads to there darkest fear lead to the middle of nowhere.

"How long do ya' want me to drive till? Is their some place that we gotta stop at" Jerry asked calmly eyeing the lifeless and pitch black night constantly playing with the high and low beams almost shining the foggy night sky as if he was trying to slice through the sky with his lights, but wasn't getting through it.

Chris turned his head aside and had the gaze of a determined captain steering their ship through rocky rushing seas.

"Drive until you see cornfields, and we'll stop there." Chris said eyeing the road with coherent eyes wondering if this was all a mental fuck that was leading him into another trap. Chris felt pushed into a corner, and nagged by the pressures he had to deal with, but he had to look at this as a good sign and smile like the gazing moon's pale face, has seen many nights go by and no one ever cared to recognize it, that was lamenting for time that he could not retrieve again.

After another fifteen more minutes of venturing through the dark and endless night they heard a long whipping row of cornfields blowing beside the road. The high beams flowed over tall and erect stocks of corn. The stocks bent over and then bungeed back up to its regular stance—the leaves around it made a fluttering noise—like a beating heart.

In the light, they almost rose five or six feet high luminously towering over them, and the further they traveled, it looked as if the stocks were about to engulf them into the abyss of corn and fertile earth.

"Here!" Chris said jolting Jerry's nerves. "Right here," he pointed, "veer off to the right and turn the car sideways making a road block with the car." The stocks were whipping harder as the wind made a rousing cull, and it blew against the top of the car. Jerry did as he ordered and slowly pressed on the brakes as he faced the front bumper near the side on the side of the road almost veering into the small valley. As he began to turn, the whispering of the wind traveled like liquid on top of the car and echoing across the windows, like all the voices of heaven's angels telling them to stop, but they didn't hear them.

The car's brakes screeched with exertion as Jerry tapped the breaks slowly and shifted the gear along into park, and turned the key off. As the car stopped, Jerry took the keys out of the ignition switch and forced the keys into his pockets. Niccolo began to scramble out of the car first naturally forcing Jerry to follow behind him. While Chris slowly flung the door open he leapt from the wide opening slowly looking both ways, thinking meticulously about which way they would be coming at him. He didn't forget about the precautions they would encounter on this transaction having everything he needed in the back of the trunk.

After a moment of checking around Chris finally walked toward the trunk of the car and stood comfortably behind as they huddled around the trunk, ready to see what he had in his trunk, clenching their shirts trying to keep their hands warm from the icy whipping wind. The mother of all trucks was arriving and this called upon the time set Jerry and Niccolo into play.

Their hearts were filled with hot air of anxiety, their organs started to bloat up as the two awakened soldiers now realized what they were seeing was like finding buried treasure in the middle of Times Square. They gently held the guns without managing to point the barrels at anyone, and all of them were falling in love with these weapons.

"Don't get too attached to them, after we use them tonight, we need to get rid of them." Jerry took quite a liking to an automatic Israeli Uzi, hat held about twenty to twenty-five rounds a clip while he brandished a silver .45 caliber pistols in his belt line. Niccolo had been fascinated with a sawed-off shotgun, the barrels were short and cut off, and the wood handle flawless, deadly like a woman hips, and could blow clear through a persons body.

As the two busied arming themselves to the teeth with extra bullets, magazines and shotgun shells, the two noticed Chris being selectively picky about choosing a weapon for himself. Glancing at each and every individual piece and brushing his hands delicately over each weapon, it was like looking through a record list, it needed to be perfect. Even though he was deadly and proficient with any weapon, Chris didn't know which one to pick, but he knew that he needed something quick and accessible.

Although something caught his eye, like a comet soaring burning the night sky he saw the weapon he wanted. A row of long buck knives were lined up neatly beside each other all equally about twelve inches long and the blades were about six inches long, all off the black market from Russia. Since he would be the subject of bait for the driver he needed to become approachable and seem less intimidating toward the driver. He grasped a small six inch blade with a rounded handle, and looked at the blade, seeing the silver reflecting a deadly beam with the light underneath the trunk light, and was comfortable with the choice he had made and before he closed the trunk he searched for a sheath to hold the blade.

As he turned the blade sideways he pushed it tight into the sheath and latched it closed with a click, and snap of the latch. He slammed the trunk down with his free hand and started away from the car and approached the two soldiers who were indulged into their weapons. They steadily calibrated their weapons, getting acquainted with their metals of death like an actor would read a script. His soldiers were armed but not yet given a post yet. The only place that his soldiers would have cover and a good firing position was inside the cornfields. He was organizing a symphony of strategic coordinates and was placing the two soldiers into action.

"The only way that you will get a good place is inside those cornfields." He pointed to each side of the field. "I want one of you to hide on the left and one of you to hide on the right. That's how we are going to corner them in."

From a distance, all of them could see headlights burning a bright cut into the night.

"Get in the fields." He yelled, and they knew that anything could happen, so they did what he told them to do.

Jerry started on his way off the left side of the road while Niccolo pushed through the corn stocks and peered out of the stocks with a quizzical nature. Chris waved, urging Niccolo to get back inside the row of corn. After a few moments went by he saw two headlights from afar heading towards them at full speed, the burning headlights seared into their retinas. Chris saw a few stocks of corn swish on both sides of the road.

If Chris had to guess who was driving the car, his assumption would have led him to think of Frank who was driving like a madman delivering A.J. fast as he could. If Frank was not conscious of his cousins would have shot him, and even though the irony would be strong, but it would be funny as hell.

As the car began to stop all but two feet away from Chris's feet, A.J. was inside the passenger seat calm and collected noticing Chris in the flourish of the light. No longer than ten seconds did the two gunmen finally emerge from their hiding places, running toward the car with mad rage, their guns pointed at the windows shouting demands of exiting the car.

The lasting impression on Frank's face was priceless. His face went from surprised to a silent stare; his eyes leveled to the brim with hate as he saw who the gunmen were. His face went from a look of surprise, but anger swept over him as his flaring nose snorted like a mad bull, and his rage was fogging up the glass window. With a soulless smirk he raised his middle finger high and pushed it against the cold glass window. Niccolo jumped back for a moment, wondering if this was his cousin or not, but to all dismay, this was Frank. Niccolo pointed his gun away from the window and motioned for his brother to do the same. Jerry was confused by his brother's orders looking like an animal that had been told to roll over looking at him with no hope. Like a confused and threatened animal, he didn't feel content to lower the shotgun from A.J.'s stomach.

Chris stood on the side watching him park on the side of the road near a ditch. Frank turned the wheels off the side of the road and pushed the small front of the car near the stocks of corn. Frank and A.J. jumped out of the car slamming the doors behind them kicking the ground sending dust around the front of their shoes. Jerry and Niccolo stood opposite on each sides of Chris. Jerry had kept his gun pointed toward A.J. His finger was itching with discomfort to pull the trigger, only his mind began to object from the thought, and rested his awaiting finger against the outside metal.

"This is it?" Frank asked with an insufficient remark as if their small rag-tag team of five was to outmatch a whole army of family soldiers? He began to doubt if he was going die. It seemed imminent now, it always dawned on him but it didn't make sense, but he could smell the raw, unprocessed aroma of death that came with the package.

Chris saw the fear enter Frank, and the fear that they might die tonight was more than he could accept, but willingly had to, and instantly forgot about in a blink of an eye. "This is more than enough. We have more balls and brains than any army put together. We don't have much time, do you have a gun?" Frank pulled up his shirttail revealing a standard pistol in his waist.

Chris called the boys' attention "Niccolo, Jerry. This is A.J. He's another recruit just like you guys. Don't worry about him, he's cool." The three stared each other down like your best friend meeting another best friend that already hate each other because of there amount of love that made them turn against new people. The three shook hands smirking coldly as they gripped each other's hands. "Let's get you fitted. Jerry, fit this guy with a new pair of *shoes.*" After they were done shaking hands Jerry ran over to the truck—his feet clapped against the ground—roosted through the ring of keys that he had left in his pockets and flipped through every single until he found the right one.

"Shoes?" A.J. thought watching Jerry walk over to the car and searching through his pockets and picking through the ring of keys. A.J. feared that the irony was none other than code, or slang that hid a very dark, shadowed message that crossed a demographic of communication. As Jerry flung the trunk open, Chris swayed A.J.'s focus away from Jerry and onto him.

"Were you asleep yet?" Chris asked, ultimately calm, with his swarthy arms giving off a dark olive tan underneath the dark sky.

"No, I haven't slept in days. I've just been waiting to see you guys' back at school. It's been hard trying to hold a table when you only have one person watching over the chairs when everyone comes, but I don't let them out of my sight." His nervous shake revealed his wavering unease.

Chris chuckled and tapped his feet in unison. "That's good...good!" He turned toward Jerry. "He watches over our territory at school." Jerry smirked and eyed A.J. with low class but A.J. took his looks with a grain of salt. His anger was flatter than a piece of marble stone being smacked by a sledgehammer that rejected it's every blow.

Niccolo finally reentered the group holding another weapon in his left hand while he maintained control of his gun with his right. He thrusted the weapon in front A.J. and he took the gun. It fit almost perfectly inside his palms like he had been born with same fitting of the gun handle. Examining the gun's every nook and cranny, A.J. checked every angle feeling around for every button that made it possible to man this object of death, and he held it idly.

Niccolo angrily pointed out the gun's mechanical features as if he was a knucklehead showing him where the safety was, and the location of bolt that cocked the gun. A.J. studiously stood watching his hands movements, wielding the gun, as King Arthur would use his sword Excalibur to destroy all his enemies—or in this case—blast them into oblivion. He watched Niccolo pull the bolt back, and watched as the first bullet was given the privilege to be the first in the chamber like the first monkey shot into space, and in this case the first bullet being shot from the gun and land in another person's body.

Although Chris could watch them for days on end, something caught his attention out of the corner of his eye. It was a light and a bright one at that; and it was about five miles away from their destination finally making their ill-wanted appearance. He could certainly put his pawns into place with Frank helping him from the cover of shadows Chris definitely had his symphony, but they weren't in play yet.

"Go! Get in the fields. And don't come out until you know something is wrong." Chris yelled, and his voice was clear and sparkling like the Mediterranean in spring, and roused his team from idling about and immediately gaining his attention.

The three dispersed from his sight like water bugs trailing in a rippled pool of water, and A.J. was treading through the cornfields—feeling the stocks pushing against his body as he saw through the thicket of corn Chris was standing still with his chest out and hands at his side as he began to wave.

The rattles of the engines lumbered along the road. The grinding squeals of the truck meant that the truck had not been too far away. There was another truck behind it that resembled a standard meat or garments delivery truck, although a rattling death screech sounded off as it came to an abrupt halt, squealing with pain one behind each other almost hitting each other's bumpers.

As Chris waved his hand high in the sky, blocking the bright lights that weighed against his eyes it gave the heavy floodlights suddenly dimmed like the sun. Not only was their one truck, there were two more trucks right behind the first one. This was proof that they weren't just carrying CD's in the trucks, they had been harboring extra soldiers in the last two cars. Like cooped up bees, they were probably stinging each other out of nervousness and hatred. It wouldn't take them long to figure out what was wrong.

The door swung open, and a driver began stooping out the vehicle door. A large, blundering man bulging from him seems as his big stocky legs shifted across the gravel road kicking up dust as he strolled across the ground. He was so fat he could have laid him on his side and rolled him along the ground.

As the driver shifted three feet the driver's fat legs stumbled out of the car as his large belly shifted with his round piggy eyes jumbled in his eye sockets.

"You need a lift?" The driver asked with a gullible grinning gape, "Or do you need jumper cables to start you back up?" The driver studied his movements but smiled as he turned around trying to get a running start on as he tried to warn the others, but this was the weakness Chris needed.

"No." Chris said evilly "I just want to borrow your truck." Time was of the essence and Chris saw the gun peeking from within his fat waist.

With the driver's back turned, Chris lowered his hand down to his sheath, pulling the button off with a quick *clack*, and thrust the blade into the driver's lower back. As if he was carving a tough male pig he pulled on the driver's shirt and pushed the blade in deeper to make him feel the pain. The driver squealed with raw emotion and confused anger as he surrendered to the pain and his hands were open and claw-like. The scream was that of his rectum being penetrated by large bamboo sticks.

Chris left the blade in his back and wrapped his hand under his left arm. With his right hand he drew the revolver from within his waistline. The sounds of charging footsteps began traveling down the road as two men with guns were sending shots without taking aim as rapid-fire streaks of bullets zipped past his head, disappearing into the night sky. As Chris palmed the sweaty hand-grip—crooking his finger in the metal trigger loop—took aim at the gunmen and pulled the trigger expecting to feel a rumble from the barrel and a hot slug.

The only thing that the gun made was a soft *click*. It was empty; the goddamn driver did not have any bullets in it he went for it.

"Son of a bitch!" Chris muttered from the thick of his teeth. The driver managed to fool him, as the driver in his pain weakly laughed—as the blood started to spread through his organs—and out from his mouth spewed blood down his fat rippled chin.

"What are you laughing at?" Chris aggregately whispered into the driver's ear. The driver's confidence shriveled as he sent the fat driver out into the hailing bullet storm. Chris watched the gunmen fall forward with the knife still in his back yelling hysterical babble of endless pain as his body was met with lightening speed as the bullets left holes in his body as if someone had been shooting nails into a live, thumping brain, killing off a human being in the worst way possible. Blood splattered—pieces of flesh and cartilage flew in midair and limped on the gravel like pieces of meat—across the ground and blood overflowed from his large fat layered body.

Their gunmen's fingers slowly stopped, and stood with fear watching their bullet-riddled driver fall to the ground like a lame animal as the shells made falling coins sounds.

As the fat drivers' body collapsed and shook the ground, a long unsuspecting rattle of bullets began splitting through the corn stocks sending off a symphony of hybrid twig snaps and quick whipping *THUMP* of high pitch C notes as the chorus of bullets began piercing the men in their arms and stomachs. Once that repetitious fury died down, fiery shotgun blasts followed drumming into the air commingling with blazing E notes of machine gun rattle. A collapsing sound of bodies fell to the ground like sacks of flower and the sounds of cut off gasps filled the air.

Chris let the gun fall from his hands as he warily peeked around the front of the engine, and looked at the dying or near dead bodies. The brothers had shot down three to five more gunmen that were lying on their backs and on their side bleeding profusely, trying to reach for their weapons. The average man would begin coughing up his dinner meal and ruin his nice black Armani and Guess suits. Then after feeling faint and spitting again after regaining consciousness another person's brain would tell them to search for his cell-phone and report an emergency, but Chris wasn't going to be lying there on the ground next to them.

Looking at them closely he almost saw an aborted infant after the baby was mutilated, nailed to the wall while shooters would continue to defile the defenseless fetus's. Although watching their skin bubble and puss with the stinger bullets implanted into their bodies, Chris did not feel pity—only immense amount of luck. Their warm thick blood caked and spread across the floor, this meant that their death was immediate, which meant no time to pray, just the afterlife or the grave. These men were fearless, like stampeding buffalo running toward the first batch of hunters only to be unexpectedly surprised with an allusive trap of hunters that did not waste a single shot.

Only Chris and his crew were going to leave there bodies spoiled, and untouched. Chris could not down these men that beat their chests in a bellicose like rage—he would be one of them.

"It was them or me!" Chris thought, and shook his head. "Like the new cliché saying, God doesn't sort them out, we do!" In that short moment of silence the four secluded shooters quietly made their way through the thickets pushing pieces of stock with their smoking barrels, while their hands wrapped around the handles and their fingers rested inside the hole.

The four did not waste time gazing at their dead victims, for their bodies were tense and enwrapped in the heat of battle. As they slowly advanced toward the second truck, something was brewing inside the trunk. There had to be more soldiers ready to be released like an epidemic. Chris walked past the near dead hit man, and then bent down, gripping his head. He looked in his eyes and then quickly broke his neck. After he saw the life drain from his eye, he noticed that their guns flew into the ditches or sprawled out in the middle of the road.

Chris picked one of their machine guns, "A man who doesn't know when to die," he said and leapt over the dead truck driver with the knife that he stuck into his back. He left the disregarded fool on the ground—a fat caricature of grotesque obesity. Before he left he hovered over his body, and pulled the knife— the blade resembled a melting blood red Popsicle, and it didn't take long for it to start melting off the stainless steel—hearing the squishing, slippery blade slide out of his wound.

With his natural nature, he pulled out a clean handkerchief from his right pant pocket and swiped the dripping blood from the silvery blade to the white handkerchief. Chris moved his jacket back where the sheath for his blade was, stuck it inside clapping it tight with a tense *click*.

After he sheathed his sword, his hand looked into the bloody handkerchief, and it exactly looked like a woman's tampon at the end of every month. This made him laugh at that sick, but funny analysis, knowing that he had seen a few of them, but would disregard that joke for the rest of the night. With disregard he crumbled the hanky and stuffed it back into his pocket, forgetting all about it.

Chris met his soldiers at the front of the second truck and silently motioned for them to move up. A.J. saw Chris's gesture and approached with a crouch like walk and jumped in front of the rumbling engine. The night sky twinkled with relentlessly bright stars, as A.J. nodded with a rather respectful, and sighed with exhaustion. Chris smiled with some relief—breathing through his nose—and slapped A.J.'s right leg. It was almost better than saying *thanks*, or anything that would alleviate the tension, but this was better than words. It was almost as if Chris was an aged and withering mentor teaching his young, strong apprentice the old and only means of survival and leadership but A.J. was getting a crash course just like anybody else, and he looked like he was taking in every dangerous bit of it.

Chris, holding the machine gun sideways against his thigh, he felt the tension running through his body, and put a hand against his chest.

A.J. saw that Jerry and Niccolo were moving forward like ghosts keeping there weapons up, smoke was still billowing from their barrels, and their wits more alive than they had ever been. Jerry—if you would have called it that—accidentally pushed his brother off but grabbed him by the shirt before he became victim to more oncoming bullets. As Jerry pulled his brother to his side, bullets flew past his head and nicked the side of the truck. The two stood together with exasperation while out of the blue Frank fell on the ground in front of them.

"You guys okay?" Chris yelled as the tough hide of the truck began taking in bullet after bullet with a loud CLANG and a whistle as they went flying into the abyss of the fields. Frank, who was starting to feel his life starting to leave him, peeked around the large frame of the engine he threw his arm out and extending his pistol outwards and dispensed two to four bullets with the steady quickness of his left trigger finger. The bullets were just warning shots as the two gunmen jumped behind the truck again with a giggling laugh that

The Disintegrating Bloodline

bordered on demonic. But they were shouting at them in another tongue, as if one of them had caught a bullet, and it wasn't English.

Chris listened to their voices, and grabbed Jerry by the collar, with a raised finger for silence. Jerry quickly stopped talking and listened.

"You can't win. Throw out your guns and give yourselves up." One of the shooters cackled in quick Sicilian from the end of the truck, pointing his machine gun outwards again shooting maniacally as the sounds of a second gunman interlaid between rapid firing shots and maniacal whooping and screaming. Chris knew that they weren't watching the other side and they could easily make their way down the side of the truck. Then they could easily neutralize the shooter's position and claim the next truck.

Chris turned and his eyes widened as he beheld a small gushing hole in his clothing. Chris brought Frank up against the edge of the truck, and grabbed his arm examining his pulsating wound. Holding his arm lightly he pushed the layers of his clothes up until he moved the sleeve over his shoulder. He saw a tear, but no entry bullet. The bullet had probably grazed the top of his shoulders, which had probably missed his head. With an extreme angst he knew that their time slot was slipping faster than a grain of sand in an hourglass of blood.

Chris let go of Frank's arm, jumped off the ground and faced A.J. He started to pull the gun from his grip.

"Give me your gun." Chris whispered with a soft puff against his cheek.

A.J. let go of the weapon, gently letting the machine gun disappear from A.J.'s palms and into Chris hands. Then Chris whispered into Niccolo's ear swaying him to give up his gun and let A.J. have the gun. Like a priest speaking into the ears of the possessed, Niccolo let his grasp of the pistol from his belt-line with quick-draw precision. He was not left defenseless. A mighty gun it was, and the large slick slide gleamed with a sugar cake sparkle.

Chris looked up and passed the shotgun into A.J.'s gaping hand. As A.J. gripped the handle and placed his other hand on the stock, it felt like he was fitting on a glove, and this glove fit. Short and stocky it was, and he snuggled it inside his palm. But the unknown power that was behind this shotgun surpassed A.J.'s thoughts, and would wake him up once he pulled the trigger.

As Chris peered around the right side of the truck, he spared no time as Chris lurched around from his hiding spot as he lurked towards the end of the truck in a hunched over combat position. The voices grew louder as more shooting came from there side, and the gunmen took there turn as they fired back on them. A.J. followed closely behind him—heart beating, his body sweating—raising his shotgun slightly crooking his finger near the trigger, ready to weigh his finger down and deal out their judgment. In that moment Chris halted, as they stood three feet away from the end of the truck, they heard the voices repeat the same deadly chant with back and forth gunplay.

Chris let his hand fall off the trigger—the momentary silence thickened with tension—as he motioned for him with his fingers to go ahead. A.J. saw his signal and nervously began to move around Chris with the gun clamped firmly inside his hands. His palms were going psychotic as he listened to the sounds of the machine guns and the pistol fire that came from both ends on the left side of the truck, hoping that they wouldn't see them. A.J. leaned around the corner and saw the two men who were involved in their violent rage shooting—his ears were now feeling the sounds shredding through his ear drums—and laughing over the rapid gunfire as the unsuspected men reloaded their guns again.

A.J. slowly turned the corner and without alarming the unsuspecting driver, A.J. charged into the driver's back feeling his body—pushing into him with the side of the gun—and sending him bouncing against the ground with a clunking sound. The shooter went flying head first—tripping along—as the first shooter knocking him over clear enough for Jerry or Niccolo to get a good shot. The two collapsed to the ground with a clattering *THUNK* as they landed against the pavement toppling on their sides, shrieking in pain.

A.J. moved forward with the gun in his hands pointing the gun straight ahead aiming at the distracted hit men. With the insides of their ashy palms they were crawling around bumping into each other as they cursed indistinguishable obscenities. The sound of the first pump echoed with a *CLICK* and slid back out with an ominous *CLACK*.

A.J.'s finger quickly fell inside hole and gently squeezed the metallic crook. A.J. felt the gun rumble in his palms, shaking his whole body—seeing the fire erupting from the barrel—as the swarm of pellets launched itself to the unsuspecting hit man sending him and the blood all over the ground, also pieces of blood against the barrel. The hit man screamed with pure pleasures of pain that every man had not wanted to feel, not only from the pellets but the simple irony was that the men had turned their attention toward one side of the truck while their enemy had a full unprotected path.

But something else turned A.J. away from the dying man. The rustling sound of fingernails scraping across the ground as the living hitman grabbed his automatic machine-gun. As A.J. pulled the pump back dispensing the spent shell from the hot chamber and pulling it back forward he aimed his weapon lower. The overriding force of the barrel pushed his body down to the ground as he huffed and puffed the last gargle of blood that could belong to him was now God's.

As A.J. finished unloading the gun, the first gunmen glanced at A.J. and jumped for his gun as the shotgun clicked a harmoniously with death sending A.J. into idle shock.

The gunmen turned around and laughed as he positioned the weapon at A.J. "Oh shit!" A.J. thought to himself, as he tried to pull the slide back, but couldn't move it as if it had just broken down on him. The gleam in the gunmen's eye burned brighter than any bulb from a flashlight or any flame from a lakefire, and it bothered A.J. so much that he couldn't function. A.J.'s heart sank to his stomach—curdling his insides—as he stared through the eyes of a cold-blooded killer, and he was locked in his burning eyes. But Inside his eyes, the fire suddenly went cold as ice as a legion of bullets began crashing into his chest and one entered into the top of his lip, sending a gush of liquid blood all over his face—layering the lower half of his face and cheek—forcing him back to the ground in slow astonishment.

A.J. regained his senses by gripping the gun and slowly watching the lifeless carcasses lie on the gravel road, and there blood covering the ground. He turned away trying to block the bullet-riddled bodies that were two feet away from him out of his mind, but as he faced Chris who was already reloading his gun placed the empty clip in his pockets. He refilled the gun with such pinnace that his hand cocked the lever so fast that A.J. could imagine motion lines floating after his arm.

Chris saw A.J. blinking his eyes, slowly recovering from his shock as he slowly pulled his gun from his hands. A.J. did not put up much of a fight since he was still in a violent trance. The rest of the team advanced after all the shooting had finally subdued, Frank was being carried over Jerry's shoulder as they saw the slumped bodies that had been torn apart by the swarms of pellets—with the air turning around them into a thick musty smell of corn and insecticide. With the numerous machine-gun shells that made the second corpse's eyes almost alive as if he was looking through a diamond, and that fire that had burned immediately was snuffed out of existence, and there was nothing else to tell about where this dead hitman was going.

As Chris gave the shotgun back to Jerry he took it slowly and reloaded it with large, red shells (about the size of a small 4 inch wide and 4 inch diameter) into the shotgun. He was not breaking a single motion of his gentle thrusts, the pump harmoniously *CLICK-CLACKED* after he loaded them into the barrel. His movements resembled a man moving a woman's pink underwear with his index and middle finger and passionately pushing into her vulva making her scream with pain. After five to nine large shells were finally stuck inside the loading bay he cocked the pump one more time and gripped the gun feeling proud that he could feel a thrill, without having to worry about if it would miss its monthly period.

It was not long until Chris's suspicions began to make sense. The soldiers were in the last truck that were stinging and striking each other from the anticipation. There had to be one last captain who was the leader.

"They are in the last truck!" Chris yelled "Tell them they've been captured, and line them up nice and slow beside the field." Chris watched as Jerry and Niccolo moved around the side of the truck, with there guns pointed upwards at the window forcing the driver out of his position. As Chris finally called A.J. over and told Frank to give him his pistol and help the others, A.J. did not want to—but he did just that—leaving Chris and Frank leaning against the truck. After he sent his men off to seize the truck he knew that Frank had been shot, not badly, but just enough to put him in a bind for a couple weeks, even though it might fucking hurt.

"You took a hell of a shot there!" Chris noticed while he searched through his pockets to get him a cigarette to try and relive his pain, or just calm his nerves.

"Damn! I can say I got proof that I was upped." Chris stuck the cigarettes in his lips as Frank continued with a solemn grunt. "That'll make for a great dinner conversation, won't it?" Frank's mouth clamped the stick in his mouth and felt the flames jolting through his body—puffing on it and relaxed again as the smoke left through the cracks of his open lips. Although the fact was he had a fucking hole in him he was lucky it wasn't resting in his head.

"Don't worry about it. Get yourself fixed up before you go home. And this won't make a conversation because no one is going to know about it." Chris's thumb weighed off the switch, and stuck his lighter back into his pocket.

"Can you walk?" Chris pulled Frank up over his shoulder, as he still held the still burning cigarette in his mouth that would have been finished more than two seconds ago. Frank felt confident to walk as Chris pulled his arm raising his body from the ground and stood him on his feet, but the bullet weakened him. Although leaning against the engine Frank accepted his decision and the two began to walk around the side of the car approaching the military lined prisoners.

Chris saw Frank leaning against the truck, obviously taking a rest from the walk. Chris saw Jerry and Niccolo lining the soldiers along the pebbled road yelling explicit demands into the young, tired, sagging faces of all the hitmen. Without their weapons, they were left defenseless with there fears waiting to be popped like a pimple. Their hands were hanging from their sides, keeping a smug grimace, but they reeked with some fear that was holding them on the edge.

Some of them were fat and pompous with large heads and flabby legs, which bulged out of their suit pants like whale's blubber. All of them were protected from the cold with long over-coats and neat pinstriped suits with a white shirt giving him another layer of protection. Although they had coats and pants covering their entire body that wouldn't protect them from the ominous fate that would force them to recognize the pain they would have to burden.

The night was cold and desolate with a ripe whipping wind that could send the devil running with icicles hanging from his hooves and jump back into hell where he belonged. As his enemies were captured and presented to him, he could feel their loyalties trembling, as they would become face to face with their consciences that were he and down a black hollow barrel.

And to his surprise and irony, a rolling fog began settling over them like a veil hiding a young virgin's face before her husband unveiled her into a new sexual life. Although they would be ultimately unveiled into the darkness, cut off short from the entire world about to be baptized with powder and pain.

The fog began slowly covering their shoes, and slowly around there sanity.

Chapter IX:

"Inside the Office of Chris Mangini"

As the fog settled over them like a clear white veil, spreading and crawling over there bodies, Chris saw one person that looked familiar to him throughout this entire line of people. A man that he would have gladly forgotten about, but because of his brother, the memory of his drug-dealing brother, was a mental cum stain on his ever-busy mind. This tall brooding figure was Carmine Pilligrino and he looked shadier—dark eyes that were palpitating red nerve endings in the whites of his eyes—but his body seemed to lump over from their last ten year visit. He did not expect to see Carmine or these *fuoriusciti*, or outlaw's as Chris liked to call them, but an urging feeling in his stomach wanted to know why this scumbag was leading these angel faces (dressed in full attire) with no facial hair. And when they looked at Chris, they averted their eyes in fear, knowing that Chris Mangini had caught them red-handed.

"Carmine! What are you doing here?" Chris asked, rather curious, trying to find out what this prick was doing. When he turned toward Carmine, he noticed that his face had been through many years of sleepless nights, with two to three shades of bags under his eyes to prove it. His dark green eyes told many stories that Chris was disgusted by, and Chris had his own to carry, but he knew firsthand what his were like.

"I'm doing what I do best. Serving my boss and making money. Are you still trying to make sure the kids are getting to school on time?" Carmine said with a smirk trying to light Chris's trail of dynamite temper and make him loose his level-headed composure by blinding him with seething anger.

"A war of words from this smart mouth prick." Chris thought as he sharpened his forked-tongue as his mind was ready to return a reply he would never forget, even after he was gone. Chris's bodyguards stood back as he

The Disintegrating Bloodline

walked opposite the men with his arms folded—his muscles tightened against his long sleeve shirt. He slashed at his reputation first leaving his secrets out for everyone to see and be ashamed of.

"Like what you do? But I forgot you were once a dope peddler, right? To those kids that come back to you with their allowances, fulfilling their need like a *candy-man*? Yeah you could say that I am still in school. I don't do what you do."

Carmine shrugged taking this insult as a farce, and glancing at a nervous soldier, smirking non-chalantly.

Carmine turned to him and scorned him like a seething bull. "So self-richeous aren't you! You're no fucking saint! At least I don't deny how I'm supposed to make a living. Unlike you, I am taken seriously." Carmine smiled and laughed with his lively, and soullessly.

Chris knew that he would be arguing with him all night before they could get the truck and leave but he knew how kill the conversation.

"Funny" Chris said, "Even I thought you had principles. You could have sold that to ten more niggers before you would take kid's money. Making boys and girls addicts before they know what a first kiss is. I am not a complete scumbag compared to you. Your brother was better than you." He stared into his eyes. The two faced each other not breaking a single composure and walked away from the firing range and let the two brothers move back in keeping them at a distance.

Chris then waved for A.J. as A.J. pushed the short, small man in front of Chris. The driver turned, but then A.J. forced the gun into the back of his head forcing him to join his company.

Chris smiled. A smile that would make anyone question why he was smiling, ultimately comforting the man. He nodded to A.J. to lower his weapon. With aggravation, A.J. lowered his weapon and let his hand fall to his side while his fingers wrapped around the gun.

"What are you carrying?" Chris asked as he got into the driver's face. He did not want to alarm him but get his attention, before their time was wasted.

"Come on. Just answer me. What are in the back of those trucks?" Chris said looking into his eyes. The driver's attention glanced toward Carmine who looked through him and his loyalty began to shake underneath his tough hide of confidence. Chris saw that he wasn't looking at him and wasn't paying attention. So, Chris decided to make him understand his wrath.

Jerry and Niccolo heard him yell, and there guns were automatically cocked making a shrilling clacking and clicking sound as the slide became the dam for the bullets and the trigger released the bullets into the air. Everyone could guess what was about to happen, but it never hits you till it actually happens.

"Hey Carmine!" Chris said very personally. Carmine looked at him with fear-filled eyes and replied with a disgusted, "I'm waiting and what the fuck do you want" attitude. "What?"

"Say hi to your brother for me." Chris said with a straightforward devilish gesture. Carmine became angered with rage as he yelled, constricted by his physical limits. "You first!"

"No." Chris replied calmly, looking into his eyes. "You first."

The silence was then broken when Jerry fired the first shot sending a culmination of pellets shredding into the boy's rib cage. In a culmination, Niccolo gripped his finger around the trigger and felt the swarm of hot bullets leave the black barrel. One after another, he turned the gun to the right sharing the hot slugs with the rest of the soldiers. The whizzing echoes of the bullets pierced their bodies as a large hammer had punctured a watermelon.

Spurts of blood began imbedding the ground after they massacred them, sending the soldiers squealing like a bleeding pigs as the pellets tore their kneecaps, heads, into the ditch, on the stocks of corn, and in the dead grass.

A.J., from his short distance could see all these men bleeding profusely, guts torn apart by shells, splintered by hot slugs, knew that it would take more than a night for there faces to dissolve from the back of his head. After the gunfire ended, Jerry and Niccolo turned around and walked away from the bodies, with their ammo spent and barrels' oozing steaming smoke.

Chris looked at the now frightened truck driver—eyelids dropped down to his cheek, his face had become flushed knowing that he could easily become one of them murdered without mercy.

"He did not matter to these people!" The truck driver thought seeing what would become of him if he kept silent, lying right next to these long forgotten boys. His eyes saw through the thin sheet of fog all of there faces, white and pale, knowing that he would become a flaccid carcass with no more intuition in life.

"Idiots," he thought "Pure dumb fucking idiots!" The truck driver's eyes were glazed over with a drunken fear and the sour taste of cringing decrepitude quivering inside his throat as he began to speak.

"I'm cccc…ccc…carrying CD's." The truck driver stuttered thinking about what they had. "Black market operating systems bootlegged CD's," his eyes couldn't stop gazing at the oozing pounds of flesh, "underground artists and commercial labels. All the cities DJ's are under the heat of the FBI. They have all gone underground."

Chris shook his head slightly listening to what he had to say. But Chris wanted to get something straight before they talked any further. Chris reached into his back pocket and held a neatly folded bill between his fingers.

"Yeah I know." Chris replied as he flipped a bill into the palm of his hand. "Are you an associate or anyone involved in the families rackets?"

The truck driver was horrified by this and immediately answered him with a point blank answer.

"No. I'm just a truck driver. I have never been apart of or affiliated with any crime until now. I grew up hard and if my father ever knew…" The truck driver did not need to go on about his personal life filibustering his way through the conversation.

"Good, let's just understand each other." Chris interjected, and then gave him the lowdown—the skinny. "I want you to keep whatever you saw tonight to yourself. Just like in a confessional. And by the way I'm Chris." Chris held out his hand with the bill tucked inside his palms. "Chris Mangini!" Chris faced the hundred-dollar bill with the numbers facing outwards letting the bill call to him, and his voice demanded his respect.

It was a small negotiation for his silence and ironically for escaping death—forcing his right hand up from his sides and gripped Chris's steady hand. Chris let the bill fall into the truck driver's palm as he looked at the bill and did not take these guys for fools. He gratefully stuck the bill in his pocket and a cloud of heat began wafting from his shirt and a fountain of sweat poured from every known orifice—anus, pits, mouth—all contracting the same leaky odor.

"I'm okay" He added, a little shaky. "Don't worry about it, I'll go home and act like this night never existed. But the next time it probably won't be me driving. After this gets out in the open the drivers will probably be killers, family enforcers and they won't hesitate to put up a fight." The driver stood very nervous wiping the sweat from his desperate palms.

"We expected the same from tonight. I guess they didn't match up didn't they?" Chris exclaimed half-heartedly and not taking amusement out of his joke. The wind made Chris's spine shiver up and down his spine as he began to speak.

"Let's go. Jerry, you follow behind in Frank's car while A.J. will stay in front of you." Chris heartily waved as Jerry forcefully grabbed the driver by the collar swinging him towards the truck and slammed him against the door. Jerry and Niccolo nodded their heads in agreement and moved to their position.

"Frank you ride with Niccolo, I want you to take the second car and me and A.J. will take the first car. Just follow us, and dispose of the other cars." Chris said without a moment of hesitation in his voice. The truck driver climbed up the rail as he gripped the door handle and closed it echoing a loud *thunk*.

As Niccolo and Frank hurried toward the door, Frank hobbled toward the second truck as he held his arm trying to suppress his pain, gritting his teeth from the painful needles running up his arms.

Frank grunted as Niccolo jumped in front of him, "You okay," like a dog that had wanted to play with his master, "Do you feel anything," gleamed with wonder but he was not going to have this.

Niccolo's eyes gleamed with amazement. Indulged by the current pain that Frank was feeling inside his arm Frank's anger was about to burst after the stupid question he had to hear. He then showed him his arm, and the blood flowed out of the wound, and as he grunted in pain, a bit of shrewd sarcasm "Yeah, It hurts!"

Then his sarcasm was in cruise control as he forced him, "Why don't you get shot and tell me what it feels like. I don't feel a thing in my arm so get in the truck and drive this fucker, okay?"

He gripped the handle and settled his right foot on top of the swinging rail as he jumped inside the truck shutting the door with a loud THUNK! Niccolo shook his head, knowing that his ignorance had gotten the best of his judgement, and slapped the inside of his palm against his forehead, and shook his head in the most embarrassed look he had ever made. The other driver jumped inside the last truck, and nodded to them, knowing that he was ready. They had already moved the two cars that they had stolen into the ditch on the other side. While they made there way out, a mighty explosion and stashing their weapons inside Chris's car, they had wiped it down for all prints, and it was totally untraceable.

They were approaching the highway towards the city. The cornfields began to slowly disappear from view as they saw the lights of the city spreading across the burning stars, but they seemed to glisten softly in the night sky. Chris did not know whether they were going to end up on the other side of the city or on the other side of Jersey. The only place Chris could take them is to the other warehouse in Brooklyn where Don Pescaro's men did their business. Before it was used for moving dope and then distributed up and down the neighborhood ghettos. But now, Chris had taken control of the warehouse and set it up lab units for burning CD's and distribute them to underground parties and let some of their European connections get in on their products. For all Chris cared, people could socialize and dance under a tree in the midst of a lightening hailstorm.

The rich kids could listen to music on their illegal CD players transporting their minds into another life outside of their nice white houses, and into the lyrics of some punk rock screaming about the separation of their parents or some other bullshit. Or they could take a rid with an emcee (Master of Ceremony) rapping about his hard times and regular bullshit about shiny medallions, women, and lots of money. They would listen to it, but would set it aside until they got a new one. Music and society aside, if the money was green that was all that mattered to Chris. He knew better than to listen to music—he thought it gave him and the product bad luck—that he pirated.

Chris knew that he couldn't keep A.J. in the dark about his operations. With A.J. on the rise he would make the Preps, outcasts, and the Bloods divert their attention towards him while he went on about the bigger operations. The point for A.J. to stay at school during the day was to keep everybody on their toes, and no one would try to pull some shit. While the three beast's road each other's back bumpers, Chris was awoken by the bright lights of the corner stores that blazed neon blue.

"Jesus!" Chris whispered, and then looked at his watch. A.J. was pushing on the beast's leash feeling the gurgling gas spew from its pipes. It growled from the restraints as A.J. looked at him and said, "What!"

Chris turned towards him and said with anxiety, "How long have I been sleeping?"

A.J. glanced back at the road, and then gave the beast more freedom to move around. "About five minutes or so!" Chris couldn't believe that he was asleep because his eyes were open the entire time watching the other beasts pass him up—Lexus's that passed by behemoth SUV's while extinct Chevy Caprice's strolled at a slow pace. Good thing Chris wasn't driving.

Chris rubbed his eyes together, feeling his glossy eyes become hazy, he knew that they needed to drop the CD's off at the warehouse, and distribute it up between the families.

In regard to the warehouse, he did not remember if it was connected or resided next to the docks. Every warehouse in Brooklyn was surely connected to a dock, and even down around the Hudson River. While everyone had a piece of the city Chris took the opportunity to take the reigns of the CD rackets—and stealing from others wasn't an unfamiliar tool to use. Chris had strict operations and no one except Chris's outfit could do with how they saw fit with it, the family soldiers were there to copy a portion and do whatever they wanted with them.

A.J.—who was handling the driving rather carefully—came to another streetlight, seeing the shining street light reveal a dark blob leaning underneath the post—Chris instructed him to make another right at another light, but then turned, A.J. honked his horn at a few pedestrians that were ran across the middle of the street as he ran over a puddle.

"He could have run over them," Chris thought and watched them slip through a line of parked cars and jumped onto the curb in a single bound. The pedestrians had crossed the street before Chris could pull on the beast's leash causing him to slow down.

Chris could see a secluded warehouse with a straight and tall barbed wire gate as a few lights tried to liven the darkened building. They were travelling along the smooth concrete top sprawling for half a mile separating him and the warehouse. Not one speck of uprooted grass anywhere to be seen—nothing is sacred, nothing is won, and all is lost to the currency of the world's greed.

Chris and A.J. felt the beast's wheels dip into the crevice entrance levitating it up along the smooth ground. As Chris forced the beast's hind wheels up the crevice he ventured through the dark and widespread area following the direction toward the light. The darkness seemed to work against them fogging the beasts' lights confusing his line of sight. The beast trembled with anticipation seeing the warehouse from afar tugging on his leash.

Chris, with his hawk-eyes saw figures rushing from a weakly lit door jumping down the steps and signaling them to keep coming. A bright floodlight instantly shined half of the area and the men in the distance waved their hands in the air beckoning them to approach the metallic opening, which would be a place for them to let the crew retrieve there stuff.

These figures were new to Chris and their appearance became fuzzier in the bright light as A.J. kept the beast on its toes steadily moving into the blinding fog light, and covered his eyes as he advanced toward the light. Warn-full about whom these men were made him more nervous, and with his large 45 caliber, he would protect himself if it came down to an ambush. A.J. flicked his bright lights on and off, shining their faces as they threw their hands up defending their eyes against the bright lights.

Chris saw a rugged man with long tailored pants and wave like hair as the beach on a raspy day. He had a straight and edgy look about him wearing a nicely fit suit but without the tie. He seemed to be unfamiliar to him as first, shutting his eyes for a moment deeply searching through his long dictionary of faces. As soon as Chris would put a name with his face then he would feel comfortable to leave the car.

Through all the chaotic experience he and his team experienced through out the night, Chris had almost forgot about all of it when he saw Benjamin. One of Don Pescaro's second hand captains and a personal friend of his. Out of all the scum Chris had seen come and go through the game, Benny, or Benjamin was one person he could trust. He had earned his respect with him after doing some odd and risky favors—not to mention trivial favors that Chris had risked his life for made quite an impression on Benjamin. Chris turned to A.J. handing him down on who he was and what "friends" he would be around.

"This guy is Benjamin Shapiro. He's a close friend of mine. Don't worry about him, just stay around us and do whatever he tells you to do. If you need to talk, just come and look for me." Chris said, and saw A.J. nodded grimly, as if he had wanted to kill him.

Unbeknownst to A.J.'s distracted eyesight, Chris leaned over and switched the bright lights off and waved to Benjamin. Over the lights, the man waved back, and knew that he was a friend—a very good friend at that.

Chris felt secure about getting out of the car, and he knew that he had to give A.J. a gun before he left. Before he left he reached toward the glove compartment and when he opened it, a loaded Llama seven shot handgun that he had never seen before, appeared to be resting peacefully, undisturbed. It was still loaded by the weight in his hands. He pulled it out, looking at it, he saw the smudges that had a large sweaty stain resonating off the handle, and saw that the serial code was scratched off. That gave a big signal to him that this gun was bought somewhere, but looking at it even longer, he then gently threw it into A.J.'s lap.

The gun fell into A.J.'s lap, and made a small CLAPPING sound as it slapped his crotch.

A.J. peered back at Chris and smirked in pain, and then picking it up, he examined it. As he stuck it inside his pantline, Chris reached across the seat and patted his shoulders, bolstering confidence. His flattery honored Chris, and saw that his determination and loyalty seemed to rub off every time he saw him—especially his edge that he always had—but the thing he could do was calm him down, and that was complementary.

Finally A.J. did the honors of pulling down the handle, putting the beast in park, and turned the key and its engine shut off with a loud KA-WOOM and it felt time to leave. They departed the beast and Chris's feet touched the ground, he slammed the door and walked toward Benjamin. Benjamin, a rather tall 6'4 brooding shoulder man, saw Chris and a great sense of relief had eased Benny's tension and A smile spread across his face—far wider than he was with A.J. collected his arms around his sweaty pin striped suit.

"Benjamin!" Chris said into his shoulder, and the two pulled each other off them. "How have you been?"

Benjamin with his wide eyes replied with his joker smile. "Since you last saw me, been busier than ever. The other families have been laying it on us pretty thick ever since we made the first strike. They try to shake up our men by getting to them at night. You evidently received the truck that was coming through Boston and Detroit."

Chris glanced back at the truck, "I guess we did," and then patted his shoulder.

Feeling the night just getting too cold for them to even stand outside, he put his arm around his shoulders, and then said to him in freezing conviction. "Come on, let's go inside." He could feel the cold air creep through his suit.

Benjamin glanced at A.J. who had loudly slammed the door. He stared coldly at A.J. and leaning over again, but had become full of fear.

"Who's the kid? Is he a recruit?" Benny asked as he returned his gaze back to the Chris, waiting for a reply.

"He's a friend of mine." Knowing that he was partially telling him the truth. "I found him, or more like he found me. He's real low key and keeps to himself. He's a stand-up guy." Chris said as an assuring poker player who was conning you to give him more money. Chris felt that he could not let him in on everything that Chris knew about him personally. Just maybe let him in on about a few things, but nothing too personal.

"Does this friend have a name?" Benny was all too cocky and he wanted them to be intimidating, but that was his front. As much of a nice guy that he was he certainly had his moments where you did not want to cross him.

Chris laughed from his joke and began to say his name, but before he began to speak A.J. interrupted their conversation.

"How are ya'? I'm Alphonse" A.J. said uncomfortably, and held a free hand up to greet Benjamin. He looked down at his hand, scoffed from A.J.'s outward gesture, and he lowered his hand back toward his side brushing the handle of the Llama handgun. He smiled his eyes revealed a sadistic and torturous look in his eyes like a schoolyard bully who had found his first murder victim. A.J. had no clue as to how his simple gesture had offended him nor did he want to encourage it either.

"Alphonse, is it? Tell me Alphonse, how did you two meet?" Benny said evilly cornering him as A.J. frightfully glanced away—feeling the presence— the man with a thousand dreams—mixed in a pot of scolding blood stew— into one nightmarish reality.

"I saw him sitting at an abandoned table, and since I needed a place to sit, and that was it." A.J. said.

"You saw him at an lunch table and he let you sit with him." Benny scoffed and continued to pursue with his question. "Great, a fucking outsider!"

He walked away, and Chris narrowed his eyes and cocked his eyebrow as they walked into the factory.

A.J. beheld the warehouse in all its amazement and it's vague surroundings. A few swinging lights were centered on several different tables giving their work situation a rather poor visibility, but the family soldiers did not care about the light, as the Desk lights were plugged through an electrical outlet shining two feet away from the desk. It was cold and dense while desks were being heated with the whirring and spinning of the individual machines, burning CD's without shame nor knowing of reason—the dim future of our lives where our minds will become trapped in its labyrinth mind.

The men that were monotonously providing the burners with the copyright CD's and filling the tray with blank CD's to burn it on. After that individual machine was taken care of they moved to another burning system which was used by businesses to copy their hardware for individual Operating Systems or a civilian. The government was taking copying all to seriously with a fine and imprison them for five years, but with the right senators and judges they would freely turn a blind eye and disregard the crime as nothing in court.

A.J. passed several tables of machines that were copying CD's, and the soldiers were working—some of them in T-shirts and jeans while some were dressed in long sleeve shirts—without a care for anything but themselves. A few more men began moving toward the delivery pod where the beasts could wait for the men to retrieve the cargo from its space giving the beast time to relax and take time to breath. A.J. watched the process for a long moment as Chris and Benjamin were leaving him in the dust. Keeping his hand away from the gun, A.J. walked a normal pace to a vibrant walk. But as he caught up with the two, small muddled screams. Frank's body was laying on an operating table with his shirt thrown covering the back of his seat to keep his back from catching cold, and a few soldiers were working on his wound.

Two skinny men in comfortable clothes swerved around A.J. as the first man with the surgical tool was concentrating on his arm while the second man was there to hold Frank down. He was like a mad bull and to keep him from rising out of the seat he could feel a small twinge of pain came from the grinding belt.

They did not appear tough to A.J. Their hands were frail; just like an artist or a musician when he was tweaking out a note that did not fit the song, but when Frank started to scream, he cringed for him but knew that it would be better for him in the long run. Frank slowly grunted from each time that they forcibly entered—cut—and threaded his skin back together. Frank looked at Frank and knew this was the damdest of all hospitals.

"This is some place you call a hospital?" Frank spit out sarcastically, and he could feel the pain surging through his system—spit formed over the leather belt as he seethed with rage but then relaxed as they finished sewing his wound back together.

Then suddenly the phone rang from halfway across the room, and someone immediately grabbed the phone before it rang another second. He turned around and squinting his eyes he focused toward Chris, Benjamin, and A.J. There was one person that they wanted to talk to would be Chris Mangini. The person who had picked up the phone did not believe that Chris Mangini was in the building, it was like a breath of fresh air had come through and given them new life.

As he set the phone down, he waved to Chris in amazement as A.J. saw the man waving and tapped Chris on the shoulder. Chris turned his head around as he squinted from his distraction. A.J. quickly raised his hand and pointed to the messenger and turned facing the messenger swinging his body sideways and saw his left arm fall to his sides, and up came the phone, holding it high enough for him to see. The message was clear.

Chris pointed to himself just to be sure if he was talking to him. The messenger urged him forward, waving the phone in his hand. Chris nodded and held a finger up, urging him to wait one more moment.

Chris turned back to Frank and saw that he wasn't taking it very well. Chris thought about it, and needed to take this call since Frank was not hurt bad.

"Don't worry. These guys know what they are doing. You just lay back while I go and see what's up. A.J. will stay with you." Chris made sure that Frank would not be left without someone watching over him. He ran about ten paces and stopped for a cool walk as he inhaling and exhaling while he received the phone from the messenger.

The messenger nodded and walked back to the rows of individual copiers. The voice took him by surprise. It was Gene and the nature of the call was not to be discussed around soldiers and captains. He put him on hold and as he pressed a few buttons he hung up the phone and watched the flashing red button appear from one of the buttons. Then in haste he asked another man if there was another phone he could talk from. The man told him that an office upstairs led to the same line.

Chris thanked the man with appreciation and headed toward a large metal staircase that overlooked the entire shady grounds, and looped around the entire building. As Chris moved up the black metallic stairs, he did not stop to breathe or take a rest and he approached an office with two large windows separated by a door in the middle. He grabbed the doorknob and moved into the dim room. Slamming the door behind him he rattled the windowpanes as he was safely inside the room.

As he spied throughout the room with his hawk eyes he saw on a desk a phone that was blinking red, and knew that the person was put on hold, waiting for him. Noticing how murky and dim the room had been he felt that it should have been clean—even though it wasn't nicer than any of the others he frequented. On the edge of a brown desk, still blinked the flashing red button with a continuing glare.

Chris picked up the black receiver and held it to his ear. With an infatuated voice he spoke into phone. On this particular occasion Chris did not care if the FBI were listening into their conversation, because no one would ever think about tapping an abandoned warehouse. They could take his words however he wanted, because he was not talking about anything they cared about, and he secretly relished the fact they tried to decode their slang. It proved that they had stamina, and he always liked to give anyone a run for their money.

"What do ya' got?" Chris asked curiously and deterred utterance.

"I looked around like you said. The birthdays I couldn't determine, like you said. Now to look through every marriage record and birth-records in the entire state of New York is a bit like trying to find a real Mickey Rooney card in a pile of fakes. You want to find out which one is real. Now you say he might be 15 or sixteen right?" Gene said exasperated, his motor mouth projected with rapidity.

"Yeah, Do you assume that he's my cousin? The one from my mothers side? The *one that will give peace to the old country?*" Chris was ready and prepared to dive further he had gone and a lot of people could be saved if this were true.

"Not if you happen to find more about him and his past. The thing is when the parents of a child dies, the living father or mother is so eager to fill the gap so that the child wouldn't go around and ask where his father or mother would be."

Gene was certainly smart for a boy his age, but Chris didn't really take his pieces of advice word for word. While most boys would be going out with their friends and watching movies in their parents' basements, all of them were taking another route by making money the easier than receive a pitiful wage after taxes come and rape his time and money out from under him. Gene could not live on a two-week salary his whole life, and knew that this was *the right way*. "

You got a point. Forget about searching through records. The next thing I'll want you to do is get a hold of our friends downtown and see if they can pull anything up on a marriage license. You can do that?" Chris's demands were heating the receiver as his heavy breathing made Gene pull the receiver off his ear and returned the blood into his ear he set the phone gently back to his ear.

Thinking about his decision, Gene paused for a moment and felt that they were going to end up falling into another dead end, but knew that he had to answer one way or the other.

Chris had left A.J. and Benjamin for more than a few minutes while Frank's wounds were being healed. A.J. felt nervous being around Benjamin as he dragged him unwillingly toward a table of opened boxes being ripped into with box cutters, ripping the flaps open they threw the paper wrapping and Styrofoam peanuts across the table like entrails wrapping around a stomach trying to find it's way back into place. The slim CD cases were laid straight up side by side with more CD cases on top of each other. When he knew that they wasn't killing anyone with packs of powder or dirty needles, and breathed easy.

Benjamin stopped in front of an unopened box and his eyes scoured for a paper cutter that was two feet away from A.J.'s hand. Benjamin forcefully pushed A.J. in the shoulder, and then pointed toward the metal slip box cover.

"Pick up that blade and cut into that box. I want to see what this is." Benjamin insisted.

At that moment when A.J. looked around him and wanted to say, "Look around you," but he kept his mouth shut and picked up the blade with his left hand and pulled the semi-heavy box towards him. As he faced the box with the flaps straight in front of him, he glanced at Benjamin for a second and positioned the blade at the other end of the flap and with extreme precision he gently forced the blade into the clear tape—holding the box with his opposite hand—he moved the box cutter down the flaps as if A.J. was in the middle of an autopsy. The stale plastic Styrofoam puffed from the box as A.J. caught a whiff of the dry inoculating fart smell of cardboard and dust-pixy particles. A.J. coughed from the annoying smell and felt his nose running.

"Stinks don't it?" Benjamin was entertained by watching him being tortured. A.J. let out a roaring cough from his mouth and he spoke, feeling his spit forming into a large milky substance, and he swallowed it with rueful disgust.

"Yeah." A.J. managed to say as he laid the blade down next to the box and opened the flaps up and creased them out for him to dig his hand far enough—feeling the Styrofoam and the paper wrapping placed around the plastic cases. Being that this was his first time at this sort of thing, he stuck his hand into the box like a bear fishing for trout; he grabbed and threw it across the table. After that A.J. did not feel scared to stick his hand inside the box again. He grabbed another handful and threw it in the same pile sending some of the peanuts rolling like dice and landed on the steel ground.

After A.J. threw a few more handfuls of Styrofoam out of the box, A.J. finally revealed what was hidden deep inside the box. Thirty-five colorful and unimaginative plastic boxes that were laid laterally on top of each other; the background was black and semi large white words were printed across the box. As he tried to see what it said, a few peanuts were covering the full title of the box. To see it, he reached it off with his fingers and held it easy enough for him and Benjamin (as he pulled his glasses out) to read it.

The box's letters blared with its white letters,

NORTON ANTIVIRUS© .50 Guardian Angel System

Under the sign it had a pair of Angel wings and a halo over a computer system. As A.J. flipped the box over, nothing was on the back of the box, just black. The both of them weren't in with computer programs and what they did so A.J. threw the box on the table.

"Are these the programs the government have been prohibiting?" A.J. asked.

"Yeah. I guess so." Benjamin ran his hand through his wavy hair as his eyes squinted with perplexing composure as he scratched his chin with annoyance. "I couldn't really tell you how it got here, its all bullshit. I'm not a fucking computer nerd, you're not a computer nerd?" He said becoming questionable and relaxed.

"No. I know how to turn one on" A.J. replied despondently, "but the finer details I'm lost. I was born around all of this technology but I don't seem to have any use for it."

Benjamin knew what he was saying. "Maybe this A.J. isn't so bad. But, what isn't he telling me?" Benny thought, "But I can't be sure though."

"Yeah." Benny said as his warm and tingly throat became hoarse from an all night drinking binge. "I know that!" As he said that the two chuckled getting a small rise out of their conversation. As Benjamin thought about it, he did not trust Chris personally, but his loyalty stood out through long lasting betrayals and quick fixes, then he was all right with him.

Although he did not want to intimidate him, being who he was, he made sure no threatening mutter entered into the conversation.

"Where are you from?" Benny asked A.J. with a levelheaded appearance breaking the iceberg, or tension that was between them.

"Appalachian. I'm not that far from the city." A.J. replied. He did not know what Benny was trying to pull.

"Appalachian huh? I'm from Mulberry Street. I never get time to sit on the porch steps anymore. The days when a kid was always found outside playing street-ball and were never inside their homes."

"I know what you're talking about right?" A.J. replied understandingly "Now kids are always inside their houses afraid to go outside."

Benny nodded, continuing with the bickering conversation. "You're right.

Not only are they stupid. They listen to that music living carefree and giving their parents a hard time. That's why kids should be slapped across the mouth once and a while. Because if you are going to have kids, you have to set that fine line of respect and love."

"And patience." A.J. added, nodding his head. Benny looked at him and knew that he had hit the nail on the head. He was wise but could he be foolish? Foolish enough of him to give up their plans and what his family's weaknesses were.

"Patience." Benjamin scoffed giving A.J. a light slap across the back for wording. "You got that right. I got two kids probably around your age, and I have to beat them just to make them do their schoolwork. They can't concentrate for long, so I have to set them back up again."

A.J. was beginning to find this conversation more and more interesting, but a little bit frightening, but interesting all the same. He began to find out how somebody like him was dealing with attention defecate disorder, and when A.J. recommended they should go and see their family doctor, Benjamin's eyes flared with anger and pushed the idea aside and told him that he did not want their kids to become addicted to that "junk."

As A.J. reassured him about its safety; they ended the conversation by jumping onto baseball. They raved on about the upcoming Yankees game. A.J. was adamant about how the Yankees were unstoppable this year. But when Benjamin mentioned the upcoming match with the Detroit Redwings, the two were butting heads. Benjamin had doubts about the Yankees beating the Redwings. They must have talked about this for more than ten minutes.

And with an aggravated sigh, swaying away from endless conversation he began to wonder about Chris and how long he was going to leave him here with this old school hood—and at the same time, two generations were communicating without yelling or raising there voices.

"Hey. Can we talk off the record?" Benjamin asked cautiously as he looked towards the window again.

A.J. was taken off guard by his question feeling a bit strange about "talking off the record" if it was so important why did they need to go off the record? But then A.J. knew that it must have been a kind of code that restricted people from spreading any rumors but that's how assassinations always began. Reluctantly A.J. went along with the conversation, it wasn't as if he had a choice or not.

"Sure. What do you want to say?" A.J. said looking uninterested but secretly wanting to hear what this old hood had to say.

"I have been thinking. Why should someone like you be restricted from the bountiful pleasures of the world? I brought Chris under my wing and now he's Captain of his own crew. I know it may seem easy, but you already know everyone involved has responsibilities. You know with the cops and federal agents we can't even shit without them knowing what we ate for dinner."

A.J. chuckled but knew that he was dead serious. But Benjamin could go on for hours talking about the expected downside, but he didn't want to waste his time and really get to the rotted core of the conversation.

"Chris is a good guy. He's done a lot of favors for us and after everything he shows us the proper respect we deserve. But who's to say that he's doing something behind our backs?"

"Why would he do something behind your backs?" A.J. replied. He wasn't sure why anyone would have a problem with Chris, and why would he be telling him of all people? If Benjamin was trying to make Chris look weak or sway his mind, this didn't do a damn thing to his loyalty. It only aggravated him and what would happen if someone would find out about the conversation. If someone overheard their conversation someone would grow suspicious, but they were just having a conversation, nothing more, and nothing less.

"This is *off the record*, right?" Benjamin whispered underneath the stacking and packaging of workers, "so just hear me out." The sounds of ripping tops traveled through A.J.'s eardrums as he listened.

"Don't think so wrong of me for saying this. But you never know who to trust out there, and we all have to protect what we have built with our lives. We just need to know that it's in good hands."

A.J. nodded quietly absorbing everything he said. His face turned pale with fright and his heart was frozen when he assumed what Benjamin was talking about. The fact that he was assuming what Chris had been doing behind their backs made A.J. loathe and despise his own curiosity. His distrust thickened and with a hate that anyone could understand, frosted over with a chill running through his spine. All A.J. wanted to do now was change the conversation and away from this man and this threatening conversation.

But when A.J. came back to his senses, he knew that he needed to get away from him, and fast. His blue eyes were bold and curious, as his lips were parched and dry. Benjamin sighed and decided to tell him something that had also been festering in his mind.

"Theirs something you should know about Chris. Whenever he is hooked onto an endless question that seems to never have an answer he keeps thinking—even if he is sitting amongst a crowd of people—a restless mind. He's obsessed with a long lost cousin that was abandoned after his aunt died, but he never knew about until a few years ago."

As A.J. heard this he was struck with feelings of guilt and compassion for Chris. To think that someone like your brother or your cousin was said to be dead but kept a secret, was more than wrong, it was devious and uncomforting.

"Kid. You speechless, you got anything to say?" Benjamin lowered his face with discreet politeness. His predator eyes forced A.J. to speak.

His voice was reassuring and calm making sure Benjamin would not suspect any weakness. A.J. said, "Sure. I'm fine. Must feel pretty bad not knowing that you have a cousin who's alive and well. He might even be your best friend?"

"Or your worst enemy!" There was a whiff of suspicion as if it was an ominous message to him as if he was a deadly apparition.

"Then that's that. There's nothing anyone can do." A.J. said nervously tapping his right foot, and shifting his body side-to-side—looking around the warehouse of mad headless chickens.

Benny scoffed from his petty bluntness even if A.J. was a kid he must have sacrificed what childhood he had left. "I hear ya. Here's to changing the subject."

A.J. agreed.

Chris very quiet and deep in thought—only the voices were drawing on web strings of conclusion—making him imagine what his cousin's hair or what his face might look like. Or what they would have in common when they would finally meet. Did he look like him or would be completely opposite—how would he react emotionally and physically. Stuck in his mind, he began drawing a picture of what he might look like. Big, round, fat, dirty face, skinny—the scenarios would be a haunting measure of his unlimited imagination—and he walked with the phone around in the dusty room toward the large smoggy window panes.

"Come on up." Chris was standing in plain sight of the glass windows. This was the perfect time he had. He had saved him from conversing with Benjamin for another second. He nodded and hung up the phone. Chris slowly faded away from the windows and hung up the phone.

A.J. did not wait as he hung up the phone and rushed toward the metallic row of stairs that led to the office where Chris had been for the last ten minutes. A.J. started up the steps with a brisk pace as he grabbed hold of the guardrail. His shoes scraped off pieces of chipped paint as his shoes clamored against the solid brass and echoed for more than ten steps.

He made his way for another seven steps as he glanced over the warehouse and turned away smiling after lucking out of packing boxes and burning CD's while he conversed with Benjamin. He did not know why Benjamin had been so eager to trust him—taking a chance on his limitations of what he could take. But he did not suspect that Chris wasn't blind to the deep-seeded mistrust and treachery of Benjamin.

When he finally reached the last step to his office he could see Chris with his back turned and A.J. turned it slowly feeling the lock muggy air pushing against him as if he were in a thick club room of high grade sweat and cum stained pants. As he pushed the door open the air puffed into his A.J.'s face as he quietly stuck his head through the widened hole.

A.J. watched Chris lean against the edge of the lighted desk.

Waving his hand Chris A.J. opened the door, and crept into the room he slowly shut the door as he slipped into the room. A.J. nodded as he moved in his seat when he sat in the chair across from him.

After a few minutes Chris smirked, leaning back and forth in his silence. He finally sighed, being able to send air into his brain so he could concentrate on other things.

Chris leaned back in his chair and saw A.J. sitting erect and edgy in the chair.

"Relax." Chris said as A.J. fell back into the chair and breathed easily.

"You all right?" Chris asked as he walked around the desk and into his seat.

"Yeah. I'm just tired." A.J. replied, resting his arms along the armrest as his eyes were a bit glazed over as he slouched down in his chair. In this dank room, the darkness could almost slip over your eyes and make you see things come alive from the walls.

"You sure? Anything else on your mind?" Chris insisted.

A.J. thought about it for a moment, but then knew that he could address. "There's something that I want to ask you?"

"Go ahead." Chris said with an easygoing voice. He returned to an upright position feeling the chair shaking like a rickety bridge as he laid his elbows against the edge of the desk.

"I saw what was inside the trucks. The prohibited CD's..." A.J. said, insinuating an odd foreboding that should have clicked with Chris.

"Really!" Chris said sarcastically. "What made you think there weren't? Did all those CD cases give it away?"

A.J. sighed and scoffed as he thought about it, and knew what he said was stupid, but it relieved a bit of tension from his soul, but then finally admitted what he really wanted to say.

"Yeah." A.J. said pushing his chest out and airing out his conscience, but then finally came out with it. "I guess that I was glad those boxes weren't filled with dope."

Chris nodded and took this close to heart since this issue had been troublesome to A.J. He remembered the night of the game.

"Ohhhh, ever since that night at the game, huh?" Chris's eyes glared with hate. "This I suppose has suppressed your fears."

"What do you mean?" A.J. replied wrapping his fingers together in a tight fist and laid his hands across his belly.

"The night you asked me if I dealt and I didn't answer. Do you remember?" Chris said, and A.J. recalled that night so clearly when he brought it up.

"I remember now. I forgot about it." A.J. said, slouching in his seat, but not looking down. Then out of curiosity Chris asked how A.J.'s family was.

"Fine, just fine."

"Have they suspected anything else?" Chris asked questionably.

A.J. slid back up setting his feet firmly pressed against the ground.

"Yeah. But they wouldn't get any funny ideas and call the police, because I'm their only son." Chris nodded and the two let a bit of silence fall and Chris took a minute to ease his assumptions.

"How many more of these trucks are we going to steal?" A.J. asked with curiosity and Chris pressed his fingers against his eyes, and then leaned against the desk with his bare hands and felt un-obligated to answer his question.

"Why? What does it mean to you?" Chris's agitation was high. "Aren't you happy with watching over the rackets at George Bradley?"

"Yeah. I guess so." A.J. replied ungratefully. "I was thinking that since I am becoming a man. And a man needs to handle his responsibilities." But he was not done he wanted to give him the truth behind how they were doing financially. A.J. took a deep breath and put his words together. He released his words like a tidal wave of slushy swamp water that had finally crashed upon the shore.

"When you asked about my parents and how they were doing financially, I was being honest. Their money situation is terrible and the only money that I ever had was in that first week. I sacrifice *my* wants for their bills. As a man I want to help them and never have to worry about money again, and fulfill my wants."

Chris sighed, lying back in his seat with his elbows resting against the armrests. Chris was all too familiar with having to scrape and scrounge for money including having to provide a safe castle for his wife and children. Chris decided to counsel and teach him everything that Chris knew. Which was too many times for him to remember. That was the only lasting memory of anger he knew.

"You want to work!" Chris finally said, who sounded as if he was on pins and needles. "Is that what you are trying to tell me? If I do this and give you the freedom you have to answer to me and keep our 'friends' happy?" A.J. looked at him, not fully comprehending what he was saying, and decided to put it in simpler terms. "What I mean is, this states, without a contract, that you will cut out whatever you get out of whatever you make and hand it to me each week."

A.J.'s head rose, his eyes were filled with joy, and smiled knowing his words as if they were beautiful music to his ears. "Yes." He replied eagerly. The fire returned to his eyes rekindling A.J.'s spirits. He was hearing words that made his day. He saw Chris leaning back and forth, back and forth figuring out what A.J. could possibly do.

"How can A.J. keep a school appearance watching over their rackets while he could work the graveyard shift?" Chris thought as he contemplated and debated this issue for ten seconds. It seemed difficult for Chris to handle even ten years ago, but he knew that he had done incredible things while he was just riding bikes. If A.J. was strong willed and could juggle two different lives at the same time, he did not doubt him.

Chris leaned forward in his seat. "Okay. If you really want more money the bigger the risks and heat you will have to deal with? The one thing you might have to stand up to the cops and federal agents. And watch how you talk and who you talk to on the phone." He pointed to the phone with his left arm and raising his index finger with a stern voice. As Chris hurried along with his wisdom, A.J. lively nodded and studying everything he said taking it into memory.

As he told A.J. of more important rules to live by his hands traveled along the desk drawer and pulled the first drawer that his hand reached for. As he told A.J. the prices that ranged on a CD was (regular music CD's were soaring up to seventy dollars per Compact Disk while a box of thirty Norton Anti-virus programs were about ten thousand, one hundred and ninety-five dollars.) He also mentioned to never save any of the information on your hard drive, because they can bring people in. Chris's hand was searching for a pen and piece of paper to list his contacts, Danny, Antony, and Giuseppe, but then felt something else.

Then Chris decided to go into the more dangerous aspect of the entire thing. "In every business deal, there will be competition always trying to get over on you."

A.J. leaned forward becoming interested in what he was saying—his hair revealed hints of brown strands. As Chris sighed he quickly reached into the open drawer and revealed a revolver, and placed it under the desk light. A.J.'s eyes widened but his body barely flinched and his heart did not take too well to this surprise.

"And that's when things may get out of hand. Not every deal will require these matters to be backed with force. Don't show them anything, if you are dealing with serious buyers set a time and place. Make it quick and don't fuck around. But just to be safe, always, until a deal is done." Chris said and closed the drawer and searched around for a pen and paper. As he opened the second drawer, his eyes saw a ballpoint pen and a clean sheet tablet lying studiously next to each other. Dust flied off the pad and into the air as his thumb and index finger against the tablet and his thumb.

After Chris threw the pen and pad across the desk Chris handed him the list.

"Take it." Chris said with a wave of his hand.

"No, no." A.J. replied, "Don't you need it?"

"No. I just found the fucker. Like I said *the more money and respect you crave will bring greater risks*. This life will *certainly* fuck you if you don't know how to act. This is the life we lead, and if we don't use our heads, we could certainly loose them."

"I'm fine," A.J. got up, fearfully, grabbing the folded piece of paper and then turned around to the door.

"One more thing," Chris shouted, as A.J. stopped with his hand around the door knob and faced him once again. Looking down at the floor, glumly, and Chris spouted off, "Don't believe what you hear. People do what they must do in order to survive."

A.J. nodded, and then left Chris with the revolver glistening underneath the shady light.

"What's with this kid?" Chris angrily murmured, knowing that A.J. had the talent, and that was his true calling. But before he jumped to anymore ideas, leaned across the desk and picked up the phone and dialed the number to each associate instructing them to arrive at the school around the first half of the lunch period. He was helping A.J. by watching his operations in the daytime while he helped in the night.

Out of the entire night he didn't want to be bothered by anybody, unless it was his wife, which he doubted would call, because she didn't know the number to this office.

Chris—in his moment of solitude—immediately gave into his weakness. Sleep. But with the certain events of the war between the families his nights were going to affect one's eyes (sort of like a walking insomniac dream) and without sleep, people started seeing things. It started with his eyes as the lids began to close on him, but as he laid back he gave into his weakness. He started to close his mouth and staring into the ceiling he slipped into a deep sleep with his eyes open, and his mind off. He felt the weight of the world starting to dissolve off his shoulders, even for an hour, it was a nirvana.

Chapter X:

"A.J.'s Watch"

Seven o'clock had came faster for everyone that it brought up many people but for Antony, Guissepe and Guido this was the exception. They decided to meet up for breakfast and each of them had long considerable showers while their eyes were coated with weariness as they ordered anything that they could afford—large plates of hot pancakes with scrambled eggs and three strips of bacon. They gave the waitress a bit extra telling her "to keep the bacon coming."

As they devoured into the pancakes, talking with food in their mouth, shredding through the drippy sunny side eggs and charcoal bacon, they gulped it down without even looking at the ends of their forks.

"If any of us gets a call like we did last night, which I doubt he would leave any of us uninformed again, each of us has to let each other know what's up." Antony watched the two look up at him as they swallowed the rest of their food, uneasily gulping their food down. "Because we can't go in their empty handed. We have to show some control over ourselves. We've been ordered to give this kid the heads up, and show him the ropes. But with the shit that's happening out there, I don't want anyone putting any ideas about who we are with."

Giuseppe's curious mind began to infiltrate the conversation. "Who are we with?" Giuseppe asked stupidly. He had glanced up and down from his plate, playing with a dangerous suggestion.

Antony looked at him, not wanting to go on with this conversation, but choked himself with the click of his teeth. Antony sighed accepting the decision to keep this disclosed from Giuseppe.

Antony had formed an allegiance with an unholy knight, a dark malevolent force that he had joined with the signature of his own blood—forsaking his life—and his soul to this creature—a wolf in sheep's clothing. But being the sly, conniving basterd that Chris Mangini was he had kept a distance from them for a year's time never really exposing them to any of their business deals, keeping them on the back burner while they pursued their own means—creating there own contacts while they had to pine for his attention.

"What time do we have to be there?" Giuseppe asked with a stifle breaking his long pensive thoughts.

Antony lowered his head low to the table and talked inside his mouth, only so they could hear. "At eleven fifty five. We got some time to kill. Let's meet at the front of the school near the commons. You know where this guy sits?"

Giuseppe nodded wiping off some yellow egg off his lips. "Yeah. He sits where Chris Mangini always sat. It's not far."

"Good." Antony muttered through his breakfast nervously tapped the morning table continuously unknowingly making shadows across the table with his hand.

"Real good." They silently agreed with this decision and Antony dispersed calling the waitress to pick up his check. He handed her fifteen dollars and told her to keep the change. Guido decided to pick up his own check while he was at it, calling her back over again giving her the amount owed and told her to keep the change too. Their waitress, who had locks of shiny black hair smiled with content, thanking them as Guido departed down the other way toward Brooklyn.

Giuseppe was the last one left at their table, and the last to be served with the third plate of bacon. Guissepe glanced at the waitress and raised an eyebrow and flashing a smile of gratitude. She winked at him and shook her hips back and forth clearly throwing the whole package at him. The waitress disappeared into the kitchen and Guissepe left the amount on the table with her tip, if he could give his *real tip* he could have, but now was not the time to think about sex.

Giuseppe departed from the diner and ventured onto the next street feeling the pockets of forced air swoosh by him as cars eagerly traveled without concern—and into the concrete jungle of a city.

The morning sun gleamed bright enough on A.J.'s house so hard that he felt like a homeless man awoken from their trashcan slumber, but the wind would definitely add the chill that was the real kicker. While in school A.J. had wanted to be out and about feeling the sun bake against his well balanced skin, letting the wind hit his face, but all he could feel was the air conditioning slap his skin. This air would only make him close his eyes, but it was a long night and he would have liked to take a dance in the darkness. As he let the time slip by his ever-present youth—dreaming about his comrades away from this boring classroom, his youthful eyes began to become a slave to staring at the clock. His eyes twitched with pulsating weariness as his eyes began to see that the last period before lunch approaching. He had been lost in his own thoughts, fighting a loosing battle with his concentration as he kept his head propped under his hand and closing his eyes he began to dose off.

But his history teachers' voice only disturbed his slumber as he heard the chalk scraped across the board. To brush up on his history lesson, A.J. began looking around for his history book. He did not have it—quite frankly, he did not need it. Because his teacher had not approached him during or before class about where he was the other day, he decided it was better to let the limping fish die. If he was, that was a good thing, if he wasn't he's have to be stuck with more work, which was more than having a bullet in the head—it was a mind numbing fuck that had the affect of a mallet over his head.

A.J. had left half an hour slip by in his next class pretending to listen to the teacher. But when he turned to the clock again, another half an hour had went by.

"Just another half an hour!" A.J. groaned, sliding back in his seat. The chair was so smooth that his butt was not cooperating as his butt inched forward in the smooth seat. A.J. tried to straighten his back against the chair but felt his back obeying the laws of gravity—which was what must come up must fall down. He stamped his legs on the ground hoisting him back up. Although jealous eyes were on him, an unfriendly heat had been coming from an area of the room.

Someone didn't like A.J. slouching lavishly as if this was a couch instead of a living room, and that was the teacher's scornful sour face as he pitted his legs upwards, and moved along the seat, feeling electricity building through his body. This was uncomfortable for A.J., so he glanced curiously around the room he saw that a boy with long, black hair and an almost girlish figure had been staring at him. His skin was so pale that it was repulsive making his hand seemed whiter than the sky. It didn't seem like he wasn't the only one, and A.J. nodded and smirked. The boy smirked with distaste as his upper lip rose and returned a friendly nod.

Many people looked at people for many reasons. If A.J. had been looking at him, it would have been a different story. He didn't like him, and A.J. couldn't figure that out. But he decided to keep away from him, for if they would meet, their fists would be taking over for the conversation—but he knew that not talking was the best solution as A.J. heard the teacher telling the class to pack their bags and get ready for the next class. With a rush of excitement, A.J. felt his back become stronger, and his will to live seemed to rush through his body again with those words. As the students forlornly tossed their text books into there bags, zipping their plastic or finely constructed notebooks together, some conversation entered the room, and Gothic kids talked to other Goths while some Preppy kids talked to other Preps—the division was so evident that it promised no change for that person at all. Only A.J. attended his own affairs, not talking to anyone else he saw in his pack two Norton-Antivirus programs and three CD's, resting inside his pack. He must have ignored bringing his books to school, and as he glanced over his shoulder, he zipped up his pack up and slung it across his shoulders.

He grabbed his notebook and eagerly waited for the bell to give him and everyone in the class the freedom to leave the classroom. As A.J. looked up and down at the clock, his patience was running short and the attractive bell let off its lulling, *bing…bing…bing…bing*! All of the students loved this sound, and when it made that sound, it was like they had finally reached their *Siddhartha*, and they could finally be reincarnated with the earth. A.J. rose from his seat as fast as he could—without writing the homework down—and moved with speed out the door.

The halls of George Bradley began filling with students from both sides of the hall—large, tall, skinny, small began pouring—as A.J. became one in the thousands of kids in this crowd—he felt that nobody was going anywhere, like convicts in a prison yard—soared down the once quiet and crowded halls. But as the once wide hall was filling up it was like all the trains were compacted into one as all of the students smells and infidelities were the only thing he could hear were there childish laughs shoot into his ear while the rambling conversations of a girls "period" problems soaked the walls, while behind him, a few Jocks were explaining about their bad LSD and Crystalmeth trip at Saturdays party. A.J. was in the thick of it now, and there was no way he could turn back or hide his ears from these conversations. He released the held air and felt the crowd growing heavier every moment, releasing a long and reeking stench that crawled up and the walls and entered the vent systems. Some made their opinions openly know about the smells.

"This fucking hall reeks man!" One Caucasian boy with freckles up and down there arms and face said, and others followed in, adding there comments which got intermingled in the crowds of growing conversations. Beside from the comments, the smell intensified as A.J.'s mouth filled with spit fill at the corners of his mouth, almost wanting to throw up. A.J. breathed out the ghastly fumes through his nose and swallowed his spit. He clenched his teeth and pushed his way through the crowd filling in from every which way as A.J. pushed through the crowds, but he had to grin and bear the everyday grind that was George Bradley.

Then while the first large mass of students headed down the hall, another large wave came from the History hall, which ran perpendicular, or a straight shot to Commons A. But with this crowd already holding up the lines, there would surely be confusion. A.J. rubbed against a few students' shoulders and began working through the amassing bodies. A.J. worked harder as more kids came from every which way. He was going hard to leave the hall as the smell of flies on fresh horse excrement followed him. At that moment, finally squeezing through the hoards of bodies, he brushed against a few people like the wind sneaking through the cracks of a window, and the fresh air of relief came when he finally found an opening out of that hellhole and left the stinking hall, but still felt it sticking on the inside of his nose, finally disappeared. He bit his tongue just to open his mouth, for he felt like he would die. Recovering from the smell, A.J. noticed beside him a high school cheerleader who had looked at him then turned, fearing that she might have angered him.

Out of kindness A.J. leaned down to her short length. "Don't worry. I won't hurt you." His whispers attracted her to look at his adoring face. She nervously laughed and spoke with courage.

"No, no. I was just looking. Theirs nothing wrong with looking, right?" She giggled glancing up at him batting her eyes seductively as she walked very closely, rubbing against his arm. Her face was clear of any freckles, virtually spotless. Her hands were tiny and hot pink nail screamed out at everyone. Her eye shadow had a loud glittering sparkle along the bottom of her cups and he didn't trust her friendly push.

A.J. tried to think about something else. He coldly moved a few inches away from her side.

"I like to look at people, and see what people want." She said.

But then A.J. caught the drift that this cheerleader was a whore. The only reason that another cheerleader would be after him now was because of Jessica. This cheerleader must have been jealous and wanted to break them apart—or just wanted A.J. to break *a piece off inside her*—but he was not going to do that. Her false appreciation disinterested him as he let her down bluntly without playing games.

"Look!" He said coldly, grabbing her attention. "I'm not single. I'm going out with someone." He looked at her one more time seeing the agonizing pain pop her lovely bubble of flirtation. She pouted her lips and her hair almost began to wilt from the rejection sadness as A.J. left her walking, by herself.

As he approached the commons, A.J. saw his table was already being occupied. He also saw someone else standing by the farthest table, with her hands resting against her jeans, and her adorable face looking out across the Commons with longing intentions, and her breast pushed out against her flaming red t-shirt, he would only be a fool to forget this beautiful girl.

It was Jessica, and without her cheerleading uniform. He didn't care what she was wearing; he truly thought that a beautiful woman could wear anything and give off sex appeal. Having a piece of her was truly heaven, and he almost questioned what did he do to deserve her? She turned her head, and her eyes glowed with joy when she ran to him like she was that day in the parking lot. Her face radiated with happiness, only when she saw A.J., and that was a fact. Throwing his books on one of the lonely tables welcoming her with open arms. Jessica wrapped her arms around his back, gripping his sweaty shirt, almost clawing through to his back with intensity.

A.J. held onto her sides while his right hand slowly almost tickling, down her sides and turning as he gave her buttocks a soft squeeze then a light slap. Her butt giggled from the unexpected gesture.

"I guess a hug wasn't enough?" Jessica's lips fell off his as whispered as A.J. still gripped her buttocks when he moved in for the kill. Their tongues started to move around each other's mouths like an Indian dance as there suctioning lips hid their exotic pleasure games. Nothing seemed to exist for them—sounds, conversations, time—had stopped, and the only thing existed was each other. But to end all good things, Jessica's lips crackled as their two protruding tongues were given a rest—as she wiped the bottom of her lips.

"I guess not." A.J. said sarcastically. He looked all around and saw that three anxious boys were waiting for him at his table. He massaged her hips as he spoke, looking into her loving eyes, not letting the moment get too he didn't hold contact with her for long.

"How have you been?" A.J. asked letting her go and picked up his book. The two started to walk side by side. They spoke very low, almost whispering to each other, admit from all the useless conversations throughout the commons.

"I've been fine. I missed seeing you for a couple days. Where have you been? I've been worried about you!" Jessica said out of sheer, pondering curiosity.

"I've been around." A.J. said turning his face the other way hiding his secretive looks, breathing out with a more relaxed untainted appearance.

"Around?" Jessica said. "What's around? You mean around the school or around the city? Tell me." Jessica asked expecting an answer. As they inched toward his table, he knew that he needed to accompany his guests.

A.J. felt that her curiosity was always a downfall, and that always ended up with him lying. He couldn't really honestly tell her what really happened, so, he gave her something to contemplate and delay her feelings.

"I got a job." A.J. said with a straight poker face and his heart on his sleeve.

"Really?" Her voice was filled with excitement. "Where is this job?" Jessica wanted to see if he was selling her the Brooklyn Bridge.

"Oh..." His mind ran a blank and was searching for ideas. "I'm working stock. You know, unloading trucks and filling out forms. It's a city job." A.J. was unsure about how long he was going to break her iceberg of questions. He was almost lying, but her large iceberg of questions that were blocking her mind began to crack and melt with assurance as she found out from the horse's mouth. She almost belched with congratulations as her worries began melting into sweet sugar of girlish feelings.

"That's great." She said tittering. "I guess we can go out on real dates then. Or when you get your license?"

A.J. glanced at the round clock above the tables and saw he had wasted five minutes. But with a grace of luck, the bell began to ring following with the chiming *bing* that let them know that the time had started for the lunch/class to start.

Before she could say another word, words she would have regretted thinking of A.J. said them for her.

The deadly chime of the bell sounded with another malevolent *bing*.

"I'll see you later. Okay?" A.J. said. The clamoring of footsteps and the passing of students became thin as everything in the universe began to start moving again—the solar system was expanding as the last and humming *bling* ended as kids became scarce and teachers were out rampant.

Jessica nodded and kissed his lips very innocent like, without the rudeness of her tongue and his eager hands touching her butt. Her lips were honey against his dry, murderous lips. After she released her golden lips, the two lovers decided to meet after school in the parking lot to accompany each other a ride home, *again*.

She willingly agreed and parted toward the other side of the commons. Shaking her hips past his table, she brought up her and hand waving as she flashed a bright big smile that she would never forget. Although she wanted to believe that her eyes were deceiving her she couldn't help but see Giuseppe, someone that didn't even go to the school was sitting at Chris's seat. Only she couldn't help but be surprised from the way the school was run. She continued on her way, shaking her hourglass hips and her small body looked like it was about to slip off—and the universe was in alignment—all eyes on the hips of an enchanting sorceress.

As soon as she disappeared around the corner, A.J. approached the table where the three had been watching A.J. and Jessica's little Kodak moment.

"I'm A.J." He said breaking the ice, but the lingering heat that was acting as if an invisible wall had made it impossible for them to respond. But after he introduced himself, Antony made himself known and after that the other two saw that he was a stand-up guy, Guido and Giuseppe shook his hand remembering who he was. A.J. remembered the cold, prepared death wish had and shuddered when he remembered the dull click from the blackened barrel nuzzling against the quarterback's throat.

Meeting each other now was good. This could form a respectable bridge of trust between each other. Seeing that there was no chair, A.J. stood pressing his knuckles against the table.

"Since everybody knows each other now. We can lay everything out on the table." A.J. said. All their eyes were on him. "I am filling in for Chris Mangini, I'm a stand up guy. And I was lucky enough to bestow such a privilege of watching over his assets while he is attending to business away from the school."

"But that doesn't mean I don't talk to him myself." He added.

Everyone looked at each other and nodded agreeing with A.J.

A.J. decided to introduce the soldiers to his product.

"We are living in a society that schools are becoming a place for profit, not for learning, I mean. The only thing that the schools are ever going to let us move in and out without any trouble, and it isn't drugs. Because, drugs are risky, a temptation to many in the past and a current epidemic that is not leaving our society anytime soon. It's been tried many times, but it never works out. Forgive me for sounding blunt that way is the easiest way to end up in jail. Not from somebody ratting anyone else out, it's the other way around."

The three of them looked at each other with confused expressions.

"But no disrespect to anyone that does. That seems like an easy way, but that's how friendships between partners turn sour from one deal. Some fuck is offered a reduced sentence, and our friends are on the hot seat because of a slithering little snake fuck. That's my bias opinion, but we'll still deal with the usual rackets. Prostitution, protection, and one more thing…"

He decided to get to the point without leaving them on edge any longer.

A.J. slung his bag from around his back laying it down in front of them. The three noticed his black pack, covered with dust from the unwashed floor as Giuseppe and Guido anticipations became sparked as they eyed his bag with a sort of fear. Antony barked, "what's inside that?" He said with blatant stupidity.

A.J. grasped the bag by its strap, flinging it to Antony with a light toss and caught it within a blink of an eye. A.J. reared his head back and flashed him his strictest expression, as if he was dead serious. If Antony would refuse to look inside his bag, their friendship and business operations would be in jeopardy.

With the bag still in his hands, Giuseppe and Guido were almost climbing the walls with anticipation. Their curiosities were begging to know what was inside his bag. As they watched Antony unzipped the bag, and peering into the bag they watched him stare long and hard as his face of tension became elated as he revealed a trusting smirk and handed the bag to Guido. Guido held the bag as if it was a baby gently holding it by the bottom of his pack. Guido's face turned to gold as he beheld the Norton Antivirus programs and the CD's with a dumb struck face.

As Guido handed the bag over to Giuseppe's eager hands, A.J. conferred with Antony.

"This is the last thing anyone, even a school system would not turn down. Only to sell this stuff, we need to find interested people with enough cash to buy this stuff. I want us to work very low key."

Antony scoffed puzzled by his vague message. "How do we let everyone know what we got?" He said with worry. "Who's going to buy something we don't even know two shits about?"

"The thing with business is. *You* have to make the public so interested that they would be kidding themselves if they didn't buy this stuff. What I also figured out is, people are always willing to try anything new be it drugs or a candy bar."

Antony looked into him and saw that he was on to something, and with an open mind, he decided to hear him out.

"Keep talking." Antony said turning sideways in his seat. He was giving him his undivided attention even though he did not want it—he was intrigued by it.

"What makes people more eager, is what they haven't been told about or what they can't have." A.J. added with intrigue. "And the only thing that *we* need to tell them, this is what *they* need. Everybody wants what they don't have or are restricted from getting, right?"

The other two turned and felt his last words hitting home. A.J. felt that he was getting somewhere. His finale was approaching.

"It's all about *wants* and *needs*. This new generation *wants* these CD's and we'll be the one supplying their *needs*. I tell everyone at this table that we are going to do pretty well out of this deal. Now, if anyone has any disagreements please say so now."

A.J. straightened his back rising like a great tower and he was just edging out the very last, fine details. This was the first brick to his concrete empire.

Now A.J. had worked through all of the plans throughout each of his classes, when he wasn't listening to his teachers. To gather all of his ideas down, he thought of a number of things that these three needed to do. All of them needed to personally spread the word to everyone, but implant it into someone so they could pass it on to the next person, but what they said would obviously be misconstrued as it was told to each person, so they expected a lot of bullshit to come there way.

What the students told he did not care, the only thing he did worry about was the fact that some teachers were bought off and others, like the tight-asses they were, were going to be a problem. "Burrow this into their heads that everyone had a price, and we can meet it. No one's soul is clean." This was a fact of life. Some people were good at hiding their weaknesses, like in an intense game of poker and some were very good at keeping a poker face. People were so good at lying that their whole life was based around lies. Only if the teachers' were so hardheaded that if money was not going to take them to be quiet, and look the other way. Violence would be the last option if they wouldn't listen, and when pressure was applied, people's poker faces would start to fold, and there strong wills would start to fold.

But this was taken into consideration, and violence would be the last and final decision. The gangs that were still on their payroll knew that Chris had not been around for the past few days, and would get cocky about not paying their dues. Their dreams of not owning up to their debts were going to be like the effect of undigested fast food—like lead in their heads.

Nothing would change while Chris was away, and A.J. had an idea to expand their business ventures, like their nefarious gambling, protection and his prostitution rackets. One of them would handle this, and would be in charge of reporting everything to A.J. Once it became known that they were carrying this product, students would be requesting for CD's and the Norton Antivirus programs. The only thing A.J. implored that the buyers be "serious about making serious purchases." A.J. also stated that they sell their products in a lump sum, getting rid of them all at once would send the police and teachers' blood pressure's sky high.

Without the interference of the teachers and the vice-principal, nothing would stand in their way. Everything seemed to be coming together; nobody could touch his carefully constructed plans.

Around them the surrounding crowds were beginning to thin out, like volcanic magma regurgitating pints of sprinkled metal shining the surface with a bluish orange. The noise of chomping mouths, lip-smacking students began to gulp down the rest of their food in a mass rush, leaving their crumbs and rubbish sprawled across the table with unfinished twenty ounce Pepsi bottles on its sides. The fizz had already been released, welcoming pounds of air, pressing against the carbonated drinks defiling every second of its flavor. It was almost time to leave the commons area and let the next bunch of kid's litter and desecrate the area benefiting no one—lacking intelligence to clean up behind them—then the crowds of students began shifting from their seats, floating from hall to hall, like a bird that had crossed it's own shadowed, paradox view of reality, unsure of any time, the students would then gather in a large pack. As if they were great migration of walking-talking birds, but were mindless, ignorant morons that did *nothing* but except to be handed everything.

A.J. felt different from the rest, and time seemed to catch up with them. The charming bell echoed its harmonious *bing*, sounding off its tortuous rapid fire ringing. Nothing made the kids angrier than to leave the only free place, away from stressful teachers pushing the boring assignments that made them hit the desk than the books.

As the massing crowds of students began migrating toward the halls like birds, A.J. felt blood rushing through his system as he told two of them to take one of the Norton Anti-virus programs to wet some of the bigger buyers appetites. And if they could showcase the program around, it would be beneficial to them. The last thing before he decided to clear out, until the next day they would meet was the matter of the prices that the Norton Anti-virus and CD's were. They did the math and understood their purpose for now. Today, they would spread the word, and tomorrow if they were approached with a deal, then they could the money that they needed.

Before A.J. decided to let them go and make their plans come true, he asked them a question that was totally out of the blue.

"Is their anyone that hated Chris Mangini or despised him? Anyone you know of?" A.J. asked. A deafening silence filled the air, although very dead, because it almost seemed that none of them wanted to answer him. A.J. did not doubt the countless people that were envious and hateful toward him.

Then as A.J. huffed out a long breath of discontent, he felt betrayed by their petrified silence—maybe, A.J. felt that this was none of his business, but he needed to know these things if he would have to *kill* the competition, or find a way to profit from them.

A.J. glanced at the mechanical time that he had been scrolling continuously, telling "it's quarter to one, let's move on." The clock had almost been laughing at him, teasing him every second—time is money, get that money." A.J. knew that the second group of kids was going to come around, and start to dig mindlessly into their lunch. He didn't want to be any later than he was, but he needed to hear his question answered. This might have put A.J. in danger, but he had no other excuse, except wanting an explanation.

A.J. sighed and began to speak again, breaking the cold silence in the entire commons. It was almost as if they were frozen inside a large hill of snow, chilling their once warm bodies, their veins filled with icy dread. With some freak occurrence, their icy dread began to melt, as the three felt comfortable to move in their seats.

"I guess that settles it!" A.J. said, rising up from the seat. "I'm sorry if I detained you from certain businesses. We all have schedules to keep, and tomorrow we'll discuss more…over lunch." A.J.'s smooth voice made them chuckle from his unnerving, sophisticated pace. Although they did not feel like chuckling, their hearts rolled over like an unturned stone as the three slowly departed, shaking their hands, thanking them for their time.

With a Norton Anti-virus package in Antony's hands, the three slowly departed from the table, their footsteps left haunting echoes throughout the commons, like crackling dead leaves. It almost seemed like they floated through the door pushing the metallic handles with a *CLUNK*, and then letting off the handle, they began to move with delicacy and shadow moving out of sight, like ghosts soldiers in the mist looking over their bodies hoping that someone would see them.

As soon as A.J. saw them disappear behind the doors and the bright sunlight glazed along the stony walkway was then kept out for good again. The large blocks that held the school together began leaving shadows as if the sun had not set yet nor had the day begun—not fast enough, although just slow enough for him. A.J. picked up his book and bag, and moved away from the tables.

A.J. contemplated many things, many which were too large to deal with right now—feeling his head was going to slide off his shoulders—he slowly moved down the center hall and past the guidance officers' room and watching his shadows travel across the floor. He felt his shadows talking to him, telling him to go this way, left, right, A.J. stared at the halls again and moved toward the next two classes before the end of the day.

It was in the car Antony's fingers were squeezing Giuseppe's ear, almost until it turned dark pink, and in his deadly grip it was starting to turn blue.

"What did I say?" Giuseppe yelled as his grip tightened, as Antony forced his head close to his ear, and gave a hard, quick underhanded slap with his left hand across his left cheek not hurting him, but just as a personal reminder.

"You listen and listen good!" Antony viciously whispered in his ear, and then proceeded with his viper tongue-lashing. "Let me remind you, don't give this fucking kid any ideas. You might cost us our asses!"

Giuseppe heard this, and screamed in betrayed agony, "I was just…"

Antony lowered his mouth, and then hissed into his ear, "Don't say anything to this kid! Leave that to me!" He threw his ear, and his whole head backwards, and his body flung against the backseat.

Giuseppe grabbed his ear out of pain, and then he groaned, feeling the

The Disintegrating Bloodline

sting of his ear leaving him, and the car starting up. They left, and Giuseppe had swallowed the pain, but he would not forget it.

Jessica took him home that very same day, but Jessica could not come inside, his house that is. She did not want to look dirty in front of his parents.

"So what!" A.J. said as an insane feeling of ecstasy surged through his mind, taking control of his lymph nodes. "You look pretty clean to me. They wouldn't care." He could not get enough of her, even if she had passionately stroked A.J. off while he rubbed her clit sensually with his middle and index finger.

"It's not that." Jessica said, pulling up her panties. "I feel dirty. I want to get a shower and look my best when I meet your parents. You know," she grinned, looking at him, "all those girly things we have to do." Jessica's tittering voice felt her stomach rumbling, but she knew it was all out of nervousness.

The thing was she had missed her period, and it frightened her to think of this. She didn't have a clue how her body was working; it felt almost as if her body was working against her. She did not want to become too worried about it, but she knew that after a while, all things would have to come to an end. With resistance in her voice, she told him tomorrow she was free to have dinner with him. He was glad and they departed with a kiss. A.J. did not want to leave but he almost wanted to go with her.

A.J. spent all night waiting on another call. But he did not get another call like he did the night before. This was puzzling for A.J. but it didn't surprise him, he had to start living by the phone calls now.

The day quickly turned to sunset, then it became night again, and another bright morning had welcomed A.J. to a fresh day with all its rays, and washing the sleep away from his eyes, but it would take a lot more for him to wake up. They had been discussing something at breakfast, but not directed toward him. He had a bit of trouble trying to awaken that morning as he had done the night before. He smiled, and acted normal. He felt safe and calm inside his own house but after he left, the pressure would rise in his chest, sending his heart up to his throat as if he could not speak in the morning. But, he had to grin and bare it.

His morning hunger faded away, very quickly, as soon as the food had hit his belly. After A.J. was done gobbling down his breakfast with an indescribable hunger, he scooted the chair back, grinding the nubs underneath the floor, creasing down his T-shirt, and approached the sink. On the other side of the kitchen, his father had just finished putting some more unclean dishes into the dishwasher, and he was just filling it back up.

Before Tony closed the door, he approached A.J. who was cleaning the runny orange color from his plate.

He observed his son, and felt that his son was acting like he was on the edge of a knife that he could not ease off of, flushing color from his face, and he wasn't his old self, something was different about him.

"Are you okay?" He asked, watching A.J. cleaning the dish and his keen ears had saved him a hammering, piercing sound sent off a wild echo that was too hard to ignore, was piercing the inside of his mind.

"Yeah. I'm fine dad." A.J. huffed letting the hot water glimmer across the plate as he began to dry it under the morning sun. His hands made movements with the sun glaring through the window lighting the sink.

His father adjusted his arm comfortably around his shoulders, nesting his warm arm hair around his young neck.

"Where were you last night?" Tony said rather uncomfortably.

A.J. immediately stopped scrubbing the dish as if the muscles in his hands had frozen from his father's words, being interrogated so early in the morning, taking him off his guard. Neither his senses, nor his brain was in tune to answer his question. His mind was scrambling for an answer, as his father's bull snorts were steaming from his nose, waiting for an answer. He was the bull when it came down to interrogation but A.J. got hold of himself, setting his mind into a calm mind state playing the Matador with his father's control.

A.J. finally came up with the idea, a plausible "story," avoiding the word, "lie."

"I went out with Jessica last night." He saw his father exhale a long laboring breath, although he felt like he had more to say, even though his harping should have taken him off guard, it proved to be a useless gesture he saw a sad bottom-of-the-barrel look swirling inside his artic blue eyes while his rather muscular formed body drifted along his life.

His voice was calm and assuring, and it was throbbing inside his heart so loudly he could feel the coursing through his system. "I want to tell you that me and my mother are here for you. You are growing into a man right before your very eyes." But his father had seen more than what he asked for—a reflected terror that it was blood red, glazing over his arctic blue eyes like that of a horrific battle.

"I want you to promise me that if you are ever in any trouble, just talk to me. Because we love you and care about you."

A.J. nodded, but almost lacked the courage to make a promise to his father, breaking that promise he would injure their relationship, and their bond. He looked into his eyes and saw that his eyes widened as if they were about to pop out of his eyeballs. But, with a charming nonchalance, he gave him a soothing answer that would either damn him later on or haunt him later in his sleep. "Sure dad! I promise."

His father's sweaty arm began to uncoil from around his cold neck leaving a sweaty impression that he could not forget. The two hugged, whole heartedly with no feelings left aside, they patted each other's back, and then went and hugged his mother goodbye.

A.J. moved away from the kitchen sink, grabbed his book bag, and made for the door. He waved to his dad and yelled him a farewell before he gripped the door handle and disappeared onto the outside world.

The sun was gleaming harder than ever on his small town that almost resembled a deserted complex when there were no cars, and all that were left was him walking down that miserable road, all by himself—it was a hard road but he had to take it either way. As A.J. made his way down the empty street, feeling bits of sun move across his face, he felt pity burrow inside his heart, not for his parents, but for himself. He pitied himself for not being able to share the best part of his life—the money, CD's, and his near success.

A.J. was just like any other boy, lying to his parents about deeds that he knew they would never approve of. But he needed to be extra careful, even on the phone. Even at school.

He did not want to put a damper on his day before it even started—but these feelings were impudent, futile to even think about, but were so close to his heart like the lies and the souls he had taken—he had the rest of the week to do that. It was quiet. Like any other morning he had been at his bus stop. But when that bus came, he began to already fade out the next group of classes, like the previous day.

A.J. was surrounded by darkness, as if a lampshade had been turned off inside his head, severing off all the main circuits leaving A.J.'s functions in a haywire. But as his eyes were becoming accustomed to the pit of darkness, he felt his shoulder being jabbed—even though it wasn't a hurtful jab, and then that prodded feeling returned again. A.J. lifted his head off the edge of the desk, and his forehead was red as if he was pushing his head against an iron grid. Swiping his head—he felt a sharp twinning *ping* as if a crooked screw had been jamming into his head. As he wiped his eyes, his mind was urging him to find out what the time was.

A.J. looked to the clock in the classroom, seeing that the second hand was slowly inching around the clock, as if someone had stopped it. But he knew that he had been in class for an hour before the first group of sheep went to feed from the troughs. A.J. scorned it, threw it a disgusted look, not expecting the clock to do the same, and laid his head back on the desk. But as he sighed something small and peculiar was pushing its way under his arm. A.J. slowly raised from the table, looked around and saw a folded note resting underneath his left shoulder.

He glanced on his side, and saw a note resting underneath his left elbow, and pondered if this note was for him. Who was he kidding, this must have been directed to someone else?

Although he wanted to believe that the note was for someone else, he glanced back around through the corner of his eye, watching him with direct eyes, telling him to look at the note. When A.J. slowly turned away, his hand began to unravel the note very slowly, unfolding the square, turning it into a rectangle, not ruining the edges, he made the rectangle turn into a small piece of note paper as a vague message that was no less than chicken scratch. He adjusted his eyes when he saw what the message said

HOW MUCH R YOUR CD'S?

A.J. scoffed considered this vague message an insult because they did not have the decency to wait until class was over, and give the teacher their time. Since this student wanted to know he didn't feel like he deserved an answer— "keep them waiting, and you'll make them go crazy until you finally deliver." Pulling his pen out of his pocket, he began to write an answer underneath his original message. He chuckled and when his teacher's back was turned, he handed the message underneath his arm, and felt it being pulled out.

A.J. saw through the corner of his eye that the kid had not taken him seriously. Because A.J. replied with

WHO WANTS TO KNOW?

The kid read the message, and with an insulted look began to scribble another message. His hand exaggerated with every movement. They did not break a single movement as A.J. saw the note being held underneath his desk, and he received the note, laughing at the sporting taunt, seeing that it was becoming less readable as his pen could scribble across the small amount of lined space

Tha FairY fucking godmother. SoMeonE who mite bee interested in your product!

A.J. saw this, and knew that he had had a customer, and he must have been pushing his buttons very well, but he was done playing these back and forth games.

He sparingly wrote another message with his dark black pen, scribbling intensely,

> Who am I speaking to?

and passed the note back to the boy. The boy looked down at the note again, and the pen scribbled faster than anyone could imagine. The note returned to A.J., and he read his response.

> I thought I was speaking 2 a business man? Why do you talk back to "the kid" Chris Mangini never would never disrespect me.

Upon reading the note, A.J. finally realized who this was. There was only one person who was called himself "The Kid." His name was Benny "The Kid" Jesowitz. It was almost like a rip off of Billy "The Kid," but he gave this name a whole new meaning. A small Jewish boy, who was tinier than A.J. was but had large muscles, ripped pecks, and a tough face, weighing in at about one hundred twenty seven pounds and half of that was pure muscle. He was a known troublemaker and a royal pain in the school's ass, not to mention all of the gangs in the school but was never tough enough to fight Chris Mangini's team. He paid him his dues, personally. He respected Gene, who he also respected because he was a Jew. He would always do odd favors for Gene and Chris, but was never seen around Gene's very own circle. You could say he was cut off from his group.

Taking this into consideration, A.J. wrote another response taking his time, making sure he was making himself clear, stating whom he was and what he wasn't going to tolerate.

> If this is the kid, why didn't U mention my Bosses name in the first place? Do you know who I am? I am Close to Chris and I don't move for anyone. I know you are respected—but respect me. I am A.J. and if you want to know prices wait till the end of class and we can talk

business in a civilized manner.

A.J. threw down his pen and looked back at the slow ticking clock. Only fifteen minutes had past while they were writing back and forth to each other. A.J. sighed in disdain, his stomach felt twisted, like a tornado that had been banging against the insides of his stomach, and had been trying to burst out of his stomach and sends his blood and guts all over the classmates. But he saw that it was the wrong time, which revealed that it was about time to go, the tornado like feeling had began to settle down, it calmed his nerves sending one last *thump* against his stomach.

A.J. must have been going insane and blind at the same time if he was reading and thinking that the clock was fifteen minutes behind. He packed his stuff and barely glanced at "the kid" wherever he was he would catch up with him.

Out of nowhere the bell rang, easing each student, giving everyone a breath of fresh air A.J. got a second head start on them walking down the halls as usual. As he treaded down the hall, it was quiet until he felt someone nipping at his heels. "Hey Kid, wait up!" A.J. slowed down for him and slowly walked beside him.

"I just want a few boxes of your product."

A.J. looked, and saw a small but rather punky boy that had arms that were shaking, twisting side to side—his misconstrued teeth gritted over his enamels—and he walked like a lurching hyena—as A.J. replied with sarcasm and continued down the hall, keeping his distance, "Oh really? I'm very a very busy guy, and I have a lot of customers waiting…."

"You don't have dick!" Benny shot at him. A.J. suddenly halted—all the bones in his body grew tense with murderous rage—standing near the entrance of the girls bathroom—he glanced over his shoulder with hatred beginning to boil over as A.J. waited for his monkey to get off his back.

"I went around and nobody has what I want. So why should I believe you?" A.J. felt this was all apparent. Like the addict that keeps begging him to give him a bit more of his "candy" but if this was the kind of fiend that kept asking for hits that he never paid for, but Benny was worse than a fiend.

"I thought you wanted to talk about business?" A.J. added with sarcasm belching the same line he had said to him. "Now, you know what you want you can't get, and by telling me that I don't have dick is also an insult. A serious businessman would hear a price, not blowing him off before he hears a price. Also mentioning names out of boastful pride is also a form of disrespect, follow me? Do you want to be known for disrespecting the wrong people?"

Benny was a stubborn son of a bitch that did not bend for anybody, and it would have been the highway for this dude only Chris had saved his ass, and he didn't want to be on his shit list. His secure voice made his words believable, and "The Kid" could smell a liar coming, and he wasn't lying.

A liar to him couldn't keep his act together, meaning that he would fidget, look down at the floor, or clench his teeth or bite his lip every once in a while. He couldn't tell by his tone nor by his eye contact because he had been straightforward, without taking a single break.

"He's not bullshitting!" "The Kid" thought to himself realizing he had found the right person to barter with. Only his eyes bothered him, as if he was looking into an enigma, wandering if his eyes lead him into a forest full of lost souls.

The long halls were beginning to load up with the same pack of kids, the hordes of mindless sheep scurrying to the troughs so they could fatten up and go nowhere. As much as he didn't want to brace the sardine hall, the odious smell of fart and armpit stench that could chip the linoleum off the walls, A.J. felt that this cutthroat would not get off him until he would give him an offer. He didn't trust him as far as he could toss him, but this jeering hyena—a laughing megalomaniac of purified muscle—decided that it was better to do this deal in front of his soldiers. He would have an excuse this time for his absence.

A.J. felt time slip through him, like strong liquor burning through his stand-alone mind, turning his fingertips numb, and gripping his hand into a fist he felt it sting as the deadly chime made A.J. know that lunch had started, and he was late again. He made his way down the hall noticing everyone, strangely enough, they noticed him on this seemingly monotonous day but he knew that something else was going to take place for him.

He saw his table occupied, heavily. He knew that they were going to give him shit about being late. Everything was in place, but he wouldn't need their opinion about doing business with this cutthroat that stunk of venom and glimmered like a lawyer's yellow teeth.

A.J. ran over to the table and sat in an opened seat throwing his bag on the ground he started with the usual *Hey*, then the *Did you guys find any customers?* For a moment, they looked at each other with there faces half cocked sideways, and minds off on a vague blur. They had nothing, and this could be a good time to say, fuck!

He looked at all of them, and knowing that no one wanted their product was unacceptable, because he knew that they weren't attracting any moths, or customers, to their new flame. While their flame hadn't even sparked fire, A.J.'s fire had been blazing, burning through the waxy candle, already attracting a customer. But he didn't know that his flame had attracted a *dangerous* moth.

"No one has found anybody? Nobody!" A.J. demanded.

The two of them shook their heads, but Giuseppe finally was the one who spoke up.

"I sold that one you gave me" After Giuseppe said his response, he felt Antony's eyes blazing against him, knowing that he should have talked, but he wasn't going to give him any problem with that.

His voice perked A.J.'s attention, almost as if his head was about to burst, his eyes wide almost popping out of his skull, and his energy was radiated by these words.

"Really!" A.J. said with a convinced voice. "Do they want more?"

Giuseppe's shoulders were lax, and he didn't want to lie, or lead him on. But the pressure of Antony's stare made him not care about what he said anymore, because the truth was stronger—even if it leads to their deaths.

"Well..." Giuseppe started to say then halted.

He then finally started to spit the words out. "They might think about it. I managed to get about three hundred dollars."

A.J. became excited by these words. No one would ever of dreamed of paying for a Norton Antivirus that was entirely absurd. If this was inflation, or just Giuseppe's extreme knack for business, he had to applaud, and thank him for it. Only the one that was more than furious was Antony, silently cursing him for having gotten A.J. ahead. But they did not show their disgust, taking it with a grain of salt.

"That's good. Who's the buyer?"

Giuseppe felt a lump catch up to his throat, as if he had been holding the words back. Everything became silent, blocking out the entire world around them.

"I'll tell you later." Giuseppe's lowered voice made him appear afraid, and that immediately lent to the subject at hand.

"Who is it?"

A.J. just looked at him, and his eyes searched his bodies and found his weakness—*scratching the neck, constant eye movement, and repeated glances behind the shoulder.* But he didn't know if he was really hiding who the person really was.

"Who is it?" A.J. persisted. Giuseppe just kept silent and looked downwards, trying not to look him in the eyes.

"Giuseppe!" A.J. shouted, with all the fury that all he could pull out from his heart. "Who is it!" Giuseppe's head turned upwards, and his face was filled with held back anger, but then when his mouth began to move and

The Disintegrating Bloodline

the spit had been cleared from his mouth, Antony broke in between their conversation, and said, "He's some bumfuck…"

A.J.'s head turned sideways, and his intimidating blue eyes sent waves of harsh messages, one of hatred and one of violence. But when he spoke, he definitely saw that he was threatening him.

"Is your name Giuseppe!" He said sarcastically with a bit of gruffness in his voice.

"No!" Antony shot back, and then added. "I was interrupting him because he forgot." Antony looked at Giussepe who added a small nod of approval, but was ultimately ashamed of it.

A.J. looked at both of them and saw two totally different things going on inside their minds. A.J. saw Antony's flaring eyes pressuring him, and Giuseppe was succumbing to his word. But what was he pressuring him not to say? While in the midst of all this, Guido was staying silent, watching with the same confusing face that he was going through.

"It's this dumb fuck from the city." Antony added, and A.J. stared at him. "He's no one important, but he's loaded so he will be sure that he will pay."

A.J. nodded, scratching his head, and then etching this situation in the back of his head, he moved on with the rest of their business. Even though he knew it had to be important for him to interrupt Giuseppe.

He decided to be up front with them, to show them that he had nothing to hide, like they did.

"I have reason to fear that someone that we might not like is taking an interest in our business." He let a moment of silence run through them, making sure he had their attention, and then he came out with it, "The Kid!"

At that moment, everyone at the table would have angrily shit in their pants from the name he had mentioned.

"You got to be fuckin' kidding me!" Antony yelled loud enough for the entire commons to hear. While a few kids turned in their seats, A.J. made a smooth hand movement telling him to calm down.

With that notion, Antony lowered his voice and began talking almost in a whisper.

"That motherfucker is a snake. I don't know how many times he had missed being buried alive by Danny Parello himself! I don't think selling anything to him is the best choice."

"We should hear what he has to say" Giuseppe said, objectively as Antony looked at him with pure distaste, as if vinegar had passed through his throat, and stayed, leaving him paralyzed with disgust.

"A.J." Guido said out of the blue, and definitely the calmer of the two. A.J. turned toward him, and motioned for him to speak. "I think that we should go with your decision—it will work out for us in the long run." A.J. nodded with compliance, but with that remark coming from Guido, and all of them began to argue.

In the midst of this useless debate that was going to accomplish nothing as A.J. slammed picked his fist up and slammed it on the table. The slam echoed across the table, like rolling thunder beating across the ground rapidly, distracting them from their useless argument. A.J. began to snort—building spit around his tongue—almost sounded like a train of anger that was beginning to overload on the overwhelming amount it was taking in.

He began to breath through his mouth again, his face began to smooth out again, and grew clouds around his eyes began to clear out for all to see.

"You can save all your bickering for later." A.J. said, levitating his hands in the air in an expressive, positive manner. "Because I told him to come by and discuss what he wants, I don't deny what you are saying about him is true. I got this shitty vibe from him too, like the prick knows everything. If he's not speaking our language, I'll brush him off. We might have to send a message to the Preps or the outcasts, see if we can get any buyers from their groups."

Suddenly Antony broke out with suppressed rage, as nothing else mattered to him.

"Don't worry. Benny could tell you anything that's up anybody's asses." Then Antony whispered without discrepancy for his honor, "the snake basterd!" Then they changed the subject.

The Commons began to settle down, after fifteen more minutes students began jumping around from one commons to the other as if demons ordered them to walk around like a homeless person, and beg for a dollar to buy more lunch. Just like mindless pigs' running back to the troughs to fatten up for the slaughter growing a gloat of a belly that glowed with that chicken-hearted yellow piss they seemed to bath in.

A.J. glanced around and saw that Benny was nowhere to be found. Maybe this was a good thing? Maybe he had forgot about the deal entirely? But he knew that was a bunch of bullshit.

Although another part of him wanted "The Kid" to buy his product, he didn't know when a deal like this would come along again. All he wanted to do was sell his product without causing trouble but trouble seemed to come to him like those moths hovering around the flame. Sometimes it was almost impossible to keep him cool from the heat that was pressing against him, and it was the middle of winter too.

As A.J. nervously spied the Commons in a quick glance, noticing students zipping back and forth, girls powdering their noses with white snow, acne faced losers getting their groins dry jerked—he clenched the table—as if lightening bolts were striking his insides over and over again—as if a monstrous spirit had entered his body and was banging his organs against the shell of his stomach. That same aching, thunderous pain he had felt before was back now, like an ulcer.

His eyes then jumped across the room and tapped the three with a quick prod—all of them beheld the most putrid and mischievous *thing*—a small but rather muscular figure strutting down hall—the three could have seen everybody else overlooking them with ease.

"Here he comes" A.J. said to all of them, with a dose of courage hitting him like morphine travelling through his veins at a doctor.

Everyone at the table had different opinions about him. Giuseppe had never met this caliber of vile scum while Antony knew him far too well, and Guido joined Antony's side on this. To Antony he was a descendant of Cain to him, a snake pre-born into evil, but that was in all in one's perspective.

"The Kid" slithered toward them with sleek and deadly force, alone like a snake waiting to shed its skin. Even though he didn't like A.J., he still did not like the fact that he was dealing with "The Kid," who would personally shed his entire face with a twelve-inch buck knife, but that wasn't to happen if "The Kid" was speaking dollars and cents.

As he came closer, Antony moved his seat away from "The Kid" as if he was a disease that would spread if he stayed where he was. He didn't trust that *snake* while he was behind his back. It would only take a second to spark his temper, and "The Kid" would cease to be.

He smiled with that devious grin, flashing his pearly lawyer teeth, and his eyes felt as if they gave off cancer, literally turning their hair gray with every glance he gave them, and A.J. rose from his seat to greet this cancerous being.

As A.J. sat down again, none of his soldiers extended their hands out to "The Kid." "The Kid" looked at them and gave them a smile. The three nodded, but didn't smile letting him know their distaste for him. Giuseppe, who acted out of sheer business, put out his hand, and "The Kid" shook it. Even if he was trying to be friendly, Antony and Guido took notice of this shaking their heads in disgust.

After the two finished shaking hands, A.J. bid him to sit down and discuss business. Seeing that there were no chairs around, A.J. felt that Antony and Guido weren't going to give up or find a seat for him. They weren't keeping a professional attitude about this, and insulting him only aggravated the situation. "The Kid" placed the chair, and rather comfortably, where his bodyguards would see them.

"Thanks for coming, and taking time out of your schedule to meet with me." A.J. said his voice was secure, almost too calm.

"Don't mention it." "The Kid" replied nonchalantly. "I apologize for the insult. My mouth seems to take over when I should use my head. You're very serious, and you are one to respect. But you are not the one they call *Death*?"

A.J. was taken off guard by the very last thing he said, and expressed it to him. A.J. saw his face and knew that *he* or this *Death* must have had a lot more influence than A.J. The name sounded more of an assassin trademark.

"You got me there!" A.J. said with a relaxed treble in his voice. "I'm not this *Death* character. This is a business deal, and we can talk business right?"

Benny's red face slowly became white red he released all that fear from his heart, and slowly returning to "The Kid" loosing some of the color in his flesh, and everything in his system started to go backwards. Almost as if his life had been holding him had been pulled out from under him, causing his blunt behavior to come out and appeared weaker when he mentioned his name.

"The Kid" had thought out everything and seemed slippery, like rain that seeped through a metal door with titanium casings. "I need thirty Norton Anti-virus programs, and ten CD's. It doesn't matter who it is, just music. My customers want to dance and get fucked up…you know, real smooth, and totally nutso."

A.J. saw his careful planning put on hold when he just remembered—the CD's were at his home, A.J. wanted to discuss a meeting place before he had figured out a price and oddly enough, numbers and math problems began to form inside A.J.'s head. Everything seemed so simple when he put his mind to the one subject that he seemed to detest. With the prices stuck to his head like Teflon, A.J. began adding the prices together, making it an even price. But something was bothering him, now and it was not Benny. It was this anonymous figure called *death*. Was this the figure that Antony did not want them to mention?

Was he a time bomb? Was he smart, methodical, smart, or was he thirsty for someone's blood? Was he the secret inside some demonic Pandora's box? A.J. couldn't answer a question that had no variable solution at the end of it. But did he really want to know? Something inside A.J. did not want to know, but the numbers began to fall into place for him.

The numbers began to fall into place like those Tetris blocks that A.J. had to send with a touch of a button in that Game boy game. The price began to form as if he had been maneuvering those blocks with the directional pad, but his mind was working over the time as he came up with about roughly thirty thousand, "without counting tax."

Since he looked like a big spender, and had an interest in buying a few boxes of his product he decided to increase the price of the Programs up to three to four hundred dollars as he realized that the more Anti-viruses he could get rid, they could ultimately sell.

"It's going to be a rough forty-thousand, easy."

"The Kid" was taken back, feeling disgusted by his figures, as if he was being cheated but he knew that if he wouldn't come away from this deal without any products for his customers, knowing he would have to battle for his prices.

"I knew that it was going to cost me something extra, but *thirty geez?*" His tone made Antony fidget, almost as if a choke collar of hatred and anger was stretching his neck, and a chain of restraint was pulling him to the back of the seat.

A.J. glanced toward Antony and gave him the most sternly shaking his head as his round dimple archaic face, and alcohol-like anxiety seething underneath his gums, eyes were surfacing over with impatience.

"I think of this as a win-win situation, because these prices won't matter how much you buy them for, but how much *you* can get for it. Because nobody else has these except for us, then you can sell it for less. You're a supplier, you can figure out the ends."

A.J. didn't know what was going to happen next. That other part of him wanted "The Kid" to refuse the deal, get angry, and leave. But he couldn't figure out why people wanted this product so much, even he installed it on his computer, but could not see what was so great about it. But it was big business, and he could do whatever he wanted with it.

It took "The Kid" a few minutes to really consider everything through. It wasn't the deal that made him consider it, but the words he used. His alluring, confident voice made everything seem okay, as if he was talking to him as a friend would. His brutally honest answer almost made him reconsider the deal, but like he said, it was a win-win situation. This Italian knew how to do business.

He knew that thirty thousand dollars wasn't easy to get, now a day. He had his own personal stash that he only knew about.

"Okay." "The Kid" said nodding his head. "I'll do it."

A.J.'s mouth almost dropped from what he had said. A.J. wanted to believe that this was a joke, and he waited for a smart remark, adding some insult, since he was investing thirty thousand dollars into a deal that felt slippery than a French whore who had just finished cleaning her pussy, reeking of wet grease and cheap Cologne. A.J. didn't like it, but he had to go along with it now.

Even though the deal felt full of holes, his words were his bond that stayed afloat in this shipwrecked sea of untrustworthiness.

"We'll arrange a drop-off wherever you want to meet at." A.J. combed his hair with his index fingers letting each individual strand of hair pass through the crevices of his fingers.

Spying the glowing numbers that read many messages, the time followed after it like a dog in heat. The glowing numbers read,

12:25.

This situation was more than perfect, his mother and father never came home for a lunch break. Everything seemed perfect, so easy.

"How about in fifty minutes? Can you gather that kind of money together by then?"

"Shit." "The Kid" said with sarcasm, glancing toward the clock, counting out the time in his head. "Sure, would it matter if I was a few minutes late, because that's a lot of fucking money to gather up." His eyes and body shifted with such calculation, trying to figure out what he was thinking, but he couldn't see through his soulless stare.

A.J. nodded with compliance, and felt a quick rush of power surge through his body, as if he was a puppeteer, pulling, jerking this schoolyard bully's every emotional string forcing him to do anything he wanted. The hard part was over, but he was not out of the woods yet. The last and hardest part was not yet set.

"But?" He added with an even sarcastic tone, as if the deal was not going to happen, with that smirk of a smile. "Where do you want to meet? We can't meet out in the parking lot, right?" His tone had almost irked everyone including A.J. to the point of bashing those pearly white fucking teeth into his skull.

A.J., who had kept his chilly rage under tight composure, a question needed to be answered.

With that question at hand, A.J. had an idea of a place to meet. A quiet, back door kind of area, somewhere easy and accessible, but not too far out of the way. A.J. just couldn't put his finger on the right place. A.J. leaned over and spoke into the closest soldier's ear and Giuseppe was asked "where a quiet, secluded, but not far out of the way place they could do business at" was.

Ripping out a piece of paper from his notebook, and closing it back up, A.J. handed him a pen and the blank paper in front of him, itching to be written on, Giuseppe thought carefully about what A.J. requested. Although many places came to mind, a more wooded area or a more convenient place stuck in his head more than anything else did. If seclusion and cover was his option, the woods were an excellent place. If time were an issue, they would have to double-time it to set up for the exchange.

Giuseppe picked up the pen and leaned low to the table with his face close to the paper. His eyes watched his words flow out of the pen across the page, noticing that his letters weren't too big nor too small, and legible to read. After he was done, he let the pen fall flat on the table and he began to crease the page just like A.J. had said to do.

He handed A.J. the paper without lifting it off the table for anyone to see as he lifted his fingers off the note, the folded page opened in his fingers, ready for A.J. to read and give his final approval. He lifted the note from the table, and slowly opened the letter, keeping the answer from all other eyes except his own.

A.J. didn't know this location, or where it was. Maybe it was someplace where A.J. wasn't accustomed to, but before he could make any final decision A.J. needed this to be approved by the rest of his soldiers. He creased the letter down again, and handed it down the line. He handed it to Guido. Guido took the paper, and opened the letter. He kept the paper low and under the table, where his eyes could only see it. Guido folded the letter up again, and nodded with a forced compliance.

Then he past the note down to Antony, and Antony took the paper with caution. Antony was always good at finding out all the nooks and crannies of New York. He handed it down, wanting to get rid of it as fast as he could, hands were tense, and relaxed as "The Kid" grabbed it from his stone like hands.

The three weren't disagreeing with him. They were just nodding to A.J. so that they saw their approval. There was a method to their silence, in which he would hear them bitch and moan on the way up in the car.

"The Kid" held the note as if it was sacred, and inside the destination wasn't concrete until he approved with the place. "The Kid" knew that they needed his approval, and he had to give him the heads up. His intense eyes grew by the yard as his eyebrows arched into flames of approval, and his stare was etched with intense pensiveness. His teeth bit nervously into his bottom lip so hard that he broke the skin off his lips.

He knew this location very well, but his senses began to warn him. He could see he was being serious, but something didn't quite win him over yet. There was the possibility of being lead into an obvious trap, where he presented the money, but then shot point blank range making pieces of brain and skull look like dripping Christmas ornaments, if he wasn't a Jew, that's what it would look like.

"Deal." "The Kid" yipped with confidence. "Can I bring someone to help me move this stuff?"

A.J. felt that over his calm securing tone "The Kid" was paranoid frightened about being lead into a trap. "Sure, bring whoever you would like. But they can't be showing any heat. This is business."

"Okay," and then "The Kid" dispersed, sliding out of the chair gracefully, and proceeded toward the front doors but turned left near the bathrooms, and headed right into the flock of students that were heading off to the other direction. He always kept his hands in his coat pockets, real shady like, with his head straighter than an arrow.

A.J. looked at the clock again.

12:30.

He knew that deadly chime would mark the end of the first lunch period. Then the sheep would start to gather in large crowds and head off to their next classes. He had to get to his house, before the bell rang.

But before he could speak, the deadly chime interrupted him. *Bing*! Then another five seconds went by, *bing*!

"We gotta go!" A.J. said over the bells taunting hymns. Then the deadly hymn finished with its *bing* as the sheep began heading back to their remaining classes or their stables in this case. A.J. did not feel like returning to those classes, and this gave him a good reason not to go. He grabbed for his books, pulled his backpack off the ground and slung it over his shoulder.

After A.J. slipped through the crowd like water travelling in between a beautiful woman's ass, he burst through the doors and the three hurried after him. They traveled down the steps of the school, and A.J. was not farther they fifteen steps away from the parking lot waiting for them. As the tips of his sneakers hovered over the curb, casting a shadow across the pavement, baking the cement ground, he was nervous, but it was like having sex—after the first time, you always know what you did wrong—but he thought he was never wrong because the sun would never tell him he was wrong. *"The son of the sun you are, and most powerful you are, born of golden dew."*

The secret location was not so much of a secret; because it was a place that everyone knew where people came when their mouths couldn't cash out for their word. When Giuseppe and the beasts entered the large foray of foliage, it almost looked as if they were in a fortress of large stocks of Bamboo and there was a large circlet where sunlight was peering through, giving light to this haunted forest. Only this would have eased A.J. and his crew they knew of the reputation built around this forest—they could feel the blurring ghosts walking on their hind legs, jumping from tree to tree.

They parked their beast of cars, a 1987 Subaru DL and a P.O.S. Ford Escort, journeyed for another mile or so until they came upon a round open ground. It had been cleared of all trees and grass had been growing in place for the trees.

"Not too bright, just enough shade, and every appropriate exit to leave from. All the back doors to a sweet deal," A.J. thought but didn't kid himself from all the genuine fail-safes that came with a good meeting place. They had only a few minutes to make everything go smooth, and in a few minutes everything could fuck up, like a broken condom on his dick—there were many things that could go wrong. A.J. didn't want that, and especially when it was time to sell his product, he was not playing around now.

But after they had set everything up for the meeting, A.J.'s nerves were starting to get the best of him—eyebrows arched, his lips were parched and scratchy, and his hands were rubbing against his pants as he was fidgeting on all sides. Although his eyes were the ones that gave him away—tapping his feet nonstop like a cowboy—A.J. nervously maneuvered the gun he had tucked inside his waist toward the front and A.J.'s nervous grip almost made him unpredictable and he was ready to pull out his gun and aim for the next person's heart if he was threatened.

In the midst, Giuseppe saw A.J., and approached him with a sidestep, "Are you okay?" A.J. didn't see him flinch or make a movement, but he could feel the ghosts in the trees, and he decided to avoid acknowledging these spirits.

"Yeah, I'm fine." A.J. was paralyzed with fear, as if he had been holding many conversations in his head, mumbling fragments of thoughts that he would have said earlier. A.J. gave him a smirk with his grimacing face of sadness.

Giuseppe spied the jet-black handle of the Llama that was pushing out of his pants, putting out his hand and said. "Let me have the gun."

A.J. looked down at the handle of his gun and spouted off in anger, "Why?"

"Because if "The Kid" sees that you have a gun he's going to get nervous. He'll expect it from me, but not from you."

A.J. felt that Giuseppe's words and intentions were true, and the pressure from these angry spirits A.J. decided to play along. A.J. slowly pulled the gun out of his belt-line by the butt keeping the barrel away from Giuseppe.

Giuseppe took the gun from his web-like grip and inspected the gun by checking the clip. It's small shiny clip revealed the greasy bullets lined up in the bright metal clip—inserting it back into the docking bay—then aimed into the woods at some pretend target, "this thing probably couldn't hit a deer point blank range," but in the distance he could see a small child's caved in face—jeering at him with the pale bitter eye socket staring—yelling without a tongue and then disappeared—her thin dry fettuccine hair falling off her head—around the large oak tree. Giuseppe blinked his eyes, and then lowered the gun, trying to grasp—if and what he just saw.

A.J. glanced to where Giuseppe was, and he watched him routinely sticking the gun into his pants. But A.J. saw his mind was on other things, and when he glanced to the never-ending thick trees—he heard a soft echoing squeal, and then his stress had been added on—making him swallow his spit—as if he was wearing a sweater in the summer time, choking him to the point where he couldn't breathe, and he didn't know how to take it off, and every time he moved his heart pulsated against his chest and sweat caked his supple forehead. But with a deep breath A.J. breathed in and breathed out, freeing his mind of everything.

"You don't mind if I hold onto it, right?" Giuseppe said, hoping that it was really okay with him. Sliding the clip back into the docking station, it made a soft *click* as he aimed the weapon away from A.J., resting his trigger finger against the side of the gun.

"Just for now." A.J. said breathing words through his teeth spraying spit from his now wet mouth.

"Yeah." Giuseppe said busily opening his belt line he steadied the gun where it could be perfectly safe and not fall through his pants and covered the gun with a quick swish of his shirttail and it was out of sight. A.J. could've done the same thing with his shirt, but whatever the case was he would *forget* everything. Then a rumbling echo pressed against the bark, shaking the very roots as the hoof beats of other beasts began to make their way through the forest.

"Get ready!" A.J. said. The sound came closer and closer, as he shook all traces of fear and anxiety from his heart.

Out of the foliage two small, shitty beasts that were obviously did not look like they had been inspected for more than five years, began lurking out of the trail of large foliage, their prostate tail pipes were swinging free and clear for all to see. Trebles of beats echoed against the windshields while long base notes hummed from the trunk. The second vehicle was the one making the entire racket, while the first vehicle was silent obviously being the leader. "The Kid" had to be in the first beast, guiding his extra back up to their place of business.

"The Kid" probably took the time to bring another car for no real reason at all. He just wanted to look tough or be expected to be walking away with boxes and boxes of products. They would be surprised by the amount of packages, and would have not a problem with their open trade.

The beasts' engines suddenly cut off with an abrupt halt, shaking the entire forest with an ear splitting *SCREECH* that almost split the entire forest as A.J. felt his courage exerting his fears out of his body—but he didn't forget that squeal. His fist clenched like a mighty rock forming from inside the womb of a cliff. Courage began to form his face into stone and his eyes had a deep will inside them.

The car-doors began to open with all the strengths of men. One was the driver, and the other was "The Kid." All he knew that "The Kid" or whatever he called himself was trouble. And like a snake the only quality it had was to be slimy—grimy, everything A.J. was not, but he could not be a hypocrite, because they were both in the same boat.

"The Kid" and the driver were talking to each other as they walked away from the vehicle with their hands tucked inside their pockets. Although the sun was shining, a whipping wind began to fill the very air they breathed, chilling their very bones. The others looked bothered by this wind shoving their hands into their pockets, hoping to block the cold air that was coming out from the top of the circlet. But A.J. was unaffected as his hands hung from his side letting the wind take its aggression on him as if grains of salt were whipping mercilessly against his skin.

As "The Kid" approached A.J. he pulled his right hand out of his pocket and smiled, greeting him with a handshake. "How *u doin*?" He said as their hands were like Teflon as they let each other's hands unwrap letting the wind brush against their palms. The hands of the driver were still inside his pockets of his leather jacket, but he nodded to him, acknowledging A.J. without having to shake his hand

"The Kid" eagerly wanted to get this deal over with, without wasting anymore of each other's time but his hand instantly dropped against his leg his breath made a misty smoke, though the sunrays would be warm and bright enough to light the end of a cigarette. The whipping wind couldn't tame the fury he was feeling, but A.J. wanted to get out of here before more time slipped by—and the demons would be narrowing in on them.

A.J. opened his mouth, sending a long line of smoke in the air. "I'm grateful that you could come and meet with me to do business. Go get the money." His driver turned around slowly, paranoid as he opened the door he pulled out a large overstuffed manila folder that looked like it was going to explode from overexposure. The contents of the folder pushed up and down against the bag, its durability looked beaten and its strings that held the flap were wearing thin.

Giussepe saw the package in the drivers' paranoid hands, and already made his way to the trunk.

"The Kid" saw the large package, and when it came closer, his eyes had then begun to feast on a box filled with black market Norton Antivirus programs with his mouth watered with the breath of stinking carrion. He wanted to get this over quickly, because the tension was killing him, and he wanted to be out of here, because this place was giving him the creeps. As Giuseppe approached A.J. with the box in his hand, "The Kid's" chauffeur halted two feet away from A.J. with the overstuffed manila folder.

The driver slowly marched toward A.J. with the beaten folder his gruff, shackled hand almost crumbled as he waved the manila folder in mid-air, and A.J. raised his right hand slowly—the driver looked as if he was going to pull it away from him, tricking A.J. into jumping up for it—as A.J. grabbed the manila folder from the driver's hands, Giuseppe handed the box to "The Kid" as if he wanted to be rid of it. As "The Kids" chauffeur took the box off his hands, A.J. nodded and finished with an "It's been good doing business with you." A.J. and Giuseppe left with the wind whipping against their faces and the sun moved northwards making shadow patterns against the ground. He said this as he and Giuseppe—his muscles pent with hatred as he slowly turned away giving "The Kid" and his chauffeur the cold shoulder. Behind them "The Kid" had already opened the package, and saw the boxes of programs and yelled with a resourceful, "Anytime!" and that were the last A.J. saw of him.

Although Giuseppe had to glance one last time he saw that they had already started toward their beast with the box in their hands.

Thirty thousand dollars felt like a lot, and A.J.'s fingers—who acted totally on impulse quickly unwrapped the thin beaten thread from around the metal latch as the bills made gangrene indentions against the sandy manila folder and opened the flap. A.J. wanted to see what thirty thousand dollars looked like, and if it looked any different than it weighed.

A.J.'s eyes beheld the glimmering stacks of bills looking never-ending as all their eyes beheld every stare. His eyes lost that glare when he felt Giuseppe trying to glance towards the bag. As he let Giuseppe glance inside the folder, his eyes sent an undeniable heat towards the bag like a child wanting to dip his hand into a pile of hot cookies. No one would touch this money until they would be protected by a safe haven, away from the car, and away from wandering eyes and ears.

Antony and Guido approached them with expectant looks, wandering what the money looked like and A.J. pulled it away before they ogled over it like women on a hot summer's day, nipples hardened against white T-shirts, and wearing tight jeans pants, making their asses pretty much known to everyone. Before they could bust a wet one,

"We'll split the product." But before they did that, they needed to count out the money. The four walked over to Antony's vehicle; Antony in the driver's seat, A.J. was riding shotgun, and Guido and Giuseppe were in the back.

A.J. decided to make this short and sweet, because all of them had things to do, and A.J. wanted to get home before his parents got their. "Since we have successfully made a fair amount of money on all of our parts, everyone has to split their own packages up so everyone here can sell this stuff on their own. I expect you guys to make your bread off the packages; you know what to do. We can expand on our rackets if we do this. But if I hear that anyone is dealing with drugs, I don't care if it's white powder, tablets, or grass, *you deal you die!*" A.J.'s gripping face made them turn sheepish whenever he had mentioned drugs, but Antony's cool face didn't really make too much sense.

"Now since I'm done spouting off," A.J. threw the bag hearing the package clamp in Antony's lap, just as Chris had done with him, he said with pride "Let's count this money." Their faces turned to gold, eyes glowed with avaricious excitement as Antony stuck his hand inside the package he pulled out five to six small stacks of bills and laid the crisp charred logs on his thighs, and counted the money in sinful bliss.

A.J. and Giuseppe was in front of his house a smell began hovering over A.J.'s lips, asserting its smell onto his clothes, and making a home inside his nostrils. For a moment he almost wanted to gag from the pain in his chest. Spit began to thicken and stick to his mouth as he tried to stuff this feeling deep down again, but they kept regurgitating on the inside of his mouth.

As A.J. began gaining control of his nerves again, he clamped his chest, feeling his heartbeat and that swift aching attack of the unknown. Then out of nowhere the driver's side door was being attacked by a tornado like wind that made the glass windows shake as the sun baked their skins.

A moment of silence passed through them, and A.J. was stuffing his money back inside the large manila folder, and tying the thread around the metallic piece.

"What do you think?" Giuseppe's condescending eyes scoured, and saw A.J. in a distant dream, watching him smile.

"What do I think what?" A.J. said, his brows began to rise across the plains of his forehead, now revealing a scar that rolled slowly across his temple like a blood red flower that grew, and somehow insanely persevering through the heat as if it had been quenching its thirst from an underground waterbed.

"What do you think about this plan? Do you think people are going to buy into this shit? Its just CD's, it's not dope." He said as his laughter burst out in a thunderous roar.

"It's not just CD's…it's a gold-mine, and our generation have been graced with the latest crave that has been deemed illegal." Giuseppe saw his scar becoming more prevalent when the sun began rolling across his forehead, revealing his long tread mark.

It almost bothered him to see how smooth and calm as a clam in a jamb of a sandcastle, and the castle began to show its flaws in A.J.'s sandcastle as if a bucket of seawater had come and seeped through and fining out its details.

"Elaborate" Giuseppe said without understand the faintest clue as to what A.J. was saying—a lost ship at sea—way out in left field.

"To you or any other *scafootz* out on the street it may be a CD. But look at the big picture here, it's not the CD itself, it's what's on the CD. The programs that we sell are deemed illegal from the government, and for them to be sold; they need to be burned onto the CD. That's just the way the government can put a choke collar on the market. Do you really think the President gives two shits about CD's? He knows that it's just business, and there's big money involved and for all we know, Congress who added this 28th amendment that all-distributing, marketing, and trading software on a Compact Disc is a crock of shit. They just wished that they had the idea that we are doing."

Giuseppe smiled, understanding everything that he said, but then something ironic popped into his head. It sounded so stupid, but he knew that he needed to get it off his chest.

"So, essentially, we're going to get killed over a bunch of CD's?" Giuseppe said with a grimacing expression but then remembered the woods, and what he saw and swooning in pain as he saw a scar next to his temple.

"What can I say? We might get caught; we might get away with it. It's all ahead of me, I can't tell you what lies ahead for us. All we have to do is do our part, and hope that we survive. Survival is what it is all about." But before they lingered a minute longer he needed to know something. The unanswered question grew in him like a sickness and the only cure was for him to get it off his chest before it clogged his veins, cutting off his mind and choke the very well of his sanity.

A.J.'s words flew from his mouth like the spit that shot out of his nose, floating in mid-air he spoke as if another weight had been lifted, but something was replaced by it.

"How did you get into my house?" A.J. said. Giuseppe turned his head away as if he was wasting time thinking about the answer.

Giuseppe's head returned from the momentary delay, with sarcasm, "I'm not telling."

A.J.'s head jerked back from the insult, and quickly realizing he was joking around, but his stern expression—tense muscles that were pulling at all his tendons—weren't kidding.

"Come on, you know how you did it so just tell me how you got in."

"Why should I?" Giuseppe's face was gleaming with that childish *I don't give a fuck* tone that was refusing to give up his secret. Even though A.J. admired this, but time was money, and now he couldn't waste another moment waiting.

"Why should you?" A.J. replied with a scoff, his stare colder than dead man's hand, "Why shouldn't I just take back my share of the money I just let you have?" He managed to con his way into his mind with the one thing that would hurt Giuseppe—his wallet.

"You know what? Don't give me any money if that's what going to make you feel better..." Giuseppe mockingly waved the money atop of A.J. as if he had no use for his money. But A.J.'s eyelids widened as if wooden splinters had just disconnected his brain making his eyes pop out of his sockets.

His voice rose as if someone was lightly plucking the strings of his patience "I just asked you a question, *how did you get in my house*!" Although he hadn't raised his voice, he was getting the point perfectly clear that he wanted a straight answer.

But when Giuseppe noticed that A.J.'s voice no longer belonged to himself, he thought him unpredictable, although he had his weapon, his ego wouldn't let him back down from an argument, somebody had to end it before it stretched on further. He was already exhaling smoke from his nostrils like a bull and his eyes were as a rabid dog possessed by boundless infectious hatred in his loins, and all the ingredients that made him powerful but deadly in every way. Only one of them had to end this tense argument, he decided to answer his question but wouldn't let him be teased.

"Alright, you want to know?" Giuseppe said as if he was in defeat.

A.J. saw his serious face peel off as he finished the sentence with his regular *know it all* tone. "How do you think I came in?" He leaned his head forward, and then continued. "I opened the door." A.J. didn't know if he was joking or being serious, he couldn't tell by that insane smile that was his personality. That just confused the shit out of A.J., and he didn't know if he could be trusted.

"What do you mean?" A.J. asked while he began to feel the heat finally start to affect his cool patience starting to affect his armpits. The ache that just seemed to fade away and then resurfaced when he had to play these mind games, which infuriated A.J. because the piercing pain began to snowball over his conscience. The ache that secretly pounded against A.J.'s skull instantly faded away like the chocolate particles finally dissolving into that milky corner where he didn't want to think about it but the spoon that stirred the enigma—the unknown force between reason and irrationality, sanity and insanity, anger and love, the devil and God, power and fear were just things that were twirling around, haunting him with every moving ripple.

"You mean you just walked through the back-door?" A.J. wanted to know more. "That's it." He grabbed the wheel pissed off, looking like his was finishing pushing smoke from his ass. Guissepe could never joke, nor talk to him when he was pissed. Because it was a lost fight with him, because it was like trying to force-feed him food and A.J. would spit it back in his face. He had guts, but his anger seemed like his faults. Although he never uttered a real threat toward his life, he knew better than that.

But before he finally left, he needed his gun that Giuseppe had kept in his pocket when he and "The Kid" had met for the last and only time. Although he would have plenty of times to speculate, there would be times for him to sleep. Now he wanted his gun.

"Can I get my piece back?" A.J. said with his hand out, making more than crystal-clear for him to understand.

Giuseppe looked around him and said to him "Yeah!" Then in a glorious mystery Giuseppe pulled out A.J.'s piece out of his shirt. His shirt revealed half of his fairly muscular ribcage as he faced the Llama butt out to him as if it was a sword that had been sinking into the depth of his quicksand pants.

A.J. retrieved the weapon, arching his hand as he gripped the black metallic pistol, feeling the hammer lock press in between the soft spot of his hand as he gripped the rest of the handle. And in that fleeting moment— where everything in reality keeps going—Giuseppe let go, and then said, "I think you need to know something."

A.J. looked at Giuseppe, whose face had become paler every second. A.J.'s face was in shock as he said, "What's the matter."

Giuseppe was frightened, and when he opened his mouth, he looked like he was about to die before he even said the words, but then when he started to talk again, "I want you to know…" A terrible silence passed through them, and his paralyzed state kept him from vocalizing what he wanted to say. "That…if you don't see me anymore, I want you to know that I was never dishonest to Chris or you."

"What are you talking about?" A.J. demanded, not knowing how to respond to this ominous gesture.

Giuseppe looked at him, and with that sour look of despair on his face, which said everything. "I'm talking about the fact that war is brewing, and like it or not, blood will be on your hands as well."

The Disintegrating Bloodline

"What are you saying?" A.J. retorted.

"What I'm saying is," He took a deep breathe and then continued, "watch the others."

Filling in the blank space of air he looked at him with his blue eyes—now filled with real first time fear, and then said, "Is it *Death*? Or Antony and Guido?"

Giuseppe breathed in and out and then said despondently, "The others, I am positive about, but *Death*…he's unstoppable. He could come at anyone any time."

Giuseppe sighed as if his mind was carrying a thousand pounds of lies, and his eyes became saddened, and it dragged him down like a ball wrapped around his legs and it was pulling down into a puddle of secrets, riddles, and enigmas.

"What the hell does he look like then? Is he "The Kid?" Is that why you didn't want to say who he was?" Then as if he was going to strike him Giuseppe's voice rose from the bowels of his soul.

"I don't know who he is! And I sure as hell guaran-fucking-tee that "The Kid" is not *Death*."

Then A.J. interrupted, "How the hell couldn't you see him? What is he, a apparition?" A.J. refusing to believe the fact that no one could keep a name withheld from anybody, but with the situation in the woods, anything could happen.

Giuseppe wanted to find the right words to describe him, or it, in this case, a thing.

"I don't really know if *he* is a *he*! I don't know if *Death* is even human."

A.J. sighed and raised his fingers across his temple rubbing the ache that stretched across his skull. "Is he such a mystery that he doesn't have a real name? I know people have nicknames."

But when the ache in his head started to deflate like a popped balloon he returned to normal again. Then after he closed his mouth, and like an opera singer who had been struggling with his vocals he spit it out full blast.

"Like I said before, he's not just apart of the gangs, he also has done several works for one of the families, but his activities have been M.I.A for a while, but I doubt he hasn't stopped his activities for anything."

Then in an ironic tone A.J. spouted, "Elaborate!" Giuseppe gave him a remarking *touché* smirk.

Giuseppe's heart collapsed when he had to muster up his last bit of dignity and describe *Death*! "Person, difficult to say," because he "liked to meet in dark alleyways. Like a kidnapper," *Death* pulled him out from the sidewalk on Mulberry Street. In a blind rush Giussepe pushed his hands away, and started to move. But as if he was entranced Guissepe heard his deal, but never saw him.

What the most fucked up thing was the fact that the sun barely touched his face. He had an arch above his lip, almost like a blade cut. Although his face was shadowed, he resembled him. And this was in the middle of a New York busy day, on fifth and seventeenth.

To Giuseppe, "he was a shadow that ran across the city walls that New York dared pay attention to," and "he seemed to have these rather charming attributes layered under a deep seeded anger that resisted to be stuffed under the rug."

"I never saw his face!" Giuseppe said feeling his head tip back, and fell against the seat like the titanic in her last few minutes of glory before it finally sunk into the abyss.

A.J. watched his every meticulous movement, trying to see through this terrified sack of shit covering his brown-nosing face with his large, mountainous hands. As his mountainous hands slide down his face, he needed to give him an answer.

"The only thing I could remember about him was this scar." Giuseppe said with his face all flustered and run-down.

"A scar?" A.J. said with a bright gleam, and a spark of interest ignited his curiosity, as his ears sharpened like a knife. "What kind of scar?"

Giuseppe rubbed his hands across his temple and down his lip.

"Yeah!" Giuseppe shouted, "a huge fucking scar across his lip, and one across the brow of his head. Like someone dropped him or something." Giuseppe began to feel his chest pulsate with every breath he took as his head was ripping in half as if Beethoven's Ode to Joy was torturing him like the main character in the movie *Clockwork Orange*. Only if he could get that goddamn racket out of his head maybe he would feel better—but he knew that it was a drumbeat before the final purging of the sins. But before he could press his fingers against his head another minute longer, the pain began coating his mind with layers and layers of petroleum jelly that would ultimately eat through his brain and leave him like a vegetable.

"Does this explain what I'm trying to say!" Giuseppe barked and then laid against the seat, filled with fear for his life, and A.J.'s as well.

Although as A.J. watched him spit out his answer a warm feeling of compensation surged through his body and a warm zealousness tried to paint a picture. He tried to imagine the person's face—no eye-color, and no clue of what his nose looked like, but everything hidden behind the shadows with a scar above his lip was far less daunting because of the less than average details.

A.J. decided to let Giuseppe go, and he felt like he was just unconcerned, bullied, or ticked off, and it was better for both of them.

"Thanks." A.J. said sincerely as he felt a warm bubble rise against his chest.

Giuseppe looked at him and felt his tongue become untangled as he opened his mouth like a baby. "You're welcome!"

"Don't worry about it. I'll see ya in a day or two, okay?"

A.J. entered his home, and leaving the curtains open he went to his room, and fell asleep. Knowing that he had his chance, and he did not regret what he was doing was more than fine it was grand, as October came and went, and November came in at full blast. He accepted it, and relished what he was doing. Living for today and dying for tomorrow.

Chapter XI:

"Bleeding Hearts and Runny Eggs"

Before everything went down, Gene had called to warn Chris of his findings. Their contact had some valuable information regarding the war of the families, and some important news of his long lost cousin, which was detrimental to handling the problems between the families. Although his voice sounded like he was truthful, Chris could tell Gene was lying, but he took it with a grain of salt, and knew that his shaky voice (pretending to sound upset) gave everything away. But Gene had to cut it short, because he had to go to Queens to see someone, and the two ended their conversation, in which he felt it would be their *last*.

Now that he didn't need to hear any of Gene's bullshit, he had felt a traitor was arising, and he never wanted to admit it, but knew that there contact was dead or hadn't existed at all. Gene might have been looking for the perfect excuse to trade sides and leave his family, but he knew sooner or later, and if the ones that were pulling the trigger would do him the honor of not killing his wife.

Chris didn't think ill of Gene or trash him even in his own mind, because anyone would do the same thing, given the right price and the right time, a person was always going to betray people, it was human nature. Falling inside his most comfy lazy-boy chair, his neck bones began to feel like jelly, causing his head to fall back lazily on the chair. As his eyelids were closing over his sight—blurring, distilling his vision of the wall, as the voice began to speak through the chipped ceiling *"The end will greet before you meet!"*—what would be the last time he would feel comfortable again. As his eyes began to turn into the back of his head, he felt a small lightweight object landing inside his lap.

Feeling this small object in his lap, he cocked his head, and his eyelids saw two doughy hands reaching out of the small-layered tablecloth that was making low oogling and crying sounds. He gently grabbed the blanket, holding it as if a feather was between his nimble fingers, and he brought it close to his chest. Looking down inside it, he saw his young six-month child Dino Mangini—fat face and chubby body—wrapped inside a small blanket.

His small wrinkly face gave off shiny glow, more than any white diamond resting inside any precipice. He had a cocky face to go along with it, as if he was saying, with his cocked head, "Yeah, I'm here. You made me, so you better get used to me." Chris wanted to talk to him like he was a person, but remembered that his child couldn't even speak yet, but their eye contact took away the words.

"Don't let anyone get one over on you. You promise."

Dino's eyes were telling him that he understood, but he let out a soft coo that almost resembled a pigeon, and his eyes light up at the sight of his father. It was like a small baby lamb staring into the eyes of a ravenous wolf that was ready to eat him up whole. But this lamb wasn't afraid of his sharp teeth or his claws, and it was as if the two suddenly became a pair, just like Chris and his son. So, like the lamb and Chris the wolf began to drift into that deep abyss that to cave in his eyes, tumbling into the darkness, he felt his eyes roll into the back of his head, and everything faded to black.

Not too long after that, Dino's eyes felt his weight over his eyes, and like that lamb resting against the wolf's belly began to close his eyes, he fell without a sound asleep into his own world next to his father.

After what had been about a half an hour that the two were resting peacefully, Chris felt the sun's penetrating rays that poured through the window, and woke him up to the sounds of the city calling to him. The honking of the horns, the common pedestrian yelling obscenities and in between that the silence that urged him to wake up. His eyes met the dark paint chipped ceiling as if it was a blurred vision of a pot-head, waking up from a long night of tripping, not remembering anything else after that. But the one thing he knew was his son was missing; he didn't feel him in his hands anymore, and he was glad.

Feeling like he was in a freakish dream, he pushed himself out of the chair, and positioned his feet on the dirty faded ground—as it blinked like an old fashioned computer screen. His body was like one big floating jelly and nothing he could do to get rid of this pounding headache and it attacked his pulsating organs sending him—grabbing his side, and then proclaimed, "Where the hell am I"

The thick walls even began to do the blinking as well—revealing his wife who was standing over a steaming stove—mumbled under his breath--walking around this nexus of his faulty mind—as if he was the living dead, rotting away his entire life searching for some source of his food. His stomach grumbled, urging his brain to get food to feed his stomach.

Although when he thought it could get any worse, his wife's humming woke him up. It was an old Sicilian sonnet that he had always heard her sing, especially, before she fell asleep he heard this painful song being sung.

He approached the kitchen hall, and saw his wife focusing every bit of her attention on that steaming pot. Her long beautiful dark hair never got in the way of her cooking, and even if she was wearing a plain old nightgown, he loved her in anything she was in. Her small fragile body didn't interfere with her large natural breasts. They were ripe all year long, and he got his use out of her all the time. He leaned against the side of the wall, and took in her dark and beautiful song, with all the sorrow and deep affection she could muster. He closed his eyes, and could see his downfall before him.

Her singing rose like the climax of a fickle opera woman, as if she was singing for him, and the city was just the audience salivating like dogs just to listen to her sing with her beautiful, clear voice. He also had a natural companionship with her; it was like that kind of relationship where you don't have to say a word, and that person will know what you are about to say. It was like fate for him to be with her, and that made it easier for him to leave without saying goodbye.

She didn't sing for long as she slowly turned feeling Chris's presence spying on her. She turned, revealing her long beautiful face as a certain glow in her eyes made her blush as soon as she saw him spying with a watchful eye.

"*Ciao Bella!*" Chris said sneakily, clapping lightheartedly as he gave her a devilish grin.

"Stop it!" Francesca screamed at him, waving him away with her right hand as if she had been caught in one of her operatic practices. He jumped off the wall, and approached her like an alpha male lion that and curled his hands around her sides, she slapped them away, playing with him childishly. But her resistance seemed to encourage him to grab onto her sides even more, and like the female lion, running from her mate's every single attempt to jump on her. She continued to stir the sauce as if he wasn't behind her, teasing him with her round mountainous butt rubbing against his crotch. Then his hands became more curious, moving from her sides to the back of her rolling butt.

His hands gently patted her large buttocks, and they jiggled like a small bowl of green jelly in his tight grip and when his fingers fell against her butt, he had the urge to squeeze them. Out of all the gold and riches in the world, it wouldn't mean as much than his supportive wife by his side, raising his young son while he was out milking the streets for all they were worth, and in return he made sure his wife and child were satisfied. Of course they didn't want his money or power, they just wanted him to be there for them, and that was all he could give them, his love and diligence for this little bit of time.

But that wasn't all he left them with, but he couldn't tell his wife what it was yet, that was until he died, which would be very soon if his assassins wouldn't have killed him.

"I need some things at the store, could you run out and get some flour and some milk, and some things for Dino." Francesca said busy in her own world, stirring the pot of sauce that was bubbling faster than Chris's blood.

Chris's heart stopped, and like a wick to a flame, his anxiety lit on fire as he heard those *fatal* words applied to the wind, and scarring his fears. He watched her stir the pot of sauce even faster—all the meat and the spatula tinkling against the pot—accentuating only those clinking sounds—his one-way trip.

The thought hit him faster than he could have imagined as Chris's body retracted off of Francesca's, only to feel rejected by her straight forth, every day question. "Like what?" Chris replied, hoping that he could talk his way out of it.

His hands fell to his sides as he moved away from her backside, as a few strands of her hair went flying out the open window, staring into a bright and painful reality that had been his punishment.

"I need some eggs, some bread, *hard* bread because that's always the best," as she continued to run down the list of food in her brain, he began to zone out momentarily watching the street becoming chilled into a long cement glacier that no one could penetrate. He saw that the sun was out, but the heat could not warm the icy wind that swept throughout their apartment. He wanted to close it, but he wanted to study the icy street a little bit longer, and see what he was missing, and the only thing that was missing to him was loyalty and friendship. "Where did it go" He wondered, "Who is going to turn on me next?" He bit his lower lip and continued to watch the street with all its mystery, and all its blood that was seeped in that concrete.

"What are you doing," Francesca said, who had turned her attention away from the pot for a moment—staring with bubbling confusion—trying to figure out what was wrong with her husband. "Are you dazing out?"

His wife's voice secreted happiness as if she was in heat, and he leaned his arm out towards her. With one quick jerking pull he reeled her into his body, like a fish caught on a rod, he held close to his chest never letting her go. "No, I'm just thinking… that's all," Chris clutched her sides in a protective manner as if he didn't want to let her go.

"About what?" Francesca said, whose lips were quivering with fear as she placed a hand against his face. Did she really want to know what he was thinking?

As Chris clutched at her sides even tighter, the blood in his veins began to increase the speed, feeling his large heart beat through his chest and against her back.

"Nothing." To his surprise, Chris also felt a quiet pain lurking in his heart, like a shadowed beast that had remained hidden inside his heart, clothed by the darkness of his torment and willingly clawing at his emotions as if it was a fine antique sofa.

Although, he didn't feel this beast lurking inside of him anymore, it was just his heart beating against her chest, and for a moment there body and soul were then connected. Then, with his wife locked in his seductive grip he began massaging her vagina. His large fingers sent her emotions sky high without actually penetrating, as she started to moan, and she bit her lip sensually as she pushed her body against his crotch. She closed her eyes as she then forced her butt against his crotch, letting go of the stirrer as half of the wooden spoon sunk into the bubbling sauce.

Francesca gripped his back, and dug her nails into his back as his fingers continued to rub for an endless five minutes as she pushed his hand away and just held each other closely. The kitchen was beginning to feel like a sunroof and as the lust climbing the roof, Chris, relinquished his deadly grip out of her box (even though he would have gladly taken this opportunity any other time) didn't want this now; he had too many things on his mind, and his wife was in need of food.

He slowly moved away, feeling her resist his departure, pushing his hand back on her crotch, and she had already finished. She kissed him, "You be back, or I'm going to have another kid without you."

Chris scoffed, and then headed out of the kitchen—past the small wooden dinner table and towards the coat rack, standing before the chipped brown door. Opening the door by the silver handle, he felt a swarm of dust brush against his cheek like the whiff of a thousand-year-old coffin that was finally unearthed from the middle ages. A stink that would have been for the people who actually opened it having to endure the smell of the mid-evil carcass, and waft in all the grade A cinnamon putrid that came inside a package deal of a coffin.

Looking about the closet, he saw an array of coats that were pushed together like an over filled club sandwich with all the lettuce and the meat falling out of the hoagie. The coat tails were like the dressing splurging in between the bread while the necks looked as if pieces of lettuce were pushed out in the front of the sandwich. A speck of moss stood out to show how the dust had become so attracted to the cotton material as he flipped through a few shades of brown overcoats, passing all the other jackets, he came across a jacket that he had always seen, but never cared to wear it before. It was a gray jacket, almost like one of those hand-me-down brands from those corner stores that got it for cheap, and one of them had suddenly ended up in his closet. He felt like he didn't need a heavy coat since the sun was out, but did not want to take the chance of catching a cold from the brisk wind.

He grabbed the coat and examined it, pressing against his chest, "Oh, what the hell." He whispered, and immediately took the coat off the aluminum wire. Sticking his hands through the hole, he smelled the stale crusty odor that lingered off the coat, but continued towards his own room. Leaving he door open, he approached his closet on the far side of the room, right next to the window, and below was the fire escape, which lead toward the alley in both directions, east and west. That's what was so great about New York because any path that you took could lead you in your able destination or to your death.

When he looked into his closet, it was like he was staring at a neat row in some uptown shopping store that divided the pants and the shirts all in a neat isle. He always made it a point to keep his closet organized, and his wife always helped if he had been focusing his attention somewhere else. Underneath the clothes was a pile of shoeboxes, all saying *Nike* or *Reebok* tennis shoes on it, while to the side a box named *Georgio Brutini* stood out. He needed that one as he leaned over picking up the box that said *Georgio Brutini* and positioned it in his left palm as the weight of the box felt like a mass damper and the box wobbling in his palm was the large concrete brick.

His right hand hovered over the box as he began to peel the top off and what his eyes beheld a small white cloth neatly wrapped around something large—like the shape of a gun—as he hovered his hand for a moment as he laid the *Brutini* box to the side and examined it for a moment. He sat on the bed, and examined it a little longer.

"What could it be?" He muttered to himself mockingly, tricking himself into believing that it was not a gun, but fell through like a ton of bricks when he *almost* believed it. He let out a long sigh as his hands dived into the box, holding the small cloth as if it was the bread of life that Jesus broke at the Last supper. Chris thought this situation was so ironic in his case, and he couldn't blame anyone except for *him*. God didn't really want him to be this way, and for his disobedience, he would accept it what he couldn't control.

Slowly unsheathing the cloth, he slowly found out that the outline had shown more than he wanted to see, and the large metallic object shined as a large .45 caliber pistol, a classic model, which dealers didn't very well sell anymore, a true and deadly beauty it was to anybody that owned it.

The pistol had a glimmering effect as he shifted the pistol inside the greasy cloth. The cold handle became very hot in his grip as he let the greasy cloth float and twirling back on the bed like a falling leaf, leaving an indention in the air, as it landed on the bed. The gun began to clamp inside his palms as if his hands were made for *this* exact gun, and strange it was for that matter, because when it wasn't loaded, it was a lot lighter. He raised the gun—the steel round barrel gleamed at the window as the sun shined along the steel metallic slide. Resting his finger against the trigger, he pretended to pull the trigger, making a small popping sound with his mouth that was almost above a whisper. He turned it toward the wall, and did it again.

The rays glazed over the gun as cinnamon would be on a sweet doughy bun and as they bounced off the metal and leaned across the floor like a shadow creeping out of the corner and saying hello in it's shadowy form. Pointing the gun towards him, he examined watching it more closely, as if he was supposed to find meaning in the cold piece of steel that was resting inside his hands.

"Bullets!" Chris muttered to himself as his thumb searched around for the small pixel button that felt rough almost like sandpaper as he pressed his thumb into the pixel releasing the clip onto the bed. The clip was lifeless when the gravity had her way, and landed lopsided like a beached whale as the gold hollow tip bullet gleamed with a sinner's smile—rippled along the top—and shined like the desert sun.

Picking up the clip with his free hand, he traipsed his finger up the clip. "Fifteen shots." He muttered to himself, as if he was reminding himself how many times he could be spared from the big D, death.

Chris, done with what he was seeing, he leaned the gleaming .45 pistol sideways, and slammed the long clip into the gun sounding off a harmonious CLICK! But before he set the gun back down in the box, he began to feel a longing towards the gun as if he didn't want to leave it back in the box before he went to the corner store. The thoughts of pain entered his mind as a hard drilling bullet pierced his skin while the pitter-patter of hitmen left his bleeding body to rot on the corner. Even though he could make a dance in his head, it was time to make his decision, and the moving sun began to tell him that time wasn't slowing down for him.

But, if he wanted to make time stop for him, he could, because he was Chris Mangini, and since he was Chris Mangini he needed to take the gun along with him. He jumped off the bed, and with his free hand he pulled up the back of his shirt a cold breeze through the room—like fecal matter from a stall. It must have been because of his wife, letting out all the heat from the kitchen and dissipating into the city streets.

With the pistol in his pant line a mystical energy moved around his room, he could feel it throughout his body, but outside his apartment time always moved faster than he wanted to, and before he knew it, he was outside the door, as the walls began to dissipate and blink into light green.

Outside Chris was holding his bag of groceries, already a few minutes away from his wife's apartment; he was walking at a mid fast pace, not too slow, and not too fast. He didn't want to attract any unwanted attention, be it from anyone, but he felt that he was being watched. The sky grew heavy and pale with a sickly whitish color, and it weighed on his conscious like a paperweight that was about the size of an incurable tumor, and it started to eat him away, piece-by-piece. He continued down the street, looking behind him, seeing nothing but the sun glowing through the gray clouds like a gaping mouth of a dragon, the sun began to swallow the sun up whole, and bits of rays began to dive under the crescent sky running away from the dragon's gaping mouth.

Chris wanted to run away from it too, and the way the sun was starting to set over the city, he knew that it would have to happen sometime. He turned his head over his shoulder as the celery leaves brushed against his face as he continued down the street, feeling the air whip behind him, almost pulling his coattail, and trying to reveal his piece. He headed on, away from the setting sun, and he felt the dragon's mouth closing in on him.

As he was slowly furthering away from the beast—whose jaws were trailing behind him as he began to feel their presence move closer toward him like the shark that was showing his fin when he smelled blood from a prey, and they were moving toward him.

In the distance his wife was leaning on the side of the door with their baby wrapped in white tablecloth, pressing against her chest. But the air felt like water as he was walking forward as he turned and heard footsteps, but he didn't see his assailants. Only he could feel the stare were hollow as the insides of a long barrel, and his stare told him everything.

"A boy?" Chris's pace quickened as he walked along as if nothing was on his mind, except for Chris.

Francesca looked like some ancient sculpture, or a great karma-sutra painting, and it only seemed like he could taste his wife through the picture without even touching the painting. Only now he did see the small white cloth that was his child. Once he was nearing the edge of the block, his wife waved to him with a great big grin on her face, but he had to get her away. Even though he was about a block away, the assassins were gaining on him with their weapons, waiting to kill him, and he mouthed the words, "Get inside!"

The last thing he saw was his wife holding his child—his babies round head glowed like a pale diamond—and all of New York to see their child—

claws dung into his body and let out an excruciating groan. Then three more bullets hit his body, and when he was trying to get up, they sent him back to the ground. Chris felt that his body was being stuck with a large hypodermic needle, filled with liquid saccharine stinging, melting his entire body from the heart and skin.

Everything seemed to black out around him as he felt another burning shell pierce his body, and groaned as he began to feel numb as the gunshots ended with the pitter-patter of running feet that marked the end with cold dead silence lurking through the streets.

Like all woman of war, their hearts were stone and bones were made of iron, and like Francesca, she was one of those women, but something from deep inside her began to pulsate against her chest. She moved up and down as she hurried towards her husband with her child buried inside her shirt—pulling her nipple out—and the crazy thing was her baby, was screaming with that loud siren of a shrill, at the top of his lungs. The white yoke and red blood intertwined as she placed that with some deranged artists panting where the brush had been washed over too much, running like the tears that were already dripping down her face.

She slowly approached her husband, feeling that smooth chilly wind and then everything became quiet as the wind breezed through her blouse, sending goosebumps all over her body. She leaned over with her baby, viewing his body as the blood was pouring onto the ground, and she gasped, trying to hold her tears in, and then spiraled into shock as she clutched his shoulders, she began to feel her heart beating, sending her emotions through her veins faster than any drug, paralyzing her down on the ground. Her heart was swelling up in her chest as she looked into his olive drab eyes, and saw that there was nothing, no life, in his once beautiful eyes

The pain in her body became unbearable as her eyes watered, and then as she saw his face, she began to finally cry. Wailing with her child, she whispered to herself in her sweet Sicilian sadness, rubbing her hands against his cheeks—looking into his now cold eyes—she joined her baby's loud wailing. Then with a free hand, she placed a hand over her face she began to sob even more, placing her nails into her cheeks, she brought her hand down, tearing into her skin, cracking her beautiful face with a small, but noticeable cuts. She could never forgive herself for sending her husband to his death, and she scorned herself begging to take its place. Then going at it again, she wanted to feel his skin peel off his face, and long marks appeared down her cheeks—huffing and puffing.

She didn't know how long she had been crying for until the police cars had finally arrived, with their round flashing lights that never wanted to end. But their weren't swarms of police cars, only a man and a woman, both in blue suits and bright metal shields stood over as her husband's bleeding body. As she focused her attention off of Chris, she wiped her tears off her face, and she became hard and tough again, as she had always been.

"Lady?" The male officer, Dean Bell belted loudly, "What's the problem?"

Francesca looked at his lips, but she couldn't discern a single word coming out of his mouth. She didn't like his snobby way he gave her almost naked body, as if he was better than she was.

He looked at Chris's body, and tapped his partner with the end of his finger, and then reached for his radio.

The lady officer, Pattie Bucci, was shocked but not surprised to see this young man's body lying in the street, bloodied up and on the verge of death like a dying fish. Only in a fleeting second, she began to question her in English so that her partner would not be asking a bunch of unnecessary questions. "Mam, what happened here?"

Francesca peered up at the lady officer, and with her puppy eyes, just staring blankly being that she was in no state to talk to the police. Only Francesca noticed the lady cop who seemed rather mannish with lips that curled upwards and horse teeth bucked out as her slim chin bone looked dislodged. A small pierced stud was on her left ear lobe definitely stood out, especially regarding her height being she was a tiny woman, she had balls the size of King Kong.

"Mam?" Pattie persisted, "What happened!"

Francesca saw her lips moving, but she still looked like a deer in headlights that never really got over being in front of the large fog lights. She was expressionless, and the way she was talking, it sounded rapid and unintelligent as she stuttered in between her voice.

"Please...help my husband please! He's dying, he's dying!" She looked at them hoping to make some kind of sense, but saw that they couldn't understand her.

The male officer, Dean, was too lost with all her words, and huffed with deep irritation and he apathetically called in for backup as she immediately took Francesca by the hand, and gently placed her inside the car while an emergency vehicle was not too far away from them.

Inside the police squad car, Francesca watched as her the female officer glanced into the rear view mirror, and saw her crying into her child. She was pitiful looking; her face was melting waxy tears along her scrunched, painful face.

"Hey!" Pattie surprised Francesca; her voice came off in a fluent Italian.

Francesca looked up, hearing music to her ears, she lit up faster—but was confused—like fireworks in the middle of winter, but before she continued Francesca interrupted her, her throat was full of spit and liquid.

"*Who are you?*" Francesca's voice sounded stuffy and raspy, still choking on her own tears as spit flew from her mouth. "*Are you going to put us in the prison?*" Her small child let out a small whelping noise, and she covered it with the blanket, and looked dreamily into his stretched, innocent eyes.

Patti peered into the rear view mirror, and chuckled from her impervious question, "*I know a lot of things about you, you are Chris Mangini's wife, you may not know me but I am a friends of your husbands. I will take care of you.*"

Francesca's interest was definitely sparked, but how could she be able to trust her? Was she a spy, and who were her friends. Francesca wanted to speak, but the female police officer interrupted her.

"*Not now,*" the female officer said cutting into her sentence, nodding toward her stupid partner still calling in the extra company, which had come in perfect timing. It usually took them about seven to eight minutes, made it in about five minutes. "*You and your son are not going to be put in prison.*" She said gently, so that she wouldn't make her mad as she tuned around, "*Too many people respect you and Chris Mangini too much, he does so much for our precinct, and we wouldn't want to soil our relationship, right?*"

Francesca saw her gleaming smile reflecting some god-awful sin that she had never spoken about and through that condescending smile Francesca had seen how a good day had been definitely ruined, by her own stupidity. But the last thing that she said, "*he does so much for the precinct*"

"What the hell did that mean?" Francesca began to think that her husband had done *personal* favors for this woman, and at that moment, she felt angry with her husband, at the whore of a female police officer, and God. How could he let this happen, she did everything right, she had a family and remained truthful to the one man she had planned to stay married to forever. But she had to remember who her husband was, and who he dealt with everyday—the lowest people on earth. He would never cheat on her for this trashy woman, who had a nose ring and skin that looked counterfeit—cheap and bruised.

"*No, but not to be too presumptuous but can we get him to the hospital. He's fucking dying!*" Francesca got down to business, because out they're bleeding in the street was her husband, and how she would handle all those questions the police would ask her. Even if Francesca didn't trust this person, she was in the company of a friend, even if she didn't like her; she had to admire out of all the trouble he did for them they finally helped him. Being that she was in a police car, she couldn't do anything about it, and the best thing was to stay quiet after this and not say a thing to the police.

Once A.J. had heard of the news that Chris had been shot, he, Frank, and Gene went to a meeting with the Underboss, and in the middle of their Saturday dinner, only something else bothered him to come home. His parents had confronted him about his long nights, and they saw his programs and his large amounts of money, which had equaled to about more than two hundred thousand dollars.

It was around four-o clock in the morning when he returned home, and came home to an empty audience. Something made him feel funny when he walked into a empty home, because a terrible silence trailed through his system that was more frightening than the moment after the empty shells in a gunfight had finally fallen. Or maybe it was the way the smoke from the barrel circled levitating in the air, leaving a pure sulfuric residue on his senses.

A.J. looked at the door puzzled, as if he was missing some extreme clue that he was failing to see, and noticed that the top hinge was broken off. He didn't know if the door would fall off if he closed the door all the way so he started to pull it toward him as he slipped in through the ajar door and heard it shut like every door he had encountered, and continued on throughout the house.

The moon had poured in through the lifeless window, shining down on the first thing on the far end of the room, the couch. He hadn't seen any sign of his parents or Jessica being home, and by the looks of it, someone had come in by force as if some great beast had charged through the door, and left muddy footprints all over the place. Then after that this beast had quietly closed the half-broken door behind him as if nothing happened? But he wasn't concerned about that now as he saw his next stop for the night, the couch and he fell on it like a ton of bricks making a loud KA-POOF on the plastic cover. His body began to feel like putty as he sank into the couch, and the roaring heater clicked on as if a ghost had been trapped inside his house. As this ghost continued to moan the ghostly whistle died down as he curled up like a little animal, and fell into a deep, deep sleep.

The morning had come faster than he thought with the rays licking his pale face he began to feel a warm SLAP press into his face. It must have been around eleven-o clock in the morning, with the way the sun was so standing against the window, and as A.J. opened his eyes—like a newborn being blinded by the first hint of light, he received another warm SLAP across his face.

"What's going on?" A.J. asked as he pulled his numb hand out of the couch, and rubbed his eyes, gently wiping off the caca in the corner of his eyes, getting his brain readjusted.

"WHERE THE HELL WERE YOU!" Jessica straddled on top of him

screamed into his face as she forced her face into his, so that he could see her.

A.J. saw her, but her face looked a bit cracked with a few pimples began to form like beehives across her chin and neck—red and already resembling an infection. She kept digging her burning crotch into him as her body weighed down on him like a snake coiling around a weak branch.

"Well, where do you think I was?" A.J. said and shrugged coldly with a sneer. "I was with the guys, we were out settling important business, remember? I left you with my parents." He smiled at her sinfully as she grabbed his hands by the wrist and threw them against the back of the armrest. A.J. was too tired to wrestle with her grip, and continued to smile.

Jessica huffed as she felt A.J.'s fire hose sinfully rub against her cold thighs. "That's not the point you dumb fuck…"

"Then what is the point, slut!" A.J. said with spite as he leaned his head forward, and then fell back, breathing in tired, incoherent anger.

Jessica looked into his eyes and suddenly remembered why he was away all that time and she wonder who she was *really on top of*? She didn't know this degrading, horrible person anymore.

Jessica looked at him as if she was about to jump out of her skin, and her eyes were about to pop out of her skull, and explode into a million pieces. Her hand slid down toward her right thigh as she huffed out another long deep sigh of suppressed anger that was about to boil over into a fit of rage. She turned her head away ruefully as if she was about to cry quivering with fear. "Your parents are at the hospital."

A.J.'s attention was now hooked, and his eyes wide, fixed on Jessica as if some apocalyptic dream he had seen in a vision had ultimately come true and as his heart sank he slowly said, not to threaten or put her on her guard. "What did you say?"

As her grip left he slowly took control as he lowered her next to him on the couch. She was an endless river of sorrow that finally released her embittered tears and left small cum dribbled marks on his couch.

As his right hand cupped around the other he saw the fear shake her quivering lips, as she began to shiver all over. "Your father had some sort of heart attack," the tears came out faster as the tears strolled down her face, endlessly, staining the plastic couch. "I couldn't help him, I had to call 911." In the middle of her agonizing cries, A.J. looked at her, and saw her make up ruining her eye shadow—turning her into a beautiful mess.

"I couldn't sleep all night," She started to say through her whimpering as she dried her baggy tea shade eyes as she smeared the day old make-up into her cheeks, "I was beginning to think that he wouldn't make it." She then lost herself in her water works, and began to cry while she spoke, "with all those tubes connected in his body, I JUST COULDN'T STAND IT." Another set of water works went off and it sounded like the wail of a child covered in their parents blood, and a portion of it crawled into its mouth, and she hadn't yet get rid of the taste. "Words weren't going to work right now."

As a matter of fact, he was out of words to say, all he could do was comfort her as she let out her tears (but she should have been the one comforting him.) The two embraced as they fell on the couch, as A.J. held onto Jessica's shivering back as if she was his single last possession in sight, and to him she was, and the two laid together in a deep sleep.

Book 2

Chapter XII:

"The Abattoir of Truth"

In room number 110, near the critical section of the hospital, a room was occupied by one ceaseless body and another weeping soul that lamented far worse, but seemed miniscule to the worker bees. They just tried to ignore it, but the ceiling paint was starting to chip away her soul. Her body was aching and the scales on her skin were falling as her pathetic soul dripped down her things. Only she hadn't bothered to dry her eyes, she had no more tears to dry. It's like they were something sacred to her, because this was the hardest thing she had ever cried about in years—to see her husband lying defenselessly on the bed—like a oozing sack of fermented jelly.

She wanted to stop crying, but the darkness was only prolonging her sadness, and it never seemed to end, or prolong the torture. She was depressed up to the top of her face; anger was beyond plausible description, suicide was an option. "Kill myself…" but not yet.

As she rose out of her chair, she shuffled in a circle as her bloodshot eyes drooped down to her dry cups as her hands shook her beaded jewelry. It made a rhythmic *rat-ta-tat-tat* sound as she continued to scream with her telepathic waves of dark, muddled fear. Mary felt like she had wanted to scream then, but couldn't hear herself. As she trudged across the room, like a weakened soldier pushing through a sea of dead bodies, and they were bringing her along with her as she made her way toward her ailing husband—the lifeless sack of shit that he had become.

Mary grabbed onto the plastic bedside, and gripped it, shaking it forcefully, as she stood over his ceaseless body, wanting to trade for his place but she didn't know what her husband would do in her situation. "Would he be worse off than me?" Mary didn't know how to answer that question, and as she relaxed her off the bendable lever, feeling the bed start to make a small dancing, and wobbled off kilter noise as she set it on her husband's hand, and gripped her husband's lifeless fingers.

They were cold, but warm as medicine pumped through his veins, feeding him, hurting him, and drugging his abilities to act as a fully functional human being at the same time. How she would love to go on about being "under the threshold of those needles that pierced his hands like curved ingrown toenails." Only she couldn't save him, and she felt her brain spinning on an axis as her world felt ultimately upside down. This was a question that entered her mind more than anything else was, but where were the answers? None to behold, but a sack of human filth that couldn't be put back together again.

Mary, with her radiant eyes, looked upon her husband's ceaseless body. "You were so strong!" She whispered, feeling those tears embedding into her skin, as the soggy tear embedded into her skin as she leaned over and pressing her lips against him she wanted him to wake up, "Just wake up!"

Nothing, and the wheels on this very fucked up clock, kept moving at it's slow annoying pace when she could feel a revelation, an apocalypse of some sort. She definitely was dreaming, but she could feel an odd sensation.

As she continued to sob over her husband, more footsteps echoed through the hall, and the steps grew louder. A wave of uneasiness crawled down her body like a dirty feeling that never wanted to leave, like sand stuck in the thickest pigments of one's crevice. Her emotions were on the edge as the pair of footsteps grew like a rash, as she gripped the hard plastic handle as her entire body felt like a thousand needles—like pincushions—pushing into the soles of her feet, and searing through her entire body. As the footsteps grew closer, a shadow loomed over the curtain as this long bleeding shadow started to bleed over, pulsating as it clouded over the little bit of light and darkness began to settle over her. Fear began to rush through her system, and her senses became queasy as she her stomach clenched, and was turning into a small bleeding grapefruit, and rocked against the top of her stomach lining. She gritted her teeth, and felt her body tighten as the shadow moved over her room like an eclipse. She wondered if she was in the presence of an angel, or maybe a demon, pulling on her body and possessing her mind with fire and fury. Mary wanted to meet her maker head on before she would give herself over to this new found power.

"Who is it?" His mother said, almost exhaling patches of cold freezing air from her lungs.

No answer. The light brightened as she turned away for a moment, trying to adjust her eyes to the bright blob, but she gulped a wad of spit, and felt the brightness close in around the room. As she faced the light again, she didn't seem afraid, but her curiosity seemed to possess her entire spinal cord, and she was stuck looking at the light.

"WHO ARE YOU!" Mary screamed into the light, hoping that someone would answer, but not a word.

As the light grew with intensity, she began to scream. Screaming, screaming, until her voice with hoarse, and tears streamed down her face as she wrapped her arms around her husband again. Suddenly, felt her entire body being rocked up and down, left to right, and a piercing sound echoed inside her ears. The rocking continued, and her delirious screaming continued. She couldn't get control of herself, her body was in a state of epilepsy, and inside her mind she was spinning out of control as her body was going with this new darkened vision.

Outside his Mary's mind, A.J. and Jessica were trying to pull his mother off the bed because she was about to pull his father's tubes out. They somehow managed to wrestle her off the bed and were pressing her against the wall. A.J. gripped her hands while she tried to force him off of her. She dragging her nails into his skin almost to the point where small scratch marks appeared on his skin, and her voice whined with intensity.

"Mom!" A.J. yelled into her face, seeing not his mother, but a mad woman—skin of an aged devil and eyes that no longer filled with life. "What's wrong?" Her eyes still closed, her body was slipping out of A.J.'s grip, and fell to the ground. They forced her back up, but the screaming continued with a high tortuous shrill. A.J. could hear his eardrums begin to echo in pain as his hand automatically rose, fingers outstretched, and then slapped her right cheek. He could feel his hand swell from the quick slap, and let his hand fall to his side limply, but regretted it immediately.

His mother whimpered in an unconscious scream, and closed her eyes.

"Don't do that!" Jessica yelled, taken back and deeply offended by his actions.

She looked at him hatefully—wide-eyed and unresponsive eyes that just had pits—equally vindictive, like he had meant to do it, but his shriveling hand knew that he had immediately regretted it, but didn't want to admit his actions. But she could see that there was no emotion in his eye, and saw that he didn't give any thought behind his actions. There was this small aching feeling in her mind that she needed to stand up for his mother, because that was just wrong.

A.J. looked down at his hand, and said, "I was just trying to wake her up."

Jessica couldn't believe she was hearing this out of A.J.'s mouth. She got into his face, only two inches away from his lips, with an explosive look in her eye she felt a sexually imperialistic rush speed through her system as she screamed, *"WHAT THE FUCK IS WRONG WITH YOU?"* A.J. felt her hot breath pushing against his face, and she knew that he was in the wrong, and he did too.

"I didn't hit her that hard!" A.J. shot back in a self-defensive reply, but then finally put everything together, and he couldn't *justify* a right reason for hitting her.

"What the fuck is wrong with you?" Jessica's lowered a few decibels after she had received A.J.'s unwanted attention, but one thing she didn't want was A.J.'s uncontrollable rage to fall upon her. But if it stopped him from hitting his mother, then she would have been glad that he hadn't hit his mother again.

A.J. turned his head, seeing his mother whimpering and crying in her delusional state, slowly pushing his feelings inward where no one could understand what he was thinking. A place of rage, confusion, isolation, a place of optimistic diligence to money, and one of murder—that was his place.

Jessica saw this confused and masked derelict, hands slowly rose up toward his face, and as she began to cup his cheek, he pulled away from her, and looked at his mother again.

A.J. ignored her for a moment, and stared at his mother, who was beginning to awake from her hellish nightmare, and she slowly fell asleep, but when she looked at him dully, she felt her eyes revealed that this boy…no, this was a man standing in front of her? When she scooted back in her chair, she felt no need to talk, but to close her eyes, and fall into some deep abyss of a slumber. Her bones limply fell into the chair, and her arms fell beside her body. But the fear of not returning from that slumber definitely did frighten her more than any other dream in the world.

"Mom, are you okay?"

Nothing. Not a single reply uttered from her lifeless, unconscious lips. All that came out was a mindless groan that was reduced to a small grumble, like one of a diseased motor engine that had been running on the last drip of oil, and had finally blown its last breath before it died.

A.J. could see that she was not dead, but all that her episode left her in was a state of rambling tangents that would amount to an unexplainable, inexplicable, language. But something made him feel like nothing had sense to him anymore, so whatever was going on, he didn't feel the need to question it. Because there would be no real answer to his curiosity, and it would never be satisfied the way he would have wanted it to be. "Will my father live?" He would ask the doctor later, but there would be no answer to that as well. Everything is a lie, and the truth is just a veil.

The Disintegrating Bloodline

Downstairs in the busy lobby of St. Anthony's hospital, nurses were rushing toward their rooms, doctors were bustling with tablets and patients to help while janitors were idly emptying large trashcans. With faces of sadness, they wished they weren't emptying people's trash and when they took one whiff of the garbage that they were unloading, they knew where they were and couldn't live a fabulous life style he would never have. They too hated the doctors, and Frank could agree with that, but when he got rid of his trash, he always shredded the evidence, no matter how big or small it was.

Frank was sitting in a large comfy chair with his feet stretching out with the top of his foot touching the coffee table. He lightly kicked it, shaking the few magazines across the glass as he flicked his watch up his wrist and saw that it had been about a half an hour that he had been sitting in that same exact seat.

Strangers with grimaces, and looking like their lives were approaching a gigantic climax in their lives. It had either involved a dying family member that had wanted to breath there last words so that they can ease there passing before they left. Dying in peace was the best way to let go of there grievances, then it was just a sad case for the person who had to be brought down by this sad situation.

"Where is this guy?" Frank said to himself, but then immediately caught himself. He found himself beginning to talk to himself *all the time* and sometimes it was just to break the uncomfortable silence in his room, and when he talked to himself, his hands shook with trembling fear. Then that made him want a fresh rolled up blunt. A blunt, (for anyone who never had the privilege or incentive to use drugs) is a large cigar wrapping that has been cut open to get rid of the tobacco, and has been replaced with marijuana. Then all you have to do is lick the edges of the blunt, wrap that around the new ingredient, which is the marijuana, and then that person would have a ready made "blunt."

It was a habit that he never liked to admit to anyone, but the only time that anyone would be worried about it if he was literally fucking everything up his business and indulged himself with Cocaine, ecstasy, heroin, crack, then he would have to be worried about himself. Even if he did marijuana once a while, it made him forget about all the shit that he had done, and hoped that God would forgive him...but that would come later or sooner if that was in his cards or not.

But who knew that somewhere in Chris's cards that if he had been shot once before, there was a certainty that the attacks would never stop.

"Shot?" Frank thought couldn't believe the travesty, but what spurned his anger more was because he didn't know who his assailants were, but he had a pretty good guess. But when he would find A.J., they would pick up from where he left off, and settle unfinished business.

He couldn't get too ahead of himself, and he had to contact Gene. But he hadn't heard from him since that Saturday. Nobody had heard from him. Not even some of his soldiers that had been stationed in the Bronx and BK (Brooklyn) had even seen him since the shooting. He might have to get in contact with one of his friends in Queens that was a regular snoop in all the boroughs. If not in Queens there was always L.I. (Long Island) Staten Island, and Harlem left. Frank didn't know before, but he figured out that Gene was the obvious traitor.

But he saw no reason that Gene would ever run to Harlem for, but sometimes as dark as he considered himself to be, he had a few "Dreads" that spot him some good Ganja, which was Jamaican marijuana. There they would let him get high at their place. Frank never really messed with things that came from the Rastafarians, because he never messed with somebody else's religion, because it didn't seem right to interject personal beliefs from other religions.

"Damn it," Frank huffed, raising his knees up, he stamped his feet on the soft carpet, flicked his wrist to see what time his watch said. The long handle was leaning past the five like a lazy bitch, and the small handle was creeping past the number three like a worker bee. It was already five fifteen and A.J. wasn't showing up. He might have been kidnapped, beaten, and left in the gutter for all he knew. He scratched his bullet wound, that had felt like it had healed up a bit, but after being hit with one bullet, he had problems with the rain when it hit his body.

"I'm getting the fuck out of here!" Frank muttered, and rose up out of the chair. He had felt the imprint of his back stick to the edge of the seat, and rise like soft fresh bread. Right now, as hungry as he was, he could eat just about anything. He would even eat pussy if it could fill his need for hunger, but that was a "sticky" issue if it came down to eating pussy. As tempting as it sounded, a regular sandwich would suffice.

As Frank shifted out of the chair, he stood towering overlooking the entire lobby, feeling a hard on creep through the right side of his groin, made him attract some attention from a woman who was carrying a Gucci purse, high heel pumps, and a dark black dress. The tall, dark haired, brown-eyed model eyed him up and down (especially gazing at his pants where the hard on was taking place), she opened her mouth, and with a smooth wick of her tongue licked her teeth. This wasn't to clean her teeth, since they were sparkling enough to blind Frank he gave her a quick wink, puckered up his lips, and blew her a soft smacking kiss. He roused a giggle out of her, and shaking her body she blew him another kiss, and kept on walking.

Frank smiled, standing where he was, not even attempting to chase after her. It was foolish, but even if he had the balls to chase after this model, he needed to see A.J. and talk to him about their plans. But that was turning into impossibility since he didn't know where the fuck he was at the present time, and wondered if his present fears had come true.

"Maybe he was stabbed and beaten up? Maybe he is dead?" On second thought, he didn't really believe that, but his mind wasn't going to leave anything to doubt. With that thought in mind, Frank was ready and about willing to walk out that automatic door. His car was just waiting for him, and he could go and check up on Chris at the other hospital. With his hands in his pockets, he moved toward the automatic door, he started out the doors as the cold breeze welcomed him toward the parking lot. Making his way out the mechanical black rimmed doors that slid open for him, Frank heard somebody calling his name out.

Turning around he felt the cool breeze touch his neck as he saw A.J. running across the lobby. He wasn't out of breath either, and to Frank, he looked like some track athlete that never seemed to get tired of running. Frank had enough time to get rid of his hard on before he left him. Frank didn't run but took long strides, making sure he wouldn't attract attention to himself; he couldn't help but let a smirk escape him, exasperated by the fact that he wasn't dead. He didn't know whether to hit him or give him a hug. One or the other, he didn't care right at that moment, he was just glad to see him.

A.J.'s speed attracted the attention of the woman at the front desk; her blue eyes shifted over her glasses and her lips turned inward towards her face so that her teeth nervously scraped along her bottom lip. She hid her head back into her computer, and put on some invisible earphone that kept her dutifully back to her job, and ignorant of everyone around her. The phone ringed, and the woman answered it without even looking back at them.

As A.J.'s speed decreased, he stood two feet away from Frank, with a small sneaky smile.

"What's up man," He put out his hand, and Frank leaned downwards and the two slammed into each other, and they quickly patted each other's back. Then their bodies rose off each other and Frank returned back to his towering statures.

"What's up?" A.J. said, looking around him, and creasing down the back of his shirt so that it would cover up most of his pant line.

"A lot. Come on, let's get outta' here where we can talk…" Then as Frank continued to talk A.J.'s face exerted an idea but couldn't get it out.

"What is it?" Frank asked, and saw A.J.'s face was sunk low, like the one of hunger and by the way he nervously shook, and Frank knew that one very well.

"Do you think that we could get something to eat?" A.J. said with some long wanting that his body lusted for. "Because I am starving, and my mother and Jessica are downstairs in the cafeteria." Frank's eyebrow rose with disapproval, but his mouth said the exact opposite.

"Well…" Frank thought about it, and food was really sounding nice to him about now. "Yeah, sure. Let's go."

Thinking of that would help matters for them, and focusing on their own agenda was the most important thing for them to do at this moment. As the elevator stopped with one last *ding*, and the doors stretched open revealing the empty space with no one in it. The two slowly walked into the gaping elevator doors, feeling the cool conditioning wind creep through their pants, and made all their hairs stand up in their place, they stood inside the belly of the elevator as it shut closed with a soft *creeeak* and shut with a dull *clunk* they started toward there descent, whether or not they would get out would matter much to them.

The ride felt longer than it took, but when A.J. had the words to answer Frank's question, he intervened when Frank was about to talk. Frank turned, and urged him to go on with what he was saying. Frank accepted this, and told him everything that Chris had planned before he was shot.

Frank was smiling again, and felt that all the information bubbling off the top of his head was about to explode. But it was probably because he was talking about Chris, which relieved some tension in him, and maybe some of the weight that was inside his soul. Only A.J. felt relieved that he was talking about him also, because it made him feel comfortable, even though he still thought someone was still listening to them.

Frank then proceeded to tell him that Chris had an invitation to the wedding of Capo Sammy DiBernardo, and how he could have a few of his boys come along. But then Frank added in the idea that since A.J. was the acting boss of the family, he could represent in his stead, and go around and 'socialize' with some of the family associates and all he had to then was be his personable and be sociable self. A.J. looked at him rather curiously, and felt a nervous cramp enter in his stomach, like a thousand cockroaches were forming in his body, and it was probably because of the lack of food he had since that morning. The eggs felt funny to him, but thinking about personal matters he also got the hint that he needed to lie to whoever he was talking to, and get whatever information he could out of them.

"What exactly do we have to do?" A.J. asked, and waited for a response. A.J. got the hint that they would probably have to put their necks on the line somehow and it all was going to be on A.J. He didn't see the point in denying what he had to do, and he had to be the boss of the family. It was so irrevocable that this was what he was put on this earth to do, but A.J. didn't see it as anything bad, but just what he had to do in order to ease his problems, and release some of his tension.

"A weddings not a bad way to release some tension, and meet a few of my fellow brethren. Not to mention the loads of alcohol." That really seemed like a dumb-ass question to think about, but he had to think about everything.

A long sigh blew from Frank lips, as if he was just getting started, and needed to refill his lungs full of oxygen again. A.J. thought he always was kind of pompous, but he began to change that opinion very quickly.

"And that's not all." Frank added, and gave off a short burp before he continued. A.J. gave a short laugh, and listened to him continue talking about the rest of their plans A.J. somehow lost himself in what he was saying, and felt that he didn't know who he was listening to anymore. But something inside his gut told him that he should listen, just for the sake of his own well being, and for his life.

A short *ding* sounded off from the elevator. The two looked up at the elevator, as they felt the short sound reawaken them to the twirling elevators slow descent. They would be approaching the cafeteria pretty soon, but it didn't feel like they were actually moving, and this had been some sort of time warp where time and space did not exist, except the conversation at hand. But that seemed to come true when Frank stopped the elevator before it reached the last floor. As he pressed the white button, the large moving freighter stopped as the reigns withheld it in midair, making A.J. and Frank shake for a second as Frank smiled deviously, and crossed his arms in a vain manner.

Frank proceeded on with the rest of his theories that had been rattling around in his brain, and A.J. noticed that he spoke with precision of an eighty-year-old man, calm and cool, without one single solitary mistake in his tone, as if he had to memorize some cryptic password only he knew. That's what made A.J. almost intimidated by Frank, but that was because he never talked a lot.

A.J. listened as Frank explained the other theory that had been rattling inside his mind like a melon baller banging against the side of his skull back and forth at full speed. The fact that he had not heard or talked to Gene since Chris's assassination bothered him the most. He put together the rumor that Gene was on the lamb because he had betrayed Chris in the process, and he was turning against them while he had the chance. With that show of disrespect towards Chris, this probably meant that their crews were going to become mortal enemies with each other. Frank had another idea to why Gene had run away, the fact that they betrayed them was a fact, but this was something bigger to why he had betrayed them.

"I can't be Chris's cousin." A.J. huffed, and shook his head.

He put his head down, sighed in a grave manner as if hope was lost already.

"Don't be too quick to deny that! We don't know *who* you are or not. So, put your head up." A.J. raised his head with some hope and easily changed the subject back to what they were talking about.

The threat of Gene was obviously real, and that meant there would be blood in the hallways, and casualties of innocent school kids would become victims of this feud. But they had no idea when he would attack. Gene was one major factor of how business was dealt with in George Bradley, and to move things in and out of the school Gene would set up most of the meeting spots, and higher whatever backup they needed. But since Gene was on the opposite side, he would very well use violence to his advantage, and scare off all the business that Chris had earned with his own sweat and tears.

Frank knew that Gene was a businessman, but he would use violence—he was a gorilla when it came to muscle, he wasn't all brains.

And this prick was going to try to degrade it piece by piece, but Frank was confident that they had enough force to kick the shit out of Gene's small little renegade army. But was he underrating what kind of force Gene had? Was this the perfect time for Gene to rise up and try to take all out that stand in his way? Did he have enough men to rise up and take over Chris's rackets? But realistically, Frank thought that they could take them on, even if he was afraid of what might happen.

After taking a deep breath, the long and what seemed like an endless conversation was finished. Even though the conversation ended, it felt like their minds had gained a whole extra fifteen hundreds pounds of stress that strained the elevator cables. A.J., who was in a trance was filled with questions of his own and didn't dare keep silent, even though the stress felt too heavy, it was game time.

"Are you sure Gene was the one that betrayed us?" A.J felt like it was a stupid and useless question after what Frank had gone into vast examination about. But it was the first question of many he would ask.

"I do!" Frank said with confidence.

"How do you know that?" A.J. replied.

"He was acting funny that night at the meeting, and I had another source look into a few things that were bothering me."

"Which was?" A.J.'s voice was assertive, demanding his answer.

Frank's eyebrows arched up across his forehead, and his eyes centered on A.J., but then glanced over and around his shoulders.

"He was acting funny that entire night at the meeting and he never called me back. Gene was looking very agitated for the past few weeks, like something was on his mind, and he didn't want to talk about it. Also, what I also found out between some of our crews and some of the Outcasts is that Gene had been withholding on large amounts of money that is supposed to be handed to Chris every other week. But as stupid as I was thinking, pushing it aside only to be letting our enemy sneak past our grasp, and I know that its all about the cousin."

A.J. couldn't believe this, because all of this sounded so repetitive from every power struggle that he had ever read in history books. "So, his betrayal is all about money and power struggle?"

"I don't know!" Frank burst out, as if he was repenting some grave sin, and slammed the white linoleum wall and felt the elevator wobbling side to side.

"How could I let him go and murder Chris! I shouldn't have been named Capo, I'm not a Captain. I'm nothing but a grunt." A.J. watched him move around like a caged animal feeling the walls aggravating his weaknesses and irritating his anger, which was sad and frightening at the same time because A.J. was stuck inside with this confused animal. But seeing Frank like this was unlike him, which made A.J. feel sorry for him.

But at the same time, A.J. remembered that all the great leaders (or malicious tyrants) of there days was always an amiable friend to his soldiers. That's one thing A.J. could never forget is History, because it always had a way to repeat itself. A.J. would rekindle his downtrodden spirit, because he didn't know how to explain it, but this was a better time than ever show him that there was hope left.

"I'm the leader." A.J. thought, knowing his full responsibility. "They have to rely on me, and I can't let Frank fall in the dumps. I need to keep him focused on something, anything except being insecure. It's all a state of mind."

Leaning off the steel bar that was jamming into his back, A.J. stood upright, and letting his arms hang down by his side, with a majestic and wise attitude. His face was hard as stone, and his gaze could also very well pierce the thickest kind of Teflon Velcro just as a bullet would try and hinder him, and a small portion of his voice bled compassion.

"You were made a Capo because Chris could trust you, and he depended on you, as he did all of us. This wasn't your fault." A.J. said, patting his back, and giving him solace from his grief.

"I don't feel like it." Frank frowned, but then turned his head in shame. "Not after this, because I don't know what the fuck is going to happen to our crew. We don't know who's going to stall us out "

At that moment, A.J.—who had never earned a rank above Capo—saw Frank in his weakest, not weak…but definitely insecure moment. Of course, being named the boss of the family, he felt like he should have been in Frank's place, but he had for some reason earned his title from Chris for some odd reason or another, and this wasn't time for him to feel sorry for himself. He had to be tough on him, just as Chris would have been, but restate the facts for him.

"You know what. If Chris didn't trust or care about you, why would he have made you a Captain then?"

Frank, who was cowering his head, thinking about what that meant to him, but knew that there was a positive side to this whole thing, and if he didn't look to both sides to this situation. Chris did care, and in that same moment, his honest smile brightened his face. But pushing that aside, A.J. raised his eyebrows very keenly, which was somewhat of a funny thing, and gave him a smug expression that was far from anything but funny.

" I know you are worried, but you can't be like this now. The only way that we will ever win is that we stick together, and not give up on each other. Our loyalty is what makes us different, and to Chris, we are the last of his followers, well including Krazy. If you know where he is, I suppose?"

"Yeah!" Frank snorted, and chuckled as if it was some small joke, but it seemed so utterly frightening to be alone. But then he stood very reassured "I know right. He's fucking around at his house, probably with a few bitches. As far as I know, he's ready and willing to do anything."

"Well, make sure he's not fucking around, because I'm ready to retaliate, and I need you in my corner. We will need more men, but I will leave that in your hands."

Frank heard this and gave an interesting smirk as he scratched his stubble chin. The small hairs breezed back on forth on his sharp fingernails, and irritated him like small pubic hairs.

"Sure, sure. I can do that. What do you want me to do about Gene?"

A.J. suddenly remembered Gene, and with that thought came about a whole new game plan.

"Now," A.J. pondered his question for a moment, and then continued on, guiding his thoughts with such precision, "something tells me that Gene is not going to show his face, because he's too smart for that. He knows that we could crush him in a moment's notice, and he's going to send his minions to attack us since we are vulnerable. So, we need protection, and try to find us some good guys that you have in your disposal, and won't be quick to change sides on us. I trust your judgement."

"Well, if you trust my judgement, how would you know if I wasn't a back-stabber, huh?" Frank said in a satirical, but felt his body tremble from the very gesture, and spurned his mind from the thought.

With that calm ocean look in his eye he said, not even phasing him.

"Because if you were the backstabber, you wouldn't have waited so long to betray Chris. Chris trusted you, and here we are."

"Interesting notion." Frank replied as his hand reached across the elevator, as if it was gravitating in middle of some hyperspace launch like from some futuristic slow motion scene. His finger pointed and pressed the small white button, which was pretty firm looking at it from a distance, glowed bright orange, and as Frank pulled his finger out of the orange creamy button, the elevator that they had been riding on was suddenly moving toward it's downward slope.

As A.J. heard the wires slowly turn, the elevator slowly shook, like it was the heart of a debilitated old man, and the two felt like they were inside it, the rocky ride that never seemed to end or start.

But something about the whole thing made them queasy, as if the rage had finally engulfed him, and they were choking off the betrayals, murders, and changes that they couldn't accept.

Twenty or even thirty minutes when Frank had stopped the elevator, Jessica and Mary did not wait for him to already order food at the hospital Subway. The restaurant felt cool and all kinds of vibes were circulating between the two, she saw this as a good time to solace her pain, and maybe give Jessica some as well. As Jessica glanced back and forth at A.J.'s mother, she felt that the silence had been too overwhelming for her. She couldn't take things being so quiet.

"Did A.J. tell you about what that doctor said?" As she finished that question, A.J.'s mother turned her head with some scorning mockery that would only amuse a reptile. "No," Her lips puckered up, then returned back to her regular dry stance, "I don't care what he has to say."

Jessica did not like this hateful tone that was coming out of this sweet lady that she had known just a night before had turned into such a total bitch, but she could understand why she was angry, but she couldn't understand why she would hate A.J. for it. She wanted to make some sense out of this maniacal babble.

"What do you mean?" Jessica asked, weary and tired, hearing, *"The truth is just a ripple in the pond of abyss,"* and pushed it back in her mind.

Mary turned, filled with the hate that she was reeking putridity. "What do you think I mean!" Mary growled back. "He lied to us about everything, and he expects me to live with it. No, not happening!"

Jessica saw the fleshy, peeling point of her words, but she had yet begun to see what was at the core of his mother.

"He doesn't expect you to live with anything that he has done." and covered her mouth as if she was going to say something else.

"Oh sure," Mary scoffed, "he's not only living in our house, and he expects us to do prison time for him. No, I just won't stand for it, I won't..." She was about to finish her sentence with, "go to jail for my son," but she knew that her son was now a corpse.

Jessica quickly glanced around the small Subway that looked a rundown crack room that had been polished over so many times that it gave off a small grayish color. Only when she heard his mother say that, the corners started to get grayer as his mother spoke these horrible words.

Jessica was really alarmed, and shocked at by his mother's cold words. She had to rid this kind of talk before it escalated to the point where neither she nor Jessica could fix it.

With her best intentions that she had for his mother, she quietly pressed on with the issue at hand, without raising her hand. "What do you mean? He never gave you any kind of trouble."

"You wouldn't know about that!" But then she sunk herself down to a point where she could attack her.

"Well, maybe you would know because you have been fucking him on a regular basis." His mother fell silent, and she quickly clamped a hand over her mouth. But what was the point in trying to keep quiet now, she had already said the unspeakable, it was too late.

Jessica turned, and looking at this woman in shock she felt this uncontrollable anger surge throughout her body, like semen soaring sky high through a mans penis, and she was about to blow it all really quick.

Jessica turned blush red as the rage surge throughout her body, and she steadily moved forward. "Excuse me, but how would you know?"

"I know what all little whores do to a good man!"

Jessica just couldn't believe, but was confused on whom this statement was directed to, and the thought of backing down wasn't her style. "I want A.J. to be successful as much as you want him to be.

"In what, being a criminal. You two are perfect together, you impetuous little cunt!"

Jessica blinked her eyes, and continued, swallowing her anger, but her mind was still burning from the insult. "But you better know something, and know it right now. Whatever you may think I am, you have another thing coming."

"I just know," Mary snorted, like some know it all, clearing her throat so that she could continue her rant. "I see how you look at him. I know how boys and girls act."

Jessica quickly noticed that this woman was clearly pissed off about a lot of things, and couldn't categorize her thoughts. Jessica thought that maybe there were some deep-seeded problems with her husband or with A.J. But there was no one to blame for this problem…just the circumstances.

"Why…" Mary started to sniffle, "Did you…?" Her throat started to clog up as tears stroked down her cheeks, and into her mouth, "have to find him instead of me?!?"

Jessica couldn't believe the audacity of this woman knowing that all her cards were on the table, and hearing this, she knew that it had been on some personal level. More tears exploded from her eyes, and streaked down her cheeks, not even trying to wipe them away, then as she turned away, a small whimpering cry bellowed from beneath her mix of confusing lamenting sounds. As a rather small family of four walked in the restaurant they somehow saw that Mary was crying, and turned toward the corner. Only Mary had not stopped crying, and while the other three members of the family sat in the booth behind them, she continued to cry at the top of her lungs.

Jessica saw something really beautiful and ugly about this woman. A woman of sorrow, pain, misery, despair, jealous, and bitterness that was waiting for death to come and take care of her. Jessica had felt this small stroke of compassion for her, and extended her hand across the table to comfort her. When Jessica laid her hand against her shoulder Mary shrugged her shoulders off and continued to cry.

Jessica drew back her hand in disgust, and set it against the table. "Fine. If that's what you want." Jessica felt that she couldn't do anymore for this woman. She began to slump down in her seat, and saw that his mother was still lost in her own dream state. Jessica couldn't stand it, and if A.J. didn't get his ass down here she was about to strangle his mother. It would take a few minutes before she cooled down, and even though she wanted to help her she didn't have the strength to help her.

Not long after the argument between Jessica and A.J.'s mother, the elevator seemed to be taking its good old time when it finally landed on the basement, and the bell set off its last ding. The small mechanical parts inside the elevator were wheeling the whole elevator off but not their individual confidence.

A.J.'s queasiness left him when the trembling finally shook the elevator, and the large metallic doors slid opened. The two standing inside the elevator were happy to get a whiff of food, and with that smell circulating through their blood, they left the elevator, and headed toward the direction of the food. Their stomachs were craving food, and their mindset was headed in that direct. Nothing would stop them from getting a nice sixteen-inch sub sandwich, but when they headed into the entrance of the Subway, A.J. halted, caught off guard, and stood for a moment in thin air.

While Frank was already standing around in the abandoned line placing his order to the cashier, A.J. saw his mother and Jessica already in a booth, and a few seats behind them were a family of four sitting inside the booths. The parents were wearing dark sunglasses and the two children, round heads and bug eyed. But when the father took his sunglasses off, his eyes were bloodshot and had a thick disturbing shade underneath his eyes. His lips were crusted, and his face was dirty and unclean. He just stared at A.J. with very innocent eyes that were scorning A.J., angering him because he had his father, and he didn't. A.J. hated the boy, and stared at him with anger.

As he began to stare for a few more seconds, the small boy beside him started yelling, "Daddy, daddy." The father looked down, and felt the small boy's grasp around his side, and pulled him up next to him on the seat.

As A.J. headed toward his mother and Jessica, who were probably but he didn't sit down. He stood and felt struck by the boy's harmless smile, and his heart clogged with the thought of tears.

When he finally approached the table he saw Jessica slumped down in the booth with her arms slumped around her sides, with no sign of life in her eyes or body. A.J. became afraid because he also saw his mother crouched up on the table, her elbows positioned against the hard plain back, and a look that reminded him of nothing, as if it was entirely empty inside his mother's eyes as if despair had already set in her thoughts.

As he sat down, Jessica's body moved back up, and a hint of life glowed from her life-struck eyes.

"Hey." A.J. whispered, and extending his hand across the table, and he grabbed hold of her lifeless hand. It was white, like the color of a pale ghost, and she had somehow been touched or disturbed by a ghostly spirit.

She looked normal, but she lacked some encouraging stamina that always made him feel better about himself, but he knew that she hated him and he hated her.

"Mom?" But when he looked at them again, there was no response coming out of there mouths, which was beginning to piss him off. The anger was beginning to fuel his system, and he snorted out an echo of his rage. His face became unexpectedly red, and a drop of sweat rolled down his forehead and formed on his bright green shirt.

"What's wrong!" A.J. asked, and felt like his speaking was doing no good. The sweat trickled down his forehead ever so fast, and his patience was beginning to go with every new trickle that formed underneath the brow of his hair.

"Why don't you just go away, and never come back." A.J.'s mother said in a malicious and with a depraved tongue. Her eyes were filled with a hate that A.J. felt like he could never get to (but couldn't even if he tried). For the most part, A.J. didn't want to run away, nor was he going to, but what she was saying right now was not making any sense.

A.J. looked into her eyes, and saw that yelling at her wouldn't work at calming her down at all. A.J. spoke slowly, taking a few more deep breaths; he wiped the top of his forehead, and said, "If I went away, and never came back, you would never see me again. Is that what you want? Do you want your only son to run away?" That was the corniest thing he had ever said, but part of that was reflecting the truth.

Mary's anger was beginning to swell, and an undeniable heat flowed under their table. "You weren't here to save your father, so you might as well leave before you cause my death." A.J. felt the heat between the two, and A.J. was utterly confused by what she was seeing.

"I don't know what you're saying." A.J. voice raised above a tremor, and started to travel around the small room, shaking its very entirety, but not A.J. The room felt like it was about to tumble down on him, but before he went underneath the rubble, he had to get down to the bottom of his mother's mind.

"*You know what I am talking about!*" Mary's harsh voice demanded everyone's attention in the room. Even the would be busy attendant behind the subway counter cleaning all the extra condiments trays glanced, but did not say a word. For a second, A.J. played around with the idea of jumping up across subway counter, and giving him one good whack across the face. But, he didn't focus on the sensation for too long as he urged her to explain.

"What do you mean?" A.J. response was low, and dull like a soft serrated blade that was meant to cut through only the smallest of wounds.

"Don't give me that shit! All your lies, all your bullshit, all your evil deeds are the things that put your father in the hospital."

"I don't know what kind of bullshit you are talking about, but what I have done and will do *did* not put him in this state." A.J. was becoming fierce, and aggressive. "It was a heart attack *plain and simple.*" His words floated under his breath so that he would not be garnering attention. A.J. watched his mother closely as she leaned in and her jagged cheekbones swung like a limp prosthetic.

"Don't you lie to me? I had every chance to call the cops on you but I didn't, if it wasn't for your father, you'd be in jail!" She spoke through her clenched teeth, and bitterness surged through her nose, and goose bumps flowed over her arm.

A.J. was left with a situation that left him defenseless, and he needed to get control of this situation. A.J.'s anger was gradually soaring through his blood, and he wanted to start yelling at her and before he would turn his rage out on her, he took a deep breath. He exhaled all rationality that would have come in handy, but as he released the words off his lips, he couldn't help but sound a bit abrasive.

"Whatever I have done…" A.J. whispered to his mother, hoping that she heard whatever he was saying, "did not put my father in the hospital. I don't know why you are attacking me? Out of all people, you would be the one who would comfort me in a time like this. *My own mother.*"

A.J.'s mother scoffed as if she had heard something funny, like it was a joke. A.J.'s face tightened like one of a rope around his neck, suffocating all forms of life from his body, and making his cheeks turn red like polished apples.

As he puffed out that last breath of sanity, the anger took a hold of him, and he went off on his rampage.

"*What's that supposed to mean, mom?*"

Mary looked at A.J., seeing that serious look in his eye, and leaned forward, encroaching on her space, only this felt dangerous, as if he was crossing some enemy line that he shouldn't have been crossing, barreling ass forward into the emotional fray of scattered shrapnel and smoke. Only A.J. was willing to take the chance. But how couldn't he know the truth if he hadn't foreseen the lies? It was like looking at blood and tasting it to see if it was ketchup, and it would either be ketchup or blood, but the two did not taste the same.

His mother began to scoff, and turn her eyes at him as if he wasn't related to her at all.

"*What is that supposed to mean!*" A.J. saw that she was now giggling, but now he wanted to laugh, laugh at how bad he had wanted to slap her across the mouth again, just as he had did—and just as hard—as he did in his father's hospital room. But he regretted ever laying a hand on his mother 's face, and if he did it again, he would never forgive himself for the rest of his life. He already did it once, and that was embarrassing enough for him, because he hadn't fully processed why he had slapped her in the first place, but now knew that it wasn't just out of impulse this time—it was going to be out of anger.

"You were such a brat when your father was around. And you lied to us, but he even lied to you!" A.J. leaned up across the table, and saw that Frank was done ordering, but A.J. watched as Frank gave him a nod, and stood, looking at the brands of potato chips a few booths away, listening to everything. As he kept on eyeing the small bags, he conspicuously glanced at them, and listened with keen ears.

"What the hell are you talking about, mom. I don't know why you are playing games with my head?" A.J. whispered to his mother who had hid her smile as if she had finally caught what he had said, and returned to her normal self.

His mother let out a great sigh, and slammed her hands against the table as if she had lost her entire mind, and in a matter of speaking, she did loose it in the small universe of her mind. "Oh, what the hell. Your father is already in a coma. He might as well die in a few days, and it might be good that you know the truth."

"Well, tell me the truth then." A.J. hissed not regretting his decision, nothing sugarcoated, but his mother didn't intend to give him anything sugar coated.

"If you insist?" His mother sneered at him, like a two-year-old child that was ready to stick her tongue out, and as if she had a axe in her hands, the butchering of the truth was about to begin. A.J. shook his head, and waited for the answer to his question. "All I will say is that I am not your real mother."

A.J.'s heart dropped to his stomach, and almost felt like he had a severe case of diarrhea, and he didn't have any hole to release the shit that was building in his stomach. His eyes were filled with tears, but he couldn't cry, and that pained him the most. It was a low blow indeed, almost sounding untrue, but it hurt all the same.

It probably wouldn't have been worse than what he was feeling right now, and that was just a major headache. Her words affected him so quickly that it equaled up to a blade digging into his stomach, and had left a nice large gaping, hole speechless and trying to think of something to say.

"How the hell could this bitch live with herself, and pretend to be my mother?" A.J. said, to himself, and quietly swallowed his own spit that was lodged up in his throat. A.J. thought it was the most perverse act anyone could do, and especially if she pretended to love him, which seemed even more strange to him. "Why can't she just say it?"

With his half ripped heart that bore the last of his dignity, he spoke with no compassion in his voice, totally indifferent, and inconsiderate of whom had taken care of him all these years, was now a total stranger. For all A.J. knew, his mother was on the streets sucking dick for cocaine or in an abandoned crack house selling herself for a hit. There was no way in hell that he didn't want to think that, but he wasn't thinking straight at all.

"Your *real* mother died when you were two years old from a fatal accident. And to not let you be without a mother, your father married me before you could talk. Do you remember that?" She was so merciless with her axe of vindictiveness that he felt the blade of her tongue tearing his body apart.

A.J. sighed, feeling his mind being put at ease, calming the thoughts of his mother being a cocaine whore definitely eased the strain off his conscience. But he had to know why she was revealing this blade now, and slashing his body, not getting to the heart of this torture. Only he couldn't remember back so far to when he was about two, because that was just like a shaded part of his life, like a ink blot on a piece of parchment paper. "Yeah..."Only he couldn't think that hard...without a tear falling down his cheek, "a part of it, but not too much."

Mary chuckled, but this was not a vindictive laugh that she had just expressed, it seemed to be a normal laugh coming from the torturer.

A.J.'s mind was at ease when he found out that his mother had died long before he ever made any assumptions about, but he didn't know what she was getting at. "So, what did that have to do with anything?"

"Oh, I just remembered when you couldn't talk. We were so afraid that you weren't going to be able to talk. We asked you all these questions," Mary let out a cough that she had caught with the inside of her palms, and wiped it across her sleeve.

Then she decided to get reminiscent with A.J., to try to make him feel bad or just rub what used to be his life in his face. "But when you spoke your first words, I grabbed your father, and told him what he said. We were so happy for you." Mary said that with a pathetic and a sense of nostalgic ness in her voice, as if that very day had been the day before.

A.J. replied and felt sadness wrap around him, "Why did you lie to me? My whole life, you lied to me! Why couldn't you and Dad just tell me?" At that moment A.J. wanted to sniffle, but he couldn't cry, even though tears were strolling down his face. He wanted to cry for himself, if he could have done that he would have been happy enough to commit suicide. As he cleaned off the cup of his eye that had been swelling up with tears, feeling enough anxiety in his system to cry, but forced it down when this *stranger* spoke.

"I don't know, your father never wanted you to think about that, because he wanted you to be happy. He personally wanted to tell you last night, but somehow, fate intervened..."

All A.J. could do was stare with his wide blue eyes, listen with disenchanted ears, he became mentally disjointed from mind to toe, and his heart was still aching with confusion.

"So I could hear it from you!" A.J. remarked with more than offended, now he was letting his rage take control of his vocal cords. "Really, I guess that I wouldn't have found out sooner or later, you heartless bitch!"

"Well..." Mary breathed in, as if she was inhaling a cigarette, and exhaled a large fill of her vanity, "That was unfair to you, but your father never wanted you to know. You would obsess about it, and you wouldn't be happy."

A.J. lost control at that point, and the words just spread from his mouth like a disease. His voice was louder than he had expected.

"You know what!" Falling deeper into anger. "How could I be happy if you always tried to kept lying to me. I know the truth now, and it's sickening!

Don't ever call me, don't speak to me, and don't even come near me ever. We're through, and don't think for one second that my father loved me instead of you!"

"Loved you…" Mary's horrible vindictive tone rose, wanting him to be angry, because she was jealous because he really loved his son more than her. A.J. knew that he wasn't talking to his mother, he was talking to a total stranger.

A.J. grabbed Jessica, and did not speak a word to her. Frank watched in horror as he slung her arm over his shoulder, and Jessica moved by his side.

"Don't walk away from me…" Mary yelled with some last fleeting hope that she could get his attention, but the only attention that she got was from the family and the employee.

"You little ingrate, is this the kind of thanks I get for all the years I took care of you. *Is this what you would do to your father?*" She intended to hurt him even more, but how much could she say in one second? Probably a lot more than she would have thought of, but more would come to mind. Her mouth was just hanging open like some kid who had just been grounded.

A.J. heard this and scoffed as if he didn't hear her walking away with scars, memories, pains, all imprinted all over his body and mind, new wounds starting to reopen. And what was holding him and Jessica's body on there feet, was it something supernatural, was it God holding them in his hands, and pushing there bodies away from this stranger.

Totally ignoring his mother he moved with Jessica out the front entrance of the Subway, and didn't look back.

"God damn you." Mary said in a heat of rage, feeling the stinky sweat of her arm grease up the table as she finally gave up her vindictive torture, and her back curled into the slippery booth like one of a snake. The silence was horrifying, and it echoed underneath the skull of her brain sending powerful shock waves of turmoil throughout the entire store.

From two or three booths diagonally away, Frank was stunned by the whole scene, and just thought, "Fuck," and walked out with a heavy heart.

"All these fucking secrets coming out at the wrong time." He thought with some magnitude that the world was coming to an end, collapsing from the inside.

"I guess everyone is damned, including me." If that was an omen cursing his own personal life, he wasn't surprised of the irony. He and A.J. were on the verge of being shot at any second, and the way things were looking now, A.J.'s personal life was crashing faster, and it was ultimately going to destroy A.J. without the help of a steady balance. But maybe, just maybe that Chris had made him look after A.J. for a reason. He stopped questioning that a long time, and slowly followed him. But the problem was he didn't have a day, he only had a minute to let the entire scene blow away, and let the dust settle. This was a total mind fuck for him, because all of this was new to him. He was feeling the debris blow over him, and all he could do was just do what he was ordered to do, protect A.J.

When the three had past through the lobby hallway, Frank had woken himself out of that time zone that was clouded by the thick musty air cloud his eyesight, and grab at his Adams' apple like a piece of hang-rope wrapped around his neck. When he felt the last bit of sunlight hit his cheeks, he couldn't help but feel refreshed, but then a bit chilly from the quick gust of wind that crept in with the pre-sunset nighttime sky. Before the sun always faded there was always a long pink and green light that hovered over the city, and sometimes at around five-o clock in the morning, it resurfaced across the sky again.

Frank had seen both of these long luscious Milky Way lights at both of these times, always stunning him every time with its dangerous beauty. He wasn't really impressed with the one in the afternoon, which would suddenly disappear not long after rush hour.

When the three moved out of the long hallway they passed by a row of sick patients sitting on a park bench with a cigarette, the smoke twirled from there index fingers, their only friends. Their nicotine and their sadness were their only company—eyelids wrinkled all over their faces, fried blood shot nerves straining their minds, their bodies human toothpicks—sending them on a one way smoking ticket to hell. But Frank couldn't do shit for these people, and the least he could do was pity them, but he didn't want to waste his pity on the near dead and the nonfunctional human beings. "If I was them, I would kill myself a long time ago."

And with this theory in mind, he walked a long side his friends, ignoring the patients pitiful faces, across the parking lot feeling the cool breeze roll over their skin, easing the tension, just for a little bit if necessary. The three were exhausted, underfed, (except for Frank) and ready to crash on the nearest couch that they could find.

Frank could see it in their eyes that they were exhausted, but he didn't know what they wanted to do after this. He didn't feel like ruining the rather calming silence, and

as they moved through the lot of vehicles, the night seemed to be creeping faster than they wanted it to. Something in their minds told them that the night would either bring them harm or nothing, but they thought that the stars were just a shiny vessel (not on the outside) but they believed that it was really hidden inside the stars. It was as if they had to find what was inside the star to really understand the stars worth, but while they ventured on earth, they had to make the present last and quench the life until there was no more life to squeeze.

Time slipped through the night like butter when three finally approached the car, passing five or ten rows of cars, twenty minutes had slipped by when Frank moved towards the car and approached the driver seat. A.J. hopped in the passenger seat, and Jessica grabbed the back seat handle. Even though A.J. offered her the front seat out of kindness, she calmly declined his offer. A.J. didn't urge her on to give her the front, even though he insisted, and jumped in the backseat with her.

"She can grab my stick!" A.J. thought, and wanted to laugh, but he quickly held that humor inside as everyone closed the doors and she slowly nestled her body against the plastic arm rest, and stared into the sky. With everybody in there seats, Frank felt for the keys inside his pockets, and with one more pat on his right thigh he heard a soft *jingle* echo from his right pant pocket. Quickly sticking his hand inside the pocket he pulled out a ring of keys that were obviously to many different things. But out of the many jagged keys that looked like keys to a personal dungeon, he found the right key for his car and positioned the long key horizontally into the ignition hole. He felt the silence turn into a small rumble when he saw Jessica sliding down the back-seat, as if she was about to burst into flames.

Frank shrugged as he shoved the key into the ignition switch, and turned it fiercely hearing the engine buzz on with a quick *rumble*, and then a *soft* purr as Jessica' deep pale eyes reflect against the rear view mirror. Then she smiled as she had been tickling her vagina, and she gave Frank a very twisted glare. "Are you okay?" Frank saw the glazed over glare in Jessica's eye, and he was sure that she knew that he knew something was going on in her mind. She wanted to turn away and blush, but something inside her told Frank that she knew something.

She puckered her lips and turned away, very confused and her eyes showed no more of despair, and her lovely slender cheeks pushed back, revealing her dimples.

Frank had seen this look often, and he didn't know what to do, but keep driving.

But as they left the parking lot, Frank smirked as if he had secretly left his mark but as the P.O.S. moved out of the parking lot, he took the first right out of the parking lot he did another quick right avoiding the big red STOP sign. Frank decelerated, easing off from thirty-five miles per hour to the fifteen miles. But what did he care, he needed to leave that place behind him, and as he pressed on the gas he turned right again making his way toward the highway.

Louis T. Bruno

"*Here I am…On the road again…Here I am…Up on the stage*" The lyric surfaced in his head like a bad dream, but it was catchy. He started to hum the lyrics as he tore the road up at sixty miles per hour, definitely trying to get a speeding ticket, which he did not need. "*Here I go…Turn the page!*" It was Metallica, an eighties heavy metal rock group, but he couldn't put a finger on the original band that played it. He would come up with the name sooner or later, but in the meantime, he had to get back to his house and stay out of sight for a while, to think and maybe talk some more business with the *new* boss of the family.

Chapter XIII:

"Transcendent Dreams and Milky Way Lights"

While Frank was driving again, he decided to give his sandwich away since he had neither had the urge to eat the rest of his sixteen-inch sub, so he gave it to Jessica and A.J. The setting sun, that had set about thirty minutes when they had been driving, had brought out the ghostly color that was largely due to that of the destructive ozone layer, expelling soft pillows that seemed to stretch as a soft green shade moved opposite of the sky. When he made the first offer, no one said a word. A.J. just shrugged it off while Jessica was already in a peaceful slumber. With that decision *going, going, and gone* Frank kept on his assigned course, and ventured down the highway at the blazing speed of sixty, then seventy miles per hour.

After the next thirty minutes or so, Frank saw the exit ramp that lead to their sanctuary, which was only forty-five minutes to an hour away from the city and fifteen to the nearest location of butt fuck nowhere. It was all that they needed before they went back to the jungle, peace and quiet. Luckily, if his parents weren't home they could probably get some well-deserved rest. But while A.J. and Jessica were already asleep, he didn't feel the need to go eighty, but he needed to exceed the speed as much as he could.

He knew that he needed to go, but he didn't know what was driving him onward. Was it some Holy Grail or the Excalibur, the mighty sword of King Arthur? Was he driving toward that? But, now, his Excalibur was "the truth," more than food or a pack of cigarettes. All he knew what to do was to survive, and like any other organic life form, survival was the basic need for anyone, and Frank knew that just as well as Chris or A.J. did.

Only when he was beginning to stare further down the road, trying to see past the long congesting darkness his car rolled over concrete like two big bare feet trampling over a bed of flowers. He couldn't wait to feel the need to get back to his own home, the warmth of his own bed and how the unmade sheets always made him feel all cozy, especially when he was dirty. "Bathe in sheets of filth." Frank thought, and the thought of going to sleep in his own bed made everything seemed less heavier, as if a less few cruel irons were brought off his back, and this cruel unusual pleasure of getting home less excruciating. He didn't know why he had this pain in his chest, and when he thought about it the creature—a small exoskeleton of a fly oozed to the back of his mind, piercing and stabbing at his nervous system. But pushing that aside, he kept on his final destination, and the second to last one for the night, his home.

Seeing that the night was beginning to take its form over the sky, he saw his last exit taking shape, and a sign came up like a shark fin rising out of the great salty sea—sending the green glitter in scattering directions as soon as Frank felt the ramp form a straight line again. He looked into the rear view mirror, and saw that not a single car light was in sight for miles, diluting and stretching everything—the time zone, sanity, and his eyes. He liked it like that. Maybe it was paranoia, maybe it was that hint of suspiciousness, but he got a little panicky when there was no one around him on an open road, and he watched in the rear view mirror as another car's bright lights came into sight. Frank relaxed, and continued on his way, but all the same, he was driving at an incredible rate of seventy miles per hour, and as he saw the next sign read,

APPALACHIAN

3 Miles

He let a great sigh of relief from his gut, and headed down the next three miles, and there was no turning back.

Walking in his house, Frank took a quick smell, and remembered the very first girl that he had in the sack. "Erica," Frank muttered remembering how she tasted like a peach and her pussy was tough and tighter than a slab of meat fat. And that's why it maybe connected to the fact that he liked it only in his bed. It was dirty and comfortable, and that brought him back to his very first girl.

As that dry connilingus smell faded away from his nostrils, A.J. and Jessica followed behind him, probably not telling that the smell was either connilingus or wouldn't have cared about Frank's keen basset-hound sense of smell.

In the dark and deserted house, Frank searched for the light around the connecting living room and kitchen. Frank's knees whacked into something, and the force shook the table making a small *jingling* sound. Navigating his body through the dark wasn't an easy thing to do, especially with all the lights out, and in his house he was always bound to knock something over in his messy unorganized house. But as he moved his hand across the darkened room, he felt his hand brush up against a smooth top. It felt like a lampshade, but he couldn't see it to really put it into perspective. And if there was a lampshade, there was a switch that could turn on the light.

Frank's fingertips graced along the plastic material, and moved his hand up the inside with the tips of his fingers. With the tips of his fingers, his hand moved forward slowly, and feeling the gritty and metallic lamp post clinging to his fingers and then he felt a little black switch that was just below the light bulb like a pricking thorn. Placing his thumb and finger in between the switch, he turned it to the left and suddenly felt the light of the world shining from that lamp, and blinding him for a moment, revealed the living room.

He turned away, seeing Jessica and A.J. holding each other, and A.J., with an enlightened voice, "We have light." The laugh revealed his loving smirk, and Frank ventured into the kitchen. On the bar table sat a folded note on the table, and seeing in the near dim kitchen the message was addressed to him personally.

Frank

It was neatly written too, it was his mother's handwriting because when she always gave him his bagged lunches (before she stopped) would always write his name on it. He was touched by what she did, because it made him feel like his parents cared about him. Brushing the idea away for a moment, he picked the note up by the corners, and gently opened the note to read what it said. It read,

Dear Frank, hope you like Tacos. They are in the fridge, just warm them up, and sprinkle whatever you like on them. Love you, Mom

Frank felt a slight pinch grab and forced him to remember but it also reminded him of what he had. It threw him a right hook, and he couldn't remember the last time he wanted to cry. He hadn't felt this way in a long time, and a cord stringing sadness in his heart, and he wiped his wet eyes. "Get a hold of yourself, you can't show any weakness…" He gripped his hand, and then slammed his hand against the table. Out of the corner of his eye, he saw two pairs of eyes silently watching, but then disappeared down the hall.

"Are you guys hungry? I could heat some Tacos up for you guys."

"Yeah, sure." Even though he could feel that he was looking into there eyes, he could feel these tainted spirits were living in the dark. "No. I'm okay."

Even though Frank could hear her rumbling stomach hunger gurgling with anticipation, he could very well feel her distaste, like hot liquid on her lips. "No. I don't want to…I feel sick. I got to keep up my girlish figure." He could hear a small *pat pat* coming from the darkened hallway.

Frank couldn't help but noticing that her stomach *was* getting a little bulgy, but he scoffed at the response, knowing that was her decision he stuck with it. "She is getting a little big in the ass and thighs." Only he didn't want to address it, being that it was such a wrong time to think about it, and should welcome the room to Jessica, so that they could get down to business.

"Do you want to sleep in the bed across from my room?" Frank asked before they lost them, and saw the look of sadness glowing from the darkness, like a leech.

"Go down the hall, and it'll be on the first door on your left."

"Okay."

While the two darkened souls were taking their time down the hall, wrapped in each other's arms, Frank hadn't left his position, standing over the sink as if he had nothing better to do than listen to the creaks in the floors. But this weird feeling had crept into his system like he wasn't alone, even though he didn't know what it was. It crept into his mind like he was about to burst one of his blood vessels, and see nothing but sprinkling bloody glitter when the creaking stopped as A.J. moved toward the door where Jessica had been sleeping. Frank knew that he was close enough to smell her perfume from all the way underneath the door, and if she was waiting for him underneath the covers naked, she was going to show him a wild night. Frank didn't *want* to know or *care* to know if she was, and he had other important things to do like smoking his cigarette and contemplating their strategy, but he would come to a plan later.

Overall, if he had to say that they really talked about any real strategy, he would have guessed that they had just made up something to talk about before they ate. But he guessed it was good because Frank was kind of nervous about the whole thing, but he had to just go with it, and let it flow. Whatever would happen would happen when it would happen. . .

"And now," Frank conjured in his head, "Time for that smoke." As he decided on that very thing, he stuck the plate that had the third taco resting on it back in the fridge. He would eat it later, probably before he went to bed, but that still wouldn't satisfy his hunger for the truth. There was no remedy for that.

As A.J. was about to open the door, he put his ear against the door, and took a minute to listen to whatever was going on in her room. There was silence and as he listened to the air traveling, scratching along the oak wood door, and traipsing the wall. His heart began to pound against the interior of his chest, and he approached the slide deck door.

"Man, should I go in or stay out?" A.J. contemplated this decision, for a moment, then a few seconds, then when it was beginning to take him longer than he expected it to be—stuck in fear—he just went with his gut decision.

A.J. gripped the round door knob that seemed darker than a glass of black Russian mixed with tar, and slowly but surely turned the knob to the right hearing the hinges give a soft squeak as he inched his body into the room. Stepping with his right foot into the door, he pushed the door slowly and wide enough so he could fit his other foot through. Seeing the outlook of the room, the bright grinning moonlight was shining though the window onto the queen size bed where Jessica was sprawled out with her left foot hanging off the bed, and a part of the moon was shining on her Achilles heel. The light was hard to follow, which was a good thing. Only he hoped that she wasn't his Achilles heel—a fear that he would become her burden—or vice versa.

The light, A.J. liked the light, but he didn't want to see *that* light. And while he was alive, he saw a different light, and it was heading him to his heaven on earth. Slowly walking through the dark room, he tried not to wake her from the deep slumber as he moved closer to the bed he saw her golden blonde hair shine and reflect something perfect and ugly, a smashed Picasso that couldn't be refused, but was deeply drawn to it.

"She looked beautiful, even in the moonlight." Sometimes when he didn't want to admit it, the passion that he had felt before turned into something more meaningful. He didn't know if it was love—he wouldn't be human if he didn't love her, but he definitely liked her too, because her body was sweating with carnal pleasure, but her heart was the conductor for her hormones to create the sweat on her body.

When he finally approached the edge of the bed, she rolled around to the other side, waving her caboose, subconsciously teasing A.J. with all the tools that all a woman had. A.J. loved it when she did that, but he remembered that when he met her, her butt was smaller than usual, but maybe she was beginning to grow a little taller and maybe she was starting to fill out. "She can't be," A.J. thought, and then laid his dirty hand on her shoulder, "the only change I see is in her tits and ass." Flushing the sexual feeling from his mind and body, he set his knee on the bed, and felt his body sink into bed like quicksand as he slowly laid his body next to hers. As he slipped his shoes off his feet, he gave them a good kick off the bed, and as they scattered in the sky at the foot of the bed.

Although they were in the dark, A.J. could see her sleeping face shining so beautifully from the help of the bright moon that was pouring in with intensity. With her rather smelly feet exposed to the air, A.J. grabbed at the pillow and pushed it away from him as he reached for the covers. Holding onto the silky linear padding, he moved it down, hovering his legs and thighs over the blanket, he slipped inside the covers, and saw that she was very well naked as he thought, caboose showing and all. The outline of her body gleamed like a ghost, and her hair shined like the very sun that was missing from the middle of the day, uplifting his spirits to the point of total mythological perfection. He felt uncomfortable wearing his pants underneath the covers, but he would slip them off sooner or later.

"Jessica?" A.J. whispered breaking through the silence that had been so consistent and to A.J. it felt rather odd in the silence of the room.

Jessica's eyeballs started to twitch and the corner of mouth started to pull back (drool already traveled down her mouth) when her lids pulled back like the very curtains that blocked the moon light. He saw the inside of her eyes, and inside those very sockets hid some deep underlying sadness that he had never seen before, plus a layer of confusion. Like he was *supposed* to see it, but how could he if he didn't take time to notice it.

"Yeah, baby?" Jessica's mouth curved when she spoke, and it sounded like a garbled murmur, but he couldn't tell the difference either way. She let out a great yawn, and stretched her hand over towards his, and clenching his hands, grabbed it and said, "What's up?"

A.J. just looked down at her, with a compassionate smirk he retorted with a soft "Nothing, I just wanted to see how you were doing."

She looked confused, like she had just gotten off the train, but she wasn't smiling in that clouded daze that came with that marijuana kick. There was no high here; just confusion rolled around a brown Philly blunt that was the result of sleep paralysis.

"Well…" Jessica swallowed a bit of her spit, let off a fresh lip smacking *clap,* "Thanks for dropping in on me. Sorry I couldn't clean up and make yourself beautiful." After she finished cleaning her lips, she began to smile, with no clerical sense, or seriousness, in her voice. When she smiled, that made him smile. There was something beautiful and innocent in those eyes that he found sexy. A.J. heard her witty comeback, and a small chuckle escaped the two lovebirds, as if they had just met each other.

He was smiling like some great fool, and Jessica chuckled from the fact that he was smiling. Jessica always saw him as this kind of serious person, but when she saw A.J. smiling, she loved him even more, because it made him feel innocent again.

But there was something on her face that looked like she was in some sort of distress. A.J.'s smile hadn't disappeared when he was speaking, and he was exactly what he was, a grinning idiot, but that grin turned into a low and lazy frown.

"Are you okay?" A.J. asked as he stared deeper into her eyes, not noticing Jessica's undoubtedly strained look of surprise on her face, "What?" Her head hadn't moved from the pillow, and this wasn't working for A.J. since his neck was hurting.

He stretched his legs out, and fixed the pillow so he could see her better. When he fixed the pillow and said with that compassionate voice, "Are you okay?"

Jessica looked at him inquisitively and said with her groggy voice, "Yeah, what do you mean, *I'm fine.*"

"I know that, but are you okay, like *okay okay*. You were pretty quiet on the way up." A.J.'s voice was rather impotent, although he was sexually strong, and he had lift off. He couldn't help it, but how could he hide it since he was sitting in the covers with his naked girlfriend, primed up and ready for more sex. It was a good time for him to take off his pants, and let her feel his Eiffel Tower poking against her body, but he didn't feel like he wanted to have sex.

Feeling his pants becoming rather annoying to his legs, he grabbed his pant button and pushed it through the small opening. Slipping his pants down his legs and kicking his jean pants down his thighs, he kicked them down toward the end of the bed, and felt the sexual feeling flow through his shaft again. It was a wrong time, but maybe they could go at it one more time before the night was over. But, A.J. was still determined to find out about Jessica's ill behavior, even if he had to suppress his manhood for a few minutes.

"What happened between you and my…" He stopped himself before he continued on saying 'my mother', he stopped and took it into consideration. His life…no, his whole childhood seemed to be built around lies, and the fact that his own father had even refused to tell him the truth was something of a backstabbing lie. He was disgusted by the whole thing, and it made him just want to hurl the entire taco on the bed. As he thought about it more it seemed almost unreal, but what was real anymore, which seemed to be the two-hundred thousand dollar question of his life.

But before he could finish his sentence, Jessica broke in at a time that seemed to be just right. "Your mother?" Jessica said with a simple attitude that made A.J. less perturbed by the whole situation.

"Yes." A.J. said, annoyed by the sound of his words. "What went on between you and her last night?"

The thought hit Jessica like a bad *WHACK* against the side of her brain, as if she had tried to forget about everything that happened. Jessica couldn't really understand why A.J. had thought nothing had gone on between them, but in all reality, something did. She spurned the whole conversation from the moment it started, but maybe it was that sad pitiful look on her face that made him seem to cling onto the situation like incurable asbestos.

"I don't know," She moved her body, her face was the epitome of incurable sadness, as she breathed out with that "I'm-not-talking-so-leave-me-alone" jerk of her body. Her face was so construed that she looked like an older woman that was unable to stay awake, and she rolled back over on her side facing A.J. with her eyes rolled downward. Her lips pouted, avoiding eye contact—staring at his small furled chest hair and if A.J. was ready or not, he was going to hear the whole truth.

"She said that she couldn't live with what you were doing anymore, and when I tried to calm her down, she went on about how I was a whore and how I was trying to ruin your life." In that instance Jessica wanted to cry, cry to A.J. about her pregnancy, and how she had been keeping it a secret. She wanted to tell him every time she saw him, but she couldn't bear to tell him now. Especially in the recent days she had been throwing up constantly. Biting her tongue, she continued adding another conjecture. "She was mad that I found him while she was crying in your room."

"My father…" A.J. interrupted, and stroked the side of her face gently with the tips of his fingers. He felt her skin and it gave him comfort that he was next to her, to know that someone cared for him as much as she did, and if she were anyone, she would have left him twenty-four hours ago.

But Jessica saw something in A.J. eyes and his cheeks felt luke-warm when she put her open palm against his cheeks, which made her quiver in her very bed, and she couldn't have sex with him now, she felt too sick.

After that momentary silence, A.J. moved his hand away from her cheek, and laid his back against the bed, and stared at the darkened ceiling, and at that moment, he wrapped his arm over his body, and buried his head in the pillow, slowly breathing against her head. She felt him cringe, but tugged her body even harder.

"Your father loved you, I could see it." Jessica tried to comfort him, he couldn't respond. "Don't worry about whatever your mother said."

"She's not my mother!" A.J. said rather coldly, "how could a mother ever think of treating me like a total piece of shit?"

His statement shocked Jessica, obviously it wasn't his tone, or the obvious strike of anger, but it was the fact that A.J. was clueless to evil, and gave him a low smirk that was wordless, but she didn't feel like getting into this shit with him.

"Get some sleep." Jessica turned her head upwards, pressing her soft silky hair against his chest and kissed him on the lips. She lowered her eyes, and pressing her right ear against his chest, she drifted to that place of darkness, dreams, and milky ways where time did not exist.

A.J. lowered his eyes, breaking through the darkness and saw the top of her golden hair shining with such brilliance in the moonlit sky. Then he felt this tingly feeling crawling over him, like hands that were dipped in ice cold water and were rubbing all over his body but his only release was to cry, and cry he did. It wasn't like a long wailing cry, but it was a whimpering cry that babes only did when they needed the warmth of their mother's arms.

Jessica, who was not even asleep by the time, slowly opened her eyes, she felt his shoulders shake. As she clenched his body, she leaned her head towards A.J.'s chest, and kissed a bunch of his hair. His whimpering continued for more than a few minutes when they both finally fell asleep, for the first time in what seemed like days and nights. It was only eight thirty—quarter to nine, but it felt like two thirty in the morning, just as the pink and green milky-way light that gave off its last bit of glamour before it disappeared over the city.

Everything was happening all at once, and the night weighed on them. Frank's mind felt like they were being forced through a tiny hourglass, landing at the bottom on the entire hill of sand. But as he laid his head back against the grainy metal chair, he felt his eyes become heavy on him, and the bright burning stars only urged his sleepy behavior. And as he closed his eyes, he felt time begin to slow down for him, and as he almost felt like he was dreaming, he felt…no, heard a voice calling out to him, "Hey?"

The voice called out to him again, then all of a sudden as he opened his eyes he was nestled inside a trash can, and a watery smell clung to the sides of the trashcan. At the end of the trashcan was Chris hunkering down on his knees, looking through a garbage can at somebody, and that somebody was him. He could smell the disgusting fumes of vile sewage that rested in the pit of his stomach, he was sleeping in the same clothes—long shirts and dark black Corduroy jeans. Before he could drive his cousin, Jerry had taken him all the way to the city, and had dropped him off in Brooklyn. He didn't care about where he was, all in all, he hadn't cared whether or not he was living at that time. He was so cold, and everything seemed so distant in the round metallic hole, suicide and despair went hand in hand when living inside a trash can—his hunger made sense as well—and the cold air made this seem like a four star room at the Marriot.

He was so distraught—he had made permanent indentions—knife marks that were starting to heal, but he kept scratching at it to never let it heal before it would finally sink into his pigmented skin.

It was when Chris held his hand out to him, and said, "What are you doing in there?" Chris had looked a little younger than he had seen him at the hospital—but with his wide-eyed and rather adventurous look—he welcomed him by the hand and helped him out of that garbage can.

Frank had said nothing to him, but he took his hand that was peering into the garbage can and as he slid out, lines of paper fell off him like leaves in the wintertime, and pieces of garbage fell off him. When he stood on his own two feet he felt the cold but warm New York breeze blanket him like a coos would do with her fancy perfume and soft but greasy kisses.

He saw that Chris had dusted off his shoulder from another piece of paper that was dangling from him like bait. But when all the paper on him was off and a refreshed look entered into Frank's face, Chris—a far better dresser than Cuomo stood back and said "Were you hiding from anyone?"

"No." Frank replied, still smelling the stench of the trash can all around him, and stretching his back out, it cracked like one of a cripple that had been touched by some magnificent force that made his back become straight again.

Chris seemed somehow oddly patient and somehow ready to start laughing at the many jokes he had rattling around in his brain. "So, what are you doin' in the trash can, you renovating the place?"

Frank somehow found the energy to laugh, even though he smelled like shit, he still had the stomach to laugh, despite that odd hollow pit in his stomach that felt like copulating cockroaches.

"No…no…" He started to sound like a broken record, but he then took a chance of not being so guarded. "Well, I was hiding from my parents, because they started to take away my privileges and everything else."

"What kind of privileges? Smoke?" Chris asked, as he pulled out a cigarette box, and started to thumb through the package. He took out a cigarette, put to his lips, and lit it with one *wick* of his lighter. He held out the box to him, but Frank declined. "I guess that be contributing to a minor," Chris huffed along with the smoke.

"They grounded me," Frank said, feeling the wind crawling up his pants,

"I'm on fucking house arrest, and took all my allowances away for an entire month."

Chris took a long drag of his cigarette—destroying half of the cigarette—and watched it float into the air. Chris took the cigarette out of his mouth, and held it rather roughly between his fingers. He turned toward Frank, and spoke with sincerity in his voice. "Yeah, is that why? Or is there something else?"

Frank, who had went through his bag of marijuana, wanted something to put in his lips, but bit the bottom of his already chapped, and bleeding lip.

"My mom and dad are going through a rough time now, and I fucked up in school. I almost killed a kid for talking shit about me." As soon as he mentioned the thought of his mother and father, he felt the urge to ask for a cigarette, but controlled his urges for a few more seconds, but felt his organs attacking his weakened body.

"Well," Chris held the cigarette to his lips, took another puff, and exhaled a long cloud of smoke into the air as if he was a big shot of a real professional. But something was off; he had the fascination of a friend, but the eyes of a clean gun barrel. He let the hand that was holding the burning stick fall to his side, and in that five-second smoking silence Chris returned with another question.

"What did you do?" Chris said, and flicked the ashes from the burning stick. They fell to the concrete like they were lead, but then disappeared like ashes from a burning smokestack.

"I…" He wanted to sway the conversation, but he felt like coming out with it. But before he decided to speak on with it, Chris intervened with his annoying impatience, "What? Cat got your tongue?"

"No." Frank retorted, feeling the urge getting to him, talking to him, whispering, *pull me out and take a hit, you know you want to!* He had to ignore it, but he wouldn't last the temptation for long. "I just stole some money from my parents, and I snuck out of my bedroom the last few nights. I already have a court statement, but the judge didn't force an ankle bracelet on me."

Chris let a small laugh escape him, and he took another puff of his cigarette. He turned toward Frank. "Sorry, but I know where this is going?"

"Where?" Frank retorted offended by this guy's unnatural behavior.

"It's obvious," Another chuckle escaped Chris as they headed down Bleaker street, and somehow, the time didn't seem important to them, "you were seeing a woman weren't you? Your *goomar!*"

Frank didn't exactly know what the fuck he was talking about, but played along with it, because of the rather frightening and terrifying look Frank saw in Chris's eye, *told* him to play along. "Yeah, that's it!"

"You didn't even know what I just said, did you?" Chris said, pulling this out of his bag of tricks, and saw Frank's lips staying motionless while he was just pain confused. Chris had a threatening look on his face, but then laughed as he started to console the frightened child. "Your broad, that's what I mean!" Chris shouted, and started to laugh, with a wolf smile, and sarcastic grin.

Frank somehow, even while the knot in his stomach had already begun to tighten around his two livers, he began to laugh realizing what he said.

Chris beckoned to his attention "Listen," and threw the cigarette to the ground, "why don't you come back to my place, and me and my wife will put some food in your stomach," and stomped on it with his slick shined classic shoes. Frank also stood for a moment, and watched as he grind his foot on the burning cigarette, and twisted his foot as if he was doing some fifty's step.

"Why are you inviting me into your home? I don't even know you man." Franks words were redundant, but Chris didn't seem to care.

"No, man." Chris dusted off his shoulder, and stepped away from him. "You can't be smelling like shit all the time. How are you going to keep fresh and clean with the ladies if you smell like shit?"

Frank didn't understand why he had stepped on his cigarette with those nice, bright shoes. Those must have cost him a fortune, but with a suit like that, he could probably afford ten more of those shoes where he came from. But he also didn't have that swanky Manhattan kind of appeal, who didn't have time to talk to no one and stayed in there own world. The air seemed to be less thick around his face, the sun seemed to peer through some overhead clouds, and he could finally breathe without almost choking on his own spit. But Frank didn't seem to care about what kind of shoes he was wearing anymore, he wanted to know who this strange, and dangerous character was.

"What's your name?" Frank asked, and saw him raise his foot off the smashed cigarette, and then he returned to that slow normal pace, as if he didn't hear Frank talking to him at all. Frank walked beside him trying to keep up to him, even though he was taking his time, Frank felt the need… no, the urge to know who he was speaking to.

"Why? What's it to you?" Chris retorted, and quickened his pace. He had a pale and disgusted look about him that said all kinds of nasty things, but it wasn't coming from his mouth, it was spurning in the deep pit of his eyes. That dangerous look when someone's paranoia is sparked, and the only thing that someone in their position could do—keep a rather brisk pace and abandon their current responsibilities. But Chris didn't seem to care about leaving Frank behind, which was strange to Frank, but it wasn't strange to Chris. This bothered Frank, especially when he should thank the *man* that pulled him out of that trash can.

But, this guy didn't look a day over thirty, but he spoke to him like he was on his level. Frank moved beside him, and continued to speak in a sorrowful and resentful tone that only wanted to him to listen to what he had to say.

"No, I didn't mean it like that, all I wanted to do say thank you to the man that got me out of that garbage can."

Chris stopped in his tracks and replied, "No problem kid. If you ever need to earn some extra money, just say the word, and I'll give you something to do."

"But what's your name?" Frank yelled out as he watched him approach the next street. "What's your name man?" Frank saw him look back with his black rooted eyes, and yelled back with all his might in the world. It sounded so loud that the entire neighborhood shook when he said it.

"I'm Chris Mangini!"

Frank heard the name, and it sent off a loud echo inside his head. It kept ringing like some redundant alarm clock chirp and he felt his knees quiver like some school boy sissy, his heart shake with fear and a long forgotten pain that had come back to haunt him. Chris Mangini was back to haunt him. But then Frank began to have a headache, and the name echoed even louder inside his brain. His name became louder as the city street walls began to rumble and water began oozing out of the cement. Pressing his hand against his skull and thumping against his face he felt like it was about to explode. And then his entire body became cold, right down to his feet, but then he felt somebody poking him. Like one of a needle poking into his shoulder, Frank immediately grabbed onto it trying to find out where it was coming from, and opened his eyes.

But then, when he opened his eyes, everything was gone, Bleaker Street (another version), the trash can, everything was gone. He couldn't believe that he went from sitting on the porch smoking a cigarette to somewhere on Bleaker Street, talking to Chris like he would be just with some regular Joe on the street. And all he had grabbed onto was a hand, and that hand belonged to A.J.

"Hey, what's up?" A.J. said, squirming from the pain and trying to fidget his fingers out of his grip. He had scared and surprised look, as if he was going to die, and he was starting on his fingers.

He felt his small fingers in the grip of his tarantula claws, and by the look on A.J.'s face; he looked as if he was about to cry from his own grip.

Frank squeezed his hand one last time to see if he was real or not, and then let his hand go. A.J.—whose body was wrapped tight—felt his blood flowing through his fingers again gently rubbing his cupped hand. He breathed into his hand, sending smoke into his palm and rising into the air.

"Nothing, I just fell asleep a few minutes ago." Frank whispered still not fully awake—even though his hands were numb and his face was cold, he was fidgeting a cigarette out of the carton. He leaned over, and grabbed the end of it with his mouth; the cigarette fell on his lap.

"A few minutes ago?" A.J. burst out, and began to laugh. It was a raucous laugh that made Frank relax, but at the same time, let him remember that he was human as well.

"It's two thirty in the morning." A.J. said, pulling a chair next to Frank. He rubbed his shoulders as he glanced at his cigarette box.

Frank saw him, and did the respectable thing a person would do. "You want one?"

A.J. caught his voice, "One what?" and turned toward him with a sparked attention in his eye. Frank wanted to laugh, but all he could get out of his cancer bearing lungs was a small cough. Effortless at his laugh, he returned him another sarcastic look, and went for his fallen cigarette.

"A cigarette!" Frank muffled with the cigarette in his mouth, and extended his lazy hand toward the table, and placing his gaunt fingers around the lighter.

"No. I don't smoke." A.J. gave a small wave, and he fell back in his seat, letting the cold air thicken on his arms like a bloody pan.

He looked at A.J., holding the lighter up to the end of the cigarette, blankly staring, and then said, "Nervous?" He flicked the lighter, and the wind blew the ignited flame out.

"What?" A.J. said.

"Nothing." Frank replied, leaning back against the chair, and he covered the end of the cigarette with his mouth as a soft *wick* escaped with a *crackle* of the flames covering the end of stick, and serving him another fresh rush of nicotine through his veins. After he inhaled the nicotine, a cloud of smoke rose from the insides of his mouth, and twirled into the dreamy starry night sky.

After a few moments of silence past between them, Frank saw that questionable look in A.J.'s eyes, and it looked like he always had on his mind, but he couldn't get out. But, he decided to indulge him since they weren't particularly doing anything.

"You got something on your mind?" Frank asked as he pulled the cigarette out of his lips, and held it between his fingers as he let his hand fall on his leg. The smoke twirled as if it was some dancing message that was an ode to the Gods of some ancient Native American tribe. A.J. couldn't help but feel entranced by this smoke, but then felt pulled away from the smoke, and responded in about less than five seconds.

"What?" A.J. spoke through his teeth, and wiped the corner of his lips.

Frank took another long puff of his cigarette, and wondered how long it would take him to keep on playing this dumb act before Frank would finish his cigarette. But, his patience was burning faster than that cigarette he was sucking on, and he huffed out with a fiery dangerousness, that ultimately gave away a fleeting impatience.

"Do you have something to say?" He was more agitated, and less calm than he had been, flicking his cigarette a part of his patience went sprawled around on the deck.

"Yeah…" A.J. was nervous more than ever because he didn't know how he would react, but he decided to confidently go with what he had to say. Bending forward in his chair, A.J. scratched the top of his head, and came out with what he had to say. "So, do you think that Gene is after Chris's long lost cousin…or, after me?"

This was an unsuspecting question, and Frank's face fell—his human skeleton was sucking up the cigarette for all it was worth. After the smoke did its dance into the sky, he replied with the most gravest of looks on his brow. "I don't know. But whatever it is, Gene is going to make his point known in the next few days. Then after that, we hit back." Frank was so confident that he looked as if he had grown older in the face, but that could be from smoking too much, but he wasn't too sure of what he was saying, just assuming.

Only A.J. saw that they had something in common now, and it wasn't the smoking. It was the look in his eye that said he was with him until the end. As he saw Frank sucking on his cigarette, he blew out another puff of smoke, and his voice became fearful, almost ominous. "But if we ever get separated, I want you to go to the nearest payphone, and call me from there. And don't go to the city or George Bradley without me, got it."

"Don't worry, I won't." A.J. had a very sarcastic tone about him, and the two let out a constrained laugh, which they should have done a long time ago to relieve a bit of their tension, or fear. Even though they had yet to see the rest of their dangerous times unfold before them, they somehow managed to let a laugh escape between them, preparing them for the hard road ahead.

"Don't worry, even if you don't have your family anymore, you have me. You can't blame yourself for what happened…life gives you some shitty cards, but *what do you do,* play with what you got. I can be your entire family, but I'm not *gonna* be your shoulder to cry on."

A.J. wanted to cry from this beautiful, very poetic line (for Frank, it was poetry). "I don't expect you to," A.J. smirked, and then leaned forward, and whispered, "you don't have any tits."

The two let out one more laugh that seemed to resemble a howl—Frank was moving off the chair, clutching his chest—A.J. slapped his knee—and then after it ended, Frank said, "I'm sorry, man. That's the only sentimental shit that's going to be said."

"Thanks," A.J. nodded his head, and he fell back into his seat. His heart was swelling with a new found respect, and he looked into the sky. The world was a dazzling bright circus, everyone showed off their bizarre oddities, with full fashion, and without discretion for class.

Chapter XIV:

"The Bear's Hibernation"

At this meeting, one of the many soldiers that arrived early was Billy Fischel, a medium sized boy who had bluish green hair, and dark crystal cat-like eyes. He was always called "crazy boy" because he had gotten that name by trying to stop a bully from hitting on his 8-year-old sister. It got so bad to the point that he had started to harass her, called her house at odd hours of the night, and one day after school he broke into their house to sexually molest her in her room. But he beat the bully so ravishly that his fist pulsated for several days, and Tylenol didn't help to swell the pain. He beat him so bad that he put him in the hospital for about two to three months giving him a broken jaw (including knocking out all of his teeth), all of his ribs. He left him with a crooked eye that made him a laughing stock of the entire school.

That was one of the many guests that were already gracing their presence of the last and final meeting Gene Dov had planned. Even though they weren't the people that you wouldn't bring to your house and have dinner with, they were the most reliable when it came down to doing any type of dirt they were experts in burglarizing, diamond heists, bookkeeping. Horrible as this sounds, they were all predominately Jewish between the ages of fifteen through twenty-five. Being that murder was always another venture, some were willing to learn and others already had that in spades.

It wasn't true to say that his crew wasn't all muscle because when Gene stepped in, he found guys that could knock holes through walls, and get your money without even laying a finger on that person. But when Joey (his main man) came into the picture, he was rumored to have taken more bullets than any other man alive, and it literally crippled him for over a year. But when he came back he disciplined himself in all kinds of weight training and rehabilitation classes, and everything that he could do to get himself walking again. After a year's worth of training, he had thirty pounds of muscles that would make anybody run in fear. He never made Joey leave his side, but when he did, he seldom brought anybody with him because the stone cold look could frighten any grown man, and his gray eyes refused to see either side, just his own.

They said he was unstoppable, and they said he was almost like some indestructible God. When he was in a fight—he was an indestructible God—but he didn't feel so tough right at that moment. Because after tonight, everything was going to change for their crew, and Gene was going to appoint him the new leader.

"This wasn't going to be a pretty, and if you can't handle it, tough shit." Gene said, and looked over toward the door where a few more reliable guys had come in, and made themselves comfortable. "You are the strongest and toughest out of all the guys in my crew."

Seeing this, he gave Joey and evil smile and said with all of his evil intentions. "You know what to do, send them."

Joey looked and saw two young bucks trying to get in however they could to the top. He didn't like when he smiled, because he didn't know what he was thinking.

Joey nodded and he gave a wave to the boys, who had a hungry look about them, and nodded to Gene, silently accepting his words. He didn't want to admit to the shit that he was going to be telling God on Judgement Day. But sometimes he kind of thought it was the loyalty that made people die for a cause or was it something deeper than that. There was religion, but fuck that! No way would he strap a bomb across his chest, and say that this was for his religion, but that's how it went on in some circles. But God did work in mysterious ways.

It was their loyalty was what would lead them to their imminent death. "Stupid kids!" Joey thought, and wandered if it was time for that drink. But, it wasn't the time, and crazy fools were what he was looking for—apes that did their bidding—and asked no questions.

Joey and Gene ended their conversation with a dose of silence, but then a few minutes later, more soldiers poured in by the dozens.

"Right on time!" Gene whispered, and his lips drew back to reveal his top teeth, all in a straight line, perfect and flawless.

All of them were tall, pale bodies with curly hair and some had tanned bodies with short hair. Some of them had green, blue, and brown eyes. Some of them were slim, some of them were fat, but they had crazy enough guts to answer Gene's call. Almost as if this was a revolution and all the kids were following them. But as they say about rats with a sinking ship, they should have been departing the ship without even taking a second thought about it.

When all the chairs seemed to be taken up, and a total of thirty bodies occupied the room, it was time for Gene to make his last words to them, give some encouraging words to them, and then make his leave. Joey knew all of these plans, like some dirty secret he shouldn't have known, but he could only blame it on the fact that he was the leader—someone had to know before everyone else did.

He saw Gene talking to the boys, wandering what in the hell lie he could think of next? "It's all right boys, I'm just gonna send you off to the killing fields while I sit back and count the money I am reaping over your dead bodies." Joey thought Gene must have been saying something similar, but he always had a way with words. The weird thing was they all had smiles on there faces, like this was some kind of game. If Gene wasn't the devil, who in God's creation was he? The reaper, an ancient demon, or some kind of supernatural freak, Joey didn't want to know, but somehow knew that he was evil, and capable of doing evil deeds, he was. But who was he to be a hypocrite, he carried out orders upon Gene's command freely, and without question. So, now was not the time to start thinking, and start doing what Gene told him to do.

Gene looked over toward him, with a sort of conniving look that of a child who had some kind of trick up his sleeve, and the only one on the inside of this verbal message was Joey. But as he coaxed him with another wave, the rest of the soldiers called him in. "Come on, Joey! Let's go, we ain't got all night."

Something on their faces knew as to why they were here, but all of them probably had some other crazy idea in their heads. But what was he going to say?

Only when Joey would stand next to his side, and stand next to him, his soldiers would take their seats, only some of them wouldn't because of the limited amount of chairs, which was fine with them, they wanted to get in on the action. Joey looked around the room and noticed that everyone down from the two young Turks to Ray Rosenthal, another enforcer that Joey had met from a few friends of his, but it seemed to him now that he was ten times more ruthless than he was. It was the fact that he had nothing to loose, and a mad gleam blazed in his eye whenever he became violent or was aroused by a simple cajoling, like a kid poking a animal when it was already down. He probably knew some amateurs that would accept money for a suicide mission, but Joey wasn't counting on it. Only there was somebody else missing, but the mass of soldiers that arrived would probably count a few people out, but he would make somebody fill them in on what they missed later.

As Joey stood next to Gene, he saw him grabbing a chair, and set a foot on top of the seat making a soft scratching sound as he was towering over the entire congregation. As their bodies disappeared in the darkness of the room, and all he could see is the heads of the soldiers. Gene took a deep breath, and looked over the crowd with a great heir about him, and began to speak.

"We are here because I told Joey that it was important, but I didn't know that everyone was going to come without a gift."

Suddenly a burst of laughter exploded from the group of soldiers. It wasn't that funny, but it was only complementary. They looked like kids again instead of killers' life seemed perverted sometimes. It only eased some of their tension, but it wouldn't ease some of the questions that were going to arise from this crowd.

But with that final look of dreading madness, he plunged into his speech with a reverence that only seemed artificial, but was real at the same time.

"Loyal soldiers and good friends, I can not thank you more than enough for coming tonight. This meeting will prove to be beneficial to every one of you in the future. First of all…all you might know that Chris has been attacked."

Joey slyly looked around and saw the wonder on all their faces, like they were seeing the Second Coming, or something so fantastic that they were just entranced by him, and even though they were afraid, they were entranced by Gene, this God among them.

"This is so great," Gene thought, looking around him, "because vanity is my friend." This only irritated Joey even more. He wondered if he saw their faces or not, but he didn't really care. He eagerly waited to hear Gene admit to the rest of his speech, and hopefully shock and amaze a few of them.

"But who attacked him, who did him in?" He looked down, and saw them nod their heads in confused puzzlement and their blank faces were filled with curious wonder. "Who done it?" They wanted to say, but the words couldn't roll off their lips. They waited for him to speak.

He took a deep breath, and then let it all out. *"I did it."*

Their faces suddenly dropped, their skin turned pale, they looked as if their eyes were about to pop out in surprise. A dead silence fell around the room, and he had waited just a few seconds longer for this to sink into their souls.

The after the momentary silence passed a long time member of Gene's crew, Richard Stein, a high moneymaker in his crew screamed, "Are you crazy!" The room echoed with his anger as a few of the soldiers' turned around, wide eye and frightened.

Gene looked down, and saw the fat stinking soldier was already sweating through his armpit, and the fat tub of lard was leaving a sourly odor in the room. The others saw him, and Gene smiled with that Cheshire cat grin.

"You're a fool." Gene said vindictively almost trying to sound jokingly, "Can't you see that *we* were being held down by Chris? He wasn't going to let us expand our influence."

Richard Stein was shocked and confused by his words, and aired out his rather dangerous opinions. "You just obliterated our influence. If Chris dies, Frank's going to wipe the floor with our faces." He pointed to a darkened spot in the wood floor, and a few soldiers beside him looked at it willfully. It was a small dark grease spot, which was black like an endless vortex but it had seeped into the wood and turned into a grayish brown puke color. "You see this spot? He's going to turn us into a fucking grease spot."

"Stop your crying!" Another voice added from another part of the heavily congested circle, and it wasn't Joey nor was it the young Turks in front of him. It was Ray Rosenthal, and his eyes squinted, making him look like a Chinese immigrant and his lips pushed together like a fish, and then released them as he talked. "Why don't you grow a pair of balls, and stand up for your crew. This is what happens when your leader has made a new decision. You follow through with it."

Joey had to give it to him for that, but the heat in the room started to heat up, and it almost congested his voice.

"Not when he's leading us to our deaths." Rich Stein shouted, almost looked as if he was about to burst into tears. He somehow saw the destruction of their clan long before these crazy maniacs were down to the last man. "This is suicide."

Then at that single moment, it's like a small itch had been growing on all of there backs when suddenly and unexpectedly a younger soldier by the name of Bobby "rough-and-tough" Berchowitz stepped up in the middle of the circle with a threatening gleam in his eye.

"Well, then suicide might work for me, but I'm not gonna let anyone take down Gene, and if anyone wants to, they are going to have to go through me. Who's with me?" Then everything seemed to be going downhill when the entire crowd clapped and cheered on "rough-and-tough" Bobby. Everything had changed for the worse, and no one with the right mind was going to go along with Richard Stein.

Poor little Rich was beginning to feel the trickle of sweat turn into a river of nausea as his head started to swirl, and then his gut began to ache when he felt all the other voices climb on top of the darkness.

"Yeah" and "fuck this guy, he's a traitor" filled the room. Then everything seemed to be tumbling down upon him as if he was underneath a mountain of hurling rocks. Their calumniating voices were flying and picking at him maliciously, like one of a bird's beak and when he tried to defend himself, his voice was muddled like a hand over a microphone. But when he looked at Gene, he saw his Cheshire cat grin glowed across his face.

With his wide teeth out Rich saw a small twinkle, a twinkle that radiated with his undaunting pride and felt six feet in the darkness and all he could do to escape it was turn around and run out the front door. But after he left where would he go, he would run out the door, and would be up shit-creek without a paddle, or in the woods for a matter of speaking. But he couldn't take the abuse anymore; he had to get out of there.

"You're all nuts!" Rich yelled out over the clamoring voices, but was getting no where. His talking would be useless as if his whistling to the wind.

He started to yell again, but his voice fell short, and all hope of getting his point across seemed hopeless. All he could easily do was just run away from the constant harboring as his nerves began to snap like twigs, and as it grew louder, he fell backwards, and landed on his back. His back made a loud *THUD* sound—as the bodies descended around him—he turned his body and crawled toward the door.

Just when the group of carnivorous soldiers saw him crawling towards the door, they walked up to him like he was a fat suckling pig, and clutched his hammy legs. Only he threw a few of them back to the floor as he turned the doorknob a breeze of cool air flowed through the door, filling the small dank room with a cool, relaxing breeze.

Rich buried his tennis shoes into the floor and he scurried out the door just like the piece of shit that he was, leaving his dignity back in the room, no honor at all. He slammed the door behind him, and ran out faster than he could think about it.

"Let him be…" Gene yelled to the crowd just as they were about to run after him. They stood like a pack of ravenous wolves that had just had the taste of his blood on their lips. They turned toward him and looked up with a confused stare.

"He can't go far. He'll be sitting out there on the stoop, crying like a little girl." Gene started to chuckle, and then a burst of laughter escaped him, and it echoed all around the cabin.

"Forget about him." Ray concurred, and turned back toward Gene. "Continue on…" Everyone turned their attention back toward Gene, as if his meaningless attraction had no satisfaction to them, and they honed their attention back to Gene.

Gene saw in all these soldiers, except for Joey, to be like sheep. And these sheep were dispensable, because if he lost one because he had more soldiers than the reserves ever had to count. But one question popped into his head, ironic as the situation was, he couldn't ignore it. "I wonder what Hitler's ego felt like when he conquered Germany?" No one could answer that question, but the only answer he could give to that was "Sure power. That's what it felt like." A perverted rush surged through his system, giving him goosebumps all over his body, a feeling of danger that told him that he was on the edge of insanity, but didn't care if he was insane or not, he was ready for war, and war he would bring.

When Rich left the room, Gene continued on with the speech, as if he didn't exist.

The night sky was thick like oil and the stars gleamed like the inside of a wax sculpture's eyeball. As Rich landed on the small dirty front porch, he was crying a mile a minute, covering the top of his eyes, hiding the tears streaking down his cheek, his shirt had left a trail of sweat all around his pits and his stomach. His stomach was starting to cave in, and his emotions did the same. He moved his arm around his body, and the first place that felt sweaty to him, he instantly began to cry again. It wasn't largely because of what happened, well…maybe it was, but he was so embarrassed and angered about his disloyalty. He covered his eyes, and a small weeping cry escaped him, hunkering down with his knees pressed to his chest.

Then out of nowhere bright lights suddenly danced along his brow, and shined over his hands. The burning light made his eyelids quiver, and his eyes burned as he put his hand out to block the ever-brightening light. But the light faded away and a car that roared like a beast moving stealthily toward a place like a predator. It past him slowly, and Rich hid his eyes, embarrassed of his incompetence. Its tinted mirrors made him shiver, frightened of its blackness. It was black as death, and as he lowered his head, the beast moved into a shaded spot where bits of the restless moon shined upon the blackened tint. Rich cleaned his eyes of the tears, and he watched the car and waited for what was about to come.

It rested for a moment, underneath the shadows, and as it rested, patiently as the small anorexic trees began whipping in the wind. Only now, the engine hadn't been turned off. For the next few seconds, Rich watched the car, but no one got out of it. It looked as if it was waiting for someone. "But who was it for?" Rich meditated about it for a few more minutes, and wiped the wet tears from his cheeks with the back of his sweaty hand.

He didn't give two shits about who it was for, he just wanted to leave then anger slipped into his heart like an unwelcome visitor, and spurned the very thought of being apart of the whole plan. Rich wasn't going to get himself killed because Gene was committing suicide, and bringing them down with him. If he were going to get himself killed, he would rather do it with his father's pistol. Suicide was looking better than disloyalty, but he shook that off like a bad habit.

But just when he couldn't feel any worse about his life, another vehicle flashed his bright lights at him, grabbing at his attention. Covering his eyes Rich muttered a feeble response that only fit his time for sarcasm. "Who's coming now? The President?"

The smaller car pulled up beside the other one, parked with the same procedure of that first car, and the lights switched off faster than the other beast. The car engine suddenly fell short, and it stopped instantly. They weren't waiting for anyone, and both doors to the front passenger side and driver's side swung open with haste, and two bodies jumped out of the car. Rich couldn't see who they were from the dark night sky, but they somehow saw him.

"Hey, Rich?" The voice reached out to him as they past the first car, which was still humming it's annoying whirring sound that only made Rich more nervous about his safety. But the voice didn't, and a matter of fact, it sounded very familiar to him, an almost calming affect.

"Yeah, who's there?" Rich burst out, not knowing how loud his voice actually sounded. It shook the very trees that stood over him, "But that must have been the wind?" Rich thought to himself petrified in and out of his own skin. Then the wind brushed over him just to tell him that he was just scared.

"It's me, Berry."

Rich took a deep breath in, and as his head fell between his hunkered knees, literally feeling the wind knocked out of him, he let out a long constrained feeling in his gut. Berry was a gunrunner and a hustler that could get you anything close to an arsenal. If his brother was along, he could see anyone anything, even a piece of shit, if that was what he was working with.

"Berry, good to see you." Rich liked Benny, 'a good kid', Rich muttered but would never join under any flag, or gang. He liked it like that, and it made a lot of sense either way.

Although he would talk to him at any other time, Rich didn't raise his head up once when he spoke, and didn't even bother to ask whose extra set of footsteps there were. That feeling of relaxation filled him, but that vibe he got from the black tinted car was something he couldn't shake off. The shadows of Benny walked right next to him, who he had barely taken notice of.

"It's a nice night huh?" Berry said, taking a notice to how Rich was acting, but it didn't faze him, he just saw him at school sometimes. Only he felt uncomfortable, and he looked up at the stars on this black cardboard sky.

"Are you okay?" Berry asked him very slowly, but not so slow so that Rich might be insulted.

Rich didn't even raise one bone in his body as he replied with a monotone voice that everyone seemed to sound like when they didn't want to be bothered.

He said, "I'm fine. Go on in, they already started." He waved them on, without a care in the world. Like the bum who had no more life left in his tired weary alcoholic strung shoes, he kept his head down waiting to be put out of his misery.

An awful sight he was, but before they decided to go in, Berry didn't seem to be done with him. "What did I miss?" Rich raised his head, and arched it up half way in mid-air with a pathetic sadness that he could bring out of him. Bloodshot eyes, wet face, his face looked pained, even though he always had a pale complexion, this was different. "Oh, a bunch of bullshit, they'll fill you in."

"Well," Benny continued to not pay it any thought, "before I forget," he turned toward his brother and motioned toward the trunk, "get the *stuff* from the trunk." His brother didn't say a word, and nodded before he ran back toward the trunk. His footsteps left a rustling sound—patches of leaves stumbled into the air with swift kicks echoing throughout the forest like raindrops as he approached the trunk and searched eagerly for the keys resting inside his pockets. As he found the keys, Berry kept talking to Rich.

"Has anything happened yet on the streets?"

Berry shook his head, and murmured underneath his breath. "Not that I've heard of."

He might as well of been talking to a wall, and the way Berry's patience was running out, it was diminishing faster than a wick on a piece of dynamite. All he needed was one more thing, and he would explode right their, but he hoped that he didn't.

Berry rubbed his upper lip—the wind added one more level of irritation—and let his hands fall to his side. When he turned around again he saw his brother closing the trunk of the car, and what lay on the ground was a big trunk load full of *stuff* that Gene had requested to the meeting. "Only the good stuff" he remembered Gene saying, and he was going to bring nothing else but *the good stuff*.

"You need to relax, take a chill pill, smoke something to calm down." Berry said nonchalantly as his brother closed the trunk he turned toward the ground, hunkered down on his knees, and grabbed the trunk by the small handlebars. The *stuff* shifted inside the crate back and forth like small-unattached parts of a toy that made small little *clink-clink* noises when it was broken. And as he approached the porch again, Berry didn't feel the need to stay out here and waste his time with this petty bullshit, and decided to push his way through.

"Well, on that note, we need to attend to our business, so…I'll talk to yea later." He said this very cold and emotionless as he walked up the steps he motioned for his brother to walk up the right side of the path telling him with a sharp glare in his eye to ignore Rich, and keep on moving. As his brother approached the front door, he balled his fist, and with a cold force about him, he slammed his fist against the door, and he repeated it two more times. A cold silence pulsed around him—travelling all around the house—as a few footsteps approached the door, he could see there pacing shadows underneath the foot of the door, moving like animals pacing around in there cages while they waited to be fed. Berry stood back for a moment, and with a prepared look on his face that meant only a gun was going to be forced into his face, he waited for the surprise greeting.

The sounds of stomping footsteps chucked around the door for a few more seconds, when it flew open, and a bright flash of light hit him in the eye. He covered his eye for a moment, and heard his brother, James, falter with weight of the trunk as the light swayed away from him. When the light faded, he saw two large boys that looked like grown men, but dressed like they were in high school. He had never met personally but he had seen before with Gene, stood with grimacing looks on their faces, there eyes bleeding a very hateful glare.

Berry moved his head pushing away the light from his eyes at all costs as he spoke with a very sarcastic, but humble voice. "Hey, guys. Get enough light in here? Enjoying the séance?"

The two boys turned toward each other, silently signaling to one another that it was okay, and moved out of the way for him. "Thanks guys. Appreciate the help." He said in a mocking tone as he pushed by them, smirking as he stood aside for Berry's brother, and as they looked out again, they saw Rich glancing inside very sheepishly. When they saw this, they slammed the door, and gave him a strong hateful glare before they closed their world off to him forever.

After they slammed the door in his face with a loud *THWACK*, shutting him out like a mother's warning to stay outside as she battled with her drunken husband. Sitting out there on that stoop only welcomed the anger into his heart, and despair was an instigator when it came down to it. These mixed emotions welcomed the darkness as it began to burn a hole in his thoughts making him ponder about what was going on inside now since Berry had stepped in.

"Fuck em'" Richard said as he spit out a-long-phlegm-like goo out of his throat. As he wiped his mouth away from the spit, he cursed the day the thought of involving himself with Gene or anyone else from his crew. He almost wanted to cry, but couldn't for fear that someone was watching him as he sat upwards—moving like he was in a rocking chair—and buried his head in between his legs, in anger. He didn't want to leave, but he felt like he had no other choice. He was going to leave in a few minutes, after he got some things straight in his mind.

The moment that the doors had shut Rich out with the shining moon and cold wind Berry didn't want to know what was happening. Images of sacrificial slaughters appeared in his head and what their ears were being intoxicated by. He could feel his heart beating in a rhythmic Congo drum beat that echoed the very fear in his system. Images of headhunters in skimpy suits and face paint, screaming for more blood. Berry could feel their pulses tapping with rage, and he could feel there primal musk resonating like a sauna, and he had been out here for too long. He decided to go in.

Berry didn't like the way their eyes were glaring at him from all around, and as his brother stood beside him with his trunk full of *stuff* that he was about to give to them, they turned back toward the figure hiding above the light. Only he needed to find Gene, but he couldn't really be sure if Gene was on the top of that chair.

"Berry, it's so good to see you." The voice said as it echoed, and everyone's heads were now turned to Berry and his brother.

Berry's ears caught the voice, and knew it as if it was his very own. It was Gene, and to clarify that in some sort of weird way, Gene jumped down off the chair and stood in the light for a moment. Berry could see that something different was in his eye, even though the look of the fat and husky slob seemed apparent, his gesture and tone seemed to be foolhardy and dangerous. Even with that cool grin that looked like he had never sweat one drop of water in his entire life, he felt that Gene was comfortable with his newfound madness. Then another thing stood out to him was the madness in his eye, an ever-bending hatred that fed his will to live, and he was ready for war. "But with who?" He thought, and then shook off these dreadful feelings.

Pushing all these what-would-be signs or assumptions to the back of his head, he looked into his direction and smiled a relaxed as he spoke with short sparseness. "So, are we ready to do business?" When he spoke, all the soldiers looked at each other with astonished paranoia, and all their faces returned a queer yet stupid look to each other.

"Fuck yeah we are!" Gene said with a triumphant yell as he moved through the circle of boys. They joined him with a rousing *"Hell yeah,"* and as they continued, they had their hands in the air screaming for a long minute. Berry had seen the insides of his palms, ashy and dirty they were, but what were his like? "So…this is what it's like dealing with the devil. A palm dirty as that would spread onto his hand, and the grains of his evil would continue onto another hand he himself would shake."

But shaking the eerie feeling off with a strong handshake, he ignored the dampness of Gene's hand, and squeezed it firmly as their fingers popped like bursting blisters off a dirty foot and their bones creaked with some unknowing pleasure. It was as if their bones had been on fire for some reason, like some great unrest had been harboring as their grip slowly eased off each other.

"You got the *stuff*?" Gene snarled in a very anxious but patient whisper of a bear's growl, before he was about to bite him.

Berry looked behind him, seeing that he had mistakenly left his brother ten feet away from, was taken back when he saw him face to face. He looked shocked, but hid his embarrassment as he waited to grab his pistol. Returning his head back toward Gene, "You bet I did," he sounded confident and cool, but underneath he could hear his heart beating rapidly. Their finger gave off a sharp snap, and pointed toward the middle of the floor where he could set the treasure chest in plain sight. The crowd of soldiers moved away as he moved the chair with one swift kick to the left leg, and set the treasure chest down on the ground.

As he bent over, he felt the weight of his back being chained to a mound of weights, and the more he leaned over he felt his back dislodging at every corner. Even though he was only around his early twenties, he felt like shit. Even though he was feeling shitty, he let the treasure chest go, and it landed with one hollow *CLUNK!* The pain left his back, and he moved backwards, watching his clockwise positions.

Berry's brother raised up from off the ground, hearing his neck creak like an old attic floor, he still looked menacing as he walked beside his brother, and folded his arms, nodded toward the case in a peaceable offering, but his own hatred did not leave him.

After the treasure chest was in the center light, a curious soldier approached the chest, but then stood back, for fear of offending Gene. But Gene gave them the go ahead to open the chest with a clear conscience, like a child seeing before him a present that he could finally open. Feeling an overwhelming feeling of anxiousness fill his chest like a balloon, he felt it popping in his system as he hunkered down on his legs, and felt around with his hands for a latch to the chest. The chest was held together by two gold latches where it held the top of the chest down, and gave the *stuff* well cover from onlookers with it's deep black color. The soldier found the latch on the right side, and heard the latch fall off with one flip of his thumb. With that one taken care, he looked for the other, found it, and repeated the same exact procedure.

With the latches off, the soldier grabbed the top of the chest, and carefully raised it up hearing the small clamoring of feet rise around his shoulders. He could feel the inside of the chest grabbing at his brain, telling him to open it, and with one quick thrust he raised the top and held the open halfway so he could see what it was. A gleam of light poured into the box, and a smile rose across his weather-beaten face. It was a smile of pure malevolence that rekindled a perverted twinkle in his eye.

He let the top fall backwards, and as it fell a luscious ray of light fell upon the contents of the crate. Loads and loads of what were long and short metallic weapons. On the top of the pile were large crafted pistols that only a military could use. There were thirty Beretta 92f, Glock 17's and 18 C fully automatic, which fired like a machine gun and had a thirty round clip with boxes of tracer. Around the sides of the crate were a sawed off 12 gauge Mossberg shotgun; it's large robust barrel was cut off at exactly eighteen inches, and the butt was cut off and a pistol grip was added onto it. It wasn't great on distance, but up close it could take out an entire crowd with one single pull of the trigger. Then underneath the pistols were five AR-15 assault rifles, which were knock-offs of the original M-16 assault rifle, and contained about six thirty-to-sixty round clips, already loaded with long stinger-tip .556 bullets, which exploded once they punctured the target. The largest weapon that they had was an AK-47 SU47, and that was the mother of all assault weapons.

"You have the cash?" Berry blurted out, reminding them about the most important part of the transaction. He hoped for their sake they didn't forget, because the weapons would gladly buy it off him for the same price he was asking for. But when Gene took his eyes off the treasure chest of glittering firearms, and faced him, he saw Gene had the outmost sincerity in his static face. "Of course, how could I forget?" His eyebrow was raised with speculation, and his face became weary.

Everyone was tense, the room was getting too congested, and he knew that all of them were about to snap if they didn't get on with their transaction. Some would even pull out guns and even if they weren't aiming at him, someone could blow another person's head off with one careless move.

Berry saw this, and instantly became calm, and put him to ease by patting him on the shoulder. "Then that's a good thing."

Gene's eyebrows crunched together, and he moved past a few gloating soldiers that were fixated dripping tenacity of the contents chest, as if they were looking at a pound of gold bars, and wanted to touch the greasy, oily machines. While Gene pushed through a few more soldiers he approached one very shady looking soldier. A rather large and gargantuan boy that had fists the size of quadruple hearts and had a face that had tattoo's of a small butterfly on his left cheek, and as his veins were bulging throughout his arm, he saw the numbers 187 in old English. As Gene hit his arm to gain his attention, he looked as if he was about to kill him. Only the mere thought of being killed was the power he had.

When the little guy could use his brains to persuade the bigger guy to work and carry out his orders, that was *real* power, and he always had that kind of persuasion. Berry saw that the bigger guy had lowered his ear to his lips, and as he covered his mouth over his ear, he glanced up toward Berry with his beaten face, and his left eye twitched with an irregular pulse. He nodded as he glanced toward the crowd, and then all around him—checking everything around him—as Gene unveiled his hand away from his ear, he began to feel around the back of his shirt tail. Out from his back of his pants was a thick envelope—fresh and untouched—that had looked like it had been treated delicately.

The envelope was partly wet from being in his back pocket the entire time, and his fat fingers made the envelope even wetter than a fourteen year old girl's iron curtain that was gleaming brighter than piece of bloody meat at the end of the month. He past it to his right hand—with one flick of his wrist—and held it out for Gene to take on his own accord. The sound of his fat sausage fingers sounded like spreading sheets of paper, and when the last bit of the envelope slid out his fingers, Gene moved back through the crowd and presented Berry the thick sweating envelope. He held it out to Berry as if he had wanted to get rid of it, but seeing how thick it was, Berry didn't mind how sweaty the envelope looked, it was the money inside was bulging through the paper, and that's all that mattered in his case.

He needed to eat most of all, and he figured he had more than enough green to split his brother's cut, and then tend to business about getting more supplies. It couldn't get any better than this.

Seeing the large envelope in front of him, in it's sweaty and alluring gleam to it in the overhead light, Berry pointed out his hand towards the envelope, and gripped the top of the envelope. Squeezing the large envelope, he felt a sudden urge of paranoia hit him about the money.

"Is it all there?" Berry said, hoping to see Gene get thrown off his high horse, and start to reveal his madness for what he saw. But the fox that Gene was, he calmly and coolly spoke with no treble in his voice, almost deadly.

"Does a pig fly? It's all there!" In that spurring taunt, Berry knew that he wasn't lying, because he would kill him if he didn't. Gene let the envelope fall out of his thick greasy hand, Berry then carefully examined the bulkiness of it (there were many ways to tell by an envelope). It looked fine to him, but for all the trouble that he went through to get those guns, he would have a lot more to worry about instead of Chris Mangini on his back.

"It's a pleasure doing business with yeah again." Berry said with delight as he cautiously patted Gene's shoulder. Gene looked at him and gave him a laid back but tense smirk, like he had wanted to attack him than shake his hand. He would have thought that it was because he had to let go of the money, but the sooner they left, the better off they would be.

The Disintegrating Bloodline

Berry didn't show any concern for the smirk, and said "I bid you all a fond farewell." Everyone in the room suddenly turned around, watching him as Berry and James headed toward the door. "Hope to see you again in the future." As if he was some gentlemen that was going to reach for his hat, he moved with a medium paced walk as he heard the midnight crickets chirping some innocent tune, but now felt like their ironic legs were singing a cautionary, yet ironic tune.

Holding the envelope in his hands, he felt the door calling him, but his legs felt restrained by some overriding force that was prohibiting his movement. Maybe it was the fact that he was nervous in a room surrounded by Gene, his army, and a trunk-load full of heavy weaponry with his back turned to them. He didn't know how his brother felt, but all he could do was keep walking. But just when they were about to leave, he heard Gene's voice call for him, "STOP!"

Berry heard this response, and slowly stopped in his tracks. He stood in his position, but then he felt tense, like he was punch drunk from over a thousand or more shots of liquor, and everything was starting to pour from his face. Berry wiped his face that was starting to pour sweat, and a secret urge wanted him to leave. Berry prepared for the next possible thing to happen, one that he had feared would happen someday or the other, and quickly prayed to God (if he had believed in him, but now was a good time to start) before he turned around.

After twenty minutes went by when Berry and his brother stepped into the house, Rich was still feeling the affects of the door being slammed in his face, in isolation from the entire scene, he looked to his watch with anxiety. The thoughts of going inside still did not seem like a good idea. He didn't like it, but he had made up his decision, and was going ahead with it. He was more nervous than a smoker that had gone forty-five minutes without his cigarette, and his hands were starting to shake. But it must have been the cold, it surely had to have been, but who could explain the emptiness that made his insides emptier than a fresh dissected corpse that had been emptied by a mortician's blade.

He palmed his hands together, and raised them against his brow, slowly trying to figure out his next decisive plan to leave the state. But when he was just thinking of the idea, the sound of a car door opening made him jump, and his heart palpitate, no flutter ten times faster than any hummingbird he could imagine made him nervous. But when he heard the car door echo with a great *SLAM*, Rich looked over toward the black car again. That was when he heard footsteps moving from around the car, and the rustling of the leaves that mans shoes made only meant that he was coming closer, he thought it was farther away for a moment, but then it came closer, and closer.

The moment came when Rich was feeling the blade being twisted in his organs, and being dragged over to the side of the building. James caught the tail end of the sounds and glanced outside the window. He had caught the tail end of the shadowy figure dragging his body outside the window. He thought his eyes were playing tricks on him, but he couldn't tell what was real in the darkness, and what wasn't. It's like being color blind, and all that he could see was a large grayish figure scurrying past the window like some fox running with some kind of pheasant in his mouth. Or, he guessed that, it was an unwanted spirit clinging onto some long dark secret always reminding them with his shady presence that he was there.

Benny moved fixated toward the window, entranced by the movement of the shadows, partly curious about what he had seen or what he thought he had seen. Even though it might have been his eyes, he believed that something was terribly wrong. Only when Gene had called out to Berry, he advanced toward the window, and curiously looked out into the darkness. "Nothing!" Benny thought to himself, but was distracted when he could hear the entire conversation that was going on around him.

As his brother had turned around, and responded to their question, he was looking out the window with a distinct composure while his brother spoke words that were none of his business to listen in on.

"What!" Berry said, biting his lip, and clenching his fists. He looked anxious as he stood with the envelope in his hands. He could see that he didn't want to be in this room, congested with paranoia and rage, because he couldn't take small spaces for too long, and with the climate increasing, he thought that someone was going to yell sooner or later.

Standing in his place, he saw Gene very nonchalantly walk in front of the crowd, trying to garner some power from the crowd that was around him. But when he saw another soldier holding a rather large cheaply made Llama handgun, which seemed to him like it was loaded. Even though it was a piece of shit, it still made him nervous. He wanted Gene to get to the fucking question out in the open so he could get the hell out of there in one piece, and without having his brother to show them what he could really do with his own pistol.

Gene took his time, but with some reservation in his voice, only he wasn't holding back on this offer. "I was wondering if you would like to join our crew?"

Berry was taken back, ultimately he was obliged by this offer, but he couldn't very well accept it, because he liked working alone, and for very good reasons.

"I work alone. I don't run with a crew." His tone was firm, and he didn't falter one bit. But he knew this wouldn't be the last of him, because when he had his mind set on something, the two could take this in dangerous directions.

Gene threw his head back and scoffed, as he began to regain control of his maniacal laughter, and then spoke calmly again. "I know that part, but you didn't even listen to what I had to say." He saw a persuasive look in his eye, but he wouldn't fall into his trap by letting him even address his offer.

"The Devil knows its own," This rather new, and charming voice, that was blank but lovely at the same time.

Berry wanted to make this very clear, and before he continued, he wanted him to hear his rebuttal before anything. "Well, I don't want to listen."

A small clamor of excitement filled the entire room, certainly making a juicy conversation amongst the ranks. Only his men's calamity was pushing Gene's anger, slowly tearing down his pride like a chisel scratching off a glob of paint on a clean window, clearly sending his anger around his head like a cloud of thunder and lightening, just waiting to electrify him at any moment.

And like a cheetah approaching a flock of gazelles, he spoke in a stealthy voice that echoed around the entire cabin. "Silence!" Everything grew quiet again, just enough for him to talk to Berry. Gene knew that having him would be a good decision, and he didn't want them to mess it up for him, and he had to coax this formidable ally into his web.

He faced Berry, and with that unseemingly calm and cool composure, he stepped two paces away from the crowd, and two feet away from Berry, but as he was about to speak, he saw the brother, James turned and faced him with his arms crossed together. Only peering out of his pant line was a gun handle, and his left hand was lazily leaning against it, as if it were a belt loop. He took full notice of it, and began to use his head to try and work out some more reasonable demands, before they left their blood on the floor.

"I think you misunderstood me," Gene said, moving a step closer to Berry, and saw James fingers moving toward the handle of the gun. "What I said was, if you were apart of our crew, you would have no responsibilities other than to yourself. You could keep your own crew, and have us behind you if you need any backup." Gene's confidence didn't seem to have any kind of affect on Berry when he responded with a sure fire confidence, sticking to his guns, even in his time of war. Berry didn't even believe in betraying his own word. "No, like *I* said, *I work alone*! You can reason with me all you want, but I don't need any protection either!"

Gene was taken back by this, and a cord of anger strummed like a mandolin, harping from the way his strings had been plucked, it was hard for him to accept his offer. Although his blood boiled, he didn't want to attack him, or put him on edge either. Only just warn him of what was going to happen if he brought his unspeakable force of nature upon him and family.

Gene saw Berry's hands were balled into a fist, and he was ready for a fight. Only Gene had to accept the decision for now, because he would intimidate him with his actions later. "Well, I respect your decision," he breathed long and hard, and he almost couldn't contain it, "and I won't argue with you. Because you seem bent to be by yourself."

Berry's posture began to lax as he loosened his tight fists, trying to intimidate Gene. He covered up the gun handle, and moved behind his brother in a regimental routine and closed the door behind him in quiet fuck you manner. The hatred didn't last for long, because Gene couldn't even begin to explain how much he hated them.

After they closed the door, Gene turned around toward his men, and saw the sad hopeless looks on their faces. Only he intended to speak the truth to his men, and rally them up for the long bloody road ahead—blood is always paved with the ignorance. "We don't need his loyalty. All I need is you brave few ready to stand with me until the end. Are you with me?" Gene shouted, and threw up his hands in a forceful manner, and the crowd of sheep screamed louder and louder, showing him the respect that he deserved.

They yelled in a rioting response, and the way there morale was, God didn't even have power over him and his wolves.

"Settle down..." Gene finally yelled, quelling down the crowd as he held his hands up in the sky, but then he slowly lowered them down, and said to the crowd. "SETTLE DOWN!" After a few more claps echoed into the distance, he spoke again real forcefully as they looked at him with excited faces, "We have lots more to talk about." As he spoke, they returned to being children again, they stood around and listened as if they were being told a mystical story of tall tales of dragons, quests, and knights. And they listened, like all dumb children would.

Outside, not even a few seconds before he had reached there car, Benny had been glancing around to see if he could see the shadowy figure that he thought he might had seen before. The more he thought about it, the more he wanted to leave. As the two approached the car, he tried to take another long glance around the corner of the wooden cabin, but couldn't see a thing. Maybe he was just seeing things, delusions of grandeur. Only this grandeur felt so real that get couldn't get it out of his mind the entire time.

Standing for a moment as his brother hurried into the driver seat, he tried to look and see if he could see anything else. With his eyes squinting down he tried to break through the darkened forest, to try and see around the side of house. Although when he tried to gaze further around the house, he saw nothing, not even one last glimpse before he left. Only he felt like something was looking at him, and as he kept his gaze fixed upon it. He felt the darkness jabbing him, making him stand in fear. The calling of Berry's voice made him turn with a mystification that shadowed over his thoughts like a fog, and this fog was so empowering that he didn't want to leave.

He jumped inside the car, and pulled the door in behind him, sounding off a great *SLAM* as the cool air conditioning hit his panicky looking face. Berry saw his brother, sweat forming at his brow, and blood shot eyes that looked fresh and new.

"Are you okay?" Berry said, fumbling with the keys, and started it up with one flick of his wrist. The engine rumbled, and sputtered for a moment as he heard his brother reply over the sputtering engine.

"I'm fine." The engine sputtered one last time, like a clogged water boat engine that was just about to die from a lack of antifreeze, and roared one more time as Berry looked at his brother and replied, breaking his concentration away from the house. "What?"

"I'm fine!"

Berry looked at his brother, and gave him a disbelieving look. "Are you sure?"

To Berry, he looked as if he had been smoking pot and dropped two tabs of Acid at the same time, and all the multicolored frightening images had just started to hit him like a tornado. Only he couldn't tell because he wasn't that much of a smoker or a hallucinogenic freak, his brother was just one weird kid. Berry was glad he wasn't, because he went to harsher places that had that happening around the corner away, and that was one reason he liked being in George Bradley. In a nutshell, he was worried about him, and that wasn't so bad sometimes, but he wasn't a sensor to anyone, including his own brother.

"You sure?" Berry said, one last time.

"Yes, I'm fine. I just thought I saw something that's all. " His tone became aggravated, and his eyes seemed to tell him that he wasn't fine. Only this was all that Berry could go with, and that was fine for now. If he would tell him, he would hear it then.

The car was rumbling with unease as he pretended to pick his hair like a monkey would. His brother pushed his arm away, and got a smug laugh, that was sorely appreciated, but meaningful at the same time.

"Okay," Berry said, putting the gear in reverse, the settling beast began to move back very slowly, and with Berry at the wheel, he would guarantee them a safe passage back home.

The beast moved backwards through the foliage, and the two brothers took there money and headed on home.

Back around the side of the house, fifteen minutes before Berry and his brother left the house, the large shadow that was *Death* had been twisting the knife ever so hard in Rich's belly. As he was about to squeal, the shadowy figure set a hand over his mouth, and pressed it firmly against his lips. His eyes widened with a frightened, petrified stance of shock. It had taken him five or ten minutes before he could suffocate him—pushing his clawing hands away—pushing him against the wall, he felt his life fade away each second he was taking it with the blade twisting inside his stomach, sending his body into tumultuous pain while he met his maker.

As the night moon gleamed with all her fury, it seemed to be red underneath, reflecting all the hatred that this shadowy figure had for him. He had never met him before in his life, but the way he was pushing his fist against his mouth, he acted as if he was killing a woman who was stuck in a hospital bed. The shadowy figure began to grunt louder and louder, grinding his teeth together as he removed the blade from his stomach. Looking at the blade, he saw this boy's blood gleam like hot butter, and felt the rush surge through him like electricity.

Rich's once creamy skin began to turn blue as the moons shiny complexion and his eyes began to roll back into his sockets, and there was no more life in Richard.

Feeling his sweaty, gritty hand pressed against the orifices necessary for respiration, he didn't feel the need to choke him anymore. Pulling his hand from around his mouth, he heard Rich's last final breath jump out of his mouth and fly into his face.

The smell was sweet, but strangely attractive as his dying body slid down the wall, and fell to the ground with his knees bending forward. But his knees began to loose balance as his lifeless body plopped over on its right side, as his body limped over.

"That was fun." The shadowy figure whispered into the night, as if he was talking to the ancient War God thanking him for the nice gift of torture he had bestowed to this weak, putrid boy. Looking upon his victim, he hunkered down on his knees, and stared at him with total disrespect and awe as if he was some game trophy, and smiled evilly without a care in the world.

Looking over his game again, he saw his wide open eyes, and shook his head clicking his tongue in a *tisk-tisk* manner, he said to the dead body, "Poor boy, you didn't even say a word?"

No response, all but the howling wind and the chirping crickets were present when he spoke. He knew that the body would easily be found behind the house and all he could do was just leaving it where it was lopsided, but that would be too sloppy just leaving it where it was. He then thought of burying the body, and that would take a shovel and bury him in a secluded area. Only where would he get the shovel, since they were out in the middle of fucking nowhere. But the possibility of a tool-shed had to be present in a rural setting just as this. He began to think that there wouldn't be any fucking tool-shed around here because they were in the middle of the fucking woods, in the middle of fucking nowhere.

He pondered this thought for a few more minutes when he heard the door close and the two pairs of footsteps send his body on high alert. He immediately tensed up and hunkered down to the ground, his back arched up with fright as he saw the first boy, which he had never seen up until now approach the driver seat, and jumped inside the car without even noticing him. He was glad, because he had always been good concealing himself in the shadows, like all the secrets that lurk around ever corner of your brain. But for every dark secret that he had in his mind, he wasn't surprised that he wasn't dead from some deadly disease. He smokes, he drank, and he didn't exercise, but still found the energy to work out and gain muscle weight. Pretty much, he was God on earth. He took life, and that was his function in this world, and gave it away.

"I've been found," *Death* would later add to Gene.

"By who?" Gene would reply when they were in the car.

"A boy, that I've never seen before. They walked in with a treasure chest."

"Are you sure it was them?" Gene replied in a worried tone.

"Yes, I'm positive." *Death* replied despondently.

"They will be taken care of, soon."

The two, Death and Gene, the bear, headed off to their cave of eternal hibernation, but they wouldn't be far away from everyone's lips.

"The strongest hide while the weak are bit by the inhabitants of the dark abyss."

Gene had no idea where this voice was coming from, but he was starting to get used to this voice.

Chapter XV:

"An Unfortunate Case"

Monday's bright and shining dawn, which would turn into another beautiful day, but would usually turn chilly in a New York minute. But like all beautiful days a lot of things could possible happen. But at eight o' clock in the morning at George Bradley, nothing was undaunted by the outside world. The kids were sitting in there clicks chewing on there morning breakfast and sipping on there sodas, jolting their brains, disintegrating their bones, rotting there teeth, and stunting there growth one sip at a time. It would take another few minutes before the next cluster of kids would come charging off the bus, and stomping towards the tables with there faces dragging down to there chins, and there eyes still encrusted in sleep. With their heads buried in their hands, trying to catch up on the next few minutes of sleep and it was eight fifteen. This gave them fifteen minutes to get to their lockers, trade off information about useless idiocy, and after they're socializing they'd head to their first class. It was even number days today, and it made no difference to the teachers, because everyday was a nightmare for their grade books (most of the freshmen and sophomore classes were failing). Regardless if it was even number days or odd days, every day was horrible trying to teach spoiled brats that wouldn't even listen. It was a fucking pain in the ass, and if the principal didn't care, the students were off in their own worlds, so they were basically left in the lurch everyday. The faculty meetings were just ridiculous—filled with maddened complaints about unruly students and expenses, which nothing would ever be accomplished from these meetings.

When the fifteen-minute bell ended, there were a few buses that came later than eight thirty, and you usually had kids of the unsavory type walking in waving these pink slips at the teachers. They couldn't do a thing but just take it, and add their name to their tardy list.

For the next fifteen minutes another flood of kids burst from the docking bay where the buses let off all the kids, and came back at around three thirty quarter to four when it was about time for them to leave. Only at eight thirty, Ray Rosenthal had strolled into the school late as usual, and bypassed the young woman behind the desk who was writing up tardy slips as if she had been handing out bad checks. They didn't mean shit to the kids who were being handed these slips, and after they turned the next corner it would probably be crumpled up and end inside the bottom of the wastebasket.

Ray headed down the long abandoned hall with a smug but busy appearance as he walked in with no book or pencil in his hand, which was a school rule that no one really paid attention to. All he had on him was long black shirt, faded out khaki pants and darkened sunglasses. They were a cheap kind that you could only find in that mechanical claw game where the prizes usually had fake Rolex's and imitation leather wallets. But he wore them as if he was the coolest dude in the hall, impressing no one but himself, and Ray enjoyed that even if that was foolish. He made his way toward the classroom, passing by a row of lockers with the classrooms were opposite to each other, and there were long rectangular windows going up alongside the doors, and a large window that could let the teachers see who was out in the halls.

He was usually sent out because the Dinello sisters, dark haired bombshells, would just be staring and making sexual expressions to him. That was when he was sent out, and the only thing he was said to his English teacher, (an did not give her his sunglasses either,) and replied, "Uh huh," and then headed off to the library, the only sanctuary he could feel keep him from going insane.

Ray walked toward the doors, looking over his shoulder for a moment (taking off his sunglasses), knowing that it was a good idea he slipped into the doors, and saw a small little advertisement desk with the schools fund-raisers slips and boxes. Next to the desk there was a tall metal detector walkway that didn't really serve any purpose but to catch kids that stole books, but he was never in the library enough that ever gave him a chance to steal a book. Walking through it he saw the large round checkout desk with a woman looking at her computer, swiping books with a piece of machinery over a small bar code, hearing the computer making a loud *beep*, signifying that the book was turned in. She laid them on a moveable cart of sorted books.

As Ray moved through the book detector, he smiled at the lady—a dorky lady with a pointed nose and thick glasses covering his face like binoculars—glancing at him but all he saw from her was a grimacing busy look. She turned back toward the next row of books, and swiped the next bar code without even noticing his entrance. Moving right a long the desk, he kept walking past a table where a boy was busily copying down notes from a book onto a piece of paper. "He was probably studying for a test," Ray thought to himself, "Sucker!" A small chuckle escaped him as he turned his head the other way, humming a nonsensical song with no rhythm, no beats or lyrics to it, just hums.

This was where books could be stored on shelves, and you could find peace inside each page. Or some swashbuckling adventure from Robinson Caruso or a sprawling fantasies epic from J.R.R. Tolkien or Stephen Edding, or a chilling, spine tingling novel from Stephen King. Yes, this was the place to hide, and how important it was to him, because they would never suspected him here. Some bad boy thug inside a library was reading a book? It was too funny for words, but Lee Harvey Oswald was found drinking a coke-cola in the book depository, although this was a different story.

He was just another body in the system, he was sure Mrs. Smith wouldn't care about where he was, and she didn't care enough to go looking for him. The mere importance of him leaving was not to be in the classroom disturbing all the girls from their class work. "Like they were even thinking about class work!" Sarcasm was his nature, and in this case, it wasn't all too far from the truth.

But before he sat down on the nearest couch, he decided to get himself a book and find what magical or real world he was missing in his life. Only he didn't know where to start. The fiction, history, science fiction or fantasy section? But that was all entwined in the same section. He wanted something with a bit of history to it. Maybe something about World War one or two, or something about the Cuban Missile Crisis?

Oh there were so many books to choose from. Only he couldn't think of an exact topic, fantasy, military, fiction, horror, or history, but he guess this could absolve him from his sins. This brought him closer to sainthood, and away from the daily evils that was around him.

Loosing himself in the shelves, he began looking for his books, and after ten minutes of loosing his thoughts in all the shelves he found the books he stumbled upon and resided toward a corner of the library. He sat at a small table surrounded by a shelf of encyclopedias on either side of him, and was a very low-key place to hide from everyone, including from his own conscience. He sat the pile of books on the table, and pulled the chair out, he began to stretch his back, and pulled one book from atop the pile. It was a book about the civil war.

He spanned from beginning of the war, when all the southern states began to recede from the union, up until the middle of the war when they invaded Gettysburg, and how they sent them running back with their tails tucked between their legs. He closed the book at about page one hundred and eighty-four, and moved onto the next book. Ray looked back to his watch, and saw that only fifteen minutes went by. Being that a usual class spanned to about an hour or two he had all the time in the world to read the rest of his books. He felt like he could put his guard down while he was reading, and as he picked up the next book; it was a thin book about the Cuban Missile Crisis.

He had taken his time with this one because this was a subject that he knew very little of. Taking notice of pictures of Kennedy and Kruschiev holding hands and smiling for the camera while the relationship in the book began to worsen for them. It reminded him of how it must have been when Chris and Gene probably joined forces, all smiles and no worries. But what if Gene wasn't the only one behind it. It didn't really make sense to him, but he felt that something big was going to happen soon. Only there hadn't been a crisis yet, and he felt like it would happen pretty soon, in George Bradley and on the street. Ray became tired of that one, closed the book on that subject, and picked up another one. It was a fantasy novel that was entitled Lord of the Rings.

Ray began the novel with due haste, as he looked back at the clock, he saw that he had taken thirty minutes on that slim book, he wanted to get started on this. He opened the book, and became enwrapped with the first sentence about the hobbits and the Ring up through the part about Tom Bombadil, the encounters with the black riders and up to the meeting with Lord Elrond and the council of the ring. As he became tired of that one he couldn't help but remember a line near the end of that chapter coming from Frodo's lips "I will take the ring to Mordor. Only I do not know the way."

Thinking about it, maybe Ray was in Mordor but didn't know it, maybe he was in Mordor and didn't know it. Maybe he was wearing the ring right at that very moment, and he didn't know what the power of the ring was doing to him. But as his heart was racing, he closed the book, and forgot all about the Ring, the Hobbits, and Tom Bombadil, although he couldn't help but feel close to the story.

Just as he was about to pick up the next book, the bell rang out of nowhere with a sudden *clang* then a *Bing...Bing...Bing...Bing!*

The library was quiet, different from inside a classroom with kids trying to sprawl through the desk lines, and pushing by him with impatience. He thought, "Maybe he should have skipped first period more?" He was really missing out on a lot of interesting stuff inside the shelves of the library. Only this was ironic in a sense that he was inside a library when he should have been learning from his teacher. But fuck it, he finally had a break from his rather long and boring day, and he couldn't help but feel obliged to do this every day.

Only this couldn't last forever, and when it came to about lunchtime it was when he would be able to pay attention, and it was not because of the food. It was because of something more sinister, or private, and thinking about it seemed like hours away. He felt a rush of anxiety surge through his hands as he clasped them together and rubbed them from its deep, numb sleep.

When he finished stretching out his hand, he closed the book, pushing it toward the middle of the table like a good meal, and thrusting the seat backwards as he stood up. He noticed that no one had been around the library to look for him, and he was happy with his decision to skip class. But he hid his excitement as he moved out of the library, not taking any notice to the woman who was shelving books onto the shelves in the fiction area, and moved through the metal detector. He felt like the alarm should have gone off because of all the information that he had racked up in his brain. "Hobbits… quest…Missile crisis…Ulysses S. Grant and Robert E. Lee"

Man, he should have been caught for his dastardly deed, but how could he deny "a good book" when he saw one? He chuckled at this, and saw that the masses of kids were flowing through the halls again as if the school was on fire, but they weren't excited, but they were stuck in this fiery depression, watching the flames swallow them up. As Ray entered into the hallway, he became another number that made no difference to the individual classrooms. Only he couldn't escape the entire day in the library that was when they would start looking for him. Oh how vice-principal "Master bitch" would very well like to get his hands on him. He laughed deep down inside about that and moved through the halls, becoming one in the system in the masses of this assembly line.

Yesterday they had very well mapped out a plan to take out A.J., and it was very intricate because they didn't know what his classes were, and they didn't feel like going through the school system to find out. But there was another way that they could hit A.J. and whoever was with him, and that time was at lunch. It was very simple. A team of two men were waiting outside for the reconnaissance of three to four men covering the corners of the A commons lunch area, since it was the biggest out of the B commons. But they would also have a few people watching the lunchrooms for their arrival just in case they wanted to show up late. All were equipped with cell phones and all with text messaging capabilities so that they could either send reports of A.J.'s whereabouts to each person at their posts. But they needed each one to identify that this was the person that they needed, or had seen, before one of them gave the go ahead to the two men team waiting outside with machine guns and automatic rifles.

It would be traumatic, it would be horrific, but war would cost the lives of the ignorant before they took the lives of their enemies. It was the cost of doing business in wartime, and they knew that they would affect a lot of lives. But if that was going to happen, it happened everywhere else, why shouldn't it happen here at George Bradley? This place was just waiting to get hit, and they wouldn't even see it coming, including the principal.

Ray made his way toward the large Commons A section of the lunch hall, and saw all the kids carrying their brown paper bags or the bright red lunch trays with sub sandwiches all wrapped up and waiting to be eaten. The smell attracted and pulled the buds of all the hungry kids, and they went flocking toward it, but Ray turned a corner passing the lonely set of tables that faced opposite the other side of the shabby unkempt senior courtyard. This was where Chris used to sit, and this was where A.J. would very well be in just a few minutes. He had to stand next to the doorway, and report of anything that might be happening. Since he would be the one that would be the one that watched the front he was the exception because if he saw him up close and personal, he didn't need to get any of the others to confirm his identity.

All of them were informed about his identity. He was a small, kind of short stocky kid, clean cut and very well dressed boy. The one thing that they needed to run with is the fact that he always sat near those tables. But if they were seen from another point of entrance, they would need other conformations, because it would also be a big indicator if Frank were right beside him. Although if they didn't see either one of them they would send a text message in one word form, "nothing" but if they suspected something, they would very well would send a longer text message saying, "I got him, look to left or right side". But they could improvise one way or another if it came down to the quickness, if one word had to suffice, one word would serve its purpose.

This was probably going to be the most devastating thing Joey had ever come up with. Ray had to admire the balls on Joey for this one, but he didn't want to jinx their chances before it had even happened.

Ray rested against the wall as he stood opposite to the large front doors, when he knew that leaning next to a phone booth and the bathroom that was sending a putrid smell from it like asbestos. They broke from that position and moved toward the wall that was right next to the phones. He sighed as covered his mouth, letting a yawn escape him, his eyes tightened like a China-man, his cheek curled backs wards as his lips settled back down making his lips move upwards, pulling up against his teeth. Feeling the wind move through his mouth he withdrew his hand from his mouth and licked his lips to get the taste of spit back in his throat. He felt if he had been in the desert, breath hot and sticky, dying of thirst, and he couldn't leave for a second to even get himself a drink. Even though water was a supplement, he needed something else to wake him up and be alert about his task. Only when he looked back to his watch, he saw that only five minutes had gone by.

Ray patted on his legs, feeling the cell phone bulge against his jeans like a mountainous rocky ledge peering out of a cliff that was peering over the Mediterranean Sea. He waited for his phone to vibrate and say in "nothing" or "nada" But that was too early, although he waited anxiously, he couldn't help but let the all knowing feeling that he wasn't going to show up be a possibility. He peered at the tables, "nothing" he muttered, and then back to the entrance "nothing!" He slammed a fist against the wall, hearing the sound echo down his legs, and making a small *ca-clunk* sound as looked upwards he saw two kids walking by glancing at him as if he was a drug dealer.

He gave them a crooked look and grunted out through his teeth, "What do you want?"

The two kids who didn't even look a day over sixteen were wearing large baggy clothes and black T-shirts—hoping to attract some kind of attention from anyone—their cheeks were impregnated with horrible acne, and that wouldn't have made any differences because they were ugly in the first place. But the one thing he was confused by was the fact that a rotund student, with long straightened hair and an enlarged chest, he couldn't tell if it was a girl or boy. Her breasts were probably smaller than her body, and that was probably hidden by all the "Baby Fat" that was bulging out of her pants. This made him think of an underground song by an underground rapper 50 Cent, who was pushing his music out on all the bootlegged CD's, like the rest of them. "*FAT, FAT! Those Twinkies got yo' ass getting FAT FAT! Bitch you grown, that ain't baby fat!*" He wanted to burst out laughing because what he was thinking was so wrong, was obviously the truth. He hid his laughter, but was utterly disgusted by the thought that that was a girl.

They kept on walking as if they didn't see him, Ray wanted to snicker, but held it back, minding his own business but taking care not to piss them off, since they saw that crazy bulldog look in his eye. They went back to there conversation about recent shows that they had been to and what bands they had just seen on the tube, and they walked a long merrily as if nothing was bothering them, knowing that he was looking at them.

Ray raised a hand to his face, and scratching what beard that he had across his chin and said through his hands, "Fuckin' chicks with dicks!" His hand fell back down to his side, and impatiently tapped his right foot, waiting for this "A.J." to arrive so they could get it over with. He began to wander if the others had seen anything…

Bobby Fischel, the second reconnaissance man, was also beginning to wander where this "A.J." was also. He had arrived at about the same exact time when Ray was walking right past the tables. Only he was right across from where the preps were. He began to think if one of the Preps knew where he was. With his rugged face, and pretty outlandish clothing, he would probably receive a glance or two if that were his true goal or not. He wouldn't let his guard down for a moment. He couldn't wait to see this finished, and get the fuck out of here.

"11:45" He saw the green back light of his LG cell phone radiate over the number as he moved his thumb over the cursor that had a small mailbox over it, and pressed down on the small cursor. The menu opened him up to a numbered list that had choices such as

1. **2 voice messages,**
2. **New Messages,**
3. **3 inbox,**
4. **9 outbox,**
5. **Saved,**
6. **Msg (Message) Setting,**
7. **Erase all,**
8. **Mail groups.**

Bobby moved the cursor over **New Message** and clicked on it with the corner left touch pad. Then it brought him to a blank screen with a box at the top of the screen that said **Send To 1**. He searched through his memory of the number that he was told to remember, and he was told to remember it with his life. He quickly put the numbers together with the click of his hand, counting them out to himself as he clicked on the upper left corner button, and saw the new options arise from the left hand corner of the screen. A highlighted option that said **Continue** was open to him, and with a click of his finger, he did just that. Then it brought him to another blank screen, and another box at the top of the screen said **Message**. He looked down at the screen, and slowly typed the message, pressing on the buttons with little enthusiasm, pressing the buttons with precision and care that his finger wouldn't make one single mistake in his message.

"Nothin'"

"**Nothin'**" He clicked on the **back** button, and leaned back against the wall with hostility as he felt the boredom already take him, but he had to think about something else so that he could think about the task at hand.

Louis T. Bruno

"I could have told him that!" Billy whispered, shaking his head with prolonged bitterness and stunted rage, and he closed the phone in vain.

So, in a few minutes, when the bell would ring, they would all meet back together in the B commons to get some lunch, and try to talk…about what they thought or just some small talk to pass what little time they had.

"What?" Billy yelled, hopefully goading the next kid to come and meet his appointed death. They ignored him as they continued down the hall, but some voices rose out of thin air saying "Fuck you, prick!" It was just some kind of response to just sound cool.

Billy looked up at the crowd with a disgusted intimidating face "Fuck you too, toe sucking fuck!" But the voice didn't reply back, it just mingled into the crowd of useless conversation and senseless noise. As the crowd of kids moved a long there way, he laid his head back against the wall, and muttered these words of utter truthful disgust. "Man, I hate this fucking place." And he believed it; he had enough hate for this place than any person had for anything in the world. No, he hated it as much as he graduated from it, he didn't give a shit. He just hated this fucking place so much. "Prison can't be this bad!"

Then when Billy looked to the left of him Bobby and Ray were treading down the hall, slowly taking their time like they didn't want to be there in the first place. It was good to see people that he knew, because if he didn't, he would have gone fucking nuts out here without someone to talk to.

He gave them a nod, and waved his hand slowly as if it was some secret message they were supposed to do when they say to each other, but it didn't mean really anything. It was just a simple wave. A small pathetic smirk came with it too, but somehow they laughed at this, because this was exactly how they all felt, but the feeling was mutual.

By the time that they had returned back to there posts, an crew of gunmen were also waiting inside a small shabby car, roasting inside like burnt turkeys whose guts were bubbling inside the bird, just begging to be let out. They waited with every solid substantial ounce of murderous rage in their bodies. They were the bringers of doom, the four horsemen of the apocalypse, and with their large assault rifles, and pump shotguns, and automatic machine guns, they were ready to hand out the punishment. Only they couldn't release there fury upon the school, and there target until the driver got the sweet text message that told them, **"GO"**, and that was when they could be let off their leash and hell would be unleashed upon George Bradley High school.

Both of the gunmen were wearing long, very black, and very noticeable trench coats. It was rather hot inside the car, but when they stepped outside, it provided a very good cover against the wind. The largest gunmen, with pale and frightening skin and a face that was so stone like that no bullet looked like it could pierce him, was gripping his automatic Mac 10 by the handle, his large foreboding finger was hovering over the trigger as he grunted impatiently. He wanted to deal out death so bad that he would kill everyone in this car right now. Although as long as he held onto his gun, he could have some more patience.

The second one with a fat and really grotesque face, was also hiding his automatic AR-15 rifle underneath his trench coat, was becoming rather impatient as well. His beady eyes had bled all the sympathy from his bones, he had seen quite a few people killed and had done a few personal deeds himself. He was the type of person that had not been bothered by the first person he had killed, if that was supposed to be a bad thing, he relished in the fact. Seeing the barrel poke out of the end of his coat, he relished the fact that they were going to become a part of history, all coming from the barrel of a gun.

Chapter XVI:

"A Procrastinating Protagonist"

The days did indeed go slower for A.J., Frank, and Jessica but they were under the large umbrella of stress that was starting to become a daunting shade of fear.

They barely left Frank's house for half of the week, and it was for those thousand and one damn good fucking reasons. They jumped between staying at Frank's and A.J.'s when they called a local master carpenter to lock the door, since it had been busted open from the police. But it was when A.J. had a dream that some dark figure was standing over him, and whispered to him, *"I am coming for you!"* Even though it was a dream, he felt like it was so real, he could feel the person's breath pushing against his face.

During that week, Frank sent a few of his guys to check on the house, and placed a few guards around A.J.'s father's room and Chris's room. Good reliable men that could withstand anyone trying to get in except it being the doctors or nurses. Also, A.J. wanted them to see if a package was still inside his closet, and asked them if it was still there. They were to stay on the couch if anyone except the master carpenter who had come to fix the doors. If it is anyone else, except for them, they were told to not take any chances.

The next morning, it was a Thursday, and it seemed that the entire week had gone by since that Sunday. Frank woke up very peacefully, and had been walking down the halls with his rather large boxer shorts on. It showed off his legs, and stopped around at his thighs. He was wearing a white tee shirt when he came upon his living room when he saw A.J. and Jessica lying on his couch, Jessica being under the covers pressed up against A.J.'s body like she was attached to him, and he still didn't know why she had to stay. She was just being too pushy to not go away from him for a few days—important business had to be handled.

As Frank slowly walked toward them, he saw that he wasn't sleeping—his tired eyes were batting endlessly, combating the shining sun—he began to push her off and she kept her eyes closed as he moved off the couch.

Those were some of the many things that he could complain about, but he didn't care about the rest at the moment, although he couldn't help but feel a bit of jealousy run through him like the venom of a scorpions juice disintegrating his system. It almost felt that it was trying to corrupt his loyalty to A.J. But he could feel the sting, the pain from this wound, but he couldn't because it hurt him inside, and used it as an escape.

Only when he saw his face, and from the bags swelling underneath his eyes with a shade of purplish black, he knew he was wide-eyed and awake, although he was in his underwear. But he could still feel the resonance of some sleep harboring around his naked chest and his hard was pushing through his underwear from that lump-of-grab-ass impeding them from all the progress that they could be getting done. Frank had to flush this jealousy out of his veins before he said something stupid. His hatred was harder to contain than his piss, but he had to remember that he was the "boss," but wondered what Chris was really thinking when he told Frank to make him boss. "I can't think that…" Frank stopped himself before he continued, and then knew it was time to call him out of the room.

With that rather smug and determined look he motioned for A.J. to get up and follow him. When Frank and A.J. were in the hallway, he heard A.J. giving him a tired manner, stretching his arms in the air. "What's up?"

But then when he would expect a cool, well-spoken soldier, was an angry pissed off boy. "What's up?" His voice was scorning, and he scoffed at a whisper, "you can't even send her away just for a few days just so we can talk business?"

A.J. shook his head, and spoke with an insulted and levelheaded tone. "No, she can't go back to school now, Gene could take her hostage."

Frank just scoffed, and then his sarcasm was more than evident, and his body leaned forward maliciously. "Are you kidding me, Gene wouldn't have the guts. He's just waiting somewhere in some fucking crack house for us to get him."

A.J.'s temper was definitely blown, but he couldn't express it through rage, all he could do was whisper and stay level head in tact. "How do we fucking know where he is? You don't know and I don't know."

Frank was more than pissed at A.J., and he didn't know where to begin. "Then why don't get up off your ass and rally up the soldiers, I know all the names, I know everything about them, I'll give them a call each and everyone of them, you just give me the word!"

A.J. just shook his head again, with that rejecting obstinate shake. "No, we wait!"

"What are you waiting for? Are you waiting until his crew comes after us, and guns every last one of us down?"

"No!" A.J. said dryly, moving away from him.

Frank then grabbed his arm, and then whispered, looking at his face. "Then what are you waiting for!" Frank's gripped intensified as his fingers coiled, suctioning around his arm.

A.J. said nothing for a moment, as he let him finish what he was saying, and calmly spoke in a professional, no nonsense voice.

"I'm waiting for a window…"

But Frank wasn't having this now; he was too pissed off to be civil. "What fucking opportunity! You can't wait till the last fucking minute! God, I thought you would have been more professional than you act."

A.J.'s temper couldn't be controlled after this insult and grabbed his arm, "If you want to be boss fine," he peeled his hand off, and left a small sweat mark on his hand. "I can't carry all this responsibility any longer; I have enough shit going on right now that you can't even imagine. My fathers almost dead, I don't…no, I don't even have a mother. Chris is in the hospital, and I can't ask him questions about how I should go about it. How do you think that feels when you have no fucking help?" A.J. was pouring his heart out for everything, his pained voice was lamenting for his life and everything that used to be his life. Frank, who looked unimpressed, felt struck by what he was saying, because somewhere buried deep inside his mind, knew that feeling, and he couldn't blame him for how he was. But he had to admit that he was disappointed that he couldn't handle the pressure, and take up his responsibilities.

Breathing in then let it out with a relaxing blow, "No, I don't know how it feels. I'm sorry about the whole thing. This whole thing with your parents couldn't have come at a worse time. But bad things happen, you're not the only one that has been lied. Think about it, but now…now is not the time for you to be slacking off. That's just waiting for trouble."

A.J. shook his head, and scoffed bewildered, "Yeah. That's for damn sure. He couldn't have just…" Before he continued on with his ranting, Frank rose off the wall, relaxed and unthreatening, he put a hand over his shoulder. But when he felt too uncomfortable—but really was pained by his emotions—A.J. defensively moved off him, and turned around, giving him the cold shoulder. Frank slowly moved his hand back to his side, and made an amiable looking expression that he meant no harm.

"I just don't want you to forget what position you were given. Chris also wanted you to have this spot, so tough-titty about your problems. He felt that you could handle it. I'll help you, but you need to make some decisions, right now."

A.J. just turned his head, trying to ignore everything that he had said, but he couldn't hold his tongue from the truth. He turned around, and faced him with wet eyes. "To tell you the truth. I don't know where to begin. Call your two best soldiers, and send them to sniff out Gene. Could you do that for me?"

When Frank saw him smiling, he let a small smirk escape him. "I wanted to talk about it sooner or later, but…"

"Don't worry about it. You had to bring it up sooner or later." Frank shook his head, and realized what he was saying was true.

"I'm sorry." A.J. said, putting out his hand, in a friendly demonstration of his forgiveness. Frank saw his hand, his palms and fingers exposed to Frank, he saw it with great admiration, and inserted his hand into A.J.'s palm. It was like two brave knights that had jousted and fought to the best of their abilities, and they had fallen into some strange stalemate where they couldn't kill each other, but were complimenting each other with a hearty handshake about their jousting skills.

Their fingers gripped around each other's, clamping their fingers, and they squeezing until it began to hurt. It was tight then it was hard enough to break both of their fingers releasing each other from their grip, both strong and steady like, and their arms fell back to their sides peacefully.

"It's okay." A.J. said, breathing out all the angst in his system, although he felt like shit, he couldn't help but feel good about himself. Just when he was feeling at his worst, he brought up a very good idea. "But I think its time we go and see Chris. I haven't seen him for the longest time." It was something cheerful to think about at that moment, but it was like he at least owed his friend that.

Frank nodded his head, and smiled as he let out a coughing laugh—his body swaying back and forth as he placed a hand over his mouth—and his eyes filled with cheerful expression. "Yeah, we should." He suddenly raised his hand, and tapped the side of his shoulders in a big brother kind of way, and suddenly rolled over the arch in the wall, and walked into the bathroom.

"I'm going to get a shower," A.J. walked beside the door, and peered into the room, catching Frank in the midst of taking off his shirt, his chest gleaming with his softly tanned body, "and then we'll go see Chris."

"Okay?" Frank said, just looking at him with his eyebrows raised in a sarcastic mock. It was then when A.J. saw that he was invading his privacy, maybe overstepping his boundaries just a little bit more than he should have. "Well, we are both in our underwear, for God's sake. How is that a problem?"

A.J. moved inside the door, and the artificial light drew less and less as he shut the door, and as he closed the door; he heard A.J. saying, almost as if he was hearing a small sexual whisper. "Damn, you look good."

Long after everyone got their show, all of them were dressed and ready to go to the hospital. When they left, and vanished out of the house, with nothing else on their minds except to see Chris.

The ride was very quiet, but they didn't feel the need to talk, because it was as if they had said everything they had wanted to say, but maybe they were really just bored with the fact that they were in a car again, which in all truth, they did. They despised being patient, but they didn't care. Not more than A.J. did, because he imagined seeing his father resting on the bed with no sign of life in his body, and what that once powerful man he knew that raised him was now a withering form of jelly. Sagging muscles and lifeless eyes, it sickened him to realize that this was his father lying in that bed. He wished it were that whore who had raised him for all these years were lying in that bed instead of his father. For all A.J. knew, maybe he wasn't even his father, but that wouldn't matter now, since he couldn't talk.

He sighed, roughly, feeling the anguish swoop him up like a hawk's talons did to a weak field mouse.

Frank looked with a curious eye, and said, "You all right?"

A.J. glanced over to Frank with a glare about him, and then turned to Jessica, and shrugged nonchalantly as he sighed. "Yeah, I'm okay."

As he fell back in his seat, Frank cocked his right eyebrow, and began to speak coolly. "Are you sure?"

A.J. looked back at him, gave him a sarcastic look, and arched his eyebrows like his in a mocking sort of way. "Yeah, I'm fine."

Frank glanced back towards the road when he accepted his answer for what it was, but didn't want to pursue the matter at all. He replied like an everyday person would do when he or she was trying to blow a situation under their mental rug. "Cool." His eyes returned to the road, and didn't offer him another glance. But A.J. felt like a woman that had somehow lost her control and let it fumble to the ground. He could see this baby bleeding and crying, wondering what was going on but couldn't communicate it other than by crying…only crying. No talking, not verbalizing, just crying.

But pushing all of these issues to the back of his mind, he decided to fall asleep and try to forget about everything, and just sleep away all his problems. But when he went to sleep a protruding headache had suddenly pulsed in his head like a migraine, almost like a veil of confusion hit his head. He detested this feeling of all the most things, but bore it as if it was a mix of tequila and scotch working on his brain. He drifted into a deep sleep, and sleep took him by the hand as he closed his eyes very slowly. Slower he began to drift, like a plane committing kamikaze into an ocean liner, every second seemed to slow down for him, and as the plan headed toward the ocean liner, his mind sunk with the deepest of all sleep he had ever felt.

Jessica was feeling the cool breeze of the air conditioner regulating her body temperature to normal, cooling her body off the hot sun while she waited for A.J. to wake up. She wanted him to sleep, because he hadn't slept for about a week, and Jessica had found some time to spare while she waited. Jessica was reading a magazine entitled "Getting ready to have a baby." The cover of the magazine had a motherly model on the cover with long red hair, a very statuesque face, blazing green eyes, and a short curved nose. Her belly was more than curved, and pushed out like a rolling mountain out of her shirt, who was probably about thirty, but it was probably make-up that made this woman seem a lot younger, but she was sure that the child wasn't all just make-up.

She had been playing around with the idea of having an abortion—while the idea burned her soul to do it, she couldn't help but feel scared about everything. She would decide to have it, but it was not going to be an easy journey for her.

Upstairs in room four hundred and twenty, Krazy had been inside the room with Chris waiting and sleeping in for about a week in the room, not doing a thing, except for feeling on his gun. Just looking at Chris's pulsating body, watching him mumble words into the room as if he was having a personal conversation. Krazy wasn't too comfortable with this idea, but it was something to do. Although during the week, his wife, with their infant child wrapped inside them, stayed on the other side of him. Krazy and her barely looked at each other, but when they did, it was just by chance. She had come in on that Monday, and stayed the entire time, but then left late that night. He hoped she would come back, because he was starting to get a little bored with nobody to talk to.

But during the middle of the week, he had become so bored that he had started to have conversations with himself. He couldn't stand it; he needed somebody to talk to for God's sake. He hadn't slept for days, and even when he started to shut his eyes, he heard a few words stumble from his lips. He suddenly opened his eyes, and looked upon Chris again. It was chilling to hear this coming from the great Chris Mangini.

"Queens…. No one…will…ever…get one on you."

Krazy's imagination was sparked, and he was filled with fright, wondering what the hell he was talking about. Should he have been taking notes, should have he been writing this down? The thought occurred to him, but he wasn't some experiment, he was just experiencing the morphine, feeling his body with dreams that he could only see.

Krazy began to watch him even more as he spoke, as he himself began to fall into a daze…

"*Ever more, ever more…your body will be ever more…join the abyss…embrace its love.*" Chris heard the words thumping inside his head, and when he opened his eyes, he was inside a dimly lit room that had a green kind of shadow around him.

"This couldn't be real." Chris thought to himself, wondering what he was doing inside this room. It was a nice, quiet office room with a few leather bound chairs on opposite sides of a lamp. On both sides of the chairs there were mountainous bookshelves filled to the brim with glowing books. Then in front of him was a long, plush couch that looked like it could belong in one of those English films. He saw a blinking lampshade, lighting the room for two seconds then disappearing and then again. It repeated a few more times, but then inside the chairs was a woman. It looked like his wife, but he couldn't see her from that distance, he had to walk across the room to get a good look at her.

He looked down, and saw that he was standing on both his feet, strong and without pain. He couldn't remember the last time he was on his feet, but it felt heavy as he walked toward the blinking lampshade.

Chris was about to approach the woman in the lampshade when he saw her face had been all misconstrued—face marked with long scratches—gargling a demented voice as a putrid green slime had been rising out of her face. An evil gleam radiated from her, giving Chris the chills. But below her, in her rocking hands, he saw a wrapped up cloth that resembled a bloody tampon, but there was something limp inside it, like a baby had been snapped in half, and it had been bleeding profusely onto the floor.

Chris didn't want to see if that was his son or not, he wanted to be out of this place, but the more he wanted to be free of this place, the thumping returned. His heart raced and his head thumped even faster with the pain, a haunting cackle filled the room. He covered his ears—the light continued flashing—as the cackling stopped, but then a message had then appeared on the wall above the couch in messy capital letters,

YOUR FAMILY'S BLOOD WILL SPILL…

Then the letters began to ooze a bloody reddish color, and the thought sickened him, more than that it terrified him to the point of belting tears. Now, he knew that in the darkest regions of his mind that he was dreaming. Nothing existed at all as his body flickered like that of a television screen, and he closed his eyes.

He couldn't take it anymore, he needed to be awake, and as the room started to shake, he felt a bright light rip through the top of the wall, clean the nightmare of this room and the light blinded him. But the blinding light had somehow brought him out of the dream world, and into reality. The one way he could tell was by the dank air that was filling up in his nose, and as he opened his eyes, he felt blinded by another light, but it wasn't so bad, this light…

As Chris began to open his eyes, he felt the back of his head scratch against a pillow, and his neck felt locked into his back. But as his bleary eyes began to see through the black light, he looked to left side, and saw through the large glass window nurses and doctors running up behind them, grabbing the nurses asses while they made there way to another dying patient's room. Everything was still hazy to him, but his mind was never clearer at that moment. He scoffed, with his over night stinky breath, and glanced to the other side. He saw his wife, dead asleep in a hunched over position that looked only to fit a hunchback up in some bell tower of France.

Chris's mouth began to slowly move, and a few dry words burst from his lips. *"Water…Water."* But he didn't hear him, his lips must have been too parched, and his throat was too dry for him to speak up. As he began to speak more, his hand felt around for the medium sized, long rectangle call button. But he couldn't feel his way around to get it. But when his hand was looking around, reaching down his bed, gripping the blanket with his cold hands trying to warm his hands up, and wake his body up to the harsh realities of his unstable condition. But when he thought he was alone, a familiar voice suddenly filled the room.

"Chris?" The voice echoed around the building, and into his ears. It sparked an image in his head, and as he turned, his bleary vision began to focus in on who was standing at the door. Three shadowy figures, one was taller than the first two that were in front of it, and none of them seemed familiar to them. But when they came closer, his blurry vision became clearer as the figures stepped out of the darkness, and their shadows trailed across the room in a cloud of mystery. As they approached him, their faces came next to his bed light, and his eyes were filled with joy when he saw the faces. A.J, Frank, and Jessica were the faces and that's who he wanted to see…

Then out of the blue, Frank's voice called out to him, waking him up from that cold dank darkness that was enveloping him. "Chris."

Frank saw him opening his eyes, and he could somehow tell that he could see them, but they didn't try to give up on him. But the way he was looking resembled a punch-drunk boxer waking out of his fifteen round fight.

Frank looked at A.J., and then he glanced at Jessica. They were all thinking the same thing, but they didn't want to say it.

"It's us," Jessica said, with her sweet charming coo. Chris couldn't keep his eyes awake. "We came to see you. A.J.'s here." Jessica grabbed A.J. by the hand, and forced him over to her side so that he could see him in the glowing light. A.J. looked down and saw Chris staring at him with a glazed look in his eye—mouth crusty from lack of water, and face already growing a four day beard—and it frightened them to think that this was there friend lying in that chair, intoxicated by morphine, drugged up to the point where he couldn't speak. A.J. began to remember how his dying grandfather looked in the hospital bed the night before he past away in the morning.

Chris then leaned up and looking at Jessica, said dreamily *"Ciao, Bella."*

She just looked at him, eyes wide and cocked her head out of confusion, like all the life had just been drained from her, and he began to ask her another rapid-fire question, without even giving her a chance to fully comprehend his words. *"Dove il ragazzo andiamo?"*

At that point, Jessica was thinking about her friend who had been suffering from cancer, and had finally died in her sleep. She was holding her hand as she let out one more breath, and her body went entirely limp in her stance. The sadness was closing in on her, and like an awful congestion, scrunched her face together as her dimples made her face resemble the Pillsbury Dough boy. But, when he began to breath out a few words, she leaned in closer and with her smile stretching across her face, she began to choke out her words. "What is it?"

Chris looked at her with a dumbfounded stare, a dead on straight forth stare that only meant certain personal anger at that moment, but she saw his mouth moving, and she leaned over to listen to him. He cleared his throat, but she could somehow feel small sprays spit puff out from out of his mouth and land on her cheek, and she finally knew what he wanted, "Water." She whispered, and then pulled herself out of his face, and pushed past A.J., clearly a woman on a mission.

"What is it?" A.J. then leaned against the hospital window as she grabbed a tall plastic cup with a straw that was probably his—even though she didn't know for sure whose cup it was—and filled the cup up halfway, she was destined to give him whatever he needed to stay alive. Holding the cup in her hand, she burst out, "he needs water, he told me!" She ran back to Chris, and held the cup to his aching lips as the water swished forward, and she pulled back, just so that he could get a taste. Chris's life looked replenished, and his lips were wet as his thirst was quenched—his eyes were welling from the blaring fluorescent light.

Chris pushed the straw out and mouthed the words, *"Thank you."* Jessica moved the cup away from his lips, and set it on the drawer next to him.

Jessica felt her heart race, and her eyelids began to wet. Not from any kind of pain that sent stimulation's of fear, but joyful stimulation's that very well filled their souls deep with appreciation and recognition that there is a God, and tears began streaming down her face—God was in every rolling tear. A.J. was thinking the same thing, but God has somehow spared him from some evil that waits for him in the afterlife. Only the sacrifice that he was making on this bed had to redeem every human being when they were suffering under physical and mental pain.

"Maybe, just maybe?" But the fact that this could have been him on the stretcher terrified him but he didn't want to imagine that this was happening to his friend, he wanted to ignore all the theories that was hurting his mind and his soul. Although seeing his friend like this, he started thinking about his father again. His own heart began to ache with the same sorrow that he should have done for his father, but he impulsively pushed Jessica's hand out of his way, and walked off toward the corner where another chair had been placed right next to the window. Grabbing the chair with his right hand, he moved past Frank who was standing at the end of the bed, and fell in the seat.

He wanted to cry, and as he placed his hands over his face, he began to weep softly. It echoed through his fingers, and shook the entire being that he was. It sounded like a cough at first, but then as he covered his eyes, it turned into a full-hearted cry. Only his tears had sifted away like salt in a hot boiling pot and he continued on for a few more minutes, but he knew that his friend was alive, and that was all that mattered.

The time had stretched from quarter to four to seven o clock already when A.J. had just sat idly watching Chris in his morphine induced state when he finally noticed the time lapse. Nurses had come and gone, Doctors checked and left, and the orange sunset bled across the white clouds. He could see that Jessica was on the other side, standing against the wall, clicking her heels together, as if she was trying to get herself out of this place and back in her bed like in "The Wizard of Oz." But she had grown weary, and tired, and clicking her heels were just becoming boring. Her car had still been at the hospital for the past week, and she needed to get it back if she could go and get herself checked tomorrow at the doctor's office. Things went along, but things were going to get dangerous.

Chapter XVII:

"The Massacre at George Bradley"

"Come on, Godsmack can not be better than Mushroomhead!" James snorted through his nose, and exhaled the disgust out of his body.

"No way!" Ann Pantoliano shouted, "Godsmack beats it on all sides."

Benny just looked at his sister, and seeing that lusty gleam in her eye, her black hair rested on her shoulder as he shook off her response, "Whatever." They had been arguing for more than fifteen minutes, when they finally ended the conversation, or just gave up. With a puff, the two fell back into silence again, just looking around waiting for Berry to show up.

Although it was a meaningless conversation, it made the time go by waiting for their big bro to get himself here, and the three could talk about normal things, but that didn't always happen. "One month, thirteen days, and…" James sighed, and then tried to forget about his mother's death, but he found out that he couldn't forget about his mother. Benny didn't want to go and get a job, so he decided to be in with his brother, being his bodyguard while he soled his goods. They had sometimes brought their goods to school with them, but these were desperate times, and this called for extreme measures. They would want to be ready if anything did happen.

"But God forbid!" Benny thought, and wanted to make the sign of the cross. All of them were Catholics, including Ann. But her lean face, hazel nut eyes, and a rather pudgy frame that deemed pretty impressive would mistake her to be Jewish. Only no one would really mistake her to be Jewish because no one really knew what a Jewish kid looked like.

"I just don't know. I mean, her breasts never stopped her from being one of the guys, but I guess that its our fault for not letting her be a woman." Benny thought to himself as he remembered that they had always given her a hard time about everything. They had especially embarrassed her about the time a guy had asked her out one time, but she was so scared that she ran away from the boy, and never spoke to him again.

"We weren't any help except for being assholes. I guess that's why she won't go out or hang out with anyone. "

They couldn't erase what they did to her, but they could somehow make up for it now, by spending some time with her, and allowing her to come a long when ever they went out, but not on their business meetings. "Maybe to a few party's or a friend's house?" Benny thought, and knew it was a good idea.

"Because our father isn't much help on that, fucking fag…going off and fucking around with women at his theatre." They were used to being ignored by him, but when it came to their sister, it was something else. They wanted her to have some fun now, meet some guys, and take it easy for a while. Even though with the rumors about shooters were spreading faster than a Heroin addict did on the search of his next fix, adrenaline pumping through his veins. Also when it came down to it, it felt like it was just adrenaline for the students to get riled up and in a fit so that they could scare them half to death. But, overall, James had a strange feeling about this one, because this seemed totally different. Since things were official between Chris and Gene, he knew that war would reach their steps.

Fifteen minutes had past by, and the sun had taken its time to leave. But, that cold air that was in New York during the winter still hadn't left yet. Although it was still cold, people were still outside. Not too many, but as A.J. and Frank made there way into the school, Frank couldn't help but get an edge from the place. As he found a parking space, he slowly put the car into park, but didn't turn the key for another ten seconds.

Both of them were unusually quiet, and they had every reason to be. They were scared, scared about what awaits inside the school for them. They weren't sure, but they were pretty damn well sure at that moment that what would be inside waiting for them.

Only they were sure that they *needed* to be inside the school, but something was bothering them, blocking them from going inside and completing the mission.

"Are you ready?" Frank said, feeling the heat of the car take it's toll on his comfort. The sweat began to form at his brow, and he began to pant like a dog that was without water, and his breath was extremely hot from the fear that they would not make it back out.

Both of them were contemplating many things, but Frank was deep in his own thoughts. He had remembered a conversation that he had had with

Jessica, but this was not to be repeated from the time they're spoken to anyone, not even A.J. It boiled on his tongue like Acid, and bubbled in his head, wanting to be let out, but he felt restrained by the very thought of speaking about it. All he heard were the last words of Jessica pounding into his mind, *"Don't tell him. Don't you tell him."*

He remembered these words, but let them slip out of his mind, and the notion of even mentioning it would mean him his life with Jessica. All he could do was keep it to himself, away from A.J. especially, but with fear of what lay inside George Bradley like a lions den, what would they find in it. Or what would find them once they were inside? The only way to find out is for them to walk inside, and see what waits for them. He started to open his mouth, and just when he was about to finish the rest of his sentence, he closed his lips before he gave away Jessica's secret, and his cover.

After two minutes Ann left the table in a furious rage, she became swarmed by her unknown emotions, stinging her heart with bitter poisonous tips, clouding her once conscious mind with thoughts of hatred for everyone, even towards her mother. "Goddamn you, and you know what, Goddamn God!" She couldn't understand why her mother had been taken from her, she felt distraught over the whole thing. When she stormed down the hall, she was breathing continuously, and as she approached the end of the hall, two fairly big black kids walked past her, not even noticing her fairly large breasts or rather plump behind. It was strange because she had been looked at numerous times by many guys, but she had never had the guts to approach them, ever since…

But things were going too fast and she couldn't find anyone else to blame it on, her father, her brothers, God? "Yes…God." Who better than to blame it on than God, and if he was so big and powerful, let her be struck down by his oh-so powerful might.

As she exhaled the momentary plight of anger, she knew that she was hungry, but she ignored that aching crunching sound in her stomach. But as the smell of the food crept into her nose, she began to feel the aching pulsing inside her stomach again, and it began to hurt her just to think about it. She wanted to make everything go away, not just for now, but she wanted to be inside a blank world with nothing inside or around her, and inside, she could paint another world for her to escape to. Where her mother, father, and her brothers could all live together again, and live happily ever after again.

She couldn't take it anymore, her body was hot, her mind was aching just like her stomach, and as she took another left she found herself in the hall across the A Commons. She could see the preps all sitting in a row, smiling, not taking notice of anyone except themselves and their own worries.

She hated them as well, and as she caught a glimpse of one of the cheerleaders, she began to spurn wild fantasies of shaven heads of cheerleaders. She imagined the looks on their faces as their pom-poms rotted away inside their hands with heartbroken tears rolling down their faces, cheeks red with embarrassment, and tied up in S&M sex acts. Their big blue eyes filled with despair that she wanted them to feel she wanted them to feel the hurt that she was feeling—all of them, all of them.

Ann paused, and took another deep breath as she headed down another hall that lead to the side of the Commons B lunch area. But something stopped her, she couldn't eat just yet, and she fell back against the metal gate.

"At least she could be alone for a few minutes." Ann thought to herself as she folded her arms, keeping her hands underneath her sweaty pits, she felt the ache go away, for a little bit, but then returned to invade her privacy.

Away from the school, Jessica was off in her car on her way towards the doctor's office… Her appointment was at twelve-o clock, but she had left around eleven. She couldn't make anywhere nearer except in the city. "St. Francis hospital in Manhattan." She kept saying to herself, but she couldn't remember the last time she was there for any kind of checkup. It might have been when she was real young, but she couldn't really place her mind in that timeframe. "Well no duh, how could she remember? She was only three years old." But the one reason why she would even go back to this place was because of that reason. No one would even remember her there, and that was good. St. Francis was a quiet low key place, and no one would remember her after she left.

When she entered into the city, she felt an odd question stir around in her mind. "What was A.J. talking about last night?" It didn't hit her last night, but it somehow hit her at that moment very quickly. What was he exactly saying?

She gave this question some thought, and just pushed it away, realizing that it wasn't any of her business. All she could do was just hope that he was okay, and just continue her course, hoping that he wasn't making any predictions of chaos that he would have to witness firsthand. And the only thing she could ponder away at all her theories she had come up with now as she saw the trade tower buildings. They were tall and magnificent soaring in the sky as they blocked most of the sun, a building that represented all of New York, and all her pride.

At that same exact moment, back at George Bradley, a few minutes before A.J. and Frank were approaching the door, Ray was standing on the opposite side of the pay phones, directly across from the gate rail where Ann had been sitting. With his hands waving down at his sides, he pretended to not notice Ann by looking both ways trying to make himself look conspicuous, "D cups, double D cups, they didn't look like C cups. And they definitely weren't E cups." Those were just incredibly fucking large. "Like the Dinello sisters." The very thought of there big tits and incestuous kissing just made him want to just whip out his dick and start jerking off about them right at that moment.

But as he turned to the right again, he saw nothing, and knew that nothing was coming. He could take a few seconds to look at this girl, just waiting for him to be taken advantage of. But, she looked familiar though, like he had seen her in one of his classes. Or maybe he had had her before in his sexual grip one time or another, and he was starting to pitch a tent in his pants just thinking about what this girl.

He was nervous, because every time he looked at her, his shaft pulsated, and when she turned away for a moment, he spied another look at her, filling up his perversity tank.

"Lord have mercy!" He whispered to himself, but felt the words actually become louder than he thought. He sounded like one of those old black ladies in those Baptist Churches, praising God at the top of their lungs, calling out to a God that would never help them. Only, he loved women, and when he saw one in front of him he couldn't help but just go crazy thinking about what there bodies looked like underneath those clothes. That tight white T-shirt that barely covered her revealing bra, and those long black wool pants that made her legs just seem more attractive, but large at the same time. The structure of a woman really fascinated Ray, and how her body looked underneath the covers was just like science of an onion. This would involve delicately peeling away the every leaf until you got down to the center of their universe—a pulsating heart that was capable of conceiving and receiving so many emotions and insights. There was something new in every woman, because no woman was ever the same. And no longer did they appreciate the inner workings of a real man anymore.

As soon as Ray frantically hit the **Send** button, the message traveled faster beyond sight and sound. The message somehow seemed to dissolve from right within Ray's phone, and landed in the Jean's phone. The two gunmen who heard the call were attracted to this sound like it had been a bird calling, their ominous message became so clear. They made no sign of excitement as the pale face driver that they had been "so aquatinted with" opened the phone, and pressed a few buttons as he was accessing the message.

Their palms gripped around the gun handles, anxiously awaiting the response that they had been waiting to hear.

The Disintegrating Bloodline

Jean's voice trembled when he read the message out loud, and as he turned around, he saw the two gunmen had two big smiles that only made a perverted S&M freak smile after he had just tortured and beat mate, looking over her bruised and cum stained body. But the driver with the red, white, and blue hair trembled of the thought of bondage wrapped women, and they had turned into the hard boiled killers that they had become from all those beatings. But was it from the beatings, or was it from the television violence?

Whatever the answer was to this mystery, he couldn't even begin to think of an answer for it—there were smarter people for that. But when he turned around, he felt the words of the hitman crawl over his shoulder like an ominous spider that was scratching its hind leg against his neck. "Leave after two minutes, and don't look back. Hope you have a great life, and say no to drugs." The tone of his voice sounded very morbid, but the last part was so sarcastic that it bordered on weird humor, and the boy with the red, white, and blue hair watched as the two gunmen left the vehicle, they walked side by side, with their matted long red hair hanging past their collars. As he saw them walking toward the school, he saw the barrels of their guns poking through the bottom of their Trenchcoats, like the blood that was going to be on the end of their shoes.

But they didn't care, they relished in the thought of killing people for a cause, but "what was the cause for?"

But he couldn't think anymore, and his stomach began to ache from the anguish in his heart. As he felt weak in his entire body, he laid his head against the wheel, and felt his tears fell against the nylon plastic, staining them from his eternal sadness, lamenting for all the boys and girls who would die for their cause. Then he began to whisper a most haunting echo that he had ever said in his entire life. "We who are about to die, salute you." Whispering this, he gave a small salute to the boys, but then laid his head against the steering wheel, wanting all the guilt in his soul to just leave him. He wanted his soul to be exercised of this eternal grief, just for a little while.

"Just for a little while." He huffed, like some dying child that was choking on it's own blood, and another tear fell against the steering wheel like a drop of blood that fell in a Holy Communion wafer. "Then I can die or pay my debt to all my friends who might die." He couldn't get over the sadness that he was so gripped by, but as he dried his eyes, and left the terrible place that was about to become a shooting range, without a trace.

A few minutes before the shooters made there way into the school, inside the city of New York's St. Francis Doctors office in Manhattan, Jessica was waiting for Doctor Rose Aprile to give her the good news or bad news if she had to say anything. She had never seen this doctor in her life, and wandered if she was up to her abilities. All these questions were bringing her down, and in those fifteen minutes the anticipation was growing inside her, just as her pre-born child had been growing for so little time. She held a hand over her stomach and wandered if anyone around her would care if she talked about it, just to get it off her mind before she found out what it would be. Jessica observed a few of the patrons, and as she thought about talking to one of these patrons, she then reconsidered her decision about talking so carefree. The doctor came out and called for her. Jessica went inside, and then found out if she was going to be a caregiver of life.

Back at the school sitting at their everyday lunch table, A.J. had become meticulously observant of the entire lunchroom. He felt calm for a few minutes, watching the kids eat there lunches without a care in the world. Then after those few minutes passed by them like sand in an hourglass, falling with rapid speed, A.J. felt edgy uncomfortable, even at his own school. He never had those problems before, but now it was like he had a death wish. But he really wished he had the cares of those children again, but having no cares would mean wasted time, and if that meant wasted time, A.J. would never had experienced what he had experienced. Only the experience felt more like a curse, dangling over him as it laughed in his face, making his anger rush into his brain, and resent those kids with all he could muster in his system.

"That's him!" A.J. burst out unexpectedly, not realizing that he was talking to himself.

"What?" Frank said, turning toward him with a confused and sour look on his face. His eyebrows creased, and that look on his face told A.J. that he wanted to know what he was talking about. "I think we are being watched."

But he couldn't see what he was talking about, only he could start believing that he was being watched. He looked down toward the quadruple doors, and where the large piece of marble block was. He didn't see a soul, no one, which was also strange because there was usually someone just traipsing around, minding there own business. But he could feel it as well—the eyes of all unwanted souls were on them.

"Are you sure?" Frank said, not taking his eyes off the doors while he spoke. His eyes were like hawks at a distance, and could see at great distance, but even though there seemed to be nothing, he seemed to feel something in his gut that something terrible was about to happen.

"Yes, I'm sure of it. Damn it, we shouldn't have come here!"

Frank rose out of his chair, "Could have told you that one," Frank croaked in a baleful voice as they made their way down towards the entrance. But they saw the two of the four doors open, and in came two brooding figures both entirely dressed in black, but had long brown Trenchcoats covering over there entire body. Frank stood still, and pretended to look off into the crowd of the Commons. While he stood next to the table, A.J. stopped in his tracks, and he couldn't help but glance down the hall, but he hid his face, as if he was trying to hide his identity.

They looked like regular everyday Gothic kids, with their everyday long red hair. Nor there round faces with blue and brown eyes, it was the look in their faces. Frank didn't like the look on their faces, and it gave him a chilling thought that they weren't here for the food or for their next class. These were the men.

Frank looked at them, and saw no change in there direction. They were here for them.

"They are here to kill him! Or both of us?" Frank thought, and tried not to admit that he saw the gun barrels poking out from the bottom of their trenchcoats before he had even thought about it. When he finally admitted to himself for noticing the barrel, he started to notice what they were carrying. He saw that they were holding them by their sides underneath the coat, and they were just biding their time for some reason, as if they were waiting for them to make the first move.

He could see the barrel of the gun, and by the looks of it, he had an AK-47 SUV.

It was just a few inches smaller than the regular AK, but it still fired the same as a regular AK-47, and it held the same rounds as the original AK-47. Either way, it still proved to be a dangerous and formable weapon in a time when accuracy meant nothing and bullets was the key to the door of unleashing the chaos. But the other gun resting inside the other assassins hands looked like an M-4 Carbine assault rifle. It's barrel was rounded and it had one up on the AK-47 in the accuracy range. One of them would make their move, and it would be one unfair fight indeed. Although he would use his surroundings to protect him from the bullets, he didn't think that he would make it out alive.

Only, when he looked at A.J., he couldn't help but hear Jessica's words, *"Don't you tell him! Or I swear…"*

Swearing wasn't necessary; her threats had meant nothing to him right about now. He needed to know the secret that Jessica carries in her belly, and how she swore not for him to tell A.J. of the news. "What better time than to tell him than now?" Just when they were about to die, of course.

He knew that right now, time was incredibly short, and everything that they had feared had come true. Two large gunmen were here to take their lives. "There's something I have to tell you." Frank whispered in a low, compunctious tone.

A.J. heard his voice, and he was filled with frightened confusion. "What is it?" As A.J. waited with short anticipation, his hand slipped around the back of his pants, grabbing onto the butt of the Beretta. Pushing it around to his side he took a short breath before he laid the big bombshell on him.

The thought of who would either draw first in this deadly show off was becoming more prominent as he wrapped his hands around the back of his shirt, and felt on the black grip of the Berreta M92F. Although Frank at any other time would have thought of a more kind way to put it to him, he knew that the gunmen were getting anxious, and he said rather directly. "Jessica's pregnant, she didn't want to tell you, but she figured she would get an abortion so she wouldn't have to take care of it."

A.J. was horrified and stunned by what he heard, and couldn't help but start to stutter when he spoke. It was like he wasn't worried about his safety more than he wanted to know about the truth. "Ar…Are you sure? Is it a boy or girl?"

"Listen," Frank ordered, not breaking his concentration off the boys. "There will be a time for answers but now *you gotta go!* Those fucks are going to kill you, now leave!"

A.J. shook his head in disagreement, but when he saw his once charming face grow cold, he grabbed him by the shirt with his right hand and flung him to the ground, and A.J. looked back at him with a painful, threatening look in his eye. But when he saw him unleash his Beretta pistol in the air, he turned to the side, and saw something rise out of the gunmen's large trenchcoats. His eyes widened with fear then his heart began to race as many thunderous claps raised around the school walls, and over his head. The loud streams of bullets echoed, breaking his hearing to a new level. Crawling for cover, he searched for Frank.

While Ann was standing around the aisle just before the shit storm happened, she wandered, "What was that boy up to carrying a phone?" She watched him disappear down the hall, fists clenched, and his pace quickened as he disappeared near the back exit. Only she didn't want to know she wanted to sulk for a few minutes. But when she saw the two boys standing at the quadruple door exit/entrance she saw something peering out of their coats, and knew that it was a large metallic weapon. "Oh my…" She watched as the two gunmen unsheathed two large metallic weapons from their coats, and were pressing the butt of the weapons against their shoulders. They aimed their weapons outwards, Ann saw the large club like hand gripping the wooden handle and inserted his finger inside the round hole that held the trigger, and released a barrage of bullets from his large fat finger. It sounded like firecrackers blowing up a dolls head, and it made her ears ring as she just stood entranced by this spectacle, frozen in time, but then when she saw the mass flood of kids making their way down the hall, she saw the terror on their faces and she knew that it was for real, all the rumors were true. This was not the time to think about anything else, she decided to run.

She turned toward the pack of kids, filed up from wall to wall on either side of the hall, running for their lives. Only she approached the crowd and pushed her way through the masses of students. Some moved out of the way for Ann, but a lot of them didn't, feeling like she was swimming in an extreme tidal wave, being pushed back by the strong current of tall, fat, small, skinny, students that had never exercised in their lives. But now they were now running, running from their comforts and into the lion's den of carnage. When Ann finally pushed her way through the sweaty, uncontrollable flood of students, she looked behind her, and saw that these kids, black and white, tall and skinny, that were once pushing her aside and making their escape, were now on the ground bleeding and pressing their hands against their bellies, trying to stop the wounds, crying and screaming with rage as they watched their blood flow like a water fountain all over the floor. These students had never felt the wrath of a hot hollow tip bullet before, and for some of them it was their time, some would just bleed to death, experiencing an excruciating pain that no one had ever felt before they died.

Only Ann was not like these sheep, she had seen what was coming, and she had made her escape. She had no friends, and it was better for her, because no one would show up for her funeral. "Better them than me!" Ann whispered, and felt her body rejecting whatever was in her stomach, curdling and bubbling, ready to soar up to her mouth, and project vomit all over the floor. But she swallowed it, and kept going. Only she felt her heart beating irregularly, and she needed a place to hide. Ann made her way though the second commons lunch room, which was now deserted leaving only for the flies to come and take their pick from any tray they choose. But that made her think of the dead bodies that would be eaten away, piece by piece, by the worms in their compact dirt grave.

She hid in a small area where it was another entrance/exit where kids could walk into the technical center tucked away from sight. Inside this small open area, there were two payphones, and she ran toward the phone. Her heart was pounding—panting large breaths as her wet hands palming the receiver, and when she pressed it against her ear, it slipped out of her grasp and slid all the way down, past her breasts, and finally stopped in midair, dangling for a moment. As she grabbed the receiver again, more of the shots rang out. With every shot, she felt like they were coming closer, and closer to her. She finally found the courage, with her nimble finger to press the numbers, 9-1-1.

Ann's emotions began to crumble at that moment—everything had just dawned on her when those fatal shots rang off into the complacent halls—when the phone began to ring, and when somebody answered she spoke, "There's dead bodies all over the floor. Get help quick…" more tears began staining her long face—then she opened her mouth, eyes closed, and mouth wide releasing a silent cry, "I don't want to die!" She couldn't find the words to speak anymore, all she could do was drop the phone, and slink down next to it, and cry, crying for what she had said about everything. She began to close her eyes, and more tears streamed down her cheeks. As she heard constant screams and some of it got into her mind but when she began to think that everything was over, she looked up and saw her brother, holding one of their guns, she stood up and hugged him. She felt better once she was here, and he accompanied her for a few minutes before he left her, just until she stopped crying.

Frank, seeing the gunmen unsheathing the AK-47 SUV from his trenchcoat, was filled with a terror that made him pull the gun twice as fast and held it high in the air as the sun bounced off the metallic pistol. A few people had seen Frank draw his gun, but when they heard the burst of shots streaming down the halls, a loud echoing scream filled the entire commons. Some got down under the tables, and some hauled ass.

Frank advanced toward them, and took his first shot. The first shot he took three seconds to aim, feeling the gun lunging upwards, and then he pulled the trigger two more times. But the next two were just to keep them busy. But when the buzzing shots of hollow tips zinged past his head, and pierced one of the Senior Courtyard windows, he quickly sidestepped to the nearest row of cover. Keeping his head down he saw that none of his shots had even intimidated them.

The shots filled him with anxiety, a rush, and he was ready. "Bastards didn't even move!"

Frank whispered, feeling the intensity surge through his system. He didn't see where they had ended up. He could feel the shots ricocheting against the brick making a *ka-shing, ka-shing, ka-shing,* and the brick plaster began to crumble. The sulfur was already on their lips and noses, now they were after blood.

The shooters eyes were glossed over with expendable hatred he saw the fear festering, he saw these kids being struck by those hot metallic bullets, sending them to the ground. They grabbed their stomachs or wherever they had been hit, screaming for their mothers and fathers—the blood was slowly dripping from their wounds, touching the floor—but would get no comfort as the shooters shot the ones that were down, tearing their legs and sides apart with each bullet. Black and white students resembled bleeding cattle, staring at the wall above them, reduced to slabs of hunkering meat. He couldn't obsess about the dead, because if he didn't use the gun in his hand—which was already starting to become attached to his nervous palm he would become like the kids lying on the ground begging to see their mothers and fathers one last time. Only he wouldn't call for his mother or father, because, he just wanted to go out in a blaze of glory.

Ironically, this was his only choice, but as he gripped that Beretta in his hand, he knew that he had strength left in his fingers, and would never give up the fight until he was shot dead, and couldn't get up to defend himself. Feeling the burning sensation arise from deep within, he saw that A.J. had jumped into the herding crowd, and saw him disappear within a matter of seconds. Knowing that he served his purpose, he was going to make this fight worth there while.

"Go, A.J. Get out while you still can." He thought drearily, but remembered who he was protecting, and now he was doing it. He didn't know if he would ever see him again, but he began to whisper the "Our Father" prayer, which he had never said until now, that prepared himself to jump out and draw there fire away from A.J., and hopefully give him time to escape.

Frank gripped his Beretta, feeling his quick trigger finger more alive than ever, and jumped out from his hiding place, holding the gun into the air without a care in the world.

Terrible screams continued as shots buzzed down the halls like mad hornets flying at top speed its stinger foaming with intensity, one-minded objects that follow their word. A.J. had regained his footing, and ducked into the flooded swarm of kids that were heading out of the Commons lunchroom and into the Courses Hall. But when he felt like he was safe inside the crowd, he quickly glanced over his shoulder. More students around him began to fall like swatted flies, and as he glanced over his shoulders, he saw the fallen students pushing their pulsating guts back into their ornery bodies.

A.J. knew the looks on their faces, instantly remembering the men in the ditches, hearing their painful cries as the bullets ripped through their flesh, popping there skins as if it was a pimple, the blood just oozing out of there wounds. Their faces were white as a sheet, but their lips had tasted their first drop of blood from their organs—their unwilling organs refused to stay inside there bodies—which meant they were in the final stage of death.

But now he couldn't hear them scream, it was like he had lost his hearing for some reason, and was just moving on basic primal motor skills.

More people were dropping, and more bullets were flying as he heard returning gunfire echoing in the Commons lunch area. "Frank?" A.J. said, as he headed past the library. Heading into the divided Courses hall, an exhilarating thought filled his heart, "Home free!" A.J. thought, whispering it, almost shouting it as he saw his exit, the light at the end of the History Hall. But the light shining through it just blinked off and on in between the mass of bodies. A.J. pushed through these kids, black and white, jock and cheerleaders all heading next to each other without hatred and without indecency towards one another. All of them headed toward their freedom.

When the crowd seemed to move forward down the hall, more echoing shots' headed toward the crowd. The zinging bee shots sounded ever so close to him and a loud repeating *rat-tat-tat* followed, and multiple *thwacks* sounded off at the end of it, like a hammer beating a nail into a piece of wood. A.J. saw that there was a less beefy shooter running down at the end of the halls with a Mac 10, pulling on the trigger, and sending more students to their deaths.

Like a bunch of confused birds that didn't know if it was Spring or Fall—trapped to stay by the confusing bright sun light that kept them in one place but the chilled wind told them to leave—only these repeating shots aimed toward the crowd forced there direction. Only he felt like he was trapped, and he couldn't escape.

"Like trapped rats!" A.J. thought to himself, but then remembered there was another way, if he avoided the halls, and continued left, he could possibly escape on the far side near the Humanities center, and head out the back where the buses were.

If he hurried he could just make it, and he made his way toward the northern most exit, he felt the chilly wind pulling the students them out, but there were teachers already guiding the massive herd of students out the backend. Some were wounded, and were receiving medical attention.

Once Frank had caught the attention of the gunmen, two minutes after A.J. had disappeared into the crowd, he squeezed his trigger, and let an amazing two shots out from his quick and deadly trigger finger. As the bullets turned away from the crowd, a bullet *whooshed* past the top of his head, and feeling that air pocket made him jump back to the stone block. The shots had stopped for a moment, but this meant that they weren't going to stop either. Frank heard the mechanical *clicks* of the AK-47 slide as he had dispensed all of his bullets, and a loud clacking sound came from the end of the hall. This either meant that he had used up all the weapons' ammo, or he had just dispensed the clip, and had armed it with even faster, armor piercing bullets. Even though the bullets were fast, he could dodge them, and lure the gunmen into their deaths.

The Disintegrating Bloodline

But just before he was about to jump out from his hiding place, he heard the gunman calling out to him, "Give it up. We are going to get you either way."

Before Frank glanced around the side, he pulled his thoughts together, and decided that he would be a sitting duck just standing around waiting to die.

"Come and get me!" He chuckled with a cajoling taunt, and thought of the irony, the blasted irony.

Frank then moved to the right side, pushing over chairs, he weaved around large round tables with fallen chairs sprawled out across the floors. He jumped over one chair, and headed toward another brick hideout. It looked like an open square that had been cut, and a table had been placed inside it. There were three on each side of the lunchroom, and the one he had known was always across from the preps. But where he was headed was across from the school theatre.

He looked over his shoulder, and saw that the gunmen were moving, in a military kind of walk, the one holding the M-4 carbine stock over his shoulder while the other was holding a pistol, high in the air, just waiting to release the shots. Frank saw his cover, and lunged for it, falling to his side. Frank felt the shots buzzing over his head, and slamming against the brick design flinging bits of chipped walls on his shoulder.

Frank looked over his shoulder, and saw the dust from the broken walls resting against his shoulders like splashes of pigeon shit. He blew it off with one quick breath and it vanished into thin air. He felt like he needed to become thin air at that exact moment, but who was to say that A.J. had been ambushed? Frank couldn't take the time to figure out that one, because now wasn't the time to *think* it was the time to *act* on his gut feelings.

But he was pinned down, like a rat trapped between getting his fucking head chopped off by the blade of some old ladies wrath or an accidental run in with a mousetrap. The bullets were coming pretty close to him right about now, and when Frank regained his senses (the left side of his body was aching), he edged his back against the stone concrete wall. He was still palming the gun as he gripped the gun, edging toward the right side of the square cover. Hearing the shots begin to zoom and buzz across his head once again, he threw his hands over his head and took for cover. Clenching his teeth Frank let out a long, belting scream that made him shake and shiver as the hot metal slugs dug through the air, and smashing against the walls, chipping pieces of brick and paint, sending the pieces of debris to the ground, feeling the cold floor pressing against his body, and feeling the debris land on his body.

But as he was about to grind through his molars, as if his teeth were about to crack, he felt that the bullets had stopped for a moment, and it sounded like a struggle. When he steadied his feet along the plaster chipped ground he peered over the black plastic, and beheld the entire scene, as he kept his head low and invisible.

But it was James who had obviously surprised the gunmen that had already spent up his AK shots were wrestling over his automatic weapon. It looked like a common man fighting with a rather large bear, and the man was winning using everything he could to bring the bear down. He couldn't hear if there were whispers, but they sounded like short grunts as the two struggled for their prize that would bring one of their lives to an end.

But it was James who had been kicking the gunmen in the groins, and was bringing him down slowly with each and every blow. Only when James thought he had the gunmen to his knees, the large burly bear elbowed him in the stomach, and threw him a quick punch across his jaw, sending the weapon flying high and away from them. James' teeth flew from his mouth with blood soaring with them, but it didn't stop his body from being useful. He lunged for the large boy's throat, and his long dirty fingers were gripping his round, fat throat. His neck was as big as a watermelon, and his face began to look like a purple Radish. His eyes were almost bulging out of his skull when his face became white as a sheet. The gunman's expressions turned cold, and his body began to fall to the ground like a lead weight. James began to feel his own body grow cold, like the reaper had left a cold shiver up his spine before he took his soul. His once strong body became weak and vulnerable as an old man, and he didn't know what the cause of this hurt was, because his life was fading with the wind.

Only he felt his life draining just as quickly, and when he peered down to see what the problem was, he saw a fountain of blood had been gushing from his stomach—even though he had barely noticed—felt the bullet wound begin to take it's toll on him. The wound that the bullet made looked like one of those fountainheads urinating endless amounts of blood like he was having kidney stones. As his body was falling down with the large brooding gunman, he felt his soul begin to leave his body.

James' body fell to the ground, and his hands left his throat, and grasped his wound. The blood splurged through his fingers, caking onto his shirt, and rolling across both down both sides of his belly. He felt his life fading, and grasping the wound with his left hand, he began to call for someone. Whether it was for his mother or for God, he was calling out to all of them, and whether they were listening or not, he was calling out to them with his blood-soaked hand. As he began to speak again, more blood came flinging from his mouth. His life was hanging by a mere thread, although he wasn't going to give up now, he wanted to see his Berry just one more time. But everything was growing cold, and the echoing screams just seemed like a memory.

From around the corner, Berry's eyes widened, and his heart filled with anguish as he watched the boy wrestling with the other gunman. He couldn't admit it, with all his might he couldn't imagine in his mind his brother lying on the ground, wounded, with the other gunmen lying across him, obviously dead. He refused to believe it. As he unfastened his backpack from across his shoulders, he unzipped his book bag, and just as when he was about to reach for his weapon, he heard a terrible gut wrenching scream bellowing from one of the boys, and fill his heart with fear. He heard one last shot.

As he pulled out a large but dependable .357 Magnum Revolver from his backpack, he looked again, hoping to find the bastards responsible. Only he saw the next gunman had killed himself against the wall—the back and top of his head were covered in blood as bits of his skull dripped off the gristle bricks.

Berry edged up off the wall, he saw that the bodies were still there, and as he wiped the tears away from his cheeks, he ran closer to the body. Hoping that it wasn't his brother he approached the body, he threw off his backpack, and fell on both knees next to the body, like he had lost all feelings in his legs. His knees ached for a moment, and as he surveyed the body, he heard a word spoken from his lips, "Berry?" A few drops of blood went flying from his mouth, as if his body was rejecting his own blood, and Berry saw that he was still alive. He saw that his brother was barely alive, but not going to last too long.

Berry was too horrified for words, but his mouth and vocals did the work for him. "Are...you...alright?" Berry didn't know where the words had formed. Looking at his face, he saw the blood pulsing from his endless panting belly, as if he was going into shock, but that same I-don't-give-a-fuck attitude was still in his eye. As he clamped his hands over the wound, Benny forcefully pushed his hands away, as if he didn't want his help at all, knowing that his fate had been sealed.

Berry looked at his hand, and saw the blood cemented into his hand and drooling inside his fingernails. He forgot everything at that moment, and a tear that he had been saving up had finally headed down his cheek, rolling off of his chin, and landing on the round pale face of his brother. The life from him was fading, but he looked like he had something more to say something.

"What is it?" Berry asked in an exasperated tone, panting out of control, as if he was bleeding from a wound himself.

Benny's voice was garbled from his own blood, but the way he was trying to speak in tongues, and every time it looked painful enough for him to just try and speak— something that everyone should be able to do—just seemed extremely difficult for Benny. But Berry was listening with an open ear, and as he lowered his ear toward his lips, and listened to him again.

"Get Ann…" A spray of blood left his mouth jumping onto his cheek, making him jump back for a moment feeling the small spray catch him by surprise.

Berry lowered his ears closely again, feeling the blood staining his cheek and listened to the rest of his garbled message.

"Out…" A wad of blood dripped down his lips as he finished the rest of his words *"of here…"* Berry then saw his brother give one last signal stretching his left hand, extending all his fingers, but then his four fingers curled, leaving all gone except his index finger. He pointed to the hall past the commons B lunch-hall.

"Thanks," He said—something that hurt him to even say before, but now seemed like the not-so-perfect time to say it, even though he felt like he should have said it many times before.

"I love you." He said, his whispering turned into a coughing cry, and held his brother's head in his hand as he kissed him on the cheek. Feeling his hair in between his fingers made him shake with anguish, as he never did before, and he cried as he walked down the hall in shame.

"Get with it, and let me die. It wasn't your fault."

"Sure it was," Berry thought rapidly, "And you just let him be wrestled to the ground until he was shot, and *oh sure that wasn't your fault!*" The thought was gut wrenching, tearing apart at his soul piece by piece as Berry continued his pace down the hall, but then stopped at the end of the Commons hall, and saw something.

Frank had already cleared out after the last shot, and was venturing into the halls where A.J. had headed. By the looks of it, half of the student body had already cleared out long after the shots had been fired—and as he hurried past the library—all he could think about was how the school had become a hellhole decorated with markings of ricochet bullets across the walls and blood that looked almost like black dye across the floors just to add to the depravity.

Entering the halls, he saw that a person at the end of the hall was holding something. The way he was standing looked like he was searching for something, and Frank watched him for a moment as he was searching through the remains of fallen victims, probably looking for A.J.

"There were more." Frank thought horrified, but then stood still as he watched the gunman leaning over, and searching the bodies. "More shooters?"

The shooter glanced at there wallets—taking whatever money was in it—and tossed there wallets to the ground meant that he hadn't found his target. In the gunman's left hand was palming a weapon, a large Mack 10 with an infrared beam on the bottom. What Frank knew of that gun was it could dispense more .45 caliber shells with one quick pull of the trigger. But when there eyes or what felt like their eyes, or their presence's met, the gunmen stood still, and just looked at Frank. The gunmen's Mack 10 and Frank's Beretta stirred in there hands, like they were deadly Pitbull dogs waiting to be unleashed on each other, and there owners weren't holding them back.

Frank was ready, and the gunman was ready.

The gunman—standing at the southern end of the History hall—rose his large Mack 10, the gun gleaming with the light as the infrared beam did its dance. His finger fell quickly upon the trigger, and a large swarm of bullets burst from the barrel—looking like flashing Christmas lights, and all heading toward Frank.

Frank, moving with a quick draw reaction, held his gun up and quickly aimed at the gunman, pulling the trigger he released a barrage of bullets, making large echoing noises against his ears. He could smell the powder—shell after shell—from the bullet like exhaust smoke from a car as he released two more shots as he ran down the hall. Frank saw that the bullets all taking there own direction across the Styrofoam wall above him, sending more pieces of the chipped wall across his the top of his hair and was released. But then Frank immediately fell on the floor, seeing that more bullets were heading his way like swarms and swarms of bees. They buzzed past him with ferocity, forcing quick burst of air over his head as he felt the gunshots immediately stop. Although he could see everything he began to feel cold, but as he could tell that none of the bullets had hit him. Frank nestled the gun to his chest; he waited for the hitman to inspect him so that he could bring the reign of terror to an end.

The footsteps were haunting, and broke no stride in his walk, as he made his way toward Frank's supposed dead body. Gripping the Mac 10 ever so tightly, he could feel the gun just heat up his entire hand, and he kept the gun pointed at Frank, ready to take him out the second if he made one single solitary move.

Frank could hear him just inches away from his body, he began to say a prayer that was more than perfect, time to say, "Hail Mary, full of grace, the lord is with thee…" He gripped his Beretta, sticking his finger into the round metallic hole. "Blessed our thou amongst women, blessed is the fruit of thy womb Jesus. Holy Mary, Mother of God, Pray for us sinners," Frank felt that remembering this now was extremely ironic, because he never thought of the fear of rotting in Hell until now. But he hoped that he had squared a few things away with God and Mary before he would meet his ultimate demise. "Now and at the hour of our death, Amen." Gritting his teeth, he prepared for the roll, but then heard a rising sound bellow from across the hall.

"FREEEZE!" The voice yelled with multiple footsteps following behind them, "DON'T MAKE A MOVE!"

Frank opened his eyes, and unclenched his teeth, this was something he had never expected to see; the boys in blue, NYPD's finest just seconds away and in the flesh. A few more policemen ran up next to the main captain. It surprised him to the point of rapture, even if he wasn't on any other occasion to see the 5-0 (or police,) he was at that moment indeed welcomed by their rather late presence. Brandishing their Glock 17 pistols, there left palms covered over their right palms real tightly, they yelled again repeating their demands with there bright blue hats tipping past there brows.

The gunmen heard the orders, and just looked at them with sheer icy hatred in his face. His partly pot-marked face seemed to grow even oilier every time the police moved up along the floor, constantly shouting the demands with even more intensity as their pistols were shaking every time they moved. He could feel his muscles swelling with fire as they continued to yell their orders, "DROP THE WEAPON, RIGHT NOW!"

But the gunmen didn't care about their orders, and as they kept advancing towards the hall, he unloaded the long clip, and threw it to the floor. As he reached into his pocket, and revealed another long clip, with shiny .45 hollow tip bullets weighing down the metallic clip. This angered the police officers even more as he lined the clip along the end of the weapon and shoved it in with one single *thwap* of his hand against the end of the clip. Then he moved the gun sideways as he cocked the mechanical slide back and it entered a bullet into the slide with a soft but loud *click-clack* sound. The policemen's hands were shaking with much rotted anxiety that there demands grew louder.

"I'M WARNING YOU!" The cop bellowed showing no mercy, but the gun was shaking nervously in their hands as sweat fell off his head.

Frank could see that they were all on edge, but when he saw their eyes widen, he knew that the gunman was up to something. Then what sounded like a thousand shots rained over his head, and some of the hot shells landed on his the side of his arm, and on his face. Frank swallowed the slight pain, and he wanted to push them off, but he had to remain dead until the firefight had ended or moved away from him. But somehow the cops had been vanquished except one that had ducked near one of the western windows across from the library.

When he saw the gunman go after the fallen cops, he fled into the library while more cops burst from around the southern end of the hallway, where the fallen students were bleeding or were now dead. He had run past them, and saw their faces, that soulless hollow stare of death. And they were now either still bleeding or had met their maker. A few other cops had run into the library, not even noticing Frank, as if he was just another dead body.

But before he could think about another single thought, Frank slowly raised up off the ground with his free hand, sending the spent shells across the floor sounding like a soft jungle with a haunting tune behind it. He could hear the shells dancing along the floor, and as he left down the hall, he made his way out of the Humanities exit, he could see many other slain bodies in the Art and English halls.

As he left through the exit, the light hit him quick and fast, blinding him with all her might giving him skin cancer each second she shined brightly upon his skin, cursing him with a plague of awful radiation. Other than today, he wouldn't have felt or thought this, but the way things were going today he would have traded this for any of the other days...

The shooting had raged on for over a half an hour when Jessica had just gotten out of the doctor's office with a whole pamphlet of information on new mothers and baby information when she found out the dreadful news. Jessica's heart sank, and her theories had horribly become true when she placed her hand over her mouth—her stale breath attached itself against her palm.

It was all over the news; the press had made it their fifteen minutes after the EMT arrived. Like the plague the news was all over it and they didn't waste any bit of time at all to keep it a secret, (all from Ann's phone call) which the press doesn't have in their criteria. But all of them, she didn't somehow doubt the way they worked.

Jessica watched it intently, and for the next few minutes, she was in shock. Not moving, not talking, just listening to the television. Learning about this in terrible, and pretty much frank, detail.

Even though she couldn't stand the media, she sometimes found herself watching the news because of the circumstances. She couldn't help it, because she needed to know what the hell was going on, she couldn't get enough of it.

Jessica's raised a suspicious eyebrow and a fell below her forehead again. She listened about how the gunmen came in and started firing upon everyone, and started shooting up and down the hallways, while another gunman was in the halls looking through wallets to take money and throw it in the wounded faces. They killed mercilessly and tried to leave no survivors.

He wasn't sure if they had explosives on them, (which were found in a janitors closet) that was all he had to say. Jessica shrugged and knew he was pretty damn sure about that.

Then a quote came to her mind that she had heard from a philosophy class. Oddly it made some sense, after now that a tragedy had happened. "In war, truth is the first casualty." It was by some Greek philosopher, and it meant that in war the truth could be changed so easily, and quickly to anyone's benefit.

But another more logical and reasonable side was telling her, "Don't trust that fat Military principal. He knows something." She knew he was grimy, and would do anything to get what he wants, only she knew he wasn't that bloodthirsty. He couldn't possibly be in cahoots with her lover's ex-partner, and start a shit storm just for them to be assassinated. Someone has to get it right up the ass, and someone would always be in the background, collecting the spoils of war.

"A Massacre in the Library?" The thought lingered over her like acid rain, tearing away at her conscience, like those particles that were tearing away at the very clouds, and filling her heart like a puddle, and the rain were drops of dread that only encouraged her grief. She never would have thought all this could happen in one single day, but as the day eventually stretched on, it would become even more intricate than she would have imagined.

Chapter XVIII:

"Scars Don't Heal"

After the last gunmen had finally met his match in the library, and eventually blew his brains out after murdering five more students and a couple of policemen, he decided to end it all. Frank couldn't believe—or even fathom—that the third gunman was just some *kid* that was toying around with a fully automatic weapon. He was a professional, and he knew that very rough, tough, and smart people had trained the third person, "Oh hell," he thought, "They might have trained all three."

Only he couldn't come to any real conclusion, because the clues were all jaded. The truth was distorted and shady, like a deep fortified jungle that was just in the peak of its tropical storm, and the fortification was clouding his path. Only the large leaves of confusion would be the problem right now, and he had to cut hard enough to get through to the truth.

"The bright shining truth is really just a lie?" He thought to himself in jest, but knew the truth would lie within the thicket of all the lies, and he had to cut, whether it were people's body parts or the clouded mystery of his bogged down mind, he would find the truth. How long would it take, and how hard would he have to struggle to find it. The truth would make a lot of sense but he was destined to find it, and just like a knight on an epic quest. This was *his* grail, his reason for going on but something else bothered him, which shook his entire being.

"A.J." He hadn't seen him for half the day, and he was going nuts worrying about him. Tearing through three boxes of cigarettes—all the way down to the cherry—sucking down each and every last cigarette he felt he had washed his mouth with tobacco. He wasn't one of the casualties, but this started to feed his fears, and this started to make him shed off his tough courageous skin and doubt began to crawl along his insides.

Frank also figured that the people who had wanted to put him out of commission and that meant they *were mortified even petrified* of what would happen if he got near the truth. Then, it would all be downhill after that. Only the truth…he could just go on and on about the truth, and he couldn't even see it right now.

He couldn't even continue his search for the truth without finding A.J. Only he wanted to send all his soldiers into every neighborhood and shoot his way to find A.J. Only if he knew A.J., he didn't know where he was. He was the Boss of the family, and the Boss was evidently missing.

Sitting in the chair of his living room, the stand in boss, was staring blankly into the television contemplating as the dark screen was rippling with a silent buzz that resembled a monks chant. He had called all his soldiers and told them to start looking for A.J. but he had such a headache that a ringing of bells and tinkling of gun shells landing across the floor echoed in his mind. Only it was like a haunting crackling sound—like the sound of a weak floorboard that he only heard in the middle of the night that was pounding in the thick of his skull. But Frank seemed to be familiar with that sound, and everything before that suddenly became so clear.

When there was time for answers, patience always came hand in hand with answers, or the truth in his case. At any other time, he would have charged into the jungle and cut through the foliage without mercy. Only they needed a clue, a clue, and he felt like a clue was somewhere was waiting for him, all he had to do was look for it. Like the secret path that could lead them through the foliage, this would lead them to there truth. "Who was the long lost cousin of Chris?"

That was the biggest damn mystery to them this entire time. Who the hell were they after that was so Goddamn special? But who were *they*? "Was it Gene or was it really Don Pescaro? *Death?*" But another question that was at the back of his mind, "What would he do that would frighten all the five families?" And that was the thing, there were so many fucking questions, Frank felt that there weren't any answers to them. It's like they were walking around blindfolded and away from the truth, only he was going a bit too far thinking about this. But after witnessing the kids being shot down like deer and without mercy is when the question of his safety occurs.

But when he thought he was listening to the impervious, dastardly silence, the phone rang. Its slow melodic sound rang into his ears—like the sound of an old lover—and amplified the weight against his eardrums. If pounds of weights could relate to how loud this buzzing was, he would definitely say that he was hearing (instead of lifting) two hundred fifty pounds banging against his ears.

Opening his eyes, he felt the afternoon sun shine upon him, and the weight of that sound inside his head had sent him dilapidating back toward the couch like a dead fish and gravity that he could use was just drained. When his back hit the puffy plastic, it made its whooping farting noise that sounded like Velcro with their naked back on it. Feeling the ring going off again, the sound made him jump out of the chair, and pick the phone up just to wonder, "Who the fuck is it, I'm trying to get some sleep!" And that he did.

But the phone rung again and it interrupted his momentary shut-eye. Giving into the piercing telephone ring, he rose up off the armchair, heading over toward the clanging phone box that gave off a harmonious ring and when he approached the ringing phone box he stopped. He picked up the phone with one fell swoop as he put the phone to his ear, and said, "Hello?" His voice was groggy—by the way his cat breath fogged over the round microphone—he could tell that he needed to brush his teeth, and wiped away the drool that was forming at the corner of his mouth.

The voice was so familiar to him, but she didn't seem to be like her usual self. "Hey, Frank, that you?"

Frank didn't know if this was Jessica or not, but he wasn't sure of how high her voice had sounded, very frightened.

"Who's this?" Frank replied with his eyebrows flaring back, with a few wild hairs sticking out from his rather straight arch, and approached the windows. Slipping an eye through the curtain, "This is Jessica, Frank. What's up?" Her voice sounded very curious, like she was itching to know something, and he didn't know what to say to her when she would say, "So where's A.J.?" Frank did not rightly know what to say, and didn't know whether he would lie or just tell her the truth. Even though her voice sounded like it beckoned for the truth, to Frank, she would not stand for it. She would say he's lying, and would just laugh at the idea first, but then her anger would get the best of her. Even though she had a desire for the truth, Frank knew that she wouldn't understand.

Frank trailed off for a moment, making a soft humming sound, likes a treble in the twinning stage, just before it was just right. Being that if he was going to lie he proceeded in a nervous walk as he thought of a reason, but then came out with it, in a wavy, unconfident voice, "he's in the bathroom."

Jessica was taken back by his response, "Are you sure?" but then continued on to ask him, "Okay…just tell him to call me back."

Frank glanced around him as a small creak of the air conditioner clicked with its *whirring* and *chavrooorrrrrr* sounds sent chills up his spine, sending his paranoia into full effect. But then his paranoia washed away, and settled in the back of his wishy-washy peninsula.

"Yeah, sure!" Frank said, and slowly hung up the phone. Stretching his back he felt all the bones in his spine crack as he leaned backwards. He felt his back grow ten times taller—his bony back stretched against his skin—and as he returned his back upright, he laughed because he always remembered his father telling him after he had given him a back breaker. "There you go, you look ten times taller now." After he laughed, he felt better, more relaxed as he returned back to the seat. Falling back into the armchair, he let the cool breeze of the air conditioner send him into a deeper state of relaxation, far more relaxed, like he had been paralyzed. But one thought kept him from being paralyzed, and it was A.J.

Shaking off the cold air, rejecting its chilly massage that it had given him, he placed his right hand over his chest. His nipples were hard, and all his hairs around it began to stick out like small blades of grass with the occasional long hair looking like a weed sticking out, Although he had some muscles to impress the girls, his back had been considerably small framed.

But the thought of lifting weights and impressing girls seemed like a far off distant memory to Frank, and he had to keep his mind onto business, dragging his spirits even further down into the dumps. And his business was trying to find A.J., because he wasn't going to find peace until his soldiers found him or A.J. would somehow give him a call, sooner or later.

"Yes, sooner or later." And just maybe, they might be contacted by the likes of some unsavory figures, like the Principal for one. Frank knew that he would call for their help since the school had been attacked, and would help organize some of the security around the school. He would test their loyalty.

As his skin shuddered off the coldness of the room, he wanted to forget all about the violence, and all about the kids lying across the floor bleeding all their life out for the world to see. Holding their hands out for God, with their blood soaked hands. It was a violation, a violation that should never be attempted or put into action again.

But the difficulty of this situation largely depends on how many people would talk, and how many would be urging to talk. There would always be a snitch at every corner; it was like a dirty quarter, and you know you can always find them. But the city lights seemed so distant to him; it's like he didn't know his own city anymore. How the changing lights hung over the cars at each street like a long single dragons claw, and the buildings towering over the city with a allure that gave New York its most noticeable footnote in history. The

The Disintegrating Bloodline

bridges that interconnected between the boroughs, and the culture that was inside the city as a whole, was that of a far off mystery to him these days.

Maybe this was the answer to all his questions, maybe it wasn't, but he definitely was becoming separated from the city, in his own mind.

But before he could forget the images of the bright New York lights and the slain kids, he heard the telephones painful ringing. Feeling the spit rolling down his cheek, he raised a hand over his face, and wiped his the spit away from his face. The wet stickiness traveled onto his hands, and he thought nothing of it as he wiped the coldness that waved through his eyelashes. Freeing his eyes from that chain, he felt the mid-afternoon sun shine across his face blinding him—the lies are always brighter than the truth.

It stung the core of his eyes, and it made him think of a time when he looked into the sun, and wanted to see the face of God. But it blinded him, and that must've been what God was like, so beautiful and blinding, and he couldn't look at it again.

Slowly walking toward the ringing annoyance, he watched the box grumble with some painful pleasure that loved to torture everyone, "What?" As Frank stopped, it rung that tortuous rung again as if it was trying to split his ears with each malignant shrill and Frank ended by pulling it up to his ear, and breathed into the phone, exhausted.

"Hello…"

Frank remained silent, and the voice echoed into the speaker, "Frank… It's me…"

Frank's attention was sparked, but a strike of paranoia was unearthed inside it. "Me who? If this is who this is, you better say you're all right." He began to slowly walk toward the curtain and peeking around curtain. He cautiously checked the left side of the curtain, checking for anything that would seem unnatural. Seeing nothing, he felt like going crazy was an understatement, but who could blame him.

"It's me…I'm okay." A moment of silence made its way through, but then the voice came back.

"Yeah, well, what's your status?" Frank said uncertain of whom he was talking to, but was listening with a clear ear in the background a soft whispering sound of another person in the background, and Frank began to think that the worst had happened.

"Yeah I'm fine. Don't worry, I won't be long till I get there!" Then just as Frank had opened his mouth, and was about to say something else, he heard the phone line go dead. Frank pulled the phone away from his ear in bewilderment and scoffed insulted, wanting to grab and his "heater" and shoot somebody. Only he didn't like that feeling, because when he had a gun, he couldn't resist the temptation to use it.

Although he looked outside for a few more seconds longer if someone else was about to get on and start listing their demands. Frank listened for a few minutes trying to think of what he was going to do, but he held onto sound came from that phone was the relapsing of the phone line begging to be placed back in its place. He would lay it down, but he already had a plan ready. He knew that someone had saved him, and when he saw him walk through that door, he hugged him, and felt that there was a bit of hope left.

After the two had embraced for another minute, A.J. introduced Frank around to his friends. Shaking Berry's hand, he saw that there was a layer of blood staining half of his hand. "Blood, but who's was it?"

Frank did not know that answer, but when it came to meeting Ann, his attention was then sparked, like a dog's prick when it has just seen something that he wanted to fuck. He saw her face, and being as though it was ugly as a donkey, he saw that the rest of her body had caught up with her womanly figure. Large plump breasts that were as round as melons and her cold nipples had been pushing out through her shirt, looking like round knobs that looked begging to be pulled by his fingers, and open the door to her innermost pleasure. Then he would to start massaging her breasts, but he was getting too carried away with himself. It had been too long since he had had a woman's organs around his penis.

Although when the two caught a second glimpse of each other, he saw some kind of disparity that was rather beautiful in her horse face. Her hands felt cold as a linoleum floor that was covered in wax, and Frank saw her cold face, but with his sly devilish attitude, he gave her a warm reaffirming smile and quick wink. She looked at him with those not so innocent eyes, and her gaze pierced him deeply. Those brown eyes withheld some hidden terror, and whatever she was thinking at that moment would have made him want to cry.

As A.J. escorted them to his couch, he began to think that maybe, just maybe that he had brought some happiness to her, especially he had felt the same way, not in his pants but unfortunately in his heart.

Everything stood still for him at that moment, and as he followed them to the couch, their words had broken his day dreaming, but it was for the better as A.J. began to start the conversation in a professional laid back voice he had learned from Chris.

Once everyone was on the couch, it seemed like everyone was starting to just talk, since all of them felt pretty uncomfortable in the room together. Frank had heard everything that they were saying, from Ann's coincidental

The Disintegrating Bloodline

watching of the one boy that had pulled out the cell phone, and "supposedly" sent the call into the two gunmen. Then Berry recounted about how his brothers' death, and how it had deeply affected him. Frank could see the tears that had stained his face, even though he probably didn't cry in front of them, he could see the rage building up in his face, and that made Frank edgy to be around, because in his voice he knew he wanted revenge. Revenge didn't mix well with professionalism, and it also got in the way of business, and this was business planning an attack. They had something going about the boy that was messing with the phone.

But the only thing he kept focusing on was Ann—quickly glancing at her—seeing her just made him feel all warm and mushy inside. He didn't like it, but he couldn't help but behold this hidden gem right in front of him—gleaming and blinding him with all her unfound beauty—unknowingly checking her pushed out breasts. Although when he became fixated on her breasts even longer, her eyes traveled over to him, exchanging a glance for more than a moment. Feeling his cover had been blown, Frank's eyes moved away from her, pretending not be looking at her, he glanced around the room, looking at the wall embarrassed from him voyeuristic behavior.

Although something inside him was telling him "get your mind out of the gutter, she's probably never had sex" but another more bolder, aggressive side burst out, "She probably was looking at you because she wants to brush her teeth with your dick." That was definitely his conscience, and all he could do was just sit there, while they all were in there own worlds, he sneakily made one more glance at Ann. But now, it seemed the other way around, she was looking at him with those devilish brown eyes, he raised his eyebrows, and mouthed the words without actually speaking.

"*Hey*" It seemed almost like a whisper, but he covered the side of his mouth—pretending to listen—to conceal his smoothness.

A strand of her black hair fell beside her left ear, and combing the strand around her ear, she covered her mouth away from the two who were talking inconsistently, and whispered, "*Hi*"

Her lips were pushed out, and in that sexy gesture, she opened her mouth to reveal her teeth and her pink tongue traveled across the top of her teeth in a sensual slide.

Frank's eyebrows raised, and a tingling sensation was traveling through his lower region. Yet he didn't want to admit to it, but he was definitely pitching a tent, and the only thing that he could whisper back was, "*Where?*"

When she was about to mouth one more word, she suddenly stopped, and they broke off communication for a moment. She turned toward Berry, and gave him a smile, but Frank played it off like it was nothing. Then the two continued onto talking, and like they didn't see them or stop them from making their secret arrangements. Once they were in the clear, she mouthed the words, *"Meet me in the bathroom."*

Frank's eyebrows rose with uncertainty, as if in jest, but saw that sensual look in her eye that she was ready to take any kind of dick, large or small, and take the pain that came along with it. And he would give her what she wanted.

Lowering her hand, she glimpsed around the room, and asked breaking through the conversation—her heart palpitating as she rocked back and forth. "Where's your bathroom?"

Both A.J.'s and Berry's heads both turned toward Ann, and A.J. looked at Frank while he gave her the directions, as if to get it exactly right. "Down the hall, and the first door on the right." Frank nodded his head with approval as she gave them all a small, but his gingerly grin could arouse certain suspicion.

The three saw her walk into the hall, shaking her rather large bottom that she had always done, and disappeared down the dark hall. Frank watched her out of the corner of his eyes, seeing the swarms of dust floating in between the added shades of setting sunlight that bled through the windows. Frank had been eyeing her for that entire time, not caring about a single thing in the world. And all he would have to do is just let the conversation dry up like a well, and when it would run dry, he would go off and dive into her naval, head and tongue first.

"Now, Frank." A.J.'s words brought his eyes away from the hallway, and he looked.

Frank's eyebrows rose—tuning into what A.J. was saying, and A.J. gave him a cocked eyebrow, and continued on, like he didn't see him make any facial expressions.

"I think that we might have found a way to find Gene."

Frank just looked at him with cynical confusion and his narrow eyes nodded sourly. A.J. could see the cynical look just start to form ideas in his head, and his lips were ready to slash it down. But, all he could say in reply was, "What is it?" Clasping his hands together, he acted calm again, hunching over resting his elbows against his knees.

"What crazy idea do you have installed for us now?" Frank contemptuous voice wanted to say underneath that calm exterior. But at this point it was better to listen then remain ignorant, to hear whatever plans they had come up with, and then go against it with full intensity.

A.J. looked at Berry, and motioning for him to lay down his plan, he did, but before Berry started he added, like an extra shot of rum and coke. "It wasn't entirely my idea, it was partly my sister's, but A.J. helped as well. Well, maybe it's all of our plan." Frank nodded at this response, and wrapped his fingers together making his hands into a fist, and rested it underneath his chin in a "I'm waiting stature". Then, Berry laid out his plan, and Frank listened, getting ready to attack everything that he might say.

Frank indeed listened, and absorbed it all like a sponge cleaning up the bottom of a blood soaked dungeon, taking all the pain from many tortured screams that gave them this lead. Like that sponge, he began to see the genius in their plan, but it was going to take a whole lot on everyone's part to try and find Gene. The plan was very simple; Berry would snoop around for Gene and ask for his loyalty. After a while, they would start to get closer to him, and he would start to trust him. Then after that they would become even closer, he would then lead him to a trap where a hitman would end his life, and this war, for good.

But Frank felt like the war was not going to end there, and Frank had to be the one that would burst their bubble today. Either way, he had to be the one that had to disagree with them, because things were not that simple.

After Berry was all done, and the wind had left him, Frank sat back in his seat and contemplated many, many things he could say to correct them. But the one thing that he was curious to ask him was ever bubbling in the front of his mind.

"Well, it's a good plan and all, but one thing is bugging me about this whole thing." Frank said, and let a long sigh. Everyone was listening and waiting for him to give his complaint, but he couldn't find the right words to say it.

"Let's say we do get him, what about the cousin? The five families are looking for him, and are bidding on who takes his life first. Do you have that worked out? Because if Gene is gone, there is a lot more happening than you think. The war's not going to end there. Because I already know that Gene is underground, and it'll take a while before he comes back up."

On the families, Berry had no answer, but he stubbornly attacked him, repulsed by his own agenda. "Underground?" Frank had the impression that he wasn't up on his game, which was a rather bad thing to be if he was a gunrunner. Which he had given them the impression when he told them about his deal with Gene, but, he was just another pawn, a smaller kink in the cog of this deal, selling hardware to survive. He didn't have anything against that, but he needed to see if he was that bent on his revenge.

"Yes, UNDERGROUND!" Frank yelled, "as *in hiding* or *out of sight* because it's going to be like chasing a ghost." Frank expected Berry to hold his mouth shut, but with a defiant outrage Berry came out with a furious response.

"Fuck you," Berry said defiantly, "I don't care where he is I am going to *kill him with my bare hands! And all his friends too!"*

"That's great," Frank replied in a sarcastic tone, fueling his anger with more procrastinating quips. "How are you going to find him if he's gone, and everyone around him is gone?"

"Maybe you should be looking harder!"

"How can we if he can't be found, *you dumb fuck!"*

Neither Berry nor Frank was being rational anymore, and as Berry rose from his place, he unsheathed the large Glock. Frank, whose reflexes matched Berry's, and saw the end of the barrel pointing into his face. Frank saw the hate in Berry's eyes, and he didn't care about death anymore.

"Go ahead! *Pull it!* Chicken shit!" Frank goaded, with his icy stare was not looking at the end of the barrel, but was looking into Berry's bleary tear-filled eyes. "You got the guts you little shit!" He goaded, almost coolly. "Kill me so that you can feel better about your brother! Just to remind you, he's dead, he's never coming back!" Frank had a death wish in his eyes, and he was drunk with anger.

"Fuck you!" Berry exclaimed, "Your time has come." Berry felt his trigger finger just begging to release a bullet that his brother couldn't do, "No, he tried…" Berry thought. His emotions were on the edge of that trigger, and his mind was off the Richter scale of reality, because Berry didn't know if he was possessed or not. All he was thinking of was his brother, and what his face looked like, pale and sad—his ghost haunting the darkest corners of his mind.

On the other end of the trigger, Frank saw his scared, intimidated voice, and saw that the gun was still he looked as nervous and scared as a first timer with a hand gun. He seemed young and inexperienced, and but his anger was hindering his professionalism. Frank didn't care about that his capriciousness at all, he wanted to see if he would have the guts to pull the trigger or not and end these haunting screams in his head. Although he was inviting death in his own home, questions were running through his head faster than he could comprehend them, but he wandered *if and when* this kid had the guts to pull the trigger. He didn't care where he would go if he pulled the trigger, but hoped it was just somewhere that he didn't have to deal with stupid assholes that couldn't keep their fingers away from the trigger.

A.J. rose up from his seat, and squeezed his hands through Berry and Frank.

"STOP!"

A.J. looked at them—but they weren't seeing past each other as the thick veil of madness between them. Gripping Berry's arm he could feel the sweat on his long arm radiating the hate that was possessing his entire arm. A.J. could feel the sweat radiating anything rational that would sway him from pointing the gun anywhere else. A.J. turned and saw Frank's fatalistic eyes, but his face was stone, as he waited for Berry to pull the trigger on the large Glock handgun. Only if A.J. didn't intervene himself in this troublesome issue, Berry's finger would fall against the trigger, and Frank's brains would end up all over his furniture and across A.J. as well.

A.J. gave one last yell, "STOP IT! This is ridiculous, we aren't here to kill each other, and yes Frank, we will need your guys," A.J. turned to Berry, hoping he was listening because he would kill him if he wasn't.

"Yes Berry. You'll have your revenge, but it will take some time. If we stick to the plan we will live to see the end of the day. But if you guys want to kill each other, go ahead. But when you come out of this shitty mood…" A.J. took a deep breath, feeling the anger leaving his body, but his blood was boiling and they didn't want to anger him.

Berry felt like lowering the gun, but he kept it pointed in between his eyes, and Frank kept his position.

A.J. continued with pain. "But if you want to swallow your pride for a few minutes, maybe you can see why we need to stick together, because if we don't, we're no better than him. We'll be like that snake fuck Gene!" A.J. exhaustedly breathed out his last word with his own patience, and turned around, laying his hand across his head.

After a few moments of silence, they began to breathe clear thoughts as Berry lowered the gun away from his face—Frank never left his angry gaze away from his face as Berry stuck the large Glock 22 back into the side of his pants. With this dangerous event squashed, and their hatred subsiding, the two in some deep introverted silence, like two warriors that had both found no reason to kill each other, left each other in uneasy peace. Then out of the silence came the loud buzzing ring of his telephone. It might have came at the right time for all of them, but it definitely made Berry jump in his place, and he gave a soft laugh of relief as he looked out the window. When Berry and Frank were finally taken care of A.J. walked toward the phone hearing it's buzzing ring give off one last *brrrring* as he raised the receiver from the box.

"Hello?" A.J. said, turning around watching Frank leave the room as he headed into the hallway. The voice burst out with extreme joy and whining pleasure, "A.J.!" A.J. knew this voice, and it brought a smile from his own worried face.

"Hey baby." A.J. added almost sympathetically before Jessica immediately cut him off with her worried questions.

"Are you okay, are you hurt, are you okay." Her voice was anxious, fearful, and curious.

Frank let an unusual chuckle escape him as he heard this, and moved out of the living room, shaking his head trying to place this situation in some unknown part of his brain where he could forget about a gun that was in his face. But the only part that burned him was the fact that a twerp put a gun in his face.

"He has balls!" Frank thought, and the smell of that made him figure that he was ready to do anything. "But now I am going to fuck his sister!" He thought, as he just remembered that this girl was in the bathroom, probably all wet and waiting for him. "And I don't even know her name!" Frank thought, as he caught a smell that that was something like unwashed, dirty dishes, and in the hallway saw someone reentering the bathroom, very quietly, and softly.

All he heard from inside the door that was a chuckle, a rather soft and cute chuckle, one that he had remembered so well, like a prisoners memories of freedoms that he had taken for granted. "All I'm gonna do is just fuck her, not torture her!" He muttered, but he guessed fucking was a form of torture, on some levels.

Only fast-forward all of that, and putting it into perspective, this all happened in a matter of ten to fifteen minutes. He didn't even know if he busted inside her, and that was an even scarier thought. Frank didn't want to think about that, more or less having his dick inside this horse. Both of them were getting dressed when his wondering eyes caught her arm, like a flash from a dying bulb.

"What?" She said in a shuddering, abashed tone as if he was looking at her on purpose.

Frank leaned back against the edge of the sink, and spied her arm once again. "Nothing, I was just looking at your arm."

Ann stopped in her tracks, and glanced down at her arm, and quickly turned her arm away as if she tried to ignore the wounds on her arms, "It's nothing. Don't worry about them." She replied in a distant and cold voice, the voice he had met her by, but her smile hadn't shown any disapproval when he shook her hand, he was sure of that. But Frank, even though when he should know when and when not to stick his nose into other people's business, was a little out of his range, but since he cared for her wanted to know a little bit more about these wounds. Even if he might get yelled at, and possibly attacked by her ever sharp fingernails, he needed to know the truth behind those wounds.

But as she gave him a rather odd smirk, one of ignorance and obstinate behavior, she tried to walk past him. As her sleeve opened revealing her shaved armpit, the sweat from the corner of her shirt had already made a small stain, giving a raunchy stench inside his nose, making all the hairs inside his nose start to shrivel and fall out from it's place. But when she was about to grab onto the door knob, his hand shot out over her left hand, and with a quick hand maneuver, as if he was trying to disarm a weapon from her hand, he turned her hands sideways and focused his eyes on the large cuts. She made a feeble attempt to break away, but the only thing she could do was whisper, "Stop it!" She cried miserably, "Stop it or I'll…" and Frank closed a hand over her mouth.

Frank looked back at her with a dead on stare expressionless, and replied, "Or you'll do what?" He made sure not to raise his voice, and whispered with a deadly, "Go and tell your brother? By all means, go ahead, because I'm not afraid of him, or you!" Frank calmed his anger down, and said in a reassuring voice, looking at her arm. "I just want to see your marks!"

She tried to pull her arm out again, but his grip only tightened as he stretched her hand out and followed his finger along her pale arm. The long, protruding wounds trailed in small directions, just avoiding her veins, and a small crust was starting to form next to them. Frank examined them with an extreme closeness, as he saw two to three marks appearing next to the larger cuts. With his other hand he placed a finger across the longer mark, the one that went across her wrist, and massaged it, almost imitating the slicing that she had done to herself.

Frank looked up at her, and said with a real disgust, "Why did you do this to yourself?" She looked up at him, not answering, and tried to pull away. But she wasn't going anywhere and Anne looked at him again. She flashed her buck teeth as she replied in a nasty and shameful tone, "I tried to commit suicide, you fuck. Are you happy now?" She said angrily, not breaking her whisper, and enwrapped in her anger, she began to whimper, and when she began to pull for her hand, Frank let it go. Realizing what the marks were, he felt shameful that he had asked her, now knowing her painful truth behind her scars, and he didn't have the urge to cry for her. It took him a moment when he could bring himself to her level and show her any compassion. As he raised a hand toward her shoulder she turned away, like A.J. had done.

All he could say in return was, "I'm sorry. I'm sorry." He saw her cover a hand over her face, and began to hide her cries, still crying inside her palmed hand.

Hearing her soft whimpering, Frank couldn't help but want to approach and comfort her. He sometimes didn't care about what that person thought of him, he wanted to give her some comfort, or peace if he could do it.

"Especially since she was such a fucking mess," Frank thought in the back of his head, but didn't want to think about anything more. In a ballsy shrug, he walked behind Ann, feeling a wave of sadness drowning her in a sea of depression and he wanted to pull her out of her drowning sea of tears. He slowly put a hand on her shoulder, but before he could even feel her shoulder again, she brushed him off again as if he didn't even exist, ad he got that impression from her instantly. But he wasn't going to stand for any of that.

As he moved in behind her, she was still whimpering with her cries sounding like echoes in a water well, and leaned his crotch against her bottom. But the way his feelings were gripping his emotions, he couldn't help but feel close to her, not just physically but emotionally. Frank lowered his chin, he slowly breathed in all the anxiety and anxiousness. Slowly exhaling his breath as he felt his chest beginning to elevate against her back, and all he could hear was her heart beating with such agony and disparity.

He whispered into her ear, very softly, rocking her back and forth in his own body as if she was a child in his arms, encouraging or uplifting words to cheer her up. "Shhhhhhhhhhhhh…" Whispering, he slowly kissed her cheek, feeling the coldness of her body begin to defrost from all it's icy layers. "Don't worry…" Frank felt her heart beat rapidly, and in some crazy or natural act, he felt no sexual pleasure at this point, and Frank thought that was a good thing, especially if his nerves were calming down.

Ann looked up to Frank, turning her straight and combed down hair across the side of Frank's shirt, feeling it create a soft scratchy sound as she looked into his eyes filled with worry, and the look of terror filled there eyes. But strangely, Frank had a plan.

Way before Berry had even approached the door, and while Frank had been in the bathroom, A.J. had called Jessica to get to the bottom of what Frank said before they departed for that short, but dangerous time. But how would he start this conversation off. Even while Jessica was still talking, he felt it was impertinent to interrupt her in the middle of her sentence. Even though she was asking him questions like, "Oh, I heard about the whole thing" and "Are you okay" over and over, but he wasn't hearing what he wanted to hear.

"I was so worried about you this morning, and you should have told me." Jessica's question was said with full simplicity, but it was overall confusing to him because he hadn't even gotten around to his side of the story. But before more time was wasted, A.J. made his first move.

"Jessica," A.J. interrupted her as she was in the middle of her sentence. A.J. took a deep breath and heard that she had stopped to let him speak, her labored breaths made A.J. more nervous to even ask her the very same question. Swallowing the last bit of respect he had for himself, he came outright with the painstaking question, just to avoid dancing around the question.

"Are you….pregnant?"

The Disintegrating Bloodline

A small gasp burst through the phone cord, like a daunting dream that had come back to haunt her had finally become true and now she couldn't escape the question now because he called her on the question, and if she lied, she would never gain his trust back.

"What?" Jessica said, unsure of what she was about to say, and then added, "What are you talking about?"

A.J. took a moment, putting all the words together not knowing if he would falter or fumble his words. He didn't care if he did, everything was still too perplexing. "Yeah, I heard that you have been pregnant for a while now, and…you…"

"What, spit it out!" Jessica said in a perplexed tone, her anger goading him on to finish his sentence.

As he breathed again, he let all the pain out. "I heard that you wanted to get an abortion, without telling me."

Jessica sighed, hearing the results of her secretive behavior, and went to calm his outrageous behavior. "Where did you hear this. I wonder who told you?"

Then A.J. replied mockingly, letting his beast take over his senses. "A little bird did as he took a shit on my shoulder, oh that was you."

Jessica controlled herself, and knew that she only told one person, and that was Frank. He must've told him, but why did he tell him. "Well, was that bird by the name of Frank, and tell me, how does it feel to be shitted on?"

A.J. began to think that she was playing with his head, and A.J. knew this was going bad. But he didn't care.

"Well, I wouldn't really know what that feels like. Maybe that's how you lied to me before I was walking into a death trap." His voice wasn't aggressive, but he was trying to communicate to her what he was thinking and feeling—and make her accept it.

Jessica sighed, feeling the resentment grip her, and her exasperated voice sounded as if she had been punched over and over in the stomach.

"I'm sorry…" She was then silenced and swallowed her own grief for those few moments. "Can we talk about this in person?"

A.J. closed his eyes, and let out a long sigh of some disbelief as he rubbed his palm over his head—the gristle inside his palm began to make the sweat undeniably hot—as he tried to figure out what the hell this was all about. But then, without thinking, he impulsively replied, rubbing the sweat into the palms of his hands, "Yeah, sure. Come over." He wasn't sure why he had invited her over to Frank's house, but he might have been curious to argue with her a little more, find out what other secrets she had been hiding.

"Okay. I'll see you in a few minutes. I love you!" She said, adding that "I love you" as an added bonus, seemed rather feeble. Only A.J. made no reply and just hung up the phone.

After Jessica hung up the phone A.J. saw that Berry was not in front of him anymore. A.J., with some nervous anxiety running throughout his body, moved out of the kitchen with the phone lowered down from his ear he saw him slamming his hand against the door hearing the insides of the wall crumble with the very power of his curled fingers, and yelling if she was done yet. A.J. watched from that distance, leaning against the hallway, he began to remember not too long ago Frank slipping into the bathroom unnoticed. If those two were in there together, he decided to stay out of it. "Just pretend that he didn't see them." But if Berry would ever point a gun into Frank's sight again, he would definitely be in for a big surprise.

As Ann slammed the door behind her, Ann saw A.J. and Berry standing at the end of the hallway, seeing her crease her T-shirt down over her pants and gave him a smile.

Turning her back away from the lightly dimmed hallway—the sun moved across her meaty body—she turned back toward the hall where A.J. was, and saw that had left her sight.

"Huh?" She thought, scratching her head, and combed a strand of hair over her two ears with her fingerprints, and made her way down the hall. Leaving the darkened hallway, she made her way toward the artificial light as it felt like she was walking through an old unkempt church with the dust forming around the glass paintings like a clinging mildew. Only a serious question surfaced in her head.

"But who was that guy in the bathroom with her? Holding her, sucking on her nipples, pushing his love stick in and out of her as if his dick was a underground measuring tool and was her vagina was the muddy ground?" It felt damn good, but she thought that the pleasure would have lasted a little longer.

And on that note she rid the thought of ever having sex with this guy, but she felt something when she looked into his large brown eyes. And that was why she didn't want to take one more glance at him and her burning flesh bubbled with the thought of his lovely arms around her body. But after she had had him, felt his bone, her skin turned back to ice, only her heart was beginning to thaw.

As Ann headed out toward the door, she glanced around for one more look, and detaching herself from her surroundings she opened the door. She slipped out the door unnoticed moving in between the cracks, and feeling her chest and legs brush against the open door, sending a small inch of pain in her system. She groaned as she grabbed the knob and pulled the door behind her as she slipped out onto the porch. Ann pulled the door shut she heard it *click* behind her, and it made her think of a fortress plank that was pushing on the other side of the door. Glancing out toward the driveway, she saw that Berry was already in the car, waiting for her arrival with his usual smug and thought-provoking stare that came with Berry's personality. As she moved closer toward the car, she could see that he was staring at her like he was ready to kill her.

"Whatever!" Ann thought, feeling that she was dangerously close to the edge of a cliff, she approached the car, grabbing onto the door handle, and entered into his piece of junk car that had no air conditioning, and not one single window barely rolled down enough to get air.

Ann saw the car and couldn't believe that her father was such a cheap-wad about things lately, but she knew that he had barely seen them for the last few days. But maybe since the shooting at the school happened that very day, she knew that they would start to see more of their father…maybe?

When the front door finally closed, and the silence fell upon the house again, A.J. left the kitchen with a sandwich—roast beef and cheddar cheese in his hand—waiting till he heard an opening of a car door, and a *slam* echoed into the air. After that he would be listening for the sound of an engine starting, and the grinding squeal of the tires peeling the pavement as the small piece of shit car would scurry down the road, and make everyone know that they had been there!

A.J. made his way into the hall again, listening ever so closely to the sounds that he wanted to hear, like a composer does when he wants to hear the notes that he had written down on the musical parchment. "A composer of death?" A.J. thought scornfully, and thought, but his thoughts were dragging him into the abyss.

Pushing his feelings aside, he waited and listened.

Like a turning cheese grater, the engine squealed as the wheels of the shitty vehicle moved down the road, and away from his house. It was safe now, and as he leaned on his shoulder against the wall, he saw through the window the car moving past the windows reflecting the sun in his eye as it blinded him. As the light left his eyes, the light reflected into the second window as the car moved away from the house, and sped down the street, giving off an exhaling sputter from the engine's tired transistor.

A.J. breathed through his nose, and relaxed his muscles. Sighing again, he saw that the door was slowly opening, and A.J. turned to look down the darkened hallway, and he heard the door opening. What he saw didn't totally take him by surprise, but when he saw Frank's body walking out from the doorway, trying to blend into the darkened hallway, he glanced down the hall, and he saw him standing with that apathetic stare, that showed no sign of remorse, which he loathed to see.

A.J. just looked at him and said, "Were you in there with her?"

Frank, who was still hiding in the darkened hallway, sarcastically, "What do you think?" Pulling his pants up, he grabbed his crotch in a mocking sexual manner. A.J. just shook his head, and was filled with dread and his serious stare pierced through the darkness, catching him even watching his disgusting gesture. A.J. was worried what would happen if he found out, but he had to make sure and see if he was not seeing right.

"Did you two fuck?" A.J. said bluntly, trying to pull him from out of the darkness. But from his adamant voice, he wasn't going to move out of the dark hallway.

"Yeah, she was basically begging for it the moment she met me."

"Frank," A.J. let a breath of anger out of his system before he spoke again, "Don't you see that if he caught you, you would really be…"

"Oh, in what, *trouble*?" Frank combatively swung, "I can handle that stupid fuck. He wouldn't shoot me, because he's too confused about getting revenge for his *dead* brother."

A.J. had enough of this, and Frank's temperamental attitude was slowly working on A.J.'s nerves. A.J. had to regain some order of respect since he was the boss, and the boss can not be spoken to with irrational behavior.

"I know that. That is easy to see, but get a grip, okay. This is no time to be thinking of pussy. Let's just watch out, okay."

Frank—lowering his eyes in resentment—could argue this till his eyes turned black and his face turned blue, but now he just didn't feel like it since he had just gotten laid.

As Frank responded, the arrogance in his voice left, but the aggravation was still strong. "Okay, I understand. Let's just stick to the plan, and I'll call up some guys. But remember this." Frank felt his body becoming more invisible with his surroundings, almost as if he had entered into the shadows himself.

Feeling his breath become sparse, he could almost feel his breath almost look as if smog of air was flowing from his mouth of how cold the hall must have been to him. "If *I* find out that he's a spy, *I'm* gonna kill him!" Frank felt the coldness blanketing him as if a malignant evil had just overshadowed him.

"I know." A.J. agreed with him. "But don't get carried away, we have much to do and to worry about."

"*You don't know the half!*" Frank thought to himself, remaining ever so still, but constant dread was ever eternal in his soul.

Frank didn't want to move out of the darkness just yet, he wanted to be inside his room for a while. But he couldn't find an answer to reply, but to stay in silence and walk toward his room.

A.J. left the hallway, and made his way into the living room, pondering the next plan of action while he chomped down on the rest of the Roast-Beef and Cheese. Gulping down the rest of the sandwich, he fell onto the couch, he closed his eyes, but saw the faces of those kids that were struck by the bullets of the assassins. "Blood across the floor, blood drooling from their mouths. Crying for their mothers and fathers…" He wanted to cry for them, but didn't know how…he didn't know them, but in a way, he did. When he was done eating he went back to his guest bed, and lying down, he closed his eyes.

He then fell asleep, and forgot all about those kids, for a while.

Chapter XIX

"The Woman Inside the Box"

When the day finally ended, the news had taken the nation off guard, like a beer bottle across the head. A wide frenzy that called to the attention of the nations' parents and children to gather around the television, and watch and talk about the horror of this awful day that innocent lives were killed so needlessly. And there was no reason for these lives to be taken, that was for sure, and A.J., Jessica, and Frank could attest to that. The whole fucking school could attest to that, including the thirty-two dead students and teachers.

Frank, A.J., and Jessica were all inside Chris's room, obviously hoping to give him some company, or trying to comfort themselves from the news blabbering heads. It was around eight-o clock when they had arrived at the hospital, and the look of the hospital had seemed dense and frigid, almost as a fresh corpse had been inside the square metallic filing system box.

"A filing system for the dead." A.J. thought, and could smell the residue of the lingering tortured souls walking from room to room, hoping to see if they could have a conversation with the near dead, just so that they could warn them of what always stays. No light at the end of the tunnel, no clearing, but the same old place that they were banished to live in for all eternity. A.J. and Frank played around with this idea, not really believing it was true or not, but Jessica still had her hopes up that she might see all her family after her life was over.

Only A.J. didn't know if that was true or not, but he didn't really know it for sure. A.J. and Jessica not speaking a word to each other and not one single breath were even drawn toward each other. The only thing that passed through them at that moment was Frank's disgusted as his angry face and his temper was definitely making his eyes and body puff with excitement.

"Trench coat Mafia!" He burst out into the room as if he was about to choke on the idea like a piece of steak, and he was about to die from it. "Trench coat Mafia?" Frank whispered under his breath, and turned to A.J. as if he was also feeling the same way about the entire thing. Even though Frank was enraged, A.J. didn't show hint of emotion, except for a nod, and then returned his attention back to the screen. It's as if Frank had forgotten all about what he had said on the elevator, but somehow lost it all in the midst of the ordeal.

Frank at the moment felt all this lodged in his throat, moved his chair away from the screen, and sat his chair next to Chris. Looking at his sleeping body, he turned toward the window, and tried to look out upon the starry night as if there was a secret message for him. But all he could see was the pitch black night that hid all the bright and shining stars that would lead there band of warriors along the path of truth, but all he could visualize was Gene's fat face sucking the meat off barbecue ribs.

He pulled his eyes away momentarily from the window, and focused it back inside the room. An overhead light was just above Chris, which gave it that fluorescent bluish color that shined in the dark room, as if there was some last bit of hope in the face of perilous times.

Hearing the news channel break off into a commercial, Frank turned back toward A.J. and Jessica who were still in opposite chairs, not even glancing at each other, like an old dysfunctional couple. Frank looked around him again, and saw that the light had flickered off and on, but then shined brighter again, filling in the desperate mood as if they were being stenciled with a pale blue marker that gave there faces that pale look of death, that blue gave them an even sadder look that only reflected their sadness like a demeaning crystal ball.

"I don't know about you but…" A.J. and Jessica turned toward him, and they gave him there full undivided attention. "I want to stay the night. Do you guys have a problem with that?"

Jessica and A.J. unwillingly glanced at each other, and A.J. turned away toward Jessica with a smirk that meant, "Whatever you want to do," And A.J. replied, "That's fine. I just hope your house is going to be okay?"

Frank responded with a complacent smirk while he said, "No, my parents are there. And all your personal stuff are there too so you don't have to worry about if any of our stuff will be stolen, and if it is, you don't have anything to be worried about."

A.J. woke up from his momentary daydream, hearing his voice turning into a low whisper, "No, I won't worry." A.J. breathed uneasily, leaned back inside the seat, and made no glance at Jessica. Frank looked at both of them, and let a small smirk of boredom escape him as he slapped his knees, trying to get his spirit motivated.

"I'm going to get some coffee."

Upon hearing him, it brought A.J. and Jessica toward each other, and A.J. looked at him and turning their heads A.J. replied with a spark in his eye. "Coffee?"

As Frank rose up off his seat, he retorted with a simplicity in his voice, "Yes. Coffee." Frank had just noticed A.J.'s face seem a bit happier at that moment and he obviously thought—that in the pits of his eyes—something was actually funny. He had brought Jessica and A.J. to bear a look at each other, and even though he didn't even intend on that, Frank felt weirdly good about that.

A.J.'s lips rose up in a questioning raise for a moment, as if he was about to chuckle. "When did you start drinking coffee?"

"When did you finally realize that?" Frank shot back sarcastically.

"I realized it when you just said it." A.J. said, with an even more all knowing grin on his face.

"Then you are exactly right."

A.J. was taken by surprise, but couldn't help but feel an odd liking toward it, as so being his inquisitive nature was taken rather strangely.

"Wait, wouldn't it equal four." Jessica blurted out unknowingly at the moronic and undeniable randomness of this statement. What she didn't really know was that it didn't really mean anything.

"No…what?" Frank looked around, grabbing at his pants, and then left the room with his pants being held by the Beretta.

Frank smiled knowing that A.J. was something special, no doubt. He had definitely seen what Chris had told him, and looking down at his body, he saw that he was right.

"For someone to question even the smallest things means that one will pick out the smallest flower out of a rose garden, and that one rose shall lead the wild to the promise land." This was rather poetic and yet whimsical at the same time, but Frank had many, many ideas and he needed to talk to A.J. about their plans for there family.

After Frank finished, he felt another embarrassing silence fill the room like a bad joke, and the weirdness was at a standstill.

As he exited the room, he glanced around the room, one last time through the darkness, enamored by its pale glint. The bright hallway was buzzing with the nurses and doctors as the small hand on a clock limped around the circle of numbers. He knew that time went faster than sand, but what he didn't know that they were one in the same.

Frank knew that they were the same encumbered by the darkness, and what might happen if he didn't go into the light for a while, madness would descend and chaos would reach around their throats. Only he didn't know what to do in there boredom, and when boredom made itself known that usually led to dry conversations and fell into the silence that came along like a crack in the floor.

The night waxed and waned on while nurses and their carts full of medicine and other medical items rushed past the rooms, flashing like twirling diamonds in the sky as doctors moved in like the wind and out with a quick breath as Frank, who was wide eye and unbearably exhausted, when he found out that Chris was going to need to stay in the hospital for at least three weeks.

"Oh great." Frank thought as he stared at this doctor, but shook his head up and down in response to his conversation. Frank's eyes bulged from dry exhaustion as the exhaustion swept over his body as the doctor kept quacking on about the medical mumbo-jumbo he just wasn't ready to hear about at this ungodly hour of two in the morning.

Before the doctor left, he could see how long his face had stretched in the mirror—his fingers fell into his cheek—and revealed a few large pimples and his week old beard. He moaned in tired agony, and then looked at the three sleeping beauties, all resting in eternal sleep. Only he could feel there dreams like a thumping heart, and all the terrible things that could lie in a human heart.

"Never more will you live …never more will you see your life as it is!" The crow screamed pounding against the walls with a hackling cackle. Chris, standing inside the room again—the room, chair, woman, began to blink off in an electrical glow and returned back to normal every two seconds. Only he saw the crow's wings flutter, and he saw its small breast fluttering rapidly. Chris clenched his fists and as the bird flew by he swung his fist at the crow, but it flew away from him in a pitiful retreat, and laughed with its cawing cackle.

Chris, standing transfixed in the room saw the bird perched on the top of the room as if he was inside a huge cage, and the only thing that was going to keep him company was this damned bird. Feeling a rage climbing through him he yelled to the bird, "What do you want? Speak now, or I'll choke you with my bear hands!"

The bird said nothing, and standing motionless, he cocked his head to the side showing off his beak like a proud schoolboy.

"Go to the box." The crow gaped with a deep demonic voice with his open beak as the winged pest flew away from the corner of the box, and disappeared until it turned into a small blip in the green puke sky that was clouding over the roofless room. His heart began to beat ten times faster than he ever felt before. It made his body ache at first, but as Chris walked across the room, he saw that everything inside the room had disappeared, and nothing except windows had appeared on either side of the room.

Moving into the center of the room, he saw a small but rather noticeable box and saw it shaking in its place.

Chris stopped, and then it did one last little jump, as he backed up, "Open the box" the demonic voice said. Chris looked into the sky, and saw the greenish sky starting to turn, like some vortex, and then he cried into the sky, "What's in it?"

The sky started to pulsate, and it sounded like it was going to drip oozing liquid with every time it talked. "The true identity of your cousin lies in that box."

Chris shook his head, and then turned around, seeing the window. "I don't want to look!" Chris yelled in pain, as he opened the windows, resisting the temptations of his own weakness.

Leaning his head forward, he saw that the mirror of the windows started to look almost bluish, as deep as the Mediterranean Ocean, the one he had used to swim in all the time, and what he saw at first, was the crystal clear reflection of his face.

Chris was as much shocked by his own reflection, but when he saw it again, the window suddenly disappeared, and Chris beheld something more disturbing. He couldn't explain it, but all he could see that a small town, like when he was born, and everything came alive. It felt familiar to him, but as he looked even harder, he saw that the people in the town looked like ghosts and when he looked harder he saw an old woman was holding something to her mouth. It was almost like a light bulb, but in her other hand was a long candlestick at the end, and a long line of smoke came out. Chris came to the realization that a woman was smoking crack, a derivative of cocaine, from a glass pipe. He could see her face as she blew out the smoke, her face skeletal and skin so clear that one brush of sandpaper could break her skin.

Chris couldn't stand it any longer, and when he felt like he was about to throw up, the pounding in his head and Chris held his hands over his ear. He let out a terribly pained scream, trying to numb the pain. The intensity was like a sword right through his genitals, and the images retching, he screamed again and all he could remember was that voice in the sky…

When Chris awoke from his slumber, his eyes were groggy, and his stomach partially swaying back and forth like he had been taking eight different shots at various times. He was breathing heavy when he focused his eyes around him, and saw A.J. and Frank leaping from their seats.

"Are you okay?" A.J. asked, gripping the handle post of the bed, almost so hard that he wanted to break it from the intensity. Frank was standing on the other side of the bed, looking upon his fallen comrade, worried.

"Are you okay? Do you need a nurse?" Frank said, reaching for the call button, but then saw Chris shaking his head, and waving for him to steady his hand. Frank was holding the receiver, and with a drop of his hat, he lowered it toward the bed and let it fall against his leg. They were flabbergasted, more like shocked, and breathing slowly they calmed themselves down knowing it was their friend, and he was alive, it wasn't like a ghost talking to them. They could feel his warmth even when he was asleep.

Chris reached for another switch that controlled the movement of the bed, and it slowly moved him up and they looked at him as if he was a king awakening from a crippling sickness; he wiped his head from the sweat that was forming underneath his hair. They saw a new life in their leaders' eyes, and sat back in their chair dumbfounded.

Chris looked at them, and said licking his dry parched lips. "What day is it?"

"It's December 1st."

Chris felt the pounding leave his head as he looked outside—drained from the amount of drugs he had been on—and thought that it should have been snowing, but it would probably snow in a few weeks. That wasn't important to him, and then motioned for them to sit back down. They didn't know what he wanted, but they would do as he motioned for them to pull their chairs forward. "Pull your chairs closer. It's been too long, too much time has been wasted."

A.J. and Frank looked back at each other, and they smirked as they pulled their chairs closer, and they saw him give a content smile. On the other side of A.J., Frank was so entranced that he was like looking at Chris as if he was sitting in front of the Pope and in this fluorescent light, and with the shadow creeping under his eye, it only made him even more terrifying—a God in the darkness.

"Too much time." Frank said, rubbing his hands together, letting the rambunctious energy flow through his veins, and energize his brain.

Chris just looked at him, and smiled, but then continued on.

"I have been dreaming, and these dreams are so life like that they have been stuffed inside my subconscious that until now, it's like a portal, you know. But an issue that has gone on for too long has been riding on cruise control, and no one has taken a step to fix the problems back home. You must know what the next obstacle you are about to face."

Chris looked at both of them, and said, "If you will listen to what I say."

"Yes." A.J. said in a honest tone, and leaned forward, "I will."

Chris gave a relaxed motioning of his hand, and said, "At ease. Just sit back and open your ears to the truth that I speak."

A.J. felt relaxed and then leaned back and crossed between each other.

"This has been the first attack, and I know that Gene has pulled the most dastardly of all tricks from his bag. He tried to kill you two in school, but he won no prizes as he commonly failed in that attempt." Looking at both of them, he sighed from the distressing news that he had seen on the television, in and out of his consciousness and breathed all his despair that he had left in his system.

"But that is old news, I have been dreaming these past few days, and even though they may be dreams, dreams aren't entirely lies. "

Frank and A.J. leaned forward, and opened their ears to their leader, and friend.

The night set in over the skies, and the morning light came protruding through like a drunk friend stumbling all across the bar floor, and spilling his drink across an unsuspecting woman's dress like the first dawn of light touching the first blade of grass. The school was swarmed with reporters, trying to get everyone's opinions but even though there charitable offerings were secretly flaming the already dampened fire, some students were willing to talk about it, but Berry would not cooperate with the reporters and there microphones. The hot microphone felt like a wet blunt that was two centimeters away from his lips.

"What do you think about what has happened?" The first reporter said, shoving the microphone into his face.

Berry didn't look at them, covering his face away from the cameras he pushed the microphone away, and just said, "No comment!"

Even though he tried to fight the first reporter off, another came from the other side screaming, "What's your name, don't you have anything to say?" It was a female reporter with large rounded breasts, a skinny body and her fingers had little to no bone on it. As her high heels clicked like horse hooves, more cameras swarmed around him like bees and Berry's other hand covered the other side of his face, unable for her or anyone else to get a good shot of him.

"Don't you have any respect!" Berry said, becoming enraged that the temptation was jolting through his fingertips. When he just about pushed the reporter he knocked the microphone away and it fell to the ground, around a few other reporters that stepped over the fallen microphone.

"Shit!" The woman said, and falling to the ground trying to grab for her microphone. The woman hoped that no one caught her sudden outburst, but she sighed in embarrassment, knowing that was a lie. She grabbed the microphone with her left hand and propped herself back on her feet, and felt something the ground crack her right index fingernail. "Damn it!" The female reporter burst out, turning her hand over, curling her fingers into her creamy milk palm, and saw her index fingernail chipped.

She saw that the boy had left them far behind, and the jackals, or the other groups of reporters were feasting on the next innocent face to interview, and make there television stations happy, filling the bellies of all the news programmers. She turned around, her lockjaw making a crooked slant—and threw a piece of hair around her left ear lobe, catching the early morning air in her nose as she regained her footing. Even though she had wanted to interview the boy that had pushed her microphone out of her hand, she somehow felt that maybe he did that for a reason. Maybe they were just being too pushy, and ordinary people were being put on the spotlight, and maybe they should just call it a day. But as she watched the group of reporters flock toward another boy, business was business, and they were asking him questions.

She shook her head, and then looked at her finger with distress "No dice!" The woman thought, and she rose up off the ground. The cameraman pointed the camera downwards, making sure he wasn't getting his reporter in the thick of her weakest moment. She straightened out her blue blouse as her cameraman beside her asked, "Are you all right?"

She ignored him, and traveled toward another girl. The cameraman just smirked with delight not taking her ignorance seriously, and followed her alongside her with the camera. It wasn't too long before the jackals started to crowd in around another victim.

Berry ran as fast as a wolf would do when stalking its prey, but in his case, he was evading the ravenous wolves nipping at his heels. He managed to escape without his head nearly bit off by the cameras, but the only thing that were stopping the wolves from following him into the school were the few policemen that were staked out beside the large pillars, and the policemen gave him a long look. Berry turned his head, and headed on into the school doors. Only then he saw a long line of kids that were being swept and checked for illegal weapons or contraband. The kids that were being checked at that moment had a sour smug and were on the brink of yelling if the policemen didn't finish. But Berry could see the same look across the cop's face, and his was as ugly as a bull dog on a bad day.

As he walked toward the line, he could hear the complaints forming underneath the breath of an large black boy getting his bags checked. Only Frank caught fragments of words that the cop must have heard, and looked towards them like a vulture would do from his high circling path when it would see a dead, dying carcass. The cop looked at them with a rather tough expression as he gave the kid his backpack. But as the black kid grabbed the pack by the strap, he walked away from him, the words that the boy had dare not utter finally sprung from his mouth as forthwith as an assassin would stick his blade into his victim. "Fuck you, pig."

Only as the cop with his far reaching keen sense of hearing he turned to catch the boy with his blue stocking cap, but the boy did not turn around when the cop cocked his head like an watchful eagle. Only this kid didn't give him so much trouble as the other boy had, and walking away with no regard for what he was doing. Although the next person calmly gave him his backpack, stretched his arms out as if they were flimsy weather-beaten limbs, and straightened his back like a rigid oak tree.

The boy let the electronic stick float above his underarms, clicking silently as it let out a small humming sound as it glided down his left leg, and then it traveled back up his right leg, and above his right underarm. He took it away from him, and swiped his bag. Only he proved no results, and handed the person the bag. Then it came time for Berry to be swiped with this electronic stick. Berry's pits started to sweat underneath him, and a nervous feeling secreted through his pits over him as he approached the policeman holding the large electronic stick.

He saw the large policeman holding the stick, and instantly thought of some character out of some science fiction character brandishing a weapon for the victim to see them in plain sight.

Berry approached, and stood two inches away from the policeman. The air between them raised an intimidating pillar of hatred with his gleaming sunglasses.

"Hi." Berry muttered, as if he was talking from his own rear, and Berry willingly took off his backpack and set it on the table. Even though his rear could have made more noise than a tiny squeak, he didn't want to be overly nice, because that would lead him to believe that he was a suspect, and unwanted attention was something he did not want on his tail right now.

As Berry waited for the police officer to finish swiping his bag down with the magical wand he felt his heart race as if he had forgotten to take something out of his bag. Although when he thought about it, he was pretty sure if he had taken all his *stuff* out of the backpack, but even a single nine millimeter, forty five shell, or any kind of bullet that had gone unseen, could bring down his card castle.

He always had disdain for authority figures, and especially since the cops came so late to help them, even though his heart demanded that he scream, "YOU FUCKING PIG," and then punch him, he took hold of his anger and listened to the policeman.

"Stretch your legs and arms please." The cop condescendingly, looking at him with impatience enwrapped around the cop's body like a tentacle of some sea serpent squeezing the life out of him.

Berry spread his legs apart, and his hands outwards, he felt like he was being experimented and stretched apart as if he was reenacting Da Vinci's human anatomy chart. Hearing the large metallic stick flow over and under his body, the small beeping sounds drove him mad—mad enough to cut his own head off, and run around in a circle like a headless chicken, spouting blood all across the floor in a kind of gory thick molten lava.

But the beeping seemed to lessen when the policeman (or "Pig" by his own standards) removed the long beeping bar away from his body, and stretched his hand out with the bag in his sweaty grip.

"Here you go!" The policeman/pig said, holding the bag out in front of him, as if he had just violated his own privacy. But Berry had to comply, and for various reasons he wasn't going to give the cop any trouble—*"real lady like,"* Berry pretended to sound like a homosexual.

Grabbing the bag from the "pig", Berry slung the backpack over his shoulder, moved past the guard. Their meeting came and went like an uncomfortable silent fart, sending everyone out of a nice room with old Victorian furniture.

As he left the guard behind him, he slung his backpack in a comfortably around his shoulders, he made his way into the school. Everything was quiet, especially all the kids since they were scared to even breathe. It had been almost three days after the massacre right in the lunchroom, and the bodies spread out, their blood staining the linoleum floor. But the police must have came through and swept the bodies up, delivering them to the morgue where the morticians could cut them open, and then explain it to all the parents that had to see there son or daughter stretched out across a cold metallic panel. Berry had to identify his brother on a metallic tray, with his father and sister. He couldn't cry, but his sister did, and his father did.

But he remembered that his brother was somewhere resting on a stretcher with his eyes closed, the umbilical cord of life permanently cut off forever, but his presence was all around him.

He shook the feeling off for now, but would ultimately have to return to it much later because they had to go to there brothers funeral. The thing that bothered him was how his father was taking this washing his mouth with whiskey and Henessey.

Berry remembered that there was one person to blame, and that was Gene. He wanted to murder him, and watch him die very slowly. Only he thought of it like a complex math question—to get from point A, he had to get to point B, and then finally point C. It wasn't that he was good at math or economy, it was just common sense to think in logical terms. Only he thought sometimes that this crazy world didn't operate on logic courses, and math didn't have anything to do with that.

"Did Gene have to shoot up the school any other day, or did he just want to see innocent people die?"

Berry sighed as he made his way toward the Commons B; he wanted to talk to someone to calm his turbulent soul. The thought of even coming back was crazy enough for him but he needed to find answers—travel to the bottom of this conundrum, while trying to keep his mind off of any unwanted questions, if he could hold all the questions down for the time being.

Even though Commons A was particularly quiet, the other half, Commons B was already filled with conversations but not too much commotion was going on. Berry heard there were no outcasts free-styling occapellas, but a terrible silence, only meant a disturbed presence, and when he saw the large group of kids in long black attire, and baggy black Jinco jeans trailing down past their shoes, and he knew he was in the right place.

From what he knew, the Outcasts were just a small piddling gang that did a few things here and there, but it's main purpose was to accept anybody, including anyone from the jocks or prep gangs, to come and be themselves in this gang of misfits, separated almost like communists. He knew that they were the cause of many fistfights, but he never knew them ordering any hit on anyone before. Berry decided to suspend his disbelief, and dive into this thing headfirst. Whether he would expect to end up hitting the bottom would be how far he would dive into this ordeal. Only feeling his body divulged into naked territory, he moved sideways, watching the group of kids standing around the table as if they had been intimidated and had seen something coming towards them, and by the looks of it, they had seen him.

Only he knew whom they were guarding, and the thought of him talking to these two just made him worry. Because they were also known to never hold a secret for long, and had no honor for anyone except for there own. As Berry swallowed this uneasy feeling, he began to see the two brothers that he had only heard of, hair brighter than the sun and eyes just as deep as the sea, and skin just a shade over a piece of paper, and body's frail as a woman's pinky finger.

The Disintegrating Bloodline

When Berry stepped closer he remembered their names, Jacob and Clifford Barley, and what a terrible, and strange name to have. He could see that they had seen him from a short distance, and if they caught sight of him now, that was a good thing.

As Berry just approached the table, a few of the kids with acne faces pushed Berry back and clutching his shirt said, "Who are you guy?" Berry quickly glanced around at the ghoulish stick figure, and felt an odious smell radiate off him as if it was cologne, "B.O. Extra creamy. Made from all the sweaty juice in your toilet." Berry thought, making an uncomfortable situation very humorous. The guard dog with the deep black *Slipknot* tee shirt gripped his shoulder even harder, but what came across surprisingly to him was the middle of his forearm. It resembled a few pot marks that looked like a large Wasps stinger had left a pulsating gaping hole, and it was oozing incredibly. But at that moment, he would have wished he was at another place and time.

"Heroin?" Berry thought, and saw that by the looks of it, they weren't old marks by a long shot.

Out of the blue, what looked a boy that was sitting down had seen the entire ordeal. The boy rose up from his seat, with a maddening gleam in his eye arms out as Berry was assaulted by another ugly face. His mouth opened, releasing his horrendous breath right into Berry's face.

"Yeah guy, who are you? You want to be a tough guy?" Berry pulled his face backwards, and forced the hand on one of the guards off his shirt. Berry couldn't stand how bad this kids breath was, and it made him think if somebody actually brushed there teeth with dog shit—brown stains and a mix of yellow painted on the two front teeth. It made him want to gag just as he thought about it even more. Berry saw his hands, and saw that his fist were layered with ashy crusted over knuckles, and his arms were covered with long marks that resembled only a knife entrance, and saw a few small holes inside the corner of his arms. He had seen these marks not just a moment ago, and put two and two together.

Maybe Heroin is what intensifies everyone's insanity, but he didn't know entirely all the details yet. But what he knew about junkies was plain and simple, "if one person was on it, there was a good clear chance that some one else was on it."

But when his eyes moved down his hands he saw that he had fingernails exceeded beyond the normal rate and the insides of his fingernails looked like layers and layers of dirt had been caked inside the crevices of his nails.

But pushing all these details in the back of his head for now (unfortunately), he stated his purpose, and hope that this meek little yapping pup would keep his distance.

"I'm Berry Pantoliano. I want to talk to Jacob Barley."

The boy, the one with his shit stained teeth and dog breath, chuckled offensively as if something upset him. Berry just looked at him, with his decisions made plainly up front, but he didn't want to listen to his request.

Moving to the side of Berry, he forced his face closer to his.

"Oh yeah Berry? I'm Clifford. Like I said you want to talk," As his head moved closer to Berry, he felt the putrid breath of his crawl out of his throat, and into the open air where Berry's nostrils were. "You got to talk to me."

Berry was repulsed by the smell again, and forcibly broke through the space between them and said, "Kid, if you don't back your stinkin' ass breath off me, we are going to have a problem."

The kid pulled his head back, but still had the cringing face of anger as he smirked, and danced around him as if he was some jester trying to antagonize him for his own sadistic pleasure. "Oh yeah?" He moved behind him, and whispered into Berry's ear, "Like I said, you got to talk to me." As the jester Clifford danced with playful glee, Berry heard a few snickering laughs around him, but they immediately fell to a hush.

Berry didn't move, despite his eagerness to lay his fist against his teeth, and the thought of these kids laughing as if this was funny, it was a temptation that he would other wise embellish with his whole heart intact. Berry rested his hands against his sides in a calm impatient manner, even though he wanted to, he was not about to miss his chance from getting his information.

"Even if it has to be at my expense." Berry thought angrily as he let out another breath of air out of his body, clenching his fist, and then relaxed.

Berry could obviously tell that this wasn't the brain of the two, this kid was surely the brawns in this gang. Even if he tried to, he probably couldn't push him into a locker if he didn't get pushed inside first.

The sight of this blue eyed freak with a face that had pot marks and incurable acne just intensified as if he was rubbing his face with his dirty hands, and this goading jester was on his last nerve.

But as the dancing monkey circled around him again, a voice rose out from the table, and the dancing monkey turned toward the sound of that voice as a Doberman Pincher or Rotweiller would respond to his master's voice.

"Stop!" The voice said in a commanding gesture, almost booming and thunderous as God himself. But Berry didn't hear a God, only Clifford did.

Berry and the boy turned toward the table, and laid his eyes to the one person that ran it all in the Outcast clique, the one who pulled all the Goths, misfits, and everyone who was an anti-socialite under his wing, Jacob Barley.

He had a frightening presence with his sandy blonde hair combed straight down with his curls on the side and rather curved out nose that made his cheekbones pulsing as if his heart was in his throat while his eccentric eyes scoured the lunchroom. Even though Jacob and Clifford weren't twins—but he couldn't exactly tell what it was, but Jacob was blessed more with the looks than did Clifford.

Jacob turned toward his brother, and motioned him with his eyebrows to return back to his seat. Clifford let out a small whine of displeasure stamping his foot against the floor sounding off a rather loud *clapping* against the dirty green linoleum floor as a soldier clicking his heels against the ground. In a disappointed gesture, Clifford looked back towards him with a grimacing and pissed off look. He headed toward the seat swallowing his pride down his throat, and sat down in his seat next to his brother very disgusted.

"You have something to say?" Jacob said with his rather attractive blue eyes reflecting a bit of innocence, but knew that this was just a front. Only Berry didn't believe this act would last too long.

"Yes." Berry said, and sat his body down in the closest chair next to him, and found one that was directly across from Jacob, face to face, eyes gazing at Clifford with endearing brotherly anger.

"I apologize for my brother, Cliff. He can be somewhat asinine at times, or all the time," After he finished his sentence, Clifford (or Cliff) glanced toward his brother with narrow eyebrows. As he breathed in, his throat made a gargling sound in the middle of his throat, as if he was choking on a hard piece of candy. When he breathed outwards, the gargling sound left his throat, and passed from him like the sound of the few drops of water twirling down a large drainage pipe.

Berry looked at him strangely, his eyebrows cocked, but as Jacob moved his tongue along the bottom of his teeth as if he was picking out a piece of popcorn, he opened his mouth making it ring out with a dull *click*. But Berry saw below him, across the top of his Adam's apple was a long but rather noticeable slash mark streaming from the left side of his neck to the right cheek bone, looking like a rather irreversible scar that made any of his look like a birth mark. But as he stared at the scar even longer, he broke his concentration, and returned to his original thought.

"Oh yeah. I want to know if you guys are accepting any newcomers."

This rose an interesting, yet formidable question for him, and as he glanced around the table, he felt that he was well protected by many of his *knights* or guards of his kingdom. Him being the king opened his mind to suspicion about what this Berry Pantoliano was hiding up his sleeve, because he knew a great deal about him too, but not personally though.

"My friend," Jacob said his voice turning into a real methodical kind of tone, raising his hands up, and proclaimed, "You are standing before the Lord of all the Goths, the misfits, and the shun upon. I am the king that holds his arms out to everyone like a loving father who accepts everyone for all there faults. What is your father's and mother's name?"

Berry felt taken back by his speech, thinking that he wasn't even hearing the full lunacy of Jacob Barley. It was his fiery glare in his eye made his speech even more chilling. Only the thing that took him off his guard from this blonde pale white boy, before he had even had a chance to speak, was his request to know his father's name. Berry was skeptic about saying a single word at first, but then ultimately put his life in God's hands, and spoke his words carefully, which sounded like water flowing down a dry riverbank.

Berry took a deep breath, and he felt rather refreshed "My mother's name is Marie, and my father's name is Joe."

When Berry was finished, he saw Jacob smirking very mischievously as if he had just said or had done something that gave him away. Berry watched him, with a careful eye. Even though he wanted to be angry, he couldn't help but feel at the mercy of this madman. At that moment, Jacob glanced around the table and pressing his elbows against the table he leaned forward so that Berry could get a look at his menacing, beautifully flawed figure's bronze skin.

"Well..." Berry was taking his good old time to just come out with what he had to say, but then he laid it heavily upon him. "Berry Pantoliano, son of Joe and Marie Pantoliano. I think you have come to be apart of our group at the wrong place at the wrong time."

"Yeah," Clifford burst out from his quiet unclean hole that was his mouth, and continued as a shower of rain spots of spit flew with his words as if he was about to cough blood. "You came in at the wrong place at the wrong time, buddy." The tone of his voice almost sounded like he was trying to imitate lines from a movie, like *Dirty Harry* or any of those Clint Eastwood Westerns. Even though Clifford took some enjoyment in this rather farce outburst, everyone was not.

Only just now seeing the bewildering narrow eyes his comrades were giving Clifford he did not want to turn his head, and see the raised eyebrows and the rather charming smile that fell flat whenever he was doing something bad. He felt like his neck had frozen stiff, but maybe he just wanted his neck to be stiff, maybe he didn't want to look, but all he couldn't stand was his harsh reprimanding in public. Clifford remembered that Jacob had always told him to shut his mouth whenever he was talking, but he couldn't help his compulsive yet erratic behavior.

Clifford turned his head away from the others, and caught the reprimanding look of his brother that he expected to see. What he saw were those same condescending blue eyes narrowed with his long streak of neatly pulled eyebrows squinting, and his bony cheeks pushed out through his skin mapping out his bony facial features.

"Keeping quiet." It sounded pretty sound, and at that moment, he knew that he wasn't supposed to have any kind of say, period. "The walking talking dummy." At that moment, he lowered his head, and breathed outwards in degrading shame for his joyful outburst.

But then he knew that there was another problem to blame for his behavior, and that was from the extreme amounts of Heroin that he had been injecting into his arms. He glanced down at his hole and exhaled, "This shit's getting to me!" He mumbled underneath his arms, but he felt that no one paid attention to what he said anyway. "When I get back home, I'll fix myself up real nice." He shuddered from the ecstasy, and silenced himself, for the rest of the conversation at least.

After Clifford lowered his head, and danced in his silent tomb, Jacob could then proceed with the rest of his thought, undisturbed and unchallenged by his brother's erratic behavior.

"So..." Jacob said, looking around his table of knights and squires, waiting for him to give them the word to beat him up, would be sadly disappointed by his call of action.

"I might have been too harsh about what I said before, Berry, son of Marie and Joe." His voice toned down from the cocky all knowing king to a personable and straight forward kind of tone, "What I meant that in this time of great change, things are rapidly changing around us. Even though some things decide to go against the way we are always familiar with, we have to adapt with the change, you understand that do you?"

Berry knew instantly what change Jacob was referring to, and there was nothing else to say except that the war between Gene and Chris's factions was on the rise. Three days ago it had come right to there own backyard, and Berry could tell that Jacob was not at all pleased with the situation. But regarding whose side he was on was up for grabs, and his soldiers would torture for the tiniest piece of information and then left like a floppy little rag doll covered in junk and sweat.

Then Berry saw his face changing from the lax face that he had seen just a moment ago, into a hard distant methodical despot that wanted no change but Berry knew that everyone wanted things to stay the same, but there was only one side that wanted change. He didn't need to think about him now because he would enwrap himself in the hatred that burned like oil in his bones.

"I know what you are, and don't try to bullshit me."

Berry just looked at him blankly, and responded with confusion in his voice. "What do you mean, bullshit, What do I have to hide?" Berry's heart began to race with the confusion, waiting for the blade of a guillotine to fall, and cut through his fake persona like a hot knife through butter. Only the pain wouldn't hurt his neck as much as much as his ego would be tortured.

"I know you run guns for anyone who will pay your wages. Word travels fast around the school, and anyone who is anyone knows already. What does someone that runs by himself want with someone like me? Do you want to become our friend and betray us for whatever we might know?" Berry cocked his head back, and felt his rage aggravated by this mad mans choice of too true words. Berry knew that denial might be the best road, but it might not since he knew what he did. But what had he caught him in, just trying to talk?

With a courageous feeling, his rebuttal was quick and clean, like a sword. "What would it have to do with my allegiance toward you. I'm a man of my word, if I say I am going to be a part of your crew, I will stay with your crew. And if you think that I can not keep up, you are sorely mistaken, *my friend*."

Berry had never heard himself take this kind of tone with any kind of leader before, and it felt good, but if they were going to play games with him, Berry's impatience was not going to keep up with this mad mans high talk.

Everyone around the table looked toward each other, and began whispering to one another in confusion, but then they faced there leader who had not broken his calm exterior, nor was he going to put his feelings in the way of business. But his calm interior was rippling with ravenous rage and his tone gave more reason to attack him, but he wasn't sure about Berry's intentions yet.

A moment of silence past through the table after the conversations were sworn away with the swipe and then there voices fell faster than a pigeon obeying mother natures laws. The silence paralyzed and cut off their vocal boxes, and as they turned toward their master and waited for his response, they saw his breath weighing heavy on his body. They knew that he was thinking heavily, like a large steam filled locomotion train, and by the look in his eye, they would suspect that his patience was running thinner than the blood of…

They wouldn't dare to think of that, because too much blood has been spilt on that rumor and more innocent people would still be paying the price for that damned rumor. The long lost cousin of Chris Mangini, and all the trouble that it was starting. Some of them believed that it was that rumor that started with Gene's dissention, but they were still debating what had really happened. They knew nothing but of the rumors of this cousin and they didn't even know if he existed or not. They didn't care at all about those affairs, but Gene was making sure that everyone in the school got the message clear that he wouldn't stop until the cousin was found, and ultimately taken care of. Only one of their greatest fears was that one of there own would lower himself to pledge his allegiance with the enemy of Chris Mangini and A.J.

"I know you have not come to pledge your allegiance. But is it something else you're looking for," He stared into Berry's eyes as if he was seeing into his soul. "Revenge…?" he continued, trying to make him unearth his true intentions. After Jacob finished his sentence, Clifford suddenly poked his head out from his arms, and eyed Berry with the all intensity in his eye.

Berry's eyes met Jacob's eyes, watching his intently, ignoring Clifford with all his patience could hold up. Only Berry acted as if he hadn't been thinking of grabbing Gene by the throat and squeezing the life from his fat face, but he also wanted to do it to Jacob and his disgusting ugly brother as well.

"No, it is not because of revenge. But the matter of my arrival has not been to join your crew. And I hoped I haven't offended you by my outburst. But what I have come for is beyond the point."

Jacob leaned forward, and chuckled with a discrepancy in his voice, as if he had seen through his very mind, frighteningly true.

"What did you come for?" Jacob said, relieving himself of the anger that he was forming like a small tumor in his organs. Berry finally felt free to tell him what he was after—the tension was blocking his blood stream and just when he was about to speak, the bell rang as he was opening his mouth. Its sadistic ringing let everyone know, if people around them were either awake or not, that it was time to move onto the first class of the day. Only a few moments after it's last *bing*, everyone else was rising from their seats with their backpacks slung across their shoulders in disgust. Only Berry knew they weren't going to there first classes.

"Let's walk and talk. Which class room are you headed to?"

Berry's guards all looked at each other, and then to Jacob in which they awaited impatiently for his response. Some of the looked eager and ready for something to get up and walk while most of them were weary and the look in there eyes said that they were ready to do anything.

"Young knight, you are more persistent than you look. Let's go!" Jacob said with rejuvenation in his system, and that Cheshire cat smile, all of his pearly white teeth making an appearance.

Berry didn't know if this was a compliment or not, but whatever it meant, it surely came out with a smiling grin of his Cheshire cat smile. Berry couldn't help but remember the cartoon *Alice in Wonderland* where the cat's body disappeared, and the last thing that Alice could see was his teeth fading into the abyss of that forest. All that was left was his evil sadistic smile, and Jacob's smile terrified Berry for some strange reason.

Once that was settled, Jacob rose out of his seat exposing himself from his protective castle, and moving around to his right cautiously, and approached Berry. His clothing line was hidden by long black baggy pants that mounted over his large Vans sneakers and the light shirt barely hid the weak forefront of his weak chest. Berry looked at him, and wandered if this guy was any kind of threat at all, even though he had a ripped, stone cut six pack. That did not deter him from his actual threat capability.

But before they could walk away, the whole crowd of kids, including his brother rose, looking like rocks rising out from beneath the ground, sending debris of dirt and dust all around them, and all of them were dressed in black. But some of them had demented visuals on them that could make your blood chill, and fill it with sickness.

One boy had a tee shirt that had a picture of a small infant child in the womb, and then underneath it in scraggily white letters said,

Dead Baby Jokes Anyone?

Berry could admit that what was on his shirt was just sick, and "distasteful" which was what his father would say, but then the others looked like they were wearing long black shirts and long black pants of chain mail suits. All of them were pale as that of a sixteen year old hookers' bottom, and there faces looked as coarse as a rocky terrain filled with pimples across the top of there cheeks, and imbedded into their small pubescent chin hairs.

When Berry and Jacob started to walk away, they were not too far behind them, like a black cloud of sickness hovered around them. As they walked down the hall, they began to talk, and headed down the hall, making their escape out toward the side doors that led to the hall, and out to a secret place where they could talk sensibly, and not palaver.

Time had sped faster than they wanted it to as the sun had then crept up over the morning sky, and everything was once foreshadowed the sun was now rising clear over the shadows—iridescent clouds began shimmering with the truth. Only A.J. was so infatuated his eye was like a pen that was taking in everything, word for word. Frank just glanced at him, and then returned his attention back to Chris. He then told them about everything in his dreams, from the crow's ominous warnings to the horrible grandmother vision but avoided revealing the temptation that he had with the box (thinking that it was probably the affect of the medicine).

Around them the whole world was moving, but Jessica was sleeping in the chair, only to awake for one moment as she eyed him every once in a while if she had been awoken by A.J. Only she was too weary to find out what he was saying, and closed her eyes again—blips of a baby appeared in her mind—dreaming of their child and the pain of his birth.

But when Chris started back up again, A.J. listened with full intensity again.

Frank should have known that Gene was a traitor a long time ago, but the question that came to his mind was, "Who was he working for?" Was it the Preps, the Bloods, or the Outcasts? Being that anyone of these groups could be the likely perpetrator, Chris assured them that this is coming from another higher power.

"Are you kidding me?" A.J. said acting surprised, but then regained his excitement. Chris nodded with a dead tired disgust on his face, as if he had just lost all ability to talk, and Frank looked at him as if he didn't believe it himself. A.J. was leaning out of his chair, and fell back in it with embarrassment.

All of them were tired, and there faces—eyes pulsating with red nerve endings and pupils dilating fresh tears of exhaustion—were proof of what tired really meant.

"No, I am not. But I am thirsty, and I need a soda pop. Go get me one."

A.J., who would get up for his mother when she woke him up in the morning, slowly rose from his chair, and stretched his arms out in front of him, "What kind of drink," hearing a few bones inside his arms click from it's incapability of being used.

Chris's eyes narrowed as if he was about to say something, but then knew this was A.J. he was talking to, not just any common hooligan off the streets with there thumbs off there ass.

"Any kind," Chris said with a bemusing smile, and then motioned with his left hand to flee.

A.J. gave him a respectful nod, and before he left he turned to Frank and said, "Do you want anything?"

Frank just nodded his head, and deliberately whispered, "No, I'm okay."

When A.J. heard his response, and processed it quite easily, he walked out of the room and the sounds of his footsteps echoed around the hallways as the sounds mingled with other noises.

Chris, as his heart started to beat, waited a few moments until he left, and let out a long contained breath that should have been let out a long time ago. Frank saw this, and his heart was filled with worry. He then began to figure out that there was more to the story than he was telling them.

"What is it? Is there more to what you are telling us?"

Chris nodded his head in complete honesty, and the way his eyes stared into his, provoked an inner fear inside Frank that he hadn't felt for a long time. It's like something was inside both of their stomachs, eating away at the insides of their souls. Frank had felt something was up with his dream, maybe with the thing about the room, but everything else seemed unfathomable.

"There is trouble back home. I saw a town in what looked liked my birthplace, I saw people's faces, and there was this old lady smoking crack from a glass pipe."

Frank shook his head, not entirely comprehending what he had said, but couldn't really understand. "What does that mean?"

Chris thought about what he was going to say in one hot minute, and that passed him by faster than he could have imagined it. Time went by so quickly when life was being detained by the needles that made him feel like less than a man. Only when his body could not be used to any sort of function, his mind was just as strong as his muscles.

But pertaining to the question, the images were burning fresh in his head like hot liquid burning, bubbling and burning, torturing his mind with fiery intensity. Only one came to mind when he saw that old woman's face magnified with his own, the desperation pouring out of her, eyes dripping sadness. He didn't know how to answer him.

"I don't know, but it is definitely a sign, and we must be careful, and watchful of everyone. Watch everyone, I mean it, everyone."

Chris sighed, fully aware of what he was talking about now. But with the way things were going, he wouldn't be surprised about a lot of things. Also he began to think this so-called war was not between the families, but maybe it was some conspiracy between the five families to over throw their clans. It was like a five hundred-pound gorilla hanging on their backs, and they didn't know how to get it off. But only they were playing dirty, because they got to one of there own, and that was Gene and somebody else. Chris was sure of that. But Chris knew that if this were the weight of Don Pescaro and the five Families, they would surely be having nervous breakdowns. This was just the work of a renegade. Chris didn't know when the weight of the families would start to fall on them, but he knew that they should get started sooner.

Chris knew that they weren't actually sending there own men to take these kids out, but Chris didn't know if these kids were actually trained by one of the families. That he would not be surprised by, but what he would be surprised to find out if…

He sighed from the aggravation, and became extremely tired. There were so many unanswered questions that made no sense, because if he found out the answer to that particular question there would be fifty more questions surrounding that answer. But he wouldn't worry about finding them, he was just so tired of searching for the truth, because now it was not in his hands.

"I don't know. But if there is trouble back home, somebody has to know. But only send family to find out, and I mean family. When you can't trust your friends, you can only turn to your family, remember that Frank. I know that A.J. is like family to me, but I don't want him to be deeper than he already is. It's cause I love him as much as a I love you, you know that, don't you?"

Frank knew those words far too well to even make a reply. He saw his eyes, and saw the determination to live radiate from his words.

"Remember that too Frank. Don't loose sight of your allegiance either, or your trust in him either. And agree with whatever decision he goes along with, but don't let him do anything by himself."

Frank just looked at him, and saw that he was growing extremely tired each second he was speaking, just as if his life was fading with each growing breath. His heartbeat raced, and when Frank set his hand over Chris's cold stone like hand, Frank nodded with a deeper appreciation for his friend and leader.

"I will." He said confidently, and when the two glanced at each other, hearing the footsteps following all too closely into the room, he shot his hand off of Chris's, when he heard A.J.'s gallivanting footsteps.

When Frank glanced around him and saw A.J. in full spirits with a cold drink in his hand. He saw that the can had been misty, and it hadn't been long since Chris set all the cards on the table for Frank. Tossing the drink into his other hand, he tapped the cold opening, making sure the fizz wouldn't explode, and loose half the drink. After he tapped on the opener, he slide his fingernail underneath the tab, and pulled it out with little to no force, like flicking a bug off his fresh unbitten arm.

When the tab broke the seal he left the tab sticking up, and a mist of twirling fizz shot out across the top and the air pushed against his arm like a gusher of water exploding into the air like a Great White rising to the surface, and forcing excess water from its blowhole.

A.J. would think of something very perverse and childish when he thought about that, but he didn't have time to think about plights of sexual thoughts. He treated every order that came from Chris like it was a message from God, and he had to carry it out to perfection. Standing beside Chris he saw his eyes yearning for the drink, but being that he was too weak to hold his arms up for long, "Can you get a straw?"

A.J. was still holding the green soda can, with a closing tightness, he stood in his place processing the information at lightening speed. He spied around the desk that had a plastic tray with a few food ridden plates that Chris or one of his guards must have ate for him in his deep sleep. It left a smell that made them think of a cafeteria floor, not outside the kitchen, but inside the steaming, pots and pans soapy smell, which was a sweet tingling disgusting smell. There were forks and knives laying across the plates, covered in a food that only resembled cafeteria style spaghetti dish that had been sitting in a freezer all night long, and then warmed up until it was mushy and warm enough to eat.

A.J. could tell from the piece of string spaghetti that had been hanging over the dish like it was a worm, but didn't want to imagine that was old cafeteria food filled with diseases and other harmful bacteria that would work his way into Chris's bodily fluids, and ultimately cripple him.

At that moment A.J. got a grip on his thoughts, and wrapped them up to the fact that the plate might have been a few days old, and it wasn't contaminated. A.J. eased his paranoia, and found a straw lying on the side of the plastic tray, with the paper already looking wet around one end of the straw. Seeing that this must have been the only straw he could find, and A.J. grabbed the straw, feeling the soft paper rub against his fingers, he shuddered from the feeling and set the can on the tray for a moment while he began to tear through the paper. Holding the paper he ripped through the seal, and pulled the paper downwards. The paper pulled halfway down from the top looked like an incredibly thin and long circumcised penis. A.J. laughed to himself, but then as the rest of the small plastic tube was becoming seen; he revealed the straws full self and with the paper in his other hand he balled the long piece of paper in his fist—squeezing it until it turned to dust.

Once when he heard the paper crinkle inside his palm, he let it go, and it fell on the tray looking like a snake's skin and the paper landed on its side. But then it fell flat looking like a card that had been squashed in between a giant's sweaty toes with fungus, and the paper had been reduced to mush like fungus. When he revealed the straw in it's original plastic form, long and naked with no color stripes running down the sides either. As he noted the specifics for some odd reason of curiosity, he grabbed the drink, and forced the plastic tube into the opening. The tube pushed upwards, riding the edge of the opening as it floated up towards the surface with it's crooked head pointed outwards.

"*Your drink, sir.*" A.J. said in a mock English accent, holding it out to Chris for him to take at his leisure.

Chris looked at him, and laughed from the rather weird gesture that reminded him of those English butlers in those Sherlock Holmes stories. Chris reached out, and took the drink from A.J.'s hands. The drink was still wet, and its perspiration was trailing down the can and leaped onto the blanket that was covering him. It left a small round spot that it looked identical to a small semen mark. Only he didn't want to think about that kind of stuff at that moment.

His eyes were filled with excitement, as a person who had been walking through the desert for hours, and when the first chance of water (or soda pop in Chris's case), the opportunity was too hard to miss.

Chris held the can out in front of his lips, and positioned the straw in front of his mouth for him to place his lips over the plastic tube. Grasping the tube with his lips, he breathed inwards inhaling the liquid through the straw sending a wave of soda against his tongue. "Ginger Ale." Chris thought, closing his eyes as he felt the liquid splash against his mouth giving his mind another pleasure that only reminded him of the crispest of water falling against his naked body, and against his face waking him up to the day that awaits him.

"Is it good?" A.J. said, watching with some strange awe about his lonely meditation that had transfigured him with calmness, and distant from the world around him.

Chris breathed inwards as he let his lips off of the straw—rolling his lips—and opened his eyes with a new taste in his mouth and a readiness to take on the world filled him with all the confidence that he needed. Only he hadn't been so transfigured that he had been ignorant of A.J.'s request.

Chris licked the corner of his mouth that had been forming with spit ever since he had drank the cool Ginger Ale that had rejuvenated his senses, and for that he was grateful in his choice of soda.

"Yes, it's good. I compliment you in your choice of soda." Chris handed him the drink, and as A.J. took it from him as he felt that the drink was already half way done. "He couldn't have finished the drink that quick." But A.J. found no reason to complain about that, maybe it was a good thing that he finished half the drink, maybe it was to let him know that he wasn't dead yet, and more alive than he thought he was.

"Why thank you." A.J. said, his voice sounding surprised but thankful, and he smiled with a content grin he placed the soda on the dresser next to the tray full of already eaten plastic cups and trays. A.J. ignored the tray again hoping to miss those ideas of the old school lunches that were just heated up from the day before, and swallowed the disgust leaving his saliva bitter. As A.J. moved around the bed, Chris took another glance at Frank, and saw that in his eyes he knew that his mission was laid out for him, and a whole new window had been opened in his mind. Also a lot of ideas had been boiling inside his brain, but they hadn't come to the surface until now.

And for that he wanted to thank Chris *milli grazie*, a thousands of times for his broad insight, and with everything laid out for him, he suddenly rose from his seat and burst out in a loud triumphant voice.

"I'll be right back," Frank said, sounding rather uncomfortable but his voice did not display that tense feeling in the pit of his stomach.

Only with his loud voice Frank caught the attention of A.J., Chris, and also Jessica, who had been aroused in her sleep with blinking eyes, and leaning out the seat with curious ears. She looked as if she had just woken up with a hangover, everything all misconstrued and squinting her eyes with the best of intentions to remember if she had done anything embarrassing, and then gave up the thought of trying, for no one that was completely wasted would ever remember what they did. Jessica looked at Frank, but could see that he did not see her with his back turned.

"What?" A.J. asked, eyes open and he moved to the edge of his seat as if he was about to follow him.

"I just have to make a phone call." Frank said, looking at A.J. and Chris. Only he could see that A.J. didn't want to go alone, but Frank had a mission. When Chris gave him that self assuring look to go and do it, Frank knew that he had to go alone, even if he didn't want to, he had to.

"Do you need any company?" A.J. said with a faint look in his eye that made A.J. ready for anything. His bottom was already off the seat, and when he was about to fall off of his seat Frank gave him a concrete answer.

"No." He said, sounding confident and detached from A.J., even though he bore no ill feelings towards him but Frank didn't want A.J. to interfere with his mission that Chris had set out for him to do. Frank was sure that each and every one of them had a quest, but with the help of Chris, now in full health to give out the orders again, Frank had a feeling that their chances were starting to change for the better.

"Okay. See you then." A.J.'s voice was tight, almost as if he had been insulted, but then laid back in his seat contemplating about who he was going to call, and why he needed to be alone. It curdled his stomach just to even think about the possibilities. *"Don't let the waves of deceit swallow you whole,"* the voice whispered to himself, and remembered what side Frank was on. So, he let the thought go, and felt his stomach untie itself from that knot he had been wrapped so tightly in.

Frank looked at them, and gave them all a farewell-for-now nod, and left the room with a clear head, and what he was about to do next was plain and simple. "All I need now is to find a pay phone." Frank said to himself as he left the room, and walked down the hall where a bunch of white and Hispanic nurses were all gathered around talking and laughing giddily about something they saw on television, lacking any recognition for reality around them. Frank ignored them, and kept on walking down the nicely painted hall, he turned at another corner and saw two open elevator doors revealing the insides of there cargo. While one was empty and a sign above it was an arrow pointing down had no people in it, he dived into the abandoned elevator and felt the doors slowly close behind him.

It was a rather comfortable rush, but he needed to get a hold of himself, and focus on his mission. When the doors finally closed he turned around to feel the emptiness of the elevator weigh down upon him. Loneliness and security, Frank loved it when he was alone, but when he saw the row of white buttons with many faded numbers from 1 to 8, he became confused for a moment, and tried to put it in perspective. He remembered that there had to be payphones located on every floor, but he might as well give A.J. a chance to talk about whatever he wanted to talk to Chris alone. As he surveyed the rows of buttons, he felt the elevator suddenly break from it's rock like position, shifting upwards slowly.

"Great." He thought as he heard elevator descending, and the light on the buttons looked like blinking Christmas lights as the illuminated and everything started to get hazy, and as a elevator pulled him upwards, he started to get a headache that didn't want to end. Only Frank felt that his headache was not attributed to anything else except to be on that, and had just remembered in the blink of an eye that he had wanted to go down, and the elevator was going upwards.

"Well, I'll see where this takes me." Frank said, and felt his body move upwards with his fears not too far away. Only he decided to let the elevator take him wherever it wanted to go, and from there, he would have to find a pay phone. But sooner than he started to think about what he was going to do, he felt the elevator come to a halt shaking his very bones, and the illuminated light stopped on the number four. When the elevator suddenly stopped, it gave a soft *ding*. This was a rather small important sound that let him know that the doors were opening, and the doors withdrew slowly revealing the next floor to him.

Chapter XX:

"A Secret in the Rabbit's Drug Den"

At the time the bell had rung, Berry and Jacob started to make there move away from there table, with his soldiers (or knights as he liked to refer them by) hovering all around them, Berry felt like they were some cloud hanging over him just waiting to pour down rains of fists if they didn't leave their masters sight for less than a minute.

Berry and Jacob, including his crowd moved down the hallway, and slipped around toward a double entrance that led to right side of the stadium, overlooking the basketball court and the other side of the gym that was opposite the other side where the freshman and sophomores sat. On the side that they were on was just extra space for any students that weren't juniors or seniors. But on the bottom where the pull out seats sprung out from one touch of a button is where the seniors and juniors sat, if that was supposed to be of any recognition. Front row seat for all the pep rallies and all the school functions that nobody really wanted to go to, if that was you were a senior that is, and in Berry's case, it felt like he would never see that day with his brother. He figured that if his brother was killed, he played with the thought that they would meet up at the end.

"Stop that!" Berry thought, and shuddered from the thought. "He would not want me to think something like that." Berry kept on following Jacob, and they kept on moving, to who the hell knows where.

As the two moved down a flight of stairs, which led to the basketball court, and whenever anybody stood in the middle of it, you could look down and see the footprints from kids in the last gym class from the weeks before. But they weren't headed to gym class or going to stand in the middle of the gym court, but to talk and Jacob knew the perfect place. Jacob and his black cloud of bodyguards moved through the other doors, and Berry didn't know where he was heading, but he didn't complain. Since they needed to be in private, they might as well as find the safest place possible to discuss hot news that had been circulating throughout the schools.

They headed down a flight of stone chipped stairs, and when they moved down the stairs, Jacob strode ahead of him as if he was trying to test him, but Berry kept up with his quickened pace. Jacob's lips smirked with bubble gum lips stretching his Cheshire cat grin, and maybe that was his aim, to scare him. When it seemed that they had been walking for forever, Berry wandered when he was going to stop, and even his knights said in an impatient tone, "Where the hell are we going?" And when Berry turned for a moment over his shoulder, he immediately identified the voice of that was from Clifford. His scratchy voice whined hoping to get some answer that got neither the attention of his brother, nor any attention of his knights. Berry felt a bit of sadness pinch him when he thought about the degrading levels of a human being could go.

"Possibly far lower than he could imagine." Berry thought as his feet kept on moving while his mind did the thinking. "To hell…maybe, just maybe?" He played around with the thought, but did not go onto think about it anymore after that.

As Jacob started to stride away from the group, he passed the auto-mechanics shop. He could hear the buzzing and whirring of the portable drills digging into the cars as students with greasy hands delved into cars, hoping to learn a trade in an honest job, but then become chop shop owners after they left.

"Such levels of corruption the young resort to become." Jacob thought, and saw his favorite spot to talk that was located across from the Junior Military Academy, which he thought was a place that only bred want-to be Nazi's, and real dick-heads that thought they were tough guys. "Just like Clifford." Berry thought, and wanted to laugh from it, but didn't, from over daunting fear.

As Jacob made his way toward the door, the sun moved over their heads and when they were covered by darkness, Berry felt comfortable to talk.

"So, what is it that you have called me here to talk about?" Jacob said, his blue eyes narrowing on Berry, waiting for an answer. Jacob tapped the person to the right of him, and put his two fingers together right up to his mouth, and made a blowing noise indicating that he wanted a smoke.

The boy (or knight) looked at him strangely at first, but then after two more seconds, the thought hit him in an instant. He reached down into his pockets and pulled out a pack of Marlboro Lights that were already open by how the box cover had been pushed back so much. Inside it were thirteen cigarettes packed against each other, sticks of death ready to be lit with a small white colored lighter. The knight held it out towards him, and Jacob grabbed the box and pulled out a cigarette. When he balanced the cigarette with his thin ashy lips, he held the lighter at the end of the cigarette and struck the flint. Jacobs thumb sent the flame rising from the small discharge, and breathed in all the tobacco that was traveling throughout his body, sending him the medication that would put him in the mood to think more properly.

"So…" Jacob said, muttering through the cloud of smoke that sifted from his mouth, and took the cigarette out of his mouth holding it in between his index and middle finger, almost ladylike. "What have we come all the way to my favorite place to talk about, Berry son of Mary and Joe Pantoliano." Jacob took another long breath of the cigarette—smoke flowed from his thin creased opening—and held out the box to Berry offering him a cigarette.

Berry saw the small box of tar, and refused his offer with a simple: "Nah, I'm fine."

Jacob nodded his head in compliance, and handed his bodyguard the cigarette box and the lighter a long with it. The boy took the pack of Marlboro's and the lighter very slowly, and stuffed it back inside his pocket. Once the Marlboro pack and lighter had disappeared from sight, Berry began to think of what kind of question that would sound appropriate to say, but he needed to get down to the nitty-gritty before they got caught by some unsuspecting teacher. The end of the cigarette was slowly burning the paper off the edges, and he used that as a time limit.

Berry cleared his throat, feeling his heart race as he had forgot the question that he wanted to ask without being forthright. Berry wanted to open his mouth, but he couldn't, and with his congested thoughts the smoke seemed to hinder him more than help him. Berry saw the ash on his end of his cigarette lessen as the fire began to tear at the paper around it. The smoke sifted from his mouth like fog on a winter morning, and the way the weather was going now, he thought that a blizzard were about to happen at any time. Only catching a cold would be the least of his problems, and if he didn't come out with something, Berry knew that Jacob might just walk away and abandon the entire thing.

Then out of the blue, the same scratchy voice that had greeted him with his uncontrollable foul breath had once again spoken out.

"What the hell man, did you go deaf all of a sudden?" Clifford said, piercing through the hovering group, like a knife scraping across the top of a wooden floor, and all of the crowds heads turned around toward the source of that sound. That was definitely a no-brainer. They cleared a path for the scratchy tone, acne filled, skeleton face, shit breathing nuisance look upon the two with his lazy left eye squinting to look at them as if he had some super powers, trying to read his mind, and get him to show his weaknesses.

"GET FUCKED you dog breath, shit stained lookin' motherfucker!" Berry thought to himself, boosting his courage, he hoped that he was reading his mind at that moment. *"Yeah, I said it. Go get fucked with a dirty dildo, and brush your teeth with Pitbull shit! I hope you are reading my mind now."*

The two eyed each other for a few seconds: Clifford's lazy eye twitched as he stared with a ravenous intensity that made Berry uneasy but it was time Berry needed to put this piece of shit down to his own level. Because if he didn't do anything now there was no telling when or if he would stop blabbering.

"No, but did you ever learn that when people aren't talking to you, you should close your mouth." It wasn't harsh, but if he hadn't said a thing, he wouldn't hear the end of it, and wouldn't appear tough to them.

"You got to have respect to get respect." He thought, and felt triumphant with that. But when Berry finished shooting back at Jacob's insane brother, Clifford's lazy eye began to twitch again, almost as if his eye was about to explode right out of his socket, and fall right in front of him. Only if that eye were to ever pop out of that socket, Berry's temptation to stomp on that eye was a growing pulse in his thoughts. But this thought was not something to toy around with for long.

Only this caught the attention of Jacob, and his voice rose up like the tide crashing against a sandy beach, howling up into the wind like a silent death call. "Well put," Jacob's tone was flat, and demeaning towards his brother. "He's never been too bright about keeping his mouth shut around guests."

His bold blue eye gazed against Clifford's one lazy and wide green eye. In the one eye he was afraid, and when he opened his mouth and started to say something, but then all that came out of his mouth was one pathetic whine from his ashy quivering lips. As his bony hands began to shake as he slapped them against his pants, trying to calm himself down.

Only it wasn't working, and as he saw his brother's demeaning eye, he heard that croaking sound coming from Jacob's throat again. He hated that beating sound that came from his throat, that gurgling blood curdling sound that made Clifford's blood shivering from the way his blood traveled through his face. It wanted him to go crazy, but that was just the missing addiction that wasn't coursing through his blood. Oh, how he wanted his Heroin who was his heroin, the love of his life and the only one who could calm him down when he was filled without her in his blood. Then again, finally beaten down by the reality of his brother's demeaning tone, he bowed his head, and began talking to himself again, in defeat.

With Jacob's brother momentarily defeated, and at a great cost to their time, Berry saw this as an important time to get the answers to the questions, because the cigarette was almost half done. "What the hell is that noise?" The question was bold, and direct, but as distracting as it sounded with that raspy sound just begging to be cleared, but maybe that had something to do with the faded slash mark across the top of his neck, just residing above his Adam's apple.

Only now, his questions needed to be answered, and he dove straight into the conversation, head first. Everyone was waiting for him to answer him.

Gene took a deep breath and tried to find the right words to say, and it came out of his mouth like a tidal wave, cleaning the tarnishes on his soul. "What I came here to ask you is…do you know about the beef between Chris Mangini's family and Gene's crew?" Berry wanted to add the word renegade after Gene, but he didn't want to send off any red alarms to anyone inside the group that sympathized with that bastard's crew.

Berry's face turned gray, and as he flicked the ashes off the end of the cigarette, he shook his head in a disagreeing manner, as if he had been offended. Jacob lowered his cigarette, and scratched the middle of his clear, pasty forehead. He looked mentally stressed as he rubbed his eyes together, trying to clear the headache from his mind.

After a momentary second of rubbing his eyes the smoke twirled around his eyes, and burned against with a rage that made his eyes water and his throat tickle with an pleasurable hatred. As he laid his thumb over his end of the cigarette flicking more ashes from his burning stick he raised his head back as he forced his curly sun blonde hair jump across of his shoulders like a dangling spider.

Looking at Berry with his bright blue-blazer eyes of judgement that made Berry uncomfortable, but it was also uncomfortable for Jacob too, because everyone that was somebody was always going to ask questions, but these were questions that he didn't know a single fucking thing about.

Finally coming out with his answer, he replied with a rather aggressive, yet calm response. "You know…" Jacob said scratching his head out of anxiety, and then breathing out in a long uncomfortable sigh, "I was once told that you should never talk about things that might offend people, because people don't know any better today about what they should and shouldn't talk about."

"Shit, he's found me out" Berry thought, feeling his heart begin to over pump a mass amount of blood into brain filling him with a striking reaction to Jacobs response. But, he didn't sense that he was a sympathizer with Gene, but he decided to stop thinking, and just get it out while he could.

"What do you mean, by what I just said right before?" Berry asked innocently, questioning his motives. Whether he was trying to sound remorseful or not, Jacob's voice remained the same, but it sounded wise in some very unapologetic way.

"Exactly…" Jacob said, raising the cigarette back toward his mouth, he inhaled one last bit of tar on the cigarette, and threw it beside his foot. After the cigarette landed on the concrete with the smoke pushing out from the paper, he raised his foot, and quickly stomped out the cigarette butt as he ground it into smoldering paper. Raising his foot off of the cigarette, he cleared his throat, but had that obvious gurgling building up in his throat.

"Well, I guess I don't have to worry about being fast today." Berry thought comfortably.

After Jacob made a loud snorting sound, and hawking up a loogie in the patch of grass right next to his foot, looking like a lob of what he would call "loogie sperm" becoming unimportant, staining the concrete, and dry out in no time at all. After he cleared his throat Jacob continued on with the rest of his sentence, if he would choke on his own spit before he even started his sentence.

"As I was saying…" He took a moment to prepare his sentence, and then burst out with… "*Exactly,* because what you just asked me now is a question that I can not answer, Berry son of Joe and Mary, and it makes me angry because everybody, including some of my knights are wondering the same thing that you asked me. But let's get some things straight, I know nothing, and even if I did, I would not tell even you or my own knights because of we will be left in the dust for even prying." He took another deep breath, and felt a trail of goosebumps popping up along his neck, making the wound in his neck ache like a frog's croak, "my God it would be catastrophic."

Berry was taken back, and certainly was filled with sorrow for what he had said; but somewhere inside was certainly forcing him to accept his answer without pitying his frail demeanor, but he couldn't help but see the confusion and anger that arose from Jacob's mouth. But two things arouse a certain sense of suspicion because he just changed the subject, and veered toward another whole subject at large. He wanted him to keep talking some more, and see if he would say anything that might give some information away.

Only as soon as he was about to go on questioning him, he burst out, "I'm sorry," sympathetically and surprisingly, "but did I offend you just now by asking that question?"

Jacob looked at him with a reverence that pinched Berry conscience attracting his attention to him, and he shook his head with confidence as he replied. "No, it's just that's the question I am being asked everyday and it is pissing me off to have every John Q student coming up to me and asking that, like I'm God or something!" He sighed as he wiped the forming sweat from his forehead, and cleared his throat from the smoke that made him gargle, but it was from that damn wound that ultimately gave him the worst problems.

Berry looked at Jacob who had swallowed the forming spit in his throat hearing him make those small but noticeable clicking noises. But before Berry could lay everything down on him Jacob interrupted as Berry opened his mouth.

"Also, I know you are asking yourself why the hell I am making that noise."

Berry was taken back, and slowly frowning he came back with a dumb, unnoticing look at his throat. Jacob could see, and knew that his clicking sound that made him feel like a ticking bullfrog that swallowed a tiny stick of dynamite.

"You know what the hell I am talking about…" Jacob felt the patch that was holding his wound together itching his throat making his breaths raspy and construed, almost like a dry cough tickling his throat.

With a constrained gesture, he moved his neck upwards, and pointed to a long faded cut that almost looked like a stretch mark that ended just right above his Adams apple. It made Berry cringe as he heard his finger hit against his neck making a soft *thwacking* sound. Berry didn't really notice it at first, but maybe the clicking sound that his throat made had something to do with the cut that was just above his Adam's apple.

"You've been trying not to look at it since you saw it." He lowered his neck as the long slice mark bulged against his bronze boned skin. "I won't tell you how I got that mark, but I will say that I got this because of what I said before. People don't know what's appropriate to say anymore, and you can put two and two together about what I said before."

Berry thought about what he had said, and it all made sense, but it clearly did not settle in until he saw that long mark in its gargantuan form. Only then Berry had then decided to change the subject.

Although Jacob had changed the subject a long time ago, Berry had not of forgotten about what Jacob had said before. "Catastrophic…to his soldiers…and…" He had forgotten part of what he had said, but the reason why those words stuck out to him was that his words had signaled a red flag—a certain memento of anxiety and paranoia, "What would happen to his knights, *if he knew?*" Berry had a suspicion growing in his mind that Jacob had known something, or was at least not telling him about it. Then with confidence building up in his gut, he came back with another question.

"Listen, I know you do not want to get involved, but the shit storm is already upon us, and if…"

Berry was about to add the word *we* at the end of his sentence, thinking about A.J. and his allegiance but stopped his mouth immediately. "I understand that you don't want to be involved."

Jacob, throughout the entire conversation said nothing, probably contemplating what he wanted to say, cocked his head upwards, and just shook his head in compliance that he understood what he was talking about, but felt the next part strike him the hardest, and unexpectedly.

"But I can't go on from here and quit now, because someone is going to say something, and I got to act on it. No hard feelings, nothing against you and your knights, trust me. But I have a problem with this person, and I think I and a few people need to handle it in whatever way needs to be dealt with, because if it's not going to be dealt with sooner or later, it's going to be contagious."

"It already is!" Jacob wanted to add, but contained himself from digging his hole even further that he had already dug up so he could lie inside, and cover himself in brown dirt and feces for the worms to feast on. The thought of it just made him shutter, but then he didn't know if he really believed in a heaven or not, but when the days would be slim, he would find out what he will believe sooner or later.

Another long silence ran through them as if they were about to draw weapons and as the silence purveyed, the group became more anxious, standing around as if they were about to piss in there pants.

"Well, Berry son of Mary and Joe." Jacob took another long uncomfortable breath as his raspy throat. "You have made your point clear to me, and for both of our sakes, we don't want to be caught by any unsuspecting teachers trying to sneak a cigarette in while the kids are busy sleeping."

Berry nodded his head, and whole heartily agreed with what he was saying, but knew that Jacob was not telling him everything, and if he was, he still knew something that he was not going to tell him. It was like 50 Cent said in a song blatantly titled "Fuck you"; a line stood out to him about this situation, and the line started out with *"Keep street shit in the street, so keep it on the low, but anybody who is somebody already know!"* Berry agreed with the last part of the line, and that was very true right at that particular moment.

Berry nodded his head, and in a disappointed good-shot-but-no-cigar kind of attitude; it was time to leave this wild goose chase before all of them got caught.

Berry raised out his hand, and said cordially, "Well...Jacob Barley, I want to thank you for answering my question, and I'll leave you to your business."

Jacob looked at him with those blazing blue eyes, and gripped his hand around his fingers. While both of them were pressing his ashy palm into each other's, clearly proclaiming there peace between each other that out of every knight that saw this handshake, one of them was disgusted by this peaceful handshake.

Like a slithering snake, Clifford watched from between two knight's shoulders with his good eye open that it boiled so much that he couldn't hear the rest of what Berry was saying, and all that he could hear was the beating of his own heart. His heart began to pulsate from his chest as he saw their hands rubbing there sweat on there hands. Once he had disappeared from sight, the meeting had only last for ten minutes, the Outcasts were still dumbstruck from the way the entire thing ended. Not with a whimper, or a bang, just a *sploooosh*. Everyone of them knew what was going on between Chris and Gene's factions, but the thing that made them worry was from what Berry had told them took them off by surprise. Even Jacob knew that Gene had recruited a few of their men for the hit on A.J. and Frank. Only another question that was on there minds was what Jacob's decision on whether bodying this man before any opposition took place against Gene. Now, Jacob even knew that they were supporting Gene out of fear, and overall Jacob knew that was the worst decision that they had ever made throughout there entire existence as a circulating gang.

If word ever got around that they helped Gene with the attempted assassination on A.J. and Frank, it would be disastrous. For all of them because if A.J. had Frank and Berry on his side, Jacob and all of them knew that it mean their lives—they were all dead men—end of story.

But the question that came out of a familiar antagonistic voice, which seemed to be the ominous voice that no one liked to hear, was from Jacob's own flesh and blood, Clifford. And with that voice, also came trouble.

"Bro!" Clifford called out from between the two soldiers, pushing his weak body through them as if he was a small piece of sperm pushing through the embryo skin, trying to reach the egg first, and hopefully redeem his brother's honor.

Jacob saw his brother, and shook his head in a disrespected manner, as if he didn't have to wait for him to say another word. Jacob gave him that long stare, as he finally stood in front of him as Clifford caught his cold, indifferent stare.

"What is it?" Jacob said, looking around at his knights, and let out a long sigh that only meant that he was tired, and no more bullshit was going to be accepted past this point. He remembered what his brother did for him, and his selfish pride was not going to fuel a war that they could not afford. It wasn't as if Clifford had come out without any physical injuries; his left eye had drooped down lazily because of the beatings that he had taken.

Jacob stood within two feet from his face, and with his ashy crusted lips, disrespectful spit poured from his mouth. "Are you just gonna' let that guy go man, he's going to come back and kill us man. Every one of us!" It was not until the last part his knights became very interested in the conversation, and there eyebrows began to slant and nub foreheads moving backwards in shock, as if this hadn't dawned on them already, but he was just stating the obvious for the other misguided sheep. Jacob saw that his knights had to know that this was nothing, but no one wanted to disagree with Clifford either, because he was insane, and no one wanted to mess with an insane person. An insane person will do anything to get their way; fight, yell, scream, and do anything to get there way just like a spoiled child would do when they wanted there favorite GI Joe doll or a Cabbage Patch doll. Only Jacob was not going to stand for his brothers ranting and ravings right now, too much shit was on the line for him to fuck it up.

"I don't care what you think we should do, you are not the leader of this brotherhood." He pushed his brother aside, and stood in front of a rather large, but acne faced boy, and looked him dead in the eye, putting a hand over his shoulder.

He said, with a painful croak. "I want you all to witness me say this now, because I don't want anyone to get anything confused, or *be* confused about what has just happened."

At that moment, everyone in the group abandoned paying attention to Clifford, as they should have done, and intensely stretched there eyelids open revealing their blistering pimples against the domes of their heads as if they were saluting his good effort.

Jacob slowly took his hand off of the knights shoulders, and the knight looked at his shoulder as if he had been touched by God, and Jacob continued on, "This boy is not our enemy. I want everyone to know this. No one touches Berry Pantoliano, do you hear me. I warn you now that if I find out from anyone that one of you harmed him or any of his family, there will be consequences, do you understand me."

Jacob felt the patch in his throat making that small clicking noise, even though it was annoying to his knights, they said nothing to anger him as he placed his right hand against his clicking throat, and heard the small clicking noise die down very slowly.

"Yes, master." A few of the soldiers said.

As the clicking noises suddenly died down in his throat he felt ready to talk again and felt cool saliva soothing the patch, which made everything so fucking complicated in the way he talked.

Clifford heard the pain that made his life miserable for Jacob, and he relished in the fact that he was in pain. He was a bit of a sadist when it came to that, but he hoped to God that he was in lots and lots of pain.

"I will make sure I will make an example out of any one of you. As much as I care for you, *the punishment* will be extreme. As far as you have come to know me, believe my words. The words are protected, but the words will not protect you."

Clifford, at this very moment, could feel every bit of his hatred burning in his system as he grabbed his chest to make the blow that Jacob had made stop just for a minute or two. "Boosting your ego, isn't it, you little bitch!" Clifford thought "I bet you would kill me if you had the chance, *your own brother?*" He could feel his heart beating against his ribs as if he had pushed his bones out of place, and as he breathed in deep, all he was thinking about was to get in his brother's face and hit him for pushing him aside. But he couldn't, he was stuck in his own hurt and anguish, rendered powerless from speaking up.

Once Jacob was done with his speech, he took a break to let the patch in his throat stop making that annoying sound, and hopefully give him the momentum at the end of his ominous warning.

"I'll make an example out of you." He said to himself, but then felt like he was some ridiculous villain out of some Scooby Doo rerun. Only he was now focused on another task, and that was full filling his need of Heroin—*Crank, Horse, Jive*—or whatever he called it, into his system. He felt a tingling chill flow up and down his arms whenever he thought about it, as if it seemed pretty sound to him for a moment. Hell, it felt right on all occasions, plus it was an addiction that he couldn't, and wouldn't kick. He had already stuck himself twice today, and he found out that he could go four times a day, just to fill his need.

"After we leave, I'll get my addiction stick from my locker, and I'll go into one of the bathrooms, and take a ride on the magic carpet." He felt corny thinking about it that way, but he didn't care about what he was doing to his body, all he needed was his "only one," his Heroin to save him from this knifing anguish. He started to get a little antsy thinking about it, and as his brother turned to him, he saw his lips moving, but he couldn't hear the words. It seemed as if someone put him on mute, and all he could do was just lip-sync what he was trying to say. It was no use to try and figure out what he was saying, and for fear that he might see what he was really thinking, what really lie in his still beating heart.

Clifford watched his lips move, and saw that he was becoming aggravated, and wanted to hear a response. Clifford thought that he must have been saying, "Do you understand?" but he wasn't sure. Only he had to take this fact into consideration that Jacob wanted to be in control, so he decided to give him the benefit of the doubt because on the inside, he never really did what his brother told him to do.

"I understand." He said, or he thought he said, but he didn't hear his lips saying these words. But when he saw his brother's defensive stare fade away, and as he shook his head toward the school he added "Let's go."

Jacob looked at him confused, but then Jacob just shook his head out of impatience, and walked away with anger. Then not too far after he left his group, his knights immediately followed after him, just looking at Jacob with a certain disdain that only held hatred in there eyes was. But they wouldn't say anything.

As they moved away Clifford yelled, "What are you looking at?" but none of them replied, and just scoffed at him as they walked away toward Jacob, who was already heading up the stairs, and less than two people were behind him as he reached the top of the hill. Clifford legs went limp, and his entire body was dead to his allegiance and saw his brother staring down the hill as if he was a hawk watching everything happening over a hundred miles. Only he knew was ignoring his own brother standing underneath the shadow, all alone and under the shadow of his own personal eclipse. He saw his brother's blonde hair blowing in the wind, and pressing against his ashy white skin as if it would come off with one single blow. Clifford wanted Jacob to look at him, and wave him on to come and follow him.

Clifford looked up at him, and then thought, "Oh, so that's how it's going to be." His mouth went dry as if he had thirsted for hours, although his mind was clear and open as the sea was at the first hint of sea sludge. Everything was so clear to him at that moment, they were to be enemies now, and he wouldn't regret it.

He saw him glance around him then caught one glance of his brother, but looked past him as if he didn't see him at all, like he had forgotten somebody. Then when his crew charged slowly up the steps, Clifford headed through the door, and looked at his brother no more.

When the doors slowly opened the bright artificial light that reflected off the slick lobby floor—rushing out of the small deathtrap—it looked like someone was acting like him on the other side of the floor almost replicating his moves. And as he glanced down at the floor, he almost felt the urge to fall over become mesmerized by the slick linoleum mirror of death. But when he brought his eyes back toward the hall, and away from the floors death-defying balance beam, he looked around the walls to find any kind of directions can give him an inkling to where they can point him in the right direction.

But what direction was right these days? To get philosophical, there were many choices but he knew that there was only one, and he knew he was too deep to turn back now.

Ignoring this thought his eyes searched endlessly across the blue tinted walls, seeing a large rectangle picture of the Hudson Bridge with the Twin Towers between a crescent moon. The buildings were a pride of New York that had outdone any size and stature of any production in America. Once he passed that picture, there was another picture of a painting that had half of a sun looking over what looked like an sunrise on a chilly Portland morning. Then there were pictures of animals that were consistently of ducks, Labrador dogs with long mangy hair, and a long straight mouth. Looking at it for a moment, he felt immersed in all the textures of the drawings; the curved motion lines, the dog's rather harmless, but amused look in his eye. When he thought about what that dog could be saying to him with that one haunting glance, he stopped thinking about it.

After he stopped looking at the pictures for a moment, shaking off that haunting vibe of death kept on moving down the hall, ignoring more of the rather positive pictures he searched for another more obvious sign that would lead him in any kind of direction toward the pay phones.

Frank turned another corner, and the smell of chlorine filled his senses, almost weakening him with a rather rancid smell he felt his body being pushed back a bit, and a large body stood in a disturbed pace. Frank saw a rather clean white coat, and a identification picture of a rather large brown cheek man with long wavy hair that almost looked like a toupee, and a small rounded nose. A certain weird feeling passed through him for a moment as he had felt the man's large gut pushing onto his shirt.

He stood back for a moment and looked upwards at the man who looked exactly like the person in the picture, although with some minor pimples trailing up and along his right cheek. It was the man's voice that took him off guard, and it was a rather hoarse and strained voice.

"Excuse me!" The doctor said, and then began to move around him in a subtle embarrassed walk, and his white cheeks pushed up in a smirk.

But Frank saw this as an opportunity to grab him, and ask where the available pay phone would be. "It wouldn't be that hard, to ask for help." Frank thought instantly, and grabbed the man's large arms. The doctor turned toward him, and looked Frank in his eyes as he said, "Can I help you?"

Frank looked him in the eyes, and stood back for a moment, as if he was about to attack him like a rabid dog. Frank thought that he wasn't grabbing him that hard, but felt the sweat forming inside the palms of his hands. He felt the blood rushing through his veins, and as he loosened his grip his hand returned to his side, and said with a constrained voice. "Do you know where the pay phones are?"

The doctor gave him a strange look, and cocked his head; his eyes narrowed, and his bushy eyebrows flailed upwards as he turned his head away, and pointed his finger down the hall, "Take a left," the doctor said in a hurry, "and take the next right. You won't be able to miss them."

Frank heard his directions, and felt like a fool for not using his own intuitions. He should have just traveled a little bit longer, but he wasn't sure, and there should have been no fault for just asking for a hand. Frank watched the doctor's hand fall back down to his side, and Frank said, earnestly and truthfully, "Thank you."

The doctor turned toward Frank one more time, and then gave him a small nod as he walked away from him, not out of ignorance or self-indulgence, but perhaps out of the smallest inkling of sincerity within this burly doctor.

The doctor walked away without even looking at him again, and as Frank was left without a clue, another hopeful thought came to his mind, and it burst from him, as if he had sprung upon an epiphany underneath a shallow rock.

"Well, that wasn't that hard." He breathed in again, and flew down the next hallway, and took that next right without question. When the blue wall suddenly turned into a shade of milky white magnesia, he saw what he was looking for, and stopped for a moment to thank someone above him for guiding him in the right direction. He looked up at the white plaster walls, and said his thanks. When he lowered his head he moved toward the first phone that he saw, picked up the receiver, pressing it against his ear, he shoved the quarters in, and dialed with the quickest touch his finger could do.

He knew whom to call, and his cousins were the best candidates for the job. "Only family." He thought as he dialed the number, and almost frantically pressing extra buttons just out of anxiety. Frank breathed in and out slowly as the dial toned ringed in his ear just like that of the tortuous bell that told everyone that class was over, and their test was going to begin.

"Class is over." Frank said to himself humorously as the dial tone ringed for another few more seconds.

Just before Frank placed his call, Jerry and Niccolo Rossi were both sitting on their couch acting bored, but really self-satisfying in their peaceful bee's nest. Jerry wanted to get a cigarette in his room, but he didn't want to get up. Whether it was out of boredom or it was just laziness, he didn't care at that point. Niccolo had mentioned earlier that he had wanted to get something to eat, but he didn't want to get up to eat either. It was as if boredom had entered into their souls, and they didn't want to even do the things that gave them pleasure. What they used to do on the streets at first felt pleasurable, almost sensual, and they wanted to get up and collect their money. But, it just felt like a job after the first few times. Of course, it paid them lots of money for there mother to pay the bills, but it was like nothing had been fun about it now—it was just business.

Nothing, nada, zip, Fin, Finito. It was just like a regular grind—everyday bullshit but tomorrow, they would have to get back in the grind making these punks squeeze a quarter out of there asses if they could shit money. But they wanted to answer a call to arms, in retaliation to the attack on Chris's life. Only they didn't know a damn thing about what was going on, because no one was really saying anything.

"I want to do something!" Jerry's voice almost sounded bored in a nutshell.

Niccolo looked at him, and said impulsively, "*Come'?*" which meant "what" in Italian.

Jerry gave him a sarcastic look and replied, "You heard me. I want to do something."

Jerry just turned his head, and looked back up at the ceiling, with its white chipped alabaster. "There are prostitutes not far from here."

Niccolo lightly shrugged, and then let out a raucous laugh that only meant that sex meant nothing to him, except for humor's sake. But, he always appreciated humor here and there. But, right now, he was actually serious.

Niccolo wiped down his face—his face was covered in sweat—as if to put his serious face back on, and replied, "No, I wished we actually got a phone call from Frank right now man."

Jerry nodded, agreeing with his brother, "Yeah, I would like to talk to him."

He stopped; obviously realizing something had been missing since that night on the docks. But, since the assassination on Chris Mangini's life, he obviously knew that a war was starting between him and the traitorous Gene. He never really liked Gene before, like the slithering snake creeping through the long blades of grass, waiting for his perfect time to strike. This was the perfect time to prove their loyalty.

"And he had made his first blow!" Jerry almost became angry, but then clenched his teeth together, as if he did not want to jinx their chances. It felt like a curse to almost breathe a word about it, because everything was taking its toll, a downward spiral into the toilet of crushed and hopeless dreams. There were rumors floating around that Chris Mangini was finally dead and the new age was seeing its end as it approached the real millennium.

But when he was just about to give up all hope, and take his own downward spiral into the depression of his own toilet, the house phone suddenly filled the apartment house like a hideous music chord. It made Jerry's heart skip a beat, and he felt his leg jump as if someone had hit it with one of those small medical hammers. Jerry's breath quickened as he turned toward his brother, Niccolo, who had not even been affected, or taken off guard by the ringing chimes.

"You want to get that?" Jerry said.

Niccolo turned toward him and his eyes rolled over to the side as he said with the same unchangeable boredom, "No…do you?"

Jerry looked at him disgusted, even though he did not want to get up, he punched his brother in the arm—not really hard enough to leave a mark—but it was hard enough to make his rather large arm shake as if he had punched

The Disintegrating Bloodline

into a body of rocks. But Niccolo laughed it off as he rose off the couch, and then brushed off his arms as if he hadn't been affected at all.

After he brushed off his shoulder, Niccolo moved with a stride as his shoulders shifted up and down, what the moolies would say a few blocks over would be a "pimp-walking." Maybe it was how he carried himself, but Jerry would let that go for now. He just wanted him to answer the phone without taking so much of his time. The ringer made it's deadly sound again, and when he finally approached the phone, it rang another time as it made Jerry push himself up along the sunken couch. He could feel his own blood rushing through his ass again as if he had been sitting on a large furnace, and it had made a real impression into his bottom, and all the way up his back. The pressure seemed to be leaving his system as he laid his hand across the worn out, cut up armrest, as the open cotton rubbed the bottom of his arms, tickling him as his fingers tapped the edge of the armrest, waiting for him to pick up the phone.

The phone rung another time and his patience were diminishing, and he couldn't wait a minute longer until that blasted ring would end.

"Will you pick up the fucking phone, please!"

"Fuck you!" Niccolo screamed from the kitchen, and with a certain amount of power behind his voice as the fourth ring died instantly, and Niccolo was off in his own world from the moment he said, "Hello?"

Jerry's head fell back on the cushion, and he yelled "Thanks, you fuck!" His voice was thankful, although he sounded sarcastic to no end, just like the brother that he was.

Suddenly, Jerry heard Niccolo's voice quieting down a whole lot more. He hadn't done that for a long time, and Jerry's ears suddenly began to tune in, hopefully to catch every word that he was saying to the person. But if Niccolo was whispering, he couldn't stand a chance to catch a word of the conversation, because he was quieter than a mouse eating a piece of cheese (when he wanted to be). But, ignorant of the possibilities of who he was talking to, Jerry just went ahead with his gut reaction, and tuned in even deeper to the conversation. Like a satellite dish, he ears were definitely catching a part of the conversation.

An **order**, according to the Webster's New World Dictionary, is a social position or rank in position. Secondly, it meant a state of peace and serenity; observance of the law; orderly conduct. It almost meant that it was a sequence or arrangements of things or events; series, succession. Another definition meant that it was a fixed or definite plan; system; law of arrangement. There were many definitions for the word order, but Jerry knew what he had to do. "Follow an order so that a sequence of events would be right." He thought to himself as Frank ended his conversation, but then before he hung up Jerry asked him if he had found anything interesting to call him back and let him know what he knew.

After being on the phone for five minutes long with both brothers, Frank had felt that there time had been held up for far too long. He had delivered his assignments to both of the brothers, and he deliberately hung up the phone. It made a rather sharp pang of a tune from the machine as a *clinkity-clink* sound of the money swirled throughout the ringing box.

Walking away from the box, he stormed back down the hallway, his heart was filled with so much energy that his walk turned into a light run. Darting down the hallways he approached the elevators, without loosing one single breath. He pressed a white button that had a black arrow that lit up faster than a Christmas light on the fritz and on the verge of exploding into a small ball of fire that would turn that tree resemble a large burning cross. But he stopped, tapping his feet against the floor and waited for the elevator to get to his floor. His breath pace began to lessen as his heart did the same as he watched the numbers on top of it slowly lighting up, almost as if someone was personally stopping at all the floors so that he couldn't get on. He began to tap his right foot rapidly—shifting his body left and right—as he waited for the elevator to stop on his floor.

But then as the neon light highlighted over the number

5

he remembered that he was on the level above where Chris was, and that was three. And he heard the machinery edging up the wires as if it was out of an old mummified tomb, and was very likely to break like a twig if it moved the wrong way. As it moved closer he heard the mechanical sounds stop letting off a screeching sound that really resembled unhealthy brakes as it stopped in front of him, and the neon light highlighted number

3

it let off a soft ding as the metallic doors suddenly slid open for him again.

After the phone line went dead for more than two seconds, Jerry slowly hung up the phone, and turned around, trying to find out where his brother disappeared off to. In his case he found him sitting in a chair, already attacking a cigarette halfway, glancing out the window in deep thought as he pulled the cigarette from his mouth, and slowly moved his thumb across the wet filter. As the burning stick moved up and shook the ashes off the stick as if he was brushing the dandruff off his hair, he rested his hand down—with the cigarette in between his index and forefinger—a long face that made him knew this was serious.

"What just happened?" Jerry exhaled a deep breath, letting off a certain amount of confusion that was twirling his system.

Niccolo caught his brother's voice, and the smoke sifted from his mouth like a fog after a hard night of rain pounding against black concrete. Only on the ground, he could see the reflection of the city's lights on the streets, reflecting the inner turmoil in his soul. "Don't ask. Don't even ask."

Jerry looked at him with his eyebrows narrowing, and turned toward the window to try and listen to the next random conversation that would pass by his alley. He licked his lips, and felt the tar clinging to the top of his mouth, like tar sticking to a piece of green grass.

"Well, we have an order." Niccolo said, as he took another puff of the cigarette, "And that's what we follow, orders," blatantly causing more damage with every breath he was taking in. Staring off at the walls, clearing his mind of all his fears and doubts, he was mentally readying himself for what he was about to follow, almost praying to God in a sense, only he wasn't going to be doing God's work. He was going to be following Frank's orders.

Jerry heard this word being told so condescendingly, but he chose to ignore it. After a while, he started to hate the idea of taking orders, but remembered that he had Frank's back, and he had a past with Frank that he could not erase with the most durable eraser on a number 2 pen. But when he thought about it, no eraser could ever forget about what he had built now, and he could feel his knuckles swelling from the shit that he had to do to get where he was. Even though he watched his brother finish the last bit of the cigarette, he didn't want to see him leave and it would be weird for him to leave without his brother beside him watching his back. Only Frank talked to him, and only him, about what he was supposed to do, not Niccolo and Frank, just him.

"Are you going to be okay without me?" Jerry asked Niccolo, who looked comfortable enough to go without any weapon at all, looked at Jerry, his brother and said in a rather calm, cool professionalism that Jerry had never heard him express before.

"Yeah, I'll be fine. We both have to do our own thing, and if we do things right, we'll see each other before the night's over."

Jerry nodded, accepting the orders that they had to follow, listening to the words that they might see each other again at the end of the day. Then

Jerry thought about it again, and remembered that if they hadn't been killed yet, Jerry began to believe that they might actually see each other again. But he guessed that they were both dead in a way, before they had even walked out the door.

"Yeah, I guess you're right." Jerry retorted, and another long silence fell in between them.

But when Jerry thought about it more deeply, the world was made up of random ass situations, and chances are if they didn't see each other before the night was over, it wasn't up to them.

"I guess we are all dead men." Jerry thought morosely, although it hurt Jerry too much to leave first, Niccolo rose from the chair with his long khaki's stretching out over his Van shoes, with the shoelaces tucked in the opposite sides of the tongue and said, "I think it's time we should leave."

Niccolo dusted off his shirt, and moved past the rather beaten down stove, and the cheap wood color finishing. He felt like his brother was going to staple his feet to the ground before they would ever leave. When he passed his brother, they did not look at each other, it wasn't out of disrespect, it was so that they wouldn't say anything more sentimental, and it just hurt them too much to say anything more. Niccolo was like that a lot of the times, but it was different now.

Jerry looked at his brother as he passed him by, and felt his words bring out the truth in this uncomfortable situation. Maybe he had to go first, because Jerry wasn't strong enough, but this entire thing felt odd to them. Even though Niccolo would never admit it, he still would dive headfirst into the storm if Frank asked them to go. But, everything was just hitting them like a major headache, and they had no Tylenol or Advil to suppress the confusion in this room.

For that, he was glad that his brother had made the first move. He smiled to himself, thanking his brother for being stronger than he was at this particular moment. He heard the door slowly close behind him, and not another word was spoken between them.

After he had heard the door slam, Jerry looked toward the door that he had watched his brother use so many times, and wanted to yell "Good luck!" But couldn't, and felt transfixed in his own sad confusion.

The words escaped him, but he couldn't stand to even breathe it beyond a whisper. And so he said it, out loud, just as he was walking down the steps. "Good luck!" He felt his eyes beginning to water up, and his throat slowly began to choke from how bad he had wanted to cry. He nose began to tickle, even though a thought of sadness was starting to poke at him, stuffing the thought away, even if it hurt him to do it.

A few hours after the meeting between Berry and Jacob Barley and the Outcasts, Berry was already off to his class that he was late for. His first class of the day was eleventh grade Math, and the teacher that was teaching it was the most boring…well, not so boring because she was old, anorexic, and would have paid money just to see if she was about to cry. He had always entertained the thought that she was some commercial Taco Bell dog always ready to explode from her mouth, "Taco Bell!" And what was even scarier was he had a dream that her head was the dog's head with a little bow tie, and she was talking to him. He had actually brought that dream back up in his mind while he was in class, just to keep his eyes open.

But then he started to hear Jacob's words coming back into his mind again, and when he was about to say something, he had almost started off saying something like "My dear lady, that answer to the problem is…" Berry, son of Joe and Mary, almost said, and stopped himself before he opened his mouth. A few kids in class saw him raising his hand, and chuckled playfully before the teacher put the "crazy eye" on them quickly ending there laughs. When everything returned to silence, Berry realized at that moment he had caught so much of his lingo that Berry started to talk like him. Everything was playing around in his mind, what had happened, and what could Berry take away from that experience.

"Well, maybe he was telling the truth?" Berry said to himself, starting the conversation in the corners of his head.

Although another more cynical and down-to-earth side was speaking to him obviously shooting down the first assumption his mind had made just before.

"Are you kidding me, I wonder what kind of shit that guy must have been telling you. I could smell the shit reeking from his very mouth. He must know something!"

"Come on." His more reasonable side, the one he thought with all the time, said to him. "Maybe he was telling the truth. You don't think he's really lying to us do you?"

His more cynical side wanted to scoff, and he responded, "Yeah right. If you start thinking people tell the truth then you really are a sucker!"

The more sane voice in his head thought about the notion, but then came back with an excellent rebuttal. "You can't say that A.J. and Frank were lying, do you?"

At that moment, his cynical side fell short. Berry guessed that his voice must have agreed with him to some extent, but then after when he thought they were done, it shot back with the same paranoid response.

"No…but watch them." It was the same repetitive shit that Berry could expect from that same cynical opinionated tone. His voice continued on, "They might pull one on us, especially that Frank kid."

Berry shook his head slowly, trying to remember what this Frank kid looked like. Then it brought him back to the gun that he had leveled toward his face so angrily, his black eyes staring him down; that hard stoic look penetrating through his eyes, and saw what was really inside him, which was his dying brother and the blood that was on his hands. Only he knew that Frank and A.J. were on his side, and he was on theirs. Berry wanted to steer clear of this assumption at all cost, but he couldn't ignore it.

"Listen. They are our only hope to even get close to Gene, to get…"

Then that cynical voice turned into a creepier voice that sent scales across his arms. "Revenge?" He sent his hand across his arm, and felt the thought of revenge becoming more and more like a good idea. Ever since he saw that man/boy/assassin (or whatever he was) kill his brother, he knew that Gene was behind it all. He had seen and packed those guns in the chest himself, and watched his brother die from those guns he had packaged. But he knew that finding someone to talk to him was not going to be easy.

Only the thought of revenge made him want to dig his fingernails into his palm, and although it hurt, it gave him some pleasure to know that he could squeeze Gene's throat and stab him with his uncut nails, just as easy as grinding his teeth. He wanted to make sure Gene would bleed all the blood from his slithering fat body.

"No. I can't think about that yet, not until I find out all the facts. If I start to obsess about the violence now, I won't be focused on finding out the rest of the pieces to this fucked up puzzle." He definitely agreed on that idea, and he knew where to go to find the rest of the pieces at the Bloods or the Preps cliques. Berry probably knew that one of the gangs, if not both, had to know something about this degrading situation. But, Berry had fists and if any pipsqueak or hard-ass wanted to give him trouble, he would show them who and what he was about. He situated his arm on the end of the desk, and pushed his chin into his wet, nervous palm. He closed his eyes just for a moment, when the teacher told them that the class was about over, he zipped up his backpack, and then considered half the morning to be a waste. Only it wasn't going to be a complete waste, he could sleep through all of his classes.

Half of the morning was about over when Berry had been striding through his classes, when about fourth period was already underway, Berry's eyes felt a thickening layer of exhaustion overtake him, and everything in his system told him that he needed to sleep. He objected to it at first, but then he gave into the temptation, and closed his eyes. Closing his eyes he slowly leaned his head forward, and curling his arm in a sideways position. Berry coyly laid his brow against the top of his arm, and slowly fell...

Suddenly, Berry was looking down into what looked like a river, and underneath him he could feel something pinching into the soles of his feet. "Grass?" He thought, and then rubbed it again to prove it. Even if it wasn't, he didn't care—this world felt nice to him. He was just wandering how in the hell he had gotten here. When he looked around, long rolling hills straight to the sky, its rolling bumps—luscious and green—were starting to warble and make the black starry night warble in itself. He was amazed with how bright the stars were, and he could see almost every pattern that he could ever think of; The Little Dipper, Orion the hunter, Scorpius, Leo the lion; all of them were blazing in the night sky as if they were just showing up for him.

But it was something about all of them, because that was just above one of the rolling hills that almost looked like a warning or a kind of message of some sort. Only he didn't pay them any mind, because nothing was as important as the lake was at that moment.

As Berry's knees clicked, he could feel his bare feet clinging into the soft muddy palate that seemed to make him feel like a kid again, dirty and carefree. He laughed, bringing him back to the days where he could feel mud oozing through his toes like jam and jelly squeezing out of two pieces of bread. It pleasured him, almost too much, and as his toes gripped into the mud, he began to see what had been attracting his eyes to the lake. When Berry finally hunkered down on his knees until his sides hurt, he lowered his face toward the blue lake, and all he could see was the water, like every same boring pond that had a few complacent frogs swimming about, poking there heads out of the water, staring judgmentally. And to Berry's surprise there were a small pond creature that always found its way into there by sheer luck. But out of the corner of Berry's eyes, he saw the moon moving through a huge massive cloud, brightening everything from the rolling hills down to the lake he was standing over. Now with the help of the light, he knew that he could probably see the lake better, and he could.

Berry decided to ignore the moon for the moment, and focused his eyes on the water in front of him.

Only he couldn't really tell by the way the moon was turning it into a greenish sort of color, gazing so bright as if he was seeing God's face. But then the water turned dark black, almost as if a dab of vanilla had been pinched into the water and then it turned the lake into a deep, dark abyss. Positioning his left hand into the mud, he leveled his hand toward the pond, his lower half moving back and forth as if he was riding a surf board, but then gained control of his movement digging his hands deeper into the oozing mud he slowly moved his hand forward. It was like some deep pool of memories that were locked underneath its calm exterior—It would either open a sea of memories, or unleash a deadly wave of forgotten troubles that should have been left alone, and locked away forever at the bottom reef. Only he didn't know how to accept it, and maybe something inside him didn't want those troubled feelings to come out.

But then he began to move back and forth again, he couldn't control his movements, his weight began to move forward again, and his hand was suddenly forced into the lake by his shaky lower half—covering his wrist in that thick delight of oozing joy.

He expected it to be cold, and for a second it was warm, almost tingling his hand like hot wax, and then it started to burn his hand and it became numb, almost like cement, and he couldn't pull or wriggle out of this deadly vagina like grip that had sucked his entire hand in. Only Berry was not enjoying this as much as anyone would think, and Berry groaned as he pulled his hand out of the deep dark lake.

When he finally pulled it out, his hand was covered in bright red, almost as if it was blood. "Blood…no?" It seemed too thick to be blood, and it had tints of purple in it, almost resembling a beat up squash.

But then the lake was calling to him again, and when he looked down he saw that the river was indeed changing from black to blood red, and almost looked like one of those crystal balls from those old shows back in fifties and sixties. And there was always some want to be host in a shitty costume that would give you some chilling anecdotes, and then once the camera moved in on the crystal ball, the red smoke then cleared from the way, and the show would then begin.

Only there was no rerun of some old, decrepit show with black and white camera shots, but just a face that was too familiar to him. But the bloody water ran over James's face, and when he looked at his hand again he saw that the purplish color had faded away, and then turned bright red again. He started to gag, he wanted to throw up, and as he turned away from the lake he crawled on his hands and knees as if his eyes had been blinded. Tears were streaming down his eyes, and when he was in a soft bunch of grass, he tried to wipe the blood off his hands, but then saw that the more he rubbed it across the grass he saw that the blood painted the green grass, a dark brownish color. But when he was about to scream, he swallowed his anxiety, and fell into the blades of grass. Then he felt something poking into his back, and as he ignored it longer, he closed his eyes and wanted to be out of this place. He wanted to be gone from this place so badly, he didn't want to be here anymore.

"Berry Pantoliano!" A voice boomed over his shoulder, and a small tap was jumping across his back. "Do you need to go to the principals office?" When he finally opened his eyes, he saw that he was still in the classroom, but his books were scattered around his desk, and bundled up papers were all scattered around him, looking like paper pigeons that had been crumpled up and piled on top of one another.

He pulled his head upward off his arm, and felt a headache surging through the forefront of his brain. It began to swell up his brain, clogging all his ability to move. But when he focused in on the teacher, he saw his arm returning back to his side, and balling up into a fist.

"Do you need to see the nurse?" Berry knew that he, Mr. O'Leary, wasn't trying to be mean or disrespectful, but Berry did not care at that moment about anything.

"No, but can you do me a favor and stop molesting me!" He lowered his head on his arm, and closed his eyes again, trying to ignore the teacher at all costs.

The teacher was taken back, and then looked around him as he heard small little snickers escaping from certain parts of the classroom. But it suddenly stopped when the teacher put his left hand on his hip, and then spoke with an enraged voice.

"I think you need to see the principal!" The teacher's hands folded together as he waited for him to move.

Berry could feel the teacher's presence still hovering over him as he let out a long sigh of displeasure. Then as he raised his head upwards, he said, "Are you still here?" His voice sounded polite, but his tone definitely meant *fuck you*. But this definitely ruffled the teacher's feathers, and then he walked away from him as he said, "Okay. If you won't move, I'm going to call the Vice Principal."

At that moment when the teacher made his way toward the phone, and upon picking up the phone, and dialing two numbers he eyed the ground as he waited for the Vice Principal to answer.

The students knew that having the Vice Principal coming to get you was never a good thing because he answered to the Principal, and they thought of him as the master's little bitch. But no one ever had any guts to stick their balls out to the Vice-Principal or the Principal, and wave it in their faces was Chris Mangini. Only Berry did not give a damn if the police came here to get him, and in remembrance of his brother he decided to antagonize the situation, because he knew his brother would have done the same.

Then with a proud boastful voice, he shouted out into the classroom as if he had nothing to loose, "Hey…" Berry waited a few moments until the teacher looked up at the phone, wearing his intimidating-tough-guy-look like a Halloween mask. "Good you're calling him because maybe he can come down here and share some of his nail polish with you."

At the moment he finished his sentence, everyone, including the few silent Goth kids burst into a raucous roar of laughter that made him at that moment free from the constraints of their rules and brought the power back into the kid's hands, but to the teacher, it was a line that was only going to make that student's life even worse.

The laughter spilled, and was shocked as he heard these inflammatory words, he instantly covered his hand over the phone, and then muttered, "Yes, get over here now!" He said into the phone, and turned to the crowd of kids who were yelling at the top of their lungs in excitement.

Thinking over his words carefully, he pushed the evil faces that these demon children were, out of his mind, and took control of his emotions. Walking up to the front of the class he looked across the class, and yelled with a great bellowing yell. "BE QUIET!"

At that moment, the heart stopping laughs of the children suddenly fell to a soft hush, as he gave them all an ominous stare, he returned to his desk—but only a few snickering had continued like the chirping of midnight crickets—and made a note of what happened. But when he moved across the room again, he faced the blackboard, and with his back turned for a moment, he felt something slightly whopping against his back. When he turned around again, he looked at the class of students (or demons in his case), and imagined halo's across the top of there heads, and there hands clasped together looking like sweet little angels.

He looked downwards, and saw a crumpled piece of paper that had obviously been what he had thrown. He faced the classroom again, and took a deep breath, and was breathing fast, feeling the anger rising through his body like steam billowing from a smoky chimney.

"Who threw that?" He surveyed the class, and then saw that no one was going to say a word, or even cock their head's to give him a head's up. Only they weren't going to tell, and he knew better than to believe that anyone would tell *him*. Kids these days were worse than they were twenty years ago. He could attest to that. "Come on, give it up."

He leaned over, and picked up the balled up piece of paper. Curious to see what was written inside, unwrapping paper as if it was shrink wrap, straightening the paper back out, the surface of the paper was rough and large creases deformed the paper's face value. Only on the paper, inside the crinkled patches, a one word message that everybody understood, "Fag!" It was written with a long free hand, and he couldn't exactly tell who had written it by the deformed paper. But, if no one was going to say a word, he ultimately could blame it on one person, and that was Berry Pantoliano. But, he decided to give them a scare, and shake there confidence up.

"Well, I guess that is detention for everybody."

A tremor of *ooh* and disappointed sighs filled the aisles of kids, but only one person was smiling, and that was Berry Pantoliano.

Then at the door, when he was just having some fun, a loud slamming sound fell against the door. And at that moment, everyone fell silent again, and when the teacher looked through the windows, he saw Mr. O'Donnell poking his head through with his long, protruding noise almost touching the window as he gave him a nod, staring at him with his frightening, intimidating eyes. But Berry didn't care. "Come on!" Berry thought readily.

Moving toward the door with the note in his hand, he opened the door, and Mr. O' Donnell poked his head through the door and said, "What do you need?"

The teacher lowered his head toward his, and whispered all the gory details to him. And when O'Donnell had heard enough, he pushed the door wide open, and called for Berry Pantoliano.

Berry knew this was coming, and felt the pressure rising inside of him. As he moved down the aisle with his backpack slung across his shoulders, there must have been people watching him from all the aisles, looking at him as if he was the first lamb to the slaughter. Only Berry didn't care, he was glad to be out of that class. As he moved out the door, O' Donnel closed the door, and he took him to his office.

It was nine thirty when Niccolo was in the subway, and one place that he knew he could find anything about anything was Brooklyn. He regretted the fact that he had to leave his brother back at the apartment, but he had to do it because his brother was just going to question it. Frank had given them an order, and they were to carry it out without each other. Only Niccolo was well armed with a Smith and Wesson revolver that they didn't use too much, but served its purpose in and out of any situation. Besides the revolver he had the choice to bring a Glock 17, but since he didn't care about what he went with, he just grabbed the first thing he saw in his brother's drawer.

The cold metallic piece chilled his lower side as he fidgeted in the rather sleek, and about to be warm subway seat that had been accompanied by the usual stinky cheese bum or sidewalk sleepwalker. Across from him was an old woman that was bundled up from head to toe and a scarf hung around her neck like a cast. But the bags around her eyes were saggy, and her whole face looked like a big oversized watermelon. Although her cheeks looked as if someone had stuck two big peaches on both sides of her face. They were red too, and her body looked as plump as a stuffed Turkey on Christmas

Eve, and her legs even resembled a turkey's legs too. Niccolo chuckled about this, and then laid back as he waited for the next stop to let him off at his destination.

"Brooklyn." He thought, and knew that there was always something going on at each corner. There were dice games at some corners, and there were Latin women always hanging around like dirty sheets. He remembered that a few of them were beautiful with their tiny bellies hanging out of their small tight shirts sticking against their hot tanned bodies. But beauty also was like a dangerous flower and the uglier the women (excessive hips and large heavy lipstick) were the only ones that would give up the poonani (Niccolo chuckled from his brother's humor) for less then fifteen dollars.

"Shit, even less than that!" But let's say he were really lucky, and one of the long legged beauties that sometimes had long jet red hair or a black crow's nest; those mysterious but incredible fuck faces that would make a person come before they even took off your clothes. They would usually be "back door beauties" that took the pain for any costs, and sucked your fingers, accentuating the pleasure.

A rather disgraceful kind of term to use, but it made all perfect sense to any Math teacher, although this had to depend on the teacher (if they were pretty fucking clueless to even put two and two together). Niccolo never really messed with those girls too much, but he would mess around with a dice game. That was his one other vice that he would have to bend the rules for, but now was not the time.

"How many *wise guys* were there still running around Brooklyn these days, and if there are, how old would they be?"

Niccolo knew that the answer to this question would ultimately be found in the streets, but he had to form his questions right about everything; about the rumors, about the families, and about the future of "our thing." Because everything depended on him finding out the best information, but he trusted his guts primordial instinct, and then the questions would come last.

He felt the cold metallic steel pushing against his back, and twisting his hand around towards his back he grabbed the butt with three free fingers, and positioned it near his right hip. The barrel pushed against his thigh, and it made his entire lower half full of goosebumps as if he had shot himself already, and could feel the bullet already burning through his skin burrowing a place inside his arteries, and no telling if he could walk straight again without limping. But as he delved deeper into this emotion, he felt the train rocking him back and forth letting him know that Brooklyn was closer than he thought.

The train's velocity began to decrease as he heard the bell making it's rather loud dinging sound while the wheels graded across the steel as it pulled up to the next stop. Then at that moment, everything that was black, became filled with artificial light that filled a few people with a small bit of hope that the ride wasn't too long. When the train's brakes let off last screech, the doors to the subway slid open on each of the train cars behind them and ahead of them. In that instant Niccolo rose out from the seat, when the seat had just been warmed by his body, but then was met with a two to three people storming toward the door, and joined the huddled group of the large oversized woman. On the other side a person who looked liked a cocaine-addicted lady with her baggy eyes, lips crusted from her teeth marks, and her long bony legs would put a chicken down to shame. Her fake mink coat barely covered her lower half of the short black dress, and black and blue marks were hidden by extremely dark bage cheek coloring. She was utterly disgusting, and when he thought he was about off the subway, more people pushed past them and blocked Niccolo's way as they pushed past him.

Anger rose through him as a oversized black person with a cheap jacket pushed past him, and didn't bother to say "excuse me." Niccolo watched the black man with murderous intent, but remembered to control his temper, and remembered where he was. Niccolo didn't blame the kid for being ignorant, he knew that the parents were to blame for that. As he left the subway, he left the thought of the boy that pushed past him on that subway, and moved on with his mind on the mission at hand sifting out the A-train behind, and heading toward his mission like a breeze in the wind.

This long isle of stalls were the place where the Bloods would do their dirty business, dark and dank it was, where the students could escape to and snort and smoke there preferred drug of choice. Berry detested drugs, and anyone that didn't like drugs, would avoid the bathrooms at all costs. That was where he was going.

He reached the stalls within ten minutes before the longhand could even touch ten till, hoping that he wouldn't run into anyone's recreational time. Even though the little hand was moving faster than he could imagine, he knew that he could release his shit before the bell rang for all the Cretans, large and small, round and skinny, ugly and pretty, and be fed out of the same trough. Although he knew that pigs didn't get such a fine selection of food, especially since the food wasn't already chewed and then poured back into the pot that was also a reason why Berry never ate the cafeteria food.

As he traveled down this dark and dank bathroom, he heard his footsteps echoing around him as that putrid stench of piss and shit hovered around the stall door, sticking to the walls and floors as if it were a drastic endemic darkness. The smell of excrement increased as he walked towards some of the stalls and took a giant, dangerous whiff.

As he took that dangerous whiff, the smell jumped into his nostrils, and hit his senses with no remorse as Berry backed away, about ready to gag from the awful smell, God how terrible it was. Covering his hand over his mouth and nostrils, he let out a solid whooping cough that probably made all the kids scatter and tense up. But when his throat became free of that toxic waft of excrement, Berry covered his nose with his shirt hopefully trying to detain the smell from entering his nostrils. He felt like one of those doctors on ER where they went into the emergency room to save some innocent victim that had either been hurt from a gang war, or just a common accident—ultimately knowing that nothing could be done. But he knew he would never become one of those doctors, and would never want to, even though he might think of it later in his life one day, he knew he would never act upon this thought, even if he did grow up.

As he set his right hand against the door, he waited for a moment as if he was trying to feel this doors pulse. But then he moved the door open as he saw the bowl with no excrement leftovers, and none receding above the water that resembled somebody's leftover breakfast. He moved silently into the stall, and immediately ripped open the buttons and sat on the white toilet seat. When he began to feel his stomach unloosen from the knot that had been with him ever since that morning, he searched for his backpack, and found a book that he had to read for one of his classes.

"Crime and punishment." It was by Dovstoesky, a thick five hundred or more page novel that he couldn't possibly tackle now, but would try to read later. He sometimes hated to read, but he decided to give this book a chance since he had a few minutes to spare. Since time was like the wind, it moved and changed faster than a leaf's skin, Berry knew that he could spend a few minutes inside this rather large and modern classic. But when he was beginning to read the first few lines of the third chapter, his attention was ultimately taken off when he heard the door open, and stayed quiet as a mouse.

Just two minutes before Berry approached the toilet, another annoying force was moving like a jaguar adrenaline, and the full fury of a ticking time bomb. Although this force were a party of two, Billy Mangamo and Terrance O' Reily, who were craving a fix of some nice "China White" or cocaine that they had bought off the nigger's before school had started. Billy usually claimed he was with the Outcasts, but the only reason he was with the Outcasts was because he could fix up and ride the "H" train with that crazy brother, Clifford. He never liked getting high with him, and that was when he met Terrance O'Reily. Terrance sometimes hung around the Preps, and he knew that the Outcasts did not like the Preps, but in Terrance's case, him and Billy had been friends for the longest time. But Billy was holding something dear to him; it was a secret, a secret that he had wanted to tell somebody since he heard it. It burned in his mind faster than the feeling of wanting to toke up, but he figured he could tell his secret later, when they were in proper surroundings.

Even though the two had wanted to cut up earlier, they knew that they wouldn't have time to get a snort or two before the masses of kids stormed through the hallways, and the teachers would be watching for kids carefully now. That would have been embarrassing if they had been caught then, and that was a waste of good fucking China not being able to smoke it. So, it was better now because fewer teachers were in their classrooms and more students were in their classrooms, and they could get a high without being bothered by anyone.

But where was the China hidden, do you ask? Because, every person that holds drugs know that they can have them for so long until being caught. It was hidden in a place that no one could even imagine putting it. The small bag of China White was tightly packed between Terrance's grundle. (Now, for people that do not know the term grundle, not the dragon from the story "Beowulf," but it was a fleshy part that is located between a man's testicles and his asshole.) The small bag could definitely fit in there, but it was uncomfortable enough that it seemed like he was wearing some kind of Maxi Pad for his period. But then he felt so comfortable with it after a while it just made him walk as if he had taken a dump in his pants. But he didn't care what anybody said about him, he just grumbled and then moved on, knowing what he knew made him better than the rest.

When Terrance and Billy were about two seconds away from the bathroom, both of them stormed into the bathroom door, anxiously pushing the brown door with intensity as they stormed into the bathroom, impatient to satisfy their cravings.

"Oh God." Terrance said as he grabbed for the button of his Khaki pants, and lowered them halfway, showing his white and blue boxers, and stuffed his right hand down the back of his pants so that he could retrieve his tightly packaged bag of fun.

"That shit was hurting my ball-sack, man." He groaned with displeasure as his hand rubbed against his chaffing balls, searching for the small bag with blind determination.

Billy Mangamo looked at him, eyes narrowed and his brows turned downwards, "Goddamn man. Just get the motherfucker out of there so we can snort this shit. I can't believe I even let you put that there man!" Billy was definitely getting jittery, just as much as Terrance was, and he saw that his hand was shaking from the anticipation. Both of them usually did this together in privacy, but they had to answer their body's call for its medication. It had been only a few hours since they had done their morning dosage, and it was already becoming a nuisance.

But it wouldn't hurt just to have a little bit more, would it?

"Come on man. Get that out of your asshole so we can do this. I don't want those fucking teachers to come in and spot us."

Billy groaned even louder as his hand withdrew from his blue and white boxers, and held out a small shining ball, shining with some evil and attracting glow with the black shadows surrounding the clear bag. They were transfixed by this rather plain looking sack that had become somewhat of an elixir f staring transfixed, and jittered with excitement almost as if they were holding the Holy Grail. Billy took his attention away from the bag, and then grabbed his hand and tried to shake the small bag out of his grip.

"Man, get that shit out there man, put it on the table."

Billy looked back at his friend Terrance, who did not see him as his friend at that moment, shook his hand away from his arm and an enraged maddening look gleamed from his eye as he timidly lowered his hand down to the sink.

"Don't touch me when I'm about to cut up the shit." Billy turned away from his friend/brother, and ignored him as he was getting into his drug mood by reaching into his side pocket, digging for another tool that he would need to open the bag.

Billy watched as his friend breathing urgently, as if he was about to collapse if he didn't get his next fix out, and ready before he could open the bag. But Terrance was starting to see that his friend was truly becoming addicted by this bullshit, and when he saw that Terrance was stuffing these things up his ass, he knew this was just going beyond having fun, this was going to become a dangerous relationship.

Billy saw that Terrance was becoming jittery, as he pulled the cutting knife out of the bag, and held the tip that was covered with white powder out for his tongue to test out the stuff. If it was good when he would say so, and when he put the knife in front of his lips, he licked it, and closed his eyes, thinking for a second.

"It's good. Ladies first." Terrance said, laughing with a rather disturbed resonance that made Billy's blood boil and bubble with anger. But then he hardened himself and wasn't offended by his comment.

"Fuck you." Billy said sounding as if he had pinched himself with his two fingers. "Lay the shit out man."

Billy waited for him to respond, but then saw him reaching into his wallet for something to cut it with, a Visa credit card or something that could line up the cocaine so they could snort it. As he held a plastic card in his hand that read in bed red letters

I'm not your boss, but *I will be* if you pay me to act like one

Billy chuckled from the card's cheap humor as he began to line the coke in a straight line across the top of the sink as if it was a snowy trench, and it was calling to him. His nerves were beginning to die down, and glanced back at his friend with a sense of ease.

"Well, here it goes." Billy puffed out the sentence with exertion, as if he was almost nearly out of breath. Taking in a breath of fresh air, he thought that it would have been the last bit of sober air that he might feel for a while, and everything else would feel like an allusion. He lowered his left nostril next to the sink, and catching a bad whiff of the inside sink before he pressed one side of his nose with his finger, as he braced himself again, snorting the long white trench of cocaine and pulled his face away from the sink.

Billy felt the drug surging through his body, twisting his mind like a wet rag until his mind went a little further and further into that growing madness he always felt before. It's like he was in a dream world where this song "White Rabbit" playing over and over inside his head, *Rememberrrrrr, what the door mouse saaaid! Free your head! Free your head! Free your head!"* and he was about to faint. This wasn't like the last time, this felt different than the regular stash they had always bought.

"Man." Billy exclaimed rather hazy as he cleared his nose with his thumb and index finger, "What the hell is this stuff?"

Terrance turned toward his friend, and smiled with a certain deviance in his eye. But he could see that his pupils were dilating, and he could tell that he was blasting off to the moon, and beyond.

"I don't know. Let me try it and find out."

Terrance made himself another line with the two credit cards, and with strategic precision hearing the two cards clanking against the sink like water leaking from a rusty pipe. Billy could see with what little vision his twisted eyes could see that Terrance was getting into the mood before he took his turn to ride the white train. Billy just hoped he did his turn before the bell rang. Billy watched as Terrance lowered his face toward the sink, placing his nose along the top of the line, and breathed in the long line of coke, taking the ride of his life.

From inside the stall, Berry could hear everything that was going on, from the time they entered, from their conversation to their loud snorts. He could tell from the way they were talking with that rather urgent and paranoid tone of voice that sounded almost like someone was in a rush to do something, or be somewhere, and he realized this was the place where they wanted to be.

"Oh my God. These guys are doing drugs here, right now." Berry was rather astonished from the chance that he had to be present to this rather chancy meeting of two dope-addicts. Berry had an image of the white rabbit running along saying to Alice "I'm late, I'm late, for a very important date." Berry could see the rabbit in the story drawing up a line of China White and Alice on the other side waiting to get high so that the white rabbit could molest poor little Alice, and take her virginity. But he felt like he had fallen in the rabbit's hole, and was hiding from the rabbit until they had left. These two boys were in his drug den, and Alice was nowhere to be found. "Probably out with the white rabbit getting fucked under a shady tree?" Berry thought, almost wanting to laugh, but knew that it was all juvenile and tasteless what he was thinking, but he wasn't born to have his head buried in the sand of lax creativity.

To anyone that didn't keep their head entrenched in the sand all the time, would have known what was going on, or had felt what was happening. It wouldn't be obvious to some people, but Berry did not want to make a move, because if he alarmed them, there was no telling what a couple of cocaine addicted freaks would do if alarmed. He wanted to listen, because this might be important. Gripping the book in his hands, he felt his asshole clenching up, and his stomach began to turn into a knot. Only Berry knew that this went on in other schools, being that Chris Mangini prohibited drugs and the selling of drugs in George Bradley, he wasn't surprised to find this happening inside their own bathrooms. But since Chris Mangini was out of the picture, he knew that the rules didn't apply when he wasn't around. Only he knew that someone had to be supplying this shit to them.

Berry knew that one of them implied that the "niggers", which either meant that they were talking about the "Bloods" or some two bit hustler. Only Berry knew that some dope heads would not go out of their way to find some shit, and if they can get some ready made China White with baking soda, they would do and pay whatever price they had to get that addiction flowing through there system.

But ignoring his thoughts for a moment, his ears tuned into the words that were crossing between the two cocaine-addicted buddies again.

Wiping the white powder away from his nose, he snorted again, cleaning his nose from the extra milky snot in his system, and said with a certain laxness in his voice, "That is some good shit." Terrance looked at Billy, and saw that he was laughing at him.

The Disintegrating Bloodline

"What's so funny?" Terrance was offended by his rather cajoling laugh that sounded more careless than comforting.

Billy controlled his laughter, and then pointed to his right cheek. "You got some shit on your cheek."

Terrance looked at him, then turning, and pushing his face into the barely lighted mirror he let a lighthearted laugh escape him, to alleviate some of the pressure that was inside him, and saw what his friend was laughing about. He had a bit of white powder right below his eye, almost as a woman's expressions would have been when she didn't powder her cheeks enough, embarrassed and astonished, but not really caring at all. He rubbed his thumb across the base of his cheek until it was gone. He looked back at his thumb, and licked the front of it with a certain curiosity in his action. Billy looked at him with a rather queer expression, and cleared his throat with a bit of unease.

"So, I know a secret." He said with a chuckle, and felt his legs almost going limp, but then leaned against the wall like a rather drunken sailor looking for a prostitute before he got back on the ship. In his case, the cocaine was the prostitute, pleasuring his senses and fucking his entire system, making his heart rate skyrocket and his nerves numb, giving him the ultimate shock ride.

While Billy was leaning against the wall, he saw that Terrance was not even glancing at him while he was drawing up another line of cocaine. "Oh really? What is it, did you find out that I fucked your mother last night?" Terrance let a conniving little snicker escape him laughing as he moved some of the white powder away from his line, and into the sink. He groaned and cursed to himself as he tried to move some of the powder with his card.

Billy looked at him, and thought about punching him in his face, but knew that he was too messed up to even raise a finger. He didn't even know why he was even talking at this moment. Maybe to kill some time and a lot of brain cells before the bell rang. That would be a kicker when the bell rang, that would end their cover, and they would soon have to disperse faster than water bugs traveling down a rocky ravine. But while they had a minute, they could just shoot the shit, talk for a minute about something that was on his mind since the shooting, and this wasn't because of the drugs. "Okay. Maybe it is." He thought, and came out with it freely.

"No, you dumb bitch!" Billy retorted, hopefully trying to get back at Terrance for his crude remark, and continued "I know where Gene is!"

Billy said this with such a free spirit in him, as if he didn't value his life, brought the attention of Terrance away from his cocaine, and upon him. Terrance was looking at his friend as if he was mad.

At that instance, Berry's mouth dropped, and his breath had fallen short.

He was so surprised that he almost dropped his book, and his asshole opened as if he was about to shit from excitement. But not only he was about to shit, but also his heart had just totally elapsed when he heard those words. When he was about to speak, he held his breath, cutting off all the oxygen in his lungs, "Yes! This is it! What dumb luck do I have getting to be front row of a crazy cokehead conversation. What a coincidence," but Berry always left coincidence aside, since the shooting.

"Say it!" Berry thought enraged, "Tell me where that son of a bitch is hiding."

At that moment, Berry instantly gripped the book out of unnerving hatred, and slowly closed the book when he thought he was breaking the book in half, and waited with an patient ear, and hateful heart.

Terrance, who took his dilated eyes away from the mirror, and zeroed in on his friend with a rather curious and doped up grin, but there was something spiteful in his eye when his shoulders went up and his hands were relaxed. "Oh, really?" He rose his head off the sink, and he snorted again, trying to comprehend what he was talking about.

"Do you know exactly where he is?" Terrance had lost all respect for him; stoic and unavoidable like an open face of cards in an undermined game of blackjack. Whether the hidden card underneath would show a winning number of two to ten, or a face card. But, like that card, Billy could not tell what was going to happen next, he was afraid to ask.

"Well…I heard a rumor where he might be." But then when Billy was continuing on with the rest of his sentence, Terrance's hands flung against his chest and clenched his shirt.

"Man," Billy said astonished and his face was crossed with confusion, "What are you—"

Then when Billy went to push his hands away, he felt his body being pushed along the floor, his feet moving backwards as if he became defenseless, limp and flaccid in his grip. But when he thought he was being pulled off the ground, his back was slammed against one of the bathroom doors, and with the equal force his back hit the door. It flew open and crashed against the bathroom with an undeniably loud sound that anyone would have heard.

Terrance breathed in hard, and exhaled out his nose like a mad dog that was already showing signs of his degeneration, and Billy could see it in his eyes. "Wait…"

"Don't you say a goddamn word about that!" Terrance angrily hissed into his ear, and then pushed him against the bar that connected the door hearing it jingle as the light around him seem to dim as he glanced over his shoulders, and then whispered venomously.

The Disintegrating Bloodline

"Don't breathe another word about any more of that shit. Because what you don't know might get you shot," Terrance moved his face closer, and pushed his lips to the tip of his earlobe, and pressed his body against Billy's. Billy had never seen his friend do anything like this, and it was starting to make him feel uncomfortable that his friend was holding him in this aggressive and sexual manner. "If he kisses me, it's over!" Berry thought, but then gave it up, because he knew however doped up he was, he wouldn't kiss him.

"I don't want you to get shot, that's all." Terrance's breath danced along his neck, and it made Billy really, really uncomfortable until he had the courage to push his friend off of him.

Still holding his friend against his door, he felt his breath move from his neck to his cheek and his lips giving Billy and rather up close and personal way of how his buddy's breathe smelled. Only his grip did not want to leave him, and with one more forceful push, his sweating hands unclenched his orange shirt. When Terrence moved back, he still had that killer gaze gleaming in his eyes, and his fingernails were balled up into his palms. The rather decrepit smell seemed to die away, and then float around there nostrils again, making Billy gag. But Terrance wasn't bothered by it.

"You don't breathe a word about this, you hear me. A lot of shit has already happened, and I don't want more to fall upon this school or our crews, you understand?" His tone sounded very much like a father's condescending voice but the way he was holding him wasn't like his father, and he knew there was some truth in what he was saying, but he replied to him in a rather frightened response.

"Yeah," he wiped his nose with his fingers, and snorted his anger back down his throat with his spit, "I understand," and fell against the bathroom separator once again with a heavy heart, and depression set in over him.

Terrance looked at Billy's body, limp and defenseless, and knew that he had understood. And the rage that gleamed brighter than the morning star with its bright red glare left Terrance, and then paranoia reentered into his system as he turned his back to his friend. He smirked as he gathered up the baggie that he had lain next to the sink with such carefree flamboyance. Only Terrance did not look at him as he began to clean up sink, turning on the water, he splashed the sink with a few handfuls of water, occasionally spilling some water over the sink and falling to the floor, drip by drip. It magnified a terror inside the silence that was making his heart beat with a morbid fear he could never imagine.

"Are you okay?" Terrance asked with a kind, but with certain paranoia crowding his system. And as Billy opened his mouth, Terrance continued on as if he wasn't there, and continued onto cleaning his face in the mirror. "Well," stretching his face, "just remember what I said," looking into his horrific anemic bloodless face, and then without even saying goodbye, he stormed out of there, and made his way toward the exit, without saying anything else.

Billy Mangamo was still lying against the bathroom divider, the feeling of euphoria was beginning to leave him, and that morbid feeling commonly called "depression" swept through him. It hit him faster than the cocaine had entered into his system and he hit his head against the back of the cold divider in confused anger.

"Damn it!" Billy whispered to himself as he rose his right hand, and slapped his left supple cheek. The slapping sound magnified like echoes inside a deep dank cave. When he was about to cry, he covered his face, inside the darkness and whispered with agony,

"Oh God. What did I do?"

There was no answer, and then he covered his face as he began to weep silently, almost as if he wasn't even crying, but sobbing. He sobbed for another minute, almost sounding like a choking cough.

Berry, who had heard everything, even his question toward God, pinched Berry's heart, leaking a bit of sympathy into his ice cold veins, and also led to a brilliant idea. "Just talk to him, and see what he has to say." One side was really leaning toward that notion, he held his breath, and then the thought crossed him that

"Don't let him know that you are here. He might get paranoid, and run away. Just let the son of a bitch dope fiend experience his downside, and then go about his business." That was his more conventional-let-me-be side, but then felt his conscience forcing its way through his mind.

"He might need help, and besides he could provide us with lots of information, important information." Berry at that instance became really frightened of how well he was hearing these questions produced in such a good vs. evil kind of way. He could definitely imagine an angel on one shoulder, giving him the smart info, and the devil on the other, giving him the sarcastic and deterring messages. Only he knew a secret, and that secret was more beneficial to him than anything else at that moment. He couldn't say that it was more important than his brother, but his brother always told him, and for some reason dug up a saying in his subconscious, "strike while the iron is hot." He had always stuck with that motto up until the shooting, maybe because he didn't really know what to do without his brother telling him what to do.

Then, he thought about what his brother would have told him in that certain time. "Talk to that guy. Get his attention before he leaves."

He was conflicted on the issue in itself, but he didn't want to spend too much time arguing within but he heard his brother saying, "strike while the iron is hot." That finally meant something to him now, and this was his time to strike while the iron was hot.

Berry quietly cleared his throat, and said…

"Are you okay?" Berry's voice was low, and it took Billy Mangamo by surprise all the same as he jumped off the divider he turned and yelled intensely as if a ghost had breathed across his neck, and left goosebumps across the back of his head and neck.

"Who are, speak now or I'll have to come in there and beat the shit out of you." Billy Mangamo's alert system was already on the fritz, staring with his dilated eyes at the line of closed stalls. Peering through the cracks, all he could see was an eclipse on the inside of the stall. He could definitely hear that voice, because it wasn't the cocaine, and it was alien to him. It was so distinct and so clear that he couldn't mistake this voice for anyone else's.

After a moment of silence the voice spoke out from the stall, rather calm and cool. "Do not worry. I understand your words completely, and I would be the same way also…if I were in your position. Listen, that drug is already messing with your brain, so why don't you just come into the stall next to me, and let's talk."

Billy began to think that it was a good idea, but "What the hell, it's good to talk to someone now a days."

"Are you there?" The voice said, "Do you want to talk?"

Billy approached the door, and entered into the stall, "Yeah. I guess it would be good to talk to someone sometimes." Standing inside the bathroom, he closed the door, and sat down on the toilet face down, and prepared for a conversation with a hallucination or his conscience, he didn't know which one it was, and if it was real, it was out of sight.

Sitting on the cold, empathetic stool, he felt speechless at the least to be able to talk to anybody, even if it was himself. But Billy daringly dove in the conversation head first, and opened up with the first question.

"Are you God?" Billy said, feeling his paranoia stack on him, giving his mind no rest from the insanity of knowing what was real.

When he expected to not hear silence, Berry's voice became very quiet, almost to where no one else could hear them except themselves.

"No, sorry to disappoint." The voice/Berry said sympathetically, "If you are paranoid, those are the drugs kicking in. You might know that more than anyone."

Berry sighed, knowing that this was true to some respects, and then retorted with a "Whatever" kind of scoff.

Berry who was gripping the book ever so tightly before, closed it with no trouble at all, and laid it on his lap. "Well tell me this…but first of all" Berry let a cough escape him, and apologized instantly, "Sorry, it stinks in here, what is your name?"

Billy knew what he was talking about, and glanced over each side of the toilet, and took a big whiff and said in a repulsed by the stinking, reeking dead carcass smell. "That's why they call this place a bathroom, cause it smells like shit. And don't worry about it, my name's Billy Mangamo."

Berry shook his head, and then smirked as if he had approved of his name "Well, I like you, I'm a *paisan* myself." A small chuckle escaped Billy, and a chuckle escaped him as well—maybe because it was from the rather sarcastic joke. But as he cleared his throat, he continued with persistence "My name is Berry Pantoliano, and I think that we have a certain interest that I may be interested in hearing."

"Oh really?" Billy said in a rather sarcastic attitude, and replied earnestly, sniffling as he wiped his nose with his forearm. "What is it that you want to hear?"

Berry turned his head towards the right side of the block, and tried to stare through the wall as if he was looking directly at this boy. Everything was building inside of him to ask this question, and he couldn't spit a word out. Then with all his might, his fingers withdrew from his palm, and trying not to yell or whisper it he said with a clear pitch that would clearly demand respect from anyone, even from his inner demons.

"Where is Gene?"

The question was daunting, and an uncomfortable pause fell between them like a veil. Although the question might have been logical to Berry, it wasn't logical to Billy, who was scratching his nuts outside of his denim pants, "Why? Did he do something to you?" The voice sounded so innocent, like a child that kept asking why had he been punished for setting off fire works in his neighbor's yard. Berry hated this tone, but then realized that he might not have remembered, or failed to remember from the shit he had been snorting. All he knew that he didn't have to be honest with some dope fiends, like the cockroaches that were fornicating without any real pleasure, just forthright business. That probably heard this through the cracks of some empty building.

Berry clenched his fingernails into his palms again, and felt the pressure rising in his system again. "Let's just say…" He paused, and wanting so bad to release everything in his system, and scream for loss of his brother. He clenched his teeth, and silently withdrew into his anger.

"Excuse me, but are you all right?" Billy said questioningly.

Berry pulled his thoughts out of his emotions, "Yeah," and retracted his fingernails out of his palm, "Yeah. I'm fine. But, let's just say that he did something very bad and I want to speak to him."

But when Billy decided to ask him who he hurt, he supposed that it was not his business to ask, and then said, "I'm sure you don't just want to speak to him, am I right or am I just imagining? But what if I'm dreaming, and I really am talking to God?"

Berry knew that the question was true, and without even thinking about what to say, he replied, "No, you're not." Berry made himself dig his fingernails out of his palm, returning them to a normal, outstretched position as blood flowed back to his veins. He could see the marks that looked like tooth marks stretching vertically up and down his palm—he wanted his palm to bleed—because anything else was better than trying to ask this dazed out coke-head where the hell Gene was hiding.

"Yes," Berry said, "back to the issue at hand. Do you know where Gene is?"

An exasperated breath left Billy's mouth, trying to believe that he couldn't try to remember, and then just spit something out.

"I was just joking man. You know, man." Then, out of some unnatural habit, he began to scratch his neck, and his chin. "You know, I got messed up when you do cocaine." The hairs across his neck made a soft itching sound of feet crushing a dry leaf. Although he didn't know why he did this sometimes, but he maybe thought that he had done it out of habitual anxiety since he had that Attention bullshit disorder. He had to be on Ritalin and everything, but he felt that this was not adrenaline running through him while more than likely on a 10 to 1 chance it was the drugs making him feel this way.

"All due respect, I think you know something. Maybe it hasn't donned on you yet, maybe it's being blocked up by all those drugs, but I know you *weren't* bullshitting what you were about to say to your friend, am I right?"

Billy felt his words being already misconstrued, changed, and then rerouted back to him with the same "Fuck you" attitude, and then given off that same condescending way that he wasn't prepared to listen to. "The Truth?" Billy whispered, rubbing his head pondering all the shit he had been through, and if this was a "trip" he was pretty fucking amazed by his creative imagination, or whatever imagination he had at the moment.

Billy considered the consequences in his decision, and knew that anyone who had betrayed another crew was a "marked man", and would be hunted forever.

After a few more minutes of badgering himself stirring his fears came to his final conclusion that when it came down to survival, it was every man for himself. "So," Billy said with a rather promising voice, "you want to know where Gene is?"

"Yes." Berry replied.

"But before I go on," Billy became weary and worrisome, and wondered what he would do to help him. "I want you to guarantee my safety, because if anyone from the "Outcasts" or anyone finds out that I said anything, I'm dead."

Berry didn't see this as a problem, only as a danger to this valuable contact because he did not know the intentions of the "Outcasts," and what there combat capabilities were when it came to retaliation.

"I give you my promise, now, talk before both of out time is surely gone by, please, before our time is surely wasted." Berry's voice insisted that it was time to leave.

"Oh no, my friend." Billy had the same sarcastic and deviant tone "I think you will be pretty surprised and pleased to hear what I have to say." He cleared his throat quietly, and began to talk about everything, everything that he could think of.

"Now, you might think that Gene had one of his own to try and kill A.J. and Frank?"

"No, I don't know who, was it Gene who called it in?"

Like an alluring smell of nicotine and marijuana leaves, this was promising to be interesting. Berry did not respond as Billy continued on with the rest of his promising question.

"Yes, but it was a well known fact that his people were not behind the trigger."

"This was just sounding better by the minute." Berry thought as he made a minor "Uh-huh, continue."

When he heard that, Billy felt that all his thoughts were caving on top of him, and he had to get out from under his thoughts that were avalanching on top of him. He had to juggle them in the right order so he wouldn't mess up, and then continued on with a more frank-and to-the-point attitude.

"Like I was saying, the trigger men that came running throughout the school were not with Gene. They were carefully hands picked by yours truly to go off into battle." He sounded like he had proved some triumphant point, but was just trying to sound important in his own little way. "But, that didn't work, and the targets got away without even a wound. This proved most disastrous with Gene's plans, and the Outcasts are the one's that shouldered all the blame for this mess. But he promised that more were to come before the leader of Chris's family is dead and in the ground. Including anyone that followed them."

Suddenly inside that odd, dark stalls everything around them grew quiet; no running of the water through sticky pipes, no drips of water were falling from the faucet. Billy felt chills crawl up and down across his arms as he took another breath before he continued.

"And that is A.J." Berry asked with some hopes of finding out something about this rather hazy information.

"Why…yes. But that is not all there is another who "they" are after." His voice grew dim and weary, and the light around them seemed to blink off and on above them darkening the room, one after the other. Berry looked up cautiously, and breathed outwards as he scratched his chin again while his dirty fingernail traipsed across a big fat pimple that was on the edge of his jaw. He scratched his fingernail directly above his left cheekbone, and burst the pimple as it oozed white puss that resembling a dead worm smashed by a car. He looked at it, and then wiped it off on his shirt as he cleared the puss from the bulging cavity.

Berry had felt this was being a little too hazy, because there were many groups out to get A.J. and Frank, he didn't really mind having a go with that Frank bastard. Feelings aside, he craved for it as if he was starved of all this information, and would grow fat upon listening to this valuable wealth. Only he had to get what he said straight first.

"Okay, just fill me in on something. *Whose they?*" He sounded rather juvenile, but he had to know the truth about everything—every little last glossy detail.

Then from the stall that Billy was in, he let a rather scoffing laugh escape him as if had known something far dangerous, although the laugh was certainly maddening, Berry was outraged as he yelled back in his defense.

"What's so fucking funny?"

His laughing ended while Billy's voice was rather hoarse he strangely found the strength to talk. "It's you. You just don't know what you have gotten yourself in do you? Who do you think could have the power to influence a juries decision, and who do you think could erase a valuable witness in a court case. Who do you think could set up an assassination of one of there own just to get rid of *bad blood?*"

Berry's voice fell short, and he didn't even want to mutter who "they" were. This was serious, because what he was saying was that either Chris's boss or one of the Five Families are responsible for this entire scheme. Even though he didn't feel surprised, he knew that there had to be something else to this too, but Berry's brain was being racked up so much that he himself felt like he was on cocaine himself.

"I get that, but why would they have a problem with him?" Berry said cautiously.

"Man, aren't you getting the picture? You need to start looking at things from a more higher perspective, because if you don't, your ass is not going to live long."

Berry, who was sitting inside the cold dank stall, exhaled the confusion and then knew that he did not want to piss this guy off, but he couldn't let him get the better hand of the conversation, "Okay, I get the picture, but I need more details."

Berry heard Billy let out a long breath through his constrained teeth, but knew that he had said too much, and from the way this kid was acting, he sounded as if he didn't understand.

"*Kid*. I gave you all the details, and if you want to know everything, go ask around. But be careful, because people around here are really anxious about all of this. But before I go, I want you to get rid of somebody for me, and you might know what I mean by that because he might go off and tell somebody."

Berry knew that this cokehead was getting too vain, because he was calling him "kid" already, but he didn't want to argue with this cokehead now. Only he wanted to leave immediately, and tell A.J. about what he had heard. "Okay, but you have to get out of here now." Berry said and then when he was about to leave the stall, Billy then decided to ask him one more thing.

"About that protection," Billy said "what are you going to do about that? Should I lay low for a while until you contact me?"

Berry was taken off guard by what he should have thought about the moment he gave him his word to protect him, but he couldn't come up with anything except for, "Yeah, just lay low for a while until I call you."

But then Billy thought that if he did not go with him now, he would not probably hear from him again. So with fear for his life, "Wait a minute. We can't because what if…"

Berry did not want to be stuck with this coke-head son of a bitch all day, but he had to find a way for him to be calm, and relax. "That's it. Tell him to go home, sack out for a while, and sniff on his stash." It wasn't a perfect plan, but he had to give him some comforting thoughts to live with while he ran and told this valuable news to A.J.

"Listen. Just go home right now, and you better arm yourself just in case anybody should come to your house."

Berry was feeling the paranoia leave his thoughts for a moment, and saw that this was a pretty sound idea. Only how was he going to call him if he didn't have a number. "Yeah, sure. Do you want my number?"

Berry then found himself looking through his back pack, and then patted the side of his pants as he pulled out a long Bic pen that had a rubber grip while the tip exposed with it's black ink overflowing all around the ball point. He shook the pen before he opened his palm to write down the number and waited as Billy Mangamo gave him his seven-digit number, and Berry closed his palm as he stuck his pen back into his pocket with a certain surge throughout his body. With his number in hand, they parted ways and Berry was the first to leave, and Billy moved after he left.

Berry moved fast, and quick as he left the bathroom with such an important task on his shoulders, he didn't even have time to think. "Deliver the message…to A.J. and Frank…and get people to protect my new contact." As he moved down the hall, passing the clinic on his right, and the now leaf filled Senior Courtyard, his mind was set ablaze, his imagination was burning up with anxiety, he felt as if he was about to fall short if he didn't get out of there. Only he was forgetting one person, Annie…and at that instant the bell rang out, sending him a reminder that his sister had not come to school that day. He was glad because he didn't have to wait for her, and he needed to get this information to A.J. and Frank without waiting for anyone.

After the bell made it's last *ding*, he soared down the hall with swift feet, and as soon as he heard the trampling in the hallways, he turned a right at the next corner, and then moved toward the quadruple doors, his freedom just waiting for him. The sunlight was waiting for him, and when he pushed through the doors, he didn't look back.

Berry thought that was the most surprising part of the entire thing. But, even though he was jacked up on Cocaine, it was like he wanted to torture him with the answer. "Coney Island?" Berry thought, but knew that it was probably a good tip-off. He just hoped it was true, because he would kill him if everything that he told him weren't true he would surely kill him, he made sure he knew that before he left.

But there was someone in one of the bathroom stalls, riding the Heroin train, and letting the needle sit in his arm, even after the poison had entered into his system, he had heard everything, and all of what Berry and Billy had said.

"Yeah!" Clifford whispered with a real slur in his voice, feeling the pain of the needle push into his arm, but wasn't paying the pain any mind, because his body was numb and his body was in the equilibrium of his zone. "I know who you really are!" He said, and then went off into a mutter as he pulled the needle out of his arm—his skin shifted back—very slowly, as if he wanted to torture himself to that extent. But as the needle left his arm, he started to rub the spot, and smiled, revealing the miniscule parts on his teeth that were clean, but the top part of his gums were still covered in greenish gangrene. "I will get you and your friend too, Billy…" He whispered, and then closed his eyes.

Chapter XXI:

"The Shadow of Morte"

After the bell rang, with its rather painful *dinging* sound aborting its last *ding*, Berry was departing from George Bradley, Niccolo was just stepping off the "A" train and walking into the Brooklyn subway. The subway reeked with some dank sewer smell that mixed in with the occasional grime that resided below the concrete. As he moved off the train, he felt the doors close behind him and almost nip at his heels.

Niccolo looked around, seeing the few occasional pedestrians bundled up in their fall leather coats and corner store beanie caps. Maybe it was him just being weird but Niccolo definitely felt a strange presence in these walls. It was a whole other ball field in Brooklyn and it would not be a surprise if you were then beat up and stabbed by fifteen to twenty different people. But he had to remember that a lot of the old timers were dead off from long time vendettas or just withered away in old age with the legends that embodied the streets and into the great unmistakable void—where the decay were screaming out in the bricks. Whether if there was anyone that would know about the troubles back home, and even though his real home was such a distant place to him now, someone else must have heard from different channels about the rumors.

But what were the rumors, the rumors of Chris's cousin that would change the course of "our things" history. Secondly, who were behind the shooting of Chris Mangini, and last but not least, who was this figure namely called "Death".

"One thing at a time," Niccolo said, hearing the words escape his lips in a soft roll, as if he was muttering random thoughts off the tip of his tongue. Even though he felt like he couldn't concentrate on one thing—he had to keep his priorities straight—and his senses alert for now as if he was in foreign territory, and it was quiet, *too quiet*. Once he left the subway with a few floating hot dog

The Disintegrating Bloodline

wrappers—that were dressed with mustard and relish—traipsing around his shoes, he kicked them off—wiping the mustard off the side of his shoes—and headed up the subway stairs with haste.

Only he had to get going, and find out who would know a few things about what was going on in the old country.

"Now, where do I start?" Niccolo stopped in his tracks, and glanced out of the corner of his eye that there was an alleyway on the right side of him. Dark and cold the wind called out to him with an errie whisper from the shadows as if the alley was a cave into a beastly creature's lair, and he had somehow awoken from its slumber. The gaping mouth of the alley was exhaling a long whistling wind that blew like a bellowing burp making his nostrils wretch, but it gave him a chill up and down his body. But it was certainly calling out to him in a malevolent whisper that did not want to go away. He listened for any kinds of footsteps, any kind of signals that would tell him that someone creeping, soft splashes signifying of lurking footsteps in the alley, watching him, waiting to make a attack.

But then it disappeared, the tinkling of the water disappeared from the alleyway, the rustling of what he heard as footsteps suddenly fell short. He dared not to look, for he shouldn't see something that he shouldn't he be watching. He felt his feet regain the strength that they had once felt before he was stopped by that awful alley and entranced by the sounds that had sent his fears to another level. With the revolver stirring in his belt line, he started away from the alleyway's gaping mouth, and started down the street with even more haste in his system, and something else, fear of the unknown.

When he left the alley behind him, he felt like he was becoming lost in his own backyard because he had no scent on his nose to find old man Fillini. While he was leaving the worst of the neighborhoods when he was approaching the nicer neighborhoods of Brooklyn that had the livable, more manageable apartments.

"This is where he must be?" Niccolo thought as he was standing in front of the apartments with his hands stuffed inside his pockets snuggled away from the whipping winds that were whipping against his face. It was already wearing down his lips, and even if he wetted it, it would wear them down to where the wind would hail against his skin, tearing through until it reached his soul.

Inside the top corner of the castle like apartment, Sergio Fillini, had already grown a white moustache in his old age and his physical features were that of a toothpick. He had been proudly walking around his small cubbyhole of a room in his underwear, already feeling the hot vapors from the shower cover his body. With his rather small and manila looking chest pushing out for a picture of his wife, rest in peace, had already departed from this world five years since he had been "retired." He smiled at her picture, the once beautiful looking woman who had shared this room with him, was crippled by lung cancer and then went into the hospital over two months in intensive care. As he passed her picture, he talked to her sometimes, but what would leave his mouth mostly was, "I hope this is what you wanted in a husband? A small scarecrow?" Even though he had a few flings in his lifetime, he had always cared for his wife more than those whores he slept with on those long Saturday nights. If he could share the same bed with her again in the afterlife, he hoped that she could forgive him for his mistakes, and they could embrace each other with the same love she had given him for so many years. But he hoped that wherever she was, Sergio hoped that she knew what was in his heart, and if she accepted that, Sergio was probably all right with God, he hoped.

He left his wife's picture once again and headed toward his wardrobe for the best outfit to take his morning stroll in. Only Sergio felt that it was too cold for him to be going out, and he felt like he shouldn't go because he might catch a cold. He had worried about being murdered for half of the time that he had been retired, *and he was worried about a cold?* But maybe this was what retirement meant, total absolution from every wise guys fear, an early retirement. Maybe he was just lucky, maybe he was just smart, but whatever it was, he had been living on thin ice most of his life, and one day that ice was going to break and swallow him up in the freezing water below him. In short, death was an inescapable beast.

But that was the chances he took with his life, and as he approached his closet, he saw a long white shirt that he had pressed himself with a little portable iron that he had worn through many occasions. He saw that it was showing wrinkles could tell by the long collar. He had become less than tired of pressing his own shirts lately, and he had gone out less because of his wrinkled shirts. But today he needed to go out because he couldn't just sit inside all day looking out the window and deciding whether or not it was a good day or not to go out and take a walk. Only then he heard the voice of his wife, forcefully intruding on his thoughts, "Go out, and get some fresh air. You are going to go into the loony bin if you don't get out of here." That usual kind voice entered his mind when he didn't have anything to do, and it usually haunted his dreams of late.

Sergio pushed the thought of his wife away again painfully and then said as he pulled a very expensive coat with a nice pair of dress pants hanging inside of it. But when he was about to move away from the closet, he saw a familiar looking face that he had never forgotten, but had just ignored for a while. It was his reflection in the mirror and he could see exactly what he was becoming. An old man with a decrepit body from the inside and with his chest already looking like a piece of decaying bread he began to see that his body was not what it used to be. He noticed his chest again, and saw that a crop of white hairs that infiltrated his black nest, and then said to make him feel better about himself.

"Yeah, I need to get out." He told this to himself with such honesty that he thought he almost felt his hair growing back, and he let a forced smirk widen across his face as if he was blowing a raspberry at himself. He let out a laugh that roused some enjoyment in his dull life, and then wondered over to his bed to get himself ready for his afternoon walk. Although he hoped that something unexpected would happen, he dressed rather slowly, accepting his old age with dread and disappointment. But he was looking forward to his walk as usual.

When Sergio was just finishing buttoning up his shirt that he had not even ironed for more than a week, and he felt rather attached to this shirt in many ways, almost like a mystical suit that knights in King Arthur's time wore to protect them from many dangerous perils. In his case, this shirt was a testament to his survival, but he didn't want to get too cocky, because there was a so-called "war" happening between the families—he just wanted to get suited up.

Only the months that passed when he heard this, no one he knew had been taken out or even shot at, and if this was a war, why weren't there people going at it—guns blazing—right in the middle of the street. Maybe there weren't a battle at all and all the things that he had heard were just pure fiction. But that was not his affairs anymore, even though he couldn't resist a good rumor or two, it still was not his affairs to meddle with anymore. But the more he thought about it, he wasn't doing anything he shouldn't have been doing. So, as he finished buttoning up his pants, he decided to look out the window and see what it was like. Sergio moved toward the small cubbyhole of the window, he moved the curtain, noticing that the white clouds were blocking the bright sun making a shadowy circle in the sky as if he could see his wife's smile in the sky. Although he couldn't imagine her face smiling and it saddened him. But as his eyes traveled down from the clouds then to his surprise saw a boy standing in front of the apartment with his hands in his pockets, looking at his window, staring as if he had nothing else better to do.

Sergio watched him for a few minutes as a feeling that he hadn't felt in a long time was creeping back into his system, fear of unexpected arrivals. He wasn't afraid for the past few years that he had been retired, but this was different, maybe this boy was his maker, and it was time for him to meet his maker. But he wasn't going to go without a fight. In the drawer below him, he had hidden a six shooter revolver in that drawer, just for safekeeping if anyone tried to send him into an early retirement. He usually kept another weapon by his bed—a small .22 caliber but when she passed on, he felt entitled to put the extra gun in the dresser next to his bed.

He moved the curtain back over the window, and then glanced down at the small drawer, grabbing the knob he pulled it out halfway, and saw the gun peeking out of the rather deserted drawer. Sergio grabbed the butt of the small metallic revolver as he kept it out of sight and hidden so that no one else would see his piece. As he moved away from the drawer, he held the pistol out in front of him, and then clicked on the small lever that forced out the cylinder. When he looked down into the round cylinders, he saw gold plated ends facing out with the numbers .357 Magnum around the bullets.

"I guess that this will have to do." He said to himself, clicking the cylinder back into place, and the barrel clicked the next bullet into the frame. With the gun locked and loaded, he stuffed his gun around his back. The feeling of having his gun back into his pants wasn't an ordinary thing because he had been without it for so long, and hadn't felt so worried for his life in a long time. But maybe this was a good exercise if he was just imagining things so that he could keep his wits alive—like a sharpened blade.

With his gun loaded and his pin striped pants already buckled up to his waist, he seemed ready to leave, except that he had forgotten his shoes and socks. He looked down at his feet, and then felt like an idiot.

"Aww, shit!" He muttered, and then moved with no hurry to another wardrobe that were filled with his black and white socks. Sergio saw that he wasn't that organized with how his socks were. A stray black sock lay across the top of the whites, and a few more popped out like worms digging through a rotting corpse. But he wasn't entirely too picky when it came to a few mismatched socks. It was the problem of having to bend over and put on the socks, which was his Achilles heel. Sergio picked the socks that were peeking out of the heap of white socks, and then headed over to the bed to put them on. But that's what he got for not remembering to put on his socks, the pain of having a bad back.

"God…" Sergio said, fixing the socks over his feet, pulling them up along his feet as if he was fixing a condom over his Johnson, and then adjusted it up to his calf. He groaned as he pulled his back upwards, and let out a breath of pain escape him as he straightened himself back on the bed. "…Damn it! This is what I get, huh? The price for becoming an old man?"

He looked up at the ceiling as if he would get a response out of his reply, and was then accompanied by silence. He leaned over again, and then fit his other sock on his other foot. He groaned even harder as he pulled the sock over his calf, and then positioned his back up again. In this time of pain, he began to hum a song that he had sung over and over when he started having arthritis in his back, "I haven't got time for the pain, I haven't got time for the pain."

When he finished pulling his socks over his calf, he rose up off the bed, in such pain that he was in, and made his way towards the door. But just as he grabbed his coat that was hanging on a separate chair, he heard a rather small knock fall upon the door. His breath stopped, and as he laid his coat back down on the chair, two more knocks fell upon the door again, almost in an identical knock. Sergio bent his right hand backward to reach the pistol, and gripped the butt with his few fingers as he said, "Who is it?"

Slowly and surely, he lifted the weapon from his pants and then slowly lowered the pistol toward his side as he heard the muffled response push through the wood, and into his sifting eardrum. "I am Niccolo. Don't worry, I'm just here about some business."

"What business do you have that it's so important to ruin my afternoon walk?" Sergio said with confusion as the weapon pressed next to his thigh, his finger warming up to the cold trigger he had been familiar with for so many years was returning to him. There was a momentary pause on the other side of the door when Sergio burst out, "I could be some crazy old man who has serrated heads on my walls?"

Sergio wanted to laugh with all his might after he finished, but all he could do was let out a puff of air from his nose travel across his whiskers, causing him to close his mouth, breathing steadily with a slight tremor in his pulse.

"Mr. Fillini," Niccolo said with impatience, "Any other day I would think that you were some crazy old man, but you were a *consigliere* to the D'Angelino family, and I need your help? Time is against us."

"Who are you with?" Sergio said, feeling the rush to pull the trigger.

"I'm with Chris Mangini."

Sergio Fillini cocked his head, his eyebrows flaring downwards in denial, hearing these words with importance knowing that this boy could not be lying, and only if he was, Sergio was already a dead man, he had a feeling today. Although he had heard many rumors regarding Chris Mangini, he could not help but feel obliged to share what he knew. But since he didn't have many visitors to see him lately he slowly slid his pistol into his back, and then with a groan he said, "Are you armed?"

Another pause had not fallen between them as Niccolo replied with a rapid-fire response. "Are you armed?"

"Are you?" Sergio shot out from nowhere and felt his finger warming the metal trigger. That dirty, greasy feeling was making an imprint on his finger that couldn't remind him of anything else except the smell of a woman's vagina after she had come all over his fingers. But women were last of his concern, long after he denied himself the sexual fantasies after his wife had died, because that would betray the thoughts of longing over his wife. But, he couldn't help the will of his imagination.

"Well, are you?" Niccolo replied.

But Niccolo added something so eloquently to the conversation that it seemed to stop Sergio's train of thought, derailing his thoughts. "Listen, by the way we are defending ourselves, it seems most likely that we both are armed. I know that we would not be fools to be without our pieces, but I'm not the one that you need to be afraid of."

From inside the cubbyhole room, Sergio was beginning to get interested, and then decided that an agreement needed to be settled before he let him into this stranger into his room. But as Sergio wanted to deny this boy permission to come in, he knew that if this was a cleaner, he was a dead man already, and that he knew a long time ago. But as he began to put his gun away, he then put his face toward the door, and said with discern. "All right, I'll let you in, but if you have a weapon, and that's if you have a weapon, we both put them away. Being that we are both men of honor, we can live by our words."

Sergio was going to do just that because he was a man of honor, the last few men of honor in his own opinion, he never talked or ratted anyone out or would lower himself for a less lengthy prison sentence. He paid the cost to be where he was, and did his time in prison, only why was he afraid now? He would keep the revolver near his side so that his hand could grab it if he needed to. "Yeah right, you were never a good shot." Sergio thought, and knew it was the truth.

Sergio knew that this boy would keep his weapon by his side, and he knew that it wasn't him he should have been worried about. When a momentarily silence had fallen between them, Sergio waited for the response of the boy on the other side to give his answer.

And like air rising through the cracks, the voice of Niccolo spoke in a faster pace, "It's away. Now, let me in, we don't have time."

Sergio took a deep breath, and as he pulled the door open, he looked at the boy, and saw his rather black olive eyes glinting at him with self-assurance, but his hands were in his coat pockets again, as if he was holding the gun in his hands there. But as Niccolo was about to walk into the room, Sergio pointed a long crooked finger to his coat "What's in your coat?"

Niccolo was taken off guard for a moment, and then realized what he was talking about; he let out a groaning huff and then pulled his hands out of his pockets. Sergio eyed his hands, with his rather whitish palms facing out

The Disintegrating Bloodline

toward him giving off a sweaty gleam that shined with the overhead bulb that almost looked like it was smoking—as if it had been dipped in hot water.

"Do you believe me now?" Niccolo said as he pulled his shirt tail up, revealing a small butt of a pistol was tightly packed inside his pants. Sergio eyed the gun and then stared with appreciation of how this boy cooperated exactly as he told him (not too many kids did as they were told.) But too many things could happen once he let him in, and there was no telling what would exactly become of his life. Only this life was unpredictable, and he knew that whatever fell upon him he had to roll with the punches and keep his feet steady against the encumbering forces at bay.

"Come on." He pulled the door open, and a whiff of fresh air whistled past Sergio as he moved out of the way for him to walk into the cubbyhole. Niccolo saw the door wide open, and now was his opportunity to shoot the shit with a real wartime *Consigliere* and hopefully get down to the bottom of this bullshit in the streets, and find his way to the truth.

As Niccolo walked into the room, Sergio Fillini shut the door and the whole world out except for this boy and his questions. But, he would have let more in than he had expected.

Once Sergio Fillini closed the door behind him, Sergio felt obligated to give this boy something to drink since he came all the way out from…"Where do you dwell?" He said with uncertainty.

Niccolo looked at him and then returned his gaze toward his room. "In Manhattan."

Sergio laughed and then said, "Oh really. Then it wasn't too far for you, was it?"

When Niccolo heard this, he felt the need to explain what took him so long. "No, the reason why it took so long was because I didn't know if you actually resided in Brooklyn. So I went around Manhattan, then the Bronx, and this was just my third stop before I decided to walk around for a while."

Even though Sergio had been standing beside his dresser listening to what he had to say with a grave and curious look in his eye he decided to make his grounds certainly open. It wasn't that he charged by the hour, but it was because he had bad hearing, and without eye contact, he could not tell what that person was saying, even with his own wife.

Niccolo was staring around the small cubbyhole room with much fascination as he tried to imagine how someone with such a name could live in such a small shabby place—one bed, a small desk, and one bathroom. But, he decided to leave his assumption out of the way until Sergio's voice rose out from the other side of the room like slow dripping water in a cavernous mouth, echoing around the walls with such command.

"Now…" Sergio almost forgot his name before it popped into his head, and it came out rather bluntly, "Niccolo."

Niccolo turned around and faced him with a rather simply like a pupil being called upon by his teacher, and awaited for him to show a bad note.

Sergio saw Niccolo's face, and wondered what kind of being could speak in such a grown up manner, but he was just guessing, and could analyze everything later.

"Do you speak Italian?" Sergio said with patience and a bit of reverence crept from his tone.

Niccolo's eyes were lit with excitement and his voice grew into a cocky eloquence as he fired back, in perfect Sicilian, "That's my native tongue."

Sergio let out a strong bursting laugh that made him seem like he was some anorexic Santa Clause on some hallucinogenic drug, and then in between his laughs he began to cough up something in his throat, that painstaking felt like death. He instantly ran into the bathroom to release the phlegm liquid that made his body into an uproar. Running into the bathroom, he kept the door open, leaned his head to where his mouth was just above the sink, and let out a long *HAWK-TOOIE* sound as the spit traveled from his lips, and landed right on the inside of the sink. Sergio felt relieved as the tickling felt relieved, for even a moment's time, and he said with his face down in the sink, "Ask away."

Niccolo, who had seen everything, was taken off guard by his demand, and just when he was about to speak he bottled his fears and pants on tight, and then replied, "What do you know about the rumors about Chris Mangini's cousin."

Sergio heard this with an attentive ear, and then as he pulled his face away from the sink, he made his way out of the bathroom, and then raised his elbow against the doorframe with an arch that he hadn't heard himself speak of in a long time. It was probably because he had somebody to talk to except himself.

"I might know some answers to your question, but I want to know what you know first." Sergio sounded pretty important then, and the bottom of his mouth lowered out making him look like a trout.

Then, when Niccolo was all out of ideas, Niccolo came back with something he never even expected to talk about, and it was himself. "I'm Niccolo Mancini, and I have a brother named Jerry Mancini. Our mother is barely trying to pay our rent, but we take care of that just fine. I won't waste time on that. Also I pledge an allegiance to Frank Beans, a close lieutenant to Chris Mangini, and when he calls upon me to go to Brooklyn and find out what I can about this bullshit between Chris Mangini and Gene." But when he was about to continue he saw Sergio's face grow ill, he then fell against the door.

Niccolo saw this, and then he spoke with a grave and worried voice, "What is it?" Sergio regained his stance, and then cursed to himself low without anyone, including Niccolo could understand.

"The boy…was that boy named Gene Dov?"

Niccolo hated to even reference his full name, because the thought that he would ever have to remember him again sickened him cause it crept back on him like an upset stomach.

Niccolo saw his face and then saw that in it he was getting somewhere, and before he could speak, Sergio raised a hand for him to be silent, and Niccolo did as he was told. Taking in his breath he then said, "About a month ago he came to me, wanting to know about Chris's cousin. Being that I did not know anything about this, he came to me with a proposition, and it was one of the most deadliest propositions I have ever heard."

Niccolo urged him to go on, and Sergio continued. "I found out the cousin's names from one of my old contacts who is connected, and when I saw him again, he proposed to me a plan to wipe out Chris's cousin, and wipe out all of his influence in New York. But this plan was not just because of his personal greed, it was because one of the families had gotten to him, and they had gotten to him good because the way this kid talked about it was as if there was a *Second Coming*."

"Second Coming?" Niccolo said with a rather curious tone, but inside, he was intimidated and more or less frightened.

"Yes, he said that after Don Pescaro would become obsolete a new power was going to rise in his stead."

Niccolo's eyes grew wide when he heard all of this, and he was beginning to feel something that he had not felt in a long time, fear. Niccolo saw it in Sergio's eyes as he spoke with a tremble. "The mask of *Morte*."

Niccolo knew in Italian, *Morte* means death, and this sounded all too much like a metaphor. Niccolo looked downwards, and then snickered about to burst into a laugh.

"What do you mean, *Morte*?"

Sergio saw the boy, and was offended by his petulance and then replied with spite. "Oh God, another peon!"

Niccolo then felt rage surge through him, "The nerve of this old man?" He thought wanting to strangle him where he stood, but then knew that he knew that he hadn't had a single idea of what he was trying to say, but as he dug, it proved to be more interesting. Like each glare of a crystal that was freshly shaven he had to inspect every gleam that came out of it. "Wait a minute, what are you talking about?"

"What I'm talking about is the hitman *Death*." Sergio presence was unsteady, and felt a chill growing up and down his spine. A form of sweat ran down his cheek when he continued. Niccolo did not want to interrupt him. "This is serious, because this…" Sergio did not know what the hell to call this thing, except for "*thing* is like a disease. It will take out everyone in its path, and by the sound of it, he wants to take out all the heads of the families all by himself, starting off with Chris Mangini and Don Pescaro."

Niccolo laid his hands on his side, his eyebrows cocked as he thought about it for a moment, and he still needed to know something before they continued onto the next subject.

"But, one thing before we continue, I'm not so clear about how Gene met this figure named *Death*." A chill rose across his arm, and then when he expected to be loaded with a story, it was the opposite.

"That I don't' know, and you might have to find that out for yourself, but there was one thing that I kept from Gene that I found out in the New York birth records."

Even though Niccolo's mind was full of doubt, Niccolo was disappointed, but then he let a rather sly smirk escape him, as if he was trying to relieve some of the stress in his system. Niccolo quickly got rid of the smile, and then said with a bit of edginess, "What did you find?"

Sergio saw him, and then moved over toward the bed with his hand on his side, and then continued on with pain, "I found in the birth records that there were *two* cousins from the same mother of deceased Cattiano."

"Two?" Niccolo thought to himself, and then motioned for him to go on.

Sergio did just that, and caught his breath as he fell down on the bed, feeling his lungs cage up against his ribs, and then looked at Niccolo with an outstretched neck. He looked at Niccolo, and Niccolo sat down in a chair that was across from him. As Niccolo found his way to the closest chair, he saw Sergio calmly popped his thumb out of place as if he was a young child playing with a deformed ligament.

"Are you sure there are two?" Niccolo said, taking his eyes off his thumb, leaning over in the chair, feeling his own body ache just watching this old man mess around with his thumb. But Niccolo knew that if he was watching this man thirty years ago, it wouldn't have been so bad, but it was just weird.

"Yes." Sergio saw his eyes, and felt another strange feeling overcome him, the feeling of being watched, or listened to. Then he began to whisper, "I had the papers but then disposed of them because things were already too hot with what happened at that school—a fucking tragedy—and I suspected that Gene was not too far away from playing a part."

"Then you suspected right," Niccolo added with a hint of despair, "Everybody should had seen that son of a bitch's true worth, and that would have been nothing. But I remembered when Chris Mangini held him in the highest respect, and welcomed him to dinners with his own family. But, I guess that's what you get when you treat a person too good, they turn on you."

"Well," Sergio interrupted, "I think that you have all that you need because I am tired and spent. I guess I didn't need to go out on a walk today. All I probably needed was somebody to talk to. It gets lonely in here." He smirked, and then let a small pained laugh escape him as he rose off the bed, and fell back on it. He huffed from the hate of being old, but it was then Niccolo had risen out of his seat, and extended his hand out to Sergio for him to grasp it. Sergio did just that, and as Niccolo pulled his body up off the bed, Sergio let a small groan as he raised his body upwards, and as he implanted his feet into the ground, Sergio's left hand fell against Niccolo's large arm.

"But I want to know one more thing." Niccolo said, his heart was pulsing with questions, "What's wrong back at home?"

"You don't want to know," Sergio was a foot taller than him, and tried to move away from him. Only Niccolo wasn't going to let him go when he had him going.

"No, I do not want to go any further until I know everything." Niccolo gripped Sergio's arm light gray arm turned bright red, almost to the point of discomfort. "I did not go all the way to hell to find out the devil was a woman, I want to know everything."

Sergio looked down at his arm, and felt the grip of Niccolo's arm take it's toll on his arms. Even though Sergio was in his old age, he had some reserved power to pull his grip off of him.

"Are you sure? Because once you know this, you got a whole new burden under your belt."

Niccolo heard these words, and then felt that he was asking for more trouble than he wanted—a round about way of finding out what he could.

"I'm sure." Niccolo said as he let the mighty grip of his fingers release Sergio from his iron clad grip. Insulted by his behavior, Sergio pushed him away as he walked over toward the bathroom with some kind of luminous feeling overcoming him, like a dark cloud of stress.

"Okay then." Niccolo watched as he stood in front of the bathroom, and heard him talk until he could talk no more.

"In the old country, a town that is not far from Palermo is being held under attack by a tyrant who wants all of Sicily. A small unnoticeable civil war has begun in the town, and everyone that defies…" He caught his breath, and as he put a hand over his chest, he continued on in a pant as if he was about to faint. "That defies the wrath of Don Mangiano, all will be obliterated. His captains are the one's that do the dirty work, but that is not all." Sergio took a moment to catch his breath, and continued with no change in his voice.

"He's in Palermo, like a snake waiting for his prey to try to kill him. I have heard that sometimes when only a brave few have gone to kill him, it is rumored that he always looks like he is sleeping with his eyes shut. But then, when those brave few approached his body, he attacks them without mercy." Sergio turned around, and demonstrated a quick thrust to what looked like above his gut and near his ribcage, (Niccolo slowly winced from his deadly touch) "and lays a knife in there guts so fast you couldn't even see it coming." He let his hand fall back to his side, and his face went pale again.

"But even worse, he cuts off his victims heads, and hangs it at the front of the town so all who oppose him can see what happens to people that want to kill him. Rome can't even stop him."

Niccolo saw that the old man's gray skin start to shrivel, and much older as he continued on with the rest. Only Niccolo didn't want to know the rest, for fear that someone might be listening, but he had to know, it was his orders to find out about everything that was going on. He would have to die right there if he had a gun pointed to his head. Only he hoped it wouldn't come down to that.

"So, what influence does he have on the families over here?" Niccolo said, hoping to see through the fog. But in this fog, Niccolo just couldn't quite see through this veil of mystery just yet. He needed to go further and ask more questions to get himself on the path of the truth.

"His influence ranges from narcotics, mostly the import of marijuana and Heroin, and sometimes a few of their soldiers come over to America, and they say *Death* is the only one that keeps in contact with the old country. The families don't even want to do business with them anymore, but they are a monopoly, and its business as usual, we usually trade burned CD's, but after that, we don't keep in contact with them as much."

"Then why don't we kill him?" Niccolo said with a curious tone as he folded his arms feeling his heart pumping with more new questions.

"That's impossible." Sergio burst from his lips, and then let out a long hard cough. "No one would dare go after him, because if he found out if it was one of us that went against him," Then Sergio's lung's felt like they were going to cave in on his entire system. He could feel the whooping cough traveling through his system, it tickled his throat as if a feather was scratching it, and he began to cough out the rest of his sentence. "It would…mean…the end!"

Niccolo saw the color in Sergio's face return to normal and then turned his back to Niccolo. Only then his breath began to sound raspy and grabbed for the door wall as he leaned forward a bit as if he was about to fall over. Instantly, Niccolo heard Sergio's breathe put him on alarm, and rising from his seat, he moved to his side, and stretched his wary hand out. Niccolo grabbed his shaky hand, and Sergio then weighed his body against the thin wall.

Why! Why won't anyone do something about this?" Niccolo's hand clenched his arm, but then he saw in Sergio's eyes something that he did not expect to see from a hardened Consigliere, despair.

Sergio's mouth twitched shook his furry white mustache, but it looked thinner up close compared from back at the other side of the room. Only Niccolo's mind became distracted by the thought that his beard might have been thinner than it had appeared to be, but he instantly put this weird physical feature out of his mind, and then fired back with his most honest and naive opinion.

"Why don't we, if our territory is under attack, why don't we fire back, and end this tyranny."

Sergio huffed, and then shook his head in a disgraceful nod. "You still don't get it, do yeah? We want to keep our business as usual, and no one really wants to deal with sending guys over there, and for what, just so we can loose good men. Shit, once you are in this life long enough, you don't sleep that much." His voice sounded so empathetic to the last detail as he pushed him away once again, and then mocked him with, "Besides, what do you think you are going to do, take the Don out all by yourself. You don't have the influence, you'll be slaughtered, and if they find out you are with a crew, no one over here is going to protect you."

At that moment, Niccolo felt that these discouraging words struck a wrong chord in his system, and for a moment, he wanted to give up all hope in his mission. But he didn't want to give up just yet, he wasn't dead, nor was this old, weak Consigliere dead either.

"Well, we'll try not to get anyone involved, and we'll…"

"There's no more time, you have to get out of here!" Sergio pushed his arm away and shuffled into the bathroom feeling the cold squares chilling through his black dress socks. He was strutting as if he was a raving lunatic, and felt as if his legs were running on a low tank of about to fall underneath him.

Niccolo didn't want to leave, but he felt that he should respect Sergio Fillini's decision, and leave. So, with no goodbye at all, he headed toward the door, and just as he clenched his hands around the doorknob, Sergio called back to him. He saw Sergio standing at the door, and then watched as his mouth moved the mustache as if it would fall off with the leaves that came with the rise of winter. Niccolo always dreaded her wind chills that gave him a cold and her snow piles that made the city harder to navigate in.

"Find the cousins, and protect them with your life. Too much is at stake for someone like you to fuck it up."

Niccolo's eyes widened, and all he could say to him was the truth. "We won't mess it up, and I will make sure that the cousin's are safe." His voice was almost too confident that it made Sergio doubt him for a second.

"But remember, after this, always look over your shoulder, because it's most likely that you will be watched, and remember that some of the families are not going to agree with what you are doing, and the closer you are getting, the closer the tension will be. But, since you are with Chris Mangini, you are backed up by Don Pescaro; but also remember that Don Pescaro is as much of a target as Chris Mangini is. Once you find the cousins, you will know what to do. And don't forget, his last name is Cattiano, and…"

"And what…" Niccolo asked, but then he saw Sergio searching through his mind for the answer, and he made a small echoing sound in his throat before he finally came out with the answer.

"He has a scar…yes…he has a scar. The cousin has a scar." Sergio let out a satisfying sigh knowing that he had done some good, and could finally sleep easy for at least a night. "But you get out of here, and don't look back."

Niccolo's mind was suddenly filled with questions about everything that he had just said, but then remembered that some answers must be found on his own.

"Okay, I will." Niccolo assured Sergio, who had seen him regain a bit of color in his face. Niccolo's mind didn't feel entirely easy about leaving, but he did feel easier about leaving his sight. Niccolo turned away, and as he reached for the doorknob, Sergio called out his name again.

"Yes?" Still clutching the doorknob, he turned around, and saw fulfillment and deep thanks when he said to him. "Thanks for coming to see me, I haven't talked to anyone in a long time."

Niccolo gave him a nod and spoke thoughtfully, "Don't worry about it. You have provided me with many answers to these questions."

Sergio's eyebrows cocked, and then he said in a rather rushing response, "Just remember my words, and don't forget to watch your back."

Niccolo started to think that Sergio was acting like a worrisome grandfather trying to repeat everything to his grandson. Only Niccolo felt that his neck was about to break if he didn't turn all the way around, feeling all the bones in his back wanting to be popped. Only for some reason he didn't want to let go of it, afraid he might be sucked into talking with Sergio longer. Involuntarily his hand started to turn the doorknob, proving to be very discomforting as he retold a rather chilling quip that meant a lot to Niccolo, and he hoped it would affect Sergio too. "You do the same."

Niccolo's hand that had been gripping the doorknob finally creaked open, and the door's resistance becomes lax as his hand forced the large piece of wood out, and then slipped through the open crack as he did not look back.

That was the last Sergio saw of Niccolo, and then felt the loneliness of the room creep over him again, as if it was trying to dampen his spirits. Only his spirits couldn't have been dampened than it was for the last five years of this room getting to him. But then he felt that his wife would have been proud of him, and for what? Maybe for getting a bit of what he knew off his chest. But, there was nothing more he could say to the boy, he had said enough, and could not give the boy anymore advice than he could give him.

"Go, boy. Go and find the cousins, maybe I can die in peace. But if not, maybe I can go standing up, like the old times?"

But then he felt a watery liquid began filling up in his groins, and the need to piss never felt so good in his life. Maybe it would sting, maybe he would cringe every second he was pissing, but whatever he would do from now on would not feel so bad to him anymore.

When Niccolo was at the bottom of the porch, the wind was growing faint and brushing against his cheeks like a woman's lips as he began to walk along the sidewalk with certain anticipation and angst, pushing him toward his next destination, his apartment. He had to go and contact his brother, and see if he found out anything. But before he could keep on walking, and forget about Sergio, he had to look one last time. Stopping in his place, he looked back up at the arch window and saw only the curtains with the light that was illuminating against the fake cotton material.

"Are you looking, old man?" He thought in the back of his head, and then knew that he wasn't going to look out his window. But then Niccolo felt a cold chill rise up his spine, and his mind was urging him to move away, quickly, for fear of darkness descending on Sergio Fillini. "We'll meet again, Sergio Fillini." With that, he nodded his head, and turned back toward the block. After that, he never looked back.

Jerry had been sitting inside the apartment for two hours, trying to think of what Frank was trying to tell him before. "Manhattan House of Magic?" The thought burned faster than the cigarette that he was smoking, and as he flicked the ashes of his cigarette into the alley, he stood on the metal rail, peering down into the alley.

"If this was my kingdom?" Jerry thought, and spied all the familiar things that were always in an alley. Trash bags with already torn up holes in them and the garbage bleeding from it as if it was a bleeding cow, but he was really just procrastinating from leaving the safety of his perch and proceeding through with his mission. Only it felt shifty to him because he didn't know what the hell a place such as "The Manhattan House of Magic" had anything to do with it.

"Whatever!" He thought, taking another puff of his cigarette, burning the paper slowly, revealing the ashes as a woman revealing her smooth shaved leg incestuously, and disintegrated into the air with a flick of his finger.

Taking another puff of his cigarette, he exhaled the intake of smoke with a smooth blow, pushing his lips outward like a bullfrog; he silently laughed at this, and then repeated the process again. It was just like fingering a woman, play with her a little bit just to make sure that she has your attention, then jab her repeatedly with your index and middle finger (not viciously) until she is begging for you to violate her with a hard protruding cock. Flicking the cigarette, he took a moment as he saw a rat jutting down the middle of the alley as if it had was following some sort of yellow brick road, and darted around a lumpy trash bag that looked like an over bloated bubble, and disappeared from sight.

But besides that, he had to get up and find out what this "Manhattan shop of magic," and see what he could find out.

"What the hell is going to happen? Is a magician going to pull Gene out a hat?" He scoffed when he thought about it, and took another puff of the cigarette—it was slowly burning in the middle. When Jerry withdrew the cigarette from his mouth he flicked the cigarette down toward the alley, he saw it fall into a small puddle, and disappear under the black water for a moment when it returned back to the top like a dead fish. Pulling himself away from his perch, he returned back into the apartment, refreshed by the cigarette, and with his naked body already inside the shower, he reached for knob that had a disintegrated "H" on it, and turned it quickly. The water hit his body faster than he had expected it to be, and jumped back for a moment, but then felt the warm tingling feeling of the jets spray against his body. The warm jets that were streaming out of the showerhead gave him a few minutes of relaxation to release him of all his responsibilities for a few minutes.

When he was finished, it gave him so much clarity and put him in the zone to do what he had to do, which was follow his orders, and find out anything about Gene's whereabouts. Jerry immediately got dressed in a rather half ass approach to it as he put on his pants on first, without any underwear on, already feeling the material grinding against his unprotected penis. He noticed in the mirror that he wore a rather long small blue and white checker shirt, light khaki jeans, which were creased at the bottom but still receded past the shoe, and a pair of tennis shoes. A good reliable pair of shoes when he thought about it, and then decided that this was his time to leave. With his clothes on, and mind alert and ready for anything, and his gun snug tightly against his hip, he moved toward the door, and said goodbye to all the things that he would miss with a low whisper.

Jerry was already on the subway, and was taking the first train out of Brooklyn, and into Manhattan. When he seated himself on what seemed like a deserted car, he slowly closed his eyes, and laid his head against the glass wall. Even though it was uncomfortable at first, he made it a place to close his eyes for a minute or two. But when he took his mind off of everything, he felt the car suddenly shake his head off the glass as he opened his eyes. Letting out a great yawn, he covered his eyes from the bright feigning light. Hints of light pushed through his fingers, agitating his eyes and causing him to sleep less.

But just when he was about to sleep, he was awoken by a voice that had sent his nerves higher than he would have imagined, and far worse than any marijuana addict. Taking his hands away from his face, he saw a sixteen-year-old girl sitting across from him in another row, with her right leg laid upon the seat. Jerry saw her gothic attire all in plain sight, the long black leather boots, with numerous buttons up and down the black material resembling something out of a science fiction movie, that rode up to her calf and a short black dress that revealed half of her albino white thigh. He looked up at her face and saw that she was plastered in make up, her eye line was sloppily drawn and a few blotted spots of makeup so that she could look older, or more attractive. Jerry saw that she was wide-eyed and wired as all hell as her fingers shook with intensity and her long fake red fingernail against her black unwashed black skirt. She smelled of some heavy perfume; it smelled sweet, but something was rotten.

"Huh?" Jerry said, wiping his long face with his hands, trying not to look at her legs, and cocked his head upwards gazing at her face.

"What's your name?" The girl said, slowly moving her hand down to her skirt, and then pulling it upwards seductively. But Jerry ignored this, and then turned his head as he said his name without looking up her skirt.

He then glanced up and down the boxcar as if he had not seen her in the first place, and then said, "Jerry."

"Oh," She shook her head chuckling, professionally, and then said, "Jerry?" Her fingers clutched on the end of her skirt, until her long red fingernail trailed across the top of her leg; her bush in full view. "You want a good time. I can show you what you are missing."

Jerry accidentally looked downwards, and saw that she was not wearing any kind of underwear, and that made Jerry feel uncomfortable and excited at the same time, as if he was some perverse little child that had never seen a woman's large flower. Only that wasn't the problem, it was the fact that this girls muff was so large that it looked scary to even look at, even though his dick was hard, it just felt wrong to him.

"Listen, how old are you?" Jerry asked her honestly.

The girl looked at him, and then let a small chuckle escape her as she slipped a finger into her naked vagina, her palm pressed against her large curly bush.

"Old enough to know what a man wants, and what you want." She began to stroke her small pushed out peach, sending spine tingling thrills throughout her body, and certainly trying to make Jerry horny enough to go along with this folly opportunity.

Then at that moment, Jerry let out a strong belly aching laugh that echoed all around the abandoned train car, and it made him laugh harder than he could have imagined, if he had really wanted to or not. But at that instant, his outrageous laughing aroused curiosity in the young preteen, and all the thrill of having sex left her. "Are you a fag or something?" She said trying to arouse anger as she withdrew the finger from her pulsating peach and closed her legs. She angrily readjusted her back against the shaky car.

Jerry heard this, controlling his belly aching laughs, letting a few more scoffs escape him. "No…" Another scoff escaped him as he controlled his mirth, "not at all. I would show you what a man is really like, except that you are too young for my taste, and for me to show you what I really want, you might have to grow some more tits and trim that bush."

The young preteen hooker suddenly lost all her sensuality and her mouth fired back, hurtfully, "Shut up! How can you say that about me…" She was yelling at the top of her lungs as a train car rolled past them, screaming as the wheels rolled along the tracks screeching and screaming with teenage frigidness. As another subway train finished on his side, another train car came screaming past her, blocking her words but leaving her face twisted with rage as she continued to mouth off to him as if he was listening to every single word she was saying. He liked when a woman got angry, because a woman always let her feelings get in the way, and he wasn't listening, so that made it the funnier.

Jerry just shook his head as he anxiously waited for his stop to arrive, and it hadn't been too long when the stop to Manhattan had arrived. The car shook with a hasty stop, screeching as loud as it could be, and Jerry felt as if it was going to tip off the tracks and it stopped with one last halt in front of a subway. Jerry noticed that there collars were bending upwards as if they were trying to impersonate the "Fonzy" on the show "Happy Days."

But they couldn't pull it off, and they just looked like worn out late thirty to forty-year-old guys that were acting like they were cool, but that wasn't happening for them. Only Jerry thought that maybe if this hooker wanted to show somebody maybe she could show them what a STD was, if they didn't know she already had.

As the train rattled to a halt, the compressors of the doors moved open, and then Jerry rose to his seat as he said, "Maybe you can show these guys what you are made of?" He spared her no mercy as he turned his back to her, and then jumped out in front of the businessmen as he forced his way through the crowd as if a host of semen were forcing there way to the center of the woman's belly. But all Jerry couldn't wait to do was just get through this crowd, and feeling the fresh air amidst all the senses of high priced colognes and decent after-shave, he felt the free air just awaiting him out of this crowd.

Jerry took the nearest exit to the surface. When he traveled up the stairs and met the surface, he was greeted with the smog filled sky; it was a toxic kind of odor that came with all the car pollution that hovered all over the city like a plague, not to mention the waste disposal problems. When he joined the large moving crowd, he started walking at a very fast pace so that he could blend in, but when he started down Fifth Avenue, he didn't see any stores that were *Manhattan Shop of Magic*. Maybe it was past the antique shops and fine pricey chocolate stores, but the only way he would find out is to travel down the city streets until he found it.

After he had been traveling for what was an exact half an hour, he looked to his watch and saw the sun trying to peer through the large rain clouds that was hovering over the large sky scraper buildings. Jerry looked upwards and hoped that the clouds would then depart, because maybe there was some hope for him and maybe he could find the *Manhattan Shop of Magic*. When he wished that the sun would push through the white acid rain clouds, but the sun became blocked by the traveling clouds, and the sun looked like it was no more. Jerry thought this was useless, because he was looking on both sides of the street but as he stopped at the next streetlight, his conspicuous behavior when all of a sudden he saw a small sign that said,

The *Manhattan Shop of Magic* has moved two stores down.

When he wanted to burst out into the street, he saw the light suddenly change from red to yellow, and then green. When the light instantly changed to green, Jerry and his crowd of floating suits and tight dresses moved across the street pushing through the other crowd as Jerry pushed his way through the crowding hordes. He jumped over the next curb feeling the stone curb pouncing against the bottom of his feet. He stood still for a moment, but then continued onward, looking up at the façade of the buildings trying to find the *Manhattan Shop of Magic* poster waiting for him.

When he passed a *Giradelli* which had round trays of chocolate around the three top layers piled like a big mountain of chocolate. And the outside of the mountain was all made out of these small chocolates that contained mass amounts of gooey sweetness and There was another store that was that of tacky lingerie store named *Lucile's sex store.* The outside window never looked as if it had never been cleaned, and the bright red lingerie that was inside the glass window looked like thrown away or discarded material for a blow out sale from a larger company.

Jerry stared and chuckled with amazement and the audacity of all the stores, and how incredibly creepy or incredibly tacky to look at, but he couldn't pull his face away.

As he passed the last two stores, he stood still and suddenly froze in his place as he saw the store that he had been looking for, the one that might lead them to all the answers.

"It *might* lead to all their answers, just *might*." Jerry thought to himself thinking that this sounded like a good idea. But as he was about to get off hand, wondrous lights appeared around the glass wall as it quickly pulled his gaze, and held his attention for more than fifteen seconds. He stared intently as he saw a lighted pair of cards flashing red and black, the color red represented the Queen of hearts, and the color black represented the King of diamonds.

As the letters flashed off and on, each word of the neon bar titled

Manhattan Shop of Magic

instantly began to light up one, word at a time, and he couldn't help but feel enthralled to stare at it with amazement and childlike wonder. He had yet to find out what the inside of the store held for him, but this life was full of surprises, maybe he would find something good, maybe he was just conned into finding this store out of loyalty? But whatever lay in this store, angel or snake, elf or troll, pharaoh or emperor, he was definitely convinced to go in and find out the doorway to hell was in this store.

He moved closer to the shop, but was ready if something was going to jump out at him. But he kept his straight posture as he conquered his sudden fear, and approached a door that had the words printed across the glass window with bright letters written across the glass door the same as the title of the store.

He was on unfamiliar territory, but he decided to play it cool, and take a peak around the store if he could, without attracting any attention.

The owner of the store, Harry Dean, with some sweat forming at his brow, had little to no customers in the morning, and especially on a shitty overcast day like this, his business day would have been usual.

"Shitty!" Harry thought, as he stared wide awake, taking his weary eyes away from the paper filled desk, his mortgage statement on the apartment that he had been paying in some shitty part of Queens where he could get away from his nagging wife and annoying kids, Jesse and Jane. They were both in their teens where the acne ran rampant and they started becoming pudgy in their stomachs and around their cheeks. His wife, Lucille Dean, whose marriage was already starting to rot away, and he had an affair with a young Latin girl, Julia Mendoza, who was about eighteen years old.

"She was just a kid! They arrest people for things like that!" Harry couldn't believe the idiotic decisions he had been making in the last few years, but after he had lucked out from getting her pregnant, he ended the affair, but she was quick to resist his decision. But the odd thing was that she had known some things about the struggles in the families, and she had found out through fucking some wiseguys, and that was more of a reason to leave her. When she found out she hadn't impregnated her, she agreed not to see him again, and they did not keep in contact with each other since then.

"That was a good thing too, I don't want to divorce my wife so she can have the kids, and I would be stuck with an extra kid." Harry knew that his wife would get the kids if they divorced, and even though their marriage was disintegrating, he wanted to stay together for Jesse and Jane. He wanted them to see that they had a healthy marriage, and didn't want to damper their spirits with his bullshit. Worse than that, his greatest fear was that he didn't want to see his family dead either.

So, when he decided to close his eyes, the little jingle that he had put on his door had moved, and watched the boy walking around, looking at all of his products. "A customer?" Harry thought with curiosity, and just before he made himself known, he walked toward the crevice where it was opened, watching him with such intensity.

As Jerry closed the door behind him, a small ding arose as that of a doorbell and another one chimed in as the door swooped behind him. As Jerry looked around the store, bundling up his hands in his pockets as if he wasn't searching for anything particular, the dank unclean piss smell hovered above him as he walked throughout the store. Jerry noticed that on the far side of the wall there was some magic merchandise that he had never heard of before. As he walked toward the shelf, his nose then turned that smell made him think of unwashed hair and dandruff.

"Mastering Hypnosis?" He reached up toward the highest wall, and picked up the book, sending dust off the shelf. Bringing it down to his level, he then flipped through it with fascination at all the pictures and some of the directions. Then totally against his nature he held it in his other hand and then continued down the wall of magician's tools. But then he stopped dead in his tracks when he saw something else that made him want to grab out and touch it.

"Disappearing cane?" He saw a box that had a man holding the opposite ends of the cane with what looked like it disappeared into, two handkerchiefs. But unfortunately withdrew his hand and kept it to his side.

There were so many things on these shelves, that were fascinating, and he thought that he would have died and went to a sort of magicians' heaven. Coming from a curious mind, he wanted to know all these secrets. But his mind was already off track, and when he was starting to look for other things, he heard a voice call out to him on the other side of the room, "Hey kid?" It was almost in a creepy kind of way as if he had been watched all this time, and taken off guard.

Jerry turned, clenching the book in his hand, and with his free hand he immediately jolted toward the butt of his weapon as he felt the grip of the gun within seconds away of his grasp, he stopped, and located this voice. It was a rather healthy looking older man, with a blue shirt on and a pouch bulging over his khaki work pants then said "You need somethin'?" He was holding a few playing cards, and this certainly peaked Jerry's attention, and wandered what this man wanted.

"Yeah," he said as he clenched the book for a moment, feeling panicked anxiety traveling through his hand, and it was telling him to relax his trigger hand. "I do." Easing the temptation of pulling his gun out, and with a breath of fresh air, he let all his thoughts go, and decided to analyze whatever else he saw later on. But, he walked over toward the strange man that was standing behind the glass counter with either all the answers or nothing but a hand full of tricks?

When Jerry reached the counter to where the tall strange man was standing, he gave him a conniving smirk that made Jerry feel rather uneasy for his life, but as he walked toward him his hand unbearable to let the gun go for a few minutes. But as he approached the counter, he knew that it was better to approach this situation calmly. He saw inside the clear see through glass were more small boxes of magician's tools that hadn't even looked like they had been touched in months. Then there was another box that said

"False Teeth" and the outside of the box had a picture of chattering teeth on it. There was a picture on the box of a woman holding them in her palm, screaming for her life, which was probably from her own stupidity believing that that they were real.

Then on the same side of the box, but on the far right side was a man with his mouth open as if he was laughing at this petrified woman's own stupidity. This rose a chuckle out of Jerry, releasing some of the tension out of his system, and suddenly stopped and stood two feet away the man and the line of "False teeth" boxes. But as he saved himself the embarrassment he looked up at the man, seeing a few impermeable scars showing on his acidic skin like a stain on tablecloth. Even though it wasn't because of his poncho, it certainly brought out a rather rotten appearance to this man's features.

"So, kid, what are you looking for?" The man said to him impatiently as he gripped the few cards in his large fingers, and then shuffled the few cards on the table as he waited for this card to give him an answer.

Jerry saw that he was shuffling the cards with certain angst, as if he had done something wrong and was trying to hide it in plain sight. But Jerry probably put two and two together that this man was nervous, and for some reason, his mind could not let it leave his mind for even a minute. Jerry knew that he needed to find something to start them on a conversation, and what he picked up might as well have been the product of his own curiosity, and that was the book about hypnotism.

"Can you tell me a little bit about hypnotism?" Jerry said, handing the book to him so that he could scan through the book and try to find out what to talk about.

The man took the book from his hand, and huffing as he opened the book he scanning through it—rage emitting through his eyes—he stared at it—boringly for a few moments. Then, as if he had found the answer he was looking for, he laid the book down on the counter he then started to paraphrase all of this confusing stuff into his own words.

He read aloud the definition of hypnotism. "Hypnotism is the state of being entranced by a certain force from another person's willpower. But in order for that person to be hypnotized, that person's body must be in total relaxation, and the hypnotized willpower must be in that person's hands, i.e., by the hypnotizer."

He sounded like some college professor, but was really being half ass about it, explaining everything that he needed to know, but he sounded too in tune to his own words, too vain about everything. But then his eyes widened and returned to normal as he felt the exhilaration of his words leave his system, he then backed off from the edge of the counter and his voice sounded so pathetic and annoyed at his question as he said. "Well, I wouldn't want to give all the secrets away." He then grabbed the book by the end of the hardcover edge, and then closed it shut, creating dust flurries around him. "Are you going to buy it?"

Jerry did not want to keep wasting this guy's time, or his own, because if he didn't know anything, he didn't want to buy this book from him. But he just remembered that he hadn't asked him anything about Gene's whereabouts and right now was probably the best time to do it, which was by buying that book.

Jerry looked down at the book, and then pretending to bust a brain cell or two trying to figure out if he wanted it, and then made his decision with a surprisingly warm smile as he responded with a positive, "Yeah. I'll take it." Jerry stopped his words, and thought he was like some sort of stockbroker, and in that instance he saw that he had awoken this man's taste for his old job, and he waved a hand toward the book.

"Sure," He said picking up the book and walking toward the other side, "right this way."

The man stood in front of the cashier, and like a man fiercely typing at his typewriter, began to dazzle away at a few buttons on this archaic cash box. Jerry saw that it had not been dusted either, and the dust from the room had wanted to make him sneeze. As Jerry held his breathe, the cash box began to make a few dings as he punched in a few numbers as the man reached over toward the other side of the counter and grabbed for a small notepad that he had kept for keeping track of his sales. And when he was done peered at Jerry with his optimistic voice and then said, "34 dollars and 24 cents!"

Jerry paused for a moment, and cringed at the beheading price that was taking a large chunk out of his system that he would need to use some other time, but was now buying it for this book. He thought about haggling, but this was going to be in a different way. Before he had taken out his wallet, he sucked in a wind full of breath, and then started off with the simplest of conversations.

"Hey man. What's your name?" Jerry said with a laid back voice, and held his hand out over the counter for him to shake it.

"My name's Henry." His voice sounded polite, but underneath the friendly gesture, there toiled many secrets.

The man looked at his hand with growing suspicion, but then firmly placed his palm into Jerry's palm, and tightly squeezing his palm, he then said his name again to make sure he was saying it right. "Harry Dean."

After they gripped each other, they let each other go, and withdrew there hands back to their sides. Once their acquaintances had been made, it was time to ask the real question, "Where was Gene?" He thought about saying it like that, but he knew the best way to put it in another way.

"Hey, do you know of any other person than Houdini that did the disappearing acts?" Jerry said very questioning and without hostility, as just two old friends would be when they were talking to one another.

Harry Dean looked at him and tried to imagine any other person who did the disappearing acts—face scrunching together in confusion—shaking his head and then said with a reaffirming voice, his face turning gray underneath the bright light. "No, I don't have any other idea except for Houdini. He was pretty good at it to until he died."

"Yeah, I guess so. Everyone has their day I guess?" Jerry said as he saw a few pixels of dust particles dancing around the top of his baldhead and two inches away from the light bulb. They laughed about the remark, as the pixels radiated some kind of diluted light that had been trying to shine through, as if a sting of electricity was going to appear like a random bolt of lightening.

Jerry's gaze focused off of the titillating light, and back to Harry Dean's shadowed face, which looked as if he had been obviously confused by the question, and couldn't get out of his mental slump. If it was time to ask him for anything, now was the time for Jerry to step up and say it.

"You know," Harry added as he stopped punching on the cash box, and scratching his chin. "I don't think there was anyone else like Houdini because all the audience in his shows were probably blinded by the allusion of his impossible feats, and when they saw one thing, he was probably safe and sound behind something else. For example…" Harry moved out of the cash registers sight, and one of his hands went digging into his pockets, and pulled out what looked like a Camel cigarette that had never been lit, and put into his mouth.

Speaking with the cigarette in his mouth, it came out with a muffling or gargling kind of sound. "Now…" Harry was reaching into his other pocket, and then revealed a small metallic object that was magnified and the light quickly blinded Jerry as he saw that it was a quarter. A plain old looking quarter and it didn't seem any different than he had seen in the bank, but he structured his words very carefully when he came up with his answer. "All an allusion?" It made him think that everything good in this world was just an allusion, and nothing can last forever.

Harry took the cigarette from his mouth, and held the two objects underneath the light. Harry looked at them with complete dumbfounded boredom as he shook his head mindlessly, but carefully trying to think what these two had in common with each other.

"What do these two things have in common?" Jerry said, reaching for the money.

But when Jerry had his hand halfway out to touch them, Harry Dean wrapped around the coin and Harry Dean's voice became sharp as a blade, "Have you no respect. Just hold on, I haven't gotten to the point yet."

"Well," Jerry thought to himself, "Why don't you get to the fucking point so I can ask you about Gene and I can get that overpriced book and we can part our fucking ways." He played with the thought of saying this, but that would do him no good. Maybe he was being impatient, and he didn't want to piss this guy off, but all he could do now was wait until his point was across. He hoped that it wouldn't take too long, because Jerry wasn't going to wait for long.

"Now, it's always in a magician's trade to create an allusion for his audience. Now, it's always has to be done precisely when the audience is off their guard, and watching something else, like a woman or a tiger. But I don't believe in that." Harry watched his new friend watching and waiting for him to make his move, and pulling the two things together, he quickly slid the cigarette into the coin, and slid it back out.

Jerry's eyes pushed upwards, and the fastness of his hand blew him away, and his mouth almost dropped if he hadn't caught the stupidity of the trick. But acting surprised for this man, he kept his eyes wide and his eyebrows arched up across his forehead like a pastel mark.

"Man!" Jerry's voice was believable and gave no hint to cynicism, and he forced himself to smile so this guy could feel like he had amazed him, but he knew he wasn't amused.

Harry Dean saw the boy smiling, and he smirked as he pulled it in and out again, as if he was trying to be humorous. When he saw that the smile was beginning to disintegrate off his face, he knew that it wasn't funny or amusing anymore. He gave off one pathetic chuckle, and then said, "You don't have to buy this, that was just an example of an allusion." Harry looked at his own product and then placed them back into his pocket.

"Well…" Jerry said, as he breathed inward, trying to find the exact words so that he could get his point across and direct. "Do you know anything about a kid that disappeared a few days ago—you know, like Houdini?"

Dean looked around, surveying his apartment, and then looked at him with his eyes narrowing. The statement was puzzling. "I don't think I know about that, maybe you should check the local police station, or the orphanage."

Jerry's emotions became enraged, and everything in his system was telling him to pull that gun out and start interrogating him. Only Jerry knew that if talking wasn't going to work, then he felt that brutal force might be necessary.

But as he stuffed that urge away, he let out another long breath, and said with a total lack of emotion "Well, I want you to remember very closely because I need to talk to this friend."

Harry shook his head, and put on his best confusing look, and continued inhaling his cigarette.

He then dropped the bomb on him, and said it with a more grave voice. "You might know his name. His name is Gene Dov."

Harry suddenly stood still and the cigarette fell out of his mouth. He reached into his pockets again, and revealed the cigarette and in his other hand wasn't a quarter this time, it was a blue Bic lighter. He gripped the lighter inside his large palms and his thumb quickly rolled over the spark. After his thumb fell over the spark, a long red flame burst from it and he took a long single puff. After half the cigarette was done he blew the smoke out in one single breath—the smoke crawled along the wall like a lifeless bug—and then said, "Yeah, what about him?"

Jerry rolled his eyes, and then said with certainty in his voice, "Would you know where he is?"

Harry's hand rose up to his brow, holding the cigarette between his two fingers, scratched the middle of his brow with his thumbnail, and felt some of his sweat jumping into his fingernail. Only this was information that he wished he didn't want to know, but how could he not know, it was all over the streets like a poka-dotted lizard just waiting to bite the first person that was just curious enough to show it attention. Only did curiosity kill the cat or did the truth become so great that it just wore down the cat so much that it inevitably killed him? Whatever the case, someone was going to go insane, and whether it was Harry Dean or a cat, it seemed that the one to go insane would be him. *"Everything leads back to the source, I tell you now."* The voice blew through Jerry's mind and Jerry began to think that this voice was sending a decoded message to a fragmented sentence.

And Harry Dean didn't want to end up dead at age fifty-five, and if there was ever a time to intervene his death, now would be his time to do it.

Harry Dean drew another puff of the cigarette, calming his nerves, and as it cleared his mind he withdrew the cigarette from his mouth and then said with a relaxed tone, "Before we start talking, I want to know what crew you are with."

Jerry didn't really know what to say, because he was just probably expecting him to give up the information just like that, but Jerry's wall was starting to loose its cement, and it started to bang together. He tightened his grip, and then said rather shadily "What does it matter to you?"

Harry just shook his head with concern and then withdrew another long breath of the cigarette, as if it was his last. "Because," Harry said, taking the nearly half done cigarette from his mouth, he rested his hand to his side, and the smoke twirled—the nicotine embedded into his skin—and above his head, disappearing to the top and into the darkness—where secrets festered above them. "I want to know that you aren't some spy that is going to use me up for my information and then come back here to kill me after its all over."

Jerry shook his head and then proceeded to ask him, "Who said anything about killing?"

At that moment, Harry let out a small laugh escape him, and then a long cough escaped his throat with a few gobs of spit traveled from the corner of his mouth and onto the white counter. Jerry looked down and saw the large gobs just resonating in the artificial sunlight, and slowly vegetating into a pile of wetness as it was exposed in the naked air. He took his eyes off the glob of spit and saw that Harry was covering his mouth and coughing out, "Sorry..." another whooping cough came soaring against the handkerchief and landed with a dull blow. Jerry dismissed it, and Harry nodded in compliance of the response, and then pulled his hand away from his mouth.

Then, in a moment of irrationality, he let this portly magician owner know who he was. "I'm with Chris Mangini."

Once those words came out, it was all over. Everything turned quiet, Harry's coughing suddenly stopped, and the handkerchief fell from his face and onto the floor. That must have been how his heart had felt like, dead and paralyzed, and his color drained from his skin making him look like a pale ghost, even though he was partly white, this made him look like Casper the friendly fucking ghost. He would be white when all the blood would leave his body, and he didn't want his fate to be sealed by another person.

Harry took one last drag of the cigarette, finishing it off with one last hit he let his arm fall to his side as if it went limp. Then Harry glanced down to his right side and then let the cigarette fall from his fingers, and saw it falling to the floor and landing hard on its side just inches away from the handkerchief. He saw the end of his smoking cigarette just waiting to burn through the piece of paper that he had carried with him for so many years. As he saw the charred end of his cigarette sending more smoke from the floor, looking like it had been dropped into the abyss, and a few bits of smoke had managed to rise out of it's large deep uninhabited system.

Harry quickly rose his foot over the flaming cigarette, and then slowly crushed the end, seeing the smoke disappear from underneath his feet, and relieved his foot off the suppressed piece of paper, and then returned his gaze back to the boy, Henry. Feeling more jacked up than a rabbit that had been shot full of chemicals and was running around in a fit, his voice grew tense and clear.

"That's good. I hoped that you weren't a spy for one of the families or from that bastard's crew. When I tell you where he is, you are never going to speak of this conversation, or even come to see me, because we never talked, we never even met. Do you understand?"

"Yes. I won't tell a single soul." Jerry said with full conviction in his voice, which ultimately surprised Jerry for a moment, actually thinking about his contract to the promise and how false it was.

"Okay…" Harry said scratching his chin and then focusing his gaze away from Jerry, "good." He gave his attention to the handkerchief that was lying at his feet. As he leaned over to pick it up, Jerry's brain pulsed with anxiety and paranoia as if he had smoked a whole line of cocaine and then tried to go to sleep. But Jerry knew that he would never stick to the promise that he made, and was just using this old man for information. But, he had to get it out of him very quickly.

When Harry returned to his view, he had stuffed the handkerchief in his pocket and then said with a sort of relief in his voice. Jerry looked at him, and awaited his response. "All I can say is that all your answers lead up to the Island, where lost dreams and Ferris wheels blaze in dazzling lights. It's not S.I. I'm talking about. I'm not sure if he might had left by now, but he would reside in a house that is low key, probably a crack house if anything."

Jerry was puzzled by all of this, and he got pretty much that a crack house was not a place he would be in either, but Gene's snake like ability to creep through anywhere didn't surprise him at all. But if this was where this bear was hiding, it was time for Gene to awake from his deep sleep, and face the music for his crimes against Chris Mangini and his clan.

"Where in Coney?" Jerry said trying to put together all the pieces to this terrible puzzle.

"I don't know. But if you don't find him there, you will definitely find someone else who will know because now is the time to stop this madness." He caught his breath and then whispered to himself. "The twins?"

Jerry looked at him, feeling the dank air rising up against his throat, and his voice grew perplexed, "What?"

Harry regained his senses and then said "Nothing." It sounded like his voice grew thin, and weary. Jerry could see some of the color returning back to old Harry Dean, but something else looked different about him too, as if relief had finally entered into his body and gave his soul the peace he deserved.

"But where is this crack house? There must be a thousand crack houses in New York alone."

Harry just looked at him, and then let out a great big sigh as he shook his head and said, "That you will have to find out on your own. Now, go. Forget that you ever came here. But one more thing!"

"What is it?" Jerry said, looking at him with his eyebrows arched high up against his brow, his eyes wide and waiting with impatience.

"Go see this Latin broad, her name's Julia Mendoza in Queens. She can give you some leads." Harry said this with some regret, but the way it sounded coming from him it was a relief to say these words.

"What is she to you?" Jerry exclaimed, knowing that with his pale skin, she could only be his girlfriend on the side.

Harry took a deep breath, and then letting the rest of the sentence flow from his lips like a sea of excruciating excrement out of his asshole of a mouth, "Let's say she was someone I was seeing on the side."

Jerry shook his head in return, and then held out his hand toward him. Harry looked at it, and then he put out his own, and gripped it.

It was like they both understood each other, and even though they just met for the first time, it felt like they had a common bond. Once they let there hands go Harry offered Jerry to take the book. Jerry refused his offer, but then Harry pushed it on him even more. But he insisted that he should, and then without another question, Jerry took the book in his hand and then as they said there last "good byes," Jerry headed toward the door with the book so tightly in his hand. That dank smell never left him, and as he was two feet away from the door. It was time to meet with Frank and his brother, to tell them everything he could understand, and about everything he couldn't understand.

Whatever his brother might have found out, he hoped that it would clarify everything that he had just heard, or just perplex it even more. But whatever the case was, he had to see Frank before the day was over, and to a payphone he had to go.

After Jerry had left, Harry Dean hoped that Chris Mangini would end the life of Gene Dov, and quickly, but if he didn't, nothing but chaos would reign the streets. Only Harry felt that chaos was already running amuck, and now grief overtook him just thinking about it. He felt like his time on this earth was already up, and even though he would have to leave his family behind, he knew that they would be taken care of with all the property that he left for them. He didn't worry about his children because he knew that they could take care of themselves. Harry knew it might hurt them, but it had to be done.

Harry cleaned off the top of his desk so that nothing was on it, except the picture of his family, and he stuffed all his papers in the third drawer, leaving his property to his wife and kids, for when his lawyer reads them his inheritance. He left them the business, and they had the choice to liquidate all the crap that he had tried to pawn off for years or keep it.

"Well, this is it." Harry pulled the slide back, and heard the mechanical click-clack sound off a thousand echoing screams as he imagined everything that would happen in his head after he pulled the trigger. The ambulance would come to pick him up, the police would call his wife and give him the bad news, and watch him being lowered into the coffin. Harry, who was loaded with a barrage of these images, looked at his family picture as he pointed the gun to his neck, feeling his neck give a rampant pulse, sending his blood rising throughout his body. He dried his eye with his free hand, and felt the light of the room being too bright against his weak eyes. To end his life much easier, he reached toward the lamp, with the gun still pointed to his neck, he shut the light off.

Darkness filled the room, and Harry couldn't see a thing, but all he could feel was the end of the gun pointing into his neck, and then felt the pulse rising through his neck. So quickly and painless it would, but rather tragic in a sense.

Then he ended his life, and Harry Dean was no more.

Chapter XXII:

"The Wheels are in Motion"

"Oh yeah!" Ann Pantoliano whispered to the silence of her room, feeling dirty inside her soft thick sheets, her wet finger was lubing her wet vagina, fantasizing about her sexual encounter with that boy she had sex with in the bathroom. "I'm a dirty bitch!" Her young supple vagina that she hadn't even shaved for at least a week could feel the hairs matting up in her pointer finger, and then in her middle finger, almost trying to replace the pleasure with the pain.

Then her excitement heightened in her body, and a cringing feeling of pleasure filled her as she was way beyond the point of moaning. She wanted to scream with ecstasy, but she hadn't taken any drugs, so this was new to her. "Fuck me…" her panting grew as she pushed her finger passed her clit, and found her pressure point, and she pushed at it, hard. "OH…FUCK," and finally until her pleasure finally reached her climax. "Fuuuuck!" She finally said, exasperated, finger still entrenched in her vagina and body partly shaking from how much she had come on her finger. It was different, but it provided her with the sexual fantasy she needed until she meet the boy again, and then she would fuck his brains out again.

Ann didn't like how she gave herself into that boy, letting him fuck her like that, pushing his penis inside her with such force, but with some odd feeling about it, that's what she loved about fucking, the pain that she had felt after it all. She felt that a crowbar had fuck her and felt a large gaping hole in her vagina. She wanted to be on top the next time, and she wanted to fuck him good. She couldn't wait. Annie just kept her finger inside her vagina, hoping to gain something more from this, but couldn't gain the same speck of pleasure that she had felt with his protruding penis that she was doing with her two fingers. But with his dick she felt like that he had parted her ovaries like Moses had parted the sea to cross over from Egypt.

But, knowing this was entirely different than parting waters, she knew that he had definitely parted her insides. She was fucking A sure of that!

With her two fingers still resting in her vagina, there was a sudden slamming sound coming from downstairs door, and she heard it close with a loud *CRACK*! Feeling the wetness beginning to attach onto her fingers, like gooey nectar dripping from a cracked honeycomb, oozing all its goodness onto the ground with a carnal pleasure Ann pulled her two fingers out of her comb. Pulling her underwear up she pushed the covers off of her body that was covering her lower half, which was already naked to begin with. She tried to flick it a few pubic hairs from around her fingers, but when she thought it was off, she felt the pubic hair still entangled on her finger. With some force she slid them off her fingers, and it landed somewhere inside her bed covers. She had thrown her pants beside her bed, and if she could find it through her pigpen of a room, clothes in one pile, notebooks and school work back into a corner where most of her bad tests went, she could obviously get up and see who it was.

Slipping on her tight white jeans, she looked in the mirror and saw that her white T-shirt didn't hide how pale she was. Disgusted with the way she looked, even more so to put herself in a hospital, but she tried to blame it on the darkness of the room, on what little light she had. She was only kidding herself, and sneered at the mirror, disgusted and reviled with a slobbering pinkish tongue.

Only she decided to give herself a break, and coiling a strand of her black hair over her ears, she sighed and then moved out the door. She heard, from the bottom of the stairs, someone moving around the kitchen, but the voice was talking to someone, and it sounded like it was taking down directions to go somewhere.

"But to where?" Ann thought, as she stood in the hall, but leaned against the stairs, trying to listen with her keen open ears. Lowering her elbows against the chestnut rail held up with large white tiles, she heard the footsteps and the voice travelling to the kitchen and the living room *STOMP-STOMP-STOMP*. She didn't have to worry about breaking it, because the large filed down chestnut could hold her body. She felt extreme pain in her shoulders, and her back silently aching from how her large agonizing breasts weighed on her shoulders, making her slump over.

The conversation suddenly ended, and blended into the darkness of the hallway, she heard some footsteps around the living room, and then that person walked out in front of the door, and she said with curiosity when she saw who was about to leave. "Berry!"

Berry, who had just memorized the directions to A.J.'s place, didn't hear Annie when she had called out to him. When he pulled the door open, he thought it sounded like a whisper, and it was. When he was about to pull the door open, he moved toward the stairway, with some speculation to what he heard, and then saw with his own eyes his sister, leaning over the railing, her white skin proving to be a disadvantage in the darkness. He cringed from how pale she was, and knew that she would need a tan, but he knew that was the last thing on her list as of now. He had to get out of here now.

"Ann?" Berry said, seeing her pale face reflect some haunting sadness of her everyday life, he knew that he couldn't bring her along with him. "I can't talk, okay! I got to go!"

Moving out the door, he made his way back toward the door, and twisting the door knob he pulled the door with such strength, hearing the door squeak like the cranking of a fart and felt the wind moving under the outside screen door, calling him to leave. But she wasn't going to let him go that easily, without some sort of explanation.

"Where are you going?" She called out to him, and setting her left hand over the rail, her face became ever more of a blotch in the thick darkness.

"Don't worry about it!" Berry said with urgency in his system, "I'll be back later!" He moved away from the stairs, and back towards the door.

Ann tapped her palm on the cold railway, and when he was about to walk out the door she knew something that would make him stop in his tracks, even if she wasn't trying to offend, she felt like he needed to be reminded. They would have buried their brother a week ago, but they waited for the rest of their family to come see him buried. "James's being buried tonight, I thought you should know!"

Berry stopped, just when he was about to open the screen door, he turned around, looking at this pathetic girl he called his sister, and saw her lips pushing out very dumb, but he knew why she had said that to him. She wanted to make him feel shitty about leaving her here, like she was some lab rat, but he knew that, in his cold pumping heart, now was not the time to bring her along. Most importantly, he didn't trust her around that Frank character. He wasn't too particularly sure of what really went on in the bathroom, whether she was in there with him or not, and knew what his answer was going to be if she bugged him about coming along.

"Thanks!" Berry said, breathing with such a force that he almost wanted to cry or just lunge and beat the shit out of her. But, then he said, while he was eyeing her, "What time is the funeral!"

Ann opened her mouth, but then hesitated to speak, whether or not it was at seven thirty or eight at night, and did not want to confuse him. They were different than most churches, and they were Catholic, but she guessed that her father wanted her son buried as soon as possible. Stop prolonging the hurt that must've been so overwhelming, but she didn't know what it was like, she was too confused about too many things, let alone be sad for James's death. She knew that he was strong, and wouldn't have wanted them to cry over his dead body, because he was alive in spirit, and he would have been in a far better place.

When she was sure and certain about the time, she came out with it. "Seven thirty!"

Berry nodded, and knew that it wouldn't have taken them long to discuss over what they had found out. Only he was not denying the fact out that he might have to miss the funeral, if it had to take longer than he expected. Only he was leaving his time frame open for this, because everything would be set in motion after this meeting. There would be five people at this meeting, including himself, and by the way Frank sounded, they were going to air out a lot of things that needed to be settled. He just needed to get their so that they could discuss the plans.

Berry turned his gaze off of Ann, and gave her the cold shoulder as he said, "I'll try to be there!"

But when he started to push the door open, he felt a strong gust of wind blowing in past him, chilling his bones, and stepping his foot out he heard Annie calling his name again, and he stopped so he could hear what she said.

"Don't *try* to be there!" Ann said defiantly, *"Just be there!"*

Berry sighed, feeling the wind creeping up his pant leg and didn't say a word, not promising her a thing, as he said, "I can't promise you!" That shut his sister up for a second, and saw this as his perfect time to leave. He pushed on, holding the door for him, and closed the screen door, leaving the door open, obviously letting her close the door. He had to get to the car, and get to A.J.'s house, where they would get this meeting over with, certainly having a few ideas of his own, but he had yet to know what the other four members had to offer. But he had one thing in mind, get his hands on Gene, and kill him. But his needs would probably come later, and that would be a lengthy process.

A.J. and Jessica were already at his house, A.J. especially felt different when he was inside it, when he was giving Berry the directions to his home. While he was talking to Berry, A.J. ran to his room, fulfilling his curiosity he looked for the box that had always grabbed his attention. Even though it was a plain brown box, it had some secret appeal to him, calling for him to open and see what was inside it. A.J. felt like if he had opened it, he would either unleash some unknown plague or just unearth a part of his childhood that would only hurt him even more. Whether this box was for good or evil, he knew that it was safe and after the meeting, he would end his hungry curiosity once and for all. Not just a second after he had gotten the phone call, he called the brother's he had sent to retrieve the information that he wanted. And by the way they sounded they had successfully found more than what he was looking for. He hung up the phone, and knew that they had to talk about this meeting in the only place that he could think of.

"In the kitchen," A.J. said, giving him the most blatant option, which seemed like the best place to hold this meeting. Frank looked at him, and then knew that there were only four chairs. But they would improvise.

"Let's get this place set up!" Frank said, and they immediately went to work. They had grabbed a few wet rags and were wiping off the top, and knew that laying out some sort of food for them to pick on was the best possible thing to do. So, none of them wouldn't be hungry while they had this meeting. A.J. told Jessica to get a bag of Snider chips that his parents always got when they went to their hometown in Pennsylvania, and he always had a craving for at any time of the day. They also had some Doritos and Frito chips, for some sort of variety, but would be a distraction for the others while A.J. and Frank could snack down on the chips. Jessica grabbed a few clean bowels, and blew into them, always superstitious of how long it had been cleaned for or not. Even if they were just cleaned, she always had to give a small blow just to keep the dust particles out of the bowl. She was just weird like that.

While she was dispensing the snack food in the round bowls while A.J. and Frank got some glasses and set them at arm's length between each seat. The crystal clear glasses had no ice in any of the glasses because they thought that if they preferred ice, they would provide that before or in the middle of the meeting. They didn't put their names on it, because there was just no need to do that, because he felt like none of them needed to be placed through rank. But A.J. and Frank needed to have the chairs where they could face them, and have the best advantage to hear them speak of what each of them found out.

Once everything was done, he needed Jessica to stay in his room while they talked over their business, and they had many things to talk about.

"When our people get here," A.J. walked toward her, and grabbed Jessica by the shoulders. "I need you to go in my room, and I will get you when we are ready!"

But before she could argue herself out of it, there was a knock on the door. A.J. looked out of the open hallway, and Frank went into the living room, and saw two cars parked out in front of his house. "They're here!" He yelled, wearily, and looked at A.J., knowing that it was time to go.

A.J. then looked at Jessica, and motioned her to go to his room. She narrowed her eyebrows at him, and moved away with her rather large breasts pushing against his chest, and leaning her head upwards, she kissed his dry lips against his and disappeared in disgust. A.J. did not care if she was mad at him or not, but he wanted to be in business mode right now. "No better time than now!" A.J. said in the silence, feeling like dog crap in between a tire. Frank turned, and smirked, seeing the disgust on his face, his smirk turned into a frown. "I know what you mean."

"Let's go!" A.J. said, and motioned for Frank to get the door. Frank let the top part of his teeth show, like it was the only glint of emotion he would show for the rest of the meeting, and as Frank approached the door, A.J. went into the kitchen, so that he could find the best seat out of the entire table. A.J. was nervous but he knew what he wanted to say. He was ready!

When everyone had taken their shoes off, headed into the kitchen, and sat in their seats, A.J. could see the two Italian boys, Jerry and Niccolo, with their short curly hair making an even bouncier presence than there jovial personalities. All of them had made their acquaintances outside but when A.J. turned toward Berry Pantoliano, closing his mouth, staring at the chips and assortment of round bowls like it was suffocating, like a patch of poisonous flowers.

A.J. calmly held out his hands, in a giving manner, and then said with a smile, waving, giving Berry his permission. "Don't worry! You can eat something."

Berry just nodded and said with a smirk, "thanks!" He reached his hand across the table, and delved his hand into the bowl.

"I haven't eaten in a while." He said as his fingers held a handful of Fritos. He opened his mouth, and they fell in his mouth in one single swoop. Then he chewed them up, the sound of the grinding corn chips making a loud *crunch-crunch-crunching* when he finally swallowed the mushy corn chips, rattling and grinding in his chomping mouth. Then after he did it, Jerry and Niccolo, moved in on the dishes of snacks as well. After they finished crunching on the corn chips and Doritos all of them then took a sip of their pop, and letting the liquid cleaning their throats, they laid it back on the table and they waited for him to start.

"This is it!" A.J. thought, and in that moment accepted who he was, "no more running away from whom I really am."

"I have called you today because we all have something in common. Some are here because we want revenge." He glanced around at each of them, starting with Berry. Berry shuddered, but still listened to him. "Some are here because of they have pledged their undying loyalty to Chris Mangini." He looked at Frank, who nodded with small smirk, and then A.J. looked to the two boys.

"Some are here because we all have pledged an allegiance. Not to our country no less, but to Chris Mangini and everyone that ever believed in defying the system, and for a cause greater than ourselves. I do have some things to talk about, because I believe that this is a time when we need to stand up, and take control of what we have been handed."

Then Niccolo broke into A.J.'s sentence and added with a resounding, "La Familigia!" He saw this boy's hair shine with the setting sun, and he revealed his teeth, dimples outshining his lips.

A.J. looked at him, knowing that it meant "family" in English nodded with a smirk, and said, "Yes! Our Familigia!" He sounded like he had said it different, but he wasn't going to let his accent stop him now.

He continued. "I have a few things that I want to say, and then I will give you your orders. One, I think some answers are somewhere in Queens. I want to find out the street hustlers that sell Llama handguns because this is another clue to how we will find out our answers in Queens."

"Why Queens?" Niccolo asked, with certain doubts about going into a place that was darker than the black of midnight.

Then Jerry burst in, knowing what he had found out could prove A.J.'s theory about Queens. "I found out a few things from my contacts that…"

A.J. then regained firm control of the conversation, looking at Jerry, signifying that his help was appreciated. "Thank you Jerry," Jerry stopped talking, "and I think that we might find some allies that can lead us in the right direction. If there aren't, then we don't have to worry about that. But make sure you have a colored friend with you to know that it's cool, and go in the day time, so that you can catch them off guard."

"I don't know any moolies," Niccolo shook his head, and then he said nothing.

But Jerry was not going to let this thing go. "Don't leave anything to doubt man!" he said with such prestige.

"No way man!" Niccolo interrupted, looking at him irritated, "How are we ever going to do that without even being able to talk to anyone in Queens, especially in places like South Jamaica?"

A.J. just looked at him, plainly, without any judgement at all—a duck in a cement pond. "Also, the second thing that is bothering me is that a crew that ran with me, Antony, Guido, and Guissepe, up until this happened, were all running with me. Giuseppe warned me that the two would be involved in this, and warned me before he disappeared on me the next few days. But

I think that those two might know something, if they are alive, so we need to find them as soon as possible. Jerry, Niccolo, and Berry will take care of this, in addition to the Queens affair. I believe these clues will lead to Gene's whereabouts."

All three of them nodded, even though they had different opinions about what they were ordered to do, they grinned and bore what responsibilities they had to do. If they were to stay faithful to Chris, then they needed to stay faithful to his successor, A.J.

A.J. nodded in approval, but then moved on with his ideas that he had. He turned to Frank, and knew that he was the best person to get in touch with Chris's contacts. "I want you to contact Benjamin Shapiro, but don't contact him when he's around the Don or anywhere else. Also, we should go to that wedding, because we might be able to finagle some information out of someone who is drunk enough to spill his guts. So, get back to that Captain and you make the arrangements."

Frank nodded, but then asked him out of curiosity, "How many should I say will be present?"

A.J. thought about it for a moment, and then counted out how many people, including himself, Jessica, Frank, Jerry, Niccolo, and Berry. "Six."

Frank nodded, "Six?" Knowing that the five people around this table made up most of those people, but he had a vague suspicion with whom the sixth person would be. "Jessica!" Frank thought, and knew that they would be left without any ass to squeeze on. But they would make do with what they saw. He just hoped there wouldn't be any fifteen-year-old-girls…he decided to stop thinking right now, just stop!

A.J. had just remembered a few more things that came to his mind, like a dead body that had just floated up to the top of the surface, bloated and puffy like, water filling the bodies with so much water no one could imagine a more simple way of dying.

"I also think that being at this wedding will also tell us what is happening in the streets and who is really against us or for us. We need to start looking out for other allies if we want more information, and reaching out to others, do all that we can to try to gain all the information we can. Reach out to other family members, and see what they might want, in exchange for whatever they may want or need. If you can pull it off that way, the old fashioned way is an alternative, and don't forget that!"

Niccolo laughed and then he said with a devious smirk, "We won't! Especially when we go talk to those *moolies*!"

A.J. had heard this word before, but he laughed all the same, to appease his guests. His hand moved off the table, quickly trailing his fingers along his belt line he felt on what was the handle of his black Llama handgun that he had since that first night he had highjack his first truck of CD's. A.J., with his fingers gripping the handle of the weapon, he pulled it out, revealing it to all of them. They stared with daunted faces, and looked at him as if he was missing a screw in his neck.

"What are you doing?" Jerry said, seeing the gun gleaming in the last glint of sunlight on the metallic silver pistol, and lowering it down to the table, he watched A.J. fall back in his seat. Then he waved it toward him with a flick of his hands, sighing as he said with a strong resilience to Jerry's stupid questions. "Take this when you ask the hustler's around Queens. I bet you will come up with something, and if it's nothing, then it will be nothing, and the city is always full of eyes and ears. Just look around and you'll see. Someone will know something!"

A.J. nodded, and then waved it again as Frank took the gun by the sides, passing it down toward Jerry and Niccolo. Both of them looked at each other, not knowing which one of them would hold the weapon Niccolo extended his hand toward the gun. He reached his hands out, resting his hand over the metallic piece, everything in him wanted to take it, but he pulled his hand away from it resting his hand against his leg, he looked to his brother. He was shaking his head, with his lips pushed out, and reached across the table as he said, "You pussy!" Jerry chuckled, but easily rousing his anger his right hand fell against the back of his head with a loud *THWACK!*

Then automatically, Jerry's grip around the handle tightened, and his finger moved inside the hole, slowly laying his finger down on the trigger. Pointing the gun at Niccolo, with an irate look in his eye said, "Don't do that!" Jerry didn't sound angered by what had happened, but what he did was more in a defense mechanism than anything else he had ever done before in his state of irritation.

Then Frank intervened in this nonsense with a "STOP!" His more than serious stare—reprimanding eyes, and unwavering crouch, looking at both of them—he spoke again, but this time, they didn't like this party-pooper behavior but he had to be serious, or Frank would kill them for sure.

"Listen to what he says!" Frank stared.

"Now," A.J. continued, looking at each of them, sighing heavily, and then continued to hear him, "I want to hear from everyone else what they have found. I have talked enough, and I think its time we find out what you three have found." A.J. sighed again, as if he had just run the Olympic races, and he was at the finish line, but he had to pass the baton to the next person, and that was Berry. Berry just looked at him, and then scratching his temple, feeling the sweat already pouring out of his pores, he said, "Okay, it all started..."

Four Coke Cola cans and a half an hour later Berry had explained

The Disintegrating Bloodline

everything. Everything from what he heard from cokehead was amazing but Frank seemed to think this boy was just a smaller portion in this story, a distraction, from what the addicted Outcast member had told them. A.J. would not leave anything to chance, coming from a cocaine fiend could be total bullshit, but for some reason, he listened to him all the same. He would not let anyone go interrupted, and when Frank looked at A.J., he motioned with his eyes to keep focused on Berry, who had been interrupted by Jerry and Niccolo. A.J. didn't want Frank to be that selfish. Frank understood that, and A.J. motioned for Jerry to tell them what he had found out.

"Well…" Jerry said, and almost stumbled over his words, trying to think of something grand, knowing that he didn't have the patience to take so much time, he decided to just come out with it.

"I went to the Manhattan Shop of Magic, like Frank told me to do, and I found out a lot of things. One thing importantly, the owner, Harry Dean, told me we should talk to some Spanish girl, Lucia Mendoza, who was probably his girlfriend on the side, knew something. I don't know what she knows, but she has to know something that is of worth."

"Yeah…right!" Frank thought, "What is she going to tell us! How many inches of all the dicks that she's sucked? Please, let someone have some crucial information so that we can get somewhere with this meeting!" Even though he wanted a lot more out of what he was hearing, he couldn't help but feel that they were wasting their time.

"Whores and crack-fiends! Where are they going to get us?" Frank just shook his head, "In lots of trouble," he continued to think, but he stopped thinking for a moment. Then A.J. gave Niccolo the chance to talk, and Frank got two more ice-cold coke cola cans from the refrigerator before Niccolo let himself explain what he found out. But since his brother didn't have the honor of meeting the old Consigliere of the D'Angelino family, and he would take his time with explaining everything he had told him, because he had much information, and many things had to be taken into account. He asked for another Coke Cola. Since he had finished his third Coke-Cola, he needed some more sugar to get his brain flowing.

When Frank had brought him his Coke, he slipping his finger inside the tap, and forced it upwards, making a shot of fizz rise up, and he wasted no time to let the mist flow out of the can. Either before he elevated the can he tipped it sideways, letting the dark liquid flow out of the cold can, and let it fall in the glass and the fizz slowly moved up the glass, slowly and surely.

"I talked to old D'Angelino boss, Sergio Fillini, who had been approached by Gene a long time ago to find the birth records of the lost cousin. After he said he found the records, he saw Gene acting as if the Second Coming of

Christ was coming." All of them were wide eyed, listening and hanging on every word that he had been saying. "Not that way, but metaphorically."

Frank nodded, and smirked with an uneasy smile, "We know," and rubbed his sweat brow with his two fingers, wanting him to end the torture of this long, expected wait.

Niccolo continued, regaining some momentum back in his system, "After he found the records, Gene wanted him to join his side when the new powers would rise up and take out Chris and Don Pescaro. But what is stopping then is the fact that this long lost cousin could stop what is happening with the Old world." He shuddered from the very words, missing what he had been away from for such a long time, the mountains, the trees, his home, what he had missed so much. "We should beware of the mask of *Morte*!"

"The mask of *Morte*?" Frank thought, and then wanted to almost spit.

"We don't know who he is, but we know that he is not our friend, and he wants to kill the long lost cousin of Chris. He is very well connected with the boy's back home. From what Sergio told me, no one will do business with the Old Guard. They're afraid to send any assassins over there, because they know they won't come back alive."

Frank shook his head and remembered the dream that Chris had, with the woman smoking on that glass pipe from a dripping candlestick.

A.J. took a deep breath, and then he said, "Who is he with?"

Jerry looked at him with confusion, "I don't know. That is yet to be seen!"

A.J. at this moment felt like he was going to die, because he feared that he was going to say his name, but he didn't want to ask what the name was. But he had to ask, because it was going to come out sooner or later.

"What is the cousin's name?" A.J. said, with a grave face.

All of them looked at A.J., and Frank just rolled his eyes, and Jerry said, "What?"

A.J. shook his head, and then lowered it, close and his voice was very agitated. "What…" A.J. controlled his temper and then continued, "is the cousin's name!"

Jerry shook his head, knowing that this shouldn't have concerned him but A.J. wanted to know, and that was his word. "There are two of them. His last name is Cattiano, but I don't know what his first name was? And I think he had a scar?"

Then, everything began to piece together in his head, and his eyebrows narrowed as he said, "Are you kidding me!"

"No," Jerry said as he shook his head, "I'm not!"

A.J. couldn't take this anymore, feeling on the scar near the top of his head, he had to know once and for all, and that box was going to hold his secret. "Excuse me!" He rose up from his chair, and then he ran to his room. He ran out of the kitchen, stomping down the hallway into the darkness of his own fears.

After he left the table, everyone faced Frank, expecting to find an answer out of him.

"What's wrong?" Berry said, and all of them did the same.

At that moment, he did not know what to say, and this was the perfect time to find out. He left their sight, and approached the door. Only as he walked down the hallway, he saw that his door was closed, and heard someone, from what sounded like things being moved around.

But when he approached the doorway, he heard a muffled crying that sounded almost subdued, but when he neared the doorway, he heard it grow louder. He didn't call out to him though but it was A.J., and at that moment, Frank just pieced together what he was probably thinking.

"His last name is Cattiano. He is Chris's long lost cousin." Frank was sure of it; no he wasn't sure, he was dead sure that he was the long lost cousin of Chris Mangini. But when he went in, he saw that Jessica was trying to comfort him as he gripped a large birth certificate. He knew why he was crying, because A.J. was in fear for his life, and he knew that Death was looking for him, and many things for him were going to get complicated, life altering. Closing the door, he walked over to A.J.'s convulsing body—shaking like a fish—and Frank gently removed the certificate out of his way.

But he couldn't say what was for sure or not, and he probably found his birth certificate that said who he was. "What a way to end someone's day," Frank thought, "or their life?"

Frank didn't know whether he had figured out a part of his past or not. But he left an open mind to everything, but in all practicality, he was really an orphan his whole life and he had no parents at all, just a child who had been taken care of by some benefactor that wanted to keep his life a secret. Only he didn't want them now, he had found some answer to his puzzle, and he had to live with it. Frank was ready for whatever he had to say whenever he came out to talk to him. So, Frank turned around, and went back into the kitchen.

He stalled him out, and told him that the meeting was over, and they would get back together some time in the next 24 hours. All of them agreed, shaking their heads with a certain distaste for what had happened, trying to think of some way to coax themselves into staying, but that wouldn't happen. This worked out for Berry because he could get to his brother's funeral, long before it had to start. Then after the three agreed to these terms, they left, quickly and quietly, not asking of A.J.'s whereabouts.

After everything was quiet again, Frank went into the living room, and heard his crying grow even louder. He closed his eyes, and waited for it to stop.

An hour had passed, Frank was dead asleep, and the air conditioner had woken him up a couple times. Only when he opened his eyes—the fuzz slowly faded away—and he saw someone standing over him. He couldn't really see from how fuzzy his eyesight was, mixed with the darkness of the night. It was like he had been staring at a computer screen all day and he was starting to see those little dust pixels dance around him as if he had seen his first sunlight. Frank cleared his eyes from the fuzziness and stared up at him with his red dilated eyes.

"Hey?" Frank said, raising off the couch, dusting off his shirt, like he had used to do. "Are you okay?"

A.J. said nothing, and shook his head. "I need to go to Sicily don't I?" He said it in a very haunting way, almost as if he was reading Frank's mind. Only Frank wanted to give him the choice to what he wanted to do. He was the boss, and he could do what he wanted to do.

"You don't have to," Frank tried to say gently, but it said it forthwith, letting him know of his options, "we can always send someone over for you!"

A.J. shook his head, and then said, "If I am his cousin, I need to take care of this myself. Myself only!"

"What do you mean!" Frank asked, "There could be a ton of kids that have your family's last name and not be related."

But A.J., looking at him with wet, dilated eyes, was set on a decision, and knew that fate couldn't have been such a coincidence. "That's true. But Chris reached out to me, you or anyone else wouldn't have done that, but he did. He knew that I was his cousin, and I have to do this!" He pulled back his hair and added, "The birth certificate pretty much signifies everything! I am doing this for all of us! I'm sure you know someone trustworthy that can give me some protection over there."

Frank lowered his head, ultimately crushed by what he was saying, had to do what he wanted him to do. That was what Chris would have wanted, but Frank didn't want this, and everything was out of his hands. He snorted, trying to hide his tears, he said, "Yeah, I can do that! I can get you some funds too. There's a whole different currency over there and…"

"You will get it done?" A.J. said, finishing his sentence. "I trust you. I'm leaving tomorrow, so you set up the entire thing." He patted his shoulders, and then walked down the hallway, back into his room.

Frank felt like a tornado had just swept through the room, feeling like his guts and body parts had been torn apart from head to toe. The overall force that A.J. had become, and he couldn't argue with a shattered mind. He grabbed the phone and made the phone calls to John Kennedy Airport, and he had gotten ticket for the next day. He had put it on his credit card for a one way ticket to Palermo, and then he called a guy that could get him some Lira. Which was the currency that they were using these days in Italy, and then he would make one more phone call to his friend the next day, to meet A.J. in the Palermo Airport.

The sun was starting to rise, and he hadn't slept one bit that whole night.

Frank had been checking the weather obsessively, and he had finished two packs of cigarettes in an hour. He had made a bet that he would have quit smoking if he had found the long lost cousin of Chris, and knew that he had found him so he could essentially start smoking again. He guessed that he never expected it to be A.J. He wanted to be drunk lying in a pool of his own vomit instead of sending the one that Chris had given the reigns to. Only A.J. specifically left him in charge of handling all their affairs while he was gone, and also told him to watch out for Jessica while he was away. But he couldn't control A.J.; he was a man now, because sometime between that hour and the night, he had accepted his destiny.

"To die?" Frank thought, but then remembered that if he were to die, he would die knowing that he had fought for what he had believed in. "God won't send my soul to Hell for sending an innocent person to the lions den?" He wanted to burst out crying from how much the pressure was on him, but then he knew that it was time to move, because he had made his plane flight for ten-o clock in the morning. It was eight already, and they knew that they had some time to get their without rushing, and he wouldn't try to hurry.

John F. Kennedy Airport was always busy. The time didn't always matter; people could be coming from China, Africa, Indonesia, it could be bustling with people trying to get from one plane or the other. But at nine forty five in the morning, it wasn't that busy, and A.J.'s plane was about to take off. They had already said their good-byes, and Frank was holding Jessica while she cried into his shoulders as he watched the plane soar off into the sky.

"The wheels are in motion" The wheels to a much bigger clock had just started for all of them, and they knew that it was time for them to go their separate ways.

But, as long as Chris was around, they would fight the good fight, and would try to bring down Gene however they could. Only this was just the beginning for their struggle. "It's only the beginning!" Frank thought, and hugged Jessica even tighter. She couldn't bear to watch, but Frank did, and he watched as it soared off into the sky.

"Wherever you go A.J." Frank thought, as he watched the plane soar off into the sky, and pass into the clouds, becoming a small object in the sky. "Let God be with you!" He felt his heart starting to beat rapidly, and he knew that life had to go on. So, he had to let him go, physically, but he wouldn't forget him, he would never forget him, and one side wanted to see him alive, but he was just hoping.

"Hope?" Frank thought, and knew it was a very good thing to believe in. "Hope in what! Hope that things might be the same, no, it won't be, ever again."

The End (And the Beginning)

Made in the USA
Lexington, KY
08 December 2011